EVERYMAN, I will go with thee,

and be thy guide,

In thy most need to go by thy side

SIR WALTER SCOTT

Born at Edinburgh in 1771. Called to the Bar,
1792; Sheriff-Depute of Selkirk, 1799; a Principal Clerk of Session, 1812. Moved to Abbotsford in 1812, and died there on 21st September
1832. Ruined in 1826 by the failure of Messrs
Constable & Ballantyne, but he worked off the
greater part of his indebtedness and his execu-
tors were able to settle the balance after his
death. Created a baronet in 1820.

SIR WALTER SCOTT

The Fair Maid
of Perth

INTRODUCTION BY
ARTHUR MELVILLE CLARK

DENT: LONDON
EVERYMAN'S LIBRARY
DUTTON: NEW YORK

NO. *132*

SBN: 460 00132 9

INTRODUCTION

SIR WALTER Scott's poetic and romantic imagination was always powerfully stimulated by places combining scenic beauty and historic interest; and it was so deeply stirred, even at the age of fifteen, when he first saw from the Wicks of Baiglie 'the matchless scene' of Perth and its county with the Tay, the 'noblest of Scottish rivers', sweeping majestically through it, that he carried the panorama in his retentive memory for over forty years, till he made it the appropriate setting for a romance in which the Highland and the Lowland ways of life met and clashed.

But for some years before he began *The Fair Maid of Perth* he had been mainly engaged on his bulky *Life of Napoleon*, which had cost him an immense amount of labour and left him on its conclusion in June 1827 feeling tired and jaded. At the same time he was much relieved and began to entertain hopes for a brighter future, despite the unusual moods of depression he occasionally recorded in his *Journal*. In the second half of 1827 he recommenced his authorship in a small way with *Tales of a Grandfather*. Before the first volume, covering the history of Scotland down to 1603, was published in December 1827 (but with 1828 on the title-page), Scott had tentatively started a new novel on 8th November, with a Scottish theme based on episodes from his own *Tales* but belonging to an earlier epoch in the story of his country than he had previously handled in fiction. The composition of the novel was 'often suspended and flung aside', while he watched and waited till he could 'hit on some quaint and clever mode of extricating 'himself from an *impasse*, or while he tried to meet or parry the captious criticism of James Ballantyne and Cadell the publisher. Nevertheless *The Fair Maid of Perth* was finished on 29th March 1828, only four and a half months after it was begun, and was published soon afterwards as the second series of *Chronicles of the Canongate*.

Scott's choice had fallen on the reign of Robert III (1390–1406). Perhaps any other period in Scottish medieval history would, alas, have afforded the same kind of picturesque turmoil and romantic drama. Be that as it may, the reign of the amiable

v

and ineffective Robert certainly provided rich opportunities
for the brilliant display of striking incidents, the skilful use of
contrasts (in characters and points of view, in social levels and
manners, in attitudes and idioms), and the interweaving of
real events and persons with imaginary. Scott took the Battle of
the Clans (Chapter XXXIV) 'as the point on which the main
incidents of a romantic narrative might be made to hinge';
and no more powerful scene of vividly imagined and swiftly
changing action, gripping and unforgettable, occurs even in
Scott himself who excelled in such passages as the Porteous
Mob in *The Heart of Midlothian*, the lists at Ashby in *Ivanhoe*,
or the Battle of Prestonpans in *Waverley*. But there was another
historical sensation in Robert III's reign of which Scott makes
almost as much use, the hugger-mugger death of the heir-
apparent to the throne, the headstrong, irresponsible and
libertine Duke of Rothsay, though it has to be admitted that
some of the mechanism in this part of the novel is more surprising than convincing. Both of the central historical episodes in
The Fair Maid might be classed as 'wildernesses in Scottish
history, through which . . . no certain paths have been laid
down from actual survey, but which are only described by
imperfect tradition'. The Duke of Rothsay's murder, if murder
it was, is one of the Scottish historical mysteries, along with
the problems of Mary and the Casket Letters or James VI and
the so-called Gowrie Conspiracy. As for the Battle of the Clans,
we are left doubtful what clans were involved and more than
doubtful about the origin of the quarrel and the consequences
of its disastrous arbitrament. It seems likely that Clan Kay
was either the great Chattan confederacy or (more probably)
the MacKintosh section of it. But no final or (in my opinion)
even plausible identification of Clan Quhele has been made; and
it is more than possible that the extermination of so many of
its champions on the North Inch at Perth was followed by the
virtual extermination of the clan itself through its break-up as
a unit and the loss of its lands and identity. Nevertheless it is
very strange that no clear tradition of the clan's disaster has
come down orally in the Highlands, where memories are long
and where even in the present day people retail particulars of
many events of two or three hundred years ago about which
the historians are silent.

The lack of documentation and accredited fact gave Scott
considerable liberty of surmise and invention. In any case he
claimed his 'own immunities' as a historical novelist, and never
hesitated to manipulate facts to secure a better effect. But such
liberties as he took in *The Fair Maid of Perth* are largely due
to the telescoping of time (which, says Dr Johnson, 'is, of all

modes of existence, most obsequious to the imagination') or else are consequential to such changes. The two historical foci of the novel, the Clan Battle and Rothsay's death, are made to coincide to within a few hours, though in fact they occurred six years apart. Indeed one might say that Scott effectively condenses the whole sixteen years of Robert III's reign into the short period between St Valentine's Day (14th February) and Palm Sunday (30th March) 1396.

But foreshortened as the historical sequence is and modified as are some of the data, the reader receives an overall impression of the reign truer than the bald truth of straight history. The central figures are brought before our eyes, as in Shakespeare's plays based on history, not merely in the scanty and jejune record of their actions without explanation or motivation, which is all that the textbooks give, but as flesh-and-blood persons with 'hands, organs, dimensions, senses, affections, passions'—as enjoying and suffering beings. Such are the kindly and dignified but feeble Robert, a portrait well worthy of its place in Scott's regal gallery; Rothsay, a spoilt Absalom who in his better moments returns his father's affection but is the reckless cause of his own ruin; the king's brother, the Duke of Albany, a subtle schemer with a long-term policy to clear the way to the throne for himself and his house; the fierce and haughty Archibald, Earl of Douglas; the knightly traitor, Sir John Ramorny; and still others with less important parts to play.

Though royalty and nobility figure so prominently in *The Fair Maid of Perth*, our sympathies, as also in *The Heart of Midlothian*, are focused on the fortunes of persons below the level of gentility. For all its coloured pictures of courtly and aristocratic life, *The Fair Maid* is a burghal story with a middle-class heroine and an artisan hero, the most active, stirring and resolute Scott ever drew, who, like his fellow townsmen, is proud both of his city and of his craft and his skill therein. It is one of Scott's superiorities to Shakespeare, whose brogues he said he was not worthy to unloose, that he presents his middling and still humbler characters with an even-handed justice, not as all virtuous and respectable by any means, but never with a superior's contempt, however genial. It never occurred to Shakespeare to suppose that there was more in the life of workaday folk, his Bottom the Weaver, his Dogberry and Verges, his Gravediggers, than matter for a smile from their betters, or that such ordinary people could do and say serious things and, if need be, sustain a tragic role. Scott never adopts the condescending *ab extra* attitude to his simple folk any more than to his gentle folk.

Both the historical and the fictitious characters in *The Fair Maid of Perth* are set in a convincingly medieval context. And how naturally and easily it is created for the reader, tangible detail after detail falling into place—dress and accoutrements, buildings and furniture, food and drink, arts and crafts, labour and play, peace and war. Moreover Scott realized that the spiritual atmosphere of his characters and events—the ideas, beliefs, conventions, superstitions, sentiments, and the manifestation of all these through the manners and customs of the age—was likewise a factor in the *milieu*. He wrote of both the physical and the spiritual accessories out of the fullness of his knowledge and the riches of his memory. He had, he justly said, one advantage over all his imitators in historical romance: 'They may do their fooling with better grace: but I, like Sir Andrew Aguecheek, do it more natural. They have to read old books and consult antiquarian collections to get their information; I write because I have long since read such works, and possess, thanks to a strong memory, the information which they have to seek for. This leads to a dragging-in of historical details by head and shoulders, so that the interest of the main piece is lost in minute descriptions of events which do not affect its progress.'

Though Scott is generally regarded as more objective than any of his brother Romantics, yet there is much more of the autobiographical and subjective lying beneath the surface than is commonly realized. And the personal story behind *The Fair Maid of Perth* will give the novel an added interest for the reader who knows the secret.

From childhood Scott had striven to be manly and to endure pain stoically. As a schoolboy he had maintained his cause with his fists, and had given and taken many a bloody nose in the 'bickers' or street fights of Edinburgh. Then or later he loved to encounter, in the words of Stevenson, 'the bright eyes of danger' as a foolhardy cragsman and a reckless horseman. Accordingly he would far rather have done things worthy to be written than write things worthy to be read—far rather have been a soldier, had his physical condition allowed, than a lawyer or a man of letters. All his sincerest admiration was for the undaunted warrior and the heroic champion; and contrariwise he despised the coward and the craven. 'It is clear to me', he noted in his *Journal*, 'that what is least forgiven in a man of any mark or likelihood is a want of that article blackguardly called *pluck*. All the fine qualities of genius cannot make amends for it. We are told the genius of poets, especially, is irreconcilable with this species of grenadier accomplishment. If so, *quel chien de génie*!' On another occasion he stated in more emphatic terms the first article in his code of honour: 'Without courage there cannot be truth; and without truth there can be no other virtue.'

It was, therefore, with bitter shame that he heard how his younger brother Daniel, whom he had extricated from various scrapes in Scotland and helped to a fresh start in 1804 under favourable auspices in Jamaica, had shown the white feather in some action against a mob of insurgent Negroes. When Daniel returned in disgrace to Scotland in 1809 he was received with compassion into his mother's house; but Walter steadily refused to see him and, on Daniel's death soon afterwards from a shattered constitution and shame, would neither wear the customary mourning for a close relative nor attend the funeral.

The 'compunctious visitings of nature', however, came quickly on the back of the final gestures of disgust. Thus Scott, when he had to speak of Daniel, called him, in a significant circumlocution, 'my late *unfortunate* relative' (for, as Chaucer says, 'pitee renneth sone in gentile herte'); he warmly interested himself in the welfare of Daniel's natural son and became the boy's kind and devoted protector after the death of old Mrs Scott in 1819; and through the rest of his life he felt a deep and painful remorse for his severity. So his 'secret motive' in *The Fair Maid* was, he confessed, 'to perform a sort of expiation to my poor brother's manes. I have now learned', he added, 'to have more tolerance and compassion than I had in those days.' The ritual of expiation was to present a faintheart, not as ludicrous, but as a human tragedy, a hero *manqué*, 'gaining for him', as the 1831 Preface to the novel says, 'something of that sympathy which is incompatible with the total absence of respect'. Conachar, however, is not Daniel Scott in a medieval throw-back and in 'the garb of old Gaul'. The young chieftain is a much more impressive personality than poor Daniel ever was. He is a much younger man, little more than a boy, of fine presence and gallant bearing; he has the behaviour and instincts of one born to lead and command; and he assumes his chiefship with dignity and can act in everything but on the one supreme occasion with all the spirit that his admiring clan could wish. Even in the tragic climax of his brief career, Conachar is provided by Scott with much more substantial reasons for his spiritual collapse than, for example, Joseph Conrad affords his Lord Jim in a comparable ordeal. Conachar in the Clan Battle discards his hauberk (which his relentless enemy Harry Gow had made) at his superstitious foster-father's earnest plea to rid himself of a veritable shirt of Nessus; he stands in the midst of a horrible and shocking slaughter which might well have daunted a far more seasoned warrior, were it Hector or Launcelot himself; and he flies from the field only at the last moment and only in the face of absolutely certain death, but not, as did Lord Jim, at the apparent cost of hundreds of other lives to save his own. Conachar's failure of nerve is both the more excusable and the more tragic. 'A roar of contumely', says Scott with his sure fusion of justice and humanity, 'pursued him as he swam across the river, although perhaps not a dozen of those who joined in it would have behaved otherwise in the like circumstances.'

But though Scott, by dignifying his coward in advance, by pleading mitigating circumstances for his collapse, and by presenting his tragedy with pity and understanding, may be said to have both forgiven Daniel and asked forgiveness for himself, he still did not regard cowardice itself as any less disgraceful. The wild shame and the despairing suicide of Conachar are in fact the final judgment on the unpardonable sin in the religion of honour. It has not, I think, been pointed out that among the revealing contrasts in a novel which is replete with them is one bearing on the presentation of Conachar. It is not the obvious one between the rivals unto death for the hand of Catharine, Conachar and Harry Gow, but the quite unstressed contrast between Conachar and Oliver Proudfute whose paths in the novel can hardly be said to cross. The bonnet-maker is a comic poltroon with the ambition to pass as a hero and with an immense admiration for the doughty Harry Gow, on whom he models himself, even to his walk and carriage, so successfully that in the dark he is poleaxed by a blow meant for the smith. His assassination comes like a bolt from the blue at the end of a chapter. It is told in the fewest possible words; and such pity as the dead man receives from his friends and neighbours has little respect in it and is in the main a backwash from the ready compassion felt for his widow and children.

ARTHUR MELVILLE CLARK.

Edinburgh, 1969.

SELECT BIBLIOGRAPHY

NOVELS AND TALES. Collected editions: *Waverley Novels* (Everyman's Library), 25 vols., 1906, etc.; Oxford edition, 24 vols., 1914, etc.

Separate Works: *Waverley, or 'Tis Sixty Years Since*, 1814; *Guy Mannering, or The Astrologer*, 1815; *The Antiquary*, 1816; *Tales of My Landlord* (first series, *The Black Dwarf* and *Old Mortality*), 1816; *Rob Roy*, 1817; *Tales of My Landlord* (second series, *The Heart of Midlothian*), 1818; *Tales of My Landlord* (third series, *The Bride of Lammermoor* and *A Legend of Montrose*), 1819; *Ivanhoe, a Romance*, 1820; *The Monastery, a Romance*, 1820; *The Abbot*, 1820; *Kenilworth, a Romance*, 1821; *The Pirate*, 1822; *The Fortunes of Nigel*, 1822; *Peveril of the Peak*, 1822; *Quentin Durward*, 1823; *St Ronan's Well*, 1824; *Redgauntlet; a tale of the eighteenth century*, 1824; *Tales of the Crusaders* (*The Betrothed* and *The Talisman*), 1825; *Woodstock: or, The Cavalier*, 1826; *Chronicles of the Canongate* (first series, *The Highland Widow, The Two Drovers*, and *The Surgeon's Daughter*), 1827; *My Aunt Margaret's Mirror, The Tapestried Chamber*, and *The Laird's Jock* (in *The Keepsake*), 1828; *Chronicles of the Canongate* (second series, *St Valentine's Day: or The Fair Maid of Perth*), 1828; *Anne of Geierstein: or The Maiden of the Mist*, 1829; *Tales of My Landlord* (fourth series, *Count Robert of Paris* and *Castle Dangerous*), 1832.

MISCELLANEOUS PROSE WORKS. Collected edition: *The Miscellaneous Prose Works of Sir Walter Scott*, 28 vols., 1834–6.

Separate Works: Contributions to *Edinburgh Review, Quarterly Review*, and *Foreign Quarterly Review* (details in Lockhart's *Life*); *Biographical Memoir of John Leyden, M.D.* (*Edinburgh Annual Register* for 1811); *The Eyrbiggia Saga* (in *Illustrations of Northern Antiquities*), 1814; articles 'Chivalry', 'Drama' and 'Romance' in *Encyclopaedia Britannica*, 1818–24; review of Jane Austen's *Emma* (*Quarterly Review*, Oct. 1815); *Historical Sketches* (*Edinburgh Annual Register*), 1814–15; *Paul's Letters to his Kinsfolk*, 1816; *Provincial Antiquities of Scotland*, 1819–26; *Description of the Regalia of Scotland*, 1819; *Account of the Coronation of George IV*, 1821; *Lives of the Novelists* (prefixed to Ballantyne's Novelist's Library), 1821–4; (Everyman's Library) 1910; *Character of the late Lord Byron* (in *Edinburgh Weekly Journal*), 1824; *Thought on the Proposed Change of Currency* from Malachi Malagrowther, 1826; *Character of Frederick, Duke of York* (*Edinburgh Weekly Journal*), 1827; *The Life of Napoleon Buonaparte*, 9 vols., 1827; *Religious Discourses, By a Layman*, 1828; *Tales of a Grandfather* (four series, 1828–31); *History of Scotland* (in Lardner's *Cabinet Cyclopaedia*), 1829–30; *Letters on Demonology and Witchcraft*, 1830; *Essays on Chivalry, Romance, and the Drama*, various eds.

LETTERS. Edited by H. J. C. Grierson, W. M. Parker, and others, 12 vols., 1932–7.

JOURNAL. Edited by D. Douglas, 2 vols., 1890; re-edited by J. G. Tait and W. M. Parker, 3 vols., 1939–46; 1 vol., 1950.

Scott edited *Minstrelsy of the Scottish Border* (1802–3; ed. T. Henderson, 1902), *Works of John Dryden* (18 vols., 1808), *Works of Jonathan Swift* (19 vols., 1814); Somers's *Tracts*, 13 vols., 1809–15, and many other works.

BIOGRAPHY. J. Hogg, *Domestic Manners and Private Life of Sir W. Scott*, 1834; 3rd ed., 1909; J. G. Lockhart, *Memoirs of The Life of Sir Walter Scott*, 7 vols., 1837–8; 10 vols., 1839; Everyman's Library, 1906; G. Saintsbury, *Sir Walter Scott*, 1897; John Buchan, *Sir Walter Scott*, 1932; Dame Una Pope Hennessy, *The Laird of Abbotsford*, 1932; H. J. C. Grierson, *Sir Walter Scott, a new Life*, 1938; Hesketh Pearson, *Walter Scott, His Life and Personality*, 1954; A. Melville Clark, *Sir Walter Scott: The Formative Years*, 1969.

BIBLIOGRAPHY. W. Ruff, *A Bibliography of the Poetical Works of Sir Walter Scott, 1796–1832*, 1938; J. C. Corson, *Bibliography of Sir Walter Scott* (critical works on Scott only), 1943; J. C. Corson, 'Sir Walter Scott' (in the *New Cambridge Bibliography of English Literature*).

THE FAIR MAID OF PERTH

PREFACE

In continuing the lucubrations of Chrystal Croftangry, it occurred that, although the press had of late years teemed with works of various descriptions concerning the Scottish Gael, no attempt had hitherto been made to sketch their manners, as these might be supposed to have existed at the period when the Statute-book, as well as the page of the chronicler, begins to present constant evidence of the difficulties to which the crown was exposed, while the haughty house of Douglas all but over-balanced its authority on the Southern border, and the North was at the same time torn in pieces by the yet untamed savageness of the Highland races, and the daring loftiness to which some of the remoter chieftains still carried their pretensions. The well-authenticated fact of two powerful clans having deputed each thirty champions to fight out a quarrel of old standing, in presence of King Robert III., his brother the Duke of Albany, and the whole court of Scotland, at Perth, in the year of grace 1396, seemed to mark with equal distinctness the rancour of these mountain-feuds, and the degraded condition of the general government of the country; and it was fixed upon accordingly as the point on which the main incidents of a romantic narrative might be made to hinge. The characters of Robert III., his ambitious brother, and his dissolute son, seemed to offer some opportunities of interesting contrast;—and the tragic fate of the heir of the throne, with its immediate consequences, might serve to complete the picture of cruelty and lawlessness.

Two features of the story of this barrier-battle on the Inch of Perth, the flight of one of the appointed champions, and the reckless heroism of a townsman, that voluntarily offered for a small piece of coin to supply his place in the mortal encounter, suggested the imaginary persons, on whom much of the novel is expended. The fugitive Celt might have been easily dealt with, had a ludicrous style of colouring been adopted; but it appeared to the author that there would be more of novelty, as well as of serious interest, if he

3

could succeed in gaining for him something of that sympathy which is incompatible with the total absence of respect. Miss Baillie had drawn a coward by nature capable of acting as a hero under the strong impulse of filial affection. It seemed not impossible to conceive the case of one constitutionally weak of nerve, being supported by feelings of honour and of jealousy up to a certain point, and then suddenly giving way, under circumstances to which the bravest heart could hardly refuse compassion.

The controversy, as to who really were the clans that figured in the barbarous conflict of the Inch, has been revived since the publication of the Fair Maid of Perth, and treated in particular at great length by Mr. Robert Mackay of Thurso, in his very curious " History of the House and Clan of Mackay." [1] Without pretending to say that he has settled any part of the question in the affirmative, this gentleman certainly seems to have quite succeeded in proving that his own worthy sept had *no* part in the transaction. The Mackays were in that age seated, as they have since continued to be, in the extreme north of the island; and their chief at the time was a personage of such importance, that his name and proper designation could not have been omitted in the early narratives of the occurrence. He on one occasion brought four thousand of his clan to the aid of the royal banner against the Lord of the Isles. This historian is of opinion that the Clan Quhele of Wyntoun were the *Camerons*, who appear to have about that period been often designated as *Macewans*, and to have gained much more recently the name of *Cameron*, i.e. *Wrynose*, from a blemish in the physiognomy of some heroic chief of the line of Lochiel. This view of the case is also adopted by Douglas in his Baronage, where he frequently mentions the bitter feuds between Clan Chattan and Clan Kay, and identifies the latter sept, in reference to the events of 1396, with the Camerons. It is perhaps impossible to clear up thoroughly this controversy, little interesting in itself, at least to readers on this side of Inverness. The names, as we have them in Wyntoun, are *Clanwhewyl* and *Clachinya*, the latter probably not correctly transcribed. In the Scoti-Chronicon they are *Clanquhele* and *Clankay*. Hector Boece writes *Clanchattan* and *Clankay*, in which he is followed by Leslie; while Buchanan disdains to disfigure his page with their Gaelic designations at all, and merely describes them as two powerful races in the wild and lawless region beyond the Grampians. Out of this jumble what Sassenach can pretend *dare lucem*? The name

[1] Edinburgh, 4to, 1829.

Clanwheill appears so late as 1594, in an act of James VI. Is it not possible that it may be, after all, a mere corruption of Clan Lochiel?

The reader may not be displeased to have Wyntoun's original rhymes:

> "A thousand and thre hunder yere,
> Nynty and sex to mak all clere—
> Of thre-score wyld Scottis men,
> Thretty agane thretty then,
> In Felny bolnit of auld Fede,[1]
> As thare fore-elders ware slane to dede:
> Tha three-score ware clannys twa,
> Clahynnhe Qwhewyl and Clachinyha:
> Of thir twa Kynnis ware tha men,
> Thretty agane thretty then:
> And thare thai had thair Chiftanys twa,
> Scha [2] Ferqwharis' son wes ane of tha,
> The tother Cristy Johnseone.
> A selcouth thing by tha was done.
> At Sanct Johnstoun besyde the Freris,
> All thai enterit in Barreris
> Wyth bow and ax, knyf and swerd,
> To deil amang thaim thair last werd.[3]
> Thare thai laid on that time sa fast,
> Quha had the ware [4] thare at the last
> I will nocht say; but quha best had,
> He was but dout bathe muth and mad,[5]
> Fifty or má ware slane that day,
> Suá few wyth lif than past away."

The Prior of Lochleven makes no mention either of the evasion of one of the Gaelic champions, or of the gallantry of the Perth artisan, in offering to take a share in the conflict. Both incidents, however, were introduced, no doubt from tradition, by the continuator of Fordun, whose narrative is in these words:—

"Anno Dom. millesimo trecentesimo nonagesimo sexto, magna pars borealis Scotiæ, trans Alpes, inquietata fuit per duos pestiferos Cateranos, et eorum sequaces, viz. Scheabeg et suos consanguinarios, qui Clankay; et Cristi-Jonson, ac suos, qui Clanquhele dicebantur; qui nullo pacto vel tractatu pacificari poterant, nullâque arte regis vel gubernatoris poterant edomari, quoadusque nobilis et industriosus D. David de Lindesay de Crawford, et dominus Thomas comes

---

[1] *i.e.* Boiled with the cruelty of an old feud.

[2] *Scha* is supposed to be *Toshach*, *i.e.* Macintosh: the father of the chief of this sept at the time was named Ferchard. In Bowar he is *Scheabeg*, *i.e.* Toshach the little.

[3] *i.e.* Fate, doom. [4] The *waur*—the worse.

[5] *Muth* and *mad*, *i.e.* exhausted both in body and in mind.

Moraviæ, diligentiam et vires apposuerunt, ac inter partes sic tractaverunt, ut coram domino rege certo die convenirent apud Perth, et alterutra pars eligeret de progenie sua triginta personas adversus triginta de parte contraria, gladiis tantùm, arcubus et sagittis, absque deploidibus, vel armaturis aliis, præter bipennes; et sic congredientes finem liti ponerent, et terra pace potiretur. Utrique igitur parti summè placuit contractus, et die Lunæ proximo ante festum Sancti Michaëlis, apud North-insulam de Perth, coram Rege et Gubernatore, et innumerabili multitudine comparentes, conflictum acerrimum inierunt: ubi de sexaginta interfecti sunt omnes, excepto uno ex parte Clankay, et undecim exceptis ex parte altera. Hoc etiam ibi accidit, quòd omnes in præcinctu belli constituti, unus eorum locum diffugii considerans, inter omnes in amnem elabitur, et aquam de Thaya natando transgreditur; à millenis insequitur, sed nusquam apprehenditur. Stant igitur partes attonitæ, tanquam non ad conflictum progressuri, ob defectum evasi: noluit enim pars integrum habens numerum sociorum consentire, ut unus de suis demeretur; nec potuit pars altera quocumque pretio alterum ad supplendum vicem fugientis inducere. Stupent igitur omnes hærentes, de damno fugitivi conquerentes. Et cùm totum illud opus cessare putaretur, ecce in medio prorupit unus stipulosus vernaculus, staturâ modicus, sed efferus, dicens; Ecce ego! quis me conducet intrare cum operariis istis ad hunc ludum theatralem? Pro dimidia enim marca ludum experiar, ultra hoc petens, ut si vivus de palæstra evasero, victum à quocumque vestrûm recipiam dum vixero: quia, sicut dicitur, 'Majorem caritatem nemo habet, quàm ut animam suam ponat quis pro amicis.' Quali mercede donabor, qui animam meam pro inimicis reipublicæ et regni pono? Quod petiit, à rege et diversis magnatibus conceditur. Cum hoc arcus ejus extenditur, et primò sagittam in partem contrariam transmittit, et unum interficit. Confestim hinc inde sagittæ volitant, bipennes librant, gladios vibrant, alterutro certant, et veluti carnifices boves in macello, sic inconsternatè ad invicèm se trucidant. Sed nec inter tantos repertus est vel unus, qui, tanquam vecors aut timidus, sive post tergum alterius declinans, seipsum à tanta cæde prætendit excusare. Iste tamen tyro superveniens finaliter illæsus exivit; et dehinc multo tempore Boreas quievit; nec ibidem fuit, ut suprà, Cateranorum excursus."

The scene is heightened with many florid additions by Boece and Leslie, and the contending savages in Buchanan utter speeches after the most approved pattern of Livy.

The devotion of the young Chief of Clan Quhele,s foster-father and foster-brethren, in the novel, is a trait of clannish fidelity, of which Highland story furnishes many examples. In the battle of Inverkeithing, between the Royalists and Oliver Cromwell's troops, a foster-father and seven brave sons are known to have thus sacrificed themselves for Sir Hector Maclean of Duart—the old man, whenever one of his boys fell, thrusting forward another to fill his place at the right hand of the beloved chief, with the very words adopted in the novel—"Another for Hector!"

Nay, the feeling could outlive generations. The late much lamented General Stewart of Garth, in his account of the battle of Killikrankie, informs us that Lochiel was attended on the field by the son of his foster-brother. "This faithful adherent followed him like his shadow, ready to assist him with his sword, or cover him from the shot of the enemy. Suddenly the chief missed his friend from his side, and turning round to look what had become of him, saw him lying on his back with his breast pierced by an arrow. He had hardly breath, before he expired, to tell Lochiel, that seeing an enemy, a Highlander in General Mackay's army, aiming at him with a bow and arrow, he sprung behind him, and thus sheltered him from instant death. This," observes the gallant David Stewart, "is a species of duty not often practised, perhaps, by our aide-de-camps of the present day."—*Sketches of the Highlanders*, Vol. I. p. 65.

I have only to add, that the Second Series of "Chronicles of the Canongate," with the Chapter Introductory which now follows, appeared in May 1828, and had a favourable reception.

Abbotsford,
Aug. 15, 1831.

INTRODUCTORY

The ashes here of murder'd Kings
Beneath my footsteps sleep;
And yonder lies the scene of death,
Where Mary learn'd to weep.

CAPTAIN MARJORIBANKS.

EVERY quarter of Edinburgh has its own peculiar boast, so that the city together combines within its precincts, (if you take the word of the inhabitants on the subject,) as much of historical interest as of natural beauty. Our claims in behalf of the Canongate are not the slightest. The Castle may excel us in extent of prospect and sublimity of site; the Calton had always the superiority of its unrivalled panorama, and has of late added that of its towers, and triumphal arches, and the pillars of its Parthenon. The High Street, we acknowledge, had the distinguished honour of being defended by fortifications, of which we can show no vestiges. We will not descend to notice the claims of more upstart districts, called Old New Town, and New New Town, not to mention the favourite Moray Place, which is the newest New Town of all.[1] We will not match ourselves except with our equals, and with our equals in age only, for in dignity we admit of none. We boast being the Court end of the town, possessing the Palace and the sepulchral remains of Monarchs, and that we have the power to excite, in a degree unknown to the less honoured quarters of the city, the dark and solemn recollections of ancient grandeur, which occupied the precincts of our venerable Abbey, from the time of St. David, till her deserted halls were once more made glad, and her long silent echoes awakened, by the visit of our present gracious Sovereign.[2]

[1] This "newest New Town," in case Mr. Croftangry's lucubrations should outlive its possession of any right to that designation, was begun, I think, in 1824, on the park and gardens attached to a quondam pretty suburban residence of the Earls of Moray—from whose different titles, and so forth, the names of the *places* and streets erected were, of course, taken. Aug. 1831.

[2] The visit of George IV. to Scotland, in August 1822, will not soon be forgotten. It satisfied many who had shared Dr. Johnson's doubts on the subject, that the old feelings of loyalty, in spite of all the derision of modern wits, continued firmly

My long habitation in the neighbourhood, and the quiet respectability of my habits, have given me a sort of intimacy with good Mrs. Policy, the housekeeper in that most interesting part of the old building, called Queen Mary's Apartments. But a circumstance which lately happened has conferred upon me greater privileges ; so that, indeed, I might, I believe, venture on the exploit of Chatelet, who was executed for being found secreted at midnight in the very bedchamber of Scotland's Mistress.

It chanced, that the good lady I have mentioned, was, in the discharge of her function, showing the apartments to a cockney from London ;—not one of your quiet, dull, commonplace visitors, who gape, yawn, and listen with an acquiescent *umph*, to the information doled out by the provincial cicerone. No such thing— this was the brisk, alert agent of a great house in the city, who missed no opportunity of doing business, as he termed it, that is, of putting off the goods of his employers, and improving his own account of commission. He had fidgeted through the suite of apartments, without finding the least opportunity to touch upon that which he considered as the principal end of his existence. Even the story of Rizzio's assassination presented no ideas to this emissary of commerce, until the housekeeper appealed, in support of her narrative, to the dusky stains of blood upon the floor.

" These are the stains," she said ; " nothing will remove them from the place—there they have been for two hundred and fifty years— and there they will remain while the floor is left standing—neither water nor any thing else will ever remove them from that spot."

Now, our cockney, amongst other articles, sold Scouring Drops, as they are called, and a stain of two hundred and fifty years' standing was interesting to him, not because it had been caused by the blood of a Queen's favourite, slain in her apartment, but because it offered so admirable an opportunity to prove the efficacy of his unequalled Detergent Elixir. Down on his knees went our friend, but neither in horror nor devotion.

" Two hundred and fifty years, ma'am, and nothing take it away ? Why, if it had been five hundred, I have something in my pocket will fetch it out in five minutes. D'ye see this elixir, ma'am ? I will show you the stain vanish in a moment."

rooted, and might be appealed to with confidence, even under circumstances apparently the most unfavourable. Who that had observed the state of public feeling with respect to this most amiable prince's domestic position at a period but a few months earlier, would have believed that he should ever witness such scenes of enthusiastic and rapturous devotion to his person, as filled up the whole panorama of his fifteen days at Edinburgh ? Aug. 1831.

Accordingly, wetting one end of his handkerchief with the all-deterging specific, he began to rub away on the planks, without heeding the remonstrances of Mrs. Policy. She, good soul, stood at first in astonishment, like the Abbess of St. Bridget's, when a profane visitant drank up the vial of brandy which had long passed muster among the relics of the cloister for the tears of the blessed saint. The venerable guardian of St. Bridget probably expected the interference of her patroness—She of Holy Rood might, perhaps, hope that David Rizzio's spectre would arise to prevent the profanation. But Mrs. Policy stood not long in the silence of horror. She uplifted her voice, and screamed as loudly as Queen Mary herself, when the dreadful deed was in the act of perpetration—

"Harrow now out! and walawa!" she cried.

I happened to be taking my morning walk in the adjoining gallery, pondering in my mind why the Kings of Scotland, who hung around me, should be each and every one painted with a nose like the knocker of a door, when lo! the walls once more re-echoed with such shrieks, as formerly were as often heard in the Scottish palaces as were sounds of revelry and music. Somewhat surprised at such an alarm in a place so solitary, I hastened to the spot, and found the well-meaning traveller scrubbing the floor like a housemaid, while Mrs. Policy, dragging him by the skirts of the coat, in vain endeavoured to divert him from his sacrilegious purpose. It cost me some trouble to explain to the zealous purifier of silk-stockings, embroidered waistcoats, broad-cloth, and deal planks, that there were such things in the world as stains which ought to remain indelible, on account of the associations with which they are connected. Our good friend viewed every thing of the kind only as the means of displaying the virtue of his vaunted commodity. He comprehended, however, that he would not be permitted to proceed to exemplify its powers on the present occasion, as two or three inhabitants appeared, who, like me, threatened to maintain the housekeeper's side of the question. He therefore took his leave, muttering that he had always heard the Scots were a nasty people, but had no idea they carried it so far as to choose to have the floors of their palaces blood-boltered, like Banquo's ghost, when to remove them would have cost but a hundred drops of the Infallible Detergent Elixir, prepared and sold by Messrs. Scrub and Rub, in five shilling and ten shilling bottles, each bottle being marked with the initials of the inventor, to counterfeit which would be to incur the pains of forgery.

Freed from the odious presence of this lover of cleanliness, my good friend Mrs. Policy was profuse in her expressions of thanks; and yet her gratitude, instead of exhausting itself in these declarations, according to the way of the world, continues as lively at this moment as if she had never thanked me at all. It is owing to her recollection of this piece of good service, that I have the permission of wandering, like the ghost of some departed gentleman-usher, through these deserted halls, sometimes, as the old Irish ditty expresses it,

Thinking upon things that are long enough ago;

and sometimes wishing I could, with the good-luck of most editors of romantic narrative, light upon some hidden crypt or massive antique cabinet, which should yield to my researches an almost illegible manuscript, containing the authentic particulars of some of the strange deeds of those wild days of the unhappy Mary.

My dear Mrs. Baliol used to sympathize with me when I regretted that all godsends of this nature had ceased to occur, and that an author might chatter his teeth to pieces by the seaside, without a wave ever wafting to him a casket containing such a history as that of Automathes; that he might break his shins in stumbling through a hundred vaults, without finding any thing but rats and mice, and become the tenant of a dozen sets of shabby tenements, without finding that they contained any manuscript but the weekly bill for board and lodging. A dairymaid of these degenerate days might as well wash and deck her dairy in hopes of finding the fairy tester in her shoe.

"It is a sad, and too true a tale, cousin," said Mrs. Baliol. "I am sure we all have occasion to regret the want of these ready supplements to a failing invention. But you, most of all, have right to complain that the fairies have not favoured your researches—you, who have shown the world that the Age of Chivalry still exists —you, the Knight of Croftangry, who braved the fury of the 'London 'prentice bold,' in behalf of the fair Dame Policy, and the memorial of Rizzio's slaughter! Is it not a pity, cousin, considering the feat of chivalry was otherwise so much according to rule—Is it not, I say, a great pity that the lady had not been a little younger, and the legend a little older?"

"Why, as to the age at which a fair dame loses the benefit of chivalry, and is no longer entitled to crave boon of brave knight, that I leave to the statutes of the Order of Errantry; but for the blood of Rizzio, I take up the gauntlet, and maintain against all and sundry, that I hold the stains to be of no modern date, but to have been actually the consequence and the record of that terrible assassination."

"As I cannot accept the challenge to the field, fair cousin, I am contented to require proof."

"The unaltered tradition of the Palace, and the correspondence of the existing state of things with that tradition."

"Explain, if you please."

"I will.—The universal tradition bears, that when Rizzio was dragged out of the chamber of the Queen, the heat and fury of the assassins, who struggled which should deal him most wounds, dispatched him at the door of the anteroom. At the door of the apartment, therefore, the greater quantity of the ill-fated minion's blood was spilled, and there the marks of it are still shown. It is reported further by historians, that Mary continued her entreaties for his life, mingling her prayers with screams and exclamations, until she knew that he was assuredly slain ; on which she wiped her eyes and said, 'I will now study revenge.'"

"All this is granted.—But the blood ? would it not wash out, or waste out, think you, in so many years ?"

"I am coming to that presently. The constant tradition of the Palace says, that Mary discharged any measures to be taken to remove the marks of slaughter, which she had resolved should remain as a memorial to quicken and confirm her purposed vengeance. But it is added, that, satisfied with the knowledge that it existed, and not desirous to have the ghastly evidence always under her eye, she caused a traverse, as it is called, (that is, a temporary screen of boards,) to be drawn along the under part of the anteroom, a few feet from the door, so as to separate the place stained with the blood from the rest of the apartment, and involve it in considerable obscurity. Now this temporary partition still exists, and by running across and interrupting the plan of the roof and cornices, plainly intimates that it has been intended to serve some temporary purpose, since it disfigures the proportions of the room, interferes with the ornaments of the ceiling, and could only have been put there for some such purpose, as hiding an object too disagreeable to be looked upon. As to the objection that the blood-stains would have disappeared in course of time, I apprehend that if measures to efface them were not taken immediately after the affair happened—if the blood, in other words, were allowed to sink into the wood, the stain would become almost indelible. Now, not to mention that our Scottish palaces were not

particularly well washed in those days, and that there were no
Patent Drops to assist the labours of the mop, I think it very
probable that these dark relics might subsist for a long course
of time, even if Mary had not desired or directed that they should be
preserved, but screened by the traverse from public sight. I know
several instances of similar blood-stains remaining for a great many
years, and I doubt whether, after a certain time, any thing can
remove them, save the carpenter's plane. If any Seneschal, by way
of increasing the interest of the apartments, had, by means of paint,
or any other mode of imitation, endeavoured to palm upon posterity
supposititious stigmata, I conceive that the impostor would have
chosen the Queen's cabinet and the bedroom for the scene of
his trick, placing his bloody tracery where it could be distinctly
seen by visitors, instead of hiding it behind the traverse in this
manner. The existence of the said traverse, or temporary partition,
is also extremely difficult to be accounted for, if the common and
ordinary tradition be rejected. In short, all the rest of this striking
locality is so true to the historical fact, that I think it may well bear
out the additional circumstance of the blood on the floor."

"I profess to you," answered Mrs. Baliol, "that I am very willing
to be converted to your faith. We talk of a credulous vulgar,
without always recollecting that there is a vulgar incredulity, which,
in historical matters, as well as in those of religion, finds it easier to
doubt than to examine, and endeavours to assume the credit of an
esprit fort, by denying whatever happens to be a little beyond the
very limited comprehension of the sceptic.—And so, that point
being settled, and you possessing, as we understand, the Open
Sesamum into these secret apartments, how, if we may ask, do you
intend to avail yourself of your privilege?—Do you propose to pass
the night in the royal bedchamber?"

"For what purpose, my dear lady?—if to improve the rheumatism, this east wind may serve the purpose."

"Improve the rheumatism—Heaven forbid! that would be worse
than adding colours to the violet. No, I mean to recommend a
night on the couch of the Rose of Scotland, merely to improve the
imagination. Who knows what dreams might be produced by a
night spent in a mansion of so many memories! For aught I know,
the iron door of the postern stair might open at the dead hour
of midnight and, as at the time of the conspiracy, forth might sally
the phantom assassins, with stealthy step and ghastly look, to renew
the semblance of the deed. There comes the fierce fanatic Ruthven
—party hatred enabling him to bear the armour which would

otherwise weigh down a form extenuated by wasting disease. See how his writhen features show under the hollow helmet, like those of a corpse tenanted by a demon, whose vindictive purpose looks out at the flashing eyes, while the visage has the stillness of death.—Yonder appears the tall form of the boy Darnley, as goodly in person as vacillating in resolution; yonder he advances with hesitating step, and yet more hesitating purpose, his childish fear having already overcome his childish passion. He is in the plight of a mischievous lad who has fired a mine, and who now, expecting the explosion in remorse and terror, would give his life to quench the train which his own hand lighted.—Yonder—yonder—But I forget the rest of the worthy cut-throats. Help me, if you can."

"Summon up," said I, "the Postulate, George Douglas, the most active of the gang. Let him arise at your call—the claimant of wealth which he does not possess—the partaker of the illustrious blood of Douglas, but which in his veins is sullied with illegitimacy. Paint him the ruthless, the daring, the ambitious—so nigh greatness, yet debarred from it—so near to wealth, yet excluded from possessing it—a political Tantalus, ready to do or dare any thing to terminate his necessities and assert his imperfect claims."

"Admirable, my dear Croftangry! But what is a Postulate?"

"Pooh, my dear madam, you disturb the current of my ideas —The Postulate was, in Scottish phrase, the candidate for some benefice which he had not yet attained—George Douglas, who stabbed Rizzio, was the Postulate for the temporal possessions of the rich Abbey of Arbroath."

"I stand informed—Come, proceed; who comes next?" continued Mrs. Baliol.

"Who comes next? Yon tall, thin-made, savage-looking man, with the petronel in his hand, must be Andrew Ker of Faldonside, a brother's son, I believe, of the celebrated Sir David Ker of Cessford; his look and bearing those of a Border freebooter; his disposition so savage, that, during the fray in the cabinet, he presented his loaded piece at the bosom of the young and beautiful Queen, that Queen also being within a few weeks of becoming a mother."

"Bravo, *beau cousin*!—Well, having raised your bevy of phantoms, I hope you do not intend to send them back to their cold beds to warm them? You will put them to some action, and since you do threaten the Canongate with your desperate quill, you surely mean to novelize, or to dramatize if you will, this most singular of all tragedies?"

"Worse—that is less interesting—periods of history have been, indeed, shown up, for furnishing amusement to the peaceable ages which have succeeded; but, dear lady, the events are too well known in Mary's days, to be used as vehicles of romantic fiction. What can a better writer than myself add to the elegant and forcible narrative of Robertson? So adieu to my vision—I awake, like John Bunyan, 'and behold it is a dream.'—Well, enough that I awake without a sciatica, which would have probably rewarded my slumbers had I profaned Queen Mary's bed, by using it as a mechanical resource to awaken a torpid imagination."

"This will never do, cousin," answered Mrs. Baliol; "you must get over all these scruples, if you would thrive in the character of a romantic historian, which you have determined to embrace. What is the classic Robertson to you? The light which he carried was that of a lamp to illuminate the dark events of antiquity; yours is a magic lantern to raise up wonders which never existed. No reader of sense wonders at your historical inaccuracies, any more than he does to see Punch in the show-box seated on the same throne with King Solomon in his glory, or to hear him hollowing out to the patriarch, amid the deluge, 'Mighty hazy weather, Master Noah.'"

"Do not mistake me, my dear madam," said I; "I am quite conscious of my own immunities as a taleteller. But even the mendacious Mr. Fagg, in Sheridan's Rivals, assures us, that though he never scruples to tell a lie at his master's command, yet it hurts his conscience to be found out. Now, this is the reason why I avoid in prudence all well-known paths of history, where every one can read the finger-posts carefully set up to advise them of the right turning; and the very boys and girls, who learn the history of Britain by way of question and answer, hoot at a poor author if he abandons the highway."

"Do not be discouraged, however, cousin Chrystal. There are plenty of wildernesses in Scottish history, through which, unless I am greatly misinformed, no certain paths have been laid down from actual survey, but which are only described by imperfect tradition, which fills up with wonders and with legends the periods in which no real events are recognized to have taken place. Even thus, as Mat Prior says—

> 'Geographers on pathless downs,
> Place elephants instead of towns.'"

"If such be your advice, my dear lady," said I, "the course of my story shall take its rise upon this occasion at a remote period of history, and in a province removed from my natural sphere of the Canongate."

It was under the influence of those feelings that I undertook the following Historical Romance, which, often suspended and flung aside, is now arrived at a size too important to be altogether thrown away, although there may be little prudence in sending it to the press.

I have not placed in the mouth of the characters the Lowland Scotch dialect now spoken, because unquestionably the Scottish of that day resembled very closely the Anglo-Saxon, with a sprinkling of French or Norman to enrich it. Those who wish to investigate the subject, may consult the Chronicles of Winton, and the History of Bruce, by Archdeacon Barbour. But supposing my own skill in the ancient Scottish were sufficient to invest the dialogue with its peculiarities, a translation must have been necessary for the benefit of the general reader. The Scottish dialect may be therefore considered as laid aside, unless where the use of peculiar words may add emphasis or vivacity to the composition.

THE FAIR MAID OF PERTH

CHAPTER I

" Behold the Tiber," the vain Roman cried,
Viewing the ample Tay from Baiglie's side ;
But where's the Scot that would the vaunt repay,
And hail the puny Tiber for the Tay ? [1]

Anonymous.

AMONG all the provinces in Scotland, if an intelligent stranger
were asked to describe the most varied and the most beautiful,
it is probable he would name the county of Perth.   A native
also of any other district of Caledonia, though his partialities
might lead him to prefer his native county in the first instance, would certainly class that of Perth in the second, and
thus give its inhabitants a fair right to plead that—prejudice
apart—Perthshire forms the fairest portion of the northern
kingdom.   It is long since Lady Mary Wortley Montague,
with that excellent taste which characterizes her writings, expressed her opinion that the most interesting district of every
country, and that which exhibits the varied beauties of natural
scenery in greatest perfection, is that where the mountains
sink down upon the champaign, or more level land.   The
most picturesque, if not the highest hills, are also to be found
in the county of Perth.   The rivers find their way out of the
mountainous region by the wildest leaps, and through the
most romantic passes connecting the Highlands with the
Lowlands.   Above, the vegetation of a happier climate and
soil, is mingled with the magnificent characteristics of mountain-
scenery, and woods, groves, and thickets in profusion, clothe

[1] Such is the author's opinion, founded perhaps on feelings of national
pride, of the relative claims of the classical river and the Scottish one.
Should he ever again be a blotter of paper, he hopes to be able to speak
on this subject the surer language of personal conviction.   Aug. 1831.

the base of the hills, ascend up the ravines, and mingle with the precipices. It is in such favoured regions that the traveller finds what the poet Gray, or some one else, has termed, Beauty lying in the lap of Terror.

From the same advantage of situation, this favoured province presents a variety of the most pleasing character. Its lakes, woods, and mountains, may vie in beauty with any that the Highland tour exhibits ; while Perthshire contains, amidst this romantic scenery, and in some places in connexion with it, many fertile and habitable tracts, which may vie with the richness of merry England herself. The country has also been the scene of many remarkable exploits and events, some of historical importance, others interesting to the poet and romancer, though recorded in popular tradition alone. It was in these vales that the Saxons of the plain, and the Gael of the mountains, had many a desperate and bloody encounter, in which it was frequently impossible to decide the palm of victory between the mailed chivalry of the Low Country, and the plaided clans whom they opposed.

Perth, so eminent for the beauty of its situation, is a place of great antiquity ; and old tradition assigns to the town the importance of a Roman foundation. That victorious nation, it is said, pretended to recognize the Tiber in the much more magnificent and navigable Tay, and to acknowledge the large level space, well known by the name of the North Inch, as having a near resemblance to their Campus Martius. The city was often the residence of our monarchs, who, although they had no palace at Perth, found the Cistercian Convent amply sufficient for the reception of their court. It was here that James the First, one of the wisest and best of the Scottish kings, fell a victim to the jealousy of the vengeful aristocracy. Here also occurred the mysterious conspiracy of Gowrie, the scene of which has only of late been effaced, by the destruction of the ancient palace in which the tragedy was acted. The Antiquarian Society of Perth, with just zeal for the objects of their pursuit, have published an accurate plan of this memorable mansion, with some remarks upon its connexion with the narrative of the plot, which display equal acuteness and candour.

One of the most beautiful points of view which Britain, or perhaps the world, can afford, is, or rather we may say was, the prospect from a spot called the Wicks of Baiglie, being a species of niche at which the traveller arrived, after a long stage from Kinross, through a waste and uninteresting country, and from which, as forming a pass over the summit of a ridgy eminence which he had gradually surmounted, he beheld, stretching beneath him, the valley of the Tay, traversed by its ample and lordly stream; the town of Perth, with its two large meadows, or Inches, its steeples, and its towers; the hills of Moncreiff and Kinnoul faintly rising into picturesque rocks, partly clothed with woods; the rich margin of the river, studded with elegant mansions; and the distant view of the huge Grampian mountains, the northern screen of this exquisite landscape. The alteration of the road, greatly, it must be owned, to the improvement of general intercourse, avoids this magnificent point of view, and the landscape is introduced more gradually and partially to the eye, though the approach must be still considered as extremely beautiful. There is still, we believe, a footpath left open, by which the station at the Wicks of Baiglie may be approached; and the traveller, by quitting his horse or equipage, and walking a few hundred yards, may still compare the real landscape with the sketch which we have attempted to give. But it is not in our power to communicate, or in his to receive, the exquisite charm which surprise gives to pleasure, when so splendid a view arises when least expected or hoped for, and which Chrystal Croftangry experienced when he beheld, for the first time, the matchless scene.[1]

Childish wonder, indeed, was an ingredient in my delight, for I was not above fifteen years old; and as this had been the first excursion which I was permitted to make on a pony of my own, I also experienced the glow of independence, mingled with that degree of anxiety which the most conceited boy feels when he is first abandoned to his own undirected counsels. I recollect pulling up the reins without meaning to do so, and gazing on the scene before me as if I had been afraid it would shift like those in a theatre before I could distinctly observe its different parts, or convince myself that what I saw was real. Since that hour, and the period is now more than fifty years past, the recollection of that inimitable landscape has possessed the strongest influence over my mind, and retained its place as a memorable thing, when much that was influential on my own fortunes has fled from my recollection. It is therefore natural, that, whilst deliberating on what might be brought

[1] Note I.—View from the Wicks of Baiglie.

forward for the amusement of the public, I should pitch
upon some narrative connected with the splendid scenery
which made so much impression on my youthful imagination,
and which may perhaps have that effect in setting off the
imperfections of the composition, which ladies suppose a
fine set of china to possess in heightening the flavour of
indifferent tea.[1]

The period at which I propose to commence, is, however,
considerably earlier than either of the remarkable historical
transactions to which I have already alluded, as the events
which I am about to recount occurred during the last years
of the fourteenth century, when the Scottish sceptre was swayed
by the gentle, but feeble hand of John, who, on being
called to the throne, assumed the title of Robert the Third.

CHAPTER II

A country lip may have the velvet touch ;
Though she's no lady, she may please as much.

DRYDEN.

PERTH, boasting, as we have already mentioned, so large
a portion of the beauties of inanimate nature, has at no
time been without its own share of those charms which
are at once more interesting and more transient. To be
called the Fair Maid of Perth, would at any period have
been a high distinction, and have inferred no mean superiority
in beauty, where there were many to claim that much-envied
attribute. But, in the feudal times, to which we now call
the reader's attention, female beauty was a quality of much
higher importance than it has been since the ideas of chivalry
have been in a great measure extinguished. The love of
the ancient cavaliers was a licensed species of idolatry,
which the love of Heaven alone was theoretically supposed
to approach in intensity, and which in practice it seldom

[1] Chrystal Croftangry expresses here the feelings of the author, as
nearly as he could recall them, after such a lapse of years. I am,
however, informed, by various letters from Perthshire, that I have
made some little mistakes about names. Sure enough the general effect
of the valley of the Tay, and the ancient town of Perth, rearing its
grey head among the rich pastures, and beside the gleaming waters
of that noblest of Scottish streams, must remain so as to justify warmer
language than Mr. Croftangry had at his command. Aug. 1831.

equalled. God and the Ladies were familiarly appealed to in the same breath; and devotion to the fair sex was as peremptorily enjoined upon the aspirant to the honour of chivalry, as that which was due to Heaven. At such a period in society, the power of beauty was almost unlimited. It could level the highest rank with that which was immeasurably inferior.

It was but in the reign preceding that of Robert III., that beauty alone had elevated a person of inferior rank and indifferent morals to share the Scottish throne;[1] and many women, less artful or less fortunate, had risen to greatness from a state of concubinage, for which the manners of the times made allowance and apology. Such views might have dazzled a girl of higher birth than Catharine or Katie Glover, who was universally acknowledged to be the most beautiful young woman of the city or its vicinity, and whose renown, as the Fair Maid of Perth, had drawn on her much notice from the young gallants of the Royal Court, when it chanced to be residing in or near Perth; insomuch, that more than one nobleman of the highest rank, and most distinguished for deeds of chivalry, were more attentive to exhibit feats of horsemanship as they passed the door of old Simon Glover, in what was called Couvrefew, or Curfew Street, than to distinguish themselves in the tournaments, where the noblest dames of Scotland were spectators of their address.

But the Glover's daughter—for, as was common with the citizens and artisans of that early period, her father, Simon, derived his sirname from the trade which he practised— showed no inclination to listen to any gallantry which came from those of a station highly exalted above that which she herself occupied; and though probably in no degree insensible to her personal charms, seemed desirous to confine her conquests to those who were within her own sphere of life. Indeed, her beauty being of that kind which we connect more with the mind than with the person, was, notwithstanding her natural kindness and gentleness of disposition, rather allied to reserve than to gaiety, even when in company with her equals; and the earnestness with which she attended upon the exercises of devotion, induced many to think that Catharine Glover nourished the private wish to retire from the world, and bury herself in the recesses of the cloister. But to such a sacrifice, should it be meditated, it was not to be expected

[1] Note II.

her father, reputed a wealthy man, and having this only child, would yield a willing consent.

In her resolution of avoiding the addresses of the gallant courtiers, the reigning Beauty of Perth was confirmed by the sentiments of her parent. "Let them go," he said; "let them go, Catharine, those gallants, with their capering horses, their jingling spurs, their plumed bonnets, and their trim mustaches; they are not of our class, nor will we aim at pairing with them. To-morrow is Saint Valentine's Day, when every bird chooses her mate; but you will not see the linnet pair with the sparrowhawk, nor the robin-redbreast with the kite. My father was an honest burgher of Perth, and could use his needle as well as I can. Did there come war to the gates of our fair burgh, down went needles, thread, and shamoy leather, and out came the good headpiece and target from the dark nook, and the long lance from above the chimney. Show me a day that either he or I were absent when the Provost made his musters! Thus we have led our lives, my girl, working to win our bread, and fighting to defend it. I will have no son-in-law that thinks himself better than me; and for these lords and knights, I trust thou wilt always remember thou art too low to be their lawful love, and too high to be their unlawful loon. And now lay by thy work, lass, for it is holytide eve, and it becomes us to go to the evening service, and pray that Heaven may send thee a good Valentine to-morrow."

So the Fair Maid of Perth laid aside the splendid hawking glove which she was embroidering for the Lady Drummond, and putting on her holyday kirtle, prepared to attend her father to the Blackfriars Monastery, which was adjacent to Couvrefew Street in which they lived. On their passage, Simon Glover, an ancient and esteemed burgess of Perth, somewhat stricken in years and increased in substance, received from young and old the homage due to his velvet jerkin and his gold chain, while the well-known beauty of Catharine, though concealed beneath her screen—which resembled the mantilla still worn in Flanders—called both obeisances and doffings of the bonnet from young and old.

As the pair moved on arm in arm, they were followed by a tall handsome young man, dressed in a yeoman's habit of the plainest kind, but which showed to advantage his fine limbs, as the handsome countenance that looked out from a quantity of curled tresses, surmounted by a small scarlet bonnet, became that species of head-dress. He had no other weapon than a staff in his hand, it not being thought fit that persons of his degree, (for he was an apprentice to the old Glover,) should appear on the street armed with sword or dagger, a privilege which the jackmen, or military retainers of the nobility, esteemed exclusively their own. He attended his master at holytide, partly in the character of a domestic, or guardian, should there be cause for his interference; but it was not difficult to discern, by the earnest attention which he paid to Catharine Glover, that it was to her, rather than to her father, that he desired to dedicate his good offices. Generally speaking, there was no opportunity for his zeal displaying itself; for a common feeling of respect induced passengers to give way to the father and daughter.

But when the steel caps, barrets, and plumes, of squires, archers, and men-at-arms, began to be seen among the throng, the wearers of these warlike distinctions were more rude in their demeanour than the quiet citizens. More than once, when from chance, or perhaps an assumption of superior importance, such an individual took the wall of Simon in passing, the Glover's youthful attendant bristled up with a look of defiance, and the air of one who sought to distinguish his zeal in his mistress's service by its ardour. As frequently did Conachar, for such was the lad's name, receive a check from his master, who gave him to understand that he did not wish his interference before he required it. "Foolish boy," he said, "hast thou not lived long enough in my shop to know that a blow will breed a brawl—that a dirk will cut the skin as fast as a needle pierces leather—that I love peace, though I never feared war, and care not which side of the causeway my daughter and I walk upon, so we may keep our road in peace and quietness?"—Conachar excused himself as zealous for his master's honour, yet was scarce able to pacify the old citizen.—"What have we to do with honour?" said Simon Glover. "If thou wouldst remain in my service, thou must think of honesty, and leave honour to the swaggering fools who wear steel at their heels and iron on their shoulders. If you wish to wear and use such garniture, you are welcome, but it shall not be in my house or in my company."

Conachar seemed rather to kindle at this rebuke than to submit to it. But a sign from Catharine, if that slight raising of her little finger was indeed a sign, had more effect than the angry reproof of his master; and the youth laid aside the military air which seemed natural to him, and relapsed into the humble follower of a quiet burgher.

Meantime the little party were overtaken by a tall young man wrapped in a cloak, which obscured or muffled a part of his face, a practice often used by the gallants of the time, when they did not wish to be known, or were abroad in quest of adventures. He seemed, in short, one who might say to the world around him, " I desire, for the present, not to be known, or addressed in my own character; but, as I am answerable to myself alone for my actions, I wear my incognito but for form's sake, and care little whether you see through it or not." He came on the right side of Catharine, who had hold of her father's arm, and slackened his pace as if joining their party.

" Good even to you, goodman."

" The same to your worship, and thanks.—May I pray you to pass on?—our pace is too slow for that of your lordship— our company too mean for that of your father's son."

" My father's son can best judge of that, old man. I have business to talk of with you and with my fair St. Catharine here, the loveliest and most obdurate saint in the calendar."

" With deep reverence, my lord," said the old man, "I would remind you that this is good St. Valentine's Eve, which is no time for business, and that I can have your worshipful commands by a serving-man as early as it pleases you to send them."

" There is no time like the present," said the persevering youth, whose rank seemed to be of a kind which set him above ceremony. " I wish to know whether the buff doublet be finished which I commissioned some time since;—and from you, pretty Catharine, (here he sank his voice to a whisper,) I desire to be informed whether your fair fingers have been employed upon it, agreeably to your promise? But I need not ask you, for my poor heart has felt the pang of each puncture that pierced the garment which was to cover it. Traitress, how wilt thou answer for thus tormenting the heart that loves thee so dearly ! "

" Let me entreat you, my lord," said Catharine, " to forego this wild talk—it becomes not you to speak thus, or me to listen. We are of poor rank, but honest manners ; and the presence of the father ought to protect the child from such expressions, even from your lordship."

This she spoke so low, that neither her father nor Conachar could understand what she said.

"Well, tyrant," answered the persevering gallant, "I will plague you no longer now, providing you will let me see you from your window to-morrow when the sun first peeps over the eastern hill, and give me right to be your Valentine for the year."

"Not so, my lord; my father but now told me that hawks, far less eagles, pair not with the humble linnet. Seek some court lady, to whom your favours will be honour; to me—your highness must permit me to speak the plain truth—they can be nothing but disgrace."

As they spoke thus, the party arrived at the gate of the church. "Your lordship will, I trust, permit us here to take leave of you?" said her father. "I am well aware how little you will alter your pleasure for the pain and uneasiness you may give to such as us; but, from the throng of attendants at the gate, your lordship may see that there are others in the church, to whom even your gracious lordship must pay respect.'

"Yes—respect; and who pays any respect to me?" said the haughty young lord. "A miserable artisan and his daughter, too much honoured by my slightest notice, have the insolence to tell me that my notice dishonours them. Well, my princess of white doe-skin and blue silk, I will teach you to rue this."

As he murmured thus, the Glover and his daughter entered the Dominican Church, and their attendant, Conachar, in attempting to follow them closely, jostled, it may be not un-willingly, the young nobleman. The gallant, starting from his unpleasing reverie, and perhaps considering this as an in-tentional insult, seized on the young man by the breast, struck him, and threw him from him. His irritated opponent recovered himself with difficulty, and grasped towards his own side, as if seeking a sword or dagger in the place where it was usually worn; but finding none, he made a gesture of dis-appointed rage, and entered the church. During the few seconds he remained, the young nobleman stood with his arms folded on his breast, with a haughty smile, as if defying him to do his worst. When Conachar had entered the church, his opponent, adjusting his cloak yet closer about his face, made a private signal by holding up one of his gloves. He was instantly joined by two men, who, disguised like himself,

had waited his motions at a little distance. They spoke together earnestly, after which the young nobleman retired in
one direction, his friends or followers going off in another.

Simon Glover, before he entered the church, cast a look
towards the group, but had taken his place among the congregation before they separated themselves. He knelt down
with the air of a man who has something burdensome on his
mind ; but when the service was ended, he seemed free from
anxiety, as one who had referred himself and his troubles to
the disposal of Heaven. The ceremony of High Mass was
performed with considerable solemnity, a number of noblemen
and ladies of rank being present. Preparations had indeed
been made for the reception of the good old King himself, but
some of those infirmities to which he was subject had
prevented Robert III. from attending the service, as was
his wont. When the congregation were dismissed, the Glover
and his beautiful daughter lingered for some time, for the
purpose of making their several shrifts in the confessionals,
where the priests had taken their places for discharging that
part of their duty. Thus it happened that the night had
fallen dark, and the way was solitary, when they returned
along the now deserted streets to their own dwelling. Most
persons had betaken themselves to home and to bed. They
who still lingered in the street were night-walkers or revellers,
the idle and swaggering retainers of the haughty nobles, who
were much wont to insult the peaceful passengers, relying on
the impunity which their master's court favour was too apt
to secure them.

It was, perhaps, in apprehension of mischief from some
character of this kind, that Conachar, stepping up to the
Glover, said, " Master, walk faster—we are dogg'd."

" Dogg'd, sayest thou ? By whom and by how many ? "

" By one man muffled in his cloak, who follows us like our
shadow."

"Then will I never mend my pace along the Couvrefew
Street, for the best one man that ever trode it."

" But he has arms," said Conachar.

" And so have we, and hands and legs and feet. Why
sure, Conachar, you are not afraid of one man ? "

" Afraid ! " answered Conachar, indignant at the insinuation ;
" you shall soon know if I am afraid."

" Now you are as far on the other side of the mark, thou
foolish boy—thy temper has no middle course ; there is no

occasion to make a brawl, though we do not run. Walk thou before with Catharine, and I will take thy place. We cannot be exposed to danger so near home as we are."

The Glover fell behind accordingly, and certainly observed a person keep so close to them, as, the time and place considered, justified some suspicion. When they crossed the street, he also crossed it, and when they advanced or slackened their pace, the stranger's was in proportion accelerated or diminished. The matter would have been of very little consequence had Simon Glover been alone ; but the beauty of his daughter might render her the object of some profligate scheme, in a country where the laws afforded such slight protection to those who had not the means to defend themselves. Conachar and his fair charge having arrived on the threshold of their own apartment, which was opened to them by an old female servant, the burgher's uneasiness was ended. Determined, however, to ascertain, if possible, whether there had been any cause for it, he called out to the man whose motions had occasioned the alarm, and who stood still, though he seemed to keep out of reach of the light. "Come, step forward, my friend, and do not play at bopeep ; knowest thou not, that they who walk like phantoms in the dark, are apt to encounter the conjuration of a quarterstaff ? Step forward, I say, and show us thy shapes, man."

"Why, so I can, Master Glover," said one of the deepest voices that ever answered question. "I can show my shapes well enough, only I wish they could bear the light something better."

"Body of me," exclaimed Simon, "I should know that voice !—And is it thou, in thy bodily person, Harry Gow ? —nay, beshrew me if thou passest this door with dry lips. What, man, curfew has not rung yet, and if it had, it were no reason why it should part father and son. Come in, man ; Dorothy shall get us something to eat, and we will jingle a can ere thou leave us. Come in, I say, my daughter Kate will be right glad to see thee."

By this time he had pulled the person, whom he welcomed so cordially, into a sort of kitchen, which served also upon ordinary occasions the office of parlour. Its ornaments were trenchers of pewter, mixed with a silver cup or two, which, in the highest degree of cleanliness, occupied a range of shelves like those of a beauffet, popularly called *the Bink*.

A good fire, with the assistance of a blazing lamp, spread light and cheerfulness through the apartment, and a savoury smell of some victuals which Dorothy was preparing, did not at all offend the unrefined noses of those whose appetite they were destined to satisfy.

Their unknown attendant now stood in full light among them, and though his appearance was neither dignified nor handsome, his face and figure were not only deserving of attention, but seemed in some manner to command it. He was rather below the middle stature, but the breadth of his shoulders, length and brawniness of his arms, and the muscular appearance of the whole man, argued a most unusual share of strength, and a frame kept in vigour by constant exercise. His legs were somewhat bent, but not in a manner which could be said to approach to deformity; on the contrary, which seemed to correspond to the strength of his frame, though it injured in some degree its symmetry. His dress was of buff-hide; and he wore in a belt around his waist a heavy broadsword, and a dirk or poniard, as if to defend his purse, which (burgher-fashion) was attached to the same cincture. The head was well proportioned, round, close cropped, and curled thickly with black hair. There was daring and resolution in the dark eye, but the other features seemed to express a bashful timidity, mingled with good-humour, and obvious satisfaction at meeting with his old friends. Abstracted from the bashful expression, which was that of the moment, the forehead of Henry Gow, or Smith, for he was indifferently so called, was high and noble, but the lower part of the face was less happily formed. The mouth was large, and well-furnished with a set of firm and beautiful teeth, the appearance of which corresponded with the air of personal health and muscular strength, which the whole frame indicated. A short thick beard, and mustaches which had lately been arranged with some care, completed the picture. His age could not exceed eight-and-twenty.

The family appeared all well pleased with the unexpected appearance of an old friend. Simon Glover shook his hand again and again, Dorothy made her compliments, and Catharine herself offered freely her hand, which Henry held in his massive grasp, as if he designed to carry it to his lips, but, after a moment's hesitation, desisted, from fear lest the freedom might be ill taken. Not that there was any resistance on the part of the little hand which lay passive in his grasp; but there

was a smile mingled with the blush on her cheek, which
seemed to increase the confusion of the gallant. Her father,
on his part, called out frankly, as he saw his friend's hesitation,—

"Her lips, man, her lips! and that's a proffer I would not
make to every one who crosses my threshold. But, by good
St. Valentine, (whose holyday will dawn to-morrow,) I am so
glad to see thee in the bonny city of Perth again, that it would
be hard to tell the thing I could refuse thee."

The Smith—for, as has been said, such was the craft of this
sturdy artisan—was encouraged modestly to salute the Fair
Maid, who yielded the courtesy with a smile of affection that
might have become a sister, saying, at the same time, "Let
me hope that I welcome back to Perth a repentant and
amended man."

He held her hand as if about to answer, then suddenly, as
one who lost courage at the moment, relinquished his grasp;
and drawing back as if afraid of what he had done, his dark
countenance glowing with bashfulness, mixed with delight, he
sat down by the fire on the opposite side from that which
Catharine occupied.

"Come, Dorothy, speed thee with the food, old woman;—
and Conachar—where is Conachar?"

"He is gone to bed, sir, with a headache," said Catharine, in
a hesitating voice.

"Go, call him, Dorothy," said the old Glover; "I will not
be used thus by him; his Highland blood, forsooth, is too
gentle to lay a trencher or spread a napkin, and he expects to
enter our ancient and honourable craft without duly waiting and
tending upon his master and teacher in all matters of lawful
obedience. Go, call him, I say; I will not be thus neglected."

Dorothy was presently heard screaming up stairs, or more
probably up a ladder, to the cockloft, to which the recusant
apprentice had made an untimely retreat; a muttered answer
was returned, and soon after Conachar appeared in the eating
apartment. There was a gloom of deep sullenness on his
haughty, though handsome features, and as he proceeded to
spread the board, and arrange the trenchers, with salt, spices,
and other condiments—to discharge, in short, the duties of a
modern domestic, which the custom of the time imposed upon
all apprentices—he was obviously disgusted and indignant with
the mean office imposed upon him. The Fair Maid of Perth
looked with some anxiety at him, as if apprehensive that his
evident sullenness might increase her father's displeasure; but

it was not till her eyes had sought out his for a second time, that Conachar condescended to veil his dissatisfaction, and throw a greater appearance of willingness and submission into the services which he was performing.

And here we must acquaint our reader, that though the private interchange of looks betwixt Catharine Glover and the young mountaineer indicated some interest on the part of the former in the conduct of the latter, it would have puzzled the strictest observer to discover whether that feeling exceeded in degree what might have been felt by a young person towards a friend and inmate of the same age, with whom she had lived on habits of intimacy.

"Thou hast had a long journey, son Henry," said Glover, who had always used that affectionate style of speech, though noways akin to the young artisan; "ay, and hast seen many a river besides Tay, and many a fair bigging besides St. Johnston."

"But none that I like half so well, and none that are half so much worth my liking," answered the Smith; "I promise you, father, that when I crossed the Wicks of Baiglie, and saw the bonny city lie stretched fairly before me like a Fairy Queen in romance, whom the Knight finds asleep among a wilderness of flowers, I felt even as a bird, when it folds its wearied wings to stoop down on its own nest."

"Aha! so thou canst play the Maker[1] yet?" said the Glover. "What, shall we have our ballets, and our roundels again? our lusty carols for Christmas, and our mirthful springs to trip it round the May-pole?"

"Such toys there may be forthcoming, father," said Henry Smith, "though the blast of the bellows and the clatter of the anvil make but coarse company to lays of minstrelsy; but I can afford them no better, since I must mend my fortune, though I mar my verses."

"Right again—my own son just," answered the Glover; "and I trust thou hast made a saving voyage of it?"

"Nay, I made a thriving one, father—I sold the steel habergeon that you wot of for four hundred marks to the English Warden of the East Marches, Sir Magnus Redman. [2]   He

---

[1] Old Scottish for *Poet*, and indeed the literal translation of the original Greek, Ποιητης.

[2] Sir Magnus Redman, sometime Governor of Berwick, fell in one of the battles on the Border which followed on the treason of the Earl of March, alluded to hereafter.

scarce scrupled a penny after I gave him leave to try a sword-dint upon it. The beggarly Highland thief who bespoke it boggled at half the sum though it had cost me a year's labour."

"What dost thou start at, Conachar?" said Simon, addressing himself, by way of parenthesis, to the mountain disciple; "wilt thou never learn to mind thy own business, without listening to what is passing round thee? What is it to thee that an Englishman thinks that cheap which a Scottishman may hold dear?"

Conachar turned round to speak, but, after a moment's consideration, looked down, and endeavoured to recover his composure, which had been deranged by the contemptuous manner in which the Smith had spoken of his Highland customer. Henry went on without paying any attention to him.

"I sold at high prices some swords and whingers when I was at Edinburgh. They expect war there; and if it please God to send it, my merchandise will be worth its price. St. Dunstan make us thankful, for he was of our craft. In short, this fellow" (laying his hand on his purse) "who, thou knowest, father, was somewhat lank and low in condition when I set out four months since, is now as round and full as a six-weeks' porker."

"And that other leathern-sheathed iron-hilted fellow who hangs beside him," said the Glover, "has he been idle all this while?—Come, jolly Smith, confess the truth—how many brawls hast thou had since crossing the Tay?"

"Nay, now you do me wrong, father, to ask me such a question" (glancing a look at Catharine) "in such a presence," answered the armourer; "I make swords, indeed, but I leave it to other people to use them. No, no—seldom have I a naked sword in my fist, save when I am turning them on the anvil or grindstone; and they slandered me to your daughter Catharine, that led her to suspect the quietest burgess in Perth of being a brawler. I wish the best of them would dare say such a word at the Hill of Kinnoul, and never a man on the green but he and I."

"Ay, ay," said the Glover, laughing, "we should then have a fine sample of your patient sufferance—Out upon you, Henry, that you will speak so like a knave to one who knows thee so well! You look at Kate, too, as if she did not know that a man in this country must make his hand keep his head, unless he will sleep in slender security. Come, come;

beshrew me if thou hast not spoiled as many suits of armour as thou hast made."

"Why, he would be a bad armourer, father Simon, that could not with his own blow make proof of his own workmanship. If I did not sometimes cleave a helmet, or strike a sword's point through a harness, I should not know what strength of fabric to give them; and might jingle together such pasteboard work as yonder Edinburgh smiths think not shame to put out of their hands."

"Aha—now would I lay a gold crown thou hast had a quarrel with some Edinburgh Burn-the-wind [1] upon that very ground?"

"A quarrel!—no, father," replied the Perth armourer, "but a measuring of swords with such a one upon St. Leonard's Crags, for the honour of my bonny city, I confess. Surely you do not think I would quarrel with a brother craftsman?"

"Ah, to a surety, no. But how did your brother craftsman come off?"

"Why, as one with a sheet of paper on his bosom might come off from the stroke of a lance—or rather, indeed, he came not off at all; for, when I left him, he was lying in the Hermit's Lodge daily expecting death, for which Father Gervis said he was in heavenly preparation."

"Well—any more measuring of weapons?" said the Glover.

"Why, truly, I fought an Englishman at Berwick besides, on the old question of the Supremacy, as they call it—I am sure you would not have me slack at that debate?—and I had the luck to hurt him on the left knee."

"Well done for St. Andrew!—to it again.—Whom next had you to deal with?" said Simon, laughing at the exploits of his pacific friend.

"I fought a Scotchman in the Torwood," answered Henry Smith, "upon a doubt which was the better swordsman, which, you are aware, could not be known or decided without a trial. The poor fellow lost two fingers."

"Pretty well for the most peaceful lad in Perth, who never touches a sword but in the way of his profession.—Well, any thing more to tell us?"

"Little—for the drubbing of a Highlandman is a thing not worth mentioning."

---

[1] *Burn-the-wind,* an old cant term for blacksmith, appears in Burns—

> "Then *Burnewin* came on like death,
>   At every chaup," &c.

"For what didst thou drub him, O man of peace?" enquired the Glover.

"For nothing that I can remember," replied the Smith, "except his presenting himself on the south side of Stirling Bridge."

"Well, here is to thee, and thou art welcome to me after all these exploits.—Conachar, bestir thee. Let the cans clink, lad, and thou shalt have a cup of the nut-brown for thyself, my boy."

Conachar poured out the good liquor for his master and for Catharine, with due observance. But that done, he set the flagon on the table, and sat down.

"How now, sirrah!—be these your manners? Fill to my guest, the worshipful Master Henry Smith."

"Master Smith may fill for himself, if he wishes for liquor," answered the youthful Celt. "The son of my father has demeaned himself enough already for one evening."

"That's well crowed for a cockerel," said Henry; "but thou art so far right, my lad, that the man deserves to die of thirst who will not drink without a cupbearer."

But his entertainer took not the contumacy of the young apprentice with so much patience.—"Now, by my honest word, and by the best glove I ever made," said Simon, "thou shalt help him with liquor from that cup and flagon, if thee and I are to abide under one roof."

Conachar arose sullenly upon hearing this threat, and, approaching the Smith, who had just taken the tankard in his hand, and was raising it to his head, he contrived to stumble against him and jostle him so awkwardly, that the foaming ale gushed over his face, person, and dress. Good-natured as the Smith, in spite of his warlike propensities, really was in the utmost degree, his patience failed under such a provocation. He seized the young man's throat, being the part which came readiest to his grasp, as Conachar arose from the pretended stumble, and pressing it severely as he cast the lad from him, exclaimed, "Had this been in another place, young gallows-bird, I had stowed the lugs out of thy head, as I have done to some of thy clan before thee."

Conachar recovered his feet with the activity of a tiger and exclaiming, "Never shall you live to make that boast again!" drew a short sharp knife from his bosom and springing on Henry Smith, attempted to plunge it into his body over the collar-bone, which must have been a mortal wound. But the object of this violence was so ready to defend himself by striking up the assailant's hand, that the blow only glanced on the bone, and scarce drew blood. To wrench the dagger from the boy's hand, and to secure him with a grasp like that of his own iron vice, was, for the powerful Smith, the work of a single moment. Conachar felt himself at once in the absolute power of the formidable antagonist whom he had provoked; he became deadly pale, as he had been the moment before glowing red, and stood mute with shame and fear, until, relieving him from his powerful hold, the Smith quietly said, "It is well for thee that thou canst not make me angry—thou art but a boy, and I, a grown man, ought not to have provoked thee. But let this be a warning."

Conachar stood an instant as if about to reply, and then left the room, ere Simon had collected himself enough to speak. Dorothy was running hither and thither for salves and healing herbs. Catharine had swooned at the sight of the trickling blood.

"Let me depart, father Simon," said Henry Smith, mournfully; "I might have guessed I should have my old luck, and spread strife and bloodshed where I would wish most to bring peace and happiness. Care not for me—look to poor Catharine; the fright of such an affray hath killed her, and all through my fault."

"Thy fault, my son!—It was the fault of yon Highland cateran,[1] whom it is my curse to be cumbered with; but he shall go back to his glens to-morrow, or taste the tolbooth of the burgh. An assault upon the life of his master's guest in his master's house!—It breaks all bonds between us. But let me see to thy wound."

"Catharine!" repeated the armourer, "look to Catharine."

"Dorothy will see to her," said Simon; "surprise and fear kill not—skenes and dirks do. And she is not more the daughter of my blood than thou, my dear Henry, art the son of my affections. Let me see the wound. The skene-occle [2] is an ugly weapon in a Highland hand."

"I mind it no more than the scratch of a wild-cat," said

---

[1] *Cateran,* or *robber,* the usual designation of the Celtic borderers on the lands of the Sassenach. The beautiful Lake of the Trosachs is supposed to have taken its name from the habits of its frequenters.

[2] *Skene-occle,* i.e. knife of the armpit—the Highlanders' stiletto.

the armourer; "and now that the colour is coming to Catharine's cheek again, you shall see me a sound man in a moment." He turned to a corner in which hung a small mirror, and hastily took from his purse some dry lint, to apply to the slight wound he had received. As he unloosed the leathern jacket from his neck and shoulders, the manly and muscular form which they displayed was not more remarkable than the fairness of his skin, where it had not, as in hands and face, been exposed to the effects of rough weather, and of his laborious trade. He hastily applied some lint to stop the bleeding, and a little water having removed all other marks of the fray, he buttoned his doublet anew, and turned again to the table where Catharine, still pale and trembling, was, however, recovered from her fainting fit.

"Would you but grant me your forgiveness for having offended you in the very first hour of my return? The lad was foolish to provoke me, and yet I was more foolish to be provoked by such as he. Your father blames me not, Catharine, and cannot you forgive me?"

"I have no power to forgive," answered Catharine, "what I have no title to resent. If my father chooses to have his house made the scene of night brawls, I must witness them— I cannot help myself. Perhaps it was wrong in me to faint and interrupt, it may be, the farther progress of a fair fray. My apology is, that I cannot bear the sight of blood."

"And this is the manner," said her father, "in which you receive my friend after his long absence? My friend, did I say? nay, my son. He escapes being murdered by a fellow whom I will to-morrow clear this house of, and you treat him as if he had done wrong in dashing from him the snake which was about to sting him!"

"It is not my part, father," returned the Maid of Perth, "to decide who had the right or wrong in the present brawl; nor did I see what happened distinctly enough, to say which was assailant, or which defender. But sure our friend, Master Henry, will not deny that he lives in a perfect atmosphere of strife, blood, and quarrels. He hears of no swordsman but he envies his reputation, and must needs put his valour to the proof. He sees no brawl but he must strike into the midst of it. Has he friends, he fights with them for love and honour—has he enemies, he fights with them for hatred and revenge. And those men who are neither his friends nor foes, he fights with them because they are on this or that side of a river. His days are days of battle, and doubtless he acts them over again in his dreams."

"Daughter," said Simon, "your tongue wags too freely. Quarrels and fights are men's business, not women's, and it is not maidenly to think or speak of them."

"But if they are so rudely enacted in our presence," said Catharine, "it is a little hard to expect us to think or speak of any thing else. I will grant you, my father, that this valiant burgess of Perth is one of the best-hearted men that draws breath within its walls—that he would walk a hundred yards out of the way rather than step upon a worm—that he would be as loath, in wantonness, to kill a spider, as if he were a kinsman to King Robert, of happy memory [1]—that in the last quarrel before his departure he fought with four butchers, to prevent their killing a poor mastiff that had misbehaved in the bull-ring, and narrowly escaped the fate of the cur that he was protecting. I will grant you also, that the poor never pass the house of the wealthy armourer but they are relieved with food and alms. But what avails all this, when his sword makes as many starving orphans and mourning widows as his purse relieves?"

"Nay, but Catharine, hear me but a word before going on with a string of reproaches against my friend, that sound something like sense, while they are, in truth, inconsistent with all we hear and see around us. What," continued the Glover, "do our King and our court, our knights and ladies, our abbots, monks, and priests themselves, so earnestly crowd to see? Is it not to behold the display of chivalry, to witness the gallant actions of brave knights in the tilt and tourney-ground, to look upon deeds of honour and glory achieved by arms and bloodshed? What is it these proud knights do, that differs from what our good Henry Gow works out in his sphere? Who ever heard of his abusing his skill and strength to do evil or forward oppression, and who knows not how often it has been employed as that of a champion in the good cause of the burgh? And shouldst not thou, of all women, deem thyself honoured and glorious, that so true a heart and so strong an arm has termed himself thy bachelor? In what do the proudest dames take their loftiest pride, save in the chivalry of their knight; and has the boldest in Scotland done more gallant deeds than my brave son Henry, though but of low degree? Is he not known to Highland and Lowland as the

[1] Note III.—Robert Bruce.

best armourer that ever made sword, and the truest soldier that ever drew one?"

"My dearest father," answered Catharine, "your words contradict themselves, if you will permit your child to say so. Let us thank God and the good saints, that we are in a peaceful rank of life, below the notice of those whose high birth, and yet higher pride, lead them to glory in their bloody works of cruelty, which haughty and lordly men term deeds of chivalry. Your wisdom will allow that it would be absurd in us to prank ourselves in their dainty plumes and splendid garments—why, then, should we imitate their full-blown vices? Why should we assume their hard-hearted pride and relentless cruelty, to which murder is not only a sport, but a subject of vainglorious triumph? Let those whose rank claims as its right such bloody homage, take pride and pleasure in it;—we, who have no share in the sacrifice, may the better pity the sufferings of the victim. Let us thank our lowliness, since it secures us from temptation.—But forgive me, father, if I have stepped over the limits of my duty, in contradicting the views which you entertain, with so many others, on these subjects."

"Nay, thou hast even too much talk for me, girl," said her father, somewhat angrily. "I am but a poor workman, whose best knowledge is to distinguish the left-hand glove from the right. But if thou wouldst have my forgiveness, say something of comfort to my poor Henry. There he sits, confounded and dismayed with all the preachment thou hast heaped together; and he, to whom a trumpet sound was like the invitation to a feast, is struck down at the sound of a child's whistle."

The armourer, indeed, while he heard the lips that were dearest to him paint his character in such unfavourable colours, had laid his head down on the table, upon his folded arms, in an attitude of the deepest dejection, or almost despair. "I would to Heaven, my dearest father," answered Catharine, "that it were in my power to speak comfort to Henry, without betraying the sacred cause of the truths I have just told you. And I may,—nay, I must have such a commission," she continued with something that the earnestness with which she spoke, and the extreme beauty of her features, caused for the moment to resemble inspiration. "The truth of Heaven," she said, in a solemn tone, "was never committed to a tongue, however feeble, but it gave a right to that tongue to announce mercy, while it declared judgment.—Arise, Henry—rise up, noble-minded, good, and generous, though widely mistaken man—Thy faults are those of this cruel and remorseless age— thy virtues all thine own."

While she thus spoke, she laid her hand upon the Smith's arm, and extricating it from under his head by a force which, however gentle, he could not resist, she compelled him to raise towards her his manly face, and the eyes into which her expostulations, mingled with other feelings, had summoned tears. "Weep not," she said, "or rather weep on—but weep as those who have hope. Abjure the sins of pride and anger, which most easily beset thee—fling from thee the accursed weapons, to the fatal and murderous use of which thou art so easily tempted."

"You speak to me in vain, Catharine," returned the armourer; "I may, indeed, turn monk and retire from the world, but while I live in it I must practise my trade; and while I form armour and weapons for others, I cannot myself withstand the temptation of using them. You would not reproach me as you do, if you knew how inseparably the means by which I gain my bread are connected with that warlike spirit which you impute to me as a fault, though it is the consequence of inevitable necessity. While I strengthen the shield or corslet to withstand wounds, must I not have constantly in remembrance the manner and strength with which they may be dealt; and when I forge the sword, and temper it for war, is it practicable for me to avoid the recollection of its use?"

"Then throw from you, my dear Henry," said the enthusiastic girl, clasping with both her slender hands the nervous strength and weight of one of the muscular armourer's, which they raised with difficulty, permitted by its owner, yet scarcely receiving assistance from his volition—"cast from you, I say, the art which is a snare to you. Abjure the fabrication of weapons which can only be useful to abridge human life, already too short for repentance, or to encourage with a feeling of safety those whom fear might otherwise prevent from risking themselves in peril. The art of forming arms, whether offensive or defensive, is alike sinful in one to whose violent and ever vehement disposition the very working upon them proves a sin and a snare. Resign utterly the manufacture of weapons of every description, and deserve the forgiveness of Heaven, by renouncing all that can lead to the sin which most easily besets you."

"And what," murmured the armourer, "am I to do for my livelihood, when I have given over the art of forging arms, for which Henry of Perth is known from the Tay to the Thames?"

"Your art itself," said Catharine, "has innocent and laudable resources. If you renounce the forging of swords and bucklers, there remains to you the task of forming the harmless spade, and the honourable as well as useful ploughshare,—of those implements which contribute to the support of life, or to its comforts. Thou canst frame locks and bars to defend the property of the weak against the stouthrief and oppression of the strong. Men will still resort to thee and repay thy honest industry——"

But here Catharine was interrupted. Her father had heard her declaim against war and tournaments with a feeling, that though her doctrines were new to him, they might not, nevertheless, be entirely erroneous. He felt, indeed, a wish that his proposed son-in-law should not commit himself voluntarily to the hazards which the daring character and great personal strength of Henry the Smith had hitherto led him to incur too readily; and so far he would rather have desired that Catharine's arguments should have produced some effect upon the mind of her lover, whom he knew to be as ductile, when influenced by his affections, as he was fierce and intractable when assailed by hostile remonstrances or threats. But her arguments interfered with his views, when he heard her enlarge upon the necessity of his designed son-in-law resigning a trade which brought in more ready income than any at that time practised in Scotland, and more profit to Henry of Perth, in particular, than to any armourer in the nation. He had some indistinct idea, that it would not be amiss to convert, if possible, Henry the Smith from his too frequent use of arms, even though he felt some pride in being connected with one who wielded with such superior excellence those weapons, which in that warlike age it was the boast of all men to manage with spirit. But when he heard his daughter recommend, as the readiest road to this pacific state of mind, that her lover should renounce the gainful trade in which he was held unrivalled, and which, from the constant private differences and public wars of the time, was sure to afford him a large income, he could withhold his wrath no longer. The daughter had scarce recommended to her lover the fabrication of the implements of husbandry, than, feeling the certainty of being right, of which in the earlier part of their debate he had been somewhat doubtful, the father broke in with—

"Locks and bars, plough-graith and harrow-teeth!—and why not grates and fire-prongs, and Culross girdles,[1] and an ass to carry the merchandise through the country—and thou for another ass to lead it by the halter? Why, Catharine, girl, has sense altogether forsaken thee, or dost thou think that in these hard and iron days, men will give ready silver for any thing save that which can defend their own life, or enable them to take that of their enemy? We want swords to protect ourselves every moment now, thou silly wench, and not ploughs to dress the ground for the grain we may never see rise. As for the matter of our daily bread, those who are strong seize it, and live; those who are weak yield it, and die of hunger. Happy is the man who, like my worthy son, has means of obtaining his living otherwise than by the point of his sword which he makes. Preach peace to him as much as thou wilt—I will never be he will say thee nay; but as for bidding the first armourer in Scotland forego the forging of swords, curtal-axes, and harness, it is enough to drive patience itself mad—Out from my sight!—and next morning I prithee remember, that shouldst thou have the luck to see Henry the Smith, which is more than thy usage of him has deserved, you see a man who has not his match in Scotland at the use of broadsword and battle-axe, and who can work for five hundred marks a-year without breaking a holyday."

The daughter, on hearing her father speak thus peremptorily, made a low obeisance, and, without further good-night, withdrew to the chamber which was her usual sleeping apartment.

CHAPTER III

Whence cometh *Smith*, be he knight, lord, or squire,
But from the smith that forged in the fire?

VERSTEGAN.

THE armourer's heart swelled big with various and contending sensations, so that it seemed as if it would burst

[1] The *girdle* is the thin plate of iron used for the manufacture of the staple luxury of Scotland, the oaten cake. The town of Culross was long celebrated for its girdles.

the leathern doublet under which it was shrouded. He arose
—turned away his head, and extended his hand towards the
Glover, while he averted his face, as if desirous that his
emotion should not be read upon his countenance.

"Nay, hang me if I bid you farewell, man," said Simon,
striking the flat of his hand against that which the armourer
expanded towards him. "I will shake no hands with you
for an hour to come at least. Tarry but a moment, man, and
I will explain all this ; and surely a few drops of blood from
a scratch, and a few silly words from a foolish wench's lips,
are not to part father and son, when they have been so long
without meeting? Stay, then, man, if ever you would wish
for a father's blessing and St. Valentine's, whose blessed eve
this chances to be."

The Glover was soon heard loudly summoning Dorothy,
and, after some clanking of keys and trampling up and down
stairs, Dorothy appeared bearing three large rummer cups of
green glass, which were then esteemed a great and precious
curiosity, and the Glover followed with a huge bottle, equal
at least to three quarts of these degenerate days.—"Here is a
cup of wine, Henry, older by half than I am myself ; my
father had it in a gift from stout old Crabbe the Flemish
engineer, who defended Perth so stoutly in the minority of
David the Second. We glovers could always do something in
war, though our connexion with it was less than yours who
work in steel and iron. And my father had pleased old
Crabbe—some other day I will tell you how, and also how
long these bottles were concealed under ground, to save them
from the reiving Southron. So I will empty a cup to the
soul's health of my honoured father—May his sins be forgiven
him ! Dorothy, thou shalt drink this pledge, and then be
gone to thy cockloft. I know thine ears are itching, girl, but
I have that to say which no one must hear save Henry Smith,
the son of mine adoption."

Dorothy did not venture to remonstrate, but taking off
her glass, or rather her goblet, with good courage, retired to
her sleeping apartment, according to her master's commands.
The two friends were left alone.

"It grieves me, friend Henry," said Simon, filling at the
same time his own glass and his guest's, "it grieves me, from
my soul, that my daughter retains this silly humour ; but also,
methinks, thou mightst mend it. Why wouldst thou come
hither clattering with thy sword and dagger, when the girl is

so silly that she cannot bear the sight of these? Dost thou
not remember that thou hadst a sort of quarrel with her even
before thy last departure from Perth, because thou wouldst
not go like **other** honest quiet burghers, but must be ever
armed, like one of the rascally jackmen [1] that wait on the
nobility? Sure it is time enough for decent burgesses to arm,
at the tolling of the common bell, which calls us out bodin in
effeir of war." [2]

"Why, my good father, that was not my fault; but I had
no sooner quitted my nag than I run hither to tell you of my
return, thinking, if it were your will to permit me, that I would
get your advice about being Mistress Catharine's Valentine
for the year; and then I heard from Mrs. Dorothy that you
were gone to hear mass at the Black Friars. So, I thought I
would follow thither, partly to hear the same mass with you,
and partly—Our Lady and St. Valentine forgive me—to look
upon one who thinks little enough of me—And, as you entered
the church, methought I saw two or three dangerous-looking
men holding counsel together, and gazing at you and at her,
and in especial Sir John Ramorny, whom I knew well enough,
for all his disguise, and the velvet patch over his eye, and
his cloak so like a serving-man's;—so methought, father Simon,
that as you were old, and yonder slip of a Highlander something too young to do battle, I would even walk quietly after
you, not doubting, with the tools I had about me, to bring
any one to reason that might disturb you in your way home.
You know that yourself discovered me, and drew me into
the house, whether I would or no; otherwise, I promise you,
I would not have seen your daughter till I had donn'd the new
jerkin which was made at Berwick after the latest cut; nor
would I have appeared before her with these weapons, which
she dislikes so much. Although, to say truth, so many are
at deadly feud with me for one unhappy chance or another,
that it is as needful for me as for any man in Scotland to go
by night with weapons about me."

"The silly wench never thinks of that," said Simon Glover;
"she never has sense to consider, that in our dear native land
of Scotland every man deems it his privilege and duty to

---

[1] Men wearing jacks, or armour.
[2] That is, not in dread of war, but in the guise which *effeirs*, or belongs,
to war; in arms, namely, offensive and defensive. "Bodin in feir of
war," a frequent term in old Scottish history and muniments, means
arrayed in warlike guise.

avenge his own wrong. But, Harry, my boy, thou art to blame for taking her talk so much to heart. I have seen thee bold enough with other wenches—wherefore so still and tongue-tied with her?"

"Because she is something different from other maidens, father Glover—because she is not only more beautiful, but wiser, higher, holier, and seems to me as if she were made of better clay than we that approach her. I can hold my head high enough with the rest of the lasses round the Maypole; but somehow, when I approach Catharine, I feel myself an earthly, coarse, ferocious creature, scarce worthy to look on her, much less to contradict the precepts which she expounds to me."

"You are an imprudent merchant, Harry Smith," replied Simon; "and rate too high the goods you wish to purchase. Catharine is a good girl, and my daughter; but if you make her a conceited ape by your bashfulness and your flattery, neither you nor I will see our wishes accomplished."

"I often fear it, my good father," said the Smith; "for I feel how little I am deserving of Catharine."

"Feel a thread's end!" said the Glover; "feel for me, friend Smith, for Catharine and me. Think how the poor thing is beset from morning to night, and by what sort of persons, even though windows be down and doors shut. We were accosted to-day by one too powerful to be named, —ay, and he showed his displeasure openly, because I would not permit him to gallant my daughter in the church itself, when the priest was saying mass. There are others scarce less reasonable. I sometimes wish that Catharine were some degrees less fair, that she might not catch that dangerous sort of admiration, or somewhat less holy, that she might sit down like an honest woman, contented with stout Henry Smith, who could protect his wife against every sprig of chivalry in the Court of Scotland."

"And if I did not," said Henry, thrusting out a hand and arm which might have belonged to a giant for bone and muscle, "I would I may never bring hammer upon anvil again! Ay, an it were come but that length, my fair Catharine should see that there is no harm in a man having the trick of defence. But I believe she thinks the whole world is one great Minster-church, and that all who live in it should behave as if they were at an eternal mass."

"Nay, in truth," said the father, "she has strange influence over those who approach her—the Highland lad, Conachar, with whom I have been troubled for these two or three years, although you may see he has the natural spirit of his people, obeys the least sign which Catharine makes him, and, indeed, will hardly be ruled by any one else in the house. She takes much pains with him to bring him from his rude Highland habits."

Here Harry Smith became uneasy in his chair, lifted the flagon, set it down, and at length exclaimed, "The devil take the young Highland whelp and his whole kindred! What has Catharine to do to instruct such a fellow as he? He will be just like the wolf-cub that I was fool enough to train to the offices of a dog, and every one thought him reclaimed, till, in an ill hour, I went to walk on the hill of Moncrieff, when he broke loose on the Laird's flock, and made a havoc that I might well have rued, had the Laird not wanted a harness at the time. And I marvel that you, being a sensible man, father Glover, will keep this Highland young fellow—a likely one, I promise you—so nigh to Catharine, as if there were no other than your daughter to serve him for a school-mistress."

"Fie, my son, fie,—now, you are jealous," said Simon, "of a poor young fellow, who, to tell you the truth, resides here, because he may not so well live on the other side of the hill."

"Ay, ay, father Simon," retorted the Smith, who had all the narrow-minded feelings of the burghers of his time, "an it were not for fear of offence, I would say that you have even too much packing and peeling with yonder loons out of burgh."

"I must get my deer-hides, buck-skins, kid-skins, and so forth, somewhere, my good Harry,—and Highlandmen give good bargains."

"They can afford them," replied Henry, dryly; "for they sell nothing but stolen gear."

"Well, well,—be that as it may, it is not my business where they get the bestial, so I get the hides. But as I was saying, there are certain considerations why I am willing to oblige the father of this young man, by keeping him here. And he is but half a Highlander neither, and wants a thought of the dour spirit of a Glune-amie;[1]—after all

[1] Note IV.—Glune-amie.

I have seldom seen him so fierce as he showed himself but now."

"You could not, unless he had killed his man," replied the Smith, in the same dry tone.

"Nevertheless, if you wish it, Harry, I'll set all other respects aside, and send the landlouper to seek other quarters to-morrow morning."

"Nay, father," said the Smith, "you cannot suppose that Harry Gow cares the value of a smithy-dander [1] for such a cub as yonder cat-a-mountain? I care little, I promise you, though all his clan were coming down the Shoegate [2] with slogan crying, and pipes playing; I would find fifty blades and bucklers would send them back faster than they came. But, to speak truth, though it is a fool's speech too—I care not to see the fellow so much with Catharine. Remember, father Glover, your trade keeps your eyes and hands close employed, and must have your heedful care, even if this lazy lurdane wrought at it, which you know yourself he seldom does."

"And that is true," said Simon; "he cuts all his gloves out for the right hand, and never could finish a pair in his life."

"No doubt, his notions of skin-cutting are rather different," said Henry. "But with your leave, father, I would only say, that work he, or be he idle, he has no bleared eyes,—no hands seared with the hot iron, and welked by the use of the fore-hammer,—no hair rusted in the smoke, and singed in the furnace, like the hide of a badger, rather than what is fit to be covered with a Christian bonnet. Now let Catharine be as good a wench as ever lived, and I will uphold her to be the best in Perth, yet she must see and know that these things make a difference betwixt man and man, and that the difference is not in my favour."

"Here is to thee, with all my heart, son Harry," said the old man, filling a brimmer to his companion, and another to himself; "I see, that good smith as thou art, thou ken'st not the mettle that women are made of. Thou must be bold, Henry; and bear thyself not as if thou wert going to the gallow-lee, but like a gay young fellow, who knows his own worth, and will not be slighted by the best grandchild Eve ever had. Catharine is a woman like her mother, and thou thinkest foolishly to suppose they are all set on what pleases

---

[1] Cinder.   [2] A principal street in Perth.

the eye. Their ear must be pleased too, man; they must know that he whom they favour is bold and buxom, and might have the love of twenty, though he is sueing for theirs. Believe an old man, women walk more by what others think than by what they think themselves; and when she asks for the boldest man in Perth, whom shall she hear named but Harry Burn-the-wind?—The best armourer that ever fashioned weapon on anvil? why, Harry Smith again—The tightest dancer at the May-pole?—why, the lusty smith—The gayest troller of ballads?—why, who but Harry Gow?—The best wrestler, sword-and-buckler player—the king of the weapon-shawing—the breaker of mad horses—the tamer of wild Highlandmen?—ever more it is thee—thee—no one but thee.—And shall Catherine prefer yonder slip of a Highland boy to *thee*?—Pshaw! she might as well make a steel gauntlet out of kid's leather. I tell thee, Conachar is nothing to her, but so far as she would fain prevent the devil having his due of him, as of other Highlandmen—God bless her, poor thing, she would bring all mankind to better thoughts if she could."

"In which she will fail to a certainty,"—said the Smith, who as the reader may have noticed, had no good-will to the Highland race. "I will wager on Old Nick, of whom I should know something, he being indeed a worker in the same element with myself, against Catharine on that debate—the devil will have the tartan; that is sure enough."

"Ay, but Catharine," replied the Glover, "hath a second thou knowest little of—Father Clement has taken the young reiver in hand, and he fears a hundred devils as little as I do a flock of geese."

"Father Clement?" said the Smith; "you are always making some new saint in this godly city of Saint Johnston. Pray, who, for a devil's drubber, may he be?—one of your hermits that is trained for the work like a wrestler for the ring, and brings himself to trim by fasting and penance—is he not?"

"No, that is the marvel of it," said Simon; "Father Clement eats, drinks, and lives much like other folks—all the rules of the church, nevertheless, strictly observed."

"Oh, I comprehend!—a buxom priest that thinks more of good living than of good life—tipples a can on Fastern's Eve, to enable him to face Lent—has a pleasant *in principio*—and confesses all the prettiest women about the town?"

"You are on the bow-hand still, Smith. I tell you, my

daughter and I could nose out either a fasting hypocrite or a full one. But Father Clement is neither the one nor the other."

"But what is he then, in Heaven's name?"

"One who is either greatly better than half his brethren of Saint Johnston put together, or so much worse than the worst of them, that it is sin and shame that he is suffered to abide in the country."

"Methinks it were easy to tell whether he be the one or the other," said the Smith.

"Content you, my friend," said Simon, "with knowing, that if you judge Father Clement by what you see him do and hear him say, you will think of him as the best and kindest man in the world, with a comfort for every man's grief, a counsel for every man's difficulty, the rich man's surest guide, and the poor man's best friend. But if you listen to what the Dominicans say of him, he is—Benedicite!—(here the Glover crossed himself on brow and bosom)—a foul heretic, who ought by means of earthly flames to be sent to those which burn eternally."

The Smith also crossed himself, and exclaimed—"Saint Mary! father Simon, and do you, who are so good and prudent that you have been called the Wise Glover of Perth, let your daughter attend the ministry of one who—the Saints preserve us!—may be in league with the foul Fiend himself? Why, was it not a priest who raised the devil in the Meal Vennel, when Hodge Jackson's house was blown down in the great wind?—did not the devil appear in the midst of the Tay, dressed in a priest's scapular, gambolling like a pellach amongst the waves, the morning when our stately bridge was swept away?"

"I cannot tell whether he did or no," said the Glover; "I only know I saw him not. As to Catharine, she cannot be said to use Father Clement's ministry, seeing her confessor is old Father Francis the Dominican, from whom she had her shrift to-day. But women will sometimes be wilful, and sure enough she consults with Father Clement more than I could wish; and yet when I have spoken with him myself, I have thought him so good and holy a man, that I could have trusted my own salvation with him. There are bad reports of him among the Dominicans, that is certain. But what have we laymen to do with such things, my son? Let us pay Mother Church her dues, give our alms, confess and do our penances duly, and the saints will bear us out."

"Ay, truly; and they will have consideration," said the Smith, "for any rash and unhappy blow that a man may deal in a fight, when his party was on defence, and standing up to him; and that's the only creed a man can live upon in Scotland, let your daughter think what she pleases. Marry, a man must know his fence, or have a short lease of his life, in any place where blows are going so rife. Five nobles to our altar have cleared me for the best man I ever had misfortune with."

"Let us finish our flask, then," said the old Glover; "for I reckon the Dominican tower is tolling midnight. And hark thee, son Henry; be at the lattice window on our east gable by the very peep of dawn, and make me aware thou art come by whistling the Smith's call gently. I will contrive that Catharine shall look out at the window, and thus thou wilt have all the privileges of being a gallant Valentine through the rest of the year; which if thou canst not use to thine own advantage, I shall be led to think, that for all thou be'st covered with the lion's hide, Nature has left on thee the long ears of the ass."

"Amen, father," said the armourer; "a hearty good-night to you; and God's blessing on your roof-tree, and those whom it covers. You shall hear the Smith's call sound by cock-crowing; I warrant I put Sir Chanticleer to shame."

So saying, he took his leave; and, though completely undaunted, moved through the deserted streets like one upon his guard, to his own dwelling, which was situated in the Mill Wynd, at the western end of Perth.

CHAPTER IV

What's all this turmoil crammed into our parts?
Faith, but the pit-a-pat of poor young hearts.

DRYDEN.

THE sturdy armourer was not, it may be believed, slack in keeping the appointment assigned by his intended father-in-law. He went through the process of his toilet with more than ordinary care, throwing, as far as he could, those points which had a military air into the shade. He was far too noted a person to venture to go entirely unarmed in a town where he had indeed many friends, but also, from the character of many of his former exploits, several deadly enemies, at whose hands, should they take him at advantage, he knew he had little mercy to expect. He therefore wore under his jerkin a *secret*, or coat of chain-mail, made so light and flexible that it interfered as little with his movements as a modern under-waistcoat, yet of such proof as he might safely depend upon, every ring of it having been wrought and joined by his own hands. Above this he wore, like others of his age and degree, the Flemish hose and doubtlet, which, in honour of the holy tide, were of the best superfine English broad cloth, light blue in colour, slashed out with black satin, and passamented (laced, that is) with embroidery of black silk. His walking boots were of cordovan leather; his cloak of good Scottish grey, which served to conceal a whinger, or *couteau de chasse*, that hung at his belt, and was his only offensive weapon, for he carried in his hand but a rod of holly. His black velvet bonnet was lined with steel, quilted between the metal and his head, and thus constituted a means of defence which might safely be trusted to.

Upon the whole, Henry had the appearance, to which he was well entitled, of a burgher of wealth and consideration, assuming, in his dress, as much consequence as he could display, without stepping beyond his own rank, and encroaching on that of the gentry. Neither did his frank and manly deportment, though indicating a total indifference to danger, bear the least resemblance to that of the bravoes or swash-bucklers of the day, amongst whom Henry was sometimes unjustly ranked by those who imputed the frays, in which he was so often engaged, to a quarrelsome and violent temper, resting upon a consciousness of his personal strength and knowledge of his weapon. On the contrary, every feature bore the easy and good-humoured expression of one who neither thought of inflicting mischief, nor dreaded it from others.

Having attired himself in his best, the honest armourer next placed nearest to his heart (which throbbed at its touch) a little gift which he had long provided for Catharine Glover, and which his quality of Valentine would presently give him the title to present, and her to receive, without regard to maidenly scruples. It was a small ruby cut into the form of a heart, transfixed with a golden arrow, and was enclosed in a small purse made of links of the finest work in steel, as if it had been designed for a hauberk to a king. Round the verge of the purse were these words—

> Love's darts
> Cleave hearts
> Through mail-shirts.

This device had cost the armourer some thought, and he was much satisfied with his composition, because it seemed to imply that his skill could defend all hearts saving his own. He wrapped himself in his cloak, and hastened through the still silent streets, determined to appear at the window appointed a little before dawn.

With this purpose he passed up the High Street,[1] and turned down the opening where Saint John's Church now stands, in order to proceed to Curfew Street;[2] when it occurred to him, from the appearance of the sky, that he was at least an hour too early for his purpose, and that it would be better not to appear at the place of rendezvous till nearer the time assigned. Other gallants were not unlikely to be on the watch as well as himself, about the house of the Fair Maid of Perth; and he knew his own foible so well, as to be sensible of the great chance of a scuffle arising betwixt them. "I have the advantage," he thought, "by my father Simon's friendship; and why should I stain my fingers with the blood of the poor creatures that are not worthy my notice, since they are so much less fortunate than myself? No—no—I will be wise for once, and keep at a distance from all temptation to a broil. They shall have no more time to quarrel with me than just what it may require for me to give the signal, and for my father Simon to answer it. I wonder how the old man will contrive to bring her to the window? I fear, if she knew his purpose, he would find it difficult to carry it into execution."

While these lover-like thoughts were passing through his brain, the armourer loitered in his pace, often turning his eyes eastward, and eyeing the firmament, in which no slight shades of grey were beginning to flicker, to announce the approach of dawn, however distant, which, to the impatience of the stout armourer, seemed on that morning to abstain longer than usual from occupying her eastern barbican. He was now passing slowly under the wall of Saint Anne's Chapel,

---

[1] Note V.—High Street.   [2] Note VI.—Curfew Street.

(not failing to cross himself and say an *ave*, as he trode the consecrated ground,) when a voice, which seemed to come from behind one of the flying buttresses of the chapel, said, "He lingers that has need to run."

"Who speaks?" said the armourer, looking around him, somewhat startled at an address so unexpected, both in its tone and tenor.

"No matter who speaks," answered the same voice. "Do thou make great speed, or thou wilt scarce make good speed. Bandy not words, but begone."

"Saint or sinner, angel or devil," said Henry, crossing himself, "your advice touches me but too dearly to be neglected. Saint Valentine be my speed!"

So saying, he instantly changed his loitering pace to one with which few people could have kept up, and in an instant was in Couvrefew Street. He had not made three steps towards Simon Glover's, which stood in the midst of the narrow street, when two men started from under the houses on different sides, and advanced, as it were by concert, to intercept his passage. The imperfect light only permitted him to discern that they wore the Highland mantle.

"Clear the way, catheran," said the armourer, in the deep stern voice which corresponded with the breadth of his chest.

They did not answer, at least intelligibly; but he could see that they drew their swords, with the purpose of withstanding him by violence. Conjecturing some evil, but of what kind he could not anticipate, Henry instantly determined to make his way through whatever odds, and defend his mistress, or at least die at her feet. He cast his cloak over his left arm as a buckler, and advanced rapidly and steadily to the two men. The nearest made a thrust at him, but Henry Smith, parrying the blow with his cloak, dashed his arm in the man's face, and tripping him at the same time, gave him a severe fall on the causeway; while almost at the same instant he struck a blow with his whinger at the fellow who was upon his right hand, so severely applied, that he also lay prostrate by his associate. Meanwhile, the armourer pushed forward in alarm, for which the circumstance of the street being guarded or defended by strangers who conducted themselves with such violence, afforded sufficient reason. He heard a suppressed whisper and a bustle under the Glover's windows—those very windows from which he had expected to be hailed by Catharine as her Valentine. He kept to the opposite side of the street, that he might reconnoitre their number and purpose. But one of the party, who were beneath the window, observing or hearing him, crossed the street also, and taking him doubtless for one of the sentinels, asked, in a whisper, "What noise was yonder, Kenneth? why gave you not the signal?"

"Villain!" said Henry "you are discovered, and you shall die the death!"

As he spoke thus, he dealt the stranger a blow with his weapon, which would probably have made his words good, had not the man, raising his arm, received on his hand the blow meant for his head. The wound must have been a severe one, for he staggered and fell with a deep groan. Without noticing him farther, Henry Smith sprung forward upon a party of men who seemed engaged in placing a ladder against the lattice window in the gable. Henry did not stop either to count their numbers or to ascertain their purpose. But crying the alarm-word of the town, and giving the signal at which the burghers were wont to collect, he rushed on the nightwalkers, one of whom was in the act of ascending the ladder. The Smith seized it by the rounds, threw it down on the pavement, and placing his foot on the body of the man who had been mounting, prevented him from regaining his feet. His accomplices struck fiercely at Henry, to extricate their companion. But his mail-coat stood him in good stead, and he repaid their blows with interest, shouting aloud, "Help, help, for bonnie St. Johnston!—Bows and blades, brave citizens! bows and blades!—they break into our houses under cloud of night."

These words, which resounded far through the streets, were accompanied by as many fierce blows, dealt with good effect among those whom the armourer assailed. In the meantime, the inhabitants of the street began to awaken and appear on the street in their shirts, with swords and targets, and some of them with torches. The assailants now endeavoured to make their escape, which all of them effected excepting the man who had been thrown down along with the ladder. Him the intrepid armourer had caught by the throat in the scuffle, and held as fast as the greyhound holds the hare. The other wounded men were borne off by their comrades.

"Here are a sort of knaves breaking peace within burgh," said Henry to the neighbours who began to assemble; "make after the rogues. They cannot all get off, for I have maimed some of them; the blood will guide you to them."

"Some Highland catherans," said the citizens,—"up, and chase, neighbours!"

"Ay, chase—chase,—leave me to manage this fellow," continued the armourer.

The assistants dispersed in different directions, their lights flashing, and their cries resounding through the whole adjacent district.

In the meantime the armourer's captive entreated for freedom, using both promises and threats to obtain it. "As thou art a gentleman," he said, "let me go, and what is past shall be forgiven."

"I am no gentleman," said Henry—"I am Hal of the Wynd, a burgess of Perth; and I have done nothing to need forgiveness."

"Villain, thou hast done thou knowest not what! But let me go, and I will fill thy bonnet with gold pieces."

"I shall fill thy bonnet with a cloven head presently," said the armourer, "unless thou stand still as a true prisoner."

"What is the matter, my son Harry?" said Simon, who now appeared at the window.—"I hear thy voice in another tone than I expected.—What is all this noise; and why are the neighbours gathering to the affray?"

"There have been a proper set of limmers about to scale your windows, father Simon; but I am like to prove godfather to one of them, whom I hold here, as fast as ever vice held iron."

"Hear me, Simon Glover," said the prisoner; "let me but speak one word with you in private and rescue me from the gripe of this iron-fisted and leaden-pated clown, and I will show thee, that no harm was designed to thee or thine; and, moreover, tell thee what will much advantage thee."

"I should know that voice," said Simon Glover, who now came to the door with a dark-lantern in his hand. "Son Smith, let this young man speak with me. There is no danger in him, I promise you. Stay but an instant where you are, and let no one enter the house, either to attack or defend. I will be answerable that this galliard meant but some Saint Valentine's jest."

So saying, the old man pulled in the prisoner and shut the door, leaving Henry a little surprised at the unexpected light in which his father-in-law had viewed the affray. "A jest!" he said; "it might have been a strange jest, if they had got into the maiden's sleeping room!—And they would have done so, had it not been for the honest friendly voice from betwixt the buttresses, which, if it were not that of the blessed Saint, (though what am I that the holy person should speak to me?) could not sound in that place without her permission and assent, and for which I will promise her a wax candle at her shrine, as long as my whinger,—and I would I had had my two-handed broadsword instead, both for the sake of St. Johnston and of the rogues—for of a certain, those whingers are pretty toys, but more fit for a boy's hand than a man's. Oh, my old two-handed Trojan, hadst thou been in my hands, as thou hang'st presently at the tester of my bed, the legs of those rogues had not carried their bodies so clean off the field.—But there come lighted torches and drawn swords.—So ho—stand!—Are you for Saint Johnston?—If friends to the bonnie burgh, you are well come."

"We have been but bootless hunters," said the townsmen. "We followed by the tracks of the blood into the Dominican burial-ground, and we started two fellows from amongst the tombs, supporting betwixt them a third, who had probably got some of your marks about him, Harry. They got to the postern gate before we could overtake them, and rang the sanctuary bell,—the gate opened, and in went they. So they are safe in girth and sanctuary, and we may go to our cold beds and warm us."

"Ay," said one of the party, "the good Dominicans have always some devout brother of their convent sitting up to open the gate of the sanctuary to any poor soul that is in trouble, and desires shelter in the church."

"Yes, if the poor hunted soul can pay for it," said another; "but, truly, if he be poor in purse as well as in spirit, he may stand on the outside till the hounds come up with him."

A third, who had been poring for a few minutes upon the ground by advantage of his torch, now looked upwards and spoke. He was a brisk, forward, rather corpulent little man, called Oliver Proudfute, reasonably wealthy, and a leading man in his craft, which was that of bonnet-makers; he, therefore, spoke as one in authority.—"Canst tell us, jolly Smith," —for they recognized each other by the lights which were brought into the streets,—"what manner of fellows they were who raised up this fray within burgh?"

"The two that I first saw," answered the armourer, "seemed to me, as well as I could observe them, to have Highland plaids about them."

"Like enough—like enough," answered another citizen, shaking his head. "It's a shame the breaches in our walls are not repaired, and that these land-louping Highland scoundrels are left at liberty to take honest men and women out of their beds any night that is dark enough."

"But look here, neighbours," said Oliver Proudfute, showing a bloody hand which he had picked up from the ground; "when did such a hand as this tie a Highlandman's brogues? It is large, indeed, and bony, but as fine as a lady's, with a ring that sparkles like a gleaming candle. Simon Glover has made gloves for this hand before now, if I am not much mistaken, for he works for all the courtiers." The spectators here began to gaze on the bloody token with various comments.

"If that is the case," said one, "Harry Smith had best show a clean pair of heels for it, since the Justiciar will scarce think the protecting a burgess's house an excuse for cutting off a gentleman's hand. There be hard laws against mutilation."

"Fie upon you, that you will say so, Michael Wabster," answered the bonnet-maker; "are we not representatives and successors of the stout old Romans, who built Perth as like to their own city as they could? And have we not charters from all our noble kings and progenitors, as being their loving liegemen? And would you have us now yield up our rights, privileges, and immunities, our outfang and infang, our hand-habend, our back-bearand, and our blood-suits, and amerciaments, escheats, and commodities, and suffer an honest burgess's house to be assaulted without seeking for redress? No—brave citizens, craftsmen, and burgesses, the Tay shall flow back to Dunkeld before we submit to such injustice!"

"And how can we help it?" said a grave old man, who stood leaning on a two-handed sword—"What would you have us do?"

"Marry, Bailie Craigdallie, I wonder that you, of all men, ask the question. I would have you pass like true men from this very place to the King's Grace's presence, raise him from his royal rest, and presenting to him the piteous case of our being called forth from our beds at this season, with little better covering than these shirts, I would show him this bloody token, and know from his Grace's own royal lips, whether it is just and honest that his loving lieges should be thus treated by the knights and nobles of his deboshed court. And this I call pushing our cause warmly."

" Warmly, sayst thou ? " replied the old burgess ; " why, so warmly, that we shall all die of cold, man, before the porter turn a key to let us into the royal presence.—Come, friends, the night is bitter—we have kept our watch and ward like men, and our jolly Smith hath given a warning to those that would wrong us, which shall be worth twenty proclamations of the King. To-morrow is a new day ; we will consult on this matter on this self-same spot, and consider what measures should be taken for discovery and pursuit of the villains. And therefore let us dismiss before the heart's-blood freeze in our veins."

" Bravo, bravo, neighbour Craigdallie—St. Johnston for ever ! "

Oliver Proudfute would still have spoken ; for he was one of those pitiless orators who think that their eloquence can overcome all inconveniences in time, place, and circumstances. But no one would listen ; and the citizens dispersed to their own houses by the light of the dawn, which began now to streak the horizon.

They were scarce gone ere the door of the Glover's house opened, and seizing the Smith by the hand, the old man pulled him in.

" Where is the prisoner ? " demanded the armourer.

" He is gone—escaped—fled—what do I know of him ? " said the Glover. " He got out at the back door, and so through the little garden.—Think not of him, but come and see the Valentine, whose honour and life you have saved this morning."

" Let me but sheathe my weapon," said the Smith—" let me but wash my hands."

" There is not an instant to lose, she is up and almost dressed.—Come on, man. She shall see thee with thy good weapon in thy hand, and with villain's blood on thy fingers, that she may know what is the value of a true man's service. She has stopped my mouth over long with her pruderies and her scruples. I will have her know what a brave man's love is worth, and a bold burgess's to boot."

CHAPTER V

Up! lady fair, and braid thy hair,
And rouse thee in the breezy air.
Up! quit thy bower, late wears the hour,
Long have the rooks caw'd round the tower.
JOANNA BAILLIE.

STARTLED from her repose by the noise of the affray, the Fair Maid of Perth had listened in breathless terror to the sounds of violence and outcry which arose from the street. She had sunk on her knees to pray for assistance, and when she distinguished the voices of neighbours and friends collected for her protection, she remained in the same posture to return thanks. She was still kneeling when her father almost thrust her champion, Henry Smith, into her apartment, the bashful lover hanging back at first, as if afraid to give offence, and, on observing her posture, from respect to her devotion.

"Father," said the armourer, "she prays—I dare no more speak to her than to a bishop when he says mass."

"Now, go thy ways, for a right valiant and courageous blockhead," said her father; and then speaking to his daughter, he added,—"Heaven is best thanked, my daughter, by gratitude shown to our fellow-creatures. Here comes the instrument by whom God has rescued thee from death, or perhaps from dishonour worse than death. Receive him, Catharine, as thy true Valentine, and him whom I desire to see my affectionate son."

"Not thus—father," replied Catharine. "I can see—can speak to no one now. I am not ungrateful—perhaps I am too thankful to the instrument of our safety; but let me thank the guardian Saint who sent me this timely relief, and give me but a moment to don my kirtle."

"Nay, God-a-mercy, wench, it were hard to deny thee time to busk thy body-clothes, since the request is the only words like a woman that thou hast uttered for these ten days.—Truly, son Harry, I would my daughter would put off being entirely a saint, till the time comes for her being canonized for Saint Catharine the Second."

"Nay, jest not, father; for I will swear she has at least one sincere adorer already, who hath devoted himself to her pleasure, so far as sinful man may.—Fare-thee-well then, for the moment, fair maiden," he concluded, raising his voice, "and Heaven send thee dreams as peaceful as thy waking thoughts. I go to watch thy slumbers, and woe with him that shall intrude on them!"

"Nay, good and brave Henry, whose warm heart is at such variance with thy reckless hand, thrust thyself into no farther quarrels to-night; but take the kindest thanks, and with these, try to assume the peaceful thoughts which you assign to me. To-morrow we will meet, that I may assure you of my gratitude —Farewell."

"And farewell, lady and light of my heart!" said the armourer, and, descending the stair which led to Catharine's apartment, was about to sally forth into the street, when the Glover caught him by the arm.

"I shall like the ruffle of to-night," said he, "better than I ever thought to do the clashing of steel, if it brings my daughter to her senses, Harry, and teaches her what thou art worth. By St. Macgrider![1] I even love these roysterers, and am sorry for that poor lover who will never wear left-handed chevron again. Ay! He has lost that which he will miss all the days of his life, especially when he goes to pull on his gloves,—ay, he will pay but half a fee to my craft in future.—Nay, not a step from this house to-night," he continued. "Thou dost not leave us, I promise thee, my son."

"I do not mean it. But I will, with your permission, watch in the street. The attack may be renewed."

"And if it be," said Simon, "thou wilt have better access to drive them back, having the vantage of the house. It is the way of fighting which suits us burghers best—that of resisting from behind stone walls. Our duty of watch and ward teaches us that trick; besides, enough are awake and astir to ensure us peace and quiet till morning. So come in this way."

So saying, he drew Henry, nothing loath, into the same apartment where they had supped, and where the old woman, who was on foot, disturbed as others had been by the nocturnal affray, soon roused up the fire.

"And now, my doughty son," said the Glover, "what liquor wilt thou pledge thy father in?"

Henry Smith had suffered himself to sink mechanically upon a seat of old black oak, and now gazed on the fire, that flashed back a ruddy light over his manly features. He muttered to

[1] A place called vulgarly Ecclesmagirdie (Ecclesia Macgirdi), not far from Perth, still preserves the memory of this old Gaelic saint from utter Lethe.

himself half audibly—" *Good* Henry—*brave* Henry—Ah ! had she but said, *dear* Henry !"

" What liquors be these ?" said the old Glover, laughing. " My cellar holds none such; but if sack, or rhenish, or wine of Gascony can serve, why, say the word and the flagon foams—that is all."

" The *kindest* thanks," said the armourer, still musing, " that's more than she ever said to me before—the *kindest* thanks—what may not that stretch to ?"

" It shall stretch like kid's leather, man," said the Glover, " if thou wilt but be ruled, and say what thou wilt take for thy morning's draught."

" Whatever thou wilt, father," answered the armourer carelessly, and relapsed into the analysis of Catharine's speech to him. " She spoke of my warm heart ; but she also spoke of my reckless hand. What earthly thing can I do to get rid of this fighting fancy ? Certainly I were best strike my right hand off, and nail it to the door of a church, that it may never do me discredit more."

" You have chopped off hands enough for one night," said his friend, setting a flagon of wine on the table. " Why dost thou vex thyself, man ? She would love thee twice as well did she not see how thou doatest upon her. But it becomes serious now. I am not to have the risk of my booth being broken, and my house plundered, by the hell-raking followers of the nobles, because she is called the Fair Maid of Perth, and please ye. No, she shall know I am her father, and will have that obedience to which law and gospel give me right. I will have her thy wife, Henry, my heart of gold—thy wife, my man of mettle, and that before many weeks are over. Come, come, here is to thy merry bridal, jolly Smith."

The father quaffed a large cup, and filled it to his adopted son, who raised it slowly to his head ; then, ere it had reached his lips, replaced it suddenly on the table and shook his head.

" Nay, if thou wilt not pledge me to such a health, I know no one who will," said Simon. " What canst thou mean, thou foolish lad ? Here has a chance happened, which in a manner places her in thy power, since from one end of the city to the other, all would cry fie on her if she should say thee nay. Here am I her father, not only consenting to the cutting out of the match, but willing to see you two as closely united together, as ever needle stitched buckskin. And with all this on thy side, fortune, father, and all, thou lookest like a distracted lover in a ballad, more like to pitch thyself into the Tay, than to woo a lass that may be had for the asking, if you can but choose the lucky minute."

"Ay, but that lucky minute, father! I question much if Catharine ever has such a moment to glance on earth and its inhabitants, as might lead her to listen to a coarse ignorant borrel man like me. I cannot tell how it is, father; elsewhere I can hold up my head like another man, but with your saintly daughter I lose heart and courage, and I cannot help thinking that it would be wellnigh robbing a holy shrine, if I could succeed in surprising her affections. Her thoughts are too much fitted for heaven to be wasted on such a one as I am."

"E'en as you like, Henry," answered the Glover. "My daughter is not courting you any more than I am—a fair offer is no cause of feud;—only if you think that I will give in to her foolish notions of a convent, take it with you that I will never listen to them. I love and honour the church," he said, crossing himself. "I pay her rights duly and cheerfully; tithes and alms, wine and wax, I pay them as justly, I say, as any man in Perth of my means doth; but I cannot afford the church my only and single ewe-lamb that I have in the world. Her mother was dear to me on earth, and is now an angel in heaven. Catharine is all I have to remind me of her I have lost; and if she goes to the cloister, it shall be when these old eyes are closed for ever, and not sooner.—But as for you, friend Gow, I pray you will act according to your own best liking. I want to force no wife on you, I promise you."

"Nay, now, you beat the iron twice over," said Henry. "It is thus we always end, father, by your being testy with me for not doing that thing in the world which would make me happiest, were I to have it in my power. Why, father, I would the keenest dirk I ever forged were sticking in my heart at this moment, if there is one single particle in it that is not more your daughter's property than my own. But what can I do? I cannot think less of her, or more of myself, than we both deserve; and what seems to you so easy and certain, is to me as difficult as it would be to work a steel hauberk out of hards of flax.—But here is to you, father," he added, in a more cheerful tone; "and here is to my fair Saint and Valentine, as I hope your Catharine will be mine for the season. And let me not keep your old head longer from the pillow, but make interest with your feather-bed till daybreak; and then you must be my guide to your daughter's chamber-door, and my apology for entering it, to bid her good-morrow, for the brightest that the sun will awaken in the city or for miles round it !"

"No bad advice, my son," said the honest Glover. "But you, what will you do? will you lie down beside me, or take a part of Conachar's bed?"

"Neither," answered Harry Gow; "I should but prevent your rest; and for me this easy-chair is worth a down bed, and I will sleep like a sentinel, with my graith about me."

As he spoke, he laid his hand on his sword.

"Nay, Heaven send us no more need of weapons.—Good-night, or rather, good-morrow, till day-peep—and the first who wakes calls up the other."

Thus parted the two burghers. The Glover retired to his bed, and, it is to be supposed, to rest. The lover was not so fortunate. His bodily frame easily bore the fatigue which he had encountered in the course of the night, but his mind was of a different and more delicate mould. In one point of view, he was but the stout burgher of his period, proud alike of his art in making weapons, and wielding them when made; his professional jealousy, personal strength, and skill in the use of arms, brought him into many quarrels, which had made him generally feared, and in some instances disliked. But with these qualities were united the simple good-nature of a child, and at the same time an imaginative and enthusiastic temper, which seemed little to correspond with his labours at the forge, or his combats in the field. Perhaps a little of the harebrained and ardent feeling which he had picked out of old ballads, or from the metrical romances which were his sole source of information or knowledge, may have been the means of pricking him on to some of his achievements, which had often a rude strain of chivalry in them; at least, it was certain that his love to the fair Catharine had in it a delicacy such as might have become the squire of low degree, who was honoured, if song speaks truth, with the smiles of the King of Hungary's daughter. His sentiments towards her were certainly as exalted as if they had been fixed upon an actual angel, which made old Simon, and others who watched his conduct, think that his passion was too high and devotional to be successful with maiden of mortal mould. They were mistaken, however. Catharine, coy and reserved as she was, had a heart which could feel and understand the nature and depth of the armourer's passion; and whether she was able to repay it or not, she had as much secret pride in the attachment of the redoubted Henry Gow, as a lady of romance may be supposed to have in the company of a tame lion, who follows to provide for and defend her. It was with sentiments of the most sincere gratitude that she recollected, as she awoke at dawn, the services of Henry during the course of the eventful night, and the first thought which she dwelt upon, was the means of making him understand her feelings.

Arising hastily from bed, and half-blushing at her own purpose—"I have been cold to him, and perhaps unjust; I will not be ungrateful," she said to herself, "though I cannot yield to his suit; I will not wait till my father compels me to receive him as my Valentine for the year; I will seek him out, and choose him myself. I have thought other girls bold, when they did something like this; but I shall thus best please my father, and but discharge the rites due to good Saint Valentine by showing my gratitude to this brave man."

Hastily slipping on her dress, which, nevertheless, was left a good deal more disordered than usual, she tripped down stairs and opened the door of the chamber, in which, as she had guessed, her lover had passed the hours after the fray. Catharine paused at the door, and became half afraid of executing her purpose, which not only permitted but enjoined the Valentines of the year to begin their connexion with a kiss of affection. It was looked upon as a peculiarly propitious omen, if the one party could find the other asleep, and awaken him or her by performance of this interesting ceremony.

Never was a fairer opportunity offered for commencing this mystic tie, than that which now presented itself to Catharine. After many and various thoughts, sleep had at length overcome the stout armourer in the chair in which he had deposited himself. His features, in repose, had a more firm and manly cast than Catharine had thought, who, having generally seen them fluctuating between shamefacedness and apprehension of her displeasure, had been used to connect with them some idea of imbecility.

"He looks very stern," she said; "if he should be angry—and then when he awakes—we are alone—if I should call Dorothy—if I should wake my father—but no! it is a thing of custom, and done in all maidenly and sisterly love and honour. I will not suppose that Henry can misconstrue it, and I will not let a childish bashfulness put my gratitude to sleep."

So saying, she tripped along the floor of the apartment with a light, though hesitating step, and a cheek crimsoned at her own purpose; and gliding to the chair of the sleeper, dropped a kiss upon his lips as light as if a rose-leaf had fallen on them. The slumbers must have been slight which such a touch could dispel, and the dreams of the sleeper must needs have been connected with the cause of the interruption, since Henry, instantly starting up, caught the maiden in his arms, and attempted to return in ecstasy the salute which had broken his repose. But Catharine struggled in his embrace; and as her efforts implied alarmed modesty, rather than maidenly coyness, her bashful lover suffered her to escape a grasp, from which twenty times her strength could not have extricated her.

"Nay, be not angry, good Henry," said Catharine, in the kindest tone, to her surprised lover. "I have paid my vows to Saint Valentine, to show how I value the mate which he has sent me for the year. Let but my father be present, and I will not dare to refuse thee the revenge you may claim for a broken sleep."

"Let not that be a hinderance," said the old Glover, rushing in ecstasy into the room—"to her, Smith—to her—strike while the iron is hot, and teach her what it is not to let sleeping dogs lie still."

Thus encouraged, Henry, though perhaps with less alarming vivacity, again seized the blushing maiden in his arms, who submitted with a tolerable grace to receive repayment of her salute, a dozen times repeated, and with an energy very different from that which had provoked such severe retaliation. At length, she again extricated herself from her lover's arms, and, as if frightened and repenting what she had done, threw herself into a seat, and covered her face with her hands.

"Cheer up, thou silly girl," said her father, "and be not ashamed that thou hast made the two happiest men in Perth, since thy old father is one of them. Never was kiss so well bestowed, and meet it is that it should be suitably returned. Look up, my darling! look up, and let me see thee give but one smile. By my honest word, the sun that now rises over our fair city shows no sight that can give me greater pleasure.—What," he continued, in a jocose tone, "thou thoughtst thou hadst Jamie Keddie's [1] ring, and couldst walk invisible? but not so, my fairy of the dawning. Just as I was about to rise, I heard thy chamber door open, and watched thee down stairs—not to protect thee against this sleepy-headed Henry, but to see with my own delighted eyes, my beloved girl do that which her father most wished.—Come, put down these foolish hands, and though thou blushest a little, it will only the better grace St. Valentine's morn, when blushes best become a maiden's cheek."

As Simon Glover spoke, he pulled away, with gentle violence, the hands which hid his daughter's face. She blushed deeply indeed, but there was more than maiden's shame in her face, and her eyes were fast filling with tears.

"What! weeping, love?" continued her father,—"nay, nay, this is more than need—Henry, help me to comfort this little fool."

Catharine made an effort to collect herself and to smile, but the smile was of a melancholy and serious cast.

"I only meant to say, father," said the Fair Maid of Perth, with continued exertion, "that in choosing Henry Gow for my Valentine, and rendering to him the rights and greeting of the morning, according to wonted custom, I meant but to show my gratitude to him for his manly and faithful service, and my obedience to you.—But do not lead him to think—and, oh, dearest father, do not yourself entertain an idea, that I meant more than what the promise to be his faithful and affectionate Valentine through the year requires of me."

"Ay—ay—ay—ay—we understand it all," said Simon, in the soothing tone which nurses apply to children—"We understand what the meaning is; enough for once; enough for once. Thou shalt not be frightened or hurried.—Loving, true, and faithful Valentines are ye, and the rest as Heaven and opportunity shall permit. Come, prithee, have done— wring not thy tiny hands, nor fear farther persecution now. Thou hast done bravely, excellently—And now, away to Dorothy, and call up the old sluggard; we must have a substantial breakfast, after a night of confusion and a morning of joy; and thy hand will be needed to prepare for us some of these delicate cakes, which no one can make but thyself; and well hast thou a right to the secret, seeing who taught

---

[1] There is a tradition that one Keddie, a tailor, found in ancient days a ring, possessing the properties of that of Gyges, in a cavern of the romantic hill of Kinnoul, near Perth.

it thee.—Ah! health to the soul of thy dearest mother," he added, with a sigh; "how blithe would she have been to see this happy St. Valentine's morning!"

Catharine took the opportunity of escape which was thus given her, and glided from the room. To Henry it seemed as if the sun had disappeared from the heaven at mid-day, and left the world in sudden obscurity. Even the high-swelled hopes with which the late incident had filled him, began to quail, as he reflected upon her altered demeanour—the tears in her eyes—the obvious fear which occupied her features —and the pains she had taken to show, as plainly as delicacy would permit, that the advances which she had made to him were limited to the character with which the rites of the day had invested him. Her father looked on his fallen countenance with something like surprise and displeasure.

"In the name of good St. John, what has befallen you, that makes you look as grave as an owl, when a lad of your spirit, having really such a fancy for this poor girl as you pretend, ought to be as lively as a lark?"

"Alas, father!" replied the crestfallen lover, "there is that written on her brow, which says she loves me well enough to be my Valentine, especially since you wish it—but not well enough to be my wife."

"Now, a plague on thee for a cold, down-hearted goose-cap," answered the father. "I can read a woman's brow as well, and better than thou; and I can see no such matter on hers. What, the foul fiend, man! there thou wast lying like a lord in thy elbow-chair, as sound asleep as a judge, when, hadst thou been a lover of any spirit, thou wouldst have been watching the east for the first ray of the sun. But there thou layest, snoring I warrant, thinking nought about her, or any thing else; and the poor girl rises at peep of day, lest any one else should pick up her most precious and vigilant Valentine, and wakes thee with a grace, which—so help me St. Macgrider!—would have put life in an anvil; and thou awakest to hone, and pine, and moan, as if she had drawn a hot iron across thy lips! I would to St. John she had sent old Dorothy on the errand, and bound thee for thy Valentine service to that bundle of dry bones, with never a tooth in her head. She were fittest Valentine in Perth for so craven a wooer."

"As to craven, father," answered the Smith, "there are twenty good cocks, whose combs I have plucked, can tell thee if I am craven or no. And Heaven knows, that I would give my good land, held by burgess' tenure, with smithy, bellows, tongs, anvil, and all, providing it would make your view of the matter the true one. But it is not of her coyness, or her blushes, that I speak; it is of the paleness which so soon followed the red, and chased it from her cheeks; and it is of the tears which succeeded. It was like the April shower stealing upon, and obscuring the fairest dawning that ever beamed over the Tay."

"Tutti taitti," replied the Glover; "neither Rome nor Perth were built in a day. Thou hast fished salmon a thousand times, and mightst have taken a lesson. When the fish has taken the fly, to pull a hard strain on the line would snap the tackle to pieces, were it made of wire. Ease your hand, man, and let him rise; take leisure, and in half-an-hour thou layest him on the bank.—There is a beginning, as fair as you could wish, unless you expect the poor wench to come to thy bedside, as she did to thy chair; and that is not the fashion of modest maidens. But observe me; after we have had our breakfast, I will take care thou hast an opportunity to speak thy mind; only beware thou be neither too backward, nor press her too hard. Give her line enough; but do not slack too fast, and my life for yours upon the issue."

"Do what I can, father," answered Henry, "you will always lay the blame on me; either that I give too much head, or that I strain the tackle. I would give the best habergeon I ever wrought, that the difficulty in truth rested with me; for there were then the better chance of its being removed. I own, however, I am but an ass in the trick of bringing about such discourse as is to the purpose for the occasion."

"Come into the booth with me, my son, and I will furnish thee with a fitting theme. Thou knowest the maiden who ventures to kiss a sleeping man, wins of him a pair of gloves. Come to my booth; thou shalt have a pair of delicate kid-skin, that will exactly suit her hand and arm.—I was thinking of her poor mother when I shaped them," added honest Simon, with a sigh; "and except Catharine, I know not the woman in Scotland whom they would fit, though I have measured most of the high beauties of the court. Come with me, I say, and thou shalt be provided with a theme to wag thy tongue upon, providing thou hast courage and caution to stand by thee in thy wooing."

CHAPTER VI

Never to man shall Catharine give her hand.
Taming of the Shrew.

THE breakfast was served, and the thin soft cakes, made of flour and honey according to the family receipt, were not only commended with all the partiality of a father and a lover, but done liberal justice to in the mode which is best proof of cake as well as pudding. They talked, jested, and laughed. Catharine, too, had recovered her equanimity where the dames and damsels of the period were apt to lose theirs—in the kitchen, namely, and in the superintendence of household affairs, in which she was an adept. I question much, if the perusal of Seneca for as long a period, would have had equal effect in composing her mind.

Old Dorothy sat down at the board-end, as was the homespun fashion of the period; and so much were the two men amused with their own conversation,—and Catharine occupied either in attending to them, or with her own reflections,—that the old woman was the first who observed the absence of the boy Conachar.

"It is true," said the Master Glover; "go call him, the idle Highland loon. He was not seen last night during the fray neither, at least I saw him not. Did any of you observe him?"

The reply was negative; and Henry's observation followed,—

"There are times when Highlanders can couch like their own deer,—ay, and run from danger too as fast. I have seen them do so myself, for the matter of that."

"—And there are times," replied Simon, "when King Arthur and his Round Table could not make stand against them. I wish, Henry, you would speak more reverently of the Highlanders. They are often in Perth, both alone and in numbers; and you ought to keep peace with them, so long as they will keep peace with you."

An answer of defiance rose to Henry's lips, but he prudently suppressed it.

"Why, thou knowest, father," he said, smiling, "that we handicrafts best love the folks we live by; now, my craft provides for valiant and noble knights, gentle squires and pages, stout men-at-arms, and others that wear the weapons which we make. It is natural I should like the Ruthvens, the Lindsays, the Ogilvys, the Oliphants, and so many others of our brave and noble neighbours, who are sheathed in steel of my making, like so many Paladins, better than those naked, snatching mountaineers, who are ever doing us wrong, especially since no five of each clan have a rusty shirt of mail as old as their *brattach*; and that is but the work of the clumsy clan-smith after all, who is no member of our honourable mystery, but simply works at the anvil, where his father wrought before him. I say, such people can have no favour in the eyes of an honest craftsman."

"Well, well," answered Simon; "I prithee let the matter rest even now, for here comes the loitering boy; and though it is a holyday morn, I want no more bloody puddings."

The youth entered accordingly. His face was pale, his eyes red; and there was an air of discomposure about his whole person. He sat down at the lower end of the table, opposite to Dorothy, and crossed himself, as if preparing for his morning's meal. As he did not help himself to any food, Catharine offered him a platter containing some of the cakes which had met with such general approbation. At first he rejected her offered kindness rather sullenly; but on her repeating the offer with a smile of good-will, he took a cake in his hand, broke it, and was about to eat a morsel, when the effort to swallow seemed almost too much for him; and though he succeeded, he did not repeat it.

"You have a bad appetite for Saint Valentine's morning, Conachar," said his good-humoured master; "and yet I think you must have slept soundly the night before, since I conclude you were not disturbed by the noise of the scuffle. Why, I thought a lively Glune-amie would have been at his master's side, dirk in hand, at the first sound of danger which arose within a mile of us."

"I heard but an indistinct noise," said the youth, his face glowing suddenly like a heated coal, "which I took for the shout of some merry revellers; and you are wont to bid me never open door or window, or alarm the house, on the score of such folly."

"Well, well," said Simon; "I thought a Highlander would have known better the difference betwixt the clash of swords and the twanging on harps, the wild war-cry and the merry hunts up. But let it pass, boy; I am glad thou art losing thy quarrelsome fashions. Eat thy breakfast, any way, as I have that to employ thee, which requires haste."

"I have breakfasted already, and am in haste myself. I am for the hills.—Have you any message to my father?"

"None," replied the Glover, in some surprise; "but art thou beside thyself, boy? or what a vengeance takes thee from the city, like the wing of the whirlwind?"

"My warning has been sudden," said Conachar, speaking with difficulty; but whether arising from the hesitation incidental to the use of a foreign language, or whether from some other cause, could not easily be distinguished. "There is to be a meeting—a great hunting——" Here he stopped.

"And when are you to return from this blessed hunting?" said his master; "that is, if I may make so bold as to ask."

"I cannot exactly answer," replied the apprentice. "Perhaps never—if such be my father's pleasure," continued Conachar, with assumed indifference.

"I thought," said Simon Glover, rather seriously, "that all this was to be laid aside, when at earnest intercession I took you under my roof. I thought that when I undertook, being very loath to do so, to teach you an honest trade, we were to hear no more of hunting, or hosting, or clan-gatherings, or any matters of the kind?"

"I was not consulted when I was sent hither," said the lad, haughtily. "I cannot tell what the terms were."

"But I can tell you, Sir Conachar," said the Glover, angrily, "that there is no fashion of honesty in binding yourself to an honest craftsman, and spoiling more hides than your own is worth; and now, when you are of age to be of some service, in taking up the disposal of your time at your pleasure, as if it were your own property, not your master's."

"Reckon with my father about that," answered Conachar; "he will pay you gallantly—a French mutton for every hide I have spoiled, and a fat cow or bullock for each day I have been absent."

"Close with him, friend Glover—close with him," said the armourer, dryly. "Thou wilt be paid gallantly at least, if not honestly. Methinks I would like to know how many purses have been emptied to fill the goat-skin sporran that is to be so free to you of its gold, and whose pasture the bullocks have been calved in, that are to be sent down to you from the Grampian passes."

"You remind me, friend," said the Highland youth,

turning haughtily towards the Smith, "that I have also a reckoning to hold with you."

"Keep at arm's-length, then," said Henry, extending his brawny arm,—"I will have no more close hugs—no more bodkin work, like last night. I care little for a wasp's sting, yet I will not allow the insect to come near me if I have warning."

Conachar smiled contemptuously, "I meant thee no harm," he said. "My father's son did thee but too much honour to spill such churl's blood. I will pay you for it by the drop, that it may be dried up, and no longer soil my fingers."

"Peace, thou bragging ape!" said the Smith; "the blood of a true man cannot be valued in gold. The only expiation would be that thou shouldst come a mile into the Low Country with two of the strongest gallo-glasses of thy clan; and while I dealt with them, I would leave thee to the correction of my apprentice, little Jankin."

Here Catharine interposed. "Peace," she said, "my trusty Valentine, whom I have a right to command; and peace you, Conachar, who ought to obey me as your master's daughter. It is ill done to awaken again on the morrow the evil which has been laid to sleep at night."

"Farewell, then, master," said Conachar, after another look of scorn at the Smith, which he only answered with a laugh. "Farewell! and I thank you for your kindness, which has been more than I deserved. If I have at times seemed less than thankful, it was the fault of circumstances, and not of my will. Catharine——" He cast upon the maiden a look of strong emotion, in which various feelings were blended. He hesitated, as if to say something, and at length turned away with the single word *farewell*. Five minutes afterwards, with Highland buskins on his feet, and a small bundle in his hand, he passed through the north gate of Perth, and directed his course to the Highlands.

"There goes enough of beggary and of pride for a whole Highland clan," said Henry. "He talks as familiarly of gold pieces as I would of silver pennies; and yet I will be sworn that the thumb of his mother's worsted glove might hold the treasure of the whole clan."

"Like enough," said the Glover, laughing at the idea; "his mother was a large-boned woman, especially in the fingers and wrist."

"And as for cattle," continued Henry, "I reckon his father and brothers steal sheep by one at a time."

"The less we say of them the better," said the Glover, becoming again grave. "Brothers he hath none; his father is a powerful man—hath long hands—reaches as far as he can, and hears farther than it is necessary to talk of him."

"And yet he hath bound his only son apprentice to a glover in Perth?" said Henry. "Why, I should have thought the Gentle Craft, as it is called, of St. Crispin, would have suited him best; and that, if the son of some great Mac or O was to become an artisan, it could only be in the craft where princes set him the example."

This remark, though ironical, seemed to awaken our friend Simon's sense of professional dignity, which was a prevailing feeling that marked the manners of the artisans of the time.

"You err, son Henry," he replied, with much gravity; "the glovers are the more honourable craft of the two, in regard they provide for the accommodation of the hands, whereas the shoemakers and cordwainers do but work for the feet." [1]

"Both equally necessary members of the body corporate," said Henry, whose father had been a cordwainer.

"It may be so, my son," said the Glover; "but not both alike honourable. Bethink you, that we employ the hands as pledges of friendship and good faith, and the feet have no such privilege. Brave men fight with their hands— cowards employ their feet in flight. A glove is borne aloft, a shoe is trampled in the mire;—a man greets a friend with his open hand; he spurns a dog, or one whom he holds as mean as a dog, with his advanced foot. A glove on the point of a spear is a sign and pledge of faith all the wide world over, as a gauntlet flung down is a gage of knightly battle; while I know no other emblem belonging to an old shoe, except that some crones will fling them after a man by way of good luck, in which practice I avow myself to entertain no confidence."

"Nay," said the Smith, amused with his friend's eloquent pleading for the dignity of the art he practised, "I am not the man, I promise you, to disparage the glover's mystery. Bethink you, I am myself a maker of gauntlets. But the dignity of your ancient craft removes not my wonder, that the father of this Conachar suffered his son to learn a trade of any kind from a Lowland craftsman, holding us, as they do,

[1] Note VII.—The Glovers.

altogether beneath their magnificent degree, and a race of contemptible drudges, unworthy of any other fate than to be ill used and plundered, as often as these bare-breeched Dunniewassals see safety and convenience for doing so."

"Ay," answered the Glover, "but there were powerful reasons for—for——" He withheld something which seemed upon his lips, and went on, "for Conachar's father acting as he did.—Well, I have played fair with him, and I do not doubt but he will act honourably by me.—But Conachar's sudden leave-taking has put me to some inconvenience. He had things under his charge. I must look through the booth."

"Can I help you, father?" said Henry Gow, deceived by the earnestness of his manner.

"You?—no,"—said Simon, with a dryness which made Henry so sensible of the simplicity of his proposal, that he blushed to the eyes at his own dulness of comprehension, in a matter where love ought to have induced him to take his cue easily up. "You, Catharine," said the Glover, as he left the room, "entertain your Valentine for five minutes, and see he departs not till my return.—Come hither with me, old Dorothy, and bestir thy limbs in my behalf."

He left the room, followed by the old woman; and Henry Smith remained with Catharine, almost for the first time in his life, entirely alone. There was embarrassment on the maiden's part, and awkwardness on that of the lover, for about a minute; when Henry, calling up his courage, pulled the gloves out of his pocket with which Simon had supplied him, and asked her to permit one who had been so highly graced that morning, to pay the usual penalty for being asleep at the moment when he would have given the slumbers of a whole twelvemonth to be awake for a single minute.

"Nay, but," said Catharine, "the fulfilment of my homage to St. Valentine infers no such penalty as you desire to pay, and I cannot therefore think of accepting them."

"These gloves," said Henry, advancing his seat insidiously towards Catharine as he spoke, "were wrought by the hands that are dearest to you; and see—they are shaped for your own." He extended them as he spoke, and taking her arm in his robust hand, spread the gloves beside it to show how well they fitted. "Look at that taper arm," he said, "look at these small fingers; think who sewed these seams of silk and gold, and think whether the glove, and the arm which alone the glove can fit, ought to remain separate, because the poor glove has had the misfortune to be for a passing minute in the keeping of a hand so swart and rough as mine."

"They are welcome as coming from my father," said Catharine; "and surely not less so as coming from my *friend*," (and there was an emphasis on the word,) "as well as my Valentine and preserver."

"Let me aid to do them on," said the Smith, bringing himself yet closer to her side; "they may seen a little over-tight at first, and you may require some assistance."

"You are skilful in such service, good Henry Gow," said the maiden, smiling, but at the same time drawing farther from her lover.

"In good faith, no," said Henry, shaking his head; "my experience has been in donning steel gauntlets on mailed knights, more than in fitting embroidered gloves upon maidens."

"I will trouble you then no further, and Dorothy shall aid me—though there needs no assistance—my father's eye and fingers are faithful to his craft; what work he puts through his hands is always true to the measure."

"Let me be convinced of it," said the Smith; "let me see that these slender gloves actually match the hands they were made for."

"Some other time, good Henry," answered the maiden, "I will wear the gloves in honour of St. Valentine, and the mate he has sent me for the season. I would to heaven I could pleasure my father as well in weightier matters—at present the perfume of the leather harms the headache I have had since morning."

"Headache! dearest maiden?" echoed her lover.

"If you call it heartache, you will not misname it," said Catharine, with a sigh, and proceeded to speak in a very serious tone. "Henry," she said, "I am going perhaps to be as bold as I gave you reason to think me this morning; for I am about to speak the first upon a subject, on which, it may well be, I ought to wait till I had to answer you. But I cannot, after what has happened this morning, suffer my feelings towards you to remain unexplained, without the possibility of my being greatly misconceived.—Nay, do not answer till you have heard me out.—You are brave, Henry, beyond most men, honest and true as the steel you work upon——"

"Stop—stop, Catharine, for mercy's sake! You never said so much that was good concerning me, save to introduce some bitter censure, of which your praises were the harbingers. I am honest, and so forth, you would say, but a hot-brained brawler, and common sworder or stabber."

"I should injure both myself and you in calling you such. No, Henry, to no common stabber, had he worn a plume in his bonnet, and gold spurs on his heels, would Catharine Glover have offered the little grace she has this day voluntarily done to you. If I have at times dwelt severely upon the proneness of your spirit to anger, and of your hand to strife, it is because I would have you, if I could so persuade you, hate in yourself the sins of vanity and wrath, by which you are most easily beset. I have spoken on the topic more to alarm your own conscience, than to express my opinion. I know as well as my father, that in these forlorn and desperate days, the whole customs of our nation, nay, of every Christian nation, may be quoted in favour of bloody quarrels for trifling causes; of the taking deadly and deep revenge for slight offences; and the slaughter of each other for emulation of honour, or often in mere sport. But I know, that for all these things we shall one day be called into judgment; and fain would I convince thee, my brave and generous friend, to listen oftener to the dictates of thy good heart, and take less pride in the strength and dexterity of thy unsparing arm."

"I am—I am convinced, Catharine," exclaimed Henry; "thy words shall henceforward be a law to me. I have done enough, far too much, indeed, for proof of my bodily strength and courage; but it is only from you, Catharine, that I can learn a better way of thinking. Remember, my fair Valentine, that my ambition of distinction in arms, and my love of strife, if it can be called such, do not fight even-handed with my reason and my milder dispositions, but have their patrons and sticklers to egg them on. Is there a quarrel,—and suppose that I, thinking on your counsels, am something loath to engage in it,—believe you I am left to decide between peace or war at my own choosing? Not so, by St. Mary! there are a hundred round me to stir me on. 'Why, how now, Smith, is thy mainspring rusted?' says one. 'Jolly Henry is deaf on the quarrelling ear this morning,' says another. 'Stand to it, for the honour of Perth,' says my Lord the Provost. 'Harry against them for a gold noble,' cries your father, perhaps. Now, what can a poor fellow do, Catharine, when all are hallooing him on in the devil's name, and not a soul putting in a word on the other side?"

"Nay, I know the devil has factors enough to utter his wares," said Catharine; "but it is our duty to despise such idle arguments, though they may be pleaded even by those to whom we owe much love and honour."

"Then there are the minstrels, with their romaunts and ballads, which place all a man's praise in receiving and repaying hard blows. It is sad to tell, Catharine, how many of my sins that blind Harry the Minstrel hath to answer for. When I hit a downright blow, it is not, (so save me, St. John!) to do any man injury, but only to strike as William Wallace struck."

The Minstrel's namesake spoke this in such a tone of rueful seriousness, that Catharine could scarce forbear smiling; but nevertheless she assured him that the danger of his own and other men's lives ought not for a moment to be weighed against such simple toys.

"Ay, but," replied Henry, emboldened by her smiles, "methinks now the good cause of peace would thrive all the better for an advocate. Suppose, for example, that when I am pressed and urged to lay hand on my weapon, I could have cause to recollect that there was a gentle and guardian angel at home, whose image would seem to whisper, 'Henry, do no violence; it is my hand which you crimson with blood—Henry, rush upon no idle danger; it is my breast which you expose to injury;' such thoughts would do more to restrain my mood, than if every monk in Perth should cry 'Hold thy hand, on pain of bell, book, and candle.'"

"If such a warning as could be given by the voice of sisterly affection can have weight in the debate," said Catharine, "do think, that in striking, you empurple this hand; that in receiving wounds, you harm this heart."

The Smith took courage at the sincerely affectionate tone in which these words were delivered.

"And wherefore not stretch your regard a degree beyond these cold limits? Why, since you are so kind and generous as to own some interest in the poor ignorant sinner before you, should you not at once adopt him as your scholar and your husband? Your father desires it; the town expects it; glovers and smiths are preparing their rejoicings; and you, only you, whose words are so fair and so kind, you will not give your consent!"

"Henry," said Catharine, in a low and tremulous voice, "believe me I should hold it my duty to comply with my father's commands, were there not obstacles invincible to the match which he proposes."

"Yet think—think but for a moment. I have little to say for myself in comparison of you, who can both read and write. But then I wish to hear reading, and could listen to your sweet voice for ever. You love music, and I have been taught to play and sing as well as some minstrels. You love to be charitable, I have enough to give, and enough to keep; as large a daily alms as a deacon gives would never be missed by me. Your father gets old for daily toil; he would live with us, as I should truly hold him for my father also. I would be as chary of mixing in causeless strife, as of thrusting my hand into my own furnace; and if there came on us unlawful violence, its wares would be brought to an ill-chosen market."

"May you experience all the domestic happiness which you can conceive, Henry,—but with some one more happy than I am!"

So spoke, or rather so sobbed, the Fair Maiden of Perth, who seemed choking in the attempt to restrain her tears.

"You hate me, then?" said the lover, after a pause.

"Heaven is my witness, No."

"Or you love some other better?"

"It is cruel to ask what it cannot avail you to know. But you are entirely mistaken."

"Yon wild-cat, Conachar, perhaps?" said Henry. "I have marked his looks——"

"You avail yourself of this painful situation to insult me, Henry, though I have little deserved it. Conachar is nothing to me, more than the trying to tame his wild spirit by instruction might lead me to take some interest in a mind abandoned to prejudices and passions, and therein, Henry, not unlike your own."

"It must then be some of these flaunting silkworm Sirs about the court," said the armourer, his natural heat of temper kindling from disappointment and vexation; "some of those who think they carry it off through the height of their plumed bonnets and the jingle of their spurs. I would I knew which it was, that, leaving his natural mates, the painted and perfumed dames of the court, comes to take his prey among the simple maidens of the burgher craft. I would I knew but his name and surname!"

"Henry Smith," said Catharine, shaking off the weakness which seemed to threaten to overpower her a moment before, "this is the language of an ungrateful fool, or rather of a frantic madman. I have told you already, there was no one who stood, at the beginning of this conference, more high in my opinion, than he who is now losing ground with every word he utters, in the tone of unjust suspicion and senseless anger. You had no title to know even what I have told you; which, I pray you to observe, implies no preference to you over others, though it disowns any preference of another to you. It is enough you should be aware that there is as insuperable an objection to what you desire, as if an enchanter had a spell over my destiny."

"Spell may be broken by true men," said the Smith. "I would it were come to that. Thorbiorn, the Danish armourer, spoke of a spell he had for making breastplates, by singing a certain song while the iron was heating. I told him that his runic rhymes were no proof against the weapons which fought at Loncarty—what farther came of it is needless to tell;—but the corslet and the wearer, and the leech who salved his wound, know if Henry Gow can break a spell or no."

Catharine looked at him as if about to return an answer little approving of the exploit he had vaunted, which the downright Smith had not recollected, was of a kind that exposed him to her frequent censure. But ere she had given words to her thoughts, her father thrust his head in at the door.

"Henry," he said, "I must interrupt your more pleasing affairs, and request you to come into my working room in all speed, to consult about certain matters deeply affecting the weal of the burgh."

Henry, making his obeisance to Catharine, left the apartment upon her father's summons. Indeed it was probably in favour of their future friendly intercourse that they were parted on this occasion, at the turn which the conversation seemed likely to take. For as the wooer had begun to hold the refusal of the damsel as somewhat capricious and inexplicable after the degree of encouragement which, in his opinion, she had afforded; Catharine, on the other hand, considered him rather as an encroacher upon the grace which she had shown him, than one whose delicacy rendered him deserving of such favour.

But there was living in their bosoms towards each other a reciprocal kindness, which on the termination of the dispute was sure to revive, inducing the maiden to forget her offended delicacy, and the lover his slighted warmth of passion.

CHAPTER VII

This quarrel may draw blood another day.
Henry IV. Part I.

THE conclave of citizens appointed to meet for investigating
the affray of the preceding evening, had now assembled. The
work-room of Simon Glover was filled to crowding by personages
of no little consequence, some of whom wore black velvet
cloaks, and gold chains around their necks. They were,
indeed, the fathers of the city; and there were bailies and
deacons in the honoured number. There was an ireful and
offended air of importance upon every brow, as they conversed
together, rather in whisper, than aloud or in detail. Busiest
among the busy, the little important assistant of the previous
night, Oliver Proudfute by name, and bonnet-maker by profession, was bustling among the crowd; much after the manner
of the sea-gull, which flutters, screams, and sputters most at
the commencement of a gale of wind, though one can hardly
conceive what the bird has better to do than to fly to its nest,
and remain quiet till the gale is over.

Be that as it may, Master Proudfute was in the midst
of the crowd, his fingers upon every one's button, and his
mouth in every man's ear, embracing such as were near to
his own stature, that he might more closely and mysteriously
utter his sentiments; and standing on tiptoe, and supporting
himself by the cloak-collars of tall men, that he might dole
out to them also the same share of information. He felt
himself one of the heroes of the affair, being conscious of
the dignity of superior information on the subject as an eye-
witness, and much disposed to push his connexion with the
scuffle a few points beyond the modesty of truth. It cannot
be said that his communications were in especial curious and
important, consisting chiefly of such assertions as these :—

"It is all true, by St. John. I was there and saw it myself
—was the first to run to the fray; and if it had not been for
me and another stout fellow, who came in about the same
time, they had broken into Simon Glover's house, cut his
throat, and carried his daughter off to the mountains. It
is too evil usage—not to be suffered, neighbour Crookshank,
—not to be endured, neighbour Glass—not to be borne,
neighbours Balneaves, Rollock, and Chrysteson. It was a
mercy that I and that stout fellow came in—Was it not,
neighbour and worthy Bailie Craigdallie?"

These speeches were dispersed by the busy bonnet-maker into sundry ears. Bailie Craigdallie, a portly guild-brother, the same who had advised the prorogation of their civic council to the present place and hour, a big, burly, good-looking man, shook the deacon from his cloak with pretty much the grace with which a large horse shrugs off the importunate fly that has beset him for ten minutes, and exclaimed, " Silence, good citizens ; here comes Simon Glover, in whom no man ever saw falsehood. We will hear the outrage from his own mouth."

Simon being called upon to tell his tale, did so with obvious embarrassment, which he imputed to a reluctance that the burgh should be put in deadly feud with any one upon his account. It was, he dared to say, a masking or revel on the part of the young gallants about court ; and the worst that might come of it would be, that he would put iron stancheons on his daughter's window, in case of such another frolic.

" Why, then, if this was a mere masking or mummery," said Craigdallie, " our townsman, Harry of the Wynd, did far wrong to cut off a gentleman's hand for such a harmless pleasantry, and the town may be brought to a heavy fine for it, unless we secure the person of the mutilator."

" Our Lady forbid ! " said the Glover. " Did you know what I do, you would be as much afraid of handling this matter, as if it were glowing iron. But, since you will needs put your fingers in the fire, truth must be spoken. And come what will, I must say, that the matter might have ended ill for me and mine, but for the opportune assistance of Henry Gow, the armourer, well known to you all."

" And mine also was not awanting," said Oliver Proudfute, " though I do not profess to be utterly so good a swordsman as our neighbour, Henry Gow.—You saw me, neighbour Glover, at the beginning of the fray ? "

" I saw you after the end of it, neighbour," answered the Glover, dryly.

" True, true ; I had forgot you were in your house while the blows were going, and could not survey who were dealing them."

" Peace, neighbour Proudfute ; I prithee, peace," said Craigdallie, who was obviously tired of the tuneless screeching of the worthy deacon.

" There is something mysterious here," said the Bailie ; " but I think I spy the secret. Our friend Simon is, as you all know, a peaceful man, and one that will rather sit down with wrong, than put a friend, or say a neighbourhood, in danger to seek his redress. Thou, Henry, who art never wanting where the burgh needs a defender, tell us what *thou* knowest of this matter."

Our Smith told his story to the same purpose which we have already related; and the meddling maker of bonnets added as before, "And thou sawest me there, honest Smith, didst thou not?"

"Not I, in good faith, neighbour," answered Henry; "but you are a little man, you know, and I might overlook you."

This reply produced a laugh at Oliver's expense, who laughed for company, but added, doggedly, "I was one of the foremost to the rescue for all that."

"Why, where wert thou, then, neighbour?" said the Smith; "for I saw you not, and I would have given the worth of the best suit of armour I ever wrought to have seen as stout a fellow as thou at my elbow."

"I was no farther off, however, honest Smith; and whilst thou wert laying on blows as if on an anvil, I was parrying those that the rest of the villains aimed at thee behind thy back; and that is the cause thou sawest me not."

"I have heard of Smiths of old time who had but one eye," said Henry. "I have two, but they are both set in my forehead, and so I could not see behind my back, neighbour."

"The truth is, however," persevered Master Oliver, "there I was, and I will give Master Bailie my account of the matter; for the Smith and I were first up to the fray."

"Enough at present," said the Bailie, waving to Master Proudfute an injunction of silence. "The precognition of Simon Glover and Henry Gow would bear out a matter less worthy of belief.—And now, my masters, your opinion what should be done. Here are all our burgher rights broken through and insulted, and you may well fancy that it is by some man of power, since no less dared have attempted such an outrage. My masters, it is hard on flesh and blood to submit to this. The laws have framed us of lower rank than the princes and nobles, yet it is against reason to suppose that we will suffer our houses to be broken into, and the honour of our women insulted, without some redress."

"It is not to be endured!" answered the citizens, unanimously.

Here Simon Glover interfered with a very anxious and ominous countenance. "I hope still that all was not meant so ill as it seemed to us, my worthy neighbours; and I for one would cheerfully forgive the alarm and disturbance to my poor house, providing the fair city were not brought into jeopardy for me. I beseech you to consider who are to be our judges that are to hear the case, and give or refuse redress. I speak among neighbours and friends, and therefore I speak openly. The King, God bless him! is so broken in mind and body, that he will but turn us over to some great man amongst his counsellors, who shall be in favour for the time—Perchance he will refer us to his brother the Duke of Albany, who will make our petition for righting of our wrongs the pretence for squeezing money out of us."

"We will none of Albany for our judge!" answered the meeting with the same unanimity as before.

"Or perhaps," added Simon, "he will bid the Duke of Rothsay take charge of it; and the wild young prince will regard the outrage as something for his gay companions to scoff at, and his minstrels to turn into song."

"Away with Rothsay! he is too gay to be our judge," again exclaimed the citizens.

Simon, emboldened by seeing he was reaching the point he aimed at, yet pronouncing the dreaded name with a half whisper, next added, "Would you like the Black Douglas better to deal with?"

There was no answer for a minute. They looked on each other with fallen countenances and blanched lips. But Henry Smith spoke out boldly, and in a decided voice, the sentiments which all felt, but none else dared give words to—

"The Black Douglas to judge betwixt a burgher and a gentleman, nay, a nobleman, for all I know or care?—The black devil of hell sooner! You are mad, Father Simon, so much as to name so wild a proposal."

There was again a silence of fear and uncertainty, which was at length broken by Bailie Craigdallie, who, looking very significantly to the speaker, replied, "You are confident in a stout doublet, neighbour Smith, or you would not talk so boldly."

"I am confident of a good heart under my doublet, such as it is, Bailie," answered the undaunted Henry; "and though I speak but little, my mouth shall never be padlocked by any noble of them all."

"Wear a thick doubtlet, good Henry, or do not speak so loud," reiterated the Bailie, in the same significant tone. "There are border men in the town who wear the Bloody Heart [1] on their shoulder.—But all this is no rede. What shall we do ? "

"Short rede, good rede," said the Smith. "Let us to our Provost, and demand his countenance and assistance."

A murmur of applause went through the party, and Oliver Proudfute exclaimed, "That is what I have been saying for this half hour, and not one of ye would listen to me. Let us go to our Provost, said I. He is a gentleman himself, and ought to come between the burgh and the nobles in all matters."

"Hush, neighbours, hush; be wary what you say or do," said a thin meagre figure of a man, whose diminutive person seemed still more reduced in size, and more assimilated to a shadow by his efforts to assume an extreme degree of humility, and make himself, to suit his argument, look meaner yet, and yet more insignificant than nature had made him.

"Pardon me," said he; "I am but a poor Pottingar. Nevertheless, I have been bred in Paris, and learned my humanities and my *cursus medendi* as well as some that call themselves learned leeches. Methinks I can tent this wound, and treat it with emollients. Here is our friend Simon Glover, who is, as you all know, a man of worship. Think you he would not be the most willing of us all to pursue harsh courses here, since his family honour is so nearly concerned ? And since he blenches away from the charge against these same revellers, consider if he may not have some good reason more than he cares to utter for letting the matter sleep. It is not for me to put my finger on the sore ; but, alack ! we all know that young maidens are what I call fugitive essences. Suppose now, an honest maiden—I mean in all innocence—leaves her window unlatched on St. Valentine's morn, that some gallant cavalier may—in all honesty, I mean—become her Valentine for the season ; and suppose the gallant be discovered, may she not scream out as if the visit were unexpected, and—and—bray all this in a mortar, and then consider, will it be a matter to place the town in feud for ? "

The Pottingar delivered his opinion in a most insinuating manner ; but he seemed to shrink into something less than

[1] The well-known cognizance of the house of Douglas.

his natural tenuity when he saw the blood rise in the old cheeks of Simon Glover, and inflame to the temples the complexion of the redoubted Smith. The last, stepping forward, and turning a stern look on the alarmed Pottingar, broke out as follows:—"Thou walking skeleton! thou asthmatic gallipot! thou poisoner by profession! If I thought that the puff of vile breath thou hast left could blight for the tenth part of a minute the fair fame of Catharine Glover, I would pound thee, quacksalver! in thine own mortar, and beat up thy wretched carrion with flower of brimstone, the only real medicine in thy booth, to make a salve to rub mangy hounds with!"

"Hold, son Henry, hold!" cried the Glover, in a tone of authority,—"no man has title to speak of this matter but me.—Worshipful Bailie Craigdallie, since such is the construction that is put upon my patience, I am willing to pursue this riot to the uttermost; and though the issue may prove that we had better have been patient, you will all see that my Catharine hath not by any lightness or folly of hers afforded grounds for this great scandal."

The Bailie also interposed. "Neighbour Henry," said he, "we came here to consult, and not to quarrel. As one of the fathers of the fair city, I command thee to forego all evil will and maltalent you may have against Master Pottingar Dwining."

"He is too poor a creature, Bailie," said Henry Gow, "for me to harbour feud with—I that could destroy him and his booth with one blow of my fore-hammer."

"Peace, then, and hear me," said the official. "We all are as much believers in the honour of the Fair Maiden of Perth, as in that of our blessed Lady." Here he crossed himself devoutly. "But touching our appeal to our Provost, are you agreed, neighbours, to put matter like this into our Provost's hand, being against a powerful noble, as is to be feared?"

"The Provost being himself a nobleman"—squeaked the Pottingar, in some measure released from his terror by the intervention of the Bailie. "God knows, I speak not to the disparagement of an honourable gentleman, whose forebears have held the office he now holds for many years——"

"By free choice of the citizens of Perth," said the Smith, interrupting the speaker with the tones of his deep and decisive voice.

"Ay, surely," said the disconcerted orator, "by the voice of the citizens. How else?—I pray you, friend Smith, interrupt me not. I speak to our worthy and eldest Bailie, Craigdallie, according to my poor mind. I say that, come amongst us how he will, still this Sir Patrick Charteris is a nobleman, and hawks will not pick hawks' eyes out. He may well bear us out in a feud with the Highlandmen, and do the part of our Provost and leader against them; but whether he that himself wears silk will take our part against broidered cloak and cloth of gold, though he may do so against tartan and Irish frieze, is something to be questioned. Take a fool's advice. We have saved our Maiden, of whom I never meant to speak harm, as truly I knew none. They have lost one man's hand, at least, thanks to Harry Smith——"

"And to me," added the little important bonnet-maker.

"And to Oliver Proudfute, as he tells us," continued the Pottingar, who contested no man's claim to glory, provided he was not himself compelled to tread the perilous paths which lead to it. "I say, neighbours, since they have left a hand as a pledge they will never come in Couvrefew Street again, why, in my simple mind, we were best to thank our stout townsman, and the town having the honour, and these rakehells the loss, that we should hush the matter up, and say no more about it."

These pacific counsels had their effect with some of the citizens, who began to nod and look exceedingly wise upon the advocate of acquiescence, with whom, notwithstanding the offence so lately given, Simon Glover seemed also to agree in opinion. But not so Henry Smith, who, seeing the consultation at a stand, took up the speech in his usual downright manner.

"I am neither the oldest nor the richest among you, neighbours, and I am not sorry for it. Years will come, if one lives to see them; and I can win and spend my penny like another, by the blaze of the furnace and the wind of the bellows. But no man ever saw me sit down with wrong done in word or deed to our fair town, if man's tongue and man's hand could right it. Neither will I sit down with this outrage, if I can help it. I will go to the Provost myself, if no one will go with me; he is a knight, it is true, and a gentleman of free and trueborn blood, as we all know, since Wallace's time, who settled his great-grandsire amongst us. But if he were the proudest nobleman in the land, he is the Provost of Perth, and for his own honour must see the freedoms and immunities of the burgh preserved—ay, and I know he will—I have made a steel doubtlet for him, and have a good guess at the kind of heart that it was meant to cover."

"Surely," said Bailie Craigdallie, "it would be to no purpose to stir at court without Sir Patrick Charteris's countenance; the ready answer would be, Go to your Provost, you borrel loons. So, neighbours and townsmen, if you will stand by my side, I and our Pottingar Dwining will repair presently to Kinfauns, with Sim Glover, the jolly Smith, and gallant Oliver Proudfute, for witnesses to the onslaught, and speak with Sir Patrick Charteris, in name of the fair town."

"Nay," said the peaceful man of medicine, "leave me behind, I pray you, I lack audacity to speak before a belted knight."

"Never regard that, neighbour, you must go," said Bailie Craigdallie. "The town hold me a hot-headed carle for a man of threescore—Sim Glover is the offended party—we all know that Harry Gow spoils more harness with his sword than he makes with his hammer—and our neighbour Proudfute,—who, take his own word, is at the beginning and end of every fray in Perth,—is of course a man of action. We must have at least one advocate amongst us for peace and quietness; and thou, Pottingar, must be the man. Away with you, sirs, get your boots and your beasts—horse and hattock,[1] I say—and let us meet at the East Port—that is, if it is your pleasure, neighbours, to trust us with the matter."

"There can be no better rede, and we will all avouch it," said the citizens. "If the Provost take our part, as the fair town hath a right to expect, we may bell-the-cat with the best of them."

"It is well, then, neighbours," answered the Bailie; "so said, so shall be done. Meanwhile, I have called the whole town-council together about this hour, and I have little doubt," looking around the company, "that as so many of them who are in this place have resolved to consult with our Provost, the rest will be compliant to the same resolution. And therefore, neighbours, and good burghers of the fair city of Perth—horse and hattock as I said before, and meet me at the East Port."

---

[1] *Horse and hattock*, the well-known cry of the fairies at mounting for a moonlight expedition, came to be familiarly adopted on any occasion of mounting.

A general acclamation concluded the sitting of this species of privy council, or Lords of the Articles; and they dispersed, the deputation to prepare for the journey, and the rest to tell their impatient wives and daughters of the measures they had taken to render their chambers safe in future, against the intrusion of gallants at unseasonable hours.

While nags are saddling, and the town-council debating, or rather putting in form what the leading members of their body had already adopted, it may be necessary, for the information of some readers, to state in distinct terms what is more circuitously intimated in the course of the former discussion.

It was the custom at this period, when the strength of the feudal aristocracy controlled the rights, and frequently insulted the privileges of the royal burghs of Scotland, that the latter, where it was practicable, often chose their Provost, or Chief Magistrate, not out of the order of the merchants, shopkeepers, and citizens, who inhabited the town itself, and filled up the roll of the ordinary magistracy, but elected to that pre-eminent state some powerful nobleman, or baron, in the neighbourhood of the burgh, who was expected to stand their friend at court in such matters as concerned their common weal, and to lead their civil militia to fight, whether in general battle or in private feud, reinforcing them with his own feudal retainers. This protection was not always gratuitous. The Provosts sometimes availed themselves of their situation to an unjustifiable degree, and obtained grants of lands and tenements belonging to the common good, or public property of the burgh, and thus made the citizens pay dear for the countenance which they afforded. Others were satisfied to receive the powerful aid of the townsmen in their own feudal quarrels, with such other marks of respect and benevolence, as the burgh over which they presided were willing to gratify them with, in order to secure their active services in case of necessity. The Baron, who was the regular protector of a royal burgh, accepted such free-will offerings without scruple, and repaid them by defending the rights of the town, by arguments in the council, and by bold deeds in the field.

The citizens of the town, or, as they loved better to call it, the Fair City of Perth, had for several generations found a protector and Provost of this kind in the knightly family of Charteris, Lords of Kinfauns, in the neighbourhood of the burgh. It was scarce a century (in the time of Robert

III.) since the first of this distinguished family had settled
in the strong castle which now belonged to them, with the
picturesque and fertile scenes adjoining to it.   But the history
of the first settler, chivalrous and romantic in itself, was
calculated to facilitate the settlement of an alien, in the land
in which his lot was cast.   We relate it as it is given by
an ancient and uniform tradition, which carries in it great
indications of truth, and is warrant enough, perhaps, for
its insertion in graver histories than the present.

During the brief career of the celebrated patriot Sir William
Wallace, and when his arms had for a time expelled the
English invaders from his native country, he is said to have
undertaken a voyage to France, with a small band of trusty
friends, to try what his presence (for he was respected through
all countries for his prowess) might do to induce the French
monarch to send to Scotland a body of auxiliary forces, or
other assistance, to aid the Scots in regaining their independence.

The Scottish Champion was on board a small vessel, and
steering for the port of Dieppe, when a sail appeared in the
distance, which the mariners regarded, first with doubt and
apprehension, and at last with confusion and dismay.   Wallace
demanded to know what was the cause of their alarm.   The
captain of the ship informed him, that the tall vessel which
was bearing down, with the purpose of boarding that which
he commanded, was the ship of a celebrated rover, equally
famed for his courage, strength of body, and successful piracies.
It was commanded by a gentleman named Thomas de
Longueville, a Frenchman by birth, but by practice one of
those pirates who called themselves friends to the sea, and
enemies to all who sailed upon that element.   He attacked
and plundered vessels of all nations, like one of the ancient
Norse Sea-kings, as they were termed, whose dominion was
upon the mountain waves.   The master added, that no
vessel could escape the rover by flight, so speedy was the
bark he commanded; and that no crew, however hardy,
could hope to resist him, when, as was his usual mode
of combat, he threw himself on board at the head of his
followers.

Wallace smiled sternly, while the master of the ship,
with alarm in his countenance, and tears in his eyes,
described to him the certainty of their being captured by
the Red Rover, a name given to De Longueville, because

he usually displayed the blood-red flag, which he had now hoisted.

" I will clear the narrow seas of this rover," said Wallace.

Then calling together some ten or twelve of his own followers, Boyd, Kerlie, Seton, and others, to whom the dust of the most desperate battle was like the breath of life, he commanded them to arm themselves, and lie flat upon the deck, so as to be out of sight. He ordered the mariners below, excepting such as were absolutely necessary to manage the vessel; and he gave the master instructions, upon pain of death, so to steer, as that, while the vessel had an appearance of attempting to fly, he should in fact permit the Red Rover to come up with them and do his worst. Wallace himself then lay down on the deck, that nothing might be seen which could intimate any purpose of resistance. In a quarter of an hour De Longueville's vessel ran on board that of the Champion, and the Red Rover, casting out grappling irons to make sure of his prize, jumped on the deck in complete armour, followed by his men, who gave a terrible shout, as if victory had been already secured. But the armed Scots started up at once, and the rover found himself unexpectedly engaged with men accustomed to consider victory as secure, when they were only opposed as one to two or three. Wallace himself rushed on the pirate captain, and a dreadful strife began betwixt them with such fury, that the others suspended their own battle to look on, and seemed by common consent to refer the issue of the strife to the fate of the combat between the two chiefs. The pirate fought as well as man could do; but Wallace's strength was beyond that of ordinary mortals. He dashed the sword from the rover's hand, and placed him in such peril, that, to avoid being cut down, he was fain to close with the Scottish Champion, in hopes of overpowering him in the grapple. In this also he was foiled. They fell on the deck, locked in each other's arms, but the Frenchman fell undermost; and Wallace, fixing his grasp upon his gorget, compressed it so closely, notwithstanding it was made of the finest steel, that the blood gushed from his eyes, nose, and mouth, and he was only able to ask for quarter by signs. His men threw down their weapons and begged for mercy, when they saw their leader thus severely handled. The victor granted them all their lives, but took possession of their vessel, and detained them prisoners.

When he came in sight of the French harbour, Wallace alarmed the place by displaying the rover's colours, as if De Longueville was coming to pillage the town. The bells were rung backward; horns were blown, and the citizens were hurrying to arms, when the scene changed. The Scottish Lion on his shield of gold was raised above the piratical flag, and announced that the Champion of Scotland was approaching, like a falcon with his prey in his clutch. He landed with his prisoner, and carried him to the court of France, where, at Wallace's request, the robberies which the pirate had committed were forgiven, and the King even conferred the honour of knighthood on Sir Thomas de Longueville, and offered to take him into his service. But the rover had contracted such a friendship for his generous victor, that he insisted on uniting his fortunes with those of Wallace, with whom he returned to Scotland, and fought by his side in many a bloody battle, where the prowess of Sir Thomas de Longueville was remarked as inferior to that of none, save of his heroic conqueror. His fate also was more fortunate than that of his patron. Being distinguished by the beauty as well as strength of his person, he rendered himself so acceptable to a young lady, heiress of the ancient family of Charteris, that she chose him for her husband, bestowing on him with her hand the fair baronial Castle of Kinfauns, and the domains annexed to it. Their descendants took the name of Charteris, as connecting themselves with their maternal ancestors, the ancient proprietors of the property, though the name of Thomas de Longueville was equally honoured amongst them; and the large two-handed sword with which he mowed the ranks of war, was, and is still, preserved among the family muniments. Another account is, that the family name of De Longueville himself was Charteris. The estate afterwards passed to a family of Blairs, and is now the property of Lord Gray.

These Barons of Kinfauns,[1] from father to son, held, for several generations, the office of Provost of Perth; the vicinity of the castle and town rendering it a very convenient arrangement for mutual support. The Sir Patrick of this history had more than once led out the men of Perth to battles and

[1] It is generally believed that the ancient Barons of Kinfauns are now represented in the male line by a once powerful branch of the name, the Charterises of Amisfield, in Dumfries-shire. The remains of the castle, close to which is their modern residence, attest the former extent of their resources.

skirmishes with the restless Highland depredators, and with other enemies, foreign and domestic. True it is, he used sometimes to be weary of the slight and frivolous complaints unnecessarily brought before him, and in which he was requested to interest himself. Hence he had sometimes incurred the charge of being too proud as a nobleman, or too indolent as a man of wealth, and one who was too much addicted to the pleasures of the field, and the exercise of feudal hospitality, to bestir himself upon all and every occasion when the Fair Town would have desired his active interference. But notwithstanding that this occasioned some slight murmuring, the citizens, upon any serious cause of alarm, were wont to rally around their Provost, and were warmly supported by him both in council and action.

CHAPTER VIII

Within the bounds of Annandale,
  The gentle Johnstones ride;
They have been there a thousand years,
  A thousand more they'll bide.

Old Ballad.

THE character and quality of Sir Patrick Charteris, the Provost of Perth, being such as we have sketched in the last chapter, let us now return to the deputation which was in the act of rendezvousing at the East Port[1] in order to wait upon that dignitary with their complaints, at Kinfauns.

And first appeared Simon Glover, on a pacing palfrey, which had sometimes enjoyed the honour of bearing the fairer person as well as the lighter weight of his beautiful daughter. His cloak was muffled round the lower part of his face, as a sign to his friends not to interrupt him by any questions while he passed through the streets, and partly, perhaps, on account of the coldness of the weather. The deepest anxiety was seated on his brow, as if the more he meditated on the matter he was engaged in, the more difficult and perilous it appeared. He only greeted by silent gestures his friends as they came to the rendezvous.

A strong black horse, of the old Galloway breed, of an under size, and not exceeding fourteen hands, but high-shouldered, strong-limbed, well-coupled, and round-barrelled,

[1] Note VIII.—East Port.

bore to the East Port the gallant Smith. A judge of the animal might see in his eye a spark of that vicious temper which is frequently the accompaniment of the form that is most vigorous and enduring ; but the weight, the hand, and the seat of the rider, added to the late regular exercise of a long journey, had subdued his stubbornness for the present. He was accompanied by the honest Bonnet-maker, who being, as the reader is aware, a little round man, and what is vulgarly called duck-legged, had planted himself like a red pincushion, (for he was wrapped in a scarlet cloak, over which he had slung a hawking-pouch,) on the top of a great saddle, which he might be said rather to be perched upon than to bestride. The saddle and the man were girthed on the ridge-bone of a great trampling Flemish mare, with a nose turned up in the air like a camel, a huge fleece of hair at each foot, and every hoof full as large in circumference as a frying-pan. The contrast between the beast and the rider was so extremely extraordinary, that whilst chance passengers contented them- selves with wondering how he got up, his friends were anticipating with sorrow the perils which must attend his coming down again ; for the high-seated horseman's feet did not by any means come beneath the laps of the saddle. He had associated himself to the Smith, whose motions he had watched for the purpose of joining him ; for it was Oliver Proudfute's opinion, that men of action showed to most advantage when beside each other ; and he was delighted when some wag of the lower class had gravity enough to cry out, without laughing outright, " There goes the pride of Perth—there go the slashing craftsmen, the jolly Smith of the Wynd, and the bold Bonnet-maker ! "

It is true, the fellow who gave this all-hail thrust his tongue in his cheek to some scapegraces like himself ; but as the Bonnet-maker did not see this by-play, he generously threw him a silver penny to encourage his respect for martialists. This munificence occasioned their being followed by a crowd of boys, laughing and hallooing, until Henry Smith, turning back, threatened to switch the foremost of them ; a resolution which they did not wait to see put in execution.

" Here are we the witnesses," said the little man on the large horse, as they joined Simon Glover at the East Port ; " but where are they that should back us ? Ah, brother Henry ! authority is a load for an ass rather than a spirited horse; it would but clog the motions of such young fellows as you and me."

"I could well wish to see you bear ever so little of that same weight, worthy Master Proudfute," replied Henry Gow, "were it but to keep you firm in the saddle; for you bounce about as if you were dancing a jig on your seat, without any help from your legs."

"Ay, ay; I raise myself in my stirrups to avoid the jolting. She is cruelly hard set this mare of mine; but she has carried me in field and forest, and through some passages that were something perilous; so Jezabel and I part not—I call her Jezabel, after the Princess of Castille."

"Isabel. I suppose you mean," answered the Smith.

"Ay—Isabel, or Jezabel,—all the same, you know. But here comes Bailie Craigdallie at last, with that poor, creeping, cowardly creature the Pottingar. They have brought two town-officers with their partisans, to guard their fair persons, I suppose.—If there is one thing I hate more than another, it is such a sneaking varlet as that Dwining!"

"Have a care he does not hear you say so," said the Smith. "I tell thee, Bonnet-maker, that there is more danger in yonder slight wasted anatomy, than in twenty stout fellows like yourself."

"Pshaw! Bully Smith, you are but jesting with me," said Oliver,—softening his voice, however, and looking towards the Pottingar, as if to discover in what limb or lineament of his wasted face and form lay any appearance of the menaced danger; and his examination reassuring him, he answered boldly, "Blades and bucklers, man, I would stand the feud of a dozen such as Dwining What could he do to any man with blood in his veins?"

"He could give him a dose of physic," answered the Smith, dryly.

They had no time for further colloquy, for Bailie Craigdallie called to them to take the road to Kinfauns, and himself showed the example. As they advanced at a leisurely pace, the discourse turned on the reception which they were to expect from their Provost, and the interest which he was likely to take in the aggression which they complained of. The Glover seemed particularly desponding, and talked more than once, in a manner which implied a wish that they would yet consent to let the matter rest. He did not speak out very plainly, however, fearful, perhaps, of the malignant interpretation which might be derived from any appearance of his flinching from the assertion of his daughter's reputation. Dwining seemed to agree with him in opinion, but spoke more cautiously than in the morning.

"After all," said the Bailie, "when I think of all the propines and good gifts which have passed from the good town to my Lord Provost's, I cannot think he will be backward to show himself. More than one lusty boat, laden with Bordeaux wine, has left the South Shore to discharge its burden under the Castle of Kinfauns. I have some right to speak of that, who was the merchant importer."

"And," said Dwining, with his squeaking voice, "I could speak of delicate confections, curious comfits, loaves of wastel bread, and even cakes of that rare and delicious condiment which men call sugar, that have gone thither to help out a bridal banquet, or a kirstening feast, or such like. But alack, Bailie Craigdallie, wine is drunk, comfits are eaten, and the gift is forgotten when the flavour is past away. Alas, neighbour! the banquet of last Christmas is gone like the last year's snow."

"But there have been gloves full of gold pieces," said the Magistrate.

"I should know that who wrought them," said Simon, whose professional recollections still mingled with whatever else might occupy his mind. "One was a hawking glove for my lady. I made it something wide. Her ladyship found no fault, in consideration of the intended lining."

"Well, go to," said Bailie Craigdallie, "the less I lie; and if these are not to the fore, it is the Provost's fault, and not the town's; they could neither be eat nor drunk in the shape in which he got them."

"I could speak of a brave armour too," said the Smith; "but, *cogan na schie!*[1] as John Highlandman says,—I think the Knight of Kinfauns will do his devoir by the burgh in peace or war; and it is needless to be reckoning the town's good deeds, till we see him thankless for them."

"So say I," cried our friend Proudfute, from the top of his mare. "We roystering blades never bear so base a mind as to count for wine and walnuts with a friend like Sir Patrick Charteris. Nay, trust me, a good woodsman like Sir Patrick will prize the right of hunting and sporting over the lands of the burgh as an high privilege, and one which, his Majesty the

[1] "Peace or war, I care not."

King's Grace excepted, is neither granted to lord nor loon save to our Provost alone."

As the Bonnet-maker spoke, there was heard on the left hand, the cry of, "*So so—waw waw—haw*," being the shout of a falconer to his hawk.

"Methinks yonder is a fellow using the privilege you mention, who, from his appearance, is neither King nor Provost," said the Smith.

"Ay, marry, I see him," said the Bonnet-maker, who imagined the occasion presented a prime opportunity to win honour. "Thou and I, jolly Smith, will prick towards him and put him to the question."

" Have with you, then," cried the Smith; and his companion spurred his mare and went off, never doubting that Gow was at his heels.

But Craigdallie caught Henry's horse by the reins. "Stand fast by the standard," he said; "let us see the luck of our light horseman. If he procures himself a broken pate, he will be quieter for the rest of the day."

"From what I already see," said the Smith, "he may easily come by such a boon. Yonder fellow, who stops so im-pudently to look at us, as if he were engaged in the most lawful sport in the world—I guess him, by his trotting hobbler, his rusty head-piece with the cock's feather, and long two-handed sword, to be the follower of some of the southland lords—men who live so near the Southron, that the black jack is never off their backs, and who are as free of their blows, as they are light in their fingers."

Whilst they were thus speculating on the issue of the rencounter, the valiant Bonnet-maker began to pull up Jezabel, in order that the Smith, who he still concluded was close behind, might overtake him, and either advance first, or at least abreast of himself. But when he saw him at a hundred yards' distance, standing composedly with the rest of the group, the flesh of the champion, like that of the old Spanish general, began to tremble, in anticipation of the dangers into which his own venturous spirit was about to involve it. Yet the con-sciousness of being countenanced by the neighbourhood of so many friends; the hopes that the appearance of such odds must intimidate the single intruder, and the shame of aban-doning an enterprise in which he had volunteered, and when so many persons must witness his disgrace, surmounted the strong inclination which prompted him to wheel Jezabel to the right about, and return to the friends whose protection he had quitted, as fast as her legs could carry them. He accordingly continued his direction towards the stranger, who increased his alarm considerably, by putting his little nag in motion, and riding to meet him at a brisk trot. On observing this apparently offensive movement, our hero looked over his left shoulder more than once, as if reconnoitring the ground for a retreat, and in the meanwhile came to a decided halt. But the Philistine was upon him ere the Bonnet-maker could decide whether to fight or fly, and a very ominous-looking Philistine he was. His figure was gaunt and lathy, his visage marked by two or three ill-favoured scars, and the whole man had much the air of one accustomed to say, "Stand and deliver," to a true man.

This individual began the discourse, by exclaiming, in tones as sinister as his looks,—"The devil catch you for a cuckoo, why do you ride across the moor to spoil my sport?"

"Worthy stranger," said our friend, in the tone of pacific remonstrance, "I am Oliver Proudfute, a burgess of Perth, and a man of substance; and yonder is the worshipful Adam Craigdallie, the oldest Bailie of the burgh, with the fighting Smith of the Wynd, and three or four armed men more, who desire to know your name, and how you come to take your pleasure over these lands belonging to the burgh of Perth— although, natheless, I will answer for them, it is not their wish to quarrel with a gentleman, or stranger, for any accidental trespass; only it is their use and wont not to grant such leave, unless it is duly asked; and—and—therefore I desire to know your name, worthy sir."

The grim and loathly aspect with which the falconer had regarded Oliver Proudfute during his harangue, had greatly disconcerted him, and altogether altered the character of the enquiry which, with Henry Gow to back him, he would probably have thought most fitting for the occasion.

The stranger replied to it, modified as it was, with a most inauspicious grin, which the scars of his visage made appear still more repulsive. "You want to know my name?—My name is the Devil's Dick of Hellgarth, well known in Annandale for a gentle Johnstone. I follow the stout Laird of Wamphray, who rides with his kinsman the redoubted Lord of Johnstone, who is banded with the doughty Earl of Douglas; and the Earl and the Lord, and the Laird and I the Esquire, fly our hawks where we find our game, and ask no man whose ground we ride over." [1]

" I will do your message, sir," replied Oliver Proudfute, meekly enough ; for he began to be very desirous to get free of the embassy which he had so rashly undertaken, and was in the act of turning his horse's head, when the Annandale man added,—

" And take you this to boot, to keep you in mind that you met the Devil's Dick, and to teach you another time to beware how you spoil the sport of any one who wears the flying spur on his shoulder."

With these words he applied two or three smart blows of his riding-rod upon the luckless Bonnet-maker's head and person. Some of them lighted upon Jezabel, who, turning sharply round, laid her rider upon the moor, and galloped back towards the party of citizens.

Proudfute, thus overthrown, begun to cry for assistance in no very manly voice, and almost in the same breath to whimper for mercy ; for his antagonist, dismounting almost as soon as he fell, offered a whinger, or large wood knife, to his throat, while he rifled the pockets of the unlucky citizen, and even examined his hawking bag, swearing two or three grisly oaths, that he would have what it contained, since the wearer had interrupted his sport. He pulled the belt rudely off, terrifying the prostrate Bonnet-maker still more by the regardless violence which he used, as, instead of taking the pains to unbuckle the strap, he drew till the fastening gave way. But apparently it contained nothing to his mind. He threw it carelessly from him, and at the same time suffered the dismounted cavalier to rise, while he himself remounted his hobbler, and looked towards the rest of Oliver's party, who were now advancing.

When they had seen their delegate overthrown, there was some laughter ; so much had the vaunting humour of the Bonnet-maker prepared his friends to rejoice, when, as Henry Smith termed it, they saw their Oliver meet with a Rowland. But when the Bonnet-maker's adversary was seen to bestride him, and handle him in the manner described, the armourer

[1] Every Scotchman must regret that the name of Johnstone should have disappeared from the peerage, and hope that ere long some one of the many claimants for the minor honours at least of the house of Annandale may make out a case to the satisfaction of the House of Lords. The great estates of the family are still nearly entire, and in worthy hands :—they have passed to a younger branch of the noble house of Hopetoun, one of the claimants of the elder titles.

could hold out no longer. "Please you, good Master Bailie, I cannot endure to see our townsman beaten and rifled, and like to be murdered before us all. It reflects upon the Fair Town; and if it is neighbour Proudfute's misfortune, it is our shame. I must to his rescue."

"We will all go to his rescue," answered Bailie Craigdallie; "but let no man strike without order from me. We have more feuds on our hands, it is to be feared, than we have strength to bring to good end. And therefore I charge you all, more especially you, Henry of the Wynd, in the name of the Fair City, that you make no stroke but in self-defence." They all advanced therefore, in a body; and the appearance of such a number drove the plunderer from his booty. He stood at gaze, however, at some distance, like the wolf, which, though it retreats before the dogs, cannot be brought to absolute flight.

Henry, seeing this state of things, spurred his horse and advanced far before the rest of the party, up towards the scene of Oliver Proudfute's misfortune. His first task was to catch Jezabel by the flowing rein, and his next to lead her to meet her discomfited master, who was crippling towards him, his clothes much soiled with his fall, his eyes streaming with tears, from pain as well as mortification, and altogether exhibiting an aspect so unlike the spruce and dapper importance of his ordinary appearance, that the honest Smith felt compassion for the little man, and some remorse at having left him exposed to such disgrace. All men, I believe, enjoy an ill-natured joke. The difference is, that an ill-natured person can drink out to very dregs the amusement which it affords, while the better moulded mind soon loses the sense of the ridiculous in sympathy for the pain of the sufferer.

"Let me pitch you up to your saddle again, neighbour," said the Smith, dismounting at the same time, and assisting Oliver to scramble into his war-saddle, as a monkey might have done.

"May God forgive you, neighbour Smith, for not backing of me! I would not have believed in it, though fifty credible witnesses had sworn it of you."

Such were the first words, spoken in sorrow more than anger, by which the dismayed Oliver vented his feelings.

"The Bailie kept hold of my horse by the bridle; and besides," Henry continued, with a smile, which even his compassion could not suppress, "I thought you would have accused me of diminishing your honour, if I brought you aid against a single man. But cheer up! the villain took foul odds of you, your horse not being well at command."

"That is true—that is true," said Oliver, eagerly catching at the apology.

"And yonder stands the faitour, rejoicing at the mischief he has done, and triumphing in your overthrow, like the King in the romance, who played upon the fiddle whilst a city was burning. Come thou with me, and thou shalt see how we will handle him—Nay, fear not that I will desert thee this time."

So saying, he caught Jezabel by the rein, and galloping alongside of her, without giving Oliver time to express a negative, he rushed towards the Devil's Dick, who had halted on the top of a rising ground at some distance. The gentle Johnstone, however, either that he thought the contest unequal, or that he had fought enough for the day, snapping his fingers, and throwing his hand out with an air of defiance, spurred his horse into a neighbouring bog, through which he seemed to flutter like a wild-duck, swinging his lure round his head, and whistling to his hawk all the while, though any other horse and rider must have been instantly bogged up to the saddle-girths.

"There goes a thorough-bred moss-trooper," said the Smith. 'That fellow will fight or flee as suits his humour, and there is no use to pursue him, any more than to hunt a wild-goose. He has got your purse, I doubt me, for they seldom leave off till they are full-handed."

"Ye—ye—yes," said Proudfute, in a melancholy tone; "he has got my purse—but there is less matter since he hath left the hawking-bag."

"Nay, the hawking-bag had been an emblem of personal victory, to be sure—a trophy, as the minstrels call it."

"There is more in it than that, friend," said Oliver, significantly.

"Why, that is well, neighbour; I love to hear you speak in your own scholarly tone again. Cheer up, you have seen the villain's back, and regained the trophies you had lost when taken at advantage."

"Ah, Henry Gow—Henry Gow!" said the Bonnet-maker, and stopped short with a deep sigh, nearly amounting to a groan.

"What is the matter?" asked his friend; "what is it you vex yourself about now?"

"I have some suspicion, my dearest friend, Henry Smith, that the villain fled for fear of you, not of me!"

"Do not think so," replied the armourer; "he saw two men and fled, and who can tell whether he fled for one or the other? Besides, he knows by experience your strength and activity; we all saw how you kicked and struggled when you were on the ground."

"Did I?" said poor Proudfute; "I do not remember it—but I know it is my best point—I am a strong dog in the loins. But did they all see it?"

"All as much as I," said the Smith, smothering an inclination to laughter.

"But thou wilt remind them of it?"

"Be assured I will," answered Henry, "and of thy desperate rally even now. Mark what I say to Bailie Craigdallie, and make the best of it."

"It is not that I require any evidence in my favour, for I am as brave by nature as most men in Perth—but only——" Here the man of valour paused.

"But only what?" enquired the stout armourer.

"But only I am afraid of being killed. To leave my pretty wife and my young family, you know, would be a sad change, Smith. You will know this when it is your own case, and will feel abated in courage."

"It is like that I may," said the armourer, musing.

"Then I am so accustomed to the use of arms, and so well breathed, that few men can match me. It's all here," said the little man, expanding his breast like a trussed fowl, and patting himself with his hands; "here is room for all the wind machinery."

"I dare say you are long-breathed—long-winded,—at least your speech bewrays——"

"My speech?—You are a wag—but I have got the stern post of a dromond brought up the river from Dundee."

"The stern post of a Drummond!" exclaimed the armourer, "conscience, man, it will put you in feud with the whole clan—not the least wrathful in the country, as I take it."

"St. Andrew, man, you put me out!—I mean a dromond, that is, a large ship. I have fixed this post in my yard, and had it painted and carved something like a Soldan or Saracen, and with him I breathe myself, and will wield my two-handed sword against him, thrust or point, for an hour together."

" That must make you familiar with the use of your weapon," said the Smith.

" Ay, marry does it—and sometimes I will place you a bonnet (an old one, most likely) on my Soldan's head, and cleave it with such a downright blow, that, in troth, the infidel has but little of his skull remaining to hist at."

"That is unlucky, for you will lose your practice," said Henry.—" But how say you, Bonnet-maker ? I will put on my head-piece and corslet one day, and you shall hew at me, allowing me my broadsword to parry and pay back ? Eh, what say you ? "

" By no manner of means, my dear friend. I should do you too much evil ; besides, to tell you the truth, I strike far more freely at a helmet or bonnet, when it is set on my wooden Soldan—then I am sure to fetch it down. But when there is a plume of feathers in it that nod, and two eyes gleaming fiercely from under the shadow of the visor, and when the whole is dancing about here and there, I acknowledge it puts out my hand of fence."

" So, if men would but stand stock still like your Soldan, you would play the tyrant with them, Master Proudfute ? "

" In time, and with practice, I conclude I might," answered Oliver.—" But here we come up with the rest of them ; Bailie Craigdallie looks angry—but it is not his kind of anger that frightens me."

You are to recollect, gentle reader, that as soon as the Bailie, and those who attended him, saw that the Smith had come up to the forlorn Bonnet-maker, and that the stranger had retreated, they gave themselves no trouble about advancing further to his assistance, which they regarded as quite insured by the presence of the redoubted Henry Gow. They had resumed their straight road to Kinfauns, desirous that nothing should delay the execution of their mission. As some time had elapsed ere the Bonnet-maker and the Smith rejoined the party, Bailie Craigdallie asked them, and Henry Smith in particular, what they meant by dallying away precious time by riding up hill after the falconer.

" By the mass, it was not my fault, Master Bailie," replied the Smith. " If ye will couple up an ordinary low-country greyhound with a highland wolf-dog, you must not blame the first of them for taking the direction in which it pleases the last to drag him on. It was so, and not otherwise, with my neighbour Oliver Proudfute. He no sooner got up from the ground, but he mounted his mare like a flash of lightning, and, enraged at the unknightly advantage which yonder rascal had taken of his stumbling horse, he flew after him like a dromedary. I could not but follow, both to prevent a second stumble, and secure our over bold friend and champion from the chance of some ambush at the top of the hill. But the villain, who is a follower of some Lord of the Marches, and wears a winged spur for his cognizance, fled from our neighbour like fire from flint."

The senior Bailie of Perth listened with surprise to the legend which it had pleased Gow to circulate; for, though not much caring for the matter, he had always doubted the Bonnet-maker's romancing account of his own exploits, which hereafter he must hold as in some degree orthodox. The shrewd old Glover looked closer into the matter.

"You will drive the poor Bonnet-maker mad," he whispered to Henry, "and set him a-ringing his clapper, as if he were a town-bell on a rejoicing day, when for order and decency it were better he were silent."

"O, by Our Lady, father," replied the Smith, "I love the poor little braggadocio, and could not think of his sitting rueful and silent in the Provost's hall, while all the rest of them, and in especial that venomous Pottingar, were telling their mind."

"Thou art even too good-natured a fellow, Henry," answered Simon. "But mark the difference betwixt these two men. The harmless little Bonnet-maker assumes the airs of a dragon, to disguise his natural cowardice; while the Pottingar wilfully desires to show himself timid, poor-spirited, and humble, to conceal the danger of his temper. The adder is not the less deadly that he creeps under a stone. I tell thee, son Henry, that for all his sneaking looks, and timorous talking, this wretched anatomy loves mischief more than he fears danger.— But here we stand in front of the Provost's castle; and a lordly place is Kinfauns, and a credit to the city it is, to have the owner of such a gallant castle for its chief magistrate."

"A goodly fortalice, indeed," said the Smith, looking at the broad winding Tay, as it swept under the bank on which the castle stood, like its modern successor, and seemed the queen of the valley, although, on the opposite side of the river, the strong walls of Elcho appeared to dispute the pre-eminence. Elcho, however, was in that age a peaceful nunnery, and the walls with which it was surrounded were the barriers of secluded vestals, not the bulwarks of an armed garrison. "'Tis a brave castle," said the armourer, again looking at the towers of Kinfauns, "and the breastplate and target of the bonnie course of the Tay. It were worth lipping a good blade, before wrong were offered to it."

The porter of Kinfauns, who knew from a distance the persons and characters of the party, had already opened the court-yard gate for their entrance, and sent notice to Sir Patrick Charteris, that the eldest Bailie of Perth, with some other good citizens, were approaching the castle. The good knight, who was getting ready for a hawking party, heard the intimation, with pretty much the same feelings that the modern representative of a burgh hears of the menaced visitation of a party of his worthy electors, at a time rather unseasonable for their reception. That is, he internally devoted the intruders to Mahound and Termagant, and outwardly gave orders to receive them with all decorum and civility; commanded the sewers to bring hot venison steaks and cold baked meats into the knightly hall with all dispatch, and the butler to broach his casks, and do his duty; for if the Fair City of Perth sometimes filled his cellar, her citizens were always equally ready to assist at emptying his flagons.

The good burghers were reverently marshalled into the hall, where the knight, who was in a riding habit, and booted up to the middle of his thighs, received them with a mixture of courtesy and patronising condescension; wishing them all the while at the bottom of the Tay, on account of the interruption their arrival gave to his proposed amusement of the morning. He met them in the midst of the hall, with bare head and bonnet in hand, and some such salutation as the following:—
" Ha, my Master Eldest Bailie, and you, worthy Simon Glover, fathers of the Fair City;—and you, my learned Pottingar;— and you, stout Smith;—and my slashing Bonnet-maker too, who cracks more sculls than he covers, how come I to have the pleasure of seeing so many friends so early? I was thinking to see my hawks fly, and your company will make the sport more pleasant—(*Aside*, I trust in Our Lady they may break their necks!)—that is, always, unless the city have any commands to lay on me—Butler Gilbert, dispatch, thou knave —But I hope you have no more grave errand than to try if the malvoisie holds its flavour?"

The city delegates answered to their Provost's civilities by inclinations and congees, more or less characteristic, of which the Pottingar's bow was the lowest, and the Smith's the least ceremonious. Probably he knew his own value as a fighting man upon occasion. To the general compliment the elder Bailie replied.

"Sir Patrick Charteris, and our noble Lord Provost," said Craigdallie, gravely, "had our errand been to enjoy the hospitality with which we have been often regaled here, our manners would have taught us to tarry till your lordship had invited us, as on other occasions. And as to hawking, we have had enough on't for one morning; since a wild fellow, who was flying a falcon hard by on the moor, unhorsed and cudgelled our worthy friend Oliver Bonnet-maker, or Proud-fute, as some men call him, merely because he questioned him, in your honour's name, and the town of Perth's, who or what he was that took so much upon him."

"And what account gave he of himself?" said the Provost. "By St. John! I will teach him to forestall my sport!"

"So please your lordship," said the Bonnet-maker, "he did take me at disadvantage. But I got on horseback again afterwards, and pricked after him gallantly. He calls himself Richard the Devil."

"How, man? he that the rhymes and romances are made on?" said the Provost. "I thought that smaik's name had been Robert."

"I trow they be different, my lord; I only graced this fellow with the full title, for indeed he called himself the Devil's Dick, and said he was a Johnstone, and a follower of the lord of that name. But I put him back into the bog, and recovered my hawking bag, which he had taken when I was at disadvantage."

Sir Patrick paused for an instant. "We have heard," said he, "of the Lord of Johnstone, and of his followers. Little is to be had by meddling with them.—Smith, tell me, did you endure this?"

"Ay, faith did I, Sir Patrick; having command from my betters not to help."

"Well, if thou satst down with it," said the Provost, "I see not why we should rise up; especially as Master Oliver Proudfute, though taken at advantage at first, has, as he has told us, recovered his reputation and that of the burgh. But here comes the wine at length. Fill round to my good friends and guests till the wine leap over the cup. Prosperity to St. Johnston, and a merry welcome to you all, my honest friends!

And now sit you to eat a morsel, for the sun is high up, and it must be long since you thrifty men have broken your fast."

"Before we eat, my Lord Provost," said the Bailie, "let us tell you the pressing cause of our coming, which as yet we have not touched upon."

"Nay, prithee, Bailie," said the Provost, "put it off till thou hast eaten. Some complaint against the rascally jackmen and retainers of the nobles, for playing at football on the streets of the burgh, or some such goodly matter."

"No, my lord," said Craigdallie, stoutly and firmly. "It is the jackmen's masters of whom we complain, for playing at football with the honour of our families, and using as little ceremony with our daughters' sleeping chambers, as if they were in a bordel at Paris. A party of reiving night-walkers,— courtiers, and men of rank, as there is but too much reason to believe,—attempted to scale the windows of Simon Glover's house last night; they stood in their defence with drawn weapons when they were interrupted by Henry Smith, and fought till they were driven off by the rising of the citizens."

"How?" said Sir Patrick, setting down the cup which he was about to raise to his head. "Cocksbody, make that manifest to me, and by the soul of Thomas of Longueville, I will see you righted with my best power, were it to cost me life and land.—Who attests this?—Simon Glover, you are held an honest and a cautious man—do you take the truth of this charge upon your conscience?"

"My lord," said Simon, "understand I am no willing complainer in this weighty matter. No damage has arisen, save to the breakers of the peace themselves. I fear only great power could have encouraged such lawless audacity; and I were unwilling to put feud between my native town and some powerful nobleman on my account. But it has been said, that if I hang back in prosecuting this complaint, it will be as much as admitting that my daughter expected such a visit, which is a direct falsehood. Therefore, my lord, I will tell your lordship what happened, so far as I know, and leave further proceeding to your wisdom." He then told, from point to point, all that he had seen of the attack.

Sir Patrick Charteris, listening with much attention, seemed particularly struck with the escape of the man who had been made prisoner. "Strange," he said, "that you did not secure him when you had him. Did you not look at him so as to know him again?"

"I had but the light of a lantern, my Lord Provost; and as to suffering him to escape, I was alone," said the Glover, "and old. But yet I might have kept him, had I not heard my daughter shriek in the upper room; and ere I had returned from her chamber, the man had escaped through the garden."

"Now, armourer, as a true man, and a good soldier," said Sir Patrick, "tell me what you know of this matter."

Henry Gow, in his own decided style, gave a brief but clear narrative of the whole affair.

Honest Proudfute being next called upon, began his statement with an air of more importance. "Touching this awful and astounding tumult within the burgh, I cannot altogether, it is true, say with Henry Gow, that I saw the very beginning. But it will not be denied that I beheld a great part of the latter end, and especially that I procured the evidence most effectual to convict the knaves."

"And what is it, man?" said Sir Patrick Charteris. "Never lose time fumbling and prating about it. What is it?"

"I have brought your lordship, in this pouch, what one of the rogues left behind him," said the little man. "It is a trophy which, in good faith and honest truth, I do confess I won not by the blade, but I claim the credit of securing it with that presence of mind which few men possess amidst flashing torches and clashing weapons. I secured it, my lord, and here it is."

So saying, he produced from the hawking pouch already mentioned, the stiffened hand which had been found on the scene of the skirmish.

"Nay, Bonnet-maker," said the Provost, "I'll warrant thee man enough to secure a rogue's hand after it is cut from the body. What do you look so busily for in your bag?"

"There should have been—there was—a ring, my lord, which was on the knave's finger. I fear I have been forgetful, and left it at home, for I took it off to show to my wife, as she cared not to look upon the dead hand, as women love not such sights. But yet I thought I had put it on the finger again. Nevertheless, it must, I bethink me, be at home. I will ride back for it, and Henry Smith will trot along with me."

"We will all trot with thee," said Sir Patrick Charteris,

"since I am for Perth myself. Look you, honest burghers and good neighbours of Perth. You may have thought me unapt to be moved by light complaints and trivial breaches of your privileges, such as small trespasses on your game, the barons' followers playing football in the street, and such like. But, by the soul of Thomas of Longueville, you shall not find Patrick Charteris slothful in a matter of this importance. —This hand," he continued, holding up the severed joint, "belongs to one who hath worked no drudgery. We will put it in a way to be known and claimed of the owner, if his comrades of the revel have but one spark of honour in them.—Hark you, Gerard—get me some half-score of good men instantly to horse, and let them take jack and spear. Meanwhile, neighbours, if feud arise out of this, as is most likely, we must come to each other's support. If my poor house be attacked, how many men will you bring to my support?"

The burghers looked at Henry Gow, to whom they instinctively turned when such matters were discussed. "I will answer," said he, "for fifty good fellows to be assembled ere the common bell has rung ten minutes; for a thousand, in the space of an hour."

"It is well," answered the gallant Provost; "and in case of need, I will come to aid the Fair City with such men as I can make. And now, good friends, let us to horse."

CHAPTER IX

If I know how to manage these affairs,
Thus thrust disorderly upon my hands—
Never believe me——

Richard II

It was early in the afternoon of St. Valentine's Day that the Prior of the Dominicans was engaged in discharge of his duties as Confessor to a penitent of no small importance. This was an elderly man, of a goodly presence, a florid and healthful cheek, the under part of which was shaded by a venerable white beard, which descended over his bosom. The large and clear blue eyes, with the broad expanse of brow, expressed dignity; but it was of a character which seemed more accustomed to receive honours voluntarily paid, than to enforce them when they were refused. The good-nature of the expression was so great as to approach to defenceless simplicity or weakness of character, unfit, it might be inferred, to repel intrusion, or subdue resistance. Amongst the grey locks of this personage was placed a small circlet or coronet of gold upon a blue fillet. His beads, which were large and conspicuous, were of native gold, rudely enough wrought, but ornamented with Scottish pearls, of rare size and beauty. These were his only ornaments; and a long crimson robe of silk, tied by a sash of the same colour, formed his attire. His shrift being finished, he arose heavily from the embroidered cushion upon which he kneeled during his confession, and by the assistance of a crutch-headed staff of ebony, moved, lame and ungracefully, and with apparent pain, to a chair of state, which, surmounted by a canopy, was placed for his accommodation by the chimney of the lofty and large apartment.

This was Robert, third of that name, and the second of the ill-fated family of Stewart, who filled the throne of Scotland. He had many virtues, and was not without talent; but it was his great misfortune, that, like others of his devoted line, his merits were not of a kind suited to the part which he was called upon to perform in life. The King of so fierce a people as the Scots then were, ought to have been warlike, prompt, and active, liberal in rewarding services, strict in punishing crimes; one whose conduct should make him feared as well as beloved. The qualities of Robert the Third were the reverse of all these. In youth he had indeed seen battles; but, without incurring disgrace, he had never manifested the chivalrous love of war and peril, or the eager desire to distinguish himself by dangerous achievements, which that age expected from all who were of noble birth, and had claims to authority.

Besides, his military career was very short. Amidst the tumult of a tournament, the young Earl of Carrick, such was then his title, received a kick from the horse of Sir James Douglas of Dalkeith; in consequence of which, he was lame for the rest of his life, and absolutely disabled from taking share either in warfare, or in the military sports and tournaments which were its image. As Robert had never testified much predilection for violent exertion, he did not probably much regret the incapacities which exempted him from these active scenes. But his misfortune, or rather its consequences, lowered him in the eyes of a fierce nobility and warlike people. He was obliged to repose the principal charge of his affairs now in one member, now in another, of his family; sometimes with the actual rank, and always with the power, of Lieutenant-general of the kingdom. His paternal affection would have induced him to use the assistance of his eldest son, a young man of spirit and talent, whom in fondness he had created Duke of Rothsay, in order to give him the present possession of a dignity next to that of the throne.[1] But the young Prince's head was too giddy, and his hand too feeble, to wield with dignity the delegated sceptre. However fond of power, pleasure was the Prince's favourite pursuit; and the court was disturbed, and the country scandalized, by the number of fugitive amours and extravagant revels, practised by him who should have set an example of order and regularity to the youth of the Kingdom.

The license and impropriety of the Duke of Rothsay's conduct was the more reprehensible in the public view, that he was a married person; although some, over whom his youth, gaiety, grace, and good temper, had obtained influence, were of opinion, that an excuse for his libertinism might be found in the circumstances of the marriage itself. They reminded each other that his nuptials were entirely conducted by his uncle, the Duke of Albany, by whose counsels the infirm and timid King was much governed at the time, and who had the character of managing the temper of his brother and sovereign, so as might be most injurious to the interests and prospects of the young heir. By Albany's machinations, the hand of the heir apparent was in a manner put up to sale, as it was understood publicly that the nobleman in Scotland who should give the largest dower to his daughter, might aspire to raise her to the bed of the Duke of Rothsay.

In the contest for preference which ensued, George, Earl of Dunbar and March, who possessed, by himself or his vassals, a great part of the eastern frontier, was preferred to other competitors; and his daughter was, with the mutual good-will of the young couple, actually contracted to the Duke of Rothsay.

[1] This creation, and that of the Dukedom of Albany, in favour of the King's brother, were the first instances of ducal rank in Scotland Buchanan mentions the innovation in terms which may be considered as showing that even he partook in the general prejudice with which that title was viewed in Scotland down to a much later period. It had, indeed, been in almost every case united with heavy misfortunes—not rarely with tragic crimes.

But there remained a third party to be consulted, and that was no other than the tremendous Archibald, Earl of Douglas, terrible alike from the extent of his lands, from the numerous offices and jurisdictions with which he was invested, and from his personal qualities of wisdom and valour, mingled with indomitable pride, and more than the feudal love of vengeance. The Earl was also nearly related to the throne, having married the eldest daughter of the reigning Monarch.

After the espousals of the Duke of Rothsay with the Earl of March's daughter, Douglas, as if he had postponed his share in the negotiation to show that it could not be concluded with any one but himself, entered the lists to break off the contract. He tendered a larger dower with his daughter Marjory than the Earl of March had proffered ; and, secured by his own cupidity and fear of the Douglas, Albany exerted his influence with the timid Monarch till he was prevailed upon to break the contract with the Earl of March, and wed his son to Marjory Douglas, a woman whom Rothsay could not love. No apology was offered to the Earl of March, excepting that the espousals betwixt the Prince and Elizabeth of Dunbar had not been approved by the States of Parliament, and that till such ratification, the contract was liable to be broken off. The Earl deeply resented the wrong done to himself and his daughter, and was generally understood to study revenge, which his great influence on the English frontier was likely to place within his power.

In the meantime, the Duke of Rothsay, incensed at the sacrifice of his hand and his inclinations to this state intrigue, took his own mode of venting his displeasure, by neglecting his wife, contemning his formidable and dangerous father-in-law, and showing little respect to the authority of the King himself, and none whatever to the remonstrances of Albany his uncle, whom he looked upon as his confirmed enemy.

Amid these internal dissensions of his family, which extended themselves through his councils and administration, introducing every where the baneful effects of uncertainty and disunion, the feeble Monarch had for some time been supported by the counsels of his Queen Annabella, a daughter of the noble house of Drummond, gifted with a depth of sagacity and firmness of mind, which exercised some restraint over the levities of a son who respected her, and sustained on many occasions the wavering resolution of her royal husband. But after her death the imbecile Sovereign resembled nothing so much as a vessel drifted from her anchors, and tossed about amidst contending currents. Abstractedly considered, Robert might be said to doat upon his son,—to entertain respect and awe for the character of his brother Albany, so much more decisive than his own,—to fear the Douglas with a terror which was almost instinctive, and to suspect the constancy of the bold but fickle Earl of March. But his feelings towards these various characters were so mixed and complicated, that from time to time they showed entirely different from what they really were ; and according to the interest which had been last exerted over his flexible mind, the King would change from an indulgent, to a strict and even cruel father—from a confiding, to a jealous brother—or from a benignant and bountiful, to a grasping and encroaching Sovereign. Like the cameleon, his feeble mind reflected the colour of that firmer character upon which at the time he reposed for counsel and assistance. And when he disused the advice of one of his family, and employed the counsel of another, it was no unwonted thing to see a total change of measures, equally disrespectable to the character of the King, and dangerous to the safety of the state.

It followed as a matter of course, that the clergy of the Catholic Church acquired influence over a man whose intentions were so excellent, but whose resolutions were so infirm. Robert was haunted, not only with a due sense of the errors he had really committed, but with the tormenting apprehensions of those peccadilloes which beset a superstitious and timid mind. It is scarcely necessary, therefore, to add, that the churchmen of various descriptions had no small influence over this easy-tempered prince, though indeed, theirs was, at that period, an influence from which few or none escaped, however resolute and firm of purpose in affairs of a temporal character.—We now return from this long digression, without which what we have to relate could not perhaps have been well understood.

The King had moved with ungraceful difficulty to the cushioned chair, which, under a state or canopy, stood prepared for his accommodation, and upon which he sank down with enjoyment, like an indolent man, who had been for some time confined to a constrained position. When seated, the gentle and venerable looks of the good old man showed benevolence. The Prior, who now remained standing opposite to the royal seat, with an air of deep deference which cloaked the natural haughtiness of his carriage, was a man betwixt forty and fifty years of age, but every one of whose hairs still retained their natural dark colour. Acute features, and a penetrating look, attested the talents by which the venerable father had acquired his high station in the community over which he presided; and, we may add, in the councils of the kingdom in whose service they were often exercised. The chief objects which his education and habits taught him to keep in view, were the extension of the dominion and the wealth of the church, and the suppression of heresy, both of which he endeavoured to accomplish by all the means which his situation afforded him. But he honoured his religion by the sincerity of his own belief, and by the morality which guided his conduct in all ordinary situations. The faults of the Prior Anselm, though they led him into grievous error, and even cruelty, were perhaps rather those of his age and profession—his virtues were his own.

"These things done," said the King, "and the lands I have mentioned secured by my gift to this monastery, you are of opinion, father, that I stand as much in the good graces of our Holy Mother Church, as to term myself her dutiful son?"

"Surely, my liege," said the Prior; "would to God that all her children brought to the efficacious sacrament of confession as deep a sense of their errors, and as much will to make amends for them. But I speak these comforting words, my liege, not to Robert King of Scotland, but only to my humble and devout penitent, Robert Stewart of Carrick."

"You surprise me, Father," answered the King; "I have little check on my conscience for aught that I have done in my kingly office, seeing that I use therein less mine own opinion than the advice of the most wise counsellors."

"Even therein lieth the danger, my liege," replied the Prior. "The Holy Father recognizes in your Grace, in every thought, word, and action, an obedient vassal of the Holy Church. But there are perverse counsellors, who obey the instinct of their wicked hearts, while they abuse the good-nature and ductility of their monarch, and, under colour of serving his temporal interests, take steps which are prejudicial to those that last to eternity."

King Robert raised himself upright in his chair, and assumed an air of authority, which, though it well became him, he did not usually display.

"Prior Anselm," he said, "if you have discovered any thing in my conduct, whether as a king or a private individual, which may call down such censures as your words intimate, it is your duty to speak plainly, and I command you to do so."

"My liege, you shall be obeyed," answered the Prior, with an inclination of the body. Then raising himself up, and assuming the dignity of his rank in the church, he said, "Hear from me the words of our Holy Father the Pope, the successor of St. Peter, to whom have descended the keys, both to bind and to unloose. 'Wherefore, O Robert of Scotland, hast thou not received into the See of St. Andrews, Henry of Wardlaw, whom the Pontiff hath recommended to fill that See? Why dost thou make profession with thy lips, of dutiful service to the Church, when thy actions proclaim the depravity and disobedience of thy inward soul? Obedience is better than sacrifice.'"

"Sir Prior," said the Monarch, bearing himself in a manner not unbecoming his lofty rank, "we may well dispense with answering you upon this subject, being a matter which concerns us and the Estates of our kingdom, but does not affect our private conscience."

"Alas," said the Prior, "and whose conscience will it concern at the last day? Which of your belted lords or wealthy burgesses will then step between their King and the penalty which he has incurred, by following of their secular policy in matters ecclesiastical? Know, mighty King, that, were all the chivalry of thy realm drawn up to shield thee from the red levin-bolt, they would be consumed like scorched parchment before the blaze of a furnace."

"Good Father Prior," said the King, on whose timorous conscience this kind of language seldom failed to make an impression, "you surely argue over rigidly in this matter. It was during my last indisposition, while the Earl of Douglas held, as Lieutenant-general, the regal authority in Scotland, that the obstruction to the reception of the Primate unhappily arose. Do not, therefore, tax me with what happened when I was unable to conduct the affairs of the kingdom, and compelled to delegate my power to another."

"To your subject, Sire, you have said enough," replied the Prior. "But, if the impediment arose during the lieutenancy of the Earl of Douglas, the Legate of his Holiness will demand wherefore it has not been instantly removed, when the King resumed in his royal hands the reins of authority? The Black Douglas can do much; more perhaps than a subject should have power to do in the kingdom of his sovereign; but he cannot stand betwixt your grace and your own conscience, or release you from the duties to the Holy Church, which your situation as a king imposes upon you."

"Father," said Robert, somewhat impatiently, "you are over peremptory in this matter, and ought at least to wait a reasonable season, until we have time to consider of some remedy. Such disputes have happened repeatedly in the reigns of our predecessors; and our royal and blessed ancestor, Saint David, did not resign his privileges as a monarch without making a stand in their defence, even though he was involved in arguments with the Holy Father himself."

"And therein was that great and good king neither holy nor saintly," said the Prior; "and therefore was he given to be a rout and a spoil to his enemies, when he raised his sword against the banners of St. Peter, and St. Paul, and St. John of Beverley, in the war, as it is still called, of the Standard. Well was it for him, that, like his namesake, the son of Jesse, his sin was punished upon earth, and not entered against him at the long and dire day of accounting."

"Well, good Prior—well—enough of this for the present. The Holy See shall, God willing, have no reason to complain of me. I take Our Lady to witness, I would not for the crown I wear take the burden of wronging our Mother Church. We have ever feared that the Earl of Douglas kept his eyes too much fixed on the fame and the temporalities of this frail and passing life, to feel altogether as he ought the claims that refer to a future world."

"It is but lately," said the Prior, "that he hath taken up forcible quarters in the Monastery of Aberbrothock, with his retinue of a thousand followers; and the abbot is compelled to furnish him with all he needs for horse and man, which the Earl calls exercising the hospitality which he hath a right to expect from the foundation to which his ancestors were contributors. Certain, it were better to return to the Douglas his lands than to submit to such exaction, which more resembles the masterful license of Highland thiggers and sorners, than the demeanour of a Christian baron."

"The Black Douglasses," said the King, with a sigh, "are a race which will not be said nay. But, Father Prior, I am myself, it may be, an intruder of this kind; for my sojourning hath been long among you, and my retinue, though far fewer than the Douglas's, are nevertheless enough to cumber you for their daily maintenance; and though our order is to send out purveyors to lessen your charge as much as may be, yet if there be inconvenience, it were fitting we should remove in time."

"Now, Our Lady forbid!" said the Prior, who, if desirous of power, had nothing meanly covetous in his temper, but was even magnificent in his generous kindness; "certainly the Dominican Convent can afford to her Sovereign the hospitality which the house offers to every wanderer of whatever condition, who will receive it at the hands of the poor servants of our patron. No, my royal liege; come with ten times your present train, they shall neither want a grain of oats, a pile of straw, a morsel of bread, nor an ounce of food, which our convent can supply them. It is one thing to employ the revenues of the Church, which are so much larger than monks ought to need or wish for, in the suitable and dutiful reception of your royal Majesty, and another to have it wrenched from us by the hands of rude and violent men, whose love of rapine is only limited by the extent of their power."

"It is well, good Prior," said the King; "and now to turn our thoughts for an instant from state affairs, can thy reverence inform us how the good citizens of Perth have begun their Valentine's Day?—Gallantly and merrily, and peacefully, I hope."

"For gallantly, my liege, I know little of such qualities. For peacefully, there were three or four men, two cruelly wounded, came this morning before daylight to ask the privilege of girth and sanctuary, pursued by a hue and cry of citizens in their shirts, with clubs, bills, Lochaber axes, and two-handed swords, crying kill and slay, each louder than another. Nay, they were not satisfied when our porter and watch told them that those they pursued had taken refuge in the Galilee of the Church;[1] but continued for some

---

[1] The *Galilee* of a Catholic Cathedral is a small side chapel to which excommunicated persons have access, though they must not enter the body of the church. Mr. Surtees suggests that the name of the place thus appropriated to the consolation of miserable penitents, was derived from the text: "Ite, nunciate fratribus meis ut eant in Galileam : ibi me videbunt." Matth. xxviii. 10. See *History of Durham*, vol. i. p. lvi. Criminals claiming sanctuary, were, for obvious reasons, accustomed to place themselves in this part of the edifice.

minutes clamouring and striking upon the postern door, demanding that the men who had offended should be delivered up to them. I was afraid their rude noise might have broken your Majesty's rest, and raised some surprise."

"My rest might have been broken," said the Monarch; "but that sounds of violence should have occasioned surprise—Alas! reverend Father, there is in Scotland only one place where the shriek of the victim, and threats of the oppressor are not heard—and that, Father, is—the grave."

The Prior stood in respectful silence, sympathizing with the feelings of a monarch, whose tenderness of heart suited so ill with the condition and manners of his people.

"And what became of the fugitives?" asked Robert, after a minute's pause.

"Surely, Sire," said the Prior, "they were dismissed, as they desired to be, before daylight; and after we had sent out to be assured that no ambush of their enemies watched them in the vicinity, they went their way in peace."

"You know nothing," enquired the King, "who the men were, or the cause of their taking refuge with you?"

"The cause," said the Prior, "was a riot with the townsmen; but how arising is not known to us. The custom of our house is to afford twenty-four hours of uninterrupted refuge in the sanctuary of St. Dominic, without asking any question at the poor unfortunates who have sought relief there. If they desire to remain for a longer space, the cause of their resorting to sanctuary must be put upon the register of the convent; and, praised be our holy Saint, many persons escape the weight of the law by this temporary protection, whom, did we know the character of their crimes, we might have found ourselves obliged to render up to their pursuers and persecutors."

As the Prior spoke, a dim idea occurred to the Monarch, that the privilege of sanctuary thus peremptorily executed, must prove a severe interruption to the course of justice through his realm. But he repelled the feeling, as if it had been a suggestion of Satan, and took care that not a single word should escape to betray to the churchman that such a profane thought had ever occupied his bosom; on the contrary, he hasted to change the subject.

"The sun," he said, "moves slowly on the index. After the painful information you have given me, I expected the Lords of my Council ere now, to take order with the ravelled affairs of this unhappy riot. Evil was the fortune which gave me rule over a people, among whom it seems to me I am in my own person the only man who desires rest and tranquillity!"

"The Church always desires peace and tranquillity," added the Prior, not suffering even so general a proposition to escape the poor King's oppressed mind, without insisting on a saving clause for the Church's honour.

"We meant nothing else," said Robert. "But, Father Prior, you will allow that the Church, in quelling strife, as is doubtless her purpose, resembles the busy housewife, who puts in motion the dust which she means to sweep away."

To this remark the Prior would have made some reply, but the door of the apartment was opened, and a gentleman usher announced the Duke of Albany.

CHAPTER X

Gentle friend!
Chide not her mirth, who was sad yesterday,
And may be so to-morrow.
                                    JOANNA BAILLIE.

THE Duke of Albany was, like his royal brother, named Robert. The Christian name of the latter had been John, until he was called to the throne; when the superstition of the times observed that the name had been connected with misfortune in the lives and reigns of John of England, John of France, and John Baliol of Scotland. It was therefore agreed, that, to elude the bad omen, the new King should assume the name of Robert, rendered dear to Scotland by the recollections of Robert Bruce. We mention this, to account for the existence of two brothers of the same Christian name in one family, which was not certainly an usual occurrence, more than at the present day.

Albany, also an aged man, was not supposed to be much more disposed for warlike enterprise than the King himself. But if he had not courage, he had wisdom to conceal and cloak over his want of that quality, which, once suspected, would have ruined all the plans which his ambition had formed. He had also pride enough to supply, in extremity, the want of real valour, and command enough over his nerves to conceal their agitation. In other respects, he was experienced in the ways of courts, calm, cool, and crafty, fixing upon the points which he desired to attain, while they were yet far removed, and never losing sight of them, though the winding paths in which he trode might occasionally seem to point to a different direction. In his person he resembled the King, for he was noble and majestic both in stature and countenance. But he had the advantage of his elder brother, in being unencumbered with any infirmity, and in every respect lighter and more active. His dress was rich and grave, as became his age and rank, and, like his royal brother, he wore no arms of any kind, a case of small knives supplying at his girdle the place usually occupied by a dagger in absence of a sword.

At the Duke's entrance the Prior, after making an obeisance, respectfully withdrew to a recess in the apartment, at some distance from the royal seat, in order to leave the conversation of the brothers uncontrolled by the presence of a third person. It is necessary to mention, that the recess was formed by a window, placed in the inner front of the monastic buildings, called the Palace, from its being the frequent residence of the Kings of Scotland, but which was, unless on such occasions, the residence of the Prior or Abbot. The window was placed over the principal entrance to the royal apartments, and commanded a view of the internal quadrangle of the convent, formed on the right hand by the length of the magnificent church, on the left by a building, containing the range of cellars, with the refectory, chapter-house, and other conventual apartments rising above them, for such existed altogether independent of the space occupied by King Robert and his attendants; while a fourth row of buildings, showing a noble outward front to the rising sun, consisted of a large *hospitium*, for the reception of strangers and pilgrims, and many subordinate offices, warehouses, and places of accommodation, for the ample stores which supplied the magnificent hospitality of the Dominican fathers. A lofty vaulted entrance led through this eastern front into the quadrangle, and was precisely opposite to the window at which Prior Anselm stood, so that he could see underneath the dark arch and observe the light which gleamed beneath it from the eastern and open portal; but, owing to the height to which he was raised, and the depth of the vaulted archway, his eye could but indistinctly reach the opposite and extended portal. It is necessary to notice these localities. We return to the conversation between the princely relatives.

"My dear brother," said the King, raising the Duke of Albany, as he stooped to kiss his hand; "my dear, dear brother, wherefore this ceremonial? Are we not both sons of the same Stewart of Scotland, and of the same Elizabeth More?"

"I have not forgot that it is so," said Albany, arising; "but I must not omit, in the familiarity of the brother, the respect that is due to the King."

"Oh, true, most true, Robin," answered the King. "The throne is like a lofty and barren rock, upon which flower or shrub can never take root. All kindly feelings, all tender affections, are denied to a monarch. A King must not fold a brother to his heart—he dare not give way to fondness for a son!"

"Such, in some respects, is the doom of greatness, Sire," answered Albany; "but Heaven, who removed to some distance from your Majesty's sphere the members of your own family, has given you a whole people to be your children."

"Alas! Robert," answered the Monarch, "your heart is better framed for the duties of a sovereign than mine. I see from the height at which fate has placed me, that multitude whom you call my children—I love them, I wish them well—but they are many, and they are distant from me. Alas! even the meanest of them has some beloved being whom he can clasp to his heart, and upon whom he can lavish the fondness of a father! But all that a King can give to a people is a smile, such as the sun bestows on the snowy peaks of the Grampian mountains, as distant and as ineffectual. Alas, Robin! our father used to caress us, and if he chid us it was with a tone of kindness; yet he was a monarch as well as I, and wherefore should not I be permitted, like him, to reclaim my poor prodigal by affection as well as severity?"

"Had affection never been tried, my liege," replied Albany, in the tone of one who delivers sentiments which he grieves to utter, "means of gentleness ought assuredly to be first made use of. Your Grace is best judge whether they have been long enough persevered in, and whether those of discouragement and restraint may not prove a more effectual corrective. It is exclusively in your royal power to take what measures with the Duke of Rothsay you think will be most available to his ultimate benefit, and that of the kingdom."

"This is unkind, brother," said the King; "you indicate the painful path which you would have me pursue, yet you offer me not your support in treading it."

"My support your Grace may ever command," replied Albany; "but would it become me, of all men on earth, to prompt to your Grace severe measures against your son and heir? Me—on whom, in case of failure—which Heaven forefend—of your Grace's family, this fatal crown might descend? Would it not be thought and said by the fiery March and the haughty Douglas, that Albany had sown dissension between his royal brother and the heir to the Scottish throne, perhaps to clear the way for the succession of his own family? —No, my liege—I can sacrifice my life to your service, but I must not place my honour in danger."

"You say true, Robin—you say very true," replied the King, hastening to put his own interpretation upon his brother's words. "We must not suffer these powerful and dangerous lords to perceive that there is aught like discord in the royal family. That must be avoided of all things; and therefore we will still try indulgent measures, in hopes of correcting the follies of Rothsay. I behold sparks of hope in him, Robin, from time to time, that are well worth cherishing. He is young—very young—a prince, and in the hey-day of his blood. We will have patience with him, like a good rider with a hot-tempered horse. Let him exhaust this idle humour, and no one will be better pleased with him than yourself. You have censured me in your kindness for being too gentle, too retired—Rothsay has no such defects."

"I will pawn my life he has not," replied Albany, dryly.

"And he wants not reflection as well as spirit," continued the poor King, pleading the cause of his son to his brother. "I have sent for him to attend council to-day, and we shall see how he acquits himself of his devoir. You yourself allow, Robin, that the Prince wants neither shrewdness nor capacity for affairs, when he is in the humour to consider them."

"Doubtless, he wants neither, my liege," replied Albany, "when he *is* in the humour to consider them."

"I say so," answered the King; "and am heartily glad that you agree with me, Robin, in giving this poor hapless young man another trial. He has no mother now to plead his cause with an incensed father. That must be remembered, Albany."

"I trust," said Albany, "the course which is most agreeable to your Grace's feelings will also prove the wisest and the best."

The Duke well saw the simple stratagem by which the King was endeavouring to escape from the conclusions of his reasoning, and to adopt, under pretence of his sanction, a course of proceeding the reverse of what it best suited him to recommend. But though he saw he could not guide his brother to the line of conduct he desired, he would not abandon the reins, but resolved to watch for a fitter opportunity of obtaining the sinister advantages to which new quarrels betwixt the King and Prince were soon, he thought, likely to give rise.

In the meantime King Robert, afraid lest his brother should resume the painful subject from which he had just escaped, called aloud to the Prior of the Dominicans, " I hear the trampling of horse. Your station commands the court-yard, reverend Father. Look from the window, and tell us who alights—Rothsay, is it not ? "

" The noble Earl of March, with his followers," said the Prior.

" Is he strongly accompanied ? " said the King. " Do his people enter the inner-gate ? "

At the same moment, Albany whispered the King, " Fear nothing—the Brandanes [1] of your household are under arms."

The King nodded thanks, while the Prior from the window answered the question he had put. " The Earl is attended by two pages, two gentlemen, and four grooms. One page follows him up the main staircase, bearing his lordship's sword. The others halt in the court, and—Benedicite, how is this?—Here is a strolling glee-woman, with her viol, preparing to sing beneath the royal windows, and in the cloister of the Dominicans, as she might in the yard of an hostelrie ! I will have her presently thrust forth."

" Not so, Father," said the King. " Let me implore grace for the poor wanderer. The Joyous Science, as they call it, which they profess, mingles sadly with the distresses to which want and calamity condemn a strolling race ; and in that they resemble a King, to whom all men cry, ' All hail ! ' while he lacks the homage and obedient affection which the

[1] The men of the Isle of Bute were called Brandanes ; from what derivation is not quite certain, though the strong probability lies with Dr. Leyden, who deduces the name from the Patron Saint of the islands in the Frith of Clyde—viz. St. Brandin. The territory of Bute was the King's own patrimony, and its natives his personal followers. The noble family of Bute, to whom the island now belongs, are an ancient illegitimate branch of the Royal house.

poorest yeoman receives from his family. Let the wanderer remain undisturbed, Father; and let her sing if she will to the yeomen and troopers in the court—it will keep them from quarrelling with each other, belonging, as they do, to such unruly and hostile masters.'

So spoke the well-meaning and feeble-minded Prince, and the Prior bowed in acquiescence. As he spoke, the Earl of March entered the hall of audience, dressed in the ordinary riding garb of the time, and wearing his poniard. He had left in the anteroom the page of honour who carried his sword. The Earl was a well-built, handsome man, fair-complexioned, with a considerable profusion of light-coloured hair, and bright blue eyes, which gleamed like those of a falcon. He exhibited in his countenance, otherwise pleasing, the marks of a hasty and irritable temper, which his situation as a high and powerful feudal lord had given him but too many opportunities of indulging.

"I am glad to see you, my Lord of March," said the King, with a gracious inclination of his person. "You have been long absent from our councils."

"My liege," answered March, with a deep reverence to the King, and a haughty and formal inclination to the Duke of Albany, "if I have been absent from your Grace's councils, it is because my place has been supplied by more acceptable, and, I doubt not, abler counsellors. And now I come but to say to your Highness, that the news from the English frontier make it necessary that I should return without delay to my own estates. Your Grace has your wise and politic brother, my Lord of Albany, with whom to consult, and the mighty and warlike Earl of Douglas to carry your councils into effect. I am of no use save in my own country; and thither, with your Highness's permission, I am purposed instantly to return, to attend my charge, as Warden of the Eastern Marches."

"You will not deal so unkindly with us, cousin," replied the gentle Monarch. "Here are evil tidings on the wind. These unhappy Highland clans are again breaking into general commotion, and the tranquillity even of our own court requires the wisest of our council to advise, and the bravest of our barons to execute, what may be resolved upon. The descendant of Thomas Randolph will not surely abandon the grandson of Robert Bruce at such a period as this?"

"I leave with him the descendant of the farfamed James

of Douglas," answered March. "It is his lordship's boast, that he never puts foot in stirrup but a thousand horse mount with him as his daily lifeguard, and I believe the monks of Aberbrothock [1] will swear to the fact. Surely, with all the Douglas's chivalry, they are fitter to restrain a disorderly swarm of Highland kerne, than I can be to withstand the archery of England, and power of Henry Hotspur? And then, here is his Grace of Albany, so jealous in his care of your Highness's person, that he calls your Brandanes to take arms, when a dutiful subject like myself approaches the court with a poor half-score of horse, the retinue of the meanest of the petty barons who own a tower and a thousand acres of barren heath. When such precautions are taken where there is not the slightest chance of peril—since I trust none was to be apprehended from me—your royal person will surely be suitably guarded in real danger."

"My Lord of March," said the Duke of Albany, "the meanest of the barons of whom you speak put their followers in arms, even when they receive their dearest and nearest friends within the iron gate of their castle; and, if it please Our Lady, I will not care less for the King's person than they do for their own. The Brandanes are the King's immediate retainers and household servants, and an hundred of them is but a small guard round his Grace, when yourself, my lord, as well as the Earl of Douglas, often ride with ten times the number."

"My lord duke," replied March, "when the service of the King requires it, I can ride with ten times as many horse as your Grace has named; but I have never done so either traitorously to entrap the King, nor boastfully to overawe other nobles."

"Brother Robert," said the King, ever anxious to be a peacemaker, "you do wrong even to intimate a suspicion of my Lord of March. And you, cousin of March, misconstrue my brother's caution.—But hark—to divert this angry parley—I hear no unpleasing touch of minstrelsy. You know the Gay Science, my Lord of March, and love it well—Step to yonder window, beside the holy Prior, at whom we make

---

[1] The complaint of the monks of Arbroath about the too great honour the Earl of Douglas had paid them in becoming their guest with a train of a thousand men, passed into a proverb, and was never forgotten when the old Scots churchmen railed at the nobility, who, in the sequel, demolished the church, out of that earnest yearning they had long felt for her goods.

no question touching secular pleasures, and you will tell us if the music and lay be worth listening to. The notes are of France, I think—My brother of Albany's judgment is not worth a cockle-shell in such matters—so you, cousin, must report your opinion whether the poor glee-maiden deserves recompense. Our son and the Douglas will presently be here, and then, when our council is assembled, we will treat of graver matters."

With something like a smile on his proud brow, March withdrew into the recess of the window, and stood there in silence beside the Prior, like one who, while he obeyed the King's command, saw through and despised the timid precaution which it implied, as an attempt to prevent the dispute betwixt Albany and himself. The tune, which was played upon a viol, was gay and sprightly in the commencement, with a touch of the wildness of the Troubadour music. But as it proceeded, the faltering tones of the instrument, and of the female voice which accompanied it, became plaintive and interrupted, as if choked by the painful feelings of the minstrel.

The offended Earl, whatever might be his judgment in such matters on which the King had complimented him, paid, it may be supposed, little attention to the music of the female minstrel. His proud heart was struggling between the allegiance he owed his Sovereign, as well as the love he still found lurking in his bosom for the person of his well-natured King, and a desire of vengeance arising out of his disappointed ambition, and the disgrace done to him by the substitution of Marjory Douglas to be bride of the heir-apparent, instead of his betrothed daughter. March had the vices and virtues of a hasty and uncertain character, and even now, when he came to bid the King adieu, with the purpose of renouncing his allegiance as soon as he reached his own feudal territories, he felt unwilling, and almost unable, to resolve upon a step so criminal and so full of peril. It was with such dangerous cogitations that he was occupied during the beginning of the glee-maiden's lay; but objects which called his attention powerfully, as the songstress proceeded, affected the current of his thoughts, and riveted them on what was passing in the court-yard of the monastery. The song was in the Provençal dialect, well understood as the language of poetry in all the courts of Europe, and particularly in Scotland. It was more simply turned, however, than was the general caste of the Sirventes, and rather resembled the *lai* of a Norman Minstrel.   It may be translated thus :

THE LAY OF POOR LOUISE,[1]

Ah, poor Louise !   The livelong day
She roams from cot to castle gay ;
And still her voice and viol say,
Ah, maids, beware the woodland way,
             Think on Louise.

Ah, poor Louise !   The sun was high,
It smirch'd her cheek, it dimm'd her eye,
The woodland walk was cool and nigh,
Where birds with chiming streamlets vie
             To cheer Louise.

Ah, poor Louise !   The savage bear
Made ne'er that lovely grove his lair ;
The wolves molest not paths so fair—
But better far had such been there
             For poor Louise.

Ah, poor Louise !   In woody wold
She met a huntsman fair and bold !
His baldrick was of silk and gold,
And many a witching tale he told
             To poor Louise.

Ah, poor Louise !   Small cause to pine
Had'st thou for treasures of the mine ;
For peace of mind, that gift divine,
And spotless innocence, were thine,
             Ah, poor Louise !

Ah, poor Louise !   Thy treasure's reft !
I know not if by force or theft,
Or part by violence, part by gift ;
But misery is all that's left
             To poor Louise.

Let poor Louise some succour have !
She will not long your bounty crave,
Or tire the gay with warning stave—
For Heaven has grace, and earth a grave
             For poor Louise.

The song was no sooner finished, than, anxious lest the dispute should be revived betwixt his brother and the Earl of March, King Robert called to the latter, "What think you of

---

[1] This lay has been set to beautiful music by a lady whose composition, to say nothing of her singing, might make any poet proud of his verses, Mrs. Robert Arkwright, born Miss Kemble.

the minstrelsy, my lord?—Methinks, as I heard it even at this distance, it was a wild and pleasing lay."

"My judgment is not deep, my lord; but the singer may dispense with my approbation, since she seems to have received that of his Grace of Rothsay—the first judge in Scotland."

"How!" said the King in alarm; "is my son below?"

"He is sitting on horseback by the glee-maiden," said March, with a malicious smile on his cheek, "apparently as much interested by her conversation as her music."

"How is this, Father Prior?" said the King. But the Prior drew back from the lattice.

"I have no will to see, my lord, things which it would pain me to repeat."

"How is all this?" said the King, who coloured deeply, and seemed about to rise from his chair; but changed his mind, as if unwilling, perhaps, to look upon some unbecoming prank of the wild young Prince, which he might not have had heart to punish with necessary severity. The Earl of March seemed to have a pleasure in informing him of that, of which doubtless he desired to remain ignorant.

"My liege," he cried, "this is better and better. The glee-maiden has not only engaged the ear of the Prince of Scotland, as well as of every groom and trooper in the court-yard, but she has riveted the attention of the black Douglas, whom we have not known as a passionate admirer of the Gay Science. But truly, I do not wonder at his astonishment, for the Prince has honoured the fair professor of song and viol with a kiss of approbation."

"How!" cried the King, "is David of Rothsay trifling with a glee-maiden, and his wife's father in presence?—Go, my good Father Abbot, call the Prince here instantly— Go, my dearest brother"——And when they had both left the room, the King continued, "Go, good cousin of March— there will be mischief, I am assured of it. I pray you go, cousin, and second my Lord Prior's prayers with my commands."

"You forget, my liege," said March, with the voice of a deeply offended person; "the father of Elizabeth of Dunbar were but an unfit intercessor between the Douglas and his royal son-in-law."

"I crave your pardon, cousin," said the gentle old man. "I own you have had some wrong—but my Rothsay will be murdered—I must go myself."

But as he arose precipitately from his chair, the poor King missed a footstep, stumbled, and fell heavily to the ground, in such a manner, that his head striking the corner of the seat from which he had risen, he became for a minute insensible. The sight of the accident at once overcame March's resentment, and melted his heart. He ran to the fallen Monarch, and replaced him in his seat, using, in the tenderest and most respectful manner, such means as seemed most fit to recall animation. Robert opened his eyes, and gazed around with uncertainty.

"What has happened?—are we alone?—who is with us?"

"Your dutiful subject, March," replied the Earl.

"Alone with the Earl of March!" repeated the King, his still disturbed intellects receiving some alarm from the name of a powerful chief, whom he had reason to believe he had mortally offended.

"Yes, my gracious liege, with poor George of Dunbar; of whom many have wished your Majesty to think ill, though he will be found truer to your royal person at the last than they will."

"Indeed, cousin, you have had too much wrong; and believe me, we shall strive to redress——"

"If your Grace thinks so, it may yet be righted," interrupted the Earl, catching at the hopes which his ambition suggested; "the Prince and Marjory Douglas are nearly related—the dispensation from Rome was informally granted—their marriage cannot be lawful—the Pope, who will do much for so godly a Prince, can set aside this unchristian union, in respect of the pre-contract. Bethink you well, my liege," continued the Earl, kindling with a new train of ambitious thoughts, to which the unexpected opportunity of pleading his cause personally had given rise,—"bethink you how you choose betwixt the Douglas and me. He is powerful and mighty, I grant. But George of Dunbar wears the keys of Scotland at his belt, and could bring an English army to the gates of Edinburgh, ere Douglas could leave the skirts of Cairntable to oppose them. Your royal son loves my poor deserted girl, and hates the haughty Marjory of Douglas. Your Grace may judge the small account in which he holds her, by his toying with a common glee-maiden even in the presence of her father."

The King had hitherto listened to the Earl's argument with the bewildered feelings of a timid horseman, borne

away by an impetuous steed, whose course he can neither
arrest nor direct. But the last words awakened in his
recollection the sense of his son's immediate danger.

"Oh, ay, most true—my son—the Douglas—Oh, my dear
cousin, prevent blood, and all shall be as you will.—Hark,
there is a tumult—that was the clash of arms?"

"By my coronet—by my knightly faith, it is true!" said
the Earl, looking from the window upon the inner square of
the convent, now filled with armed men and brandished
weapons, and resounding with the clash of armour. The
deep-vaulted entrance was crowded with warriors at its farthest
extremity, and blows seemed to be in the act of being exchanged betwixt some who were endeavouring to shut the
gate, and others who contended to press in.

"I will go instantly," said the Earl of March, "and soon
quell this sudden broil—Humbly, I pray your Majesty to think
on what I have had the boldness to propose."

"I will—I will, fair cousin," said the King, scarce knowing
to what he pledged himself—"Do but prevent tumult and
bloodshed!"

CHAPTER XI

Fair is the damsel, passing fair—
Sunny at distance gleams her smile;
Approach—the cloud of woful care
Hangs trembling in her eye the while.

                    LUCINDA, *a Ballad.*

WE must here trace, a little more correctly, the events
which had been indistinctly seen from the window of the
royal apartments, and yet more indistinctly reported by those
who witnessed them. The glee-maiden, already mentioned,
had planted herself, where a rise of two large broad steps,
giving access to the main gateway of the royal apartments,
gained her an advantage of a foot and a half in height over
those in the court, of whom she hoped to form an audience.
She wore the dress of her calling, which was more gaudy than
rich, and showed the person more than did the garb of other
females. She had laid aside an upper mantle, and a small
basket which contained her slender stock of necessaries, and
a little French spaniel dog sat beside them, as their protector.
An azure-blue jacket, embroidered with silver, and sitting
close to the person, was open in front, and showed several

waistcoats of different-coloured silks, calculated to set off the symmetry of the shoulders and bosom, and remaining open at the throat. A small silver chain worn around her neck, involved itself amongst these brilliant-coloured waistcoats, and was again produced from them, to display a medal of the same metal, which intimated, in the name of some court or guild of minstrels, the degree she had taken in the Gay or Joyous Science. A small scrip, suspended over her shoulders by a blue silk riband, hung on her left side.

Her sunny complexion, snow-white teeth, brilliant black eyes, and raven locks, marked her country lying far in the south of France, and the arch smile and dimpled chin bore the same character. Her luxuriant raven locks, twisted around a small gold bodkin, were kept in their position by a net of silk and gold. Short petticoats, deep-laced with silver, to correspond with the jacket, red stockings which were visible so high as near the calf of the leg, and buskins of Spanish leather, completed her adjustment, which, though far from new, had been saved as an untarnished holiday suit, which much care had kept in good order. She seemed about twenty-five years old ; but perhaps fatigue and wandering had anticipated the touch of time, in obliterating the freshness of early youth.

We have said the glee-maiden's manner was lively, and we may add, that her smile and repartee were ready. But her gaiety was assumed, as a quality essentially necessary to her trade, of which it was one of the miseries, that the professors were obliged frequently to cover an aching heart with a compelled smile. This seemed to be the case with Louise, who, whether she was actually the heroine of her own song, or whatever other cause she might have for sadness, showed at times a strain of deep melancholy thought, which interfered with and controlled the natural flow of lively spirits, which the practice of the Joyous Science especially required. She lacked also, even in her gayest sallies, the decided boldness and effrontery of her sisterhood, who were seldom at a loss to retort a saucy jest, or turn the laugh against any who interrupted or interfered with them.

It may be here remarked, that it was impossible that this class of women, very numerous in that age, could bear a character generally respectable. They were, however, protected by the manners of the time ; and such were the immunities they possessed by the rights of chivalry, that nothing was more rare than to hear of such errant damsels sustaining injury or wrong, and they passed and repassed safely, where armed travellers would probably have encountered a bloody opposition. But though licensed and protected in honour of their tuneful art, the wandering minstrels, male or female, like similar ministers to the public amusement, the itinerant musicians, for instance, and strolling comedians of our own day, led a life too irregular and precarious, to be accounted a creditable part of society. Indeed, among the stricter Catholics, the profession was considered as unlawful.

Such was the damsel, who, with viol in hand, and stationed on the slight elevation we have mentioned, stepped forward to the bystanders and announced herself as a mistress of the Gay Science, duly qualified by a brief from a Court of Love and Music held at Aix, in Provence, under the countenance of the flower of chivalry, the gallant Count Aymer; who now prayed that the cavaliers of merry Scotland, who were known over the wide world for bravery and courtesy, would permit a poor stranger to try whether she could afford them any amusement by her art.—The love of song was like the love of fight, a common passion of the age, which all at least affected, whether they were actually possessed by it or no; therefore the acquiescence in Louise's proposal was universal. At the same time, an aged, dark-browed monk who was among the bystanders, thought it necessary to remind the glee-maiden, that, since she was tolerated within these precincts, which was an unusual grace, he trusted nothing would be sung or said inconsistent with the holy character of the place.

The glee-maiden bent her head low, shook her sable locks, and crossed herself reverentially, as if she disclaimed the possibility of such a transgression, and then began the song of Poor Louise, which we gave at length in the last chapter.

Just as she commenced, she was stopped by a cry of " Room—room—place for the Duke of Rothsay ! "

"Nay, hurry no man on my score," said a gallant young cavalier, who entered on a noble Arabian horse, which he managed with exquisite grace, though by such slight handling of the reins, such imperceptible pressure of the limbs and sway of the body, that to any eye save that of an experienced horseman, the animal seemed to be putting forth his paces for his own amusement, and thus gracefully bearing forward a rider who was too indolent to give himself any trouble about the matter.

The Prince's apparel, which was very rich, was put on with slovenly carelessness. His form, though his stature was low, and his limbs extremely slight, was elegant in the extreme; and his features no less handsome. But there was on his brow a haggard paleness, which seemed the effect of care or of dissipation, or of both these wasting causes combined. His eyes were sunk and dim, as from late indulgence in revelry on the preceding evening, while his cheek was inflamed with unnatural red, as if either the effect of the Bacchanalian orgies had not passed away from the constitution, or a morning draught had been resorted to, in order to remove the effects of the night's debauchery.

Such was the Duke of Rothsay, and heir of the Scottish crown, a sight at once of interest and compassion. All unbonneted, and made way for him, while he kept repeating carelessly, "No haste—no haste—I shall arrive soon enough at the place I am bound for.—How's this—a damsel of the Joyous Science? Ay, by St. Giles! and a comely wench to boot. Stand still, my merry-men; never was minstrelsy marred for me.—A good voice, by the mass! Begin me that lay again, sweetheart."

Louise did not know the person who addressed her; but the general respect paid by all around, and the easy and indifferent manner in which it was received, showed her she was addressed by a man of the highest quality. She recommenced her lay, and sung her best accordingly; while the young Duke seemed thoughtful and rather affected towards the close of the ditty. But it was not his habit to cherish such melancholy affections. "This is a plaintive ditty, my nut-brown maid," said he, chucking the retreating glee-maiden under the chin, and detaining her by the collar of her dress, which was not difficult, as he sat on horseback so close to the steps on which she stood. "But I warrant me you have livelier notes at will, *ma bella tenebrosa*; ay, and canst sing in bower as well as wold, and by night as well as day."

"I am no nightingale, my lord," said Louise, endeavouring to escape a species of gallantry which ill-suited the place and circumstances, a discrepancy to which he who addressed it to her seemed contemptuously indifferent.

"What hast thou there, darling?" he added, removing his hold from her collar, to the scrip which she carried.

Glad was Louise to escape his grasp, by slipping the knot of the riband, and leaving the little bag in the Prince's hand, as, retiring back beyond his reach, she answered, "Nuts, my lord, of the last season."

The Prince pulled out a handful of nuts accordingly. "Nuts, child!—they will break thine ivory teeth—hurt thy pretty voice," said Rothsay, cracking one with his teeth, like a village schoolboy.

"They are not the walnuts of my own sunny clime, my lord," said Louise; "but they hang low, and are within the reach of the poor."

"You shall have something to afford you better fare, poor wandering ape," said the Duke, in a tone in which feeling predominated more than in the affected and contemptuous gallantry of his first address to the glee-maiden.

At this moment, as he turned to ask an attendant for his purse, the Prince encountered the stern and piercing look of a tall black man, seated on a powerful iron-grey horse, who had entered the court with attendants while the Duke of Rothsay was engaged with Louise, and now remained stupified and almost turned to stone by his surprise and anger at this unseemly spectacle. Even one who had never seen Archibald, Earl of Douglas, called the Grim, must have known him by his swart complexion, his gigantic frame, his buff-coat of bull's-hide, and his air of courage, firmness, and sagacity, mixed with indomitable pride. The loss of an eye in battle, though not perceptible at first sight, as the ball of the injured organ remained similar to the other, gave yet a stern immovable glare to the whole aspect.

The meeting of the royal son-in-law with his terrible step-father, was in circumstances which arrested the attention of all present; and the bystanders waited the issue with silence and suppressed breath, lest they should lose any part of what was to ensue.

When the Duke of Rothsay saw the expression which occupied the stern features of Douglas, and remarked that the Earl did not make the least motion towards respectful, or even civil salutation, he seemed determined to show him how little respect he was disposed to pay to his displeased looks. He took his purse from his chamberlain.

"Here, pretty one," he said, "I give thee one gold piece for the song thou hast sung me, another for the nuts I have stolen from thee, and a third for the kiss thou art about to give me. For know, my pretty one, that when fair lips (and thine for fault of better may be called so) make sweet music for my pleasure, I am sworn to St. Valentine to press them to mine."

"My song is recompensed nobly"—said Louise shrinking back; "my nuts are sold to a good market—farther traffic, my lord, were neither befitting you nor beseeming me."

"What! you coy it, my nymph of the highway?" said the Prince, contemptuously. "Know, damsel, that one asks you a grace who is unused to denial."

"It is the Prince of Scotland"—"the Duke of Rothsay,"—said the courtiers around, to the terrified Louise, pressing forward the trembling young woman: "you must not thwart his humour."

"But I cannot reach your lordship," she said timidly, "you sit so high on horseback."

"If I must alight," said Rothsay, "there shall be the heavier penalty—What does the wench tremble for? Place thy foot on the toe of my boot, give me hold of thy hand—Gallantly done!" He kissed her as she stood thus suspended in the air, perched upon his foot, and supported by his hand; saying, "There is thy kiss, and there is my purse to pay it; and to grace thee farther, Rothsay will wear thy scrip for the day." He suffered the frightened girl to spring to the ground, and turned his looks from her to bend them contemptuously on the Earl of Douglas, as if he had said, "All this I do in despite of you and of your daughter's claims."

"By St. Bride of Douglas!" said the Earl, pressing towards the Prince, "this is too much, unmannered boy, as void of sense as honour! You know what considerations restrain the hand of Douglas, else had you never dared——"

"Can you play at spang-cockle, my lord?" said the Prince, placing a nut on the second joint of his forefinger and spinning it off by a smart application of the thumb. The nut struck on Douglas's broad breast, who burst out into a dreadful exclamation of wrath, inarticulate, but resembling the growl of a lion in depth and sternness of expression. "I cry your pardon, most mighty lord," said the Duke of Rothsay, scornfully, while all around trembled; "I did not conceive my pellet could have wounded you, seeing you wear a buff-coat. Surely, I trust, it did not hit your eye?"

The Prior, despatched by the King, as we have seen in the last chapter, had by this time made way through the crowd, and laying hold on Douglas's rein, in a manner that made it impossible for him to advance, reminded him that the Prince was the son of his Sovereign, and the husband of his daughter.

"Fear not, Sir Prior," said Douglas. "I despise the childish boy too much to raise a finger against him. But I will return insult for insult.—Here, any of you who love the Douglas,—spurn me this quean from the Monastery gates; and let her be so scourged that she may bitterly remember to the last day of her life, how she gave means to an unrespective boy to affront the Douglas!"

Four or five retainers instantly stepped forth to execute commands which were seldom uttered in vain, and heavily would Louise have atoned for an offence of which she was alike the innocent, unconscious, and unwilling instrument, had not the Duke of Rothsay interfered.

"Spurn the poor glee-woman!" he said in high indignation; "scourge her for obeying my commands!—Spurn thine own oppressed vassals, rude Earl—scourge thine own faulty hounds—but beware how you touch so much as a dog that Rothsay hath patted on the head, far less a female whose lips he hath kissed!"

Before Douglas could give an answer, which would certainly have been in defiance, there arose that great tumult at the outward gate of the Monastery, already noticed, and men both on horseback and on foot began to rush headlong in, not actually fighting with each other, but certainly in no peaceable manner.

One of the contending parties, seemingly, were partisans of Douglas, known by the cognizance of the Bloody Heart, the other were composed of citizens of the town of Perth. It appeared they had been skirmishing in earnest when without the gates, but, out of respect to the sanctified ground, they lowered their weapons when they entered, and confined their strife to a war of words and mutual abuse.

The tumult had this good effect, that it forced asunder, by the weight and press of numbers, the Prince and Douglas, at a moment when the levity of the former, and the pride of the latter, were urging both to the utmost extremity. But now peacemakers interfered on all sides. The Prior and the Monks threw themselves among the multitude, and commanded peace in the name of Heaven, and reverence to their sacred walls, under penalty of excommunication; and their expostula-

tions began to be listened to. Albany, who was despatched by
his royal brother at the beginning of the fray, had not arrived
till now on the scene of action. He instantly applied himself to
Douglas, and in his ear conjured him to temper his passion.

"By St. Bride of Douglas, I will be avenged!" said the
Earl. "No man shall brook life after he has passed an affront
on Douglas."

"Why so you may be avenged in fitting time," said Albany;
"but let it not be said, that, like a peevish woman, the Great
Douglas could choose neither time nor place for his vengeance.
Bethink you, all that we have laboured at is like to be upset
by an accident. George of Dunbar hath had the advantage
of an audience with the old man; and though it lasted but
five minutes, I fear it may endanger the dissolution of your
family match, which we brought about with so much difficulty.
The authority from Rome has not yet been obtained."

"A toy!" answered Douglas, haughtily,—"they dare not
dissolve it."

"Not while Douglas is at large, and in possession of his
power," answered Albany. "But, noble Earl, come with me,
and I will show you at what disadvantage you stand."

Douglas dismounted, and followed his wily accomplice in
silence. In a lower hall they saw the ranks of the Brandanes
drawn up, well-armed in caps of steel and shirts of mail.
Their captain, making an obeisance to Albany, seemed to
desire to address him

"What now, MacLouis?" said the Duke.

"We are informed the Duke of Rothsay has been insulted,
and I can scarce keep the Brandanes within door."

"Gallant MacLouis," said Albany, 'and you, my trusty
Brandanes, the Duke of Rothsay, my princely nephew, is as
well as a hopeful gentleman can be. Some scuffle there has
been, but all is appeased." He continued to draw the Earl
of Douglas forward. "You see, my lord," he said in his ear,
"that if the word *arrest* was to be once spoken, it would be
soon obeyed, and you are aware your attendants are few for
resistance."

Douglas seemed to acquiesce in the necessity of patience
for the time. "If my teeth," he said, "should bite through
my lips, I will be silent till it is the hour to speak out."

George of March, in the meanwhile, had a more easy task
of pacifying the Prince. "My Lord of Rothsay," he said,
approaching him with grave ceremony, "I need not tell you

that you owe me something for reparation of honour, though I blame not you personally for the breach of contract which has destroyed the peace of my family. Let me conjure you by what observance your Highness may owe an injured man, to forego for the present this scandalous dispute."

"My lord, I owe you much," replied Rothsay; "but this haughty and all-controlling lord has wounded mine honour."

"My lord, I can but add, your royal father is ill—hath swooned with terror for your Highness's safety."

"Ill!" replied the Prince—"the kind, good old man—swooned, said you, my Lord of March?—I am with him in an instant."

The Duke of Rothsay sprung from his saddle to the ground, and was dashing into the palace like a greyhound, when a feeble grasp was laid on his cloak, and the faint voice of a kneeling female exclaimed, "Protection, my noble Prince!—Protection for a helpless stranger!"

"Hands off, stroller!" said the Earl of March, thrusting the supplicant glee-maiden aside.

But the gentler Prince paused. "It is true," he said, "I have brought the vengeance of an unforgiving devil upon this helpless creature. O Heaven! what a life is mine, so fatal to all who approach me!—What to do in the hurry?—She must not go to my apartments—And all my men are such born reprobates.—Ha! thou at mine elbow, honest Harry Smith? What dost thou here?"

"There has been something of a fight, my lord," answered our acquaintance the Smith, "between the townsmen and the Southland loons who ride with the Douglas; and we have swinged them as far as the Abbey-gate."

"I am glad of it—I am glad of it. And you beat the knaves fairly?"

"Fairly, does your Highness ask?" said Henry. "Why, ay! We were stronger in numbers, to be sure; but no men ride better armed than those who follow the Bloody Heart. And so in a sense we beat them fairly; for as your Highness knows, it is the Smith who makes the man-at-arms, and men with good weapons are a match for great odds."

While they thus talked, the Earl of March, who had spoken with some one near the palace gate, returned in anxious haste. "My Lord Duke!—My Lord Duke!—Your father is recovered, and if you haste not speedily, my Lord of Albany and the Douglas will have possession of his royal ear."

"And if my royal father is recovered," said the thoughtless Prince, "and is holding, or about to hold, council with my gracious uncle and the Earl of Douglas, it befits neither your lordship nor me to intrude till we are summoned. So there is time for me to speak of my little business with mine honest armourer here."

"Does your Highness take it so?" said the Earl, whose sanguine hopes of a change of favour at court had been too hastily excited, and were as speedily checked,—"Then so let it be for George of Dunbar."

He glided away with a gloomy and displeased aspect; and thus out of the two most powerful noblemen in Scotland, at the time when the aristocracy so closely controlled the throne, the reckless heir-apparent had made two enemies; the one by scornful defiance, and the other by careless neglect. He heeded not the Earl of March's departure, however, or rather he felt relieved from his importunity.

The Prince went on in indolent conversation with our armourer, whose skill in his art had made him personally known to many of the great lords about the court.

"I had something to say to thee, Smith—Canst thou take up a fallen link in my Milan hauberk?"

"As well, please your Highness, as my mother could take up a stitch in the nets she wove—The Milaner shall not know my work from his own."

"Well, but that was not what I wished of thee just now," said the Prince, recollecting himself; "this poor glee-woman, good Smith, she must be placed in safety. Thou art man enough to be any woman's champion, and thou must conduct her to some place of safety."

Henry Smith was, as we have seen, sufficiently rash and daring when weapons were in question. But he had also the pride of a decent burgher, and was unwilling to place himself in what might be thought equivocal circumstances by the sober part of his fellow-citizens.

"May it please your Highness," he said, "I am but a poor craftsman. But though my arm and sword are at the King's service, and your Highness's, I am, with reverence, no squire of dames. Your Highness will find, among your own retinue, knights and lords willing enough to play Sir Pandarus of Troy—it is too knightly a part for poor Hal of the Wynd."

"Umph—hah!"—said the Prince. "My purse, Edgar"— (his attendant whispered him)—"True, true, I gave it to the poor wench.—I know enough of your craft, Sir Smith, and of craftsmen in general, to be aware that men lure not hawks with empty hands; but I suppose my word may pass for the price of a good armour, and I will pay it thee with thanks to boot, for this slight service."

"Your Highness may know other craftsmen," said the Smith; "but, with reverence, you know not Henry Gow. He will obey you in making a weapon, or in welding one, but he knows nothing of this petticoat service."

"Hark thee, thou Perthshire mule," said the Prince, yet smiling, while he spoke, at the sturdy punctilio of the honest burgher,—"the wench is as little to me as she is to thee. But in an idle moment, as you may learn from those about thee, if thou sawest it not thyself, I did her a passing grace, which is likely to cost the poor wretch her life. There is no one here whom I can trust to protect her against the discipline of belt and bow-string, with which the Border brutes who follow Douglas will beat her to death, since such is his pleasure."

"If such be the case, my liege, she has a right to every honest man's protection; and since she wears a petticoat,— though I would it were longer, and of a less fanciful fashion,—I will answer for her protection as well as a single man may. But where am I to bestow her?"

"Good faith, I cannot tell," said the Prince. "Take her to Sir John Ramorny's lodging—But, no—no—he is ill at ease, and besides, there are reasons—take her to the devil if thou wilt, but place her in safety, and oblige David of Rothsay."

"My noble Prince," said the Smith, "I think—always with reverence—that I would rather give a defenceless woman to the care of the devil than of Sir John Ramorny. But though the devil be a worker in fire like myself, yet I know not his haunts, and with aid of Holy Church hope to keep him on terms of defiance. And, moreover, how I am to convey her out of this crowd, or through the streets, in such a mumming habit, may be well made a question."

"For the leaving the convent," said the Prince, "this good monk, (seizing upon the nearest by his cowl,) Father Nicholas or Boniface——"

"Poor brother Cyprian, at your Highness's command," said the father.

"Ay, ay, brother Cyprian," continued the Prince, "yes. Brother Cyprian shall let you out at some secret passage which he knows of, and I will see him again to pay a Prince's thanks for it."

The churchman bowed in acquiescence, and poor Louise, who, during this debate, had looked from the one speaker to the other, hastily said, " I will not scandalize this good man with my foolish garb—I have a mantle for ordinary wear."

" Why, there, Smith, thou hast a friar's hood and a woman's mantle to shroud thee under. I would all my frailties were as well shrouded ! Farewell, honest fellow ; I will thank thee hereafter."

Then, as if afraid of farther objection on the Smith's part, he hastened into the palace.

Henry Gow remained stupified at what had passed, and at finding himself involved in a charge at once inferring much danger, and an equal risk of scandal, both which, joined to a principal share which he had taken, with his usual forward-ness, in the fray, might, he saw, do him no small injury in the suit he pursued most anxiously. At the same time, to leave a defenceless creature to the ill usage of the barbarous Galwegians, and licentious followers of the Douglas, was a thought which his manly heart could not brook for an instant.

He was roused from his reverie by the voice of the Monk, who, sliding out his words with the indifference which the holy fathers entertained, or affected, towards all temporal matters, desired them to follow him. The Smith put himself in motion, with a sigh much resembling a groan, and, without appearing exactly connected with the Monk's motions, he followed him into a cloister, and through a postern door, which, after looking once behind him, the priest left ajar. Behind them followed Louise, who had hastily assumed her small bundle, and, calling her little four-legged companion, had eagerly followed in the path which opened an escape from what had shortly before seemed a great and inevitable danger.

CHAPTER XII

Then up and spak the auld gudewife,
And wow ! but she was grim :
" Had e'er your father done the like,
It had been ill for him "

LUCKY TRUMBULL.

THE party were now, by a secret passage, admitted within the church, the outward doors of which, usually left open, had been closed against every one in consequence of the recent tumult, when the rioters of both parties had endeavoured to rush into it for other purposes than those of devotion. They traversed the gloomy aisles, whose arched roof resounded to the heavy tread of the armourer, but was silent under the sandal'd foot of the Monk, and the light step of poor Louise, who trembled excessively, as much from fear as cold. She saw that neither her spiritual nor temporal conductor looked kindly upon her. The former was an austere man, whose aspect seemed to hold the luckless wanderer in some degree of horror, as well as contempt; while the latter, though, as we have seen, one of the best-natured men living, was at present grave to the pitch of sternness, and not a little displeased with having the part he was playing forced upon him, without, as he was constrained to feel, a possibility of his declining it.

His dislike at his task extended itself to the innocent object of his protection, and he internally said to himself, as he surveyed her scornfully,—" A proper queen of beggars to walk the streets of Perth with, and I a decent burgher! This tawdry minion must have as ragged a reputation as the rest of her sisterhood, and I am finely sped if my chivalry in her behalf comes to Catharine's ears. I had better have slain a man, were he the best in Perth ; and, by hammer and nails, I would have done it on provocation, rather than convoy this baggage through the city."

Perhaps Louise suspected the cause of her conductor's anxiety, for she said, timidly and with hesitation, " Worthy sir, were it not better I should stop one instant in that chapel, and don my mantle?"

" Umph, sweetheart, well proposed," said the armourer ; but the Monk interfered, raising at the same time the finger of interdiction.

"The Chapel of Holy St. Madox is no tiring-room for jugglers and strollers to shift their trappings in. I will presently show thee a vestiary more suited to thy condition."

The poor young woman hung down her humbled head, and turned from the chapel door which she had approached, with the deep sense of self-abasement. Her little spaniel seemed to gather from his mistress's looks and manner, that they were unauthorized intruders on the holy ground which they trode, and hung his ears, and swept the pavement with his tail, as he trotted slowly and close to Louise's heels.

The Monk moved on without a pause. They descended a

broad flight of steps, and proceeded through a labyrinth of subterranean passages, dimly lighted. As they passed a low-arched door, the Monk turned, and said to Louise, with the same stern voice as before,—" There, daughter of folly, there is a robing-room, where many before you have deposited their vestments ! "

Obeying the least signal with ready and timorous acquiescence, she pushed the door open, but instantly recoiled with terror It was a charnel-house, half filled with dry skulls and bones.

" I fear to change my dress there, and alone—But if you, father, command it, be it as you will."

" Why, thou child of vanity, the remains on which thou lookest are but the earthly attire of those who, in their day, led or followed in the pursuit of worldly pleasure. And such shalt thou be, for all thy mincing and ambling, thy piping and thy harping ; thou, and all such ministers of frivolous and worldly pleasure, must become like these poor bones, whom thy idle nicety fears and loathes to look upon."

" Say not with idle nicety, reverend father," answered the glee-maiden, " for Heaven knows, I covet the repose of these poor bleached relics ; and if by stretching my body upon them, I could, without sin, bring my state to theirs, I would choose that charnel-heap for my place of rest, beyond the fairest and softest couch in Scotland."

" Be patient, and come on," said the Monk, in a milder tone ; " the reaper must not leave the harvest-work till sunset gives the signal that the day's toil is over."

They walked forward. Brother Cyprian, at the end of a long gallery, opened the door of a small apartment, or perhaps a chapel, for it was decorated with a crucifix, before which burned four lamps. All bent and crossed themselves ; and the priest said to the minstrel maiden, pointing to the crucifix, " What says that emblem ? "

" That HE invites the sinner as well as the righteous to approach."

" Ay, if the sinner put from him his sin," said the Monk, whose tone of voice was evidently milder. " Prepare thyself here for thy journey."

Louise remained an instant or two in the chapel, and presently reappeared in a mantle of coarse grey cloth, in which she had closely muffled herself, having put such of her more gaudy habiliments as she had time to take off, in the little basket which had before held her ordinary attire.

The Monk presently afterwards unlocked a door which led to the open air. They found themselves in the garden which surrounded the monastery of the Dominicans. "The southern gate is on the latch, and through it you can pass unnoticed," said the Monk. "Bless thee, my son; and bless thee too, unhappy child. Remembering where you put off your idle trinkets, may you take care how you again resume them!"

"Alas, father!" said Louise, "if the poor foreigner could supply the mere wants of life by any more creditable occupation, she has small wish to profess her idle art. But——"

But the Monk had vanished, nay, the very door through which she had just passed appeared to have vanished also, so curiously was it concealed beneath a flying buttress, and among the profuse ornaments of Gothic architecture. "Here is a woman let out by this private postern, sure enough," was Henry's reflection. "Pray Heaven the good fathers never let any in! The place seems convenient for such games at bopeep.—But, benedicite, what is to be done next? I must get rid of this quean as fast as I can; and I must see her safe. For let her be at heart what she may, she looks too modest, now she is in decent dress, to deserve the usage which the wild Scot of Galloway, or the Devil's legion from the Liddell, are like to afford her."

Louise stood as if she waited his pleasure which way to go. Her little dog, relieved by the exchange of the dark subterranean vault for the open air, sprung in wild gambols through the walks, and jumped upon its mistress; and even, though more timidly, circled close round the Smith's feet, to express its satisfaction to him also, and conciliate his favour.

"Down, Charlot, down!" said the glee-maiden. "You are glad to get into the blessed sunshine; but where shall we rest at night, my poor Charlot?"

"And now, mistress," said the Smith,—not churlishly, for it was not in his nature, but bluntly, as one who is desirous to finish a disagreeable employment,—"which way lies your road?"

Louise looked on the ground, and was silent. On being again urged to say which way she desired to be conducted, she again looked down, and said, she could not tell.

"Come, come," said Henry, "I understand all that—I

have been a *galliard*—a reveller in my day—but it's best to be plain. As matters are with me now, I am an altered man for these many, many months; and so, my quean, you and I must part sooner than perhaps a light-o'-love such as you expected to part with—a likely young fellow."

Louise wept silently, with her eyes still cast on the ground, as one who felt an insult which she had not a right to complain of. At length, perceiving that her conductor was grown impatient, she faltered out, "Noble sir——"

"*Sir* is for a knight," said the impatient burgher, "and *noble* is for a baron. I am Harry of the Wynd, an honest mechanic, and free of my guild."

"Good craftsman, then," said the minstrel woman, "you judge me harshly, but not without seeming cause. I would relieve you immediately of my company, which, it may be, brings little credit to good men, did I but know which way to go."

"To the next wake or fair, to be sure," said Henry, roughly, having no doubt that this distress was affected for the purpose of palming herself upon him, and perhaps dreading to throw himself into the way of temptation; "and that is the feast of St. Madox, at Auchterarder. I warrant thou wilt find the way thither well enough."

"Aftr—Auchter—" repeated the glee-maiden, her southern tongue in vain attempting the Celtic accentuation. "I am told my poor lays will not be understood if I go nearer to yon dreadful range of mountains."

"Will you abide, then, in Perth?"

"But where to lodge?" said the wanderer.

"Why, where lodged you last night?" replied the Smith. "You know where you came from surely, though you seem doubtful where you are going?"

"I slept in the hospital of the Convent. But I was only admitted upon great importunity, and I was commanded not to return."

"Nay, they will never take you in with the ban of the Douglas upon you, that is even too true. But the Prince mentioned Sir John Ramorny's—I can take you to his lodgings through by-streets—though it is short of an honest burgher's office, and my time presses."

"I will go any where—I know I am a scandal and incumbrance. There was a time when it was otherwise—But this Ramorny, who is he?"

"A courtly knight, who lives a jolly bachelor's life, and is Master of the Horse, and privado, as they say, to the young Prince."

"What! to the wild, scornful young man who gave occasion to yonder scandal?—Oh, take me not thither, good friend! Is there no Christian woman, who would give a poor creature rest in her cowhouse, or barn, for one night? I will be gone with early daybreak. I will repay her richly. I have gold—and I will repay you too, if you will take me where I may be safe from that wild reveller, and from the followers of that dark Baron, in whose eye was death."

"Keep your gold for those who lack it, mistress," said Henry, "and do not offer to honest hands the money that is won by violing, and tabouring, and toe-tripping, and perhaps worse pastimes. I tell you plainly, mistress, I am not to be fooled. I am ready to take you to any place of safety you can name, for my promise is as strong as an iron shackle. But you cannot persuade me that you do not know what earth to make for. You are not so young in your trade as not to know there are hostelries in every town, much more in a city like Perth, where such as you may be harboured for your money, if you cannot find some gulls, more or fewer, to pay your lawing. If you have money, mistress, my care about you need be the less; and truly I see little but pretence in all that excessive grief, and fear of being left alone, in one of your occupation."

Having thus, as he conceived, signified that he was not to be deceived by the ordinary arts of a glee-maiden, Henry walked a few paces sturdily, endeavouring to think he was doing the wisest and most prudent thing in the world. Yet he could not help looking back to see how Louise bore his departure, and was shocked to observe that she had sunk upon a bank, with her arms resting on her knees, and her head on her arms, in a situation expressive of the utmost desolation.

The Smith tried to harden his heart. "It is all a sham," he said; "the gouge knows her trade—I'll be sworn, by Saint Ringan."

At the instant, something pulled the skirts of his cloak; and, looking round, he saw the little spaniel, who immediately, as if to plead his mistress's cause, got on his hind-legs and began to dance, whimpering at the same time, and looking back to Louise, as if to solicit compassion for his forsaken owner.

"Poor thing," said the Smith, "there may be a trick in this too, for thou dost but as thou art taught.—Yet, as I promised to protect this poor creature, I must not leave her in a swoon, if it be one, were it but for manhood's sake."

Returning, and approaching his troublesome charge, he was at once assured, from the change of her complexion, either that she was actually in the deepest distress, or had a power of dissimulation beyond the comprehension of man— or woman either.

"Young woman," he said, with more of kindness than he had hitherto been able even to assume, "I will tell you frankly how I am placed. This is St. Valentine's Day, and by custom, I was to spend it with my fair Valentine. But blows and quarrels have occupied all the morning, save one poor half hour. Now, you may well understand where my heart and my thoughts are, and where, were it only in mere courtesy, my body ought to be."

The glee-maiden listened, and appeared to comprehend him.

"If you are a true lover, and have to wait upon a chaste Valentine, God forbid that one like me should make a disturbance between you! Think about me no more. I will ask of that great river to be my guide to where it meets the ocean, where I think they said there was a seaport; I will sail from thence to La Belle France, and will find myself once more in a country, in which the roughest peasant would not wrong the poorest female."

"You cannot go to Dundee to-day," said the Smith. "The Douglas people are in motion on both sides of the river, for the alarm of the morning has reached them ere now; and all this day, and the next, and the whole night which is between, they will gather to their leader's standard, like Highlandmen at the fiery cross. Do you see yonder five or six men, who are riding so wildly on the other side of the river? These are Annandale men; I know them by the length of their lances, and by the way they hold them. An Annandale man never slopes his spear backwards, but always keeps the point upright, or pointed forward."

"And what of them?" said the glee-maiden. "They are men-at-arms and soldiers—They would respect me for my viol and my helplessness."

"I will say them no scandal," answered the Smith. "If you were in their own glens, they would use you hospitably, and you would have nothing to fear; but they are now on an expedition. All is fish that comes to their net. There are amongst them who would take your life for the value of your gold ear-rings. Their whole soul is settled in their eyes to see prey, and in their hands to grasp it. They have no ears either to hear lays of music, or listen to prayers for mercy. Besides, their leader's order is gone forth concerning you, and it is of a kind sure to be obeyed. Ay, great lords are sooner listened to if they say, 'Burn a church,' than if they say, 'Build one.'"

"Then," said the glee-woman, "I were best sit down and die."

"Do not say so," replied the Smith. "If I could but get you a lodging for the night, I would carry you the next morning to Our Lady's Stairs, from whence the vessels go down the river for Dundee, and would put you on board with some one bound that way, who should see you safely lodged where you would have fair entertainment and kind usage."

"Good—excellent—generous man!" said the glee-maiden, "do this, and if the prayers and blessings of a poor unfortunate should ever reach Heaven, they will rise thither in thy behalf. We will meet at yonder postern door, at whatever time the boats take their departure."

"That is at six in the morning, when the day is but young."

"Away with you, then, to your Valentine;—and if she loves you, oh, deceive her not!"

"Alas, poor damsel! I fear it is deceit hath brought thee to this pass. But I must not leave you thus unprovided. I must know where you are to pass the night."

"Care not for that," replied Louise—"the heavens are clear —there are bushes and boskets enough by the river side; Charlot and I can well make a sleeping-room of a green arbour for one night; and to-morrow will, with your promised aid, see me out of reach of injury and wrong. Oh, the night soon passes away when there is hope for to-morrow!—Do you still linger, with your Valentine waiting for you? Nay, I shall hold you but a loitering lover, and you know what belongs to a minstrel's reproaches."

"I cannot leave you, damsel," answered the armourer, now completely melted. "It were mere murder to suffer you to pass the night exposed to the keenness of a Scottish blast in February. No, no—my word would be ill kept in this manner; and if I should incur some risk of blame, it is but just penance for thinking of thee, and using thee, more according to my own prejudices, as I now well believe, than thy merits. Come with me, damsel—thou shalt have a sure and honest lodging for the night, whatsoever may be the consequence. It would be an evil compliment to my Catharine, were I to leave a poor creature to be starved to death, that I might enjoy her company an hour sooner."

So saying, and hardening himself against all anticipations of the ill consequences or scandal which might arise from such a measure, the manly-hearted Smith resolved to set evil report at defiance, and give the wanderer a night's refuge in his own house. It must be added, that he did this with extreme reluctance, and in a sort of enthusiasm of benevolence.

Ere our stout son of Vulcan had fixed his worship on the Fair Maid of Perth, a certain natural wildness of disposition had placed him under the influence of Venus, as well as that of Mars; and it was only the effect of a sincere attachment which had withdrawn him entirely from such licentious pleasures. He was therefore justly jealous of his newly-acquired reputation for constancy, which his conduct to this poor wanderer must expose to suspicion—a little doubtful, perhaps, of exposing himself too venturously to temptation—and moreover in despair to lose so much of St. Valentine's Day, which custom not only permitted, but enjoined him to pass beside his mate for the season. The journey to Kinfauns, and the various transactions which followed, had consumed the day, and it was now nearly even-song time.

As if to make up by a speedy pace for the time he was compelled to waste upon a subject so foreign to that which he had most at heart, he strode on through the Dominican's gardens, entered the town, and casting his cloak around the lower part of his face, and pulling down his bonnet to conceal the upper, he continued the same celerity of movement through by-streets and lanes, hoping to reach his own house in the Wynd without being observed. But when he had continued his rate of walking for ten minutes, he began to be sensible it might be too rapid for the young woman to keep up with him. He accordingly looked behind him with a degree of angry impatience, which soon turned into compunction, when he saw that she was almost utterly exhausted by the speed which she had exerted.

"Now, marry, hang me up for a brute," said Henry to himself. "Was my own haste ever so great, could it give that poor creature wings? And she loaded with baggage too! I am an ill-nurtured beast, that is certain, wherever women are in question; and always sure to do wrong when I have the best will to act right.—Hark thee, damsel; let me carry these things for thee. We shall make better speed that I do so."

Poor Louise would have objected, but her breath was too much exhausted to express herself; and she permitted her good-natured guardian to take her little basket, which when the dog beheld, he came straight before Henry, stood up, and shook his fore-paws, whining gently, as if he too wanted to be carried.

"Nay, then, I must needs lend thee a lift too," said the Smith, who saw the creature was tired.

"Fie, Charlot!" said Louise; "thou knowest I will carry thee myself."

She endeavoured to take up the little spaniel, but it escaped from her; and going to the other side of the Smith, renewed its supplication that he would take it up.

"Charlot's right," said the Smith; "he knows best who is ablest to bear him. This lets me know, my pretty one, that you have not been always the bearer of your own mail— Charlot can tell tales."

So deadly a hue came across the poor glee-maiden's countenance as Henry spoke, that he was obliged to support her, lest she should have dropped to the ground. She recovered again, however, in an instant or two, and with a feeble voice, requested her guide would go on.

"Nay, nay," said Henry, as they began to move, "keep hold of my cloak, or my arm, if it helps you forward better. A fair sight we are; and had I but a rebeck or a guitar at my back, and a jackanapes on my shoulder, we should seem as joyous a brace of strollers as ever touched string at a castle gate.—'Snails!" he ejaculated internally, "were any neighbour to meet me with this little harlotry's basket at my back, her dog under my arm, and herself hanging on my cloak, what could they think but that I had turned mumper in good earnest? I would not for the best harness I ever laid hammer on, that any of our long-tongued neighbours met me in this guise; it were a jest would last from St. Valentine's Day to next Candlemas."

Stirred by these thoughts, the Smith, although at the risk of making much longer a route which he wished to traverse as swiftly as possible, took the most indirect and private course which he could find in order to avoid the main streets, still crowded with people, owing to the late scene of tumult and agitation. But unhappily his policy availed him nothing; for in turning into an alley he met a man with his cloak muffled around his face, from a desire like his own to pass unobserved, though the slight insignificant figure, the spindle-shanks, which showed themselves beneath the mantle, and the small dull eye that blinked over its upper folds, announced the Pottingar as distinctly as if he had carried his sign in front of his bonnet. His unexpected and most unwelcome presence overwhelmed the Smith with confusion. Ready evasion was not the property of his bold, blunt temper; and knowing this man to be a curious observer, a malignant tale-bearer, and by no means well disposed to himself in particular, no better hope occurred to him than that the worshipful apothecary would give him some pretext to silence his testimony, and secure his discretion, by twisting his neck round.

Bur far from doing or saying any thing which could warrant such extremities, the Pottingar, seeing himself so close upon his stalwart townsman that recognition was inevitable, seemed determined it should be as slight as possible; and without appearing to notice any thing particular in the company or circumstances in which they met, he barely slid out these words as he passed him, without even a glance towards his companion after the first instant of their meeting,—"A merry holiday to you once more, stout Smith. What! thou art bringing thy cousin, pretty Mrs. Joan Letham, with her mail, from the water-side—fresh from Dundee, I warrant? I heard she was expected at the old cordwainer's."

As he spoke thus, he looked neither right nor left, and exchanging a "Save you!" with a salute of the same kind which the Smith rather muttered than uttered distinctly, he glided forward on his way like a shadow.

"The foul fiend catch me, if I can swallow that pill," said Henry Smith, "how well soever it may be gilded. The knave has a shrewd eye for a kirtle, and knows a wild-duck from a tame, as well as e'er a man in Perth—He were the last in the Fair City to take sour plums for pears, or my round-about Cousin Joan for this piece of fantastic vanity. I fancy his bearing was as much as to say, I will not see what you might wish me blind to—and he is right to do so, as he might easily purchase himself a broken pate by meddling with my matters—and so he will be silent for his own sake. But whom have we next—By St. Dunstan! the chattering, bragging, cowardly knave, Oliver Proudfute!"

It was, indeed, the bold Bonnet-maker whom they next encountered, who, with his cap on one side, and trolling the ditty of

"Thou art over long at the pot, Tom, Tom,"

gave plain intimation that he had made no dry meal.

"Ha! my jolly Smith," he said, "have I caught thee in the manner?—What, can the true steel bend?—Can Vulcan, as the minstrel says, pay Venus back in her own coin?—Faith, thou wilt be a gay Valentine before the year's out, that begins with the holiday so jollily."

"Hark ye, Oliver," said the displeased Smith, "shut your eyes and pass on, crony. And hark ye again, stir not your tongue about what concerns you not, as you value having an entire tooth in your head."

"I betray counsel?—I bear tales, and that against my brother martialist?—I scorn it—I would not tell it even to my timber Soldan!"—Why, I can be a wild galliard in a corner as well as thou, man—And now I think on't, I will go with thee somewhere, and we will have a rouse together, and thy Dalilah shall give us a song. Ha! said I not well?"

"Excellently," said Henry, longing the whole time to knock his brother martialist down, but wisely taking a more peaceful way to rid himself of the incumbrance of his presence— "Excellently well!—I may want thy help, too—for here are five or six of the Douglasses before us—they will not fail to try to take the wench from a poor burgher like myself, so I will be glad of the assistance of a tearer such as thou art."

"I thank ye—I thank ye," answered the Bonnet-maker; "but were I not better run, and cause ring the common bell, and get my great sword?"

"Ay, ay—run home as fast as you can, and say nothing of what you have seen."

"Who, I?—Nay, fear me not. Pah! I scorn a tale-bearer."

"Away with you, then;—I hear the clash of armour."

This put life and mettle into the heels of the Bonnet-maker, who, turning his back on the supposed danger, set off at a pace which the Smith never doubted would speedily bring him to his own house.

"Here is another chattering jay to deal with," thought the Smith; "but I have a hank over him too. The minstrels have a fabliau of a daw with borrowed feathers,—why, this Oliver is the very bird, and, by St. Dunstan, if he lets his chattering tongue run on at my expense, I will so pluck him as never hawk plumed a partridge. And this he knows."

As these reflections thronged on his mind, he had nearly reached the end of his journey; and, with the glee-maiden still hanging on his cloak, exhausted, partly with fear, partly with fatigue, he at length arrived at the middle of the Wynd, which was honoured with his own habitation, and from which, in the uncertainty that then attended the application of surnames, he derived one of his own appellatives. Here, on ordinary days, his furnace was seen to blaze, and four half-stripped knaves stunned the neighbourhood with the clang of hammer and stithy. But St. Valentine's holiday was an excuse for these men of steel having shut the shop, and for the present being absent on their own errands of devotion or pleasure. The house which adjoined to the smithy called Henry its owner; and though it was small, and situated in a narrow street, yet, as there was a large garden with fruit-trees behind it, it constituted upon the whole a pleasant dwelling. The Smith, instead of knocking or calling, which would have drawn neighbours to doors and windows, drew out a pass-key of his own fabrication, then a great and envied curiosity, and opening the door of his house, introduced his companion into his habitation.

The apartment which received Henry and the glee-maiden was the kitchen, which served amongst those of the Smith's station for the family sitting-room, although one or two individuals, like Simon Glover, had an eating-room apart from that in which their victuals were prepared. In the corner of this apartment, which was arranged with an unusual attention to cleanliness, sat an old woman, whose neatness of attire, and the precision with which her scarlet plaid was drawn over her head, so as to descend to her shoulders on each side, might have indicated a higher rank than that of Luckie Shoolbred, the Smith's housekeeper. Yet such and no other was her designation; and not having attended mass in the morning, she was quietly reposing herself by the side of the fire, her beads, half told, hanging over her left arm; her prayers, half said, loitering upon her tongue; her eyes, half closed, resigning themselves to slumber, while she expected the return of her foster-son, without being able to guess at what hour it was likely to happen. She started up at the sound of his entrance, and bent her eye upon his companion, at first with a look of the utmost surprise, which gradually was exchanged for one expressive of great displeasure.

"Now the Saints bless mine eyesight, Henry Smith!"—she exclaimed, very devoutly.

"Amen, with all my heart. Get some food ready presently, good nurse, for I fear me this traveller hath dined but lightly."

"And again I pray that Our Lady would preserve my eyesight from the wicked delusions of Satan!"

"So be it, I tell you, good woman. But what is the use of all this pattering and prayering? Do you not hear me? or will you not do as I bid you?"

"It must be himself, then, whatever is of it! But oh! it is more like the foul Fiend in his likeness, to have such a baggage hanging upon his cloak.—O Harry Smith, men called you a wild lad for less things! But who would ever have thought that Harry would have brought a light leman under the roof that sheltered his worthy mother, and where his own nurse has dwelt for thirty years!"

"Hold your peace, old woman, and be reasonable," said the Smith. "This glee-woman is no leman of mine, nor of any other person that I know of; but she is going off for Dundee to-morrow by the boats, and we must give her quarters till then."

"Quarters!" said the old woman. "You may give quarters to such cattle if you like it yourself, Harry Wynd; but the same house shall not quarter that trumpery quean and me, and of that you may assure yourself."

"Your mother is angry with me," said Louise, misconstruing the connexion of the parties. "I will not remain to give her any offence. If there is a stable or a cowhouse, an empty stall will be bed enough for Charlot and me."

"Ay, ay; I am thinking it is the quarters you are best used to," said Dame Shoolbred.

"Hark ye, Nurse Shoolbred," said the Smith. "You know I love you for your own sake, and for my mother's; but by St. Dunstan, who was a saint of my own craft, I will have the command of my own house; and if you leave me without any better reason but your own nonsensical suspicions, you must think how you will have the door open to you when you return; for you shall have no help of mine, I promise you."

"Aweel, my bairn, and that will never make me risk the honest name I have kept for sixty years. It was never your mother's custom, and it shall never be mine, to take up with ranters, and jugglers, and singing women ; and I am not so far to seek for a dwelling, that the same roof should cover me and a tramping princess like that."

With this the refractory gouvernante began in great hurry to adjust her tartan mantle for going abroad, by pulling it so far forwards as to conceal the white linen cap, the edges of which bordered her shrivelled but still fresh and healthful countenance. This done, she seized upon a staff, the trusty companion of her journeys, and was fairly trudging towards the door, when the Smith stepped between her and the passage.

"Wait at least, old woman, till we have cleared scores. I owe you for fee and bountith."

"An' that's e'en a dream of your own fool's head. What fee or bountith am I to take from the son of your mother, that fed, clad, and bielded me as if I had been a sister ?"

"And well you repay it, nurse, leaving her only child at his utmost need."

This seemed to strike the obstinate old woman with compunction. She stopped and looked at her master and the minstrel alternately ; then shook her head, and seemed about to resume her motion towards the door.

"I only receive this poor wanderer under my roof," urged the Smith, "to save her from the prison and the scourge."

"And why should you save her ?" said the inexorable Dame Shoolbred. "I dare say she has deserved them both as well as ever thief deserved a hempen collar."

"For aught I know she may, or she may not. But she cannot deserve to be scourged to death, or imprisoned till she is starved to death ; and that is the lot of them that the Black Douglas bears maltalent against."

"And you are going to thraw the Black Douglas, for the sake of a glee-woman ? This will be the worst of your feuds yet.—Oh, Henry Gow, there is as much iron in your head as in your anvil !"

"I have sometimes thought this myself, Mistress Shoolbred ; but if I do get a cut or two on this new argument, I wonder who is to cure them, if you run away from me like a scared wild-goose ? Ay, and moreover, who is to receive my bonny bride, that I hope to bring up the Wynd one of these days ?"

"Ah, Harry, Harry," said the old woman, shaking her head,

"this is not the way to prepare an honest man's house for a young bride—you should be guided by modesty and discretion, and not by chambering and wantonness."

"I tell you again, this poor creature is nothing to me. I wish her only to be safely taken care of; and I think the boldest Borderman in Perth will respect the bar of my door as much as the gate of Carlisle Castle.—I am going down to Sim Glover's—I may stay there all night, for the Highland cub is run back to the hills, like a wolf-whelp as he is, and so there is a bed to spare, and father Simon will make me welcome to the use of it. You will remain with this poor creature, feed her, and protect her during the night, and I will call on her before day; and thou mayst go with her to the boat thyself an thou wilt, and so thou wilt set the last eyes on her at the same time I shall."

"There is some reason in that," said Dame Shoolbred; "though why you should put your reputation in risk for a creature that would find a lodging for a silver twopence and less matter, is a mystery to me."

"Trust me with that, old woman, and be kind to the girl."

"Kinder than she deserves, I warrant you; and truly, though I little like the company of such cattle, yet I think I am less like to take harm from her than you—unless she be a witch, indeed, which may well come to be the case, as the devil is very powerful with all this wayfaring clanjamfray."

"No more a witch than I am a warlock," said the honest Smith; "a poor broken-hearted thing, that, if she hath done evil, has dreed a sore weird for it. Be kind to her—And you, my musical damsel—I will call on you to-morrow morning, and carry you to the water-side. This old woman will treat you kindly, if you say nothing to her but what becomes honest ears."

The poor minstrel had listened to this dialogue, without understanding more than its general tendency; for, though she spoke English well, she had acquired the language in England itself, and the northern dialect was then, as now, of a broader and harsher character. She saw, however, that she was to remain with the old lady, and meekly folding her arms on her bosom, bent her head with humility. She next looked towards the Smith with a strong expression of thankfulness, then raising her eyes to heaven, took his passive hand, and seemed about to kiss the sinewy fingers, in token of deep and affectionate gratitude. But Dame Shoolbred did not give license to the stranger's mode of expressing her feelings. She thrust in between them, and pushing poor Louise aside, said, " No, no, I'll have none of that work. Go into the chimney-nook, mistress, and when Harry Smith's gone, if you must have hands to kiss, you shall kiss mine as long as you like.—And you, Harry, away down to Sim Glover's, for if pretty Mistress Catharine hears of the company you have brought home, she may chance to like them as little as I do.—What's the matter now?—is the man demented?—are you going out without your buckler, and the whole town in misrule?"

"You are right, dame," said the armourer; and throwing the buckler over his broad shoulders, he departed from his house without abiding farther question.

CHAPTER XIII

How in the noon of night that pibroch thrills,
Savage and shrill! But with the breath which fills
Their mountain pipe, so fill the mountaineers
With the fierce native daring which instils
The stirring memory of a thousand years.

BYRON.

WE must now leave the lower parties in our historical drama, to attend to the incidents which took place among those of a higher rank and greater importance.

We pass from the hut of an armourer, to the council-room of a monarch; and resume our story just when, the tumult beneath being settled, the angry chieftains were summoned to the royal presence. They entered, displeased with and lowering upon each other, each so exclusively filled with his own fancied injuries, as to be equally unwilling and unable to attend to reason or argument. Albany alone, calm and crafty, seemed prepared to use their dissatisfaction for his own purposes, and turn each incident as it should occur to the furtherance of his own indirect ends.

The King's irresolution, although it amounted even to timidity, did not prevent his assuming the exterior bearing becoming his situation. It was only when hard pressed, as in the preceding scene, that he lost his apparent composure. In general, he might be driven from his purpose, but seldom from his dignity of manner. He received Albany, Douglas, March, and the Prior, (those ill-assorted members of his motley council,) with a mixture of courtesy and loftiness, which reminded each haughty peer that he stood in the presence of his Sovereign, and compelled him to do the beseeming reverence.

Having received their salutations, the King motioned them to be seated; and they were obeying his commands when Rothsay entered. He walked gracefully up to his father, and, kneeling at his footstool, requested his blessing. Robert, with an aspect in which fondness and sorrow were ill disguised, made an attempt to assume a look of reproof, as he laid his hand on the youth's head, and said, with a sigh, "God bless thee, my thoughtless boy, and make thee a wiser man in thy future years!"

"Amen, my dearest father!" said Rothsay, in a tone of feeling such as his happier moments often evinced. He then kissed the royal hand, with the reverence of a son and a subject; and instead of taking a place at the council board, remained standing behind the King's chair, in such a position that he might, when he chose, whisper into his father's ear.

The King next made a sign to the Prior of St. Dominic to take his place at the table, on which there were writing materials, which, of all the subjects present, Albany excepted, the churchman was alone able to use.[1] The King then opened the purpose of their meeting, by saying, with much dignity,

"Our business, my lords, respected these unhappy dissensions in the Highlands, which, we learn by our latest messengers, are about to occasion the waste and destruction of the country, even within a few miles of this our own court. But near as this trouble is, our ill fate, and the instigations of wicked men, have raised up one yet nearer, by throwing strife and contention among the citizens of Perth and those attendants who follow your lordships, and others our knights and nobles. I must first, therefore, apply to yourselves, my lords, to know why our court is disturbed by such unseemly contendings, and by what means they ought to be repressed?—

[1] Mr. Chrystal Croftangry had not, it must be confessed, when he indited this sentence, exactly recollected the character of Rothsay, as given by the Prior of Lochleven.

"A seemly person in stature
Cunnand into letterature."

B. ix. cap. 23.

Brother of Albany, do you tell us first your sentiments on this matter."

"Sir, our royal Sovereign and brother," said the Duke, "being in attendance on your Grace's person when the fray began, I am not acquainted with its origin."

"And for me," said the Prince, "I heard no worse war-cry than a minstrel wench's ballad, and saw no more dangerous bolts flying than hazel nuts."

"And I," said the Earl of March, "could only perceive that the stout citizens of Perth had in chase some knaves who had assumed the Bloody Heart on their shoulders. They ran too fast to be actually the men of the Earl of Douglas."

Douglas understood the sneer, but only replied to it by one of those withering looks with which he was accustomed to intimate his mortal resentment. He spoke, however, with haughty composure.

"My liege," he said, "must of course know it is Douglas who must answer to this heavy charge; for when was there strife or bloodshed in Scotland, but there were foul tongues to asperse a Douglas or a Douglas's man, as having given cause to them? We have here goodly witnesses. I speak not of my Lord of Albany, who has only said that he was, as well becomes him, by your Grace's side. And I say nothing of my Lord of Rothsay, who, as befits his rank, years. and understanding, was cracking nuts with a strolling musician, —He smiles—Here he may say his pleasure—I shall not forget a tie which he seems to have forgotten. But here is my Lord of March, who saw my followers flying before the clowns of Perth! I can tell that Earl, that the followers of the Bloody Heart advance or retreat, when their chieftain commands, and the good of Scotland requires."

"And I can answer"—exclaimed the equally proud Earl of March, his blood rushing into his face, when the King interrupted him—

"Peace! angry lords," said the King, "and remember in whose presence you stand!—And you, my Lord of Douglas, tell us, if you can, the cause of this mutiny, and why your followers, whose general good services we are most willing to acknowledge, were thus active in private brawl?"

"I obey, my lord," said Douglas, slightly stooping a head that seldom bent. "I was passing from my lodgings in the Carthusian Convent, through the High Street of Perth, with a few of my ordinary retinue, when I beheld some of the baser sort of citizens crowding around the Cross, against which there was nailed this placard, and that which accompanies it."

He took from a pocket in the bosom of his buff-coat, a human hand and a piece of parchment. The King was shocked and agitated.

"Read," he said, "good Father Prior, and let that ghastly spectacle be removed."

The Prior read a placard to the following purpose :—

"Inasmuch as the house of a citizen of Perth was assaulted last night, being St. Valentine's Eve, by a sort of disorderly night-walkers, belonging to some company of the strangers now resident in the Fair City : And whereas this hand was struck from one of the lawless limmers in the fray that ensued, the Provost and Magistrates have directed that it should be nailed to the Cross, in scorn and contempt of those by whom such brawl was occasioned. And if any one of knightly degree shall say that this our act is wrongfully done, I, Patrick Charteris of Kinfauns, knight, will justify this cartel in knightly weapons, within the barrace ; or, if any one of meaner birth shall deny what is here said, he shall be met with by a citizen of the Fair City of Perth, according to his degree. And so God and St. John protect the Fair City !"

"You will not wonder, my lord," resumed Douglas, "that when my almoner had read to me the contents of so insolent a scroll, I caused one of my squires to pluck down a trophy so disgraceful to the chivalry and nobility of Scotland. Whereupon, it seems some of these saucy burghers took license to hoot and insult the hindmost of my train, who wheeled their horses on them, and would soon have settled the feud, but for my positive command that they should follow me in as much peace as the rascally vulgar would permit. And thus they arrived here in the guise of flying men, when, with my command to repel force by force, they might have set fire to the four corners of this wretched borough, and stifled the insolent churls, like malicious fox-cubs in a burning brake of furze."

There was a silence when Douglas had done speaking, until the Duke of Rothsay answered, addressing his father—

"Since the Earl of Douglas possesses the power of burning the town where your Grace holds your court, so soon as the Provost and he differ about a night riot, or the terms of a cartel, I am sure we ought all to be thankful that he has not the will to do so."

"The Duke of Rothsay," said Douglas, who seemed resolved to maintain command of his temper, "may have reason to thank Heaven in a more serious tone than he now uses, that the Douglas is as true as he is powerful. This is a time when the subjects in all countries rise against the law; we have heard of the insurgents of the Jacquerie in France; and of Jack Straw, and Hob Miller, and Parson Ball, among the Southron, and we may be sure there is fuel enough to catch such a flame, were it spreading to our frontiers. When I see peasants challenging noblemen, and nailing the hands of the gentry to their city Cross, I will not say I *fear* mutiny—for that would be false—but I foresee, and will stand well prepared for it."

"And why does my Lord Douglas say," answered the Earl of March, "that this cartel has been done by churls? I see Sir Patrick Charteris' name there, and he, I ween, is of no churl's blood. The Douglas himself, since he takes the matter so warmly, might lift Sir Patrick's gauntlet without soiling of his honour."

"My Lord of March," replied Douglas, "should speak but of what he understands. I do no injustice to the descendant of the Red Rover, when I say he is too slight to be weighed with the Douglas. The heir of Thomas Randolph might have a better claim to his answer."

"And, by my honour, it shall not miss for want of my asking the grace," said the Earl of March, pulling his glove off.

"Stay, my lord," said the King. "Do us not so gross an injury as to bring your feud to mortal defiance here; but rather offer your ungloved hand in kindness to the noble Earl, and embrace in token of your mutual fealty to the crown of Scotland."

"Not so, my liege," answered March; "your Majesty may command me to return my gauntlet, for that and all the armour it belongs to are at your command, while I continue to hold my Earldom of the crown of Scotland—but when I clasp Douglas, it must be with a mailed hand. Farewell, my liege. My counsels here avail not, nay, are so unfavourably received, that perhaps farther stay were unwholesome for my safety. May God keep your Highness from open enemies and treacherous friends!—I am for my castle of Dunbar, from whence I think you will soon hear news. Farewell to you, my Lords of Albany and Douglas; you are playing a high game, look you play it fairly—Farewell, poor thoughtless Prince, who art sporting like a fawn within spring of a tiger!—Farewell all—George of Dunbar sees the evil he cannot remedy.— Adieu, all."

The King would have spoken, but the accents died on his tongue, as he received from Albany a look cautioning him to forbear. The Earl of March left the apartment, receiving the mute salutations of the members of the council whom he had severally addressed, excepting from Douglas alone, who returned to his farewell speech a glance of contemptuous defiance.

"The recreant goes to betray us to the Southron," he said; "his pride rests on his possessing that sea-worn Hold [1] which can admit the English into Lothian.—Nay, look not alarmed, my liege, I will hold good what I say—nevertheless, it is yet time. Speak but the word, my liege—say but 'Arrest him,' and March shall not yet cross the Earn on his traitorous journey."

"Nay, gallant Earl," said Albany, who wished rather that the two powerful lords should counterbalance each other, than that one should obtain a decisive superiority, "that were too hasty counsel. The Earl of March came hither on the King's warrant of safe-conduct, and it may not consist with my royal brother's honour to break it. Yet, if your lordship can bring any detailed proof——"

Here they were interrupted by a flourish of trumpets.

"His Grace of Albany is unwontedly scrupulous to-day," said Douglas; "but it skills not wasting words—the time is past—these are March's trumpets, and I warrant me he rides at flight-speed so soon as he passes the South Port. We shall hear of him in time; and if it be as I have conjectured, he shall be met with though all England backed his treachery."

"Nay, let us hope better of the noble Earl," said the King, no way displeased that the quarrel betwixt March and Douglas had seemed to obliterate the traces of the disagreement betwixt Rothsay and his father-in-law; "he hath a fiery, but not a sullen temper—In some things he has been—I will not say wronged—but disappointed—and something is to be allowed to the resentment of high blood armed with great power. But,

[1] The Castle of Dunbar.

thank Heaven, all of us who remain are of one sentiment, and, I may say, of one house ; so that, at least, our councils cannot now be thwarted with disunion.—Father Prior, I pray you take your writing materials, for you must as usual be our clerk of council.—And now to business, my lords—and our first object of consideration must be this Highland cumber."

"Between the Clan Chattan and the Clan Quhele," said the Prior ; "which, as our last advices from our brethren at Dunkeld inform us, is ready to break out into more formidable warfare than has yet taken place between these sons of Belial, who speak of nothing else than of utterly destroying one another. Their forces are assembling on each side, and not a man, claiming in the tenth degree of kindred, but must repair to the Brattach [1] of his tribe, or stand to the punishment of fire and sword. The fiery cross hath flitted about like a meteor in every direction, and awakened strange and unknown tribes beyond the distant Murray Frith—may Heaven and St. Dominic be our protection ! But if your lordships cannot find remedy for evil, it will spread broad and wide, and the patrimony of the Church must in every direction be exposed to the fury of these Amalekites, with whom there is as little devotion to Heaven, as there is pity or love to their neighbours —may Our Lady be our guard !—We hear some of them are yet utter heathens, and worship Mahound and Termagaunt."

"My lords and kinsmen," said Robert, "ye have heard the urgency of this case, and may desire to know my sentiments before you deliver what your own wisdom shall suggest. And, in sooth, no better remedy occurs to me, than to send two commissioners, with full power from us to settle such debates as be among them ; and at the same time to charge them, as they shall be answerable to the law, to lay down their arms, and forbear all practices of violence against each other."

"I approve of your Grace's proposal," said Rothsay ; "and I trust the good Prior will not refuse the venerable station of envoy upon this peacemaking errand. And his reverend brother, the Abbot of the Carthusian convent, must contend for an honour which will certainly add two most eminent recruits to the large army of martyrs, since the Highlanders little regard the distinction betwixt clerk and layman, in the ambassadors whom you send to them."

---

[1] Standard—literally cloth. The Lowland language still retains the word *brat*, which, however, is only now applicable to a child's pinafore, or a coarse towel. To such mean offices may words descend.

"My royal Lord of Rothsay," said the Prior, "if I am destined to the blessed crown of martyrdom, I shall be doubtless directed to the path by which I am to attain it. Meantime, if you speak in jest, may Heaven pardon you, and give you light to perceive that it were better buckle on your arms to guard the possessions of the Church, so perilously endangered, than to employ your wit in taunting her ministers and servants."

"I taunt no one, Father Prior," said the youth, yawning; "nor have I much objection to taking arms, excepting that they are a somewhat cumbrous garb, and in February a furred mantle is more suiting to the weather than a steel corslet. And it irks me the more to put on cold harness in this nipping weather, that, would but the Church send a detachment of their saints, (and they have some Highland ones well known in this district, and doubtless used to the climate,) they might fight their own battles, like merry St. George of England. But I know not how it is, we hear of their miracles when they are propitiated, and of their vengeance, if any one trespasses on their patrimonies, and these are urged as reasons for extending their lands by large largesses; and yet if there come down but a band of twenty Highlanders, bell, book, and candle make no speed, and the belted baron must be fain to maintain the Church in possession of the lands which he has given to her, as much as if he himself still enjoyed the fruits of them."

"Son David," said the King, "you give an undue license to your tongue."

"Nay, sir, I am mute," replied the Prince. "I had no purpose to disturb your Highness, or displease the Father Prior, who, with so many miracles at his disposal, will not face, as it seems, a handful of Highland caterans."

"We know," said the Prior, with suppressed indignation, "from what source these vile doctrines are derived, which we hear with horror from the tongue that now utters them. When princes converse with heretics, their minds and manners are alike corrupted. They show themselves in the streets as the companions of maskers and harlots, and in the council as the scorners of the Church and of holy things."

"Peace, good father!" said the King. "Rothsay shall make amends for what he has idly spoken. Alas! let us take counsel in friendly fashion, rather than resemble a mutinous crew of mariners in a sinking vessel, when each is more intent on quarrelling with his neighbours, than in assisting the exertions of the forlorn master for the safety of the ship.—My Lord of Douglas, your house has been seldom to lack, when the crown of Scotland desired either wise counsel or manly achievement; I trust you will help us in this strait?"

"I can only wonder that the strait should exist, my lord," answered the haughty Douglas. "When I was intrusted with the lieutenancy of the kingdom, there were some of these wild clans came down from the Grampians. I troubled not the council about the matter, but made the Sheriff, Lord Ruthven, get to horse with the forces of the Carse—the Hays, the Lindsays, the Ogilvies, and other gentlemen. By St. Bride! when it was steel coat to frieze mantle, the thieves knew what lances were good for, and whether swords had edges or no. There were some three hundred of their best bonnets, besides that of their chief, Donald Cormac,[1] left on the moor of Thorn, and in Rochinroy Wood; and as many were gibbeted at Houghman Stairs, which has still the name from the hangman work that was done there. This is the way men deal with thieves in my country; and if gentler methods will succeed better with these Earish knaves, do not blame Douglas for speaking his mind.—You smile, my Lord of Rothsay. May I ask how I have a second time become your jest, before I have replied to the first which you passed on me?"

"Nay, be not wrathful, my good Lord of Douglas," answered the Prince; "I did but smile to think how your princely retinue would dwindle, if every thief were dealt with as the poor Highlanders at Houghman Stairs."

The King again interfered, to prevent the Earl from giving an angry reply. "Your lordship," said he to Douglas, "advises wisely, that we should trust to arms when these men come out against our subjects on the fair and level plain; but the difficulty is to put a stop to their disorders while they continue to lurk within their mountains. I need not tell you that the Clan Chattan, and the Clan Quhele, are great confederacies, consisting each of various tribes, who are banded together, each to support their own separate league, and who of late have had dissensions which have drawn blood wherever they have met, whether individually or in bands. The whole country is torn to pieces by their restless feuds."

"I cannot see the evil of this," said the Douglas, "the

[1] Some authorities place this skirmish so late as 1443.

ruffians will destroy each other, and the deer of the Highlands will increase as the men diminish. We shall gain as hunters the exercise we lose as warriors."

"Rather say that the wolves will increase as the men diminish," replied the King.

"I am content," said Douglas; "better wild wolves than wild Caterans. Let there be strong forces maintained along the Earish frontier, to separate the quiet from the disturbed country. Confine the fire of civil war within the Highlands; let it spend its uncontrolled fury, and it will be soon burnt out for want of fuel. The survivors will be humbled, and will be more obedient to a whisper of your Grace's pleasure, than their fathers, or the knaves that now exist, have been to your strictest commands."

"This is wise but ungodly counsel," said the Prior, shaking his head; "I cannot take it upon my conscience to recommend it. It is wisdom, but it is the wisdom of Achitophel, crafty at once and cruel."

"My heart tells me so"—said the King, laying his hand on his breast; "my heart tells me, that it will be asked of me at the awful day, 'Robert Stewart, where are the subjects I have given thee?' it tells me, that I must account for them all, Saxon and Gael, Lowland, Highland, and Border man; that I will not be required to answer for those alone who have wealth and knowledge, but for those also who were robbers because they were poor, and rebels because they were ignorant."

"Your Highness speaks like a Christian King," said the Prior; "but you bear the sword as well as the sceptre, and this present evil is of a kind which the sword must cure."

"Hark ye, my lords," said the Prince, looking up as if a gay thought had suddenly struck him,—"Suppose we teach these savage mountaineers a strain of chivalry? It were no hard matter to bring these two great commanders, the captain of the Clan Chattan, and the chief of the no less doughty race of the Clan Quhele, to defy each other to mortal combat. They might fight here in Perth—we would lend them horse and armour: thus their feud would be stanched by the death of one, or probably both, of the villains, (for I think both would break their necks in the first charge,) my father's godly desire of saving blood would be attained, and we should have the pleasure of seeing such a combat between two salvage knights, for the first time in their lives wearing breeches, and mounted on horses, as has not been heard of since the days of King Arthur."

"Shame upon you, David!" said the King. "Do you make the distress of your native country, and the perplexity of our councils, a subject for buffoonery?"

"If you will pardon me, royal brother," said Albany, "I think, that though my princely nephew hath started this thought in a jocular manner, there may be something wrought out of it, which might greatly remedy this pressing evil."

"Good brother," replied the King, "it is unkind to expose Rothsay's folly by pressing further his ill-timed jest. We know the Highland clans have not our customs of chivalry, nor the habit or mode of doing battle which these require"

"True, your Grace," answered Albany; "yet I speak not in scorn, but in serious earnest. True, the mountaineers have not our forms and mode of doing battle in the lists, but they have those which are as effectual to the destruction of human life; and so that the mortal game is played, and the stake won and lost, what signifies it whether these Gael fight with sword and lance, as becomes belted knights, or with sand-bags, like the crestless churls of England, or butcher each other with knives and skeans, in their own barbarous fashion? Their habits, like our own, refer all disputed rights and claims to the decision of battle. They are as vain, too, as they are fierce; and the idea that these two clans would be admitted to combat in presence of your Grace and of your court, will readily induce them to refer their difference to the fate of battle, even were such rough arbitrement less familiar to their customs, and that in any such numbers as shall be thought most convenient. We must take care that they approach not the court, save in such a fashion and number that they shall not be able to surprise us; and that point being provided against, the more that shall be admitted to combat upon either side, the greater will be the slaughter among their bravest and most stirring men, and the more the chance of the Highlands being quiet for some time to come."

"This were a bloody policy, brother," siad the King; "and again I say, that I cannot bring my conscience to countenance the slaughter of these rude men, that are so little better than so many benighted heathens."

"And are their lives more precious," asked Albany, "than those of nobles and gentlemen who by your Grace's license are so frequently admitted to fight in barrace, either for the satisfying of disputes at law, or simply to acquire honour?"

The King, thus hard pressed, had little to say against a custom so engrafted upon the laws of the realm and the usages of chivalry, as the trial by combat; and he only replied, "God knows, I have never granted such license as you urge me with, unless with the greatest repugnance; and that I never saw men have strife together to the effusion of blood, but I could have wished to appease it with the shedding of my own."

"But, my gracious lord," said the Prior, "it seems that if we follow not some such policy as this of my Lord of Albany, we must have recourse to that of the Douglas; and, at the risk of the dubious event of battle, and with the certainty of losing many excellent subjects, do, by means of the Lowland swords, that which these wild mountaineers will otherwise perform with their own hand.—What says my Lord of Douglas to the policy of his Grace of Albany?"

"Douglas," said the haughty lord, "never counselled that to be done by policy which might be attained by open force. He remains by his opinion, and is willing to march at the head of his own followers, with those of the Barons of Perthshire and the Carse; and either bring these Highlanders to reason or subjection, or leave the body of a Douglas among their savage wildernesses."

"It is nobly spoken, my Lord of Douglas," said Albany; "and well might the King rely upon thy undaunted heart, and the courage of thy resolute followers. But see you not how soon you may be called elsewhere, where your presence and services are altogether indispensable to Scotland and her Monarch? Marked you not the gloomy tone in which the fiery March limited his allegiance and faith to our Sovereign here present, to that space for which he was to remain King Robert's vassal? And did not you yourself suspect that he was plotting a transference of his allegiance to England? —Other chiefs, of subordinate power and inferior fame, may do battle with the Highlanders; but if Dunbar admit the Percies and their Englishmen into our frontiers, who will drive them back if the Douglas be elsewhere?"

"My sword," answered Douglas, "is equally at the service of his Majesty, on the frontier, or in the deepest recesses of the Highlands. I have seen the backs of the proud Percy and George of Dunbar ere now, and I may see them again.

And, if it is the King's pleasure I should take measures against this probable conjunction of stranger and traitor, I admit that, rather than trust to an inferior or feebler hand the important task of settling the Highlands, I would be disposed to give my opinion in favour of the policy of my Lord of Albany, and suffer those savages to carve each other's limbs, without giving barons and knights the trouble of hunting them down."

"My Lord of Douglas," said the Prince, who seemed determined to omit no opportunity to gall his haughty father-in-law, "does not choose to leave to us Lowlanders even the poor crumbs of honour which might be gathered at the expense of the Highland kerne, while he, with his Border chivalry, reaps the full harvest of victory over the English. But Percy hath seen men's backs as well as Douglas; and I have known as great wonders as that he who goes forth to seek such wool should come back shorn."

"A phrase," said Douglas, "well becoming a prince, who speaks of honour with a wandering harlot's scrip in his bonnet, by way of favour."

"Excuse it, my lord," said Rothsay; "men who have matched unfittingly become careless in the choice of those whom they love *par amours*. The chained dog must snatch at the nearest bone."

"Rothsay, my unhappy son!" exclaimed the King, "art thou mad? or wouldst thou draw down on thee the full storm of a king and father's displeasure?"

"I am dumb," returned the Prince, "at your Grace's command."

"Well then, my Lord of Albany," said the King, "since such is your advice, and since Scottish blood must flow, how, I pray you, are we to prevail on these fierce men to refer their quarrel to such a combat as you propose?"

"That, my liege," said Albany, "must be the result of more mature deliberation. But the task will not be difficult. Gold will be needful to bribe some of the bards, and principal counsellors and spokesmen. The chiefs, moreover, of both these leagues must be made to understand, that, unless they agree to this amicable settlement——"

"*Amicable*, brother!" said the King, with emphasis.

"Ay, amicable, my liege," replied his brother, "since it is better the country were placed in peace, at the expense of losing a score or two of Highland kernes, than remain at war till as many thousands are destroyed by sword, fire, famine, and all the extremities of mountain battle. To return to the purpose; I think that the first party to whom the accommodation is proposed will snatch at it eagerly; that the other will be ashamed to reject an offer to rest the cause on the swords of their bravest men; that the national vanity, and factious hate to each other, will prevent them from seeing our purpose in adopting such a rule of decision; and that they will be more eager to cut each other to pieces, than we can be to halloo them on.—And now, as our councils are finished, so far as I can aid, I will withdraw."

"Stay yet a moment," said the Prior, "for I also have a grief to disclose, of a nature so black and horrible, that your Grace's pious heart will hardly credit its existence; and I state it mournfully, because, as certain as that I am an unworthy servant of St. Dominic, it is the cause of the displeasure of Heaven against this poor country; by which our victories are turned into defeat, our gladness into mourning, our councils distracted with disunion, and our country devoured by civil war."

"Speak, reverend Prior," said the King; "assuredly if the cause of such evils be in me, or in my house, I will take instant care to their removal."

He uttered these words with a faltering voice, and eagerly waited for the Prior's reply, in the dread, no doubt, that it might implicate Rothsay in some new charge of folly or vice. His apprehensions perhaps deceived him, when he thought he saw the churchman's eye rest for a moment on the Prince, before he said, in a solemn tone,—"Heresy, my noble and gracious liege, heresy is among us. She snatches soul after soul from the congregation, as wolves steal lambs from the sheepfold."

"There are enough of shepherds to watch the fold," answered the Duke of Rothsay. "Here are four convents of regular monks alone, around this poor hamlet of Perth, and all the secular clergy besides. Methinks a town so well garrisoned should be fit to keep out an enemy."

"One traitor in a garrison, my lord," answered the Prior, "can do much to destroy the security of a city which is guarded by legions; and if that one traitor is, either from levity, or love of novelty, or whatever other motive, protected and fostered by those who should be most eager to expel him from the fortress, his opportunities of working mischief will be incalculably increased."

"Your words seem to aim at some one in this presence, Father Prior," said the Douglas; "if at me, they do me foul wrong. I am well aware that the Abbot of Aberbrothock hath made some ill-advised complaints, that I suffered not his beeves to become too many for his pastures, or his stock of grain to burst the girnels of the Monastery, while my followers lacked beef, and their horses corn. But bethink you, the pastures and cornfields which produced that plenty, were bestowed by my ancestors on the house of Aberbrothock, surely not with the purpose that their descendant should starve in the midst of it; and neither will he, by St. Bride! But for heresy and false doctrine," he added, striking his large hand heavily on the council-table, "who is it that dare tax the Douglas? I would not have poor men burned for silly thoughts; but my hand and sword are ever ready to maintain the Christian faith."

"My lord, I doubt it not," said the Prior; "so hath it ever been with your most noble house. For the Abbot's complaints, they may pass to a second day. But what we now desire, is a commission to some noble lord of state, joined to others of Holy Church, to support by strength of hand, if necessary, the enquiries which the reverend official of the bounds, and other grave prelates, my unworthy self being one, are about to make into the cause of the new doctrines, which are now deluding the simple, and depraving the pure and precious faith, approved by the Holy Father and his reverend predecessors."

"Let the Earl of Douglas have a royal commission to this effect," said Albany; "and let there be no exception whatever from his jurisdiction, saving the royal person. For my own part, although conscious that I have neither in act nor thought received or encouraged a doctrine which Holy Church hath not sanctioned, yet I should blush to claim an immunity under the blood royal of Scotland, lest I should seem to be seeking refuge against a crime so horrible."

"I will have nought to do with it"—said Douglas; "to march against the English, and the Southron traitor March, is task enough for me. Moreover, I am a true Scotsman, and will not give way to aught that may put the Church of Scotland's head farther into the Roman yoke, or make the baron's coronet stoop to the mitre and cowl. Do you, therefore, most noble Duke of Albany, place your own name in the commission; and I pray your Grace so to mitigate the zeal of the men of Holy Church, who may be associated with you, that there be no over zealous dealings; for the smell of a fagot on the Tay would bring back the Douglas from the walls of York."

The Duke hastened to give the Earl assurance, that the commission should be exercised with lenity and moderation.

"Without a question," said King Robert, "the commission must be ample; and did it consist with the dignity of our crown, we would not ourselves decline its jurisdiction. But we trust, that while the thunders of the Church are directed against the vile authors of these detestable heresies, there shall be measures of mildness and compassion taken with the unfortunate victims of their delusions."

"Such is ever the course of Holy Church, my lord," said the Prior of St. Dominic's.

"Why, then, let the commission be expedited with due care, in name of our brother Albany, and such others as shall be deemed convenient," said the King.—"And now once again let us break up our council; and, Rothsay, come thou with me, and lend me thine arm,—I have matter for thy private ear."

"Ho, la!"—here exclaimed the Prince, in the tone in which he would have addressed a managed horse.

"What means this rudeness, boy?" said the King; "wilt thou never learn reason and courtesy?"

"Let me not be thought to offend, my liege," said the Prince; "but we are parting without learning what is to be done in the passing strange adventure of the dead hand, which the Douglas hath so gallantly taken up. We shall sit but uncomfortably here at Perth, if we are at variance with the citizens."

"Leave that to me," said Albany. "With some little grant of lands and money, and plenty of fair words, the burghers may be satisfied for this time; but it were well that the barons and their followers, who are in attendance on the court, were warned to respect the peace within burgh."

"Surely, we would have it so," said the King; "let strict orders be given accordingly."

"It is doing the churls but too much grace," said the Douglas; "but be it at your Highness's pleasure. I take leave to retire."

"Not before you taste a flagon of Gascon wine, my lord?" said the King.

"Pardon," replied the Earl, "I am not athirst, and I drink not for fashion, but either for need or for friendship." So saying he departed.

The King, as if relieved by his absence, turned to Albany, and said, "And now, my lord, we should chide this truant Rothsay of ours; yet he hath served us so well at council, that we must receive his merits as some atonement for his follies."

"I am happy to hear it," answered Albany, with a countenance of pity and incredulity, as if he knew nothing of the supposed services.

"Nay, brother, you are dull," said the King, "for I will not think you envious. Did you not note that Rothsay was the first to suggest the mode of settling the Highlands, which your experience brought indeed into better shape, and which was generally approved of—and even now we had broken up, leaving a main matter unconsidered, but that he put us in mind of the affray with the citizens?"

"I nothing doubt, my liege," said the Duke of Albany, with the acquiescence which he saw was expected, "that my royal nephew will soon emulate his father's wisdom."

"Or," said the Duke of Rothsay, "I may find it easier to borrow from another member of my family, that happy and comfortable cloak of hypocrisy which covers all vices, and then it signifies little whether they exist or not."

"My Lord Prior," said the Duke, addressing the Dominican, "we will for a moment pray your reverence's absence. The King and I have that to say to the Prince, which must have no further audience, not even yours."

The Dominican bowed and withdrew.

When the two royal brothers and the Prince were left together, the King seemed in the highest degree embarrassed and distressed; Albany sullen and thoughtful; while Rothsay himself endeavoured to cover some anxiety under his usual appearance of levity. There was a silence of a minute. At length Albany spoke.

"Royal brother," he said, "my princely nephew entertains with so much suspicion any admonition coming from my mouth, that I must pray your Grace yourself to take the trouble of telling him what it is most fitting he should know."

"It must be some unpleasing communication indeed, which my Lord of Albany cannot wrap up in honied words," said the Prince.

"Peace with thine effrontery, boy," answered the King, passionately. "You asked but now of the quarrel with the citizens—Who caused that quarrel, David?—what men were those who scaled the window of a peaceful citizen and liegeman, alarmed the night with torch and outcry, and subjected our subjects to danger and affright?"

"More fear than danger, I fancy," answered the Prince; "but how can I of all men tell who made this nocturnal disturbance?"

"There was a follower of thine own there," continued the King; "a man of Belial, whom I will have brought to condign punishment."

"I have no follower, to my knowledge, capable of deserving your Highness's displeasure," answered the Prince.

"I will have no evasions, boy—Where wert thou on St. Valentine's Eve?"

"It is to be hoped that I was serving the good Saint, as a man of mould might," answered the young man, carelessly.

"Will my royal nephew tell us how his Master of the Horse was employed upon that holy Eve?" said the Duke of Albany.

"Speak, David,—I command thee to speak," said the King.

"Ramorny was employed in my service—I think that answer may satisfy my uncle."

"But it will not satisfy me," said the angry father. "God knows, I never coveted man's blood, but that Ramorny's head I will have, if law can give it. He has been the encourager and partaker of all thy numerous vices and follies. I will take care he shall be so no more.—"Call MacLouis, with a guard."

"Do not injure an innocent man," interposed the Prince, desirous at every sacrifice to preserve his favourite from the menaced danger,—"I pledge my word that Ramorny was employed in business of mine, therefore could not be engaged in this brawl."

"False equivocator that thou art!" said the King, presenting to the Prince a ring, "behold the signet of Ramorny, lost in the infamous affray! It fell into the hands of a follower of the Douglas, and was given by the Earl to my brother. Speak not for Ramorny, for he dies; and go thou from my presence, and repent the flagitious councils which could make thee stand before me with a falsehood in thy mouth.—Oh, shame, David, shame! as a son, thou hast lied to thy father; as a knight, to the head of thy order."

The Prince stood mute, conscience-struck, and self-convicted. He then gave way to the honourable feelings which at bottom he really possessed, and threw himself at his father's feet.

"The false knight," he said, "deserves degradation, the disloyal subject death; but, oh! let the son crave from the father pardon for the servant who did not lead him into guilt, but who reluctantly plunged himself into it at his command! Let me bear the weight of my own folly, but spare those who have been my tools, rather than my accomplices. Remember, Ramorny was preferred to my service by my sainted mother."

"Name her not, David, I charge thee!" said the King; "she is happy that she never saw the child of her love stand before her doubly dishonoured, by guilt and by falsehood."

"I am indeed unworthy to name her," said the Prince: "and yet, my dear father, in her name I must petition for Ramorny's life."

"If I might offer my counsel," said the Duke of Albany, who saw that a reconciliation would soon take place betwixt the father and son, "I would advise that Ramorny be dismissed from the Prince's household and society, with such further penalty as his imprudence may seem to merit. The public will be contented with his disgrace, and the matter will be easily accommodated or stifled, so that his Highness do not attempt to screen his servant."

"Wilt thou, for my sake, David," said the King, with a faltering voice, and the tear in his eye, "dismiss this dangerous man? for my sake, who could not refuse thee the heart out of my bosom?"

"It shall be done, my father—done instantly," the Prince replied; and seizing the pen, he wrote a hasty dismissal of Ramorny from his service, and put it into Albany's hands. "I would I could fulfil all your wishes as easily, my royal father," he added, again throwing himself at the King's feet, who raised him up, and fondly folded him in his arms.

Albany scowled, but was silent; and it was not till after the space of a minute or two, that he said, "This matter being so happily accommodated, let me ask if your Majesty is pleased to attend the Even-song service in the chapel?"

"Surely," said the King. "Have I not thanks to pay to God, who has restored union to my family? You will go with us, brother?"

"So please your Grace to give me leave of absence—No,"

said the Duke. "I must concert with the Douglas, and others, the manner in which we may bring these Highland vultures to our lure."

Albany retired to think over his ambitious projects, while the father and son attended divine service, to thank God for their happy reconciliation.

CHAPTER XIV

> Will you go to the Hielands, Lizzy Lyndesay,
>   Will you go to the Hielands wi' me?
> Will you go to the Hielands, Lizzy Lyndesay,
>   My bride and my darling to be?
>
> *Old Ballad.*

A FORMER chapter opened in the royal confessional; we are now to introduce our readers to a situation somewhat similar, though the scene and persons were very different. Instead of a Gothic and darkened apartment in a monastery, one of the most beautiful prospects in Scotland lay extended beneath the hill of Kinnoul, and at the foot of a rock which commanded the view in every direction, sat the Fair Maid of Perth, listening in an attitude of devout attention to the instructions of a Carthusian monk, in his white gown and scapular, who concluded his discourse with prayer, in which his proselyte devoutly joined.

When they had finished their devotions, the priest sat for some time with his eyes fixed on the glorious prospect, of which even the early and chilly season could not conceal the beauties, and it was some time ere he addressed his attentive companion.

"When I behold," he said at length, "this rich and varied land, with its castles, churches, convents, stately palaces, and fertile fields, these extensive woods, and that noble river, I know not, my daughter, whether most to admire the bounty of God or the ingratitude of man. He hath given us the beauty and fertility of the earth, and we have made the scene of his bounty a charnel-house and a battle-field. He hath given us power over the elements, and skill to erect houses for comfort and defence, and we have converted them into dens for robbers and ruffians."

"Yet surely, my Father, there is room for comfort," replied Catharine, "even in the very prospect we look upon. Yonder four goodly convents, with their churches, and their towers, which tell the citizens with brazen voice, that they should think on their religious duties ;—their inhabitants, who have separated themselves from the world, its pursuits and its pleasures, to dedicate themselves to the service of Heaven, —all bear witness, that if Scotland be a bloody and a sinful land, she is yet alive and sensible to the claims which religion demands of the human race."

"Verily, daughter," answered the priest, "what you say seems truth ; and yet, nearly viewed, too much of the comfort you describe will be found delusive. It is true, there was a period in the Christian world, when good men, maintaining themselves by the work of their hands, assembled together, not that they might live easily or sleep softly, but that they might strengthen each other in the Christian faith, and qualify themselves to be teachers of the word to the people. Doubtless there are still such to be found in the holy edifices on which we now look. But it is to be feared that the love of many has waxed cold. Our churchmen have become wealthy, as well by the gifts of pious persons as by the bribes which wicked men have given in their ignorance, imagining that they can purchase that pardon by endowments to the church, which Heaven has only afforded to sincere penitents. And thus, as the Church waxeth rich, her doctrines have unhappily become dim and obscure, as a light is less seen if placed in a lamp of chased gold, than beheld through a screen of glass. God knows, if I see these things and mark them, it is from no wish of singularity, or desire to make myself a teacher in Israel ; but because the fire burns in my bosom, and will not permit me to be silent. I obey the rules of my order, and withdraw not myself from its austerities. Be they essential to our salvation, or be they mere formalities, adopted to supply the want of real penitence and sincere devotion, I have promised, nay vowed, to observe them ; and they shall be respected by me the more, that otherwise I might be charged with regarding my bodily ease, when Heaven is my witness how lightly I value what I may be called on to act or suffer, if the purity of the Church could be restored, or the discipline of the priesthood replaced in its primitive simplicity."

"But, my father," said Catharine, "even for these opinions men term you a Lollard and a Wickliffite, and say it is your desire to destroy churches and cloisters, and restore the religion of Heathenesse."

"Even so, my daughter, am I driven to seek refuge in hills and rocks, and must be presently contented to take my flight amongst the rude Highlanders, who are thus far in a more gracious state than those I leave behind me, that theirs are crimes of ignorance, not of presumption. I will not omit to take such means of safety and escape from their cruelty, as Heaven may open to me; for, while such appear, I shall account it a sign that I have still a service to accomplish. But when it is my Master's pleasure, he knows how willingly Clement Blair will lay down a vilified life upon earth, in humble hope of a blessed exchange hereafter.—But wherefore dost thou look northward so anxiously, my child?—thy young eyes are quicker than mine—dost thou see any one coming?"

"I look, Father, for the Highland youth, Conachar, who will be thy guide to the hills, where his father can afford thee a safe, if a rude retreat. This he has often promised, when we spoke of you and of your lessons—I fear he is now in company where he will soon forget them."

"The youth hath sparkles of grace in him," said Father Clement; "although those of his race are usually too much devoted to their own fierce and savage customs, to endure with patience either the restraints of religion or those of the social law.—Thou hast never told me, daughter, how, contrary to all the usages either of the burgh or of the mountains, this youth came to reside in thy father's house?"

"All I know touching that matter," said Catharine, "is, that his father is a man of consequence among those hill men, and that he desired as a favour of my father, who hath had dealings with them in the way of his merchandise, to keep this youth for a certain time; and that it is only two days since they parted, as Conachar was to return home to his own mountains."

"And why has my daughter," demanded the priest, "maintained such a correspondence with this Highland youth, that she should know how to send for him when she desired to use his services in my behalf? Surely, this is much influence for a maiden to possess over such a wild colt as this youthful mountaineer."

Catharine blushed, and answered with hesitation, "If I have had any influence with Conachar, Heaven be my witness I have only exerted it to enforce upon his fiery temper compliance with the rules of civil life. It is true, I have long expected that you, my Father, would be obliged to take to flight, and I therefore had agreed with him that he should meet me at this place, as soon as he should receive a message from me with a token, which I yesterday despatched. The messenger was a light-footed boy of his own clan, whom he used sometimes to send on errands into the Highlands."

"And am I then to understand, daughter, that this youth, so fair to the eye, was nothing more dear to you, than as you desired to enlighten his mind and reform his manners?"

"It is so, my Father, and no otherwise," answered Catharine; "and perhaps I did not do well to hold intimacy with him, even for his instruction and improvement. But my discourse never led farther."

"Then have I been mistaken, my daughter; for I thought I had seen in thee of late some change of purpose, and some wishful regards looking back to this world, of which you were at one time resolved to take leave."

Catharine hung down her head, and blushed more deeply than ever, as she said, "Yourself, Father, were used to remonstrate against my taking the veil."

"Nor do I now approve of it, my child," said the priest. "Marriage is an honourable state, appointed by Heaven as the regular means of continuing the race of man; and I read not in the Scriptures, what human inventions have since affirmed, concerning the superior excellence of a state of celibacy. But I am jealous of thee, my child, as a father is of his only daughter, lest thou shouldst throw thyself away upon some one unworthy of thee. Thy parent, I know, less nice in thy behalf than I am, countenances the addresses of that fierce and riotous reveller, whom they call Henry of the Wynd. He is rich, it may be; but a haunter of idle and debauched company—a common prize-fighter, who has shed human blood like water. Can such a one be a fit mate for Catharine Glover?—And yet report says they are soon to be united."

The Fair Maid of Perth's complexion changed from red to pale, and from pale to red, as she hastily replied, "I think not of him; though it is true some courtesies have passed betwixt us of late, both as he is my father's friend, and as being, according to the custom of the time, my Valentine."

"Your Valentine, my child?" said Father Clement. "And can your modesty and prudence have trifled so much with the delicacy of your sex, as to place yourself in such a relation to such a man as this artificer?—Think you that this Valentine, a godly saint and Christian bishop, as he is said to have been, ever countenanced a silly and unseemly custom, more likely to have originated in the heathen worship of Flora or Venus, when mortals gave the names of deities to their passions, and studied to excite instead of restraining them?"

"Father," said Catharine, in a tone of more displeasure that she had ever before assumed to the Carthusian, "I know not upon what ground you tax me thus severely for complying with a general practice, authorized by universal custom, and sanctioned by my father's authority. I cannot feel it kind that you put such misconstruction upon me."

"Forgive me, daughter," answered the priest, mildly, "if I have given you offence. But this Henry Gow, or Smith, is a forward, licentious man, to whom you cannot allow any uncommon degree of intimacy and encouragement, without exposing yourself to worse misconstruction,—unless, indeed, it be your purpose to wed him, and that very shortly."

"Say no more of it, my Father," said Catharine. "You give me more pain than you would desire to do; and I may be provoked to answer otherwise than as becomes me. Perhaps I have already had cause enough to make me repent my compliance with an idle custom. At any rate, believe that Henry Smith is nothing to me; and that even the idle intercourse arising from St. Valentine's Day, is utterly broken off."

"I am rejoiced to hear it, my daughter," replied the Carthusian; "and must now prove you on another subject, which renders me most anxious on your behalf. You cannot yourself be ignorant of it, although I could wish it were not necessary to speak of a thing so dangerous, even before these surrounding rocks, cliffs, and stones. But it must be said.— Catharine, you have a lover in the highest rank of Scotland's sons of honour?"

"I know it, Father," answered Catharine, composedly. "I would it were not so."

"So would I also," said the priest, "did I see in my daughter only the child of folly, which most young women are at her age, especially if possessed of the fatal gift of beauty. But as thy charms, to speak the language of an idle world, have attached to thee a lover of such high rank, so I know that thy virtue and wisdom will maintain the influence over the Prince's mind which thy beauty hath acquired."

"Father," replied Catharine, "the Prince is a licentious

gallant, whose notice of me tends only to my disgrace and ruin. Can you, who seemed but now afraid that I acted imprudently in entering into an ordinary exchange of courtesies with one of my own rank, speak with patience of the sort of correspondence which the heir of Scotland dares to fix upon me? Know, that it is but two nights since he, with a party of his debauched followers, would have carried me by force from my father's house, had I not been rescued by that same rash-spirited Henry Smith,—who, if he be too hasty in venturing on danger on slight occasion, is always ready to venture his life in behalf of innocence, or in resistance of oppression. It is well my part to do him that justice."

"I should know something of that matter," said the monk, "since it was my voice that sent him to your assistance. I had seen the party as I passed your door, and was hastening to the civil power in order to raise assistance, when I perceived a man's figure coming slowly towards me. Apprehensive it might be one of the ambuscade, I stepped behind the buttresses of the chapel of St. John, and seeing from a nearer view, that it was Henry Smith, I guessed which way he was bound, and raised my voice in an exhortation, which made him double his speed."

"I am beholden to you, Father," said Catharine; "but all this, and the Duke of Rothsay's own language to me, only show that the Prince is a profligate young man, who will scruple no extremities which may promise to gratify an idle passion, at whatever expense to its object. His emissary, Ramorny, has even had the insolence to tell me, that my father shall suffer for it, if I dare to prefer being the wife of an honest man, to becoming the loose paramour of a married prince. So I see no other remedy than to take the veil, or run the risk of my own ruin and my poor father's. Were there no other reason, the terror of these threats, from a man so notoriously capable of keeping his word, ought as much to prevent my becoming the bride of any worthy man, as it should prohibit me from unlatching his door to admit murderers.—Oh, good Father! what a lot is mine! and how fatal am I likely to prove to my affectionate parent, and to any one with whom I might ally my unhappy fortunes!"

"Be yet of good cheer, my daughter," said the monk; "there is comfort for thee even in this extremity of apparent distress. Ramorny is a villain, and abuses the ear of his patron. The Prince is unhappily a dissipated and idle youth;

but, unless my grey hairs have been strangely imposed on, his character is beginning to alter. He hath been awakened to Ramorny's baseness, and deeply regrets having followed his evil advice. I believe, nay, I am well convinced, that his passion for you has assumed a nobler and purer character, and that the lessons he has heard from me on the corruptions of the church, and of the times, will, if enforced from your lips, sink deeply into his heart, and perhaps produce fruits, for the world to wonder as well as rejoice at. Old prophecies have said, that Rome shall fall by the speech of a woman."

"These are dreams, Father," said Catharine; "the visions of one whose thoughts are too much on better things, to admit his thinking justly upon the ordinary affairs of earth. When we have looked long at the sun, every thing else can only be seen indistinctly."

"Thou art over hasty, my daughter," said Clement, "and thou shalt be convinced of it. The prospects which I am to open to thee were unfit to be exposed to one of a less firm sense of virtue, or a more ambitious temper. Perhaps it is not fit that, even to you, I should display them; but my confidence is strong in thy wisdom and thy principles. Know, then, that there is much chance that the Church of Rome will dissolve the union which she has herself formed, and release the Duke of Rothsay from his marriage with Marjory Douglas."

Here he paused.

"And if the Church hath power and will to do this," replied the maiden, "what influence can the divorce of the Duke from his wife produce on the fortunes of Catharine Glover?"

She looked at the priest anxiously as she spoke, and he had some apparent difficulty in framing his reply, for he looked on the ground while he answered her.

"What did beauty do for Catharine Logie? Unless our fathers have told us falsely, it raised her to share the throne of David Bruce."

"Did she live happy, or die regretted, good Father?" asked Catharine, in the same calm and steady tone.

"She formed her alliance, from temporal, and perhaps criminal ambition," replied Father Clement; "and she found her reward in vanity and vexation of spirit. But had she wedded with the purpose that the believing wife should convert the unbelieving, or confirm the doubting, husband, what then had been her reward? Love and honour upon earth, and an inheritance in Heaven with Queen Margaret, and those heroines who have been the nursing mothers of the Church."

Hitherto Catharine had sat upon a stone beside the priest's feet, and looked up to him as she spoke or listened; but now, as if animated by calm, yet settled feelings of disapprobation, she rose up, and extending her hand towards the monk as she spoke, addressed him with a countenance and voice which might have become a cherub, pitying, and even as much as possible sparing, the feelings of the mortal whose errors he is commissioned to rebuke.

"And is it even so?" she said, "and can so much of the wishes, hopes, and prejudices of this vile world, affect him who may be called to-morrow to lay down his life for opposing the corruptions of a wicked age and backsliding priesthood? Can it be the severely virtuous Father Clement, who advises his child to aim at, or even to think of, the possession of a throne and a bed, which cannot become vacant but by an act of crying injustice to the present possessor? Can it be the wise reformer of the church who wishes to rest a scheme, in itself so unjust, upon a foundation so precarious? Since when is it, good Father, that the principal libertine has altered his morals so much, to be likely to court in honourable fashion the daughter of a Perth artisan? Two days must have wrought this change; for only that space has passed since he was breaking into my father's house at midnight, with worse mischief in his mind than that of a common robber. And think you, that if Rothsay's heart could dictate so mean a match, he could achieve such a purpose without endangering both his succession and his life, assailed by the Douglas and March at the same time, for what they must receive as an act of injury and insult to both their houses? Oh! Father Clement, where was your principle, where your prudence, when they suffered you to be bewildered by so strange a dream, and placed the meanest of your disciples in the right thus to reproach you?"

The old man's eyes filled with tears, as Catharine, visibly and painfully affected by what she had said, became at length silent.

"By the mouths of babes and sucklings," he said, "hath He rebuked those who would seem wise in their generation. I thank Heaven, that hath taught me better thoughts than my own vanity suggested, through the medium of so kind a monitress.—Yes, Catharine, I must not hereafter wonder or exclaim, when I see those whom I have hitherto judged too harshly, struggling for temporal power, and holding all the while the language of religious zeal. I thank thee, daughter, for thy salutary admonition, and I thank Heaven that sent it by thy lips, rather than those of a sterner reprover."

Catharine had raised her head to reply, and bid the old man, whose humiliation gave her pain, be comforted, when her eyes were arrested by an object close at hand. Among the crags and cliffs which surrounded this place of seclusion, there were two which stood in such close contiguity, that they seemed to have been portions of the same rock, which, rended by lightning or by an earthquake, now exhibited a chasm of about four feet in breadth, betwixt the masses of stone. Into this chasm an oak-tree had thrust itself, in one of the fantastic frolics which vegetation often exhibits in such situations. The tree, stunted and ill-fed, had sent its roots along the face of the rock in all directions to seek for supplies, and they lay like military lines of communication, contorted, twisted, and knotted like the immense snakes of the Indian archipelago. As Catharine's look fell upon the curious complication of knotty branches and twisted roots, she was suddenly sensible that two large eyes were visible among them, fixed and glaring at her, like those of a wild animal in ambush. She started, and without speaking, pointed out the object to her companion, and looking herself with more strict attention, could at length trace out the bushy red hair and shaggy beard, which had hitherto been concealed by the drooping branches and twisted roots of the tree.

When he saw himself discovered, the Highlander, for such he proved, stepped forth from his lurking-place, and, stalking forward, displayed a colossal person, clothed in purple, red, and green-checked plaid, under which he wore a jacket of bull's hide. His bow and arrows were at his back, his head was bare, and a large quantity of tangled locks, like the glibbs of the Irish, served to cover the head, and supplied all the purposes of a bonnet. His belt bore a sword and dagger, and he had in his hand a Danish pole-axe, more recently called a Lochaber axe. Through the same rude portal advanced —one by one—four men more, of similar size, and dressed and armed in the same manner.

Catharine was too much accustomed to the appearance of

the inhabitants of the mountains so near to Perth, to permit herself to be alarmed, as another Lowland maiden might have been on the same occasion. She saw with tolerable composure these gigantic forms arrange themselves in a semi-circle around and in front of the Monk and herself, all bending upon them in silence their large fixed eyes, expressing, as far as she could judge, a wild admiration of her beauty. She inclined her head to them, and uttered imperfectly the usual words of a Highland salutation. The elder and leader of the party returned the greeting, and then again remained silent and motionless. The monk told his beads; and even Catharine began to have strange fears for her personal safety, and anxiety to know whether they were to consider themselves at personal freedom. She resolved to make the experiment, and moved forward as if to descend the hill; but when she attempted to pass the line of Highlanders, they extended their pole-axes betwixt each other, so as effectually to occupy each opening through which she could have passed.

Somewhat disconcerted, yet not dismayed, for she could not conceive that any evil was intended, she sat down upon one of the scattered fragments of rock, and bade the monk, standing by her side, be of good courage.

"If I fear," said Father Clement, "it is not for myself; for whether I be brained with the axes of these wild men, like an ox when, worn out by labour, he is condemned to the slaughter, or whether I am bound with their bowstrings, and delivered over to those who will take my life with more cruel ceremony, it can but little concern me, if they suffer thee, dearest daughter, to escape uninjured."

"We have neither of us," replied the Maiden of Perth, "any cause for apprehending evil; and here comes Conachar, to assure us of it."

Yet as she spoke, she almost doubted her own eyes; so altered were the manner and attire of the handsome, stately, and almost splendidly dressed youth, who, springing like a roebuck from a cliff of considerable height, lighted just in front of her. His dress was of the same tartan worn by those who had first made their appearance, but closed at the throat and elbows with a necklace and armlets of gold. The hauberk which he wore over his person, was of steel, but so clearly burnished, that it shone like silver. His arms were profusely ornamented, and his bonnet, besides the eagle's feather marking the quality of chief, was adorned with a chain of gold, wrapt several times around it, and secured by a large clasp, glistening with pearls. His brooch, by which the tartan mantle, or plaid, as it is now called, was secured on the shoulder, was also of gold, large and curiously carved. He bore no weapon in his hand, excepting a small sapling stick, with a hooked head. His whole appearance and gait, which used formerly to denote a sullen feeling of conscious degradation, was now bold, forward and haughty; and he stood before Catharine with smiling confidence, as if fully conscious of his improved appearance, and waiting till she should recognize him.

"Conachar," said Catharine, desirous to break this state of suspense, "are these your father's men?"

"No, fair Catharine," answered the young man. "Conachar is no more, unless in regard to the wrongs he has sustained, and the vengeance which they demand. I am Ian Eachin MacIan, son to the Chief of the Clan Quhele. I have moulted my feathers, as you see, when I changed my name. And for these men, they are not my father's followers, but mine. You see only one half of them collected; they form a band consisting of my foster father and eight sons, who are my bodyguard, and the children of my belt, who breathe but to do my will. But Conachar," he added, in a softer tone of voice, "lives again so soon as Catharine desires to see him; and while he is the young Chief of the Clan Quhele to all others, he is to her as humble and obedient as when he was Simon Glover's apprentice. See, here is the stick I had from you when we nutted together in the sunny braes of Lednoch, when Autumn was young in the year that is gone. I would not exchange it, Catharine, for the truncheon of my tribe."

While Eachin thus spoke, Catharine began to doubt in her own mind whether she had acted prudently in requesting the assistance of a bold young man, elated, doubtless, by his sudden elevation from a state of servitude, to one which she was aware gave him extensive authority over a very lawless body of adherents.

"You do not fear me, fair Catharine?" said the young Chief, taking her hand. "I suffered my people to appear before me for a few minutes, that I might see how you could endure their presence; and methinks you regarded them as if you were born to be a chieftain's wife."

"I have no reason to fear wrong from Highlanders," said

Catharine, firmly; "especially as I thought Conachar was with them. Conachar has drunk of our cup, and eaten of our bread; and my father has often had traffic with Highlanders, and never was there wrong or quarrel betwixt him and them."

"No?" replied Hector, for such is the Saxon equivalent for Eachin, "what! never when he took the part of the Gow Chrom," (the bandy-legged Smith,) "against Eachin MacIan? —Say nothing to excuse it, and believe it will be your own fault if I ever again allude to it. But you had some command to lay upon me—speak, and you shall be obeyed."

Catharine hastened to reply; for there was something in the young Chief's manner and language, which made her desire to shorten the interview.

"Eachin," she said, "since Conachar is no longer your name, you ought to be sensible that in claiming, as I honestly might, a service from my equal, I little thought that I was addressing a person of such superior power and consequence. You, as well as I, have been obliged to the religious instruction of this good man. He is now in great danger; wicked men have accused him with false charges, and he is desirous to remain in safety and concealment till the storm shall pass away."

"Ha! the good Clerk Clement? Ay, the worthy clerk did much for me, and more than my rugged temper was capable to profit by. I will be glad to see any one in the town of Perth persecute one who hath taken hold of MacIan's mantle!"

"It may not be safe to trust too much to that," said Catharine. "I nothing doubt the power of your tribe, but when the Black Douglas takes up a feud, he is not to be scared by the shaking of a Highland plaid."

The Highlander disguised his displeasure at this speech with a forced laugh.

"The sparrow," he said, "that is next the eye, seems larger than the eagle that is perched on Ben-goile. You fear the Douglasses most, because they sit next to you. But be it as you will—You will not believe how wide our hills, and vales, and forests, extend beyond the dusky barrier of yonder mountains, and you think all the world lies on the banks of the Tay. But this good Clerk shall see hills that could hide him were all the Douglasses on his quest—ay, and he shall see men enough also, to make them glad to get once more southward of the Grampians.—And wherefore should you not go with the good man? I will send a party to bring him in safety from Perth, and we will set up the old trade beyond Loch Tay—only no more cutting out of gloves for me. I will find your father in hides, but I will not cut them, save when they are on the creatures' backs."

"My father will come one day and see your housekeeping, Conachar—I mean, Hector.—But times must be quieter, for there is feud between the town's-people and the followers of the noblemen, and there is speech of war about to break out in the Highlands."

"Yes, by Our Lady Catharine! and were it not for that same Highland war, you should not thus put off your Highland visit, my pretty mistress. But the race of the hills are no longer to be divided into two nations. They will fight like men for the supremacy, and he who gets it will deal with the King of Scotland as an equal, not as a superior. Pray that the victory may fall to MacIan, my pious St. Catharine, for thou shalt pray for one who loves thee dearly."

"I will pray for the right," said Catharine; "or rather, I will pray that there be peace on all sides.—Farewell, kind and excellent Father Clement; believe I shall never forget thy lessons—remember me in thy prayers.—But how wilt thou be able to sustain a journey so toilsome?"

"They shall carry him if need be," said Hector, "if we go far without finding a horse for him. But you, Catharine—it is far from hence to Perth. Let me attend you thither as I was wont."

"If you were as you were wont, I would not refuse your escort. But gold brooches and bracelets are perilous company, when the Liddesdale and Annandale lancers are riding as throng upon the highway as the leaves at Hallowmass; and there is no safe meeting betwixt Highland tartans and steel jackets."

She hazarded this remark, as she somewhat suspected, that, in casting his slough, young Eachin had not entirely surmounted the habits which he had acquired in his humbler state, and that, though he might use bold words, he would not be rash enough to brave the odds of numbers, to which a descent into the vicinity of the city would be likely to expose him. It appeared that she judged correctly; for, after a farewell, in which she compounded for the immunity of her lips, by permitting him to kiss her hand, she returned towards Perth, and could obtain at times, when she looked back, an occasional glance of the Highlanders, as, winding through the most concealed and impracticable parts, they bent their way towards the North.

She felt in part relieved from her immediate anxiety, as the distance increased betwixt her and these men, whose actions were only directed by the will of their chief, and whose chief was a giddy and impetuous boy. She apprehended no insult on her return to Perth, from the soldiery of any party whom she might meet; for the rules of chivalry were in those days a surer protection to a maiden of decent appearance, than an escort of armed men, whose cognizance might not be acknowledged as friendly by any other party whom they might chance to encounter. But more remote dangers pressed on her apprehension. The pursuit of the licentious Prince was rendered formidable by threats which his unprincipled counsellor, Ramorny, had not shunned to utter against her father, if she persevered in her coyness. These menaces, in such an age, and from such a character, were deep grounds for alarm; nor could she consider the pretensions to her favour which Conachar had scarce repressed during his state of servitude, and seemed now to avow boldly, as less fraught with evil, since there had been repeated incursions of the Highlanders into the very town of Perth, and citizens had, on more occasions than one, been made prisoners, and carried off from their own houses, or had fallen by the claymore in the very streets of their city. She feared, too, her father's importunity on behalf of the Smith, of whose conduct on St. Valentine's day unworthy reports had reached her; and whose suit, had he stood clear in her good opinion, she dared not listen to, while Ramorny's threats of revenge upon her father rung on her ear. She thought on these various dangers with the deepest apprehension, and an earnest desire to escape from them and herself, by taking refuge in the cloister; but saw no possibility of obtaining her father's consent to the only course from which she expected peace and protection.

In the course of these reflections, we cannot discover that she very distinctly regretted that her perils attended her because she was the *Fair Maid of Perth*; this was one point which marked that she was not yet altogether an angel; and perhaps it was another, that, in despite of Henry Smith's real or supposed delinquencies, a sigh escaped from her bosom, when she thought upon St. Valentine's dawn.

CHAPTER XV

O for a draught of power to steep
The soul of agony in sleep!

BERTHA.

WE have shown the secrets of the confessional; those of the sick chamber are not hidden from us. In a darkened apartment, where salves and medicines showed that the leech had been busy in his craft, a tall thin form lay on a bed, arrayed in a nightgown belted around him, with pain on his brow, and a thousand stormy passions agitating his bosom. Every thing in the apartment indicated a man of opulence and of expense. Henbane Dwining, the apothecary, who seemed to have the care of the patient, stole with a crafty and cat-like step from one corner of the room to another, busying himself with mixing medicines and preparing dressings. The sick man groaned once or twice, on which the leech, advancing to his bedside, asked whether these sounds were a token of the pain of his body, or of the distress of his mind.

"Of both, thou poisoning varlet," said Sir John Ramorny; "and of being encumbered with thy accursed company."

"If that is all, I can relieve your knighthood of one of these ills by presently removing myself elsewhere. Thanks to the feuds of this boisterous time, had I twenty hands, instead of these two poor servants of my art, (displaying his skinny palms,) there is enough of employment for them; well requited employment, too, where thanks and crowns contend which shall best pay my services; while you, Sir John, wreak upon your chirurgeon the anger you ought only to bear against the author of your wound."

"Villain, it is beneath me to reply to thee," said the patient; "but every word of thy malignant tongue is a dirk, inflicting wounds which set all the medicines of Arabia at defiance."

"Sir John, I understand you not; but if you give way to these tempestuous fits of rage, it is impossible but fever and inflammation must be the result."

"Why then dost thou speak in a sense to chafe my blood? Why dost thou name the supposition of thy worthless self having more hands than nature gave thee, while I, a knight and gentleman, am mutilated like a cripple?"

"Sir John," replied the chirurgeon, "I am no divine, nor a mainly obstinate believer in some things which divines tell us. Yet I may remind you that you have been kindly dealt with; for if the blow which has done you this injury had lighted on your neck, as it was aimed, it would have swept your head from your shoulders, instead of amputating a less considerable member."

"I wish it had, Dwining—I wish it had lighted as it was addressed. I should not then have seen a policy, which had spun a web so fine as mine, burst through by the brute force of a drunken churl. I should not have been reserved to see horses which I must not mount—lists which I must no longer enter—splendours which I cannot hope to share— or battles which I must not take part in. I should not, with a man's passions for power and for strife, be set to keep place among the women, despised by them, too, as a miserable impotent cripple, unable to aim at obtaining the favour of the sex."

"Supposing all this to be so, I will yet pray of your knight-hood to remark," replied Dwining, still busying himself with arranging the dressings of the wounds, "that your eyes, which you must have lost with your head, may, being spared to you, present as rich a prospect of pleasure as either ambition, or victory in the lists or in the field, or the love of woman itself, could have proposed to you."

"My sense is too dull to catch thy meaning, leech," replied Ramorny. "What is this precious spectacle reserved to me in such a shipwreck?"

"The dearest that mankind knows," replied Dwining; and then, in the accent of a lover who utters the name of his beloved mistress, and expresses his passion for her in the very tone of his voice, he added the word "REVENGE!"

The patient had raised himself on his couch to listen with some anxiety for the solution of the physician's enigma. He laid himself down again as he heard it explained, and after a short pause, asked, "In what Christian college learned you this morality, good Master Dwining?"

"In no Christian college," answered his physician; "for though it is privately received in most, it is openly and manfully adopted in none. But I have studied among the sages of Granada, where the fiery-souled Moor lifts high his deadly dagger as it drops with his enemy's blood, and avows the doctrine which the pallid Christian practises, though coward-like he dare not name it."

"Thou art then a more high-souled villain than I deemed thee" said Ramorny.

"Let that pass," answered Dwining. "The waters that are the stillest, are also the deepest ; and the foe is most to be dreaded who never threatens till he strikes. You knights and men-at-arms go straight to your purpose with sword in hand. We, who are clerks, win our access with a noiseless step and an indirect approach, but attain our object not less surely."

"And I," said the knight, "who have trod to my revenge with a mailed foot, which made all echo around it, must now use such a slipper as thine ? Ha !"

"He who lacks strength," said the wily mediciner, "must attain his purpose by skill."

"And tell me sincerely, mediciner, wherefore thou wouldst read me these devil's lessons ? Why wouldst thou thrust me faster or farther on to my vengeance, than I may seem to thee ready to go of my own accord ? I am old in the ways of the world, man ; and I know that such as thou do not drop words in vain, or thrust themselves upon the dangerous confidence of men like me, save with the prospect of advancing some purpose of their own. What interest hast thou in the road, whether peaceful or bloody, which I may pursue on these occurrents ?"

"In plain dealing, Sir Knight, though it is what I seldom use," answered the leech, "my road to revenge is the same with yours."

"With mine, man ?" said Ramorny, with a tone of scornful surprise. "I thought it had been high beyond thy reach. Thou aim at the same revenge with Ramorny !"

"Ay, truly," replied Dwining ; "for the smithy churl under whose blow you have suffered, has often done me despite and injury. He has thwarted me in council, and despised me in action. His brutal and unhesitating bluntness is a living reproach to the subtlety of my natural disposition. I fear him, and I hate him."

"And you hope to find an active coadjutor in me ?" said Ramorny, in the same supercilious tone as before. "But know, the artisan fellow is too low in degree, to be to me either the object of hatred or of fear. Yet he shall not escape. We hate not the reptile that has stung us, though we might shake it off the wound, and tread upon it. I know the ruffian of old as a stout man-at-arms, and a pretender, as I have heard, to the favour of the scornful puppet, whose beauties, forsooth, spurred us to our wise and hopeful attempt. —Fiends, that direct this nether world ! by what malice have ye decided that the hand which has couched a lance against the bosom of a prince, should be struck off like a sapling, by the blow of a churl, and during the turmoil of a midnight riot!—Well, mediciner, thus far our courses hold together, and I bid thee well believe that I will crush for thee this reptile mechanic. But do not thou think to escape me, when that part of my revenge is done, which will be most easily and speedily accomplished."

"Not, it may be, altogether so easily accomplished," said the apothecary ; "for if your knighthood will credit me, there will be found small ease or security in dealing with him. He is the strongest, boldest, and most skilful swordsman in Perth, and all the country around it."

"Fear nothing ; he shall be met with had he the strength of Sampson. But then, mark me ! Hope not thou to escape my vengeance, unless thou become my passive agent in the scene which is to follow. Mark me, I say once more. I have studied at no Moorish college, and lack some of thy unbounded appetite for revenge, but yet I will have my share of vengeance.—Listen to me, mediciner, while I shall thus far unfold myself; but beware of treachery, for powerful as thy fiend is, thou hast taken lessons from a meaner devil than mine. Hearken—the master whom I have served through vice and virtue, with too much zeal for my own character perhaps, but with unshaken fidelity to him—the very man, to soothe whose frantic folly I have incurred this irreparable loss, is, at the prayer of his doating father, about to sacrifice me, by turning me out of his favour, and leaving me at the mercy of the hypocritical relative, with whom he seeks a precarious reconciliation at my expense. If he perseveres in this most ungrateful purpose, thy fiercest Moors, were their complexion swarthy as the smoke of hell, shall blush to see their revenge outdone ! But I will give him one more chance for honour and safety, before my wrath shall descend on him in unrelenting and unmitigated fury.— There, then, thus far thou hast my confidence—Close hands on our bargain—close hands, did I say ?—where is the hand that should be the pledge and representative of Ramorny's plighted word ! is it nailed on the public pillory, or flung as offal to the houseless dogs, who are even now snarling over it ? Lay thy finger on the mutilated stump then, and swear to be a faithful actor in my revenge, as I shall be in yours.—How now, Sir Leech, look you pale—you, who say to Death, stand back or advance, can you tremble to think of him or to hear him named? I have not mentioned your fee, for one who loves revenge for itself, requires no deeper bribe—yet, if broad lands and large sums of gold can increase thy zeal in a brave cause, believe me, these shall not be lacking."

"They tell for something in my humble wishes," said Dwining; "the poor man in this bustling world is thrust down like a dwarf in a crowd, and so trodden under foot—the rich and powerful rise like giants above the press, and are at ease, while all is turmoil around them."

"Then shalt thou rise above the press, mediciner, as high as gold can raise thee. This purse is weighty, yet it is but an earnest of thy guerdon."

"And this Smith? my noble benefactor"—said the leech, as he pouched the gratuity—"This Henry of the Wynd, or whatever is his name—would not the news that he hath paid the penalty of his action, assuage the pain of thy knighthood's wound better than the balm of Mecca with which I have salved it?"

"He is beneath the thoughts of Ramorny; and I have no more resentment against him than I have ill-will at the senseless weapon which he swayed. But it is just thy hate should be vented upon him. Where is he chiefly to be met with?"

"That also I have considered," said Dwining. "To make the attempt by day in his own house, were too open and dangerous, for he hath five servants who work with him at the stithy, four of them strong knaves, and all loving to their master. By night were scarce less desperate, for he hath his doors strongly secured with bolt of oak and bar of iron, and ere the fastenings of his house could be forced, the neighbourhood would rise to his rescue, especially as they are still alarmed by the practice on St. Valentine's Even."

"O ay, true, mediciner," said Ramorny, "for deceit is thy nature even with me—thou knewest my hand and signet, as thou said'st, when that hand was found cast out on the street, like the disgusting refuse of a shambles,—why, having such knowledge, went'st thou with these jolter-headed citizens to consult that Patrick Charteris, whose spurs should be hacked off from his heels for the communion which he holds with paltry burghers, and whom thou brought'st here with the fools to do dishonour to the lifeless hand, which, had it held its wonted place, he was not worthy to have touched in peace, or faced in war?"

"My noble patron, as soon as I had reason to know you had been the sufferer, I urged them with all my powers of persuasion to desist from prosecuting the feud, but the swaggering Smith, and one or two other hot heads, cried out for vengeance. Your knighthood must know this fellow calls himself bachelor to the Fair Maiden of Perth, and stands upon his honour to follow up her father's quarrel; but I have forestalled his market in that quarter, and that is something in earnest of revenge."

"How mean you by that, Sir Leech?" said the patient.

"Your knighthood shall conceive," said the mediciner, "that this Smith doth not live within compass, but is an outlier and a galliard. I met him myself on St. Valentine's day, shortly after the affray between the townsfolk and the followers of Douglas. Yes, I met him sneaking through the lanes and by-passages with a common minstrel wench, with her messan and her viol on his one arm, and her buxom self hanging upon the other. What thinks your honour? Is not this a trim squire, to cross a prince's love with the fairest girl in Perth, strike off the hand of a knight and baron, and become gentleman-usher to a strolling glee-woman, all in the course of the same four-and-twenty hours?"

"Marry, I think the better of him that he is so much of a gentleman's humour, clown though he be," said Ramorny. "I would he had been a precisian instead of a galliard, and I should have had better heart to aid thy revenge;—and such revenge! revenge on a smith—in the quarrel of a pitiful manufacturer of rotten cheverons! Pah!—And yet it shall be taken in full. Thou hast commenced it, I warrant me, by thine own manœuvres."

"In a small degree only"—said the apothecary;—"I took care that two or three of the most notorious gossips in Curfew Street, who liked not to hear Catharine called the Fair Maid of Perth, should be possessed of this story of her faithful Valentine. They opened on the scent so keenly, that, rather than doubt had fallen on the tale, they would have vouched for it as if their own eyes had seen it. The lover came to her father's within an hour after, and your worship may think what a reception he had from the angry Glover, for the damsel herself would not be looked upon. And thus your honour sees I had a foretaste of revenge. But I trust to receive the full draught from the hands of your lordship, with whom I am in a brotherly league, which——"

"Brotherly!" said the Knight, contemptuously. "But be it so, the priests say we are all of one common earth. I cannot tell—there seems to me some difference; but the better mould shall keep faith with the baser, and thou shalt have thy revenge. Call thou my page hither."

A young man made his appearance from the anteroom upon the physician's summons.

"Eviot," said the knight, "does Bonthron wait? and is he sober?"

"He is as sober as sleep can make him after a deep drink," answered the page.

"Then fetch him hither, and do thou shut the door."

A heavy step presently approached the apartment, and a man entered, whose deficiency of height seemed made up in breadth of shoulders and strength of arm.

"There is a man thou must deal upon, Bonthron," said the knight.

The man smoothed his rugged features, and grinned a smile of satisfaction.

"That mediciner will show thee the party. Take such advantage of time, place, and circumstance, as will ensure the result; and mind you come not by the worst, for the man is the fighting Smith of the Wynd."

"It will be a tough job," growled the assassin; "for if I miss my blow, I may esteem myself but a dead man. All Perth rings with the Smith's skill and strength."

"Take two assistants with thee," said the Knight.

"Not I," said Bonthron. "If you double any thing, let it be the reward."

"Account it doubled," said his master; "but see thy work be thoroughly executed."

"Trust me for that, Sir Knight—seldom have I failed."

"Use this sage man's directions," said the wounded knight, pointing to the physician. "And hark thee—await his coming forth—and drink not till the business be done."

"I will not," answered the dark satellite; "my own life depends on my blow being steady and sure. I know whom I have to deal with."

"Vanish, then, till he summons you, and have axe and dagger in readiness."

Bonthron nodded and withdrew.

"Will your knighthood venture to intrust such an act to a single hand?" said the mediciner, when the assassin had left the room. "May I pray you to remember that yonder party did, two nights since, baffle six armed men?"

"Question me not, Sir Mediciner; a man like Bonthron, who knows time and place, is worth a score of confused revellers.—Call Eviot—thou shalt first exert thy powers of healing, and do not doubt that thou shalt, in the farther work, be aided by one who will match thee in the art of sudden and unexpected destruction."

The page Eviot again appeared at the mediciner's summons, and at his master's sign assisted the chirurgeon in removing the dressings from Sir John Ramorny's wounded arm. Dwining viewed the naked stump with a species of professional satisfaction, enhanced, no doubt, by the malignant pleasure which his evil disposition took in the pain and distress of his fellow-creatures. The knight just turned his eye on the ghastly spectacle, and uttered, under the pressure of bodily pain or mental agony, a groan which he would fain have repressed.

"You groan, sir," said the leech, in his soft insinuating tone of voice, but with a sneer of enjoyment, mixed with scorn, curling upon his lip, which his habitual dissimulation could not altogether disguise—"You groan—but be comforted. This Henry Smith knows his business—his sword is as true to its aim as his hammer to the anvil. Had a common swordsman struck this fatal blow, he had harmed the bone and damaged the muscles, so that even my art might not have been able to repair them. But Henry Smith's cut is clean, and as sure as that with which my own scalpel could have made the amputation. In a few days you will be able, with care and attention to the ordinances of medicine, to stir abroad."

"But my hand—the loss of my hand——"

"It may be kept secret for a time," said the mediciner; "I have possessed two or three tattling fools, in deep confidence, that the hand which was found was that of your knighthood's groom, Black Quentin, and your knighthood knows that he has parted for Fife, in such sort as to make it generally believed."

"I know well enough," said Ramorny, "that the rumour may stifle the truth for a short time. But what avails this brief delay?"

"It may be concealed till your knighthood retires for a

time from the court, and then, when new accidents have darkened the recollection of the present stir, it may be imputed to a wound received from the shivering of a spear, or from a crossbow bolt. Your slave will find a suitable device, and stand for the truth of it."

"The thought maddens me," said Ramorny, with another groan of mental and bodily agony. "Yet I see no better remedy."

"There is none other," said the leech, to whose evil nature his patron's distress was delicious nourishment. "In the meanwhile it is believed you are confined by the consequences of some bruises, aiding the sense of displeasure at the Prince's having consented to dismiss you from his household, at the remonstrance of Albany ; which is publicly known."

"Villain, thou rack'st me!" exclaimed the patient.

"Upon the whole, therefore," said Dwining, "your knighthood has escaped well, and, saving the lack of your hand, a mischance beyond remedy, you ought rather to rejoice than complain ; for no barber-chirurgeon in France or England could have more ably performed the operation than this churl with one downright blow."

"I understand my obligation fully," said Ramorny, struggling with his anger, and affecting composure ; "and if Bonthron pays him not with a blow equally downright, and rendering the aid of the leech unnecessary, say that John of Ramorny cannot requite an obligation."

"That is spoke like yourself, noble knight !" answered the mediciner. "And let me further say, that the operator's skill must have been vain, and the hemorrhage must have drained your life-veins, but for the bandages, the cautery, and the styptics, applied by the good monks, and the poor service of your humble vassal, Henbane Dwining."

"Peace !" exclaimed the patient, "with thy ill-omened voice, and worse-omened name !—Methinks, as thou mentionest the tortures I have undergone, my tingling nerves stretch and contract themselves as if they still actuated the fingers that once could clutch a dagger !"

"That," explained the leech, "may it please your knighthood, is a phenomenon well known to our profession. There have been those among the ancient sages who have thought that there still remained a sympathy between the severed nerves, and those belonging to the amputated limb ; and that the several fingers are seen to quiver and strain, as corresponding with the impulse which proceeds from their sympathy with the energies of the living system. Could we recover the hand from the Cross, or from the custody of the Black Douglas, I would be pleased to observe this wonderful operation of occult sympathies. But I fear me, one might as safely go to wrest the joint from the talons of an hungry eagle."

"And thou mayst as safely break thy malignant jests on a wounded lion, as on John of Ramorny!" said the knight, raising himself in uncontrollable indignation. "Caitiff, proceed to thy duty; and remember, that if my hand can no longer clasp a dagger, I can command an hundred."

"The sight of one drawn and brandished in anger were sufficient," said Dwining, "to consume the vital powers of your chirurgeon. But who then," he added, in a tone partly insinuating, partly jeering, "who would then relieve the fiery and scorching pain which my patron now suffers, and which renders him exasperated even with his poor servant for quoting the rules of healing, so contemptible, doubtless, compared with the power of inflicting wounds?"

Then, as daring no longer to trifle with the mood of his dangerous patient, the leech addressed himself seriously to salving the wound, and applied a fragrant balm, the odour of which was diffused through the apartment, while it communicated a refreshing coolness, instead of the burning heat; a change so gratifying to the fevered patient, that, as he had before groaned with agony, he could not now help sighing for pleasure, as he sank back on his couch to enjoy the ease which the dressing bestowed.

"Your knightly lordship now knows who is your friend," said Dwining; "had you yielded to rash impulse, and said, 'Slay me this worthless quacksalver,' where, within the four seas of Britain, would you have found the man to have ministered to you as much comfort?"

"Forget my threats, good leech," said Ramorny, "and beware how you tempt me. Such as I brook not jests upon our agony. See thou keep thy scoffs, to pass upon misers[1] in the hospital."

Dwining ventured to say no more, but poured some drops from a phial which he took from his pocket, into a small cup of wine allayed with water.

---

[1] That is, miserable persons, as used in Spenser, and other writers of his time; though the sense is now restricted to those who are covetous.

"This draught," said the man of art, "is medicated to produce a sleep which must not be interrupted."

"For how long will it last?" asked the knight.

"The period of its operation is uncertain—perhaps till morning."

"Perhaps for ever," said the patient. "Sir Mediciner, taste me that liquor presently, else it passes not my lips."

The leech obeyed him with a scornful smile. "I would drink the whole with readiness; but the juice of this Indian gum will bring sleep on the healthy man as well as upon the patient, and the business of the leech requires me to be a watcher."

"I crave your pardon, Sir Leech," said Ramorny, looking downwards, as if ashamed to have manifested suspicion.

"There is no room for pardon where offence must not be taken," answered the mediciner. "An insect must thank a giant that he does not tread on him. Yet, noble knight, insects have their power of harming as well as physicians. What would it have cost me, save a moment's trouble, so to have drugged that balm, as should have made your arm rot to the shoulder joint, and your life-blood curdle in your veins to a corrupted jelly? What is there that prevented me to use means yet more subtle, and to taint your room with essences, before which the light of life twinkles more and more dimly, till it expires, like a torch amidst the foul vapours of some subterranean dungeon? You little estimate my power, if you know not that these, and yet deeper modes of destruction, stand at command of my art.[1] But a physician slays not the patient by whose generosity he lives, and far less will he, the breath of whose nostrils is the hope of revenge, destroy the vowed ally who is to favour his pursuit of it.— Yet one word;—should a necessity occur for rousing yourself, —for who in Scotland can promise himself eight hours' uninterrupted repose?—then smell at the strong essence con-

---

[1] The extent to which the science of poisoning was carried in the middle ages on the continent, is well known. The hateful practice was more and more refined, and still more generally adopted, afterwards; and, we are told, among other instances of diabolical cunning, of gloves which could not be put on without inflicting a mortal disease, of letters which, on being opened, diffused a fatal vapour, &c. &c. Voltaire justly and candidly mentions it as a distinguishing characteristic of the British, that political poisonings make little, if any, figure in their history

tained in this pouncet-box.—And now, farewell, Sir Knight; and if you cannot think of me as a man of nice conscience, acknowledge me at least as one of reason and of judgment."

So saying, the mediciner left the room; his usual mean and shuffling gait elevating itself into something more noble, as conscious of a victory over his imperious patient.

Sir John Ramorny remained sunk in unpleasing reflections, until he began to experience the incipient effects of his soporific draught. He then roused himself for an instant, and summoned his page.

"Eviot! what ho! Eviot!—I have done ill to unbosom myself so far to this poisonous quacksalver—Eviot!"

The page entered.

"Is the mediciner gone forth?"

"Yes, so please your knighthood."

"Alone, or accompanied?"

"Bonthron spoke apart with him, and followed him almost immediately—by your lordship's command, as I understood him."

"Lack-a-day, yes!—he goes to seek some medicaments—he will return anon. If he be intoxicated, see he comes not near my chamber, and permit him not to enter into converse with any one. He raves when drink has touched his brain. He was a rare fellow, before a Southron bill laid his brain-pan bare; but since that time he talks gibberish whenever the cup has crossed his lips.—Said the leech aught to you, Eviot?"

"Nothing, save to reiterate his commands that your honour be not disturbed."

"Which thou must surely obey," said the knight. "I feel the summons to rest, of which I have been deprived since this unhappy wound—At least, if I have slept it has been but for a snatch. Aid me to to take off my gown, Eviot."

"May God and the saints send you good rest, my lord," said the page, retiring after he had rendered his wounded master the assistance required.

As Eviot left the room, the knight, whose brain was becoming more and more confused, muttered over the page's departing salutation.

"God—saints—I *have* slept sound under such a benison. But now—methinks if I awake not to the accomplishment of my proud hopes of power and revenge, the best wish for me is, that the slumbers which now fall around my head, were the forerunners of that sleep which shall return my borrowed powers to their original non-existence—I can argue it no farther."

Thus speaking, he fell into a profound sleep.

CHAPTER XVI

On Fastern's E'en when we war fou.

Scots Song.

THE night which sunk down on the sick-bed of Ramorny, was not doomed to be a quiet one. Two hours had passed since curfew-bell, then rung at seven o'clock at night, and in those primitive times all were retired to rest, excepting such whom devotion, or duty, or debauchery, made watchers; and the evening being that of Shrovetide, or, as it was called in Scotland, Fastern's E'en,[1] the vigils of gaiety were by far the most frequented of the three.

The common people had, throughout the day, toiled and struggled at football; the nobles and gentry had fought cocks, and hearkened to the wanton music of the minstrel; while the citizens had gorged themselves upon pancakes fried in lard, and brose, or brewis—the fat broth, that is, in which salted beef had been boiled, poured upon highly-toasted oatmeal, a dish which even now is not ungrateful to simple old-fashioned Scottish palates. These were all exercises and festive dishes proper to the holiday. It was no less a solemnity of the evening, that the devout Catholic should drink as much good ale and wine as he had means to procure; and, if young and able, that he should dance at the ring, or figure among the morrice-dancers, who, in the city of Perth, as elsewhere, wore a peculiarly fantastic garb, and distinguished themselves by their address and activity. All this gaiety took place under the prudential consideration, that the long term of Lent, now approaching, with its fasts and deprivations, rendered it wise for mortals to cram as much idle and sensual

---

[1] *Fastern's E'en*, the evening before the commencement of the fast,—*Anglicé – Shrove-tide*, the season of being shriven, or of confession and absolution, before beginning the penance of Lent. The cockfights, &c., still held at this period, are relics of the Catholic carnival that preceded the weeks of abstinence.

indulgence as they could into the brief space which intervened before its commencement.

The usual revels had taken place, and in most parts of the city were succeeded by the usual pause. A particular degree of care had been taken by the nobility, to prevent any renewal of discord betwixt their followers and the citizens of the town ; so that the revels had proceeded with fewer casualties than usual, embracing only three deaths, and certain fractured limbs, which, occurring to individuals of little note, were not accounted worth enquiring into. The Carnival was closing quietly in general, but in some places the sport was still kept up.

One company of revellers, who had been particularly noticed and applauded, seemed unwilling to conclude their frolic. The Entry, as it was called, consisted of thirteen persons, habited in the same manner, having doublets of chamois leather sitting close to their bodies, curiously slashed and laced. They wore green caps with silver tassels, red ribands, and white shoes, had bells hung at their knees and around their ankles, and naked swords in their hands. This gallant party, having exhibited a sword-dance before the King, with much clashing of weapons, and fantastic interchange of postures, went on gallantly to repeat their exhibition before the door of Simon Glover, where, having made a fresh exhibition of their agility, they caused wine to be served round to their own company and the bystanders, and with a loud shout drank to the health of the Fair Maid of Perth. This summoned old Simon to the door of his habitation, to acknowledge the courtesy of his countrymen, and in his turn to send the wine around in honour of the Merry Morrice-Dancers of Perth.

"We thank thee, Father Simon," said a voice, which strove to drown in an artificial squeak the pert conceited tone of Oliver Proudfute. "But a sight of thy lovely daughter had been more sweet to us young bloods, than a whole vintage of Malvoisie."

"I thank you, neighbours, for your good-will," replied the Glover. "My daughter is ill at ease, and may not come forth into the cold night air—but if this gay gallant, whose voice methinks I should know, will go into my poor house, she will charge him with thanks for the rest of you."

"Bring them to us at the hostelrie of the Griffin," cried the rest of the ballet to their favoured companion ; for there will we ring-in Lent, and have another rouse to the health of the lovely Catharine."

"Have with you in half an hour," said Oliver, "and see who will quaff the largest flagon, or sing the loudest glee. Nay, I will be merry, in what remains of Fastern's Even, should Lent find me with my mouth closed for ever."

"Farewell, then," cried his mates in the morrice; "farewell, slashing Bonnet-maker, till we meet again."

The morrice-dancers accordingly set out upon their further progress, dancing and caroling as they went along to the sound of four musicians, who led the joyous band, while Simon Glover drew their Coryphæus into his house, and placed him in a chair by his parlour fire.

"But where is your daughter?" said Oliver. "She is the bait for us brave blades."

"Why, truly, she keeps her apartment, neighbour Oliver; and, to speak plainly, she keeps her bed."

"Why, then will I up stairs to see her in her sorrow—you have marred my ramble, Gaffer Glover, and you owe me amends—a roving blade like me—I will not lose both the lass and the glass.—Keeps her bed, does she?

> "My dog and I we have a trick
> To visit maids when they are sick;
> When they are sick and like to die,
> O thither do come my dog and I.
>
> "And when I die, as needs must hap,
> Then bury me under the good ale-tap;
> With folded arms there let me lie
> Cheek for jowl, my dog and I."

"Canst thou not be serious for a moment, neighbour Proudfute?" said the Glover; "I want a word of conversation with you."

"Serious?" answered the visitor; "why, I have been serious all this day—I can hardly open my mouth, but something comes out about death, a burial, or suchlike—the most serious subjects that I wot of."

"St. John, man!" said the Glover, "art thou fey?"

"No, not a whit—it is not my own death which these gloomy fancies foretell—I have a strong horoscope, and shall live for fifty years to come. But it is the case of the poor fellow—the Douglasman, whom I struck down at the fray of St. Valentine's—he died last night—it is that which weighs on my conscience, and awakens sad fancies. Ah, Father Simon, we martialists that have spilt blood in our choler, have dark thoughts at times—I sometimes wish that my knife had cut nothing but worsted thrums."

"And I wish," said Simon, "that mine had cut nothing but buck's leather, for it has sometimes cut my own fingers. But thou mayst spare thy remorse for this bout; there was but one man dangerously hurt at the affray, and it was he from whom Henry Smith hewed the hand, and he is well recovered. His name is Black Quentin, one of Sir John Ramorny's followers. He has been sent privately back to his own country of Fife."

"What, Black Quentin?—why, that is the very man that Henry and I, as we ever keep close together, struck at in the same moment, only my blow fell somewhat earlier. I fear further feud will come of it, and so does the Provost.—And is he recovered? Why, then, I will be jovial, and since thou wilt not let me see how Kate becomes her night-gear, I will back to the Griffin to my morrice-dancers."

"Nay, stay but one instant. Thou art a comrade of Henry Wynd, and hast done him the service to own one or two deeds, and this last among others. I would thou couldst clear him of other charges, with which fame hath loaded him."

"Nay, I will swear by the hilt of my sword, they are as false as hell, Father Simon. What—blades and targets! shall not men of the sword stick together?"

"Nay, neighbour Bonnet-maker, be patient; thou mayst do the Smith a kind turn, an thou takest this matter the right way. I have chosen thee to consult with anent this matter—not that I hold thee the wisest head in Perth, for should I say so I should lie."

"Ay, ay," answered the self-satisfied Bonnet-maker; "I know where you think my fault lies—you cool heads think we hot heads are fools—I have heard men call Henry Wynd such a score of times."

"Fool enough and cool enough may rhyme together passing well," said the Glover; "but thou art good-natured, and I think lovest this crony of thine. It stands awkwardly with us and him just now," continued Simon. "Thou knowest there hath been some talk of marriage between my daughter Catharine and Henry Gow?"

"I have heard some such song since St. Valentine's Morn—Ah! he that shall win the Fair Maid of Perth must be a happy man—and yet marriage spoils many a pretty fellow. I myself somewhat regret——"

"Prithee, truce with thy regrets for the present, man," interrupted the Glover, somewhat peevishly. "You must know, Oliver, that some of these talking women, who I think make all the business of the world their own, have accused Henry of keeping light company with glee-women and such-like. Catharine took it to heart; and I held my child insulted, that he had not waited upon her like a Valentine, but had thrown himself into unseemly society on the very day when, by ancient custom, he might have had an opportunity to press his interest with my daughter. Therefore when he came hither late on the evening of St. Valentine's, I, like a hasty old fool, bid him go home to the company he had left, and denied him admittance. I have not seen him since, and I begin to think that I may have been too rash in the matter. She is my only child, and the grave should have her sooner than a debauchee. But I have hitherto thought I knew Henry Gow as if he were my son. I cannot think he would use us thus, and it may be there are means of explaining what is laid to his charge. I was led to ask Dwining, who is said to have saluted the Smith while he was walking with this choice mate—If I am to believe his words, this wench was the Smith's cousin, Joan Letham. But thou knowest that the potter-carrier ever speaks one language with his visage, and another with his tongue—Now, thou, Oliver, hast too little wit—I mean, too much honesty—to belie the truth, and as Dwining hinted that thou also hadst seen her——"

"I see her, Simon Glover! Will Dwining say that I saw her?"

"No, not precisely that—but he says you *told* him you had met the Smith thus accompanied."

"He lies, and I will pound him into a gallipot!" said Oliver Proudfute.

"How? Did you never tell him then of such a meeting?"

"What an if I did?" said the Bonnet-maker. "Did not he swear that he would never repeat again to living mortal what I communicated to him? and therefore, in telling the occurrent to you he hath made himself a liar."

"Thou didst not meet the Smith, then," said Simon, "with such a loose baggage as fame reports?"

"Lack-a-day, not I—perhaps I did, perhaps I did not. Think, Father Simon—I have been a four-years' married man, and can you expect me to remember the turn of a glee-woman's ankle, the trip of her toe, the lace upon her petticoat, and such toys? No, I leave that to unmarried wags, like my gossip Henry."

"The upshot is then," said the Glover, much vexed, "you *did* meet him on St. Valentine's day walking the public streets——"

"Not so, neighbour; I met him in the most distant and dark lane in Perth, steering full for his own house, with bag and baggage, which, as a gallant fellow, he carried in his arms, the puppy dog on one, and the jilt herself (and to my thought she was a pretty one) hanging upon the other."

"Now, by good St. John," said the Glover, "this infamy would make a Christian man renounce his faith, and worship Mahound in very anger! But he has seen the last of my daughter. I would rather she went to the wild Highlands with a barelegged cateran, than wed with one who could at such a season, so broadly forget honour and decency— Out upon him!"

"Tush! tush! father Simon," said the liberal-minded Bonnet-maker; "you consider not the nature of young blood. Their company was not long, for—to speak truth, I did keep a little watch on him—I met him before sunrise, conducting his errant damsel to the Lady's Stairs, that the wench might embark on the Tay from Perth; and I know for certainty, (for I made enquiry,) that she sailed in a gabbart for Dundee. So you see it was but a slight escape of youth."

"And he came here," said Simon, bitterly, "beseeching for admittance to my daughter, while he had his harlot awaiting him at home! I had rather he had slain a score of men!—It skills not talking, least of all to thee, Oliver Proudfute, who, if thou art not such a one as himslf, would fain be thought so. But——"

"Nay, think not of it so seriously," said Oliver, who began to reflect on the mischief his tattling was likely to occasion to his friend, and on the consequences of Henry Gow's displeasure, when he should learn the disclosure which he had made rather in vanity of heart than in evil intention. "Consider," he continued, "that there are follies belonging to youth. Occasion provokes men to such frolics, and confession wipe them off. I care not if I tell thee, that though my wife be as goodly a woman as the city has, yet I myself——"

"Peace, silly braggart," said the Glover, in high wrath;
"thy loves and thy battles are alike apocryphal. If thou must
needs lie, which I think is thy nature, canst thou invent
no falsehood that may at least do thee some credit? Do I
not see through thee, as I could see the light through the
horn of a base lantern? Do I not know, thou filthy weaver
of rotten worsted, that thou durst no more cross the threshold
of thy own door, if thy wife heard of thy making such a
boast, than thou darest cross naked weapons with a boy of
twelve years old, who has drawn a sword for the first time
of his life? By St. John, it were paying you for your tale-
bearing trouble, to send thy Maudie word of thy gay brags."

The Bonnet-maker, at this threat, started as if a crossbow
bolt had whizzed past his head when least expected. And
it was with a trembling voice that he replied, "Nay, good
Father Glover, thou takest too much credit for thy grey
hairs. Consider, good neighbour, thou art too old for a
young martialist to wrangle with. And in the matter of my
Maudie, I can trust thee, for I know no one who would be
less willing than thou to break the peace of families."

"Trust thy coxcomb no longer with me," said the incensed
Glover; "but take thyself, and the thing thou call'st a head,
out of my reach, lest I borrow back five minutes of my youth,
and break thy pate!"

"You have had a merry Fastern's Even, neighbour," said
the Bonnet-maker, "and I wish you a quiet sleep; we shall
meet better friends to-morrow."

"Out of my doors to-night!" said the Glover. "I am
ashamed so idle a tongue as thine should have power to
move me thus." "Idiot—beast—loose-tongued coxcomb!"
he exclaimed, throwing himself into a chair, as the Bonnet-
maker disappeared; "that a fellow made up of lies should
not have had the grace to frame one when it might have
covered the shame of a friend! And I—what am I, that
I should, in my secret mind, wish that such a gross insult
to me and my child had been glossed over? Yet such was
my opinion of Henry, that I would have willingly believed
the grossest figment the swaggering ass could have invented.
Well!—it skills not thinking of it. Our honest name must
be maintained, though every thing else should go to ruin."

While the Glover thus moralised on the unwelcome con-
firmation of the tale he wished to think untrue, the expelled
morrice-dancer had leisure, in the composing air of a cool

and dark February night, to meditate on the consequences of the Glover's unrestrained anger.

"But it is nothing," he bethought himself, "to the wrath of Henry Wynd, who hath killed a man for much less than placing displeasure betwixt him and Catharine, as well as her fiery old father. Certainly I were better have denied every thing. But the humour of seeming a knowing gallant (as in truth I am) fairly overcame me. Were I best go to finish the revel at the Griffin?—But then Maudie will rampauge on my return,—ay, and this being holiday even, I may claim a privilege.—I have it—I will not to the Griffin—I will to the Smith's, who must be at home, since no one hath seen him this day amid the revel. I will endeavour to make peace with him, and offer my intercession with the Glover. Harry is a simple downright fellow, and though I think he is my better in a broil, yet in discourse I can turn him my own way. The streets are now quiet—the night, too, is dark, and I may step aside if I meet any rioters. I will to the Smith's, and, securing him for my friend, I care little for old Simon. Saint Ringan bear me well through this night, and I will clip my tongue out ere it shall run my head into such peril again! Yonder old fellow, when his blood was up, looked more like a carver of buff-jerkins than a clipper of kid-gloves."

With these reflections, the puissant Oliver walked swiftly, yet with as little noise as possible, towards the wynd in which the Smith, as our readers are aware, had his habitation. But his evil fortune had not ceased to pursue him. As he turned into the High, or principal street, he heard a burst of music very near him, followed by a loud shout.

"My merry mates, the morrice-dancers," thought he; "I would know old Jeremy's rebeck among an hundred. I will venture across the street ere they pass on—if I am espied, I shall have the renown of some private quest, which may do me honour as a roving blade."

With these longings for distinction among the gay and gallant, combated, however, internally, by more prudential considerations, the Bonnet-maker made an attempt to cross the street. But the revellers, whoever they might be, were accompanied by torches, the flash of which fell upon Oliver, whose light-coloured habit made him the more distinctly visible. The general shout of "A prize, a prize," overcame the noise of the minstrel, and before the Bonnet-maker could determine whether it were better to stand or fly, two active young men, clad in fantastic masking habits, resembling wild men, and holding great clubs, seized upon him, saying, in a tragical tone, "Yield thee, man of bells and bombast; yield thee, rescue or no rescue, or truly thou art but a dead morrice-dancer."

"To whom shall I yield me?" said the Bonnet-maker, with a faltering voice; for though he saw he had to do with a party of mummers who were a-foot for pleasure, yet he observed, at the same time, that they were far above his class, and he lost the audacity necessary to support his part in a game where the inferior was likely to come by the worst.

"Dost thou parley, slave?" answered one of the maskers; "and must I show thee that thou art a captive, by giving thee incontinently the bastinado?"

"By no means, puissant man of Ind," said the Bonnet-maker; "lo, I am conformable to your pleasure."

"Come, then," said those who had arrested him, "come and do homage to the Emperor of Mimes, King of Caperers, and Grand Duke of the Dark Hours, and explain by what right thou art so presumptuous as to prance and jingle, and wear out shoe-leather within his dominions, without paying him tribute. Know'st thou not thou hast incurred the pains of high treason?"

"That were hard, methinks," said poor Oliver, "since I knew not that his Grace exercised the government this evening. But I am willing to redeem the forfeit, if the purse of a poor Bonnet-maker may, by the mulct of a gallon of wine, or some such matter."

"Bring him before the Emperor," was the universal cry; and the morrice-dancer was placed before a slight, but easy and handsome figure of a young man, splendidly attired, having a cincture and tiara of peacock's feathers, then brought from the East as a marvellous rarity; a short jacket and under-dress of leopard's skin fitted closely the rest of his person, which was attired in flesh-coloured silk, so as to resemble the ordinary idea of an Indian prince. He wore sandals, fastened on with ribands of scarlet silk, and held in his hand a sort of fan, such as ladies then used, composed of the same feathers, assembled into a plume or tuft.

"What mister wight have we here," said the Indian chief, "who dares to tie the bells of a morrice on the ankles of a dull ass?—Hark ye, friend, your dress should make you a subject of ours, since our empire extends over all Merryland, including mimes and minstrels of every description.—What, tongue-tied? He lacks wine—minister to him our nutshell full of sack."

A huge calabash full of sack was offered to the lips of the supplicant, while this prince of revellers exhorted him,—

"Crack me this nut, and do it handsomely, and without wry faces."

But, however Oliver might have relished a moderate sip of the same good wine, he was terrified at the quantity he was required to deal with. He drank a draught, and then entreated for mercy.

"So please your princedom, I have yet far to go, and if I were to swallow your grace's bounty, for which accept my dutiful thanks, I should not be able to stride over the next kennel."

"Art thou in case to bear thyself like a galliard? Now, cut me a caper—ha! one—two—three—admirable!—again—give him the spur—(here a satellite of the Indian gave Oliver a slight touch with his sword)—Nay, that is best of all—he sprang like a cat in a gutter! Tender him the nut once more—nay, no compulsion, he has paid forfeit, and deserves not only free dismissal but reward. Kneel down, kneel, and arise Sir Knight of the Calabash! What is thy name? And one of you lend me a rapier."

"Oliver, may it please your honour—I mean your princi-pality."

"Oliver, man? nay, then thou art one of the Douze peers [1] already, and fate has forestalled our intended promotion. Yet rise up, sweet Sir Oliver Thatchpate, Knight of the honourable order of the Pumpkin—Rise up, in the name of Nonsense, and begone about thine own concerns, and the devil go with thee."

So saying, the prince of the revels bestowed a smart blow with the flat of the weapon across the Bonnet-maker's shoulders, who sprung to his feet with more alacrity of motion than he had hitherto displayed, and, accelerated by the laugh and halloo which arose behind him, arrived at the Smith's house before he stopped, with the same speed with which a hunted fox makes for his den.

It was not till the affrighted Bonnet-maker had struck a blow on the door, that he recollected he ought to have

[1] The *twelve* peers of Charlemagne, immortal in romance.

bethought himself beforehand in what manner he was to present himself before Henry, and obtain his forgiveness for his rash communications to Simon Glover. No one answered to his first knock, and, perhaps, as these reflections arose, in the momentary pause of recollection which circumstances permitted, the perplexed Bonnet-maker might have flinched from his purpose, and made his retreat to his own premises, without venturing upon the interview which he had purposed. But a distant strain of minstrelsy revived his apprehensions of falling once more into the hands of the gay maskers from whom he had escaped, and he renewed his summons on the door of the Smith's dwelling, with a hurried, though faltering hand. He was then appalled by the deep, yet not unmusical voice of Henry Gow, who answered from within,—"Who calls at this hour?—and what is it that you want?"

"It is I—Oliver Proudfute," replied the Bonnet-maker; "I have a merry jest to tell you, gossip Henry."

"Carry thy foolery to some other market. I am in no jesting humour," said Henry. "Go hence—I will see no one to-night."

"But, gossip—good gossip," answered the martialist without, "I am beset with villains, and beg the shelter of your roof!"

"Fool that thou art!" replied Henry; "no dunghill cock, the most recreant that has fought this Fastern's Eve, would ruffle his feathers at such a craven as thou!"

At this moment another strain of minstrelsy, and, as the Bonnet-maker conceived, one which approached much nearer, goaded his apprehensions to the uttermost; and in a voice, the tones of which expressed the undisguised extremity of instant fear, he exclaimed,—

"For the sake of our old gossipred, and for the love of Our blessed Lady, admit me, Henry, if you would not have me found a bloody corpse at thy door, slain by the bloody-minded Douglasses!"

"That would be a shame to me," thought the good-natured Smith; "and sooth to say, his peril may be real. There are roving hawks that will strike at a sparrow as soon as a heron."

With these reflections, half-muttered, half-spoken, Henry undid his well-fastened door, proposing to reconnoitre the reality of the danger before he permitted his unwelcome guest to enter the house. But as he looked abroad to ascertain how matters stood, Oliver bolted in like a scared deer into a thicket, and harboured himself by the Smith's kitchen fire, before Henry could look up and down the lane, and satisfy himself there were no enemies in pursuit of the apprehensive fugitive. He secured his door, therefore, and returned into the kitchen, displeased that he had suffered his gloomy solitude to be intruded upon by sympathizing with apprehensions, which he thought he might have known were so easily excited as those of his timid townsman.

"How now?" he said, coldly enough, when he saw the Bonnet-maker calmly seated by his hearth. "What foolish revel is this, Master Oliver?—I see no one near to harm you."

"Give me a drink, kind gossip," said Oliver; "I am choked with the haste I have made to come hither."

"I have sworn," said Henry, "that this shall be no revel night in this house—I am in my workday clothes, as you see, and keep fast, as I have reason, instead of holiday. You have had wassail enough for the holiday evening, for you speak thick already—If you wish more ale or wine you must go elsewhere."

"I have had over much wassail already," said poor Oliver, "and have been wellnigh drowned in it.—That accursed calabash!—A draught of water, kind gossip—you will not surely let me ask for that in vain? or, if it is your will, a cup of cold small ale."

"Nay, if that be all," said Henry, "it shall not be lacking. But it must have been much which brought thee to the pass of asking for either."

So saying, he filled a quart flagon from a barrel that stood nigh, and presented it to his guest. Oliver eagerly accepted it, raised it to his head with a trembling hand, imbibed the contents with lips which quivered with emotion, and, though the potation was as thin as he had requested, so much was he exhausted with the combined feelings of alarm and of former revelry, that when he placed the flagon on the oak table, he uttered a deep sigh of satisfaction, and remained silent.

"Well, now you have had your draught, gossip," said the Smith, "what is it you want? Where are those that threatened you? I could see no one."

"No—but there were twenty chased me into the wynd," said Oliver. "But when they saw us together, you know they lost the courage that brought all of them upon one of us."

"Nay, do not trifle, friend Oliver," replied his host; "my mood lies not that way."

"I jest not, by St. John of Perth. I have been stayed and foully outraged (gliding his hand sensitively over the place affected) by mad David of Rothsay, roaring Ramorny, and the rest of them. They made me drink a firkin of Malvoisie."

"Thou speakest folly, man—Ramorny is sick nigh to death, as the potter-carrier every where reports; they and he cannot surely rise at midnight to do such frolics."

"I cannot tell," replied Oliver; "but I saw the party by torchlight, and I can make bodily oath to the bonnets I made for them since last Innocent's. They are of a quaint device, and I should know my own stitch."

"Well, thou mayst have had wrong," answered Henry. "If thou art in real danger, I will cause them get a bed for thee here. But you must fill it presently, for I am not in the humour of talking."

"Nay, I would thank thee for my quarters for a night, only my Maudie will be angry—that is, not angry, for that I care not for—but the truth is, she is over anxious on a revel night like this, knowing my humour is like thine, for a word and a blow."

"Why, then, go home," said the Smith, "and show her that her treasure is in safety, Master Oliver—the streets are quiet—and, to speak a blunt word, I would be alone."

"Nay, but I have things to speak with thee about of moment," replied Oliver, who, afraid to stay, seemed yet unwilling to go. "There has been a stir in our city council about the affair of St. Valentine's Even. The Provost told me not four hours since, that the Douglas and he had agreed that the feud should be decided by a yeoman on either part, and that our acquaintance, the Devil's Dick, was to wave his gentry, and take up the cause for Douglas and the nobles, and that you or I should fight for the Fair City. Now, though I am the elder burgess, yet I am willing, for the love and kindness we have always borne to each other, to give thee the precedence, and content myself with the humbler office of stickler."

Henry Smith, though angry, could scarce forbear a smile.

"If it is that which breaks thy quiet, and keeps thee out of thy bed at midnight, I will make the matter easy. Thou shalt not lose the advantage offered thee. I have fought a score of duels—far, far too many. Thou hast, I think, only encountered with thy wooden Soldan—it were unjust—unfair—unkind—in me to abuse thy friendly offer. So go home, good fellow, and let not the fear of losing honour disturb thy slumbers. Rest assured that thou shalt answer the challenge, as good right thou hast, having had injury from this rough-rider."

"Gramercy, and thank thee kindly," said Oliver, much embarrassed by his friend's unexpected deference; "thou art the good friend I have always thought thee. But I have as much friendship for Henry Smith, as he for Oliver Proudfute. I swear by St. John, I will not fight in this quarrel to thy prejudice. So, having said so, I am beyond the reach of temptation, since thou wouldst not have me mansworn, though it were to fight twenty duels."

"Hark thee," said the Smith, "acknowledge thou art afraid, Oliver; tell the honest truth, at once, otherwise I leave thee to make the best of thy quarrel."

"Nay, good gossip," replied the Bonnet-maker, "thou knowest I am never afraid. But, in sooth, this is a desperate ruffian; and as I have a wife—poor Maudie, thou knowest—and a small family, and thou——"

"And I," interrupted Henry, hastily, "have none, and never shall have."

"Why, truly—such being the case—I would rather thou fought'st this combat than I."

"Now, by our holidame, gossip," answered the Smith, "thou art easily gulled! Know, thou silly fellow, that Sir Patrick Charteris, who is ever a merry man, hath but jested with thee. Dost thou think he would venture the honour of the city on thy head? or that I would yield thee the precedence in which such a matter was to be disputed? Lack-a-day, go home, let Maudie tie a warm night-cap on thy head; get thee a warm breakfast, and a cup of distilled waters, and thou wilt be in case to-morrow to fight thy wooden dromond, or Soldan, as thou call'st him, the only thing thou wilt ever lay downright blow upon."

"Ay, say'st thou so, comrade?" answered Oliver, much relieved, yet deeming it necessary to seem in part offended. "I care not for thy dogged humour; it is well for thee thou canst not wake my patience to the point of falling foul. Enough—we are gossips, and this house is thine. Why should the two best blades in Perth clash with each other? What! I know thy rugged humour, and can forgive it.—But is the feud really soldered up?"

"As completely as ever hammer fixed rivet," said the Smith. "The town hath given the Johnston a purse of gold, for not ridding them of a troublesome fellow called Oliver Proudfute, when he had him at his mercy; and this purse of gold buys for the Provost the Sleepless Isle, which the King grants him, for the King pays all in the long run. And thus, Sir Patrick gets the comely Inch, which is opposite to his dwelling, and all honour is saved on both sides, for what is given to the Provost, is given, you understand, to the town. Besides all this, the Douglas hath left Perth to march against the Southron, who, men say, are called into the Marches by the false Earl of March. So the Fair City is quit of him and his cumber."

"But, in St. John's name, how came all that about," said Oliver, "and no one spoken to about it?"

"Why, look thee, friend Oliver, this I take to have been the case. The fellow whom I cropped of a hand, is now said to have been a servant of Sir John Ramorny's, who hath fled to his motherland of Fife, to which Sir John himself is also to be banished, with full consent of every honest man. Now, any thing which brings in Sir John Ramorny, touches a much greater man—I think Simon Glover told as much to Sir Patrick Charteris. If it be as I guess, I have reason to thank Heaven, and all the saints, I stabbed him not upon the ladder when I made him prisoner."

"And I too thank Heaven, and all the saints, most devoutly," said Oliver. "I was behind thee, thou knowest, and——"

"No more of that, if thou be'st wise—There are laws against striking princes," said the Smith; "best not handle the horseshoe till it cools. All is hushed up now."

"If this be so," said Oliver, partly disconcerted, but still more relieved, by the intelligence he received from his better informed friend, "I have reason to complain of Sir Patrick Charteris for jesting with the honour of an honest burgess, being, as he is, Provost of our town."

"Do, Oliver; challenge him to the field, and he will bid his yeomen loose his dogs on thee.—But come, night wears apace, will you be shogging?"

"Nay, I had one word more to say to thee, good gossip. But first, another cup of your cold ale."

"Pest on thee, for a fool! Thou makest me wish thee where cold liquors are a scarce commodity.—There, swill the barrelful an thou wilt."

Oliver took the second flagon, but drank, or rather seemed to drink, very slowly, in order to gain time for considering how he should introduce his second subject of conversation, which seemed rather delicate for the Smith's present state of irritability. At length, nothing better occurred to him than to plunge into the subject at once, with, "I have seen Simon Glover to-day, gossip."

"Well," said the Smith, in a low, deep, and stern tone of voice, "and if thou hast, what is that to me?"

"Nothing—nothing," answered the appalled Bonnet-maker. "Only I thought you might like to know that he questioned me close, if I had seen thee on St. Valentine's day, after the uproar of the Dominicans', and in what company thou wert."

"And I warrant thou told'st him thou met'st me with a glee-woman, in the mirk loaning yonder?"

"Thou know'st, Henry, I have no gift at lying; but I made it all up with him."

"As how, I pray you?" said the Smith.

"Marry, thus—Father Simon, said I, you are an old man, and know not the quality of us, in whose veins youth is like quicksilver. You think now, he cares about this girl, said I, and, perhaps, that he has her somewhere here in Perth in a corner? No such matter; I know, said I, and I will make oath to it, that she left his house early next morning for Dundee. Ha! have I helped thee at need?"

"Truly, I think thou hast, and if any thing could add to my grief and vexation at this moment, it is, that when I am so deep in the mire, an ass like thee should place his clumsy hoof on my head, to sink me entirely. Come, away with thee, and mayst thou have such luck as thy meddling humour deserves, and then, I think, thou wilt be found with a broken neck in the next gutter—Come, get you out, or I will put you to the door with head and shoulders forward."

"Ha, ha!" exclaimed Oliver, laughing with some constraint; "thou art such a groom! But in sadness, gossip Henry, wilt thou not take a turn with me to my own house, in the Meal Venall?"

"Curse thee, no," answered the Smith.

"I will bestow the wine on thee, if thou wilt go," said Oliver.

"I will bestow the cudgel on thee, if thou stay'st," said Henry.

"Nay, then, I will don thy buff-coat and cap of steel, and walk with thy swashing step, and whistling thy pibroch of, 'Broken Bones at Loncarty;' and if they take me for thee, there dare not four of them come near me."

"Take all, or any thing thou wilt, in the fiend's name! only be gone."

"Well, well, Hal, we shall meet when thou art in better humour," said Oliver, who had put on the dress.

"Go—and may I never see thy coxcombly face again!"

Oliver at last relieved his host by swaggering off, imitating, as well as he could, the sturdy step and outward gesture of his redoubted companion, and whistling a pibroch, composed on the rout of the Danes of Loncarty, which he had picked up from its being a favourite of the Smith's, whom he made a point of imitating as far as he could. But as the innocent, though conceited fellow, stepped out from the entrance of the wynd, where it communicated with the High Street, he received a blow from behind, against which his head-piece was no defence, and he fell dead upon the spot; an attempt to mutter the name of Henry, to whom he always looked for protection, quivering upon his dying tongue.

CHAPTER XVII

Nay, I will fit you for a young prince.

FALSTAFF.

WE return to the revellers, who had, half an hour before, witnessed, which such boisterous applause, Oliver's feat of agility, being the last which the poor Bonnet-maker was ever to exhibit, and at the hasty retreat which had followed it, animated by their wild shout. After they had laughed their fill, they passed on their mirthful path, in frolic and jubilee, stopping and frightening some of the people whom they met; but, it must be owned, without doing them any serious injury, either in their persons or feelings. At length, tired with his rambles, their chief gave a signal to his merrymen to close around him.

"We, my brave hearts and wise counsellors, are," he said, "the real King [1] over all in Scotland that is worth command-

[1] The Scottish Statute Book affords abundant evidence of the extravagant and often fatal frolics practised among our ancestors under the

ing. We sway the hours when the wine-cup circulates, and when beauty becomes kind, when Frolic is awake, and Gravity snoring upon his pallet. We leave to our vicegerent, King Robert, the weary task of controlling ambitious nobles, gratifying greedy clergymen, subduing wild Highlanders, and composing deadly feuds. And since our empire is one of joy and pleasure, meet it is that we should meet with all our forces, to the rescue of such as own our sway, when they chance, by evil fortune, to become the prisoners of care and hypochondriac malady. I speak in relation chiefly to Sir John, whom the vulgar call Ramorny. We have not seen him since the onslaught of Curfew Street, and though we know he was some deal hurt in that matter, we cannot see why he should not do homage in leal and duteous sort.— Here, you, our Calabash King-at-arms, did you legally summon Sir John to his part of this evening's revels?"

"I did, my lord."

"And did you acquaint him that we have for this night suspended his sentence of banishment, that since higher powers have settled that part, we might at least take a mirthful leave of an old friend?"

"I so delivered it, my lord," answered the mimic herald.

"And sent he not a word in writing, he that piques himself upon being so great a clerk?"

"He was in bed, my lord, and I might not see him. So far as I hear, he hath lived very retired, harmed with some bodily bruises, malecontent with your Highness's displeasure, and doubting insult in the streets, he having had a narrow escape from the burgesses, when the churls pursued him and his two servants into the Dominican Convent. The servants, too, have been removed to Fife, lest they should tell tales."

"Why, it was wisely done," said the Prince,—who, we need not inform the intelligent reader, had a better title to be so called, than arose from the humours of the evening,—"it was prudently done to keep light-tongued companions out of the way. But Sir John's absenting himself from our solemn revels, so long before decreed, is flat mutiny, and disclamation of allegiance. Or, if the knight be really the prisoner of

personages elected to fill the high offices of *Quene of May*, Prince of Yule (Christmas), Abbot of Unreason, &c. &c., corresponding to the Boy Bishop of England and the French *Abbé de Liesse*, or *Abbas Letitiæ*. Shrovetide was not less distinguished by such mumming dignitaries.

illness and melancholy, we must ourself grace him with a visit, seeing there can be no better cure for those maladies than our own presence, and a gentle kiss of the calabash.—Forward, ushers, minstrels, guard, and attendants! Bear on high the great emblem of our dignity—Up with calabash, I say! and let the merry-men who carry these firkins, which are to supply the wine-cup with their life-blood, be chosen with regard to their state of steadiness. Their burden is weighty and precious, and if the fault is not in our eyes, they seem to us to reel and stagger more than were desirable. Now, move on, sirs, and let our minstrels blow their blithest and boldest."

On they went with tipsy mirth and jollity, the numerous torches flashing their red light against the small windows of the narrow streets, from whence nightcapped householders, and sometimes their wives to boot, peeped out by stealth to see what wild wassail disturbed the peaceful streets at that unwonted hour. At length the jolly train halted before the door of Sir John Ramorny's house, which a small court divided from the street.

Here they knocked, thundered, and hollowed, with many denunciations of vengeance against the recusants, who refused to open the gates. The least punishment threatened was imprisonment in an empty hogshead, within the Massamore [1] of the Prince of Pastimes' feudal palace, videlicet, the ale-cellar. But Eviot, Ramorny's page, heard and knew well the character of the intruders who knocked so boldly, and thought it better, considering his master's condition, to make no answer at all, in hopes that the revel would pass on, than to attempt to deprecate their proceedings, which he knew would be to no purpose. His master's bedroom looking into a little garden, his page hoped he might not be disturbed by the noise; and he was confident in the strength of the outward gate, upon which he resolved they should beat till they tired themselves, or till the tone of their drunken humour should change. The revellers accordingly seemed likely to exhaust themselves in the noise they made by shouting and beating the door, when their mock Prince (alas! too really such)

---

[1] The *Massamore*, or *Massy More*, the principal dungeon of the feudal castle, is supposed to have derived its name from our intercourse with the Eastern nations at the time of the Crusades. Dr. Jamieson quotes an old Latin Itinerary: "Proximus est carcer subterraneus, sive, ut *Mauri* appellant, *Mazmorra*."

upbraided them as lazy and dull followers of the god of wine and of mirth.

"Bring forward," he said, "our key—yonder it lies, and apply it to this rebellious gate."

The key he pointed at was a large beam of wood, left on one side of the street, with the usual neglect of order characteristic of a Scottish borough of the period.

The shouting men of Ind instantly raised it in their arms, and, supporting it by their united strength, ran against the door with such force, that hasp, hinge, and staple jingled, and gave fair promise of yielding. Eviot did not choose to wait the extremity of this battery; he came forth into the court, and after some momentary questions for form's sake, caused the porter to undo the gate, as if he had for the first time recognized the midnight visitors.

"False slave of an unfaithful master," said the Prince, "where is our disloyal subject, Sir John Ramorny, who has proved recreant to our summons?"

"My lord," said Eviot, bowing at once to the real and to the assumed dignity of the leader; "my master is just now very much indisposed—he has taken an opiate—and—your Highness must excuse me if I do my duty to him in saying, he cannot be spoken with without danger of his life."

"Tush! tell me not of danger, Master Teviot—Cheviot—Eviot—what is it they call thee?—But show me thy master's chamber, or rather undo me the door of his lodging, and I will make a good guess at it myself.—Bear high the calabash, my brave followers, and see that you spill not a drop of the liquor, which Dan Bacchus has sent for the cure of all diseases of the body, and cares of the mind. Advance it, I say, and let us see the holy rind which encloses such precious liquor."

The Prince made his way into the house accordingly, and, acquainted with its interior, ran up stairs, followed by Eviot, in vain imploring silence, and, with the rest of the rabble rout, burst into the room of the wounded master of the lodging.

He who has experienced the sensation of being compelled to sleep in spite of racking bodily pains, by the administration of a strong opiate, and of having been again startled by noise and violence, out of the unnatural state of insensibility in which he had been plunged by the potency of the medicine, may be able to imagine the confused and alarmed state of Sir John Ramorny's mind, and the agony of his body, which acted and re-acted upon each other. If we add to these feelings the consciousness of a criminal command, sent forth and in the act of being executed, it may give us some idea of an awakening, to which, in the mind of the party, eternal sleep would be a far preferable doom. The groan which he uttered as the first symptom of returning sensation, had something in it so terrific, that even the revellers were awed into momentary silence; and as, from the half-recumbent posture in which he had gone to sleep, he looked around the room, filled with fantastic shapes, rendered still more so by his disturbed intellects, he muttered to himself,—

"It is thus then, after all, and the legend is true! These are fiends, and I am condemned for ever! The fire is not external, but I feel it—I feel it at my heart—burning as if the seven times heated furnace were doing its work within!"

While he cast ghastly looks around him, and struggled to recover some share of recollection, Eviot approached the Prince, and falling on his knees, implored him to allow the apartment to be cleared.

"It may," he said, "cost my master his life."

"Never fear, Cheviot," replied the Duke of Rothsay; "were he at the gates of death, here is what should make the fiends relinquish their prey.—Advance the calabash, my masters."

"It is death for him to taste it in his present state," said Eviot; "if he drinks wine he dies."

"Some one must drink it for him, he shall be cured vicariously—and may our great Dan Bacchus deign to Sir John Ramorny the comfort, the elevation of heart, the lubrication of lungs, and lightness of fancy, which are his choicest gifts, while the faithful follower, who quaffs in his stead, shall have the qualms, the sickness, the racking of the nerves, the dimness of the eyes, and the throbbing of the brain, with which our great master qualifies gifts which would else make us too like the gods.—What say you, Eviot? will you be the faithful follower that will quaff in your lord's behalf, and as his representative? Do this, and we will hold ourselves contented to depart, for, methinks, our subject doth look something ghastly."

"I would do any thing in my slight power," said Eviot, "to save my master from a draught which may be his death, and your Grace from the sense that you had occasioned it. But here is one who will perform the feat of good-will, and thank your Highness to boot."

" Whom have we here ? " said the Prince, "a butcher—and
I think fresh from his office. Do butchers ply their craft
on Fastern's Eve? Foh, how he smells of blood ! "

This was spoken of Bonthron, who, partly surprised at the
tumult in the house, where he had expected to find all dark
and silent, and partly stupid through the wine, which the
wretch had drunk in great quantities, stood in the threshold
of the door, staring at the scene before him, with his buff-coat
splashed with blood, and a bloody axe in his hand, exhibiting
a ghastly and disgusting spectacle to the revellers, who felt,
though they could not tell why, fear as well as dislike at his
presence.

As they approached the calabash to this ungainly and
truculent-looking savage, and as he extended a hand soiled,
as it seemed, with blood, to grasp it, the Prince called out,—

" Down stairs with him ! let not the wretch drink in our
presence ; find him some other vessel than our holy calabash,
the emblem of our revels—a swine's trough were best, if it
could be come by. Away with him ! let him be drenched
to purpose, in atonement for his master's sobriety.—Leave
me alone with Sir John Ramorny and his page ; by my honour,
I like not yon ruffian's looks."

The attendants of the Prince left the apartment, and Eviot
alone remained.

" I fear," said the Prince, approaching the bed in different
form from that which he had hitherto used—" I fear, my dear
Sir John, that this visit has been unwelcome ; but it is your
own fault. Although you know our old wont, and were
yourself participant of our schemes for the evening, you have
not come near us since St. Valentine's—it is now Fastern's
Even, and the desertion is flat disobedience and treason to
our kingdom of mirth, and the statutes of the calabash."

Ramorny raised his head, and fixed a wavering eye upon
the Prince ; then signed to Eviot to give him something to
drink. A large cup of ptisan was presented by the page,
which the sick man swallowed with eager and trembling haste.
He then repeatedly used the stimulating essence left for the
purpose by the leech, and seemed to collect his scattered
senses.

" Let me feel your pulse, dear Ramorny," said the Prince ;
" I know something of that craft.—How ? Do you offer me
the left hand, Sir John ?—that is neither according to the rules
of medicine nor of courtesy."

" The right has already done its last act in your Highness's service," muttered the patient, in a low and broken tone.

" How mean you by that ? " said the Prince, " I am aware thy follower, Black Quentin, lost a hand ; but he can steal with the other as much as will bring him to the gallows, so his fate cannot be much altered."

" It is not that fellow who has had the loss in your Grace's service—it is I—John of Ramorny."

" You ! " said the Prince ; " you jest with me, or the opiate still masters your reason."

" If the juice of all the poppies in Egypt were blended in one draught," said Ramorny, " it would lose influence over me, when I look upon this." He drew his right arm from beneath the cover of the bed-clothes, and extending it towards the Prince, wrapped as it was in dressings, " Were these un done and removed," he said, " your Highness would see that a bloody stump is all that remains of a hand ever ready to un- sheath the sword at your Grace's slightest bidding."

Rothsay started back in horror. " This," he said, " must be avenged ! "

" It is avenged in small part," said Ramorny ; " that is, I thought I saw Bonthron but now—or was it that the dream of hell that first arose in my mind when I awakened, summoned up an image so congenial ? Eviot, call the miscreant,—that is, if he is fit to appear."

Eviot retired, and presently returned with Bonthron, whom he had rescued from the penance, to him no unpleasing in- fliction, of a second calabash of wine, the brute having gorged the first without much apparent alteration in his demeanour.

" Eviot," said the Prince, " let not that beast come nigh me. My soul recoils from him in fear and disgust ; there is something in his looks alien from my nature, and which I shudder at as at a loathsome snake, from which my instinct revolts."

" First hear him speak, my lord," answered Ramorny , " unless a wine-skin were to talk, nothing could use fewer words.—Hast thou dealt with him, Bonthron ? "

The savage raised the axe which he still held in his hand, and brought it down again edgeways.

" Good. How knew you your man ?—the night, I am told, is dark."

" By sight and sound, garb, gait, and whistle."

" Enough, vanish !—and, Eviot, let him have gold and wine

to his brutish contentment.—Vanish!—and go thou with him."

"And whose death is achieved?" said the Prince, released from the feelings of disgust and horror under which he suffered while the assassin was in presence. "I trust this is but a jest? Else must I call it a rash and savage deed. Who hast had the hard lot to be butchered by that bloody and brutal slave?"

"One little better than himself," said the patient; "a wretched artisan, to whom, however, fate gave the power of reducing Ramorny to a mutilated cripple—a curse go with his base spirit!—his miserable life is but to my revenge what a drop of water would be to a furnace. I must speak briefly, for my ideas again wander; it is only the necessity of the moment which keeps them together, as a thong combines a handful of arrows. You are in danger, my lord— I speak it with certainty—you have braved Douglas, and offended your uncle—displeased your father—though that were a trifle, were it not for the rest."

"I am sorry I have displeased my father," said the Prince, (entirely diverted from so insignificant a thing as the slaughter of an artisan, by the more important subject touched upon,) "if indeed it be so. But if I live, the strength of the Douglas shall be broken, and the craft of Albany shall little avail him!"

"Ay—if—if. My lord," said Ramorny, "with such opposites as you have, you must not rest upon if or but—you must resolve at once to slay or be slain."

"How mean you, Ramorny? your fever makes you rave," answered the Duke of Rothsay.

"No, my lord," said Ramorny, "were my frenzy at the highest, the thoughts that pass through my mind at this moment would qualify it. It may be that regret for my own loss has made me desperate; that anxious thoughts for your Highness's safety have made me nourish bold designs; but I have all the judgment with which Heaven has gifted me, when I tell you, that if ever you would brook the Scottish crown, nay, more, is ever you would see another Saint Valentine's Day, you must——"

"What is it that I must do, Ramorny?"—said the Prince, with an air of dignity; "nothing unworthy of myself, I hope?"

"Nothing, certainly, unworthy or misbecoming a Prince of

Scotland, if the blood-stained annals of our country tell the tale truly; but that which may well shock the nerves of a prince of mimes and merry-makers."

"Thou art severe, Sir John Ramorny," said the Duke of Rothsay, with an air of displeasure; "but thou hast dearly bought a right to censure us by what thou hast lost in our cause."

"My Lord of Rothsay," said the knight, "the chirurgeon who dressed this mutilated stump, told me that the more I felt the pain his knife and brand inflicted, the better was my chance of recovery. I shall not, therefore, hesitate to hurt your feelings, while by doing so I may be able to bring you to a sense of what is necessary for your safety. Your Grace has been the pupil of mirthful folly too long; you must now assume manly policy, or be crushed like a butterfly, on the bosom of the flower you are sporting on."

"I think I know your cast of morals, Sir John; you are weary of merry folly,—the churchmen call it vice,—and long for a little serious crime. A murder, now, or a massacre, would enhance the flavour of debauch, as the taste of the olive gives zest to wine. But my worst acts are but merry malice; I have no relish for the bloody trade, and abhor to see or hear of its being acted even on the meanest caitiff. Should I ever fill the throne, I suppose, like my father before me, I must drop my own name, and be dubbed Robert, in honour of the Bruce—well, an if it be so—every Scots lad shall have his flagon in one hand, and the other around his lass's neck, and manhood shall be tried by kisses and bumpers, not by dirks and dourlachs; and they shall write on my grave, 'Here lies Robert, fourth of his name. He won not battles like Robert the First. He rose not from a count to a king like Robert the Second. He founded not churches like Robert the Third, but was contented to live and die King of good fellows!' Of all my two centuries of ancestors, I would only emulate the fame of

'Old King Coul,
Who had a brown bowl.'"

"My gracious lord," said Ramorny, "let me remind you, that your joyous revels involve serious evils. If I had lost this hand in fighting to attain for your Grace some important advantage over your too powerful enemies, the loss would never have grieved me. But to be reduced from helmet and steel-coat, to biggen and gown, in a night-brawl——"

"Why, there again now, Sir John "—interrupted the reckless Prince—" How canst thou be so unworthy as to be for ever flinging thy bloody hand in my face, as the ghost of Gaskhall threw his head at Sir William Wallace ? [1] Bethink thee, thou art more unreasonable than Fawdyon himself; for wight Wallace had swept his head off in somewhat a hasty humour, whereas I would gladly stick thy hand on again, were that possible. And, hark thee, since that cannot be, I will get thee such a substitute as the steel hand of the old Knight of Carselogie, with which he greeted his friends, caressed his wife, braved his antagonists, and did all that might be done by a hand of flesh and blood, in offence or defence. Depend on it, John Ramorny, we have much that is superfluous about us. Man can see with one eye, hear with one ear, touch with one hand, smell with one nostril; and why we should have two of each, (unless to supply an accidental loss or injury,) I for one am at a loss to conceive."

Sir John Ramorny turned from the Prince with a low groan.

"Nay, Sir John," said the Duke, "I am quite serious. You know the truth touching the legend of Steelhand of Carselogie better than I, since he was your own neighbour. In his time, that curious engine could only be made in Rome; but I will wager an hundred merks with you, that, let the Perth armourer have the use of it for a pattern, Henry of the Wynd will execute as complete an imitation as all the smiths in Rome could accomplish, with all the cardinals to bid a blessing on the work."

"I could venture to accept your wager, my lord," answered Ramorny, bitterly, "but there is no time for foolery.—You have dismissed me from your service, at command of your uncle ? "

"At command of my father," answered the Prince.

"Upon whom your uncle's commands are imperative," replied Ramorny. "I am a disgraced man, thrown aside, as I may now fling away my right hand glove, as a thing useless. Yet my head might help you, though my hand be gone. Is your Grace disposed to listen to me for one word of serious import ?—for I am much exhausted, and feel my force sinking under me."

[1] The passage referred to is perhaps the most poetical one in Blind Harry's Wallace. Book v., v. 180—220.

"Speak your pleasure," said the Prince; "thy loss binds me to hear thee; thy bloody stump is a sceptre to control me. Speak, then, but be merciful in thy strength of privilege."

"I will be brief, for mine own sake as well as thine; indeed I have but little to say. Douglas places himself immediately at the head of his vassals. He will assemble, in the name of King Robert, thirty thousand Borderers, whom he will shortly after lead into the interior, to demand that the Duke of Rothsay receive, or rather restore, his daughter to the rank and privileges of his Duchess. King Robert will yield to any conditions which may secure peace—What will the Duke do?"

"The Duke of Rothsay loves peace," said the Prince, haughtily; "but he never feared war. Ere he takes back yonder proud peat to his table and his bed, at the command of her father, Douglas must be King of Scotland."

"Be it so—but even this is the less pressing peril, especially as it threatens open violence, for the Douglas works not in secret."

"What is there which presses, and keeps us awake at this late hour? I am a weary man, thou a wounded one, and the very tapers are blinking, as if tired of our conference."

"Tell me, then, who is it that rules this kingdom of Scotland?" said Ramorny.

"Robert, third of the name," said the Prince, raising his bonnet as he spoke; "and long may he sway the sceptre!"

"True, and amen," answered Ramorny; "but who sways King Robert, and dictates almost every measure which the good King pursues?"

"My Lord of Albany, you would say," replied the Prince. "Yes, it is true my father is guided almost entirely by the counsels of his brother; nor can we blame him in our consciences, Sir John Ramorny, for little help hath he had from his son."

"Let us help him now, my lord," said Ramorny. "I am possessor of a dreadful secret—Albany hath been trafficking with me, to join him in taking your Grace's life! He offers full pardon for the past—high favour for the future."

"How, man—my life? I trust, though, thou dost only mean my kingdom? It were impious!—he is my father's brother —they sat on the knees of the same father—lay in the bosom of the same mother—Out on thee, man! what follies they make thy sick-bed believe!"

"Believe, indeed!" said Ramorny. "It is new to me to be termed credulous. But the man through whom Albany communicated his temptations, is one whom all will believe, so soon as he hints at mischief—even the medicaments which are prepared by his hands have a relish of poison."

"Tush! such a slave would slander a saint," replied the Prince. "Thou art duped for once, Ramorny, shrewd as thou art. My uncle of Albany is ambitious, and would secure for himself and for his house, a larger portion of power and wealth than he ought in reason to desire. But to suppose he would dethrone or slay his brother's son—Fie, Ramorny! put me not to quote the old saw, that evil doers are evil dreaders—It is your suspicion, not your knowledge, which speaks."

"Your Grace is fatally deluded—I will put it to an issue. The Duke of Albany is generally hated for his greed and covetousness—Your Highness is, it may be, more beloved than——"

Ramorny stopped, the Prince calmly filled up the blank—"More beloved than I am honoured? It is so I would have it, Ramorny."

"At least," said Ramorny, "you are more beloved than you are feared, and that is no safe condition for a prince. But give me your honour and knightly word that you will not resent what good service I shall do in your behalf, and lend me your signet to engage friends in your name, and the Duke of Albany shall not assume authority in this court, till the wasted hand which once terminated this stump shall be again united to the body, and acting in obedience to the dictates of my mind."

"You would not venture to dip your hands in royal blood?" said the Prince, sternly.

"Fie, my lord—at no rate—blood need not be shed; life may, nay, will, be extinguished of itself. For want of trimming it with fresh oil, or screening it from a breath of wind, the quivering light will die in the socket. To suffer a man to die is not to kill him."

"True—I had forgot that policy. Well, then, suppose my uncle Albany does not continue to live—I think that must be the phrase—Who then rules the court of Scotland?"

"Robert the Third, with consent, advice, and authority of the most mighty David, Duke of Rothsay, Lieutenant of the kingdom, and ALTER EGO; in whose favour, indeed, the good

King, wearied with the fatigues and troubles of sovereignty, will, I guess, be well disposed to abdicate. So long live our brave young monarch, King David the Third!

> ' *Ille, manu fortis,*
> *Anglis ludebit in hortis.*' "

"And our father and predecessor," said Rothsay, "will he continue to live to pray for us, as our beadsman, by whose favour he holds the privilege of laying his grey hairs in the grave as soon and no earlier, than the course of nature permits? —or must he also encounter some of those negligences, in consequence of which men cease to continue to live, and exchange the limits of a prison, or of a convent resembling one, for the dark and tranquil cell, where the priests say that the wicked cease from troubling, and the weary are at rest?"

"You speak in jest, my lord," replied Ramorny; "to harm the good old King were equally unnatural and impolitic."

"Why shrink from that, man, when thy whole scheme," answered the Prince, in stern displeasure, "is one lesson of unnatural guilt, mixed with short-sighted ambition?—If the King of Scotland can scarcely make head against his nobles, even now when he can hold up before them an unsullied and honourable banner, who would follow a prince that is blackened with the death of an uncle, and the imprisonment of a father? Why, man, thy policy were enough to revolt a heathen divine, to say nought of the council of a Christian nation.—Thou wert my tutor, Ramorny, and perhaps I might justly upbraid thy lessons and example, for some of the follies which men chide in me. Perhaps, if it had not been for thee, I had not been standing at midnight in this fool's guise, (looking at his dress,) to hear an ambitious profligate propose to me the murder of an uncle, the dethroning of the best of fathers. Since it is my fault, as well as thine, that has sunk me so deep in the gulf of infamy, it were unjust that thou alone shouldst die for it. But dare not to renew this theme to me, on peril of thy life! I will proclaim thee to my father—to Albany—to Scotland— throughout its length and breadth! As many market crosses as are in the land, shall have morsels of the traitor's carcass, who dare counsel such horrors to the Heir of Scotland!—Well hope I, indeed, that the fever of thy wound, and the intoxicating influence of the cordials which act on thy infirm brain, have this night operated on thee, rather that any fixed purpose."

"In sooth, my lord," said Ramorny, "if I have said any thing which could so greatly exasperate your Highness, it must have been by excess of zeal, mingled with imbecility of understanding. Surely I, of all men, am least likely to propose ambitious projects with a prospect of advantage to myself! Alas! my only future views must be to exchange lance and saddle for the breviary and the confessional. The convent of Lindores must receive the maimed and impoverished Knight of Ramorny, who will there have ample leisure to meditate upon the text, 'Put not thy faith in princes.'"

"It is a goodly purpose," said the Prince, "and we will not be lacking to promote it. Our separation, I thought, would have been but for a time—It must now be perpetual. Certainly, after such talk as we have held, it were meet that we should live asunder. But the convent of Lindores, or whatever other house receives thee, shall be richly endowed and highly favoured by us.—And now, Sir John of Ramorny, sleep—sleep—and forget this evil-omened conversation, in which the fever of disease and of wine has rather, I trust, held colloquy, than your own proper thoughts.—Light to the door, Eviot."

A call from Eviot summoned the attendants of the Prince, who had been sleeping on the staircase and hall, exhausted by the revels of the evening.

"Is there none amongst you sober?" said the Duke of Rothsay, disgusted by the appearance of his attendants.

"Not a man—not a man," answered the followers, with a drunken shout; "we are none of us traitors to the Emperor of Merry-makers!"

"And are all of you turned into brutes, then?" said the Prince.

"In obedience and imitation of your Grace," answered one fellow; "or, if we are a little behind your Highness, one pull at the pitcher will——"

"Peace, beast!" said the Duke of Rothsay; "are there none of you sober, I say?"

"Yes, my noble liege," was the answer; "here is one false brother, Watkins the Englishman."

"Come hither then, Watkins, and aid me with a torch—give me a cloak, too, and another bonnet, and take away this trumpery," throwing down his coronet of feathers; "I would I could throw off all my follies as easily.—English Wat, attend me alone, and the rest of you end your revelry, and doff your mumming habits. The holytide is expended, and the Fast has begun."

"Our monarch has abdicated sooner than usual this night," said one of the revel rout; but as the Prince gave no encouragement, such as happened for the time to want the virtue of sobriety, endeavoured to assume it as well as they could, and the whole of the late rioters began to adopt the appearance of a set of decent persons, who, having been surprised into intoxication, endeavour to disguise their condition by assuming a double portion of formality of behaviour. In the interim, the Prince, having made a hasty reform in his dress, was lighted to the door by the only sober man of the company, but, in his progress thither, had well-nigh stumbled over the sleeping bulk of the brute Bonthron.

"How now—is that vile beast in our way once more?" he said, in anger and disgust. "Here, some of you, toss this caitiff into the horse-trough, that for once in his life he may be washed clean."

While the train executed his commands, availing themselves of a fountain which was in the outer court, and while Bonthron underwent a discipline which he was incapable of resisting, otherwise than by some inarticulate groans and snorts, like those of a dying boar, the Prince proceeded on his way to his apartments, in a mansion called the Constable's lodgings, from the house being the property of the Earls of Errol. On the way, to divert his thoughts from the more unpleasing matters, the Prince asked his companion how he came to be sober, when the rest of the party had been so much overcome with liquor.

"So please your honour's Grace," replied English Wat, "I confess it was very familiar in me to be sober when it was your Grace's pleasure that your train should be mad drunk; but in respect they were all Scottishmen but myself, I thought it argued no policy in getting drunken in their company; seeing that they only endure me even when we are all sober, and if the wine were uppermost, I might tell them a piece of my mind, and be paid with as many stabs as there are skenes in the good company."

"So it is your purpose never to join any of the revels of our household?"

"Under favour, yes; unless it be your Grace's pleasure that the residue of your train should remain one day sober, to admit Wil Watkins to get drunk without terror of his life."

"Such occasion may arrive.—Where dost thou serve, Watkins?"

"In the stable, so please you."

"Let our chamberlain bring thee into the household, as a yeoman of the night-watch. I like thy favour, and it is something to have one sober fellow in the house, although he is only such through the fear of death. Attend, therefore, near our person, and thou shalt find sobriety a thriving virtue."

Meantime a load of care and fear added to the distress of Sir John Ramorny's sick chamber. His reflections, disordered as they were by the opiate, fell into great confusion when the Prince, in whose presence he had suppressed its effect by strong resistance, had left the apartment. His consciousness, which he had possessed perfectly during the interview, began to be very much disturbed. He felt a general sense that he had incurred a great danger; that he had rendered the Prince his enemy, and that he had betrayed to him a secret which might affect his own life. In this state of mind and body, it was not strange that he should either dream, or else that his diseased organs should become subject to that species of phantasmagoria which is excited by the use of opium. He thought that the shade of Queen Annabella stood by his bedside, and demanded the youth whom she had placed under his charge, simple, virtuous, gay, and innocent.

"Thou hast rendered him reckless, dissolute, and vicious," said the shade of pallid Majesty. "Yet I thank thee, John of Ramorny, ungrateful to me, false to thy word, and treacherous to my hopes. Thy hate shall counteract the evil which thy friendship has done to him. And well do I hope, that, now thou art no longer his counsellor, a bitter penance on earth may purchase my ill-fated child pardon and acceptance in a better world."

Ramorny stretched out his arms after his benefactress, and endeavoured to express contrition and excuse; but the countenance of the apparition became darker and sterner, till it was no longer that of the late Queen, but presented the gloomy and haughty aspect of the Black Douglas—then the timid and sorrowful face of King Robert, who seemed to

mourn over the approaching dissolution of his royal house—
and then a group of fantastic features, partly hideous, partly
ludicrous, which moped, and chattered, and twisted themselves
into unnatural and extravagant forms, as if ridiculing his
endeavour to obtain an exact idea of their lineaments.

CHAPTER XVIII

A purple land, where law secures not life.

BYRON.

THE morning of Ash Wednesday arose pale and bleak, as
usual at this season in Scotland, where the worst and most in-
clement weather often occurs in the early spring months. It
was a severe day of frost, and the citizens had to sleep away the
consequences of the preceding holiday's debauchery. The
sun had therefore risen for an hour above the horizon, before
there was any general appearance of life among the inhabitants
of Perth, so that it was some time after daybreak, when a
citizen, going early to mass, saw the body of the luckless
Oliver Proudfute lying on its face, across the kennel, in the
manner in which he had fallen, under the blow, as our readers
will easily imagine, of Anthony Bonthron, the " boy of the
belt," that is, the executioner of the pleasure, of John of
Ramorny.

This early citizen was Allan Griffin, so termed because he
was master of the Griffin inn ; and the alarm which he raised
soon brought together, first straggling neighbours, and by and
by a concourse of citizens. At first, from the circumstance of
the well-known buff-coat, and the crimson feather in the head-
piece, the noise arose that it was the stout Smith that lay there
slain. This false rumour continued for some time ; for the
host of the Griffin, who himself had been a magistrate, would
not permit the body to be touched or stirred till Bailie
Craigdallie arrived, so that the face was not seen.

" This concerns the Fair City, my friends," he said ; " and
if it is the stout Smith of the Wynd who lies here, the man
lives not in Perth, who will not risk land and life to avenge
him. Look you, the villains have struck him down behind
his back, for there is not a man within ten Scotch miles of
Perth, gentle or semple, Highland or Lowland, that would
have met him face to face with such evil purpose. Oh, brave

men of Perth! the flower of your manhood has been cut down, and that by a base and treacherous hand!"

A wild cry of fury arose from the people, who were fast assembling.

"We will take him on our shoulders," said a strong butcher; "we will carry him to the King's presence at the Dominican Convent."

"Ay, ay," answered a blacksmith, "neither bolt nor bar shall keep us from the King; neither monk nor mass shall break our purpose. A better armourer never laid hammer on anvil!"

"To the Dominicans! to the Dominicans!" shouted the assembled people.

"Bethink you, burghers," said another citizen, "our King is a good King, and loves us like his children. It is the Douglas and the Duke of Albany that will not let good King Robert hear the distresses of his people."

"Are we to be slain in our own streets for the King's softness of heart?" said the butcher. "The Bruce did otherwise. If the King will not keep us, we will keep ourselves. Ring the bells backward, every bell of them that is made of metal. Cry, and spare not, St. Johnston's hunt is up!"[1]

"Ay," cried another citizen, "and let us to the holds of Albany and the Douglas, and burn them to the ground. Let the fires tell far and near, that Perth knew how to avenge her stout Henry Gow! He has fought a score of times for the Fair City's right—let us show we can fight once to avenge his wrong. Hallo! ho! brave citizens, St. Johnston's hunt is up!"

This cry, the well-known rallying word amongst the inhabitants of Perth, and seldom heard but on occasions of general uproar, was echoed from voice to voice; and one or two neighbouring steeples, of which the enraged citizens possessed themselves, either by consent of the priests, or in spite of their opposition, began to ring out the ominous alarm notes, in which, as the ordinary succession of the chimes were reversed, the bells were said to be rung backward.

Still, as the crowd thickened, and the roar waxed more universal and louder, Allan Griffin, a burly man, with a deep voice, and well respected among high and low, kept his station as he bestrode the corpse, and called loudly to the multitude to keep back, and wait the arrival of the magistrates.

[1] Note IX.—St. Johnston's Hunt is up.

"We must proceed by order in this matter, my masters; we must have our magistrates at our head. They are duly chosen and elected in our town-hall, good men and true every one; we will not be called rioters, or idle perturbators of the king's peace. Stand you still, and make room, for yonder comes Bailie Craigdallie, ay, and honest Simon Glover, to whom the Fair City is so much bounden. Alas, alas, my kind townsmen! his beautiful daughter was a bride yesternight—this morning the Fair Maid of Perth is a widow before she has been a wife!"

This new theme of sympathy increased the rage and sorrow of the crowd the more, as many women now mingled with them, who echoed back the alarm cry to the men.

"Ay, ay, St. Johnston's hunt is up! For the Fair Maid of Perth and the brave Henry Gow! Up, up, every one of you, spare not for your skin-cutting! To the stables!—to the stables!—when the horse is gone the man-at-arms is useless—cut off the grooms and yeomen; lame, maim, and stab the horses; kill the base squires and pages. Let these proud knights meet us on their feet if they dare!"

"They dare not, they dare not," answered the men; "their strength is in their horses and armour; and yet the haughty and ungrateful villains have slain a man whose skill as an armourer was never matched in Milan or Venice. To arms! to arms, brave burghers! St. Johnston's hunt is up!"

Amid this clamour, the magistrates and superior class of inhabitants with difficulty obtained room to examine the body, having with them the town-clerk to take an official protocol, or, as it is still called, a precognition, of the condition in which it was found. To these delays the multitude submitted, with a patience and order which strongly marked the national character of a people, whose resentment has always been the more deeply dangerous, that they will, without relaxing their determination of vengeance, submit with patience to all delays which are necessary to ensure its attainment. The multitude, therefore, received their magistrates with a loud cry, in which the thirst of revenge was announced, together with the deferential welcome to the patrons by whose direction they expected to obtain it in right and legal fashion.

While these accents of welcome still rung above the crowd, who now filled the whole adjacent streets, receiving and circulating a thousand varying reports, the fathers of the city caused the body to be raised and more closely examined; when it was instantly perceived, and the truth publicly announced, that not the armourer of the Wynd, so highly, and according to the esteemed qualities of the time, so justly popular among his fellow-citizens; but a man of far less general estimation, though not without his own value in society, lay murdered before them—the brisk Bonnet-maker, Oliver Proudfute. The resentment of the people had so much turned upon the general opinion, that their frank and brave champion, Henry Gow, was the slaughtered person, that the contradiction of the report served to cool the general fury, although, if poor Oliver had been recognized at first, there is little doubt that the cry of vengeance would have been as unanimous, though not probably so furious, as in the case of Henry Wynd.[1] The first circulation of the unexpected intelligence even excited a smile among the crowd, so near are the confines of the ludicrous to those of the terrible.

"The murderers have without doubt taken him for Henry Smith," said Griffin, "which must have been a great comfort to him in the circumstances."

But the arrival of other persons on the scene soon restored its deeply tragic character.

CHAPTER XIX

Who's that that rings the bell?—Diablos, ho?
The town will rise.——
OTHELLO, *Act* 2. *Scene* 3.

THE wild rumours which flew through the town, speedily followed by the tolling of the alarm bells, spread general consternation. The nobles and knights, with their followers, gathered in different places of rendezvous, where a defence could best be maintained; and the alarm reached the royal residence, where the young Prince was one of the first to appear to assist, if necessary, in the defence of the old King. The scene of the preceding night ran in his recollection; and, remembering the blood-stained figure of Bonthron, he conceived, though indistinctly, that the ruffian's action had been connected with this uproar. The subsequent and more interesting discourse with Sir John Ramorny had, however,

[1] Note X.—Henry Smith or Wynd.

been of such an impressive nature, as to obliterate all traces of what he had vaguely heard of the bloody act of the assassin, excepting a confused recollection that some one or other had been slain. It was chiefly on his father's account that he had assumed arms with his household train, who, clad in bright armour, and bearing lances in their hands, made now a figure very different from that of the preceding night, when they appeared as intoxicated Bacchanalians. The kind old monarch received this mark of filial attachment with tears of gratitude, and proudly presented his son to his brother Albany, who entered shortly afterwards. He took them each by the hand.

"Now are we three Stewarts," he said, "as inseparable as the holy Trefoil; and, as they say the wearer of that sacred herb mocks at magical delusion, so we, while we are true to each other, may set malice and enmity at defiance."

The brother and son kissed the kind hand which pressed theirs, while Robert III. expressed his confidence in their affection. The kiss of the youth was, for the time, sincere; that of the brother was the salute of the apostate Judas.

In the meantime the bell of Saint John's church alarmed, amongst others, the inhabitants of Curfew Street. In the house of Simon Glover, old Dorothy Glover, as she was called, (for she also took name from the trade she practised, under her master's auspices,) was the first to catch the sound. Though somewhat deaf upon ordinary occasions, her ear for bad news was as sharp as a kite's scent for carrion; for Dorothy, otherwise an industrious, faithful, and even affectionate creature, had that strong appetite for collecting and retailing sinister intelligence, which is often to be marked in the lower classes. Little accustomed to be listened to, they love the attention which a tragic tale ensures to the bearer, and enjoy, perhaps, the temporary equality to which misfortune reduces those who are ordinarily accounted their superiors. Dorothy had no sooner possessed herself of a slight packet of the rumours which were flying abroad, than she bounced into her master's bedroom, who had taken the privilege of age and the holytide to sleep longer than usual.

"There he lies, honest man!" said Dorothy, half in a screeching, and half in a wailing tone of sympathy,—"There he lies; his best friend slain, and he knowing as little about it as the babe new born that kens not life from death."

"How now!" said the Glover, starting up out of his

bed,—" What is the matter, old woman? is my daughter well?"

" Old woman!" said Dorothy, who, having her fish hooked, chose to let him play a little. " I am not so old," said she, flouncing out of the room, " as to bide in the place till a man rises from his naked bed——"

And presently she was heard at a distance in the parlour beneath, melodiously singing to the scrubbing of her own broom.

" Dorothy—screechowl—devil,—say but my daughter is well!"

" I *am* well, my father." answered the Fair Maid of Perth, speaking from her bedroom, " perfectly well; but what, for Our Lady's sake, is the matter? The bells ring backward, and there is shrieking and crying in the streets."

" I will presently know the cause.—Here, Conachar, come speedily and tie my points.—I forgot—the Highland loon is far beyond Fortingall.—Patience, daughter, I will presently bring you news."

" Ye need not hurry yourself for that, Simon Glover," quoth the obdurate old woman ; " the best and the worst of it may be tauld before you could hobble over your door-stane. I ken the haill story abroad ; for, thought I, our goodman is so wilful, that he'll be for banging out to the tuilzie, be the cause what it like ; and sae I maun e'en stir my shanks, and learn the cause of all this, or he will hae his auld nose in the midst of it, and maybe get it nipt off before he knows what for."

" And what *is* the news, then, old woman?" said the impatient Glover, still busying himself with the hundred points or latchets which were the means of attaching the doublet to the hose.

Dorothy suffered him to proceed in his task, till she conjectured it must be nearly accomplished ; and foresaw that, if she told not the secret herself, her master would be abroad to seek in person for the cause of the disturbance. She, therefore, hollowed out—" Aweel, aweel, ye canna say it is my fault, if you hear ill news before you have been at the morning mass. I would have kept it from ye till ye had heard the priest's word ; but since you must hear it, you have e'en lost the truest friend that ever gave hand to another, and Perth maun mourn for the bravest burgher that ever took a blade in hand!"

"Harry Smith! Harry Smith!" exclaimed the father and the daughter at once.

"Oh, ay, there ye hae it at last," said Dorothy; "and whase fault was it but your ain?—ye made such a piece of work about his companying with a glee-woman, as if he had companied with a Jewess!"

Dorothy would have gone on long enough, but her master exclaimed to his daughter, who was still in her own apartment, "It is nonsense, Catharine—all the dotage of an old fool. No such thing has happened. I will bring you the true tidings in a moment;" and snatching up his staff, the old man hurried out past Dorothy, and into the street, where the throng of people were rushing towards the High Street. Dorothy, in the meantime, kept muttering to herself, "Thy father is a wise man, take his ain word for it. He will come next by some scathe in the hobbleshow, and then it will be, Dorothy, get the lint, and, Dorothy, spread the plaster; but now it is nothing but nonsense, and a lie, and impossibility, that can come out of Dorothy's mouth—Impossible! Does auld Simon think that Harry Smith's head was as hard as his smithy, and a haill clan of Highlandmen dinging at him?"

Here he was interrupted by a figure like an angel, who came wandering by her with wild eye, cheek deadly pale, hair dishevelled, and an apparent want of consciousness, which terrified the old woman out of her discontented humour.

"Our Lady bless my bairn!" said she. "What look you sae wild for?"

"Did you not say some one was dead?" said Catharine, with a frightful uncertainty of utterance, as if her organs of speech and hearing served her but imperfectly.

"Dead, hinny! Ay, ay, dead eneugh; ye'll no hae him to gloom at ony mair."

"Dead!" repeated Catharine, still with the same uncertainty of voice and manner. "Dead—slain, and by Highlanders?"

"I'se warrant by Highlanders,—the lawless loons. Wha is it else that kills maist of the folks about, unless now and then when the burghers take a tirrivie, and kill ane another, or whiles that the knights and nobles shed blood? But I'se uphauld it's been the Highlandmen this bout. The man was no in Perth laird or loon, durst have faced Henry Smith man to man. There's been sair odds against him; ye'll see that when it's looked into."

"Highlanders!" repeated Catharine, as if haunted by some

idea which troubled her senses. "Highlanders!—Oh, Cona-char! Conachar!"

"Indeed, and I daresay you have lighted on the very man, Catharine. They quarrelled, as you saw, on the St. Valentine's Even, and had a warstle. A Highlandman has a long memory for the like of that. Gie him a cuff at Martinmas, and his cheek will be tingling at Whitsunday. But what could have brought down the lang-legged loons to do their bloody wark within burgh?"

"Woe's me, it was I," said Catharine; "it was I brought the Highlanders down—I that sent for Conachar—ay, they have lain in wait—but it was I that brought them within reach of their prey. But I will see with my own eyes—and then—something we will do. Say to my father I will be back anon."

"Are ye distraught, lassie?" shouted Dorothy, as Catharine made past her towards the street door. "You would not gang into the street with the hair hanging down your haffets in that guise, and you kenn'd for the Fair Maid of Perth?—Mass, but she's out in the street, come o't what like, and the auld Glover will be as mad as if I could withhold her, will she nill she, flyte she fling she.—This is a brave morning for an Ash-Wednesday! —What's to be done? If I were to seek my master among the multitude, I were like to be crushed beneath their feet, and little moan made for the old woman—And am I to run after Catharine, who ere this is out of sight, and far lighter of foot than I am?—so I will just down the gate to Nicol Barber's, and tell him a' about it."

While the trusty Dorothy was putting her prudent resolve into execution, Catharine ran through the streets of Perth in a manner, which at another moment would have brought on her the attention of every one, who saw her hurrying on with a reckless impetuosity, wildly and widely different from the ordinary decency and composure of her step and manner, and without the plaid, scarf, or mantle, which "women of good," of fair character and decent rank, universally carried around them, when they went abroad. But distracted as the people were, every one enquiring or telling the cause of the tumult, and most recounting it different ways, the negligence of her dress, and discomposure of her manner, made no impression on any one; and she was suffered to press forward on the path she had chosen, without attracting more notice than the other females, who, stirred by anxious curiosity or fear, had come out to enquire the cause of an alarm so general—it might be to seek for friends, for whose safety they were interested.

As Catharine passed along, she felt all the wild influence of the agitating scene, and it was with difficulty she forbore from repeating the cries of lamentation and alarm, which were echoed around her. In the meantime, she rushed rapidly on, embarrassed like one in a dream, with a strange sense of dreadful calamity, the precise nature of which she was unable to define, but which implied the terrible consciousness that the man who loved her so fondly, whose good qualities she so highly esteemed, and whom she now felt to be dearer than perhaps she would before have acknowledged to her own bosom, was murdered, and most probably by her means. The connexion betwixt Henry's supposed death, and the descent of Conachar and his followers, though adopted by her in a moment of extreme and engrossing emotion, was sufficiently probable to have been received for truth, even if her understanding had been at leisure to examine its credibility. Without knowing what she sought, except the general desire to know the worst of the dreadful report, she hurried forward to the very spot, which of all others her feelings of the preceding day would have induced her to avoid.

Who would, upon the evening of Shrove-tide, have persuaded the proud, the timid, the shy, the rigidly decorous Catharine Glover, that before mass on Ash-Wednesday, she should rush through the streets of Perth, making her way amidst tumult and confusion, with her hair unbound, and her dress disarranged, to seek the house of that same lover, who, she had reason to believe, had so grossly and indelicately neglected and affronted her, as to pursue a low and licentious amour! Yet so it was; and her eagerness taking, as if by instinct, the road which was most free, she avoided the High Street, where the pressure was greatest, and reached the wynd by the narrow lanes on the northern skirt of the town, through which Henry Smith had formerly escorted Louise. But even these comparatively lonely passages were now astir with passengers, so general was the alarm. Catharine Glover made her way through them, however, while such as observed her looked on each other, and shook their heads in sympathy with her distress. At length, without any distinct idea of her own purpose, she stood before her lover's door, and knocked for admittance.

The silence which succeeded the echoing of her hasty summons increased the alarm, which had induced her to take this desperate measure.

"Open,—open, Henry!" she cried. "Open, if you yet live!—Open, if you would not find Catharine Glover dead upon your threshold!"

As she cried thus franticly, to ears which she was taught to believe were stopped by death, the lover she invoked opened the door in person, just in time to prevent her sinking on the ground. The extremity of his ecstatic joy upon an occasion so unexpected, was qualified only by the wonder which forbade him to believe it real, and by his alarm at the closed eyes, half-opened and blanched lips, total absence of complexion, and apparently total cessation of breathing.

Henry had remained at home, in spite of the general alarm, which had reached his ears for a considerable time, fully determined to put himself in the way of no brawls that he could avoid; and it was only in compliance with a summons from the Magistrates, which, as a burgher, he was bound to obey, that, taking his sword and a spare buckler from the wall, he was about to go forth, for the first time unwillingly, to pay his service, as his tenure bound him.

"It is hard," he said, "to be put forward in all the town feuds, when the fighting work is so detestable to Catharine. I am sure there are enough of wenches in Perth, that say to their gallants, 'Go out—do your devoir bravely, and win your lady's grace;' and yet they send not for their lovers, but for me, who cannot do the duties of a man to protect a minstrel woman, or of a burgess who fights for the honour of his town, but this peevish Catharine uses me as if I were a brawler and bordeller!"

Such were the thoughts which occupied his mind, when, as he opened his door to issue forth, the person dearest to his thoughts, but whom he certainly least expected to see was present to his eyes, and dropped into his arms.

His mixture of surprise, joy, and anxiety, did not deprive him of the presence of mind which the occasion demanded. To place Catharine Glover in safety, and recall her to herself, was to be thought of before rendering obedience to the summons of the Magistrates, however pressingly that had been delivered. He carried his lovely burden, as light as a feather, yet more precious than the same quantity of purest gold, into a small bedchamber which had been his mother's. It was the most fit for an invalid, as it looked into the garden, and was separated from the noise of the tumult.

"Here, Nurse—Nurse Shoolbred—come quick—come for death and life—here is one wants thy help!"

Up trotted the old dame. "If it should but prove any one that will keep thee out of the scuffle"—for she also had been aroused by the noise,—but what was her astonishment, when, placed in love and reverence on the bed of her late mistress, and supported by the athletic arms of her foster son, she saw the apparently lifeless form of the Fair Maid of Perth. "Catharine Glover!" she said; "and, Holy Mother—a dying woman, as it would seem!"

"Not so, old woman," said her foster son; "the dear heart throbs—the sweet breath comes and returns! Come thou, that may aid her more meetly than I—bring water—essences—whatever thy old skill can devise. Heaven did not place her in my arms to die, but to live for herself and me!"

With an activity which her age little promised, Nurse Shoolbred collected the means of restoring animation; for, like many women of the period, she understood what was to be done in such cases, nay, possessed a knowledge of treating wounds of an ordinary description, which the war-like propensities of her foster son kept in pretty constant exercise.

"Come now," she said, "son Henry, unfold your arms from about my patient—though she is worth the pressing—and set thy hands at freedom to help me with what I want.— Nay, I will not insist on your quitting her hand, if you will beat the palm gently, as the fingers unclose their clenched grasp."

"*I* beat her slight beautiful hand!" said Henry; "you were as well bid me beat a glass cup with a fore-hammer, as tap her fair palm with my horn-hard fingers.—But the fingers do unfold, and we will find a better way than beating;" and he applied his lips to the pretty hand whose motion indicated returning sensation. One or two deep sighs succeeded, and the Fair Maid of Perth opened her eyes, fixed them on her lover, as he kneeled by the bedside, and again sunk back on the pillow. As she withdrew not her hand from her lover's hold or from his grasp, we must in charity believe that the return to consciousness was not so complete as to make her aware that he abused the advantage, by pressing it alternately to his lips and his bosom. At the same time we are compelled to own, that the blood was colouring in her cheek, and that her breathing was deep and regular, for a minute or two during this relapse.

The noise at the door began now to grow much louder, and Henry was called for by all his various names, of Smith, Gow, and Hal of the Wynd, as heathens used to summon their deities by different epithets. At last, like Portuguese Catholics when exhausted with entreating their saints, the crowd without had recourse to vituperative exclamations.

" Out upon you, Henry ! You are a disgraced man, man-sworn to your burgher-oath, and a traitor to the Fair City, unless you come instantly forth ! "

It would seem that Nurse Shoolbred's applications were now so far successful, that Catharine's senses were in some measure restored ; for turning her face more towards that of her lover, than her former posture permitted, she let her right hand fall on his shoulder, leaving her left still in his possession, and seeming slightly to detain him, while she whispered, " Do not go, Henry—stay with me—they will kill thee, these men of blood."

It would seem that this gentle invocation, the result of finding the lover alive whom she expected to have only recognized as a corpse, though it was spoken so low as scarcely to be intelligible, had more effect to keep Henry Wynd in his present posture, than the repeated summons of many voices from without had to bring him down stairs.

" Mass, townsmen," cried one hardy citizen to his com-panions, " the saucy Smith but jests with us ! Let us into the house, and bring him out by the lug and the horn."

" Take care what you are doing," said a more cautious assailant. " The man that presses on Henry Gow's retirement may go into his house with sound bones, but will return with ready-made work for the surgeon.—But here comes one has good right to do our errand to him, and make the recreant hear reason on both sides of his head."

The person of whom this was spoken was no other than Simon Glover himself. He had arrived at the fatal spot where the unlucky Bonnet-maker's body was lying, just in time to discover, to his great relief, that when it was turned with the face upwards by Bailie Craigdallie's orders, the features of the poor braggart Proudfute were recognized, when the crowd expected to behold those of their favourite champion Henry Smith. A laugh, or something approaching to one, went among those who remembered how hard Oliver had struggled to obtain the character of a fighting man, however foreign to his nature and disposition, and remarked now, that he had met with a mode of death much better suited to his pretensions than to his temper. But this tendency to ill-timed mirth, which savoured of the rudeness of the times, was at once hushed by the voice, and cries, and exclamations of a woman, who struggled through the crowd, screaming at the same time, —" Oh, my husband !—my husband ! "

Room was made for the sorrower, who was followed by two or three female friends. Maudie Proudfute had been hitherto only noticed as a good-looking, black-haired woman, believed to be *dink* and disdainful to those whom she thought meaner or poorer than herself, and lady and empress over her late husband, whom she quickly caused to lower his crest when she chanced to hear him crowing out of season But now, under the influence of powerful passion, she assumed a far more imposing character.

" Do you laugh," she said, " you unworthy burghers of Perth, because one of your own citizens has poured his blood into the kennel ?—or do you laugh because the deadly lot has lighted on my husband ? How has he deserved this ?—Did he not maintain an honest house by his own industry, and keep a creditable board, where the sick had welcome, and the poor had relief ? Did he not lend to those who wanted,— stand by his neighbours as a friend, keep counsel and do justice like a magistrate ? "

" It is true, it is true," answered the assembly ; " his blood is our blood, as much as if it were Henry Gow's."

" You speak truth, neighbours," said Bailie Craigdallie ; " and this feud cannot be patched up as the former was— citizen's blood must not flow unavenged down our kennels, as if it were ditchwater, or we shall soon see the broad Tay crimsoned with it. But this blow was never meant for the poor man on whom it has unhappily fallen. Every one knew what Oliver Proudfute was, how wide he would speak, and how little he would do. He has Henry Smith's buff-coat, target, and head-piece. All the town know them as well as I do ; there is no doubt on't. He had the trick, as you know, of trying to imitate the Smith in most things. Some one, blind with rage, or perhaps through liquor, has stricken the innocent Bonnet-maker, whom no man either hated or feared, or indeed cared either much or little about, instead of the stout Smith, who has twenty feuds upon his hands."

"What then is to be done, Bailie?" cried the multitude.

"That, my friends, your magistrates will determine for you, as we shall instantly meet together when Sir Patrick Charteris cometh here, which must be anon. Meanwhile, let the chirurgeon Dwining examine that poor piece of clay, that he may tell us how he came by his fatal death; and then let the corpse be decently swathed in a clean shroud, as becomes an honest citizen, and placed before the high altar in the church of St. John, the patron of the Fair City. Cease all clamour and noise, and every defensible man of you, as you would wish well to the Fair Town, keep his weapons in readiness, and be prepared to assemble on the High Street, at the tolling of the common bell from the Town-House, and we will either revenge the death of our fellow-citizen, or else we shall take such fortune as Heaven will send us. Meanwhile avoid all quarrelling with the knights and their followers, till we know the innocent from the guilty—But wherefore tarries this knave Smith? He is ready enough in tumults when his presence is not wanted, and lags he now when his presence may serve the Fair City?—What ails him, doth any one know? Hath he been upon the frolic last Fastern's Even?"

"Rather he is sick or sullen, Master Bailie," said one of the city's mairs, or sergeants; "for though he is within door, as his knaves report, yet he will neither answer to us nor admit us."

"So please your worship, Master Bailie," said Simon Glover, "I will go myself to fetch Henry Smith. I have some little difference to make up with him. And blessed be Our Lady, who hath so ordered it, that I find him alive, as a quarter of an hour since I could never have expected!"

"Bring the stout Smith to the Council-house," said the Bailie, as a mounted yeoman pressed through the crowd, and whispered in his ear,—"Here is a good fellow, who says the knight of Kinfauns is entering the port."

Such was the occasion of Simon Glover presenting himself at the house of Henry Gow at the period already noticed.

Unrestrained by the considerations of doubt and hesitation which influenced others, he repaired to the parlour; and having overheard the bustling of Dame Shoolbred, he took the privilege of intimacy to ascend to the bedroom, and, with the slight apology of—"I crave your pardon, good neighbour," he opened the door, and entered the apartment, where a singular and unexpected sight awaited him. At the sound of his voice, May Catharine experienced a revival much speedier than Dame Shoolbred's restoratives had been able to produce; and the paleness of her complexion changed into a deep glow of the most lovely red. She pushed her lover from her with both her hands, which, until this minute, her want of consciousness, or her affliction, awakened by the events of the morning, had wellnigh abandoned to his caresses. Henry Smith, bashful as we know him, stumbled as he rose up; and none of the party were without a share of confusion, excepting Dame Shoolbred, who was glad to make some pretext to turn her back to the others, in order that she might enjoy a laugh at their expense, which she felt herself utterly unable to restrain, and in which the Glover, whose surprise, though great, was of short duration, and of a joyful character, sincerely joined.

"Now, by good St. John," he said, "I thought I had seen a sight this morning that would cure me of laughter, at least till Lent was over; but this would make me curl my cheek, if I were dying. Why, here stands honest Henry Smith, who was lamented as dead, and toll'd out for from every steeple in town, alive, merry, and, as it seems from his ruddy complexion, as like to live as any man in Perth. And here is my precious daughter, that yesterday would speak of nothing but the wickedness of the wights that haunt profane sports, and protect glee-maidens—Ay, she who set St. Valentine and St. Cupid both in defiance,—here she is, turned a glee-maiden herself, for what I can see! Truly, I am glad to see that you, my good Dame Shoolbred, who give way to no disorder, have been of this loving party."

"You do me wrong, my dearest father," said Catharine, as if about to weep. "I came here with far different expectations than you suppose. I only came because—because——"

"Because you expected to find a dead lover," said her father, "and you have found a living one, who can receive the tokens of your regard, and return them. Now, were it not a sin, I could find in my heart to thank Heaven, that thou hast been surprised at last into owning thyself a woman—Simon Glover is not worthy to have an absolute saint for his daughter. —Nay, look not so piteously, nor expect condolence from me! Only I will try not to look merry, if you will be pleased to stop your tears, or confess them to be tears of joy."

"If I were to die for such a confession," said poor Catharine, "I could not tell what to call them. Only believe, dear father, and let Henry believe, that I would never have come hither, unless—unless——"

"Unless you had thought that Henry could not come to you," said her father. "And now, shake hands in peace and concord, and agree as Valentines should. Yesterday was Shrovetide, Henry—We will hold that thou hast confessed thy follies, hast obtained absolution, and art relieved of all the guilt thou stoodest charged with."

"Nay, touching that, father Simon," said the Smith, "now that you are cool enough to hear me, I can swear on the Gospels, and I can call my nurse, Dame Shoolbred, to witness——"

"Nay, nay," said the Glover, "but wherefore rake up differences, which should all be forgotten?"

"Hark ye, Simon!—Simon Glover!" This was now echoed from beneath.

"True, son Smith," said the Glover, seriously, "we have other work in hand. You and I must to the council instantly. Catharine shall remain here with Dame Shoolbred, who will take charge of her till we return; and then, as the town is in misrule, we two, Harry, will carry her home, and they will be bold men that cross us."

"Nay, my dear father," said Catharine, with a smile, "now you are taking Oliver Proudfute's office. That doughty burgher is Henry's brother-at-arms."

Her father's countenance grew dark.

"You have spoke a stinging word, daughter; but you know not what has happened. Kiss him, Catharine, in token of forgiveness."

"Not so," said Catharine; "I have done him too much grace already. When he has seen the errant damsel safe home, it will be time enough to claim his reward."

"Meantime," said Henry, "I will claim, as your host, what you will not allow me on other terms."

He folded the fair maiden in his arms, and was permitted to take the salute which she had refused to bestow.

As they descended the stair together, the old man laid his hand on the Smith's shoulder, and said, "Henry, my dearest wishes are fulfilled; but it is the pleasure of the saints that it should be in an hour of difficulty and terror."

"True," said the Smith; "but thou knowest, father, if our riots be frequent at Perth, at least they seldom last long."

Then, opening a door which led from the house into the smithy, "Here, comrades," he cried, "Anton, Cuthbert, Dingwell, and Ringan! Let none of you stir from the place till I return. Be as true as the weapons I have taught you to forge; a French crown and a Scotch merry-making for you, if you obey my command. I leave a mighty treasure in your charge. Watch the doors well—let little Jannekin scout up and down the wynd, and have your arms ready if any one approaches the house. Open the doors to no man, till Father Glover or I return; it concerns my life and happiness."

The strong swarthy giants to whom he spoke, answered, "Death to him who attempts it!"

"My Catharine is now as safe," said he to her father, "as if twenty men garrisoned a royal castle in her cause. We shall pass most quietly to the Council-house by walking through the garden."

He led the way through a little orchard accordingly, where the birds, which had been sheltered and fed during the winter by the good-natured artisan, early in the season as it was, were saluting the precarious smiles of a February sun, with a few faint and interrupted attempts at melody

"Hear these mistrels, father," said the Smith; "I laughed at them this morning in the bitterness of my heart, because the little wretches sung, with so much of winter before them. But now, methinks, I could bear a blithe chorus, for I have my Valentine as they have theirs; and whatever ill may lie before me for to-morrow, I am to-day the happiest man in Perth, city or county, burgh or landward."

"Yet I must allay your joy," said the old Glover, "though, Heaven knows, I share it.—Poor Oliver Proudfute, the inoffensive fool that you and I knew so well, has been found this morning dead in the streets."

"Only dead drunk, I trust?" said the Smith; "nay, a caudle and a dose of matrimonial advice will bring him to life again."

"No, Henry, no. He is slain—slain with a battle-axe, or some such weapon."

"Impossible!" replied the Smith; "he was light-footed enough, and would not for all Perth have trusted to his hands, when he could extricate himself by his heels."

"No choice was allowed him. The blow was dealt in the very back of his head; he who struck must have been a shorter man than himself, and used a horseman's battle-axe, or some such weapon, for a Lochaber-axe must have struck the upper part of his head—But there he lies dead, brained, I may say, by a most frightful wound."

"This is inconceivable," said Henry Wynd. "He was in my house at midnight, in a morricer's habit; seemed to have been drinking, though not to excess. He told me a tale of having been beset by revellers, and being in danger; but, alas! you know the man; I deemed it was a swaggering fit, as he sometimes took when he was in liquor; and, may the Merciful Virgin forgive me! I let him go without company, in which I did him inhuman wrong. Holy St. John be my witness! I would have gone with any helpless creature; and far more with him, with whom I have so often sat at the same board, and drunken of the same cup. Who, of the race of man, could have thought of harming a creature so simple, and so unoffending, excepting by his idle vaunts!"

"Henry, he wore thy head-piece, thy buff-coat, thy target—How came he by these?"

"Why, he demanded the use of them for the night, and I was ill at ease, and well pleased to be rid of his company; having kept no holiday, and being determined to keep none, in respect of our misunderstanding."

"It is the opinion of Bailie Craigdallie, and all our sagest counsellors, that the blow was intended for yourself, and that it becomes you to prosecute the due vengeance of our fellow-citizen, who received the death which was meant for you."

The Smith was for some time silent. They had now left the garden, and were walking in a lonely lane, by which they meant to approach the Council-house of the burgh, without being exposed to observation of idle enquiry.

"You are silent, my son, yet we two have much to speak of," said Simon Glover. "Bethink thee that this widowed woman Maudlin, if she should see cause to bring a charge against any one for the wrong done to her and her orphan children, must support it by a champion, according to law and custom; for be the murderer who he may, we know enough of these followers of the nobles to be assured, that the party suspected will appeal to the combat, in derision, perhaps, of those whom they will call the cowardly burghers. While we are men with blood in our veins, this must not be, Henry Wynd."

"I see where you would draw me, father," answered Henry,

dejectedly; "and St. John knows I have heard a summons to battle as willingly as war-horse ever heard the trumpet. But bethink you, father, how I have lost Catharine's favour repeatedly, and have been driven wellnigh to despair of ever regaining it, for being, if I may say so, even too ready a man of my hands. And here are all our quarrels made up, and the hopes, that seemed this morning removed beyond earthly prospect, have become nearer and brighter than ever; and must I, with the dear one's kiss of forgiveness on my lips, engage in a new scene of violence, which you are well aware will give her the deepest offence?"

"It is hard for me to advise you, Henry," said Simon; "but this I must ask you—Have you, or have you not, reason to think, that this poor unfortunate Oliver has been mistaken for you?"

"I fear it too much," said Henry. "He was thought something like me, and the poor fool had studied to ape my gestures and manner of walking, nay, the very airs which I have the trick of whistling, that he might increase a resemblance which has cost him dear. I have ill-willers enough, both in burgh and landward, to owe me a shrewd turn; and he, I think, could have none such."

"Well, Henry, I cannot say but my daughter will be offended. She has been much with Father Clement, and has received notions about peace and forgiveness, which methinks suit ill with a country where the laws cannot protect us, unless we have spirit to protect ourselves. If you determine for the combat, I will do my best to persuade her to look on the matter as the other good womanhood in the burgh will do; and if you resolve to let the matter rest— the man who has lost his life for yours remaining unavenged— the widow and the orphans without any reparation for the loss of a husband and father—I will then do you the justice to remember, that I, at least, ought not to think the worse of you for your patience, since it was adopted for love of my child. But, Henry, we must in that case remove our- selves from bonny St. Johnston, for here we will be but a disgraced family."

Henry groaned deeply, and was silent for an instant, then replied, "I would rather be dead than dishonoured, though I should never see her again! Had it been yester evening, I would have met the best blade among these men-at-arms as blithely as ever I danced at a May-pole. But to-day, when she had first as good as said, 'Henry Smith, I love thee!'—Father Glover, it is very hard. Yet it is all my own fault! This poor unhappy Oliver! I ought to have allowed him the shelter of my roof, when he prayed me in his agony of fear; or, had I gone with him, I should then have prevented or shared his fate. But I taunted him, ridiculed him, loaded him with maledictions, though the saints know they were uttered in idle peevishness of impatience. I drove him out from my doors, whom I knew so helpless, to take the fate which was perhaps intended for me. I must avenge him, or be dishonoured for ever. See, father—I have been called a man hard as the steel I work in—Does burnished steel ever drop tears like these? —Shame on me that I should shed them!"

"It is no shame, my dearest son," said Simon; "thou art as kind as brave, and I have always known it. There is yet a chance for us. No one may be discovered to whom suspicion attaches, and where none such is found, the combat cannot take place. It is a hard thing to wish that the innocent blood may not be avenged. But if the perpetrator of this foul murder be hidden for the present, thou wilt be saved from the task of seeking that vengeance which Heaven, doubtless, will take at its own proper time."

As they spoke thus, they arrived at the point of the High Street where the Council-House was situated. As they reached the door, and made their way through the multitude who thronged the street, they found the avenues guarded by a select party of armed burghers, and about fifty spears belonging to the Knight of Kinfauns, who, with his allies the Grays, Blairs, Moncrieffs, and others, had brought to Perth a considerable body of horse, of which these were a part. So soon as the Glover and Smith presented themselves, they were admitted to the chamber in which the magistrates were assembled.

CHAPTER XX

A woman wails for justice at the gate,
A widow'd woman, wan and desolate.

BERTHA.

THE Council-room of Perth [1] presented a singular spectacle. In a gloomy apartment, ill and inconveniently lighted by two

[1] See Note XI.—The Council-room.

windows of different form and of unequal size, were assembled, around a large oaken table, a group of men, of whom those who occupied the higher seats were merchants, that is, guild brethren, or shopkeepers, arrayed in decent dresses becoming their station, but most of them bearing, like the Regent York, "signs of war around their aged necks;" gorgets, namely, and baldricks, which sustained their weapons. The lower places around the table were occupied by mechanics and artisans, the presidents, or deacons, as they were termed, of the working classes, in their ordinary clothes, somewhat better arranged than usual. These too wore pieces of armour of various descriptions. Some had the black jack, or doublet, covered with small plates of iron of a lozenge shape, which, secured through the upper angle, hung in rows above each, and which, swaying with the motion of the wearer's person, formed a secure defence to the body. Others had buff-coats, which, as already mentioned, could resist the blow of a sword, and even a lance's point, unless propelled with great force. At the bottom of the table, surrounded as it was with this varied assembly, sat Sir Louis Lundin; no military man, but a priest and a parson of St. John's, arrayed in his canonical dress, and having his pen and ink before him. He was town-clerk of the burgh, and, like all the priests of the period, (who were called from that circumstance the Pope's knights,) received the honourable title of *Dominus*, contracted into Dom, or Dan, or translated into Sir, the title of reverence due to the secular chivalry.

On an elevated seat, at the head of the council board, was placed Sir Patrick Charteris, in complete armour, brightly burnished; a singular contrast to the motley mixture of warlike and peaceful attire exhibited by the burghers, who were only called to arms occasionally. The bearing of the Provost, while it completely admitted the intimate connexion which mutual interests had created betwixt himself, the burgh, and the magistracy, was at the same time calculated to assert the superiority, which, in virtue of gentle blood and chivalrous rank, the opinions of the age assigned to him over the members of the assembly in which he presided. Two squires stood behind him, one of them holding the knight's pennon, and another his shield, bearing his armorial distinctions, being a hand holding a dagger, or short sword, with the proud motto, *This is my charter*. A handsome page displayed the long sword of his master, and another bore his lance; all which chivalrous emblems and appurtenances were the more scrupulously exhibited, that the dignitary to whom they belonged was engaged in discharging the office of a burgh magistrate. In his own person the Knight of Kinfauns appeared to affect something of state and stiffness, which did not naturally pertain to his frank and jovial character.

"So, you are come at length, Henry Smith and Simon Glover," said the Provost. "Know that you have kept us waiting for your attendance. Should it so chance again while we occupy this place, we will lay such a fine on you as you will have small pleasure in paying. Enough—make no excuses. They are not asked now, and another time they will not be admitted. Know, sirs, that our reverend clerk hath taken down in writing, and at full length, what I will tell you in brief, that you may see what is to be required of you, Henry Smith, in particular. Our late fellow-citizen, Oliver Proudfute, hath been found dead in the High Street, close by the entrance into the Wynd. It seemeth he was slain by a heavy blow with a short axe, dealt from behind and at unawares; and the act by which he fell can only be termed a deed of foul and forethought murder. So much for the crime. The criminal can only be indicated by circumstances. It is recorded in the protocol of the Reverend Sir Louis Lundin, that divers well-reputed witnesses saw our deceased citizen, Oliver Proudfute, till a late period, accompanying the Entry of the morrice-dancers,[1] of whom he was one, as far as the house of Simon Glover, in Curfew Street, where they again played their pageant. It is also manifested, that at this place he separated from the rest of the band, after some discourse with Simon Glover, and made an appointment to meet with the others of his company at the sign of the Griffin, there to conclude the holiday.—Now, Simon, I demand of you whether this be truly stated, so far as you know? and further, what was the purport of the defunct Oliver Proudfute's discourse with you?"

"My Lord Provost and very worshipful Sir Patrick," answered Simon Glover, "you and this honourable council shall know, that, touching certain reports which had been made of the conduct of Henry Smith, some quarrel had arisen between myself and another of my family, and the said Smith here present. Now, this our poor fellow-citizen, Oliver Proudfute, having been active in spreading these reports, as indeed his element lay in such gossipred, some words passed

[1] See Note XII.—Morrice-Dancers.

betwixt him and me on the subject; and, as I think, he left me with the purpose of visiting Henry Smith, for he broke off from the morrice-dancers, promising, as it seems, to meet them, as your honour has said, at the sign of the Griffin, in order to conclude the evening. But what he actually did, I know not, as I never again saw him in life."

"It is enough," said Sir Patrick, "and agrees with all that we have heard.—Now, worthy sirs, we next find our poor fellow-citizen environed by a set of revellers and maskers, who had assembled in the High Street, by whom he was shamefully ill-treated, being compelled to kneel down in the street, and there to quaff huge quantities of liquor against his inclination, until at length he escaped from them by flight. This violence was accomplished with drawn swords, loud shouts and imprecations, so as to attract the attention of several persons, who, alarmed by the tumult, looked out from their windows, as well as of one or two passengers, who, keeping aloof from the light of the torches, lest they also had been maltreated, beheld the usage which our fellow-citizen received in the High Street of the burgh. And although these revellers were disguised, and used vizards, yet their disguises were well known, being a set of quaint masking habits, prepared some weeks ago by command of Sir John Ramorny, Master of the Horse to his Royal Highness the Duke of Rothsay, Prince Royal of Scotland."

A low groan went through the assembly.

"Yes; so it is, brave burghers," continued Sir Patrick; "our enquiries have led us into conclusions both melancholy and terrible. But as no one can regret the point at which they seem likely to arrive more than I do, so no man living can dread its consequences less. It is even so—various artisans employed upon the articles, have described the dresses prepared for Sir John Ramorny's mask as being exactly similar to those of the men by whom Oliver Proudfute was observed to be maltreated. And one mechanic, being Wingfield the feather-dresser, who saw the revellers when they had our fellow-citizen within their hands, remarked that they wore the cinctures and coronals of painted feathers, which he himself had made by the order of the Prince's Master of the Horse.

"After the moment of his escape from these revellers, we lose all trace of Oliver; but we can prove that the maskers went to Sir John Ramorny's, where they were admitted, after some show of delay. It is rumoured, that thou, Henry

Smith, sawest our unhappy fellow-citizen after he had been in the hands of these revellers—What is the truth of that matter?"

"He came to my house in the Wynd," said Henry, "about half an hour before midnight; and I admitted him, something unwillingly, as he had been keeping carnival while I remained at home; and there is ill talk, says the proverb, betwixt a full man and a fasting."

"And in which plight seemed he when thou didst admit him?" said the Provost.

"He seemed," answered the Smith, "out of breath, and talked repeatedly of having been endangered by revellers. I paid but small regard, for he was ever a timorous chicken-spirited, though well-meaning man, and I held that he was speaking more from fancy than reality. But I shall always account it for foul offence in myself, that I did not give him my company, which he requested; and if I live, I will found masses for his soul, in expiation of my guilt."

"Did he describe those from whom he received the injury?" said the Provost.

"Revellers in masking habits," replied Henry.

"And did he intimate his fear of having to do with them on his return?" again demanded Sir Patrick.

"He alluded particularly to his being waylaid, which I treated as visionary, having been able to see no one in the lane."

"Had he then no help from thee of any kind whatsoever?" said the Provost.

"Yes, worshipful," replied the Smith; "he exchanged his morrice dress for my head-piece, buff-coat, and target, which I hear were found upon his body; and I have at home his morrice-cap and bells, with the jerkin and other things pertaining. He was to return my garb of fence, and get back his own masking suit this day, had the saints so permitted."

"You saw him not then afterwards?"

"Never, my lord."

"One word more," said the Provost. "Have you any reason to think that the blow which slew Oliver Proudfute was meant for another man?"

"I have," answered the Smith; "but it is doubtful, and may be dangerous to add such a conjecture, which is besides only a supposition."

"Speak it out, on your burgher faith and oath—For whom, think you, was the blow meant?"

"If I must speak," replied Henry, "I believe Oliver Proudfute received the fate which was designed for myself; the rather that, in his folly, Oliver spoke of trying to assume my manner of walking, as well as my dress."

"Have you feud with any one, that you form such an idea?" said Sir Patrick Charteris.

"To my shame and sin be it spoken, I have feud with Highland and Lowland, English and Scot, Perth and Angus. I do not believe poor Oliver had feud with a new-hatched chicken. —Alas! he was the more fully prepared for a sudden call!"

"Hark ye, Smith," said the Provost,—"Answer me distinctly—Is there cause of feud between the household of Sir John Ramorny and yourself?"

"To a certainty, my lord, there is. It is now generally said, that Black Quentin, who went over Tay to Fife some days since, was the owner of the hand which was found in Couvrefew Street upon the eve of St. Valentine. It was I who struck off that hand with a blow of my good sword. As this Black Quentin was a chamberlain of Sir John, and much trusted, it is like there must be feud between me and his master's dependents."

"It bears a likely front, Smith," said Sir Patrick Charteris. —"And now, good brothers and wise magistrates, there are two suppositions, each of which leads to the same conclusion. The maskers who seized our fellow-citizen, and misused him in a manner of which his body retains some slight marks may have met with their former prisoner as he returned homewards, and finished their ill usage by taking his life. He himself expressed to Henry Gow fears that this would be the case. If this be really true, one or more of Sir John Ramorny's attendants must have been the assassins. But I think it more likely that one or two of the revellers may have remained on the field, or returned to it, having changed perhaps their disguise, and that to those men (for Oliver Proudfute, in his own personal appearance, would only have been a subject of sport) his apparition in the dress, and assuming, as he proposed to do, the manner, of Henry Smith, was matter of deep hatred; and that seeing him alone, they had taken, as they thought, a certain and safe mode to rid themselves of an enemy so dangerous as all men know Henry Wynd is accounted by those that are his unfriends. The same train of reasoning, again, rests the guilt with the household of Sir John Ramorny. How think you, sirs? Are we not free to charge the crime upon them?"

The Magistrates whispered together for several minutes, and then replied by the voice of Bailie Craigdallie,—"Noble Knight, and our worthy Provost,—we agree entirely in what your wisdom has spoken concerning this dark and bloody matter; nor do we doubt your sagacity in tracing to the fellowship and the company of John Ramorny of that Ilk, the villainy which hath been done to our deceased fellow-citizen, whether in his own character and capacity, or as mistaking him for our brave townsman, Henry of the Wynd. But Sir John, in his own behalf, and as the Prince's Master of the Horse, maintains an extensive household; and as of course the charge will be rebutted by a denial, we would ask, how we shall proceed in that case?—It is true, could we find law for firing the lodging, and putting all within it to the sword, the old proverb of 'short rede, good rede,' might here apply; for a fouler household of defiers of God, destroyers of men, and debauchers of women, are nowhere sheltered than are in Ramorny's band. But I doubt that this summary mode of execution would scarce be borne out by the laws; and no tittle of evidence which I have heard will tend to fix the crime on any single individual or individuals."

Before the Provost could reply, the Town-Clerk arose, and stroking his venerable beard, craved permission to speak, which was instantly granted. "Brethren," he said, "as well in our father's time as ours, hath God, on being rightly appealed to, condescended to make manifest the crimes of the guilty, and the innocence of those who may have been rashly accused. Let us demand from our Sovereign Lord, King Robert, who, when the wicked do not interfere to pervert his good intentions, is as just and clement a Prince as our annals can show in their long line, in the name of the Fair City, and of all the commons in Scotland, that he give us, after the fashion of our ancestors, the means of appealing to Heaven for light upon this dark murder. We will demand the proof by *bier-right*, often granted in the days of our Sovereign's ancestors, approved of by bulls and decretals, and administered by the great Emperor Charlemagne in France, by King Arthur in Britain, and by Gregory the Great, and the mighty Achaius, in this our land of Scotland."

"I have heard of the bier-right, Sir Louis," quoth the Provost, "and I know we have it in our charters of the Fair

City; but I am something ill-learned in the ancient laws, and would pray you to inform us more distinctly of its nature."

"We will demand of the King," said Sir Louis Lundin, "my advice being taken, that the body of our murdered fellow-citizen be transported into the High Church of St. John,[1] and suitable masses said for the benefit of his soul, and for the discovery of his foul murder. Meantime we shall obtain an order that Sir John Ramorny give up a list of such of his household as were in Perth in the course of the night between Fastern's Even and this Ash-Wednesday, and become bound to present them on a certain day and hour, to be early named, in the High Church of St. John; there one by one to pass before the bier of our murdered fellow-citizen, and in the form prescribed to call upon God and His saints to bear witness that he is innocent of the acting, art or part, of the murder. And credit me, as has been indeed proved by numerous instances, that if the murderer shall endeavour to shroud himself by making such an appeal, the antipathy which subsists between the dead body, and the hand which dealt the fatal blow that divorced it from the soul, will awaken some imperfect life, under the influence of which the veins of the dead man will pour forth at the fatal wounds the blood which has been so long stagnant in the veins. Or, to speak more certainly, it is the pleasure of Heaven, by some hidden agency which we cannot comprehend, to leave open this mode of discovering the wickedness of him who has defaced the image of his Creator."

"I have heard this law talked of," said Sir Patrick, "and it was enforced in the Bruce's time. This surely is no unfit period to seek, by such a mystic mode of enquiry, the truth, to which no ordinary means can give us access, seeing that a general accusation of Sir John's household would full surely be met by a general denial. Yet, I must crave farther of Sir Louis, our reverend town-clerk, how we shall prevent the guilty person from escaping in the interim?"

"The burghers will maintain a strict watch upon the wall, drawbridges shall be raised, and portcullises lowered, from sunset to sunrise, and strong patrols maintained through the night. This guard the burghers will willingly maintain, to secure against the escape of the murderer of their townsman."

The rest of the counsellors acquiesced, by word, sign, and look, in this proposal.

[1] See Note XIII.—Church of St. John.

"Again," said the Provost, "what if any one of the suspected household refuse to submit to the ordeal of bier-right?"

"He may appeal to that of combat," said the reverend city scribe, "with an opponent of equal rank; because the accused person must have his choice, in the appeal to the judgment of God, by what ordeal he will be tried. But if he refuses both, he must be held as guilty, and so punished."

The sages of the council unanimously agreed with the opinion of their Provost and Town-Clerk, and resolved, in all formality, to petition the King, as a matter of right, that the murder of their fellow-citizen should be enquired into according to this ancient form, which was held to manifest the truth, and received as matter of evidence in case of murder, so late as towards the end of the seventeenth century. But before the meeting dissolved, Bailie Craigdallie thought it meet to enquire, who was to be the champion of Maudie, or Magdalen Proudfute, and her two children.

"There need be little enquiry about that," said Sir Patrick Charteris; "we are men, and wear swords, which should be broken over the head of any one amongst us, who will not draw it in behalf of the widow and orphans of our murdered fellow-citizen, and in brave revenge of his death. If Sir John Ramorny shall personally resent the enquiry, Patrick Charteris of Kinfauns will do battle with him to the outrance, whilst horse and man may stand, or spear and blade hold together. But in case the challenger be of yeomanly degree, well wot I that Magdalen Proudfute may choose her own champion among the bravest burghers of Perth, and shame and dishonour were it to the Fair City for ever, could she light upon one who were traitor and coward enough to say her nay! Bring her hither, that she may make her election."

Henry Smith heard this with a melancholy anticipation that the poor woman's choice would light upon him, and that his recent reconciliation with his mistress would be again dissolved, by his being engaged in a fresh quarrel, from which there lay no honourable means of escape, and which, in any other circumstances, he would have welcomed as a glorious opportunity of distinguishing himself, both in sight of the court and of the city. He was aware that, under the tuition of Father Clement, Catharine viewed the ordeal of battle rather as an insult to religion, than an appeal to the Deity, and did not consider it as reasonable, that superior strength of arm, or skill of weapon, should be resorted to as the proof of moral guilt or innocence. He had, therefore, much to fear from her peculiar opinions in this particular, refined as they were beyond those of the age she lived in.

While he thus suffered under these contending feelings, Magdalen, the widow of the slaughtered man, entered the court, wrapt in a deep mourning veil, and followed and supported by five or six women of good, (that is, of respectability,) dressed in the same melancholy attire. One of her attendants held an infant in her arms, the last pledge of poor Oliver's nuptial affections. Another led a little tottering creature of two years, or thereabouts, which looked with wonder and fear, sometimes on the black dress in which they had muffled him, and sometimes on the scene around him.

The assembly rose to receive the melancholy group, and saluted them with an expression of the deepest sympathy, which Magdalen, though the mate of poor Oliver, returned with an air of dignity, which she borrowed, perhaps, from the extremity of her distress. Sir Patrick Charteris then stepped forward, and with the courtesy of a knight to a female, and of a protector to an oppressed and injured widow, took the poor woman's hand, and explained to her briefly, by what course the city had resolved to follow out the vengeance due for her husband's slaughter.

Having, with a softness and gentleness which did not belong to his general manner, ascertained that the unfortunate woman perfectly understood what was meant, he said aloud to the assembly, "Good citizens of Perth, and freeborn men of guild and craft, attend to what is about to pass, for it concerns your rights and privileges. Here stands Magdalen Proudfute, desirous to follow forth the revenge due for the death of her husband, foully murdered, as she sayeth, by Sir John Ramorny, Knight, of that Ilk, and which she offers to prove, by the evidence of bier-right, or by the body of a man. Therefore, I, Patrick Charteris, being a belted knight and freeborn gentleman, offer myself to do battle in her just quarrel, whilst man and horse may endure, if any one of my degree shall lift my glove.—How say you, Magdalen Proudfute, will you accept me for your champion?"

The widow answered with difficulty,—"I can desire none nobler."

Sir Patrick then took her right hand in his, and, kissing her forehead, for such was the ceremony, said solemnly,—"So

may God and St. John prosper me at my need, as I will do
my devoir as your champion, knightly, truly, and manfully.
Go now, Magdalen, and choose at your will among the
burgesses of the Fair City, present or absent, any one
upon whom you desire to rest your challenge, if he against
whom you bring plaint shall prove to be beneath my degree."

All eyes were turned to Henry Smith, whom the general
voice had already pointed out as in every respect the fittest to
act as champion on the occasion.   But the widow waited not for
the general prompting of their looks.   As soon as Sir Patrick
had spoken, she crossed the floor to the place where, near
the bottom of the table, the armourer stood among the men
of his degree, and took him by the hand:—

"Henry Gow, or Smith," she said, "good burgher and
craftsman, my—my——"

Husband, she would have said, but the word would not
come forth ; she was obliged to change the expression.

"He who is gone, loved and prized you over all men ;
therefore meet it is that thou shouldst follow out the quarrel
of his widow and orphans."

If there had been a possibility, which in that age there
was not, of Henry's rejecting or escaping from a trust for
which all men seemed to destine him, every wish and idea
of retreat was cut off, when the widow began to address
him ; and a command from Heaven could hardly have made
a stronger impression than did the appeal of the unfortunate
Magdalen.   Her allusion to his intimacy with the deceased
moved him to the soul.   During Oliver's life, doubtless, there
had been a strain of absurdity in his excessive predilection
for Henry, which, considering how very different they were
in character, had in it something ludicrous.   But all this
was now forgotten, and Henry, giving way to his natural
ardour, only remembered that Oliver had been his friend
and intimate ; a man who had loved and honoured him as
much as he was capable of entertaining such sentiments for
any one ; and above all, that there was much reason to suspect
that the deceased had fallen victim to a blow meant for Henry
himself.

It was, therefore, with an alacrity which, the minute
before, he could scarce have commanded, and which seemed
to express a stern pleasure, that, having pressed his lips to
the cold brow of the unhappy Magdalen, the armourer
replied,—

"I, Henry the Smith, dwelling in the Wynd of Perth, good man and true, and freely born, accept the office of champion to this widow Magdalen, and these orphans, and will do battle in their quarrel to the death, with any man whomsoever of my own degree, and that so long as I shall draw breath. So help me at my need God and good St. John!"

There arose from the audience a half-suppressed cry, expressing the interest which the persons present took in the prosecution of the quarrel, and their confidence in the issue.

Sir Patrick Charteris then took measures for repairing to the King's presence, and demanding leave to proceed with enquiry into the murder of Oliver Proudfute, according to the custom of bier-right, and, if necessary, by combat.

He performed this duty, after the Town-Council had dissolved, in a private interview between himself and the King, who heard of this new trouble with much vexation, and appointed next morning, after mass, for Sir Patrick and the parties interested, to attend his pleasure in council. In the meantime, a royal pursuivant was despatched to the Constable's lodgings, to call over the roll of Sir John Ramorny's attendants, and charge him, with his whole retinue, under high penalties, to abide within Perth, until the King's pleasure should be farther known.

CHAPTER XXI

In God's name, see the lists and all things fit;
There let them end it—God defend the right!
Henry IV. Part II.

In the same Council-room of the conventual palace of the Dominicans, King Robert was seated with his brother Albany, whose affected austerity of virtue, and real art and dissimulation, maintained so high an influence over the feeble-minded monarch. It was indeed natural, that one who seldom saw things according to their real forms and outlines, should view them according to the light in which they were presented to him by a bold astucious man, possessing the claim of such near relationship.

Ever anxious on account of his misguided and unfortunate son, the King was now endeavouring to make Albany coincide in opinion with him, in exculpating Rothsay from any part in the death of the Bonnet-maker, the precognition concerning which had been left by Sir Patrick Charteris for his Majesty's consideration.

"This is an unhappy matter, brother Robin," he said, "a most unhappy occurrence; and goes nigh to put strife and quarrel betwixt the nobility and the commons here, as they have been at war together in so many distant lands. I see but one cause of comfort in the matter; and that is, that Sir John Ramorny having received his dismissal from the Duke of Rothsay's family, it cannot be said that he or any of his people, who may have done this bloody deed, (if it has truly been done by them,) have been encouraged or hounded out upon such an errand by my poor boy. I am sure, brother, you and I can bear witness, how readily, upon my entreaties, he agreed to dismiss Ramorny from his service, on account of that brawl in Curfew Street."

"I remember his doing so," said Albany; "and well do I hope that the connexion betwixt the Prince and Ramorny has not been renewed since he seemed to comply with your Grace's wishes."

"Seemed to comply?—The connexion renewed?" said the King; "what mean you by these expressions, brother? Surely, when David promised to me, that if that unhappy matter of Curfew Street were but smothered up and concealed, he would part with Ramorny, as he was a counsellor thought capable of involving him in similar fooleries, and would acquiesce in our inflicting on him either exile, or such punishment as it should please us to impose—surely you cannot doubt that he was sincere in his professions, and would keep his word? Remember you not, that when you advised that a heavy fine should be levied upon his estate in Fife in lieu of banishment, the Prince himself seemed to say, that exile would be better for Ramorny, and even for himself?"

"I remember it well, my royal brother. Nor, truly, could I have suspected Ramorny of having so much influence over the Prince, after having been accessary to placing him in a situation so perilous, had it not been for my royal kinsman's own confession, alluded to by your Grace, that, if suffered to remain at court, he might still continue to influence his conduct. I then regretted I had advised a fine in place of exile. But that time is passed, and now new mischief has occurred, fraught with much peril to your Majesty, as well as to your royal heir, and to the whole kingdom."

"What mean you, Robin?" said the weak-minded King. "By the tomb of our parents! by the soul of Bruce, our immortal ancestor! I entreat thee, my dearest brother, to take compassion on me. Tell me what evil threatens my son, or my kingdom?"

The features of the King, trembling with anxiety, and his eyes brimful of tears, were bent upon his brother, who seemed to assume time for consideration ere he replied.

"My lord, the danger lies here. Your Grace believes that the Prince had no accession to this second aggression upon the citizens of Perth—the slaughter of this bonnet-making fellow, about whose death they clamour, as a set of gulls about their comrade, when one of the noisy brood is struck down by a boy's shaft."

"Their lives," said the King, "are dear to themselves and their friends, Robin."

"Truly, ay, my liege; and they make them dear to us too, ere we can settle with the knaves for the least blood-witt.—But, as I said, your Majesty thinks the Prince had no share in this last slaughter: I will not attempt to shake your belief in that delicate point, but will endeavour to believe along with you. What you think is rule for me. Robert of Albany will never think otherwise than Robert of broad Scotland."

"Thank you, thank you," said the King, taking his brother's hand. "I knew I might rely that your affection would do justice to poor heedless Rothsay, who exposes himself to so much misconstruction that he scarcely deserves the sentiments you feel for him."

Albany had such an immovable constancy of purpose, that he was able to return the fraternal pressure of the King's hand, while tearing up by the very roots the hopes of the indulgent, fond old man.

"But, alas!" the Duke continued with a sigh, "this burly intractable Knight of Kinfauns, and his brawling herd of burghers, will not view the matter as we do. They have the boldness to say, that this dead fellow had been misused by Rothsay and his fellows, who were in the street in mask and revel, stopping men and women, compelling them to dance, or to drink huge quantities of wine, with other follies needless to recount; and they say, that the whole party repaired to Sir John Ramorny's and broke their way into the house, in order to conclude their revel there; thus affording good reason to judge, that the dismissal of Sir John from the Prince's service was but a feigned stratagem to deceive the public. And hence, they urge, that if ill were done that night, by Sir John Ramorny or his followers, much it is to be thought that the Duke of Rothsay must have at least been privy to, if he did not authorize it."

"Albany, this is dreadful!" said the King; "would they make a murderer of my boy? would they pretend my David would soil his hands in Scottish blood, without having either provocation or purpose? No, no—they will not invent calumnies so broad as these, for they are flagrant and incredible."

"Pardon, my liege," answered the Duke of Albany; "they say the cause of quarrel which occasioned the riot in Curfew Street, and its consequences, were more proper to the Prince than to Sir John; since none suspects, far less believes, that that hopeful enterprise was conducted for the gratification of the Knight of Ramorny."

"Thou drivest me mad, Robin!" said the King.

"I am dumb," answered his brother; "I did but speak my poor mind according to your royal order."

"Thou meanest well, I know," said the King; "but instead of tearing me to pieces with the display of inevitable calamities, were it not kinder, Robin, to point me out some mode to escape from them?"

"True, my liege; but as the only road of extrication is rough and difficult, it is necessary your Grace should be first possessed with the absolute necessity of using it, ere you hear it even described. The chirurgeon must first convince his patient of the incurable condition of a shattered member, ere he venture to name amputation, though it be the only remedy."

The King at these words was roused to a degree of alarm and indignation, greater than his brother had deemed he could be awakened to.

"Shattered and mortified member! my Lord of Albany? Amputation the only remedy!—These are unintelligible words, my lord.—If thou appliest them to our son Rothsay, thou must make them good to the letter, else mayst thou have bitter cause to rue the consequence."

"You construe me too literally, my royal liege," said Albany. "I spoke not of the Prince in such unbeseeming terms; for I call Heaven to witness, that he is dearer to me as the son of a well-beloved brother, than had he been son of my own. But I spoke in regard to separating him from the follies and vanities of life, which holy men say are like to mortified members, and ought, like them, to be cut off and thrown from us, as things which interrupt our progress in better things."

"I understand—thou wouldst have this Ramorny, who hath been thought the instrument of my son's follies, exiled from court," said the relieved monarch, "until these unhappy scandals are forgotten, and our subjects are disposed to look upon our son with different and more confiding eyes."

"That were good counsel, my liege; but mine went a little —a very little—farther. I would have the Prince himself removed for some brief period from court."

"How, Albany! part with my child, my first-born, the light of my eyes, and—wilful as he is—the darling of my heart!— Oh, Robin! I cannot, and I will not."

"Nay, I did but suggest, my lord—I am sensible of the wound such a proceeding must inflict on a parent's heart, for am I not myself a father?" And he hung his head, as if in hopeless despondency.

"I could not survive it, Albany. When I think that even our own influence over him, which, sometimes forgotten in our absence, is ever effectual whilst he is with us, is by your plan to be entirely removed, what perils might he not rush upon? I could not sleep in his absence—I should hear his death-groan in every breeze; and you, Albany, though you conceal it better, would be nearly as anxious."

Thus spoke the facile monarch, willing to conciliate his brother and cheat himself, by taking it for granted that an affection, of which there were no traces, subsisted betwixt the uncle and nephew.

"Your paternal apprehensions are too easily alarmed, my lord," said Albany. "I do not propose to leave the disposal of the Prince's motions to his own wild pleasure. I understand that the Prince is to be placed for a short time under some becoming restraint—that he should be subjected to the charge of some grave counsellor, who must be responsible both for his conduct and his safety, as a tutor for his pupil."

"How! a tutor? and at Rothsay's age?" exclaimed the King; "he is two years beyond the space to which our laws limit the term of nonage."

"The wiser Romans," said Albany, "extended it for four

years after the period we assign; and, in common sense, the right of control ought to last till it be no longer necessary, and so the time ought to vary with the disposition. Here is young Lindsay, the Earl of Crawford, who they say gives patronage to Ramorny on this appeal—He is a lad of fifteen, with the deep passions and fixed purpose of a man of thirty; while my royal nephew, with much more amiable and noble qualities both of head and heart, sometimes shows, at twenty-three years of age, the wanton humours of a boy, towards whom restraint may be kindness.—And do not be discouraged that it is so, my liege, or angry with your brother for telling the truth; since the best fruits are those that are slowest in ripening, and the best horses such as give most trouble to the grooms who train them for the field or lists."

The Duke stopped, and after suffering King Robert to indulge for two or three minutes in a reverie which he did not attempt to interrupt, he added, in a more lively tone,—"But, cheer up, my noble liege; perhaps the feud may be made up without farther fighting or difficulty. The widow is poor, for her husband, though he was much employed, had idle and costly habits. The matter may be therefore redeemed for money, and the amount of an assythment may be recovered out of Ramorny's estate."

"Nay, that we will ourselves discharge," said King Robert, eagerly catching at the hope of a pacific termination of this unpleasing debate. "Ramorny's prospects will be destroyed by his being sent from court, and deprived of his charge in Rothsay's household; and it would be ungenerous to load a falling man.—But here comes our secretary, the Prior, to tell us the hour of council approaches.—Good-morrow, my worthy father."

"Benedicite, my royal liege," answered the Abbot.

"Now, good father," continued the King, "without waiting for Rothsay, whose accession to our counsels we will ourselves guarantee, proceed we to the business of our kingdom. What advices have you from the Douglas?"

"He has arrived at his Castle of Tantallon, my liege, and has sent a post to say, that though the Earl of March remains in sullen seclusion in his fortress of Dunbar, his friends and followers are gathering and forming an encampment near Coldingham, where it is supposed they intend to await the arrival of a large force of English, which

Hotspur and Sir Ralph Percy are assembling on the English frontier."

"That is cold news," said the King; "and may God forgive George of Dunbar!"—The Prince entered as he spoke, and he continued—"Ha! thou art here at length, Rothsay;—I saw thee not at mass."

"I was an idler this morning," said the Prince, "having spent a restless and feverish night."

"Ah, foolish boy!" answered the King; "hadst thou not been over restless on Fastern's Eve, thou hadst not been feverish on the night of Ash-Wednesday."

"Let me not interrupt your prayers, my liege," said the Prince lightly. "Your Grace was invoking Heaven in behalf of some one—an enemy doubtless, for these have the frequent advantage of your orisons."

"Sit down and be at peace, foolish youth!" said his father, his eye resting at the same time on the handsome face and graceful figure of his favourite son. Rothsay drew a cushion near to his father's feet, and threw himself carelessly down upon it, while the King resumed.

"I was regretting that the Earl of March, having separated warm from my hand with full assurance that he should receive compensation for every thing which he could complain of as injurious, should have been capable of caballing with Northumberland against his own country—Is it possible he could doubt our intentions to make good our word?"

"I will answer for him, No," said the Prince; "March never doubted your Highness's word. Marry, he may well have made question whether your learned counsellors would leave your Majesty the power of keeping it."

Robert the Third had adopted to a great extent the timid policy, of not seeming to hear expressions, which, being heard, required, even in his own eyes, some display of displeasure. He passed on, therefore, in his discourse, without observing his son's speech; but in private, Rothsay's rashness augmented the displeasure which his father began to entertain against him.

"It is well the Douglas is on the marches," said the King. "His breast, like those of his ancestors, has ever been the best bulwark of Scotland."

"Then woe betide us if he should turn his back to the enemy," said the incorrigible Rothsay.

"Dare you impeach the courage of Douglas?" replied the King, extremely chafed.

"No man dare question the Earl's courage," said Rothsay; "it is as certain as his pride;—But his luck may be something doubted."

"By Saint Andrew, David!" exclaimed his father, "thou art like a screech-owl—every word thou sayest betokens strife and calamity."

"I am silent, father," answered the youth.

"And what news of our Highland disturbances?" continued the King, addressing the Prior.

"I trust they have assumed a favourable aspect," answered the clergyman. "The fire which threatened the whole country is likely to be drenched out by the blood of some forty or fifty kerne; for the two great confederacies have agreed, by solemn indenture of arms, to decide their quarrel with such weapons as your Highness may name, and in your royal presence, in such place as shall be appointed, on the 30th of March next to come, being Palm Sunday; the number of combatants being limited to thirty on each side, and the fight to be maintained to extremity, since they affectionately make humble suit and petition to your Majesty, that you will parentally condescend to wave for the day your royal privilege of interrupting the combat, by flinging down of truncheon, or crying of Ho! until the battle shall be utterly fought to an end."

"The wild savages!" exclaimed the King; "would they limit our best and dearest royal privilege, that of putting a stop to strife, and crying truce to battle?—Will they remove the only motive which could bring me to the butcherly spectacle of their combat?—Would they fight like men, or like their own mountain wolves?"

"My lord," said Albany; "the Earl of Crawford and I had presumed, without consulting you, to ratify that preliminary for the adoption of which we saw much and pressing reason."

"How! the Earl of Crawford!" said the King. "Methinks he is a young counsellor on such grave occurrents."

"He is," replied Albany, "notwithstanding his early years, of such esteem among his Highland neighbours, that I could have done little with them but for his aid and influence."

"Hear this, young Rothsay!" said the King reproachfully to his heir.

"I pity Crawford, Sire," replied the Prince. "He has

too early lost a father, whose counsels would have better become such a season as this."

The King turned next towards Albany with a look of triumph, at the filial affection which his son displayed in his reply.

Albany proceeded without emotion. " It is not the life of these Highlandmen, but their death, which is to be profitable to the commonwealth of Scotland; and truly it seemed to the Earl of Crawford and myself most desirable that the combat should be a strife of extermination."

" Marry," said the Prince, " if such be the juvenile policy of Lindsay, he will be a merciful ruler some ten or twelve years hence! Out upon a boy, that is hard of heart before he has hair upon his lip! Better he had contented himself with fighting cocks on Fastern's Even, than laying schemes for massacring men on Palm Sunday, as if he were backing a Welsh main, where all must fight to death."

" Rothsay is right, Albany," said the King; " it were unlike a Christian Monarch to give way in this point. I cannot consent to see men battle until they are all hewn down like cattle in the shambles. It would sicken me to look at it, and the warder would drop from my hand for mere lack of strength to hold it."

" It would drop unheeded," said Albany. " Let me entreat your Grace to recollect, that you only give up a royal privilege, which, exercised, would win you no respect, since it would receive no obedience. Were your Majesty to throw down your warder when the war is high, and these men's blood is hot, it would meet no more regard than if a sparrow should drop among a herd of battling wolves the straw which he was carrying to his nest. Nothing will separate them but the exhaustion of slaughter; and better they sustain it at the hands of each other, than from the swords of such troops as might attempt to separate them at your Majesty's commands. An attempt to keep the peace by violence, would be construed into an ambush laid for them; both parties would unite to resist it,—the slaughter would be the same, and the hoped-for results of future peace would be utterly disappointed."

" There is even too much truth in what you say, brother Robin," replied the flexible King. " To little purpose is it to command what I cannot enforce; and, although I have the unhappiness to do so each day of my life, it were needless to give such a very public example of royal impotency, before the crowds who may assemble to behold this spectacle. Let these savage men, therefore, work their bloody will to the uttermost upon each other; I will not attempt to forbid what I cannot prevent them from executing.—Heaven help this wretched country! I will to my oratory and pray for her, since to aid her by hand and head is alike denied to me. Father Prior, I pray the support of your arm."

"Nay, but, brother," said Albany, "forgive me if I remind you, that we must hear the matter between the citizens of Perth and Ramorny, about the death of a townsman——"

"True, true—" said the Monarch, reseating himself; "more violence—more battle—Oh, Scotland! Scotland! if the best blood of thy bravest children could enrich thy barren soil, what land on earth would excel thee in fertility! When is it that a white hair is seen on the beard of a Scottish man, unless he be some wretch like thy sovereign, protected from murder by impotence, to witness the scenes of slaughter to which he cannot put a period?—Let them come in—delay them not. They are in haste to kill, and grudge each other each fresh breath of their Creator's blessed air. The demon of strife and slaughter hath possessed the whole land!"

As the mild Prince threw himself back on his seat, with an air of impatience and anger not very usual with him, the door at the lower end of the room was unclosed, and, advancing from the gallery into which it led, (where in perspective was seen a guard of the Bute-men, or Brandanes, under arms,) came, in mournful procession, the widow of poor Oliver, led by Sir Patrick Charteris, with as much respect as if she had been a lady of the first rank. Behind them came two women of good, the wives of magistrates of the city, both in mourning garments, one bearing the infant, and the other leading the elder child. The Smith followed in his best attire, and wearing over his buff-coat a scarf of crape. Bailie Craigdallie, and a brother magistrate, closed the melancholy procession, exhibiting similar marks of mourning.

The good King's transitory passion was gone the instant he looked on the pallid countenance of the sorrowing widow, and beheld the unconsciousness of the innocent orphans who had sustained so great a loss; and when Sir Patrick Charteris had assisted Magdalen Proudfute to kneel down, and, still holding her hand, kneeled himself on one knee, it was with a sympathetic tone that King Robert asked her name and business. She made no answer, but muttered something, looking towards her conductor.

"Speak for the poor woman, Sir Patrick Charteris," said the King, "and tell us the cause of her seeking our presence."

"So please you, my liege," answered Sir Patrick, rising up, "this woman, and these unhappy orphans, make plaint to your Highness upon Sir John Ramorny of Ramorny, Knight, that by him, or by some of his household, her umquhile husband, Oliver Proudfute, freeman and burgess of Perth, was slain upon the streets of the city on the Eve of Shrove Tuesday, or morning of Ash Wednesday."

"Woman," replied the King, with much kindness, "thou art gentle by sex, and shouldst be pitiful even by thy affliction ; for our own calamity ought to make us—nay, I think it doth make us—merciful to others. Thy husband hath only trodden the path appointed to us all."

"In his case," said the widow, "my liege must remember it has been a brief and a bloody one."

"I agree he hath had foul measure. But since I have been unable to protect him, as I confess was my royal duty, I am willing, in atonement, to support thee and these orphans, as well, or better, than you lived in the days of your husband ; only do thou pass from this charge, and be not the occasion of spilling more life. Remember, I put before you the choice betwixt practising mercy and pursuing vengeance, and that betwixt plenty and penury."

"It is true, my liege, we are poor," answered the widow with unshaken firmness ; "but I and my children will feed with the beasts of the field, ere we live on the price of my husband's blood. I demand the combat by my champion, as you are belted knight and crowned King."

"I knew it would be so !" said the King, aside to Albany. "In Scotland, the first words stammered by an infant, and the last uttered by a dying greybeard, are—'combat—blood —revenge.'—It skills not arguing further. Admit the defendants."

Sir John Ramorny entered the apartment. He was dressed in a long furred robe such as men of quality wore when they were unarmed. Concealed by the folds of drapery, his wounded arm was supported by a scarf, or sling of crimson silk, and with the left arm he leaned on a youth, who, scarcely beyond the years of boyhood, bore on his brow the deep impression of early thought, and premature passion. This was that celebrated Lindsay, Earl of Crawford, who, in his afterdays, was known by the epithet of the Tiger Earl,[1] and who ruled the great and rich valley of Strathmore with the absolute power and unrelenting cruelty of a feudal tyrant. Two or three gentlemen, friends of the Earl, or of his own, countenanced Sir John Ramorny by their presence on this occasion. The charge was again stated, and met by a broad denial on the part of the accused; and in reply the challengers offered to prove their assertion by an appeal to the ordeal of bier-right.

"I am not bound," answered Sir John Ramorny, "to submit to this ordeal, since I can prove, by the evidence of my late royal master, that I was in my own lodgings, lying on my bed, ill at ease, while this Provost and these Bailies pretend I was committing a crime to which I had neither will nor temptation. I can therefore be no just object of suspicion."

"I can aver," said the Prince, "that I saw and conversed with Sir John Ramorny about some matters concerning my own household, on the very night when this murder was a-doing. I therefore know that he was ill at ease, and could nor in person commit the deed in question. But I know nothing of the employment of his attendants, and will not take it upon me to say that some of them may not have been guilty of the crime now charged on them."

Sir John Ramorny had, during the beginning of this speech, looked round with an air of defiance, which was somewhat disconcerted by the concluding sentence of Rothsay's speech. "I thank your Highness," he said, with a smile, "for your cautious and limited testimony in my behalf. He was wise who wrote, 'Put not your faith in Princes.'"

"If you have no other evidence of your innocence, Sir John Ramorny," said the King, "we may not, in respect to your followers, refuse to the injured widow and orphans, the complainers, the grant of a proof by ordeal of bier-right, unless any of them should prefer that of combat. For yourself, you are, by the Prince's evidence, freed from the attaint."

"My liege," answered Sir John, "I can take warrant upon myself for the innocence of my household and followers."

[1] Sir David Lyndsaye, first Earl of Crawford, and brother-in-law to Robert III.

"Why so a monk or a woman might speak," said Sir Patrick Charteris. "In knightly language, wilt thou, Sir John de Ramorny, do battle with me in the behalf of thy followers?"

"The Provost of Perth had not obtained time to name the word combat," said Ramorny, "ere I would have accepted it. But I am not at present fit to hold a lance."

"I am glad of it, under your favour, Sir John—There will be the less bloodshed," said the King. "You must therefore produce your followers according to your steward's household book, in the great church of St. John, that, in presence of all whom it may concern, they may purge themselves of this accusation. See that every man of them do appear at the time of High Mass, otherwise your honour may be sorely tainted."

"They shall attend to a man," said Sir John Ramorny. Then bowing low to the King, he directed himself to the young Duke of Rothsay, and making a deep obeisance, spoke so as to be heard by him alone. "You have used me generously, my lord!—One word of your lips could have ended this controversy, and you have refused to speak it!"—

"On my life," whispered the Prince, "I spake as far as the extreme verge of truth and conscience would permit. I think thou couldst not expect I should frame lies for thee; —and after all, John, in my broken recollections of that night, I do bethink me of a butcherly-looking mute, with a curtal-axe, much like such a one as may have done yonder night-job?—Ha! have I touched you, Sir Knight?"—

Ramorny made no answer, but turned away as precipitately as if some one had pressed suddenly on his wounded arm, and regained his lodgings with the Earl of Crawford; to whom, though disposed for any thing rather than revelry, he was obliged to offer a splendid collation, to acknowledge in some degree his sense of the countenance which the young noble had afforded him.

CHAPTER XXII

In pottingry he wrocht great pyne;
He murdreitmony in medecyne.

DUNBAR.

WHEN, after an entertainment the prolonging of which was like torture to the wounded knight, the Earl of Crawford at length took horse, to go to his distant quarters in the Castle of Dupplin, where he resided as a guest, the Knight of Ramorny retired into his sleeping apartment, agonized by pains of body and anxiety of mind. Here he found Henbane Dwining, on whom it was his hard fate to depend for consolation in both respects. The physician, with his affectation of extreme humility, hoped he saw his exalted patient merry and happy.

" Merry as a mad dog!" said Ramorny, "and happy as the wretch whom the cur hath bitten, and who begins to feel the approach of the ravening madness. That ruthless boy, Crawford, saw my agony, and spared not a single carouse. I must do him *justice*, forsooth! If I had done justice to him and to the world, I had thrown him out of window, and cut short a career, which, if he grow up as he has begun, will prove a source of misery to all Scotland, but especially to Tayside.— Take heed as thou undoest the ligatures, chirurgeon; the touch of a fly's wing on that raw glowing stump were like a dagger to me."

" Fear not, my noble patron," said the leech, with a chuckling laugh of enjoyment, which he vainly endeavoured to disguise under a tone of affected sensibility. " We will apply some fresh balsam, and—he, he, he!—relieve your knightly honour of the irritation which you sustain so firmly."

" Firmly, man?" said Ramorny, grinning with pain; " I sustain it as I would the scorching flames of purgatory—the bone seems made of red-hot iron—thy greasy ointment will hiss as it drops upon the wound—And yet it is December's ice, compared to the fever-fit of my mind!"

" We will first use our emollients upon the body, my noble patron," said Dwining; " and then, with your knighthood's permission, your servant will try his art on the troubled mind— though I fain hope even the mental pain also may in some degree depend on the irritation of the wound, and that, abated as I trust the corporeal pangs will soon be, perhaps the stormy feelings of the mind may subside of themselves."

" Henbane Dwining," said the patient, as he felt the pain of his wound assuaged, "thou art a precious and invaluable leech, but some things are beyond thy power. Thou canst stupify my bodily sense of this raging agony, but thou canst not teach me to bear the scorn of the boy whom I have brought up ;—whom I loved, Dwining—for I did love him—dearly love him ! The worst of my ill deeds have been to flatter his vices—and he grudged me a word of his mouth, when a word would have allayed this cumber ! He smiled, too—I saw him smile, when yon paltry Provost, the companion and patron of wretched burghers, defied me, whom this heartless Prince knew to be unable to bear arms.—Ere I forget or forgive it, thou thyself shalt preach up the pardoning of injuries !—And then the care for to-morrow—Think'st thou, Henbane Dwining, that, in very reality, the wounds of the slaughtered corpse will gape, and shed tears of fresh blood at the murderer's approach ? "

" I cannot tell, my lord, save by report," said Dwining, " which avouches the fact."

" The brute Bonthron," said Ramorny, " is startled at the apprehension of such a thing, and speaks of being rather willing to stand the combat. What think'st thou ?—he is a fellow of steel."

" It is the armourer's trade to deal with steel," replied Dwining.

" Were Bonthron to fall it would little grieve me," said Ramorny ; " though I should miss an useful hand."

" I well believe your lordship will not sorrow as for that you lost in Curfew Street—Excuse my pleasantry—he, he, he !—But what are the useful properties of this fellow Bonthron ? "

" Those of a bull-dog," answered the knight ; " he worries without barking."

" You have no fear of his confessing ? " said the physician.

" Who can tell what the dread of approaching death may do ? " replied the patient. " He has already shown a timorousness entirely alien from his ordinary sullenness of nature ; he that would scarce wash his hands after he had slain a man, is now afraid to see a dead body bleed."

" Well," said the leech, " I must do something for him if I can, since it was to further my revenge that he struck yonder downright blow, though by ill luck it lighted not where it was intended."

" And whose fault was that, timid villain," said Ramorny, " save thine own, who marked a rascal deer for a buck of the first head ? "

" Benedicite, noble sir," replied the mediciner ; " would you have me, who know little save of chamber practice, be as skilful of woodcraft as your noble self, or tell hart from hind, doe from roe, in a glade at midnight? I misdoubted me little when I saw the figure run past us to the Smith's habitation in the wynd, habited like a morrice-dancer; and yet my mind partly misgave me whether it was our man, for methought he seemed less of stature. But when he came out again, after so much time as to change his dress, and swaggered onwards with buff-coat and steel-cap, whistling after the armourer's wonted fashion, I do own I was mistaken, *super totam materiem*, and loosed your knighthood's bull-dog upon him, who did his devoir most duly, though he pulled down the wrong deer. Therefore, unless the accursed Smith kill our poor friend stone-dead on the spot, I am determined, if art may do it, that the ban-dog Bonthron shall not miscarry."

"It will put thine art to the test, man of medicine," said Ramorny; "for know, that having the worst of the combat, if our champion be not killed stone-dead in the lists, he will be drawn forth of them by the heels, and without further ceremony knitted up to the gallows, as convicted of the murder; and when he hath swung there like a loose tassel for an hour or so, I think thou wilt hardly take it in hand to cure his broken neck."

"I am of a different opinion, may it please your knighthood," answered Dwining, gently. "I will carry him off from the very foot of the gallows into the land of faery, like King Arthur, or Sir Huon of Bordeaux, or Ugero the Dane; or I will, if I please, suffer him to dangle on the gibbet for a certain number of minutes, or hours, and then whisk him away from the sight of all, with as much ease as the wind wafts away the withered leaf."

"This is idle boasting, Sir Leech," replied Ramorny. "The whole mob of Perth will attend him to the gallows, each more eager than another to see the retainer of a nobleman die, for the slaughter of a cuckoldly citizen. There will be a thousand of them round the gibbet's foot."

"And were there ten thousand," said Dwining, "shall I, who am a high clerk, and have studied in Spain, and Araby itself, not be able to deceive the eyes of this hoggish herd of citizens, when the pettiest juggler that ever dealt in legerdemain can gull even the sharp observation of your most intelligent knighthood? I tell you, I will put the change on them as if I were in possession of Keddie's ring."

"If thou speakest truth," answered the knight, "and I think thou darest not palter with me on such a theme, thou must have the aid of Satan, and I will have nought to do with him. I disown and defy him."

Dwining indulged in his internal chuckling laugh when he heard his patron testify his defiance of the foul Fiend, and saw him second it by crossing himself. He composed himself, however, upon observing Ramorny's aspect become very stern, and said, with tolerable gravity, though a little interrupted by the effort necessary to suppress his mirthful mood,—

"Confederacy, most devout sir; confederacy is the soul of jugglery. But—he, he, he!—I have not the honour to be—he, he!—an ally of the gentleman of whom you speak— in whose existence I am—he, he!—no very profound believer, though your knightship, doubtless, hath better opportunities of acquaintance."

"Proceed, rascal, and without that sneer, which thou mayst otherwise dearly pay for."

"I will, most undaunted," replied Dwining. "Know that I have my confederate too, else my skill were little worth."

"And who may that be, pray you?"

"Stephen Smotherwell, if it like your honour, lockman of this Fair City. I marvel your knighthood knows him not."

"And I marvel thy knaveship knows him not on pro- fessional acquaintance," replied Ramorny; "but I see thy nose is unslit, thy ears yet uncropped, and if thy shoulders are scarred or branded, thou art wise for using a high-collared jerkin."

"He, he! your honour is pleasant," said the mediciner. "It is not by personal circumstances that I have acquired the intimacy of Stephen Smotherwell, but on account of a certain traffic betwixt us, in which, an't please you, I exchange certain sums of silver for the bodies, heads, and limbs, of those who die by aid of friend Stephen."

"Wretch!" exclaimed the knight with horror, "is it to compose charms and forward works of witchcraft, that you trade for these miserable relics of mortality?"

"He, he, he!—No, an it please your knighthood," answered the mediciner, much amused with the ignorance of his patron; "but we, who are knights of the scalpel, are accustomed to practise careful carving of the limbs of defunct persons, which we call dissection, whereby we discover, by examination of a dead member, how to deal with one belonging to a living man, which hath become diseased through injury or otherwise. Ah! if your honour saw my poor laboratory, I could show you heads and hands, feet and lungs, which have been long supposed to be rotting in the mould. The skull of Wallace, stolen from London Bridge; the heart of Sir Simon Fraser,[1] that never feared man; the lovely skull of the fair Katie Logie [2]—Oh, had I but had the fortune to have preserved the chivalrous hand of mine honoured patron!"

"Out upon thee, slave!—Thinkest thou to disgust me with thy catalogue of horrors?—Tell me at once where thy discourse drives. How can thy traffic with the hangdog executioner be of avail to serve me, or to help my servant Bonthron?"

"Nay, I do not recommend it to your knighthood, save in an extremity," replied Dwining. "But we will suppose the battle fought, and our cock beaten. Now we must first possess him with the certainty, that, if unable to gain the day, we will at least save him from the hangman, provided he confess nothing which can prejudice your knighthood's honour."

"Ha!—ay, a thought strikes me," said Ramorny. "We can do more than this—we can place a word in Bonthron's mouth that will be troublesome enough to him whom I am bound to curse, for being the cause of my misfortune. Let us to the ban-dog's kennel, and explain to him what is to be done in every view of the question. If we can persuade him to stand the bier-ordeal, it may be a mere bugbear, and in that case we are safe. If he take the combat, he is fierce as a baited bear, and may, perchance, master his opponent; then we are more than safe—we are revenged. If Bonthron himself is vanquished, we will put thy device in exercise; and if thou canst manage it cleanly, we may dictate his confession, take the advantage of it, as I will show thee on further conference, and make a giant stride towards satisfaction for my wrongs.—Still there remains one hazard. Suppose our mastiff mortally wounded in the lists, who shall prevent his growling out some species of confession different from what we would recommend?"

"Marry, that can his mediciner," said Dwining. "Let me wait on him, and have the opportunity to lay but a

---

[1] The famous ancestor of the Lovats, slain at Halidon Hill.
[2] The beautiful mistress of David II.

finger on his wound, and trust me he shall betray no confidence."

"Why, there's a willing fiend, that needs neither pushing nor prompting!" said Ramorny.

"As I trust I shall need neither in your knighthood's service."

"We will go indoctrinate our agent," continued the Knight. "We shall find him pliant; for hound as he is, he knows those who feed from those who browbeat him; and he holds a late royal master of mine in deep hate for some injurious treatment and base terms which he received at his hand. I must also farther concert with thee the particulars of thy practice, for saving the ban-dog from the hands of the herd of citizens."

We leave this worthy pair of friends to their secret practices, of which we shall afterwards see the results. They were, although of different qualities, as well matched for device and execution of criminal projects, as the greyhound is to destroy the game which the slowhound raises, or the slowhound to track the prey which the gazehound discovers by the eye. Pride and selfishness were the characteristics of both; but from the difference of rank, education, and talents, they had assumed the most different appearance in the two individuals.

Nothing could less resemble the high-blown ambition of the favourite courtier, the successful gallant, and the bold warrior, than the submissive unassuming mediciner, who seemed even to court and delight in insult; whilst, in his secret soul, he felt himself possessed of a superiority of knowledge,—a power, both of science and of mind, which placed the rude nobles of the day infinitely beneath him. So conscious was Henbane Dwining of this elevation, that, like a keeper of wild beasts, he sometimes adventured, for his own amusement, to rouse the stormy passions of such men as Ramorny, trusting, with his humble manner, to elude the turmoil he had excited, as an Indian boy will launch his light canoe, secure from its very fragility, upon a broken surf, in which the boat of an argosy would be assuredly dashed to pieces. That the feudal baron should despise the humble practitioner in medicine, was a matter of course; but Ramorny felt not the less the influence which Dwining exercised over him, and was in the encounter of their wits often mastered by him, as the most eccentric efforts of a fiery horse are overcome by a boy of twelve years old, if he has been bred to the arts of the manege. But the contempt of Dwining for Ramorny was far less qualified. He regarded the knight, in comparison with himself, as scarcely rising above the brute creation; capable indeed of working destruction, as the bull with his horns, or the wolf with his fangs, but mastered by mean prejudices, and a slave to priestcraft, in which phrase Dwining included religion of every kind. On the whole, he considered Ramorny as one whom nature had assigned to him as a serf, to mine for the gold which he worshipped, and the avaricious love of which was his greatest failing, though by no means his worst vice. He vindicated this sordid tendency in his own eyes, by persuading himself that it had its source in the love of power.

"Henbane Dwining," he said, as he gazed in delight upon the hoards which he had secretly amassed, and which he visited from time to time, "is no silly miser, that doats on those pieces for their golden lustre; it is the power with which they endow the possessor, which makes him thus adore them. What is there that these put not within your command? Do you love beauty, and are mean, deformed, infirm, and old?—here is a lure the fairest hawk of them all will stoop to. Are you feeble, weak, subject to the oppression of the powerful?—here is that will arm in your defence those more mighty than the petty tyrant whom you fear. Are you splendid in your wishes, and desire the outward show of opulence?—this dark chest contains many a wide range of hill and dale, many a fair forest full of game; the allegiance of a thousand vassals. Wish you for favour in courts, temporal or spiritual?—the smiles of kings, the pardon of popes and priests for old crimes, and the indulgence which encourages priest-ridden fools to venture on new ones,—all these holy incentives to vice may be purchased for gold. Revenge itself, which the gods are said to reserve to themselves, doubtless because they envy humanity so sweet a morsel—revenge itself is to be bought by it. But it is also to be won by superior skill, and that is the nobler mode of reaching it. I will spare, then, my treasure for other uses, and accomplish my revenge gratis: or rather I will add the luxury of augmented wealth to the triumph of requited wrongs."

Thus thought Dwining, as, returned from his visit to Sir John Ramorny, he added the gold he had received for his various services to the mass of his treasure; and having gloated over the whole for a minute or two, turned the key on his concealed treasure-house, and walked forth on his visits to his patients, yielding the wall to every man whom he met, and bowing and doffing his bonnet to the poorest burgher that owned a petty booth, nay, to the artificers who gained their precarious bread by the labour of their welked hands.

"Caitiffs," was the thought of his heart, while he did such obeisance, "base, sodden-witted mechanics! did you know what this key could disclose, what foul weather from Heaven would prevent your unbonneting? what putrid kennel in your wretched hamlet, would be disgusting enough to make you scruple to fall down and worship the owner of such wealth? But I will make you feel my power, though it suits my humour to hide the source of it. I will be an incubus to your city, since you have rejected me as a magistrate. Like the nightmare, I will hag-ride ye, yet remain invisible myself, —This miserable Ramorny, too, he who, in losing his hand. has, like a poor artisan, lost the only valuable part of his frame, *he* heaps insulting language on me, as if any thing which *he* can say had power to chafe a constant mind like mine! Yet while he calls me rogue, villain, and slave, he acts as wisely as if he should amuse himself by pulling hairs out of my head, while my hand had hold of his heart-strings. Every insult I can pay back instantly by a pang of bodily pain or mental agony—and—he! he!—I run no long accounts with his knighthood, that must be allowed."

While the mediciner was thus indulging his diabolical musing, and passing, in his creeping manner, along the street, the cry of females was heard behind him.

"Ay, there he is, Our Lady be praised!—there is the most helpful man in Perth," said one voice.

"They may speak of knights and kings for redressing wrongs, as they call it—but give me worthy Master Dwining the pottercarrier, cummers," replied another.

At the same moment the leech was surrounded, and taken hold of by the speakers, good women of the Fair City.

"How now—what's the matter?" said Dwining, "whose cow has calved?"

"There is no calving in the case," said one of the women, "but a poor fatherless wean dying; so come awa' wi' you, for our trust is constant in you, as Bruce said to Donald of the Isles."

"*Opiferque per orbem dicor*," said Henbane Dwining. "What is the child dying of?"

"The croup—the croup," screamed one of the gossips; "the innocent is rouping like a corbie."

"*Cynanche trachealis*—that disease makes brief work. Show me the house instantly," continued the mediciner, who was in the habit of exercising his profession liberally, not-withstanding his natural avarice, and humanely, in spite of his natural malignity. As we can suspect him of no better principle, his motive most probably may have been vanity and the love of his art.

He would nevertheless have declined giving his attendance in the present case, had he known whither the kind gossips were conducting him, in time sufficient to frame an apology. But ere he guessed where he was going the leech was hurried into the house of the late Oliver Proudfute, from which he heard the chant of the women, as they swathed and dressed the corpse of the umquhile Bonnet-maker, for the ceremony of next morning; of which chant, the following verses may be received as a modern imitation.

I

Viewless Essence, thin and bare,
Wellnigh melted into air ;
Still with fondness hovering near
The earthly form thou once didst wear;

2

Pause upon thy pinion's flight,
Be thy course to left or right ;
Be thou doom'd to soar or sink,
Pause upon the awful brink.

3

To avenge the deed expelling
Thee untimely from thy dwelling,
Mystic force thou shalt retain
O'er the blood and o'er the brain.

4

When the form thou shalt espy
That darken'd on thy closing eye ;
When the footstep thou shalt hear,
That thrill'd upon thy dying ear ;

5

Then strange sympathies shall wake,
The flesh shall thrill, the nerves shall quake
The wounds renew their clotter'd flood,
And every drop cry blood for blood !

Hardened as he was, the physician felt reluctance to pass the threshold of the man to whose death he had been so directly, though, so far as the individual was concerned, mistakingly accessary.

"Let me pass on, women," he said, "my art can only help the living—the dead are past our power."

"Nay, but your patient is up stairs—the youngest orphan——"

Dwining was compelled to go into the house. But he was surprised, when, the instant he stepped over the threshold, the gossips, who were busied with the dead body, stinted suddenly in their song, while one said to the others,—

"In God's name, who entered?—that was a large gout of blood!"

"Not so," said another voice, "it is a drop of the liquid balm."

"Nay, cummer, it was blood—Again I say, who entered the house even now?"

One looked out from the apartment into the little entrance, where Dwining, under pretence of not distinctly seeing the trap-ladder by which he was to ascend into the upper part of this house of lamentation, was delaying his progress purposely, disconcerted with what had reached him of the conversation.

"Nay, it is only worthy Master Henbane Dwining," answered one of the sibyls.

"Only Master Dwining?" replied the one who had first spoken, in a tone of acquiescence; "our best helper in need? —then it must have been balm sure enough."

"Nay," said the other, "it may have been blood neverthe-less—for the leech, look you, when the body was found, was commanded by the magistrates to probe the wound with his instruments, and how could the poor dead corpse know that that was done with good purpose?"

"Ay, truly, cummer; and as poor gossip Oliver often mistook friends for enemies while he was in life, his judgment cannot be thought to have mended now."

Dwining heard no more, being now forced up stairs into a species of garret, where Magdalen sat on her widowed bed, clasping to her bosom her infant, which, already black in the face, and uttering the gasping crowing sound, which gives the popular name to the complaint, seemed on the point of rendering up its brief existence. A Dominican monk sat near the bed, holding the other child in his arms, and seeming from time to time to speak a word or two of spiritual consolation, or intermingle some observation on the child's disorder.

The mediciner cast upon the good father a single glance, filled with that ineffable disdain which men of science entertain against interlopers. His own aid was instant and efficacious ; he snatched the child from the despairing mother, stripped its throat, and opened a vein, which, as it bled freely, relieved the little patient instantaneously. In a brief space every dangerous symptom disappeared, and Dwining, having bound up the vein, replaced the infant in the arms of the half distracted mother.

The poor woman's distress for her husband's loss, which had been suspended during the extremity of the child's danger, now returned on Magdalen with the force of an augmented torrent, which has borne down the dam-dike that for a while interrupted its waves.

" Oh, learned sir," she said, " you see a poor woman of her that you once knew a richer—But the hands that restored this bairn to my arms must not leave this house empty. Generous, kind Master Dwining, accept of his beads—they are made of ebony and silver—he aye liked to have his things as handsome as any gentleman—and liker he was in all his ways to a gentleman than any one of his standing, and even so came of it."

With these words, in a mute passion of grief she pressed to her breast and to her lips the chaplet of her deceased husband, and proceeded to thrust it into Dwining's hands.

" Take it," she said, " for the love of one who loved you well.—Ah ! he used ever to say, if ever man could be brought back from the brink of the grave, it must be by Master Dwining's guidance.—And his ain bairn is brought back this blessed day, and he is lying there stark and stiff, and kens naething of its health and sickness ! O, woe is me, and wala wa !—But take the beads, and think on his puir soul, as you put them through your fingers ; he will be freed from purgatory the sooner that good people pray to assoilzie him."

" Take back your beads, cummer—I know no legerdemain —can do no conjuring tricks," said the mediciner, who, more moved than perhaps his rugged nature had anticipated, endeavoured to avoid receiving the ill-omened gift. But his last words gave offence to the churchman, whose presence he had not recollected when he uttered them.

"How now, Sir Leech!" said the Dominican; "do you call prayers for the dead juggling tricks? I know that Chaucer, the English Maker, says of you mediciners, that your study is but little on the Bible. Our mother, the Church, hath nodded of late, but her eyes are now opened to discern friends from foes; and be well assured——"

"Nay, reverend father," said Dwining, "you take me at too great advantage. I said I could do no miracles, and was about to add, that as the church certainly could work such conclusions, those rich beads should be deposited in your hands, to be applied as they may best benefit the soul of the deceased."

He dropped the beads into the Dominican's hand, and escaped from the house of mourning.

"This was a strangely timed visit," he said to himself, when he got safe out of doors. "I hold such things cheap as any can; yet, though it is but a silly fancy, I am glad I saved the squalling child's life.—But I must to my friend Smotherwell, whom I have no doubt to bring to my purpose in the matter of Bonthron; and thus on this occasion I shall save two lives, and have destroyed only one."

CHAPTER XXIII

Lo! where he lies embalmed in gore,
His wound to Heaven cries;
The floodgates of his blood implore
For vengeance from the skies.
URANUS AND PSYCHE.

THE High Church of St. John in Perth, being that of the patron saint of the burgh, had been selected by the Magistrates as that in which the community was likely to have most fair play for the display of the ordeal. The churches and convents of the Dominicans, Carthusians, and others of the regular clergy, had been highly endowed by the king and nobles, and therefore it was the universal cry of the city-council, that "their ain good auld St. John," of whose good graces they thought themselves sure, ought to be fully confided in, and preferred to the new patrons, for whom the Dominicans, Carthusians, Carmelites, and others, had founded newer seats around the Fair City. The disputes between the regular and secular clergy added to the jealousy which dictated this choice of the spot in which Heaven was to display a species of miracle, upon a direct appeal to the divine decision in a case of doubtful guilt; and the town-clerk was as anxious that the church of St. John should be preferred, as if there had been a faction in the body of saints for and against the interests of the beautiful town of Perth.

Many, therefore, were the petty intrigues entered into and disconcerted, for the purpose of fixing on the church. But the Magistrates, considering it as a matter touching in a close degree the honour of the city, determined, with judicious confidence in the justice and impartiality of their patron, to confide the issue to the influence of St. John.

It was, therefore, after high mass had been performed, with the greatest solemnity of which circumstances rendered the ceremony capable, and after the most repeated and fervent prayers had been offered to Heaven by the crowded assembly, that preparations were made for appealing to the direct judgment of Heaven on the mysterious murder of the unfortunate Bonnet-maker.

The scene presented that effect of imposing solemnity, which the rites of the Catholic church are so well qualified to produce. The eastern window, richly and variously painted, streamed down a torrent of chequered light upon the high altar. On the bier placed before it were stretched the mortal remains of the murdered man, his arms folded on his breast, and his palms joined together, with the fingers pointed upwards, as if the senseless clay was itself appealing to Heaven for vengeance against those who had violently divorced the immortal spirit from its mangled tenement.

Close to the bier was placed the throne, which supported Robert of Scotland, and his brother Albany. The Prince sat upon a lower stool, beside his father; an arrangement which occasioned some observation, as Albany's seat being little distinguished from that of the King, the heir-apparent, though of full age, seemed to be degraded beneath his uncle in the sight of the assembled people of Perth. The bier was so placed, as to leave the view of the body it sustained open to the greater part of the multitude assembled in the church.

At the head of the bier stood the Knight of Kinfauns, the challenger, and at the foot the young Earl of Crawford, as representing the defendant. The evidence of the Duke of Rothsay in expurgation, as it was termed, of Sir John Ramorny, had exempted him from the necessity of attendance as a party subjected to the ordeal; and his illness served as a reason for his remaining at home. His household, including those who, though immediately in waiting upon Sir John, were accounted the Prince's domestics, and had not yet received their dismissal, amounted to eight or ten persons, most of them esteemed men of profligate habits, and who might therefore be deemed capable, in the riot of a festival evening, of committing the slaughter of the Bonnet-maker. They were drawn up in a row on the left side of the church and wore a species of white cassock, resembling the dress of a penitentiary. All eyes being bent on them, several of this band seemed so much disconcerted, as to excite among the spectators strong prepossessions of their guilt. The real murderer had a countenance incapable of betraying him,— a sullen, dark look, which neither the feast nor wine-cup could enliven, and which the peril of discovery and death could not render dejected.

We have already noticed the posture of the dead body. The face was bare, as were the breast and arms. The rest of the corpse was shrouded in a winding-sheet of the finest linen, so that, if blood should flow from any place which was covered, it could not fail to be instantly manifest.

High mass having been performed, followed by a solemn invocation to the Deity, that he would be pleased to protect the innocent, and make known the guilty, Eviot, Sir John Ramorny's page, was summoned to undergo the ordeal.[1] He advanced with an ill-assured step. Perhaps he thought his internal consciousness that Bonthron must have been the assassin, might be sufficient to implicate him in the murder, though he was not directly accessory to it. He paused before the bier; and his voice faltered, as he swore by all that was created in seven days, and seven nights, by heaven, by hell, by his part of paradise, and by the God and author of all, that he was free and sackless of the bloody deed done upon the corpse before which he stood, and on whose breast he made the sign of the cross, in evidence of the appeal. No consequences ensued. The body remained stiff as before; the curdled wounds gave no sign of blood.

The citizens looked on each other with faces of blank

[1] Note XIV.—Ordeal by Fire.

disappointment. They had persuaded themselves of Eviot's guilt; and their suspicions had been confirmed by his irresolute manner. Their surprise at his escape was therefore extreme. The other followers of Ramorny took heart, and advanced to take the oath, with a boldness which increased, as one by one they performed the ordeal, and were declared, by the voice of the judges, free and innocent of every suspicion attaching to them on account of the death of Oliver Proudfute.

But there was one individual, who did not partake that increasing confidence. The name of "Bonthron—Bonthron!" sounded three times through the aisles of the church; but he who owned it acknowledged the call no otherwise than by a sort of shuffling motion with his feet, as if he had been suddenly affected with a fit of the palsy.

"Speak, dog," whispered Eviot, "or prepare for a dog's death!"

But the murderer's brain was so much disturbed by the sight before him, that the judges, beholding his deportment, doubted whether to ordain him to be dragged before the bier, or to pronounce judgment in default; and it was not until he was asked for the last time, whether he would submit to the ordeal, that he answered, with his usual brevity,—

"I will not;—what do I know what juggling tricks may be practised to take a poor man's life?—I offer the combat to any man who says I harmed that dead body."

And, according to usual form, he threw his glove upon the floor of the church.

Henry Smith stepped forward, amidst the murmured applauses of his fellow-citizens, which even the august presence could not entirely suppress; and lifting the ruffian's glove, which he placed in his bonnet, laid down his own in the usual form, as a gage of battle. But Bonthron raised it not.

"He is no match for me," growled the savage, "nor fit to lift my glove. I follow the Prince of Scotland, in attending on his Master of Horse. This fellow is a wretched mechanic."

Here the Prince interrupted him. "Thou follow *me*, caitiff! I discharge thee from my service on the spot.— Take him in hand, Smith, and beat him as thou didst never thump anvil!—The villain is both guilty and recreant. It sickens me even to look at him; and if my royal father will be ruled by me, he will give the parties two handsome Scottish axes, and we will see which of them turns out the best fellow before the day is half an hour older."

This was readily assented to by the Earl of Crawford and Sir Patrick Charteris, the god-fathers of the parties, who, as the combatants were men of inferior rank, agreed that they should fight in steel caps, buff jackets, and with axes; and that as soon as they could be prepared for the combat.

The lists were appointed in the Skinners' Yards,[1] a neighbouring space of ground, occupied by the corporation from which it had the name, and who quickly cleared a space of about thirty feet by twenty-five, for the combatants. Thither thronged the nobles, priests, and commons,—all excepting the old King, who, detesting such scenes of blood, retired to his residence, and devolved the charge of the field upon the Earl of Errol, Lord High Constable, to whose office it more particularly belonged. The Duke of Albany watched the whole proceeding with a close and wary eye. His nephew gave the scene the heedless degree of notice which corresponded with his character.

When the combatants appeared in the lists, nothing could be more striking than the contrast betwixt the manly, cheerful countenance of the Smith, whose sparkling bright eye seemed already beaming with the victory he hoped for, and the sullen, downcast aspect of the brutal Bonthron, who looked as if he were some obscene bird, driven into sunshine out of the shelter of its darksome haunts. They made oath severally, each to the truth of his quarrel; a ceremony which Henry Gow performed with serene and manly confidence—Bonthron with a dogged resolution, which induced the Duke of Rothsay to say to the High Constable, "Didst thou ever, my dear Errol, behold such a mixture of malignity, cruelty, and I think fear, as in that fellow's countenance?"

"He is not comely," said the Earl, "but a powerful knave, as I have seen."

"I'll gage a hogshead of wine with you, my good lord, that he loses the day. Henry the armourer is as strong as he, and much more active. And then look at his bold bearing! There is something in that other fellow that is

[1] Note XV.—Skinners' Yards.

loathsome to look upon. Let them yoke presently, my dear Constable, for I am sick of beholding him."

The High Constable then addressed the widow, who, in her deep weeds, and having her children still beside her, occupied a chair within the lists :—" Woman, do you willingly accept of this man, Henry the Smith, to do battle as your champion in this cause?"

"I do—I do, most willingly," answered Magdalen Proudfute; "and may the blessing of God and St. John give him strength and fortune, since he strikes for the orphan and fatherless!"

"Then I pronounce this a fenced field of battle," said the Constable aloud. "Let no one dare, upon peril of his life, to interrupt this combat by word, speech, or look.—Sound trumpets, and fight, combatants!"

The trumpets flourished, and the combatants, advancing from the opposite ends of the lists, with a steady and even pace, looked at each other attentively, well skilled in judging from the motion of the eye, the direction in which a blow was meditated. They halted opposite to, and within reach of, each other, and in turn made more than one feint to strike, in order to ascertain the activity and vigilance of the opponent. At length, whether weary of these manœuvres, or fearing lest in a contest so conducted, his unwieldy strength would be foiled by the activity of the Smith, Bonthron heaved up his axe for a downright blow, adding the whole strength of his sturdy arms to the weight of the weapon in its descent. The Smith, however, avoided the stroke by stepping aside ; for it was too forcible to be controlled by any guard which he could have interposed. Ere Bonthron recovered guard, Henry struck him a sideling blow on the steel head-piece, which prostrated him on the ground.

"Confess, or die," said the victor, placing his foot on the body of the vanquished, and holding to his throat the point of the axe, which terminated in a spike or poniard.

"I will confess," said the villain, glaring wildly upward on the sky. "Let me rise."

"Not till you have yielded," said Harry Smith.

"I do yield," again murmured Bonthron, and Henry proclaimed aloud that his antagonist was defeated.

The Dukes of Rothsay and Albany, the High Constable, and the Dominican Prior, now entered the lists, and addressing Bonthron, demanded if he acknowledged himself vanquished.

"I do," answered the miscreant.

"And guilty of the murder of Oliver Proudfute?"

"I am—but I mistook him for another."

"And whom didst thou intend to slay?" said the Prior. "Confess, my son, and merit thy pardon in another world; for with this thou hast little more to do."

"I took the slain man," answered the discomfited combatant, "for him whose hand has struck me down, whose foot now presses me."

"Blessed be the saints!" said the Prior; "now all those who doubt the virtue of the holy ordeal, may have their eyes opened to their error. Lo, he is trapped in the snare which he laid for the guiltless."

"I scarce ever saw the man before," said the Smith. "I never did wrong to him or his.—Ask him, an it please your reverence, why he should have thought of slaying me treacherously."

"It is a fitting question," answered the Prior.—"Give glory where it is due, my son, even though it is manifested by thy shame. For what reason wouldst thou have waylaid this armourer, who says he never wronged thee?"

"He had wronged him whom I served," answered Bonthron; "and I meditated the deed by his command."

"By whose command?" asked the Prior.

Bonthron was silent for an instant, then growled out,—"He is too mighty for me to name."

"Hearken, my son," said the churchman; "tarry but a brief hour, and the mighty and the mean of this earth shall to thee alike be empty sounds. The sledge is even now preparing to drag thee to the place of execution. Therefore, son, once more I charge thee to consult thy soul's weal by glorifying Heaven, and speaking the truth. Was it thy master, Sir John Ramorny, that stirred thee to so foul a deed?"

"No," answered the prostrate villain, "it was a greater than he." And at the same time he pointed with his finger to the Prince.

"Wretch!" said the astonished Duke of Rothsay; "do you dare to hint that *I* was your instigator?"

"You yourself, my lord," answered the unblushing ruffian.

"Die in thy falsehood, accursed slave!" said the Prince; and, drawing his sword, he would have pierced his calumniator, had not the Lord High Constable interposed with word and action.

"Your Grace must forgive my discharging mine office—this caitiff must be delivered into the hands of the executioner. He is unfit to be dealt with by any other, much less by your Highness."

"What! noble Earl," said Albany, aloud, and with much real or affected emotion, "would you let the dog pass alive from hence, to poison the people's ears with false accusations against the Prince of Scotland?—I say, cut him to mammocks upon the spot!"

"Your Highness will pardon me," said the Earl of Errol; "I must protect him till his doom is executed."

"Then let him be gagged instantly," said Albany.—"And you, my royal nephew, why stand you there fixed in astonishment? Call your resolution up—speak to the prisoner—swear—protest by all that is sacred that you knew not of this felon deed.—See how the people look on each other, and whisper apart! My life on't that this lie spreads faster than any gospel truth.—Speak to them, royal kinsman, no matter what you say, so you be constant in denial."

"What, sir," said Rothsay, starting from his pause of surprise and mortification, and turning haughtily towards his uncle; "would you have me gage my royal word against that of an abject recreant? Let those who *can* believe the son of their sovereign, the descendant of Bruce, capable of laying ambush for the life of a poor mechanic, enjoy the pleasure of thinking the villain's tale true."

"That will not I for one," said the Smith, bluntly. "I never did aught but what was in honour towards his royal Grace the Duke of Rothsay, and never received unkindness from him, in word, look, or deed; and I cannot think he would have given aim to such base practice."

"Was it in honour that you threw his Highness from the ladder in Curfew Street, upon St. Valentine's Eve?" said Bonthron; "or think you the favour was received kindly or unkindly?"

This was so boldly said, and seemed so plausible, that it shook the Smith's opinion of the Prince's innocence.

"Alas, my lord," said he, looking sorrowfully towards Rothsay, "could your Highness seek an innocent fellow's life for doing his duty by a helpless maiden?—I would rather have died in these lists, than live to hear it said of the Bruce's heir!"

"Thou art a good fellow, Smith," said the Prince; "but

I cannot expect thee to judge more wisely than others.—
Away with that convict to the gallows, and gibbet him
alive an you will, that he may speak falsehood and spread
scandal on us to the last prolonged moment of his existence!"

So saying, the Prince turned away from the lists, dis-
daining to notice the gloomy looks cast towards him, as the
crowd made slow and reluctant way for him to pass, and
expressing neither surprise nor displeasure at a deep hollow
murmur, or groan, which accompanied his retreat. Only
a few of his own immediate followers attended him from
the field, though various persons of distinction had come
there in his train. Even the lower class of citizens ceased
to follow the unhappy Prince, whose former indifferent
reputation had exposed him to so many charges of impropriety and levity, and around whom there seemed now
darkening suspicions of the most atrocious nature.

He took his slow and thoughtful way to the church of
the Dominicans; but the ill news, which fly proverbially
fast, had reached his father's place of retirement before he
himself appeared. On entering the palace and enquiring
for the King, the Duke of Rothsay was surprised to be
informed that he was in deep consultation with the Duke
of Albany, who, mounting on horseback as the Prince left
the lists, had reached the convent before him. He was about
to use the privilege of his rank and birth, to enter the royal
apartment, when MacLewis, the commander of the guard
of Brandanes, gave him to understand, in the most respectful
terms, that he had special instructions which forbade his
admittance.

"Go at least, MacLewis, and let them know that I wait
their pleasure," said the Prince. "If my uncle desires to
have the credit of shutting the father's apartment against
the son, it will gratify him to know that I am attending in the
outer hall like a lackey."

"May it please you," said MacLewis, with hesitation, "if
your Highness would consent to retire just now, and to
wait a while in patience, I will send to acquaint you when the
Duke of Albany goes; and I doubt not that his Majesty will
then admit your Grace to his presence. At present, your
Highness must forgive me,—it is impossible you can have
access."

"I understand you, MacLewis; but go, nevertheless, and
obey my commands."

The officer went accordingly, and returned with a message, that the King was indisposed, and on the point of retiring to his private chamber; but that the Duke of Albany would presently wait upon the Prince of Scotland.

It was, however, a full half hour ere the Duke of Albany appeared,—a period of time which Rothsay spent partly in moody silence, and partly in idle talk with MacLewis and the Brandanes, as the levity or irritability of his temper obtained the ascendant.

At length the Duke came, and with him the Lord High Constable, whose countenance expressed much sorrow and embarrassment.

"Fair kinsman," said the Duke of Albany, "I grieve to say that it is my royal brother's opinion, that it will be best, for the honour of the royal family, that your Royal Highness do restrict yourself for a time to the seclusion of the High Constable's lodgings,[1] and accept of the noble Earl here present for your principal, if not sole companion, until the scandals which have been this day spread abroad, shall be refuted, or forgotten."

"How is this, my Lord of Errol?" said the Prince, in astonishment. "Is your house to be my jail, and is your lordship to be my jailer?"

"The saints forbid, my lord," said the Earl of Errol; "but it is my unhappy duty to obey the commands of your father, by considering your Royal Highness for some time as being under my ward."

"The Prince—the heir of Scotland, under the ward of the High Constable!—What reason can be given for this? Is the blighting speech of a convicted recreant of strength sufficient to tarnish my royal escutcheon?"

"While such accusations are not refuted and denied, my kinsman," said the Duke of Albany, "they will contaminate that of a monarch."

"Denied, my lord!" exclaimed the Prince; "by whom are they asserted? save by a wretch too infamous, even by his own confession, to be credited for a moment, though a beggar's character, not a prince's, were impeached.—Fetch him hither,—let the rack be shown to him; you will soon hear him retract the calumny which he dared to assert."

"The gibbet has done its work too surely to leave Bonthron

sensible to the rack," said the Duke of Albany. "He has been executed an hour since."

"And why such haste, my lord?" said the Prince; "know you it looks as if there were practice in it, to bring a stain on my name?"

"The custom is universal—the defeated combatant in the ordeal of battle is instantly transferred from the lists to the gallows.—And yet, fair kinsman," continued the Duke of Albany, "if you had boldly and strongly denied the imputation, I would have judged right to keep the wretch alive for further investigation; but as your Highness was silent, I deemed it best to stifle the scandal in the breath of him that uttered it."

"Saint Mary, my lord, but this is too insulting! Do you, my uncle and kinsman, suppose me guilty of prompting such an useless and unworthy action, as that which the slave confessed?"

"It is not for me to bandy question with your Highness; otherwise I would ask, whether you also mean to deny the scarce less unworthy, though less bloody attack, upon the house in Couvrefew Street?—Be not angry with me, kinsman; but, indeed, your sequestering yourself for some brief space from the court, were it only during the King's residence in this city, where so much offence has been given, is imperiously demanded."

Rothsay paused when he heard this exhortation; and looking at the Duke in a very marked manner, replied,—

"Uncle, you are a good huntsman. You have pitched your toils with much skill; but you would have been foiled, notwithstanding, had not the stag rushed among the nets of free-will. God speed you, and may you have the profit by this matter which your measures deserve. Say to my father, I obey his arrest.—My Lord High Constable, I wait only your pleasure to attend you to your lodgings. Since I am to lie in ward, I could not have desired a kinder or more courteous warden."

The interview between the uncle and nephew being thus concluded, the Prince retired with the Earl of Errol to his apartments; the citizens whom they met in the streets passing to the further side, when they observed the Duke of Rothsay, to escape the necessity of saluting one whom they had been taught to consider as a ferocious as well as unprincipled libertine. The constable's lodgings received the owner and his princely guest, both glad to leave the streets, yet neither feeling easy in the situation which they occupied with regard to each other within doors.

We must return to the lists after the combat had ceased, and when the nobles had withdrawn. The crowds were now separated into two distinct bodies. That which made the smallest in number, was at the same time the most distinguished for respectability, consisting of the better class of inhabitants of Perth, who were congratulating the successful champion, and each other, upon the triumphant conclusion to which they had brought their feud with the courtiers. The magistrates were so much elated on the occasion, that they entreated Sir Patrick Charteris's acceptance of a collation in the Town-hall. To this, Henry, the hero of the day, was of course invited, or he was rather commanded to attend. He listened to the summons with great embarrassment, for it may be readily believed his heart was with Catharine Glover. But the advice of his father Simon decided him. That veteran citizen had a natural and becoming deference for the magistracy of the Fair City; he entertained a high estimation of all honours which flowed from such a source, and thought that his intended son-in-law would do wrong not to receive them with gratitude.

"Thou must not think to absent thyself from such a solemn occasion, son Henry," was his advice. "Sir Patrick Charteris is to be there himself, and I think it will be a rare occasion for thee to gain his good-will. It is like he may order of thee a new suit of harness; and I myself heard worthy Bailie Craigdallie say, there was a talk of furbishing up the city's armoury. Thou must not neglect the good trade, now that thou takest on thee an expensive family."

"Tush, father Glover," answered the embarrassed victor, "I lack no custom—and thou knowest there is Catharine, who may wonder at my absence, and have her ear abused once more by tales of glee-maidens, and I wot not what."

"Fear not for that," said the Glover, "but go, like an obedient burgess, where thy betters desire to have thee. I do not deny that it will cost thee some trouble to make thy peace with Catharine about this duel; for she thinks herself wiser in such matters than King and Council, Kirk and Canons, Provost and Bailies. But I will take up the quarrel with her myself, and will so work for thee, that though she may receive thee to-morrow with somewhat of a chiding, it shall melt into tears and smiles, like an April morning, that begins with a mild shower. Away with thee then, my son, and be constant to the time, to-morrow morning after mass."

The Smith, though reluctantly, was obliged to defer to the reasoning of his proposed father-in-law, and, once determined to accept the honour destined for him by the fathers of the city, he extricated himself from the crowd, and hastened home to put on his best apparel; in which he presently afterwards repaired to the Council-house, where the ponderous oak table seemed to bend under the massy dishes of choice Tay salmon, and delicious sea-fish from Dundee, being the dainties which the fasting season permitted, whilst neither wine, ale, nor metheglin, were wanting to wash them down. The waits, or minstrels of the burgh, played during the repast, and in the intervals of the music, one of them recited with emphasis, a long poetical account of the battle of Blackearn-side, fought by Sir William Wallace, and his redoubted captain and friend, Thomas of Longueville, against the English general, Seward—a theme perfectly familiar to all the guests, who, nevertheless, more tolerant than their descendants, listened as if it had all the zest of novelty. It was complimentary to the ancestor of the Knight of Kinfauns doubtless, and to other Perthshire families, in passages which the audience applauded vociferously, whilst they pledged each other in mighty draughts, to the memory of the heroes who had fought by the side of the Champion of Scotland. The health of Henry Wynd was quaffed with repeated shouts, and the Provost announced publicly, that the magistrates were consulting how they might best invest him with some distinguished privilege, or honorary reward, to show how highly his fellow-citizens valued his courageous exertions.

"Nay, take it not thus, an it like your worships," said the Smith, with his usual blunt manner, "lest men say that valour must be rare in Perth, when they reward a man for fighting for the right of a forlorn widow. I am sure there are many scores of stout burghers in the town who would have done this day's dargue, as well or better than I. For, in good sooth, I ought to have cracked yonder fellow's head-piece, like an earthen pipkin—ay, and would have done it too, if it had not been one which I myself tempered for Sir John Ramorny. But an the Fair City think my service of any worth, I will conceive it far more than acquitted by any aid which you may afford from the Common Good, to the support of the widow Magdalen and her poor orphans."

"That may well be done," said Sir Patrick Charteris, "and yet leave the Fair City rich enough to pay her debts to Henry Wynd, of which every man of us is a better judge than himself, who is blinded with an unavailing nicety, which men call modesty.—And if the burgh be too poor for this, the Provost will bear his share. The Rover's golden angels have not all taken flight yet."

The beakers were now circulated, under the name of a cup of comfort to the widow, and anon flowed around once more to the happy memory of the murdered Oliver, now so bravely avenged. In short, it was a feast so jovial, that all agreed nothing was wanting to render it perfect, but the presence of the Bonnet-maker himself, whose calamity had occasioned the meeting, and who had usually furnished the standing jest at such festive assemblies. Had his attendance been possible, it was dryly observed by Bailie Craigdallie, he would certainly have claimed the success of the day, and vouched himself the avenger of his own murder.

At the sound of the vesper bell the company broke up, some of the graver sort going to evening prayers, where, with half-shut eyes and shining countenances, they made a most orthodox and edifying portion of a Lenten congregation; others to their own homes, to tell over the occurrences of the fight and feast, for the information of the family circle; and some, doubtless, to the licensed freedoms of some tavern, the door of which Lent did not keep so close shut as the forms of the Church required. Henry returned to the Wynd, warm with the good wine and the applause of his fellow-citizens, and fell asleep to dream of perfect happiness and Catharine Glover.

We have said that when the combat was decided, the spectators were divided into two bodies. Of these, when the more respectable portion attended the victor in joyous procession, much the greater number, or what might be termed the rabble, waited upon the subdued and sentenced Bonthron, who was travelling in a different direction, and for a very opposite purpose. Whatever may be thought of the comparative attractions of the house of mourning and of feasting under other circumstances, there can be little doubt which would draw most visitors, when the question is, whether we would witness miseries which we are not to share, or festivities of which we are not to partake. Accordingly, the tumbril in which the criminal was conveyed to execution, was attended by far the greater proportion of the inhabitants of Perth.

A friar was seated in the same car with the murderer, to whom he did not hesitate to repeat, under the seal of confession, the same false asseveration which he had made upon the place of combat, which charged the Duke of Rothsay with being director of the ambuscade by which the unfortunate Bonnet-maker had suffered. The same falsehood he disseminated among the crowd, averring, with unblushing effrontery, to those who were nighest to the car, that he owed his death to his having been willing to execute the Duke of Rothsay's pleasure. For a time he repeated these words, sullenly and doggedly, in the manner of one reciting a task, or a liar who endeavours by reiteration to obtain a credit for his words, which he is internally sensible they do not deserve. But when he lifted up his eyes, and beheld in the distance the black outline of a gallows, at least forty feet high, with its ladder and its fatal cord, rising against the horizon, he became suddenly silent, and the friar could observe that he trembled very much.

"Be comforted, my son," said the good priest, "you have confessed the truth, and received absolution. Your penitence will be accepted according to your sincerity ; and though you have been a man of bloody hands and cruel heart, yet, by the Church's prayers, you shall be in due time assoilzied from the penal fires of purgatory."

These assurances were calculated rather to augment than to diminish the terrors of the culprit, who was agitated by doubts whether the mode suggested for his preservation from death would to a certainty be effectual, and some suspicion whether there was really any purpose of employing them in his favour ; for he knew his master well enough to be aware of the indifference with which he would sacrifice one, who might on some future occasion be a dangerous evidence against him.

His doom, however, was sealed, and there was no escaping from it. They slowly approached the fatal tree, which was erected on a bank by the river's side, about half a mile from the walls of the city ; a site chosen that the body of the wretch, which was to remain food for the carrion crows, might be seen from a distance in every direction. Here the priest delivered Bonthron to the executioner, by whom he was assisted up the ladder, and to all appearance despatched according to the usual forms of the law. He seemed to struggle for life for a minute, but soon after hung still and inanimate. The executioner, after remaining upon duty for more than half an hour, as if to permit the last spark of life to be extinguished, announced to the admirers of such spectacles, that the irons for the permanent suspension of the carcass not having been got ready, the concluding ceremony of disembowelling the dead body, and attaching it finally to the gibbet, would be deferred till the next morning at sunrise.

Notwithstanding the early hour which he had named, Master Smotherwell had a reasonable attendance of rabble at the place of execution, to see the final proceedings of justice with its victim. But great was the astonishment and resentment of these amateurs, to find that the dead body had been removed from the gibbet. They were not, however, long at a loss to guess the cause of its disappearance. Bonthron had been the follower of a Baron whose estates lay in Fife, and was himself a native of that province. What was more natural than that some of the Fife men, whose boats were frequently plying on the river, should have clandestinely removed the body of their countryman from the place of public shame? The crowd vented their rage against Smotherwell, for not completing his job on the preceding evening; and had not he and his assistant betaken themselves to a boat, and escaped across the Tay, they would have run some risk of being pelted to death. The event, however, was too much in the spirit of the times to be much wondered at. Its real cause we shall explain in the following chapter.

CHAPTER XXIV

"Let gallows gape for dogs, let men go free."
                                        Henry V.

THE incidents of a narrative of this kind must be adapted to each other, as the wards of a key must tally accurately with those of the lock to which it belongs. The reader, however gentle, will not hold himself obliged to rest satisfied with the mere fact that such and such occurrences took place, which is, generally speaking, all that in ordinary life he can know of what is passing around him; but he is desirous, while reading for amusement, of knowing the interior movements occasioning the course of events. This is a legitimate and reasonable curiosity; for every man hath a right to open and examine the mechanism of his own watch, put together for his proper use, although he is not permitted to pry into the interior of the timepiece, which, for general information, is displayed on the town-steeple.

It would be, therefore, uncourteous to leave my readers under any doubt concerning the agency which removed the assassin Bonthron from the gallows; an event which some of the Perth citizens ascribed to the foul Fiend himself, while others were content to lay it upon the natural dislike of Bonthron's countrymen of Fife to see him hanging on the river side, as a spectacle dishonourable to their province.

About midnight succeeding the day when the execution had taken place, and while the inhabitants of Perth were deeply buried in slumber, three men, muffled in their cloaks, and bearing a dark lantern, descended the alleys of a garden which led from the house occupied by Sir John Ramorny, to the banks of the Tay, where a small boat lay moored to a landing-place, or little projecting pier. The wind howled in a low and melancholy manner through the leafless shrubs and bushes; and a pale moon *waded*, as it is termed in Scotland, amongst drifting clouds, which seemed to threaten rain. The three individuals entered the boat with great precaution, to escape observation. One of them was a tall powerful man; another short and bent downwards; the third middle-sized, and apparently younger than his companions, well made, and active. Thus much the imperfect light could discover. They seated themselves in the boat, and unmoored it from the pier.

"We must let her drift with the current till we pass the bridge, where the burghers still keep guard; and you know the proverb—A Perth arrow hath a perfect flight," said the most youthful of the party, who assumed the office of helmsman, and pushed the boat off from the pier; whilst the others took the oars, which were muffled, and rowed with all precaution, till they attained the middle of the river; they then ceased their efforts, lay upon their oars, and trusted to the steersman for keeping her in mid-channel.

In this manner they passed unnoticed or disregarded

beneath the stately Gothic arches of the old bridge, erected by the magnificent patronage of Robert Bruce in 1329, and carried away by an inundation in 1621. Although they heard the voices of a civic watch, which, since these disturbances commenced, had been nightly maintained in that important pass, no challenge was given; and when they were so far down the stream as to be out of hearing of these guardians of the night, they began to row, but still with precaution, and to converse, though in a low tone.

"You have found a new trade, comrade, since I left you," said one of the rowers to the other. "I left you engaged in tending a sick knight, and I find you employed in purloining a dead body from the gallows."

"A living body, so please your squirehood, Master Buncle; or else my craft hath failed of its purpose."

"So I am told, Master Pottercarrier; but saving your clerkship, unless you tell me your trick, I will take leave to doubt of its success."

"A simple toy, Master Buncle, not likely to please a genius so acute as that of your valiancie. Marry, thus it is. This suspension of the human body, which the vulgar call hanging, operates death by apoplexia,—that is, the blood being unable to return to the heart by the compression of the veins, it rushes to the brain, and the man dies. Also, and as an additional cause of dissolution, the lungs no longer receive the needful supply of the vital air, owing to the ligature of the cord around the thorax; and hence the patient perishes."

"I understand that well enough—But how is such a revulsion of blood to the brain to be prevented, Sir Mediciner?" said the third person, who was no other than Ramorny's page, Eviot.

"Marry, then," replied Dwining, "hang me the patient up in such fashion that the carotid arteries shall not be compressed, and the blood will not determine to the brain, and apoplexia will not take place; and again, if there be no ligature around the thorax, the lungs will be supplied with air, whether the man be hanging in the middle heaven, or standing on the firm earth."

"All this I conceive," said Eviot; "but how these precautions can be reconciled with the execution of the sentence of hanging, is what my dull brain cannot comprehend."

" Ah ! good youth, thy valiancie hath spoiled a fair wit. Hadst thou studied with me, thou shouldst have learned things more difficult than this. But here is my trick. I get me certain bandages, made of the same substance with your young valiancie's horse-girths, having especial care that they are of a kind which will not shrink on being strained, since that would spoil my experiment. One loop of this substance is drawn under each foot, and returns up either side of the leg to a cincture, with which it is united ; these cinctures are connected by divers straps down the breast and back, in order to divide the weight, and there are sundry other conveniences for easing the patient ; but the chief is this. The straps, or ligatures, are attached to a broad steel collar, curving outwards, and having a hook or two, for the better security of the halter, which the friendly executioner passes around that part of the machine, instead of applying it to the bare throat of the patient. Thus, when thrown off from the ladder, the sufferer will find himself suspended, not by his neck, if it please you, but by the steel circle which supports the loops in which his feet are placed, and on which his weight really rests, diminished a little by similar supports under each arm. Thus, neither vein nor windpipe being compressed, the man will breathe as free, and his blood, saving from fright and novelty of situation, will flow as temperately as your valiancie's, when you stand up in your stirrups to view a field of battle."

" By my faith, a quaint and rare device ! " quoth Buncle.

" Is it not ? " pursued the leech, " and well worth being known to such mounting spirits as your valiancies, since there is no knowing to what height Sir John Ramorny's pupils may arrive ; and if these be such, that it is necessary to descend from them by a rope, you may find my mode of management more convenient than the common practice. Marry, but you must be provided with a high-collared doublet, to conceal the ring of steel ; and above all, such a *bonus socius* as Smotherwell to adjust the noose."

" Base poison-vender," said Eviot, " men of our calling die on the field of battle ! "

" I will save the lesson, however," replied Buncle, " in case of some pinching occasion. —But what a night the bloody hangdog Bonthron must have had of it, dancing a pavise in mid air to the music of his own shackles, as the night wind swings him that way and this ! "

" It were an alms deed to leave him there," said Eviot ; " for his descent from the gibbet will but encourage him to new murders. He knows but two elements—drunkenness and bloodshed."

" Perhaps Sir John Ramorny might have been of your opinion," said Dwining ; " but it would first have been necessary to cut out the rogue's tongue, lest he had told strange tales from his airy height. And there are other reasons that it concerns not your valiancies to know. In truth, I myself have been generous in serving him, for the fellow is built as strong as Edinburgh Castle, and his anatomy would have matched any that is in the chirurgical hall of Padua.—But tell me, Master Buncle, what news bring you from the doughty Douglas ? "

" They may tell that know," said Buncle. " I am the dull ass that bears the message, and kens nought of its purport. The safer for myself perhaps. I carried letters from the Duke of Albany and from Sir John Ramorny to the Douglas, and he looked black as a northern tempest when he opened them—I brought them answers from the Earl, at which they smiled like the sun when the harvest storm is closing over him. Go to your Ephemerides, leech, and conjure the meaning out of that."

" Methinks I can do so without much cost of wit," said the chirurgeon ; " but yonder I see in the pale moonlight our dead-alive. Should he have screamed out to any chance passenger, it were a curious interruption to a night-journey to be hailed from the top of such a gallows as that.—Hark, methinks I do hear his groans amid the whistling of the wind and the creaking of the chains. So—fair and softly— make fast the boat with the grappling—and get out the casket with my matters—we would be better for a little fire, but the light might bring observation on us.—Come on, my men of valour, march warily, for we are bound for the gallows foot— Follow with the lantern—I trust the ladder has been left.

> ' Sing, three merry-men, and three merry-men,
>   And three merry-men are we,
> Thou on the land, and I on the sand,
>   And Jack on the gallows tree.' "

As they advanced to the gibbet, they could plainly hear groans, though uttered in a low tone. Dwining ventured to give a low cough once or twice, by way of signal ; but receiving no answer, "We had best make haste," said he to his companions, "for our friend must be *in extremis*, as he gives no answer to the signal which announces the arrival of help.— Come, let us to the gear. I will go up the ladder first and cut the rope. Do you two follow, one after another, and take fast hold of the body, so that he fall not when the halter is unloosed. Keep sure gripe, for which the bandages will afford you convenience. Bethink you, that though he plays an owl's part to-night, he hath no wings, and to fall out of a halter may be as dangerous as to fall into one."

While he spoke thus with sneer and gibe, he ascended the ladder, and having ascertained that the men-at-arms who followed him had the body in their hold, he cut the rope, and then gave his aid to support the almost lifeless form of the criminal.

By a skilful exertion of strength and address, the body of Bonthron was placed safely on the ground, and the faint, yet certain existence of life having been ascertained, it was thence transported to the river side, where, shrouded by the bank, the party might be best concealed from observation, while the leech employed himself in the necessary means of recalling animation, with which he had taken care to provide himself.

For this purpose he first freed the recovered person from his shackles, which the executioner had left unlocked on purpose, and at the same time disengaged the complicated envelopes and bandages by which he had been suspended. It was some time ere Dwining's efforts succeeded ; for in despite of the skill with which his machine had been constructed, the straps designed to support the body, had stretched so considerably as to occasion the sense of suffocation becoming extremely overpowering. But the address of the surgeon triumphed over all obstacles ; and after sneezing and stretching himself, with one or two brief convulsions, Bonthron gave decided proofs of reanimation, by arresting the hand of the operator as it was in the act of dropping strong waters on his breast and throat ; and, directing the bottle which contained them to his lips, he took, almost perforce, a considerable gulp of the contents.

" It is spiritual essence, double distilled," said the astonished operator, " and would blister the throat, and burn the stomach of any other man. But this extraordinary beast is so unlike all other human creatures, that I should not wonder if it brought him to the complete possession of his faculties."

Bonthron seemed to confirm this; he started with a strong convulsion, sat up, stared around, and indicated some consciousness of existence.

"Wine—wine," were the first words which he articulated.

The leech gave him a draught of medicated wine, mixed with water. He rejected it, under the dishonourable epithet of "kennel-washings," and again uttered the words—"Wine—wine."

"Nay, take it to thee, i' the devil's name," said the leech, "since none but he can judge of thy constitution."

A draught, long and deep enough to have discomposed the intellects of any other person, was found effectual in recalling those of Bonthron to a more perfect state; though he betrayed no recollection of where he was or what had befallen him, and in his brief and sullen manner, asked why he was brought to the river side at this time of night.

"Another frolic of the wild Prince, for drenching me as he did before—Nails and blood, but I would——"

"Hold thy peace," interrupted Eviot, "and be thankful, I pray you, if you have any thankfulness in you, that thy body is not crow's meat, and thy soul in a place where water is too scarce to duck thee."

"I begin to bethink me," said the ruffian; and raising the flask to his mouth, which he saluted with a long and hearty kiss, he set the empty bottle on the earth, dropped his head on his bosom, and seemed to muse for the purpose of arranging his confused recollections.

"We can abide the issue of his meditations no longer," said Dwining, "he will be better after he has slept.—Up, sir! you have been riding the air these some hours—try if the water be not an easier mode of conveyance.—Your valours must lend me a hand. I can no more lift this mass, than I could raise in my arms a slaughtered bull."

"Stand upright on thine own feet, Bonthron, now we have placed thee upon them," said Eviot.

"I cannot," answered the patient. "Every drop of blood tingles in my veins as if it had pin-points and my knees refuse to bear their burden. What can be the meaning of all this? This is some practice of thine, thou dog leech!"

"Ay, ay, so it is, honest Bonthron," said Dwining, "a practice thou shalt thank me for, when thou comest to learn it. In the meanwhile, stretch down in the stern of that boat, and let me wrap this cloak about thee." Assisted into the boat accordingly, Bonthron was deposited there as conveniently as things admitted of. He answered their attentions with one or two snorts resembling the grunt of a boar, who has got some food particularly agreeable to him.

"And now, Buncle," said the chirurgeon, "your valiant squireship knows your charge. You are to carry this lively cargo by the river to Newburgh, where you are to dispose of him as you wot of; meantime, here are his shackles and bandages, the marks of his confinement and liberation. Bind them up together, and fling them into the deepest pool you pass over; for, found in your possession, they might tell tales against us all. This low, light breath of wind from the west, will permit you to use a sail as soon as the light comes in, and you are tired of rowing.—Your other valiancy, Master Page Eviot, must be content to return to Perth with me a-foot, for here severs our fair company.—Take with thee the lantern, Buncle, for thou wilt require it more than we, and see thou send me back my flasket."

As the pedestrians returned to Perth, Eviot expressed his belief that Bonthron's understanding would never recover the shock which terror had inflicted upon it, and which appeared to him to have disturbed all the faculties of his mind, and in particular his memory.

"It is not so, an it please your pagehood," said the leech. "Bonthron's intellect, such as it is, hath a solid character—it will but vacillate to and fro like a pendulum which hath been put in motion, and then will rest in its proper point of gravity. Our memory is, of all our powers of mind, that which is peculiarly liable to be suspended. Deep intoxication or sound sleep alike destroy it, and yet it returns when the drunkard becomes sober, or the sleeper is awakened. Terror sometimes produces the same effects. I knew at Paris a criminal condemned to die by the halter, who suffered the sentence accordingly, showing no particular degree of timidity upon the scaffold, and behaving and expressing himself as men in the same condition are wont to do. Accident did for him what a little ingenious practice hath done for our amiable friend from whom we but now parted. He was cut down, and given to his friends before life was extinct, and I had the good fortune to restore him. But though he recovered in other particulars, he remembered but little of his trial and sentence. Of his confession on the morning of his execution—he! he! he!—(in his usual chuckling manner)—he remembered him not a word. Neither of leaving the prison—nor of his passage to the Greve, where he suffered—nor of the devout speeches with which he—he! he!—edified—he! he! he!—so many good Christians—nor of ascending the fatal tree, nor of taking the fatal leap, had my revenant the slightest recollection.[1]—But here we reach the point where we must separate; for it were unfit, should we meet any of the watch, that we be found together, and it were also prudent that we enter the city by different gates. My profession forms an excuse for my going and coming at all times. Your valiant pagehood will make such explanation as may seem sufficing."

"I shall make my will a sufficient excuse if I am interrogated," said the haughty young man. "Yet I will avoid interruption, if possible. The moon is quite obscured, and the road as black as a wolf's mouth."

"Tut," said the physician, "let not your valour care for that; we shall tread darker paths ere it be long."

Without enquiring into the meaning of these evil-boding sentences, and indeed hardly listening to them in the pride and recklessness of his nature, the page of Ramorny parted from his ingenious and dangerous companion; and each took his own way.

CHAPTER XXV

"The course of true love never did run smooth."

SHAKSPEARE.

THE ominous anxiety of our armourer had not played him false. When the good Glover parted with his intended son-in-law, after the judicial combat had been decided, he found, what he indeed had expected, that his fair daughter was in no favourable disposition towards her lover. But although he perceived that Catharine was cold, restrained, collected, had cast away the appearance of mortal passion, and listened with a reserve, implying contempt, to the most splendid description he could give her of the combat in the Skinners' Yards, he

---

[1] An incident precisely similar to that in the text actually occurred, within the present century, at Oxford, in the case of a young woman who underwent the last sentence of the law for child-murder. A learned professor of that university has published an account of his conversation with the girl after her recovery.

was determined not to take the least notice of her altered manner, but to speak of her marriage with his son Henry as a thing which must of course take place. At length, when she began, as on a former occasion, to intimate, that her attachment to the armourer did not exceed the bounds of friendship,—that she was resolved never to marry,—that the pretended judicial combat was a mockery of the divine will, and of human laws,—the Glover not unnaturally grew angry.

"I cannot read thy thoughts, wench; nor can I pretend to guess under what wicked delusion it is that you kiss a declared lover,—suffer him to kiss you,—run to his house when a report is spread of his death, and fling yourself into his arms when you find him alone. All this shows very well in a girl prepared to obey her parents in a match sanctioned by her father; but such tokens of intimacy, bestowed on one whom a young woman cannot esteem, and is determined not to marry, are uncomely and unmaidenly. You have already been more bounteous of your favours to Henry Smith, than your mother, whom God assoilzie, ever was to me before I married her. I tell thee, Catharine, this trifling with the love of an honest man, is what I neither can, will, nor ought to endure. I have given my consent to the match, and I insist it shall take place without delay; and that you receive Henry Wynd to-morrow, as a man whose bride you are to be with all despatch."

"A power more potent than yours, father, will say no," replied Catharine.

"I will risk it; my power is a lawful one, that of a father over a child, and an erring child," answered her father. "God and man allow of my influence."

"Then, may Heaven help us!" said Catharine: "for if you are obstinate in your purpose, we are lost."

"We can expect no help from Heaven," said the Glover, "when we act with indiscretion. I am clerk enough myself to know that; and that your causeless resistance to my will is sinful, every priest will inform you. Ay, and more than that, you have spoken degradingly of the blessed appeal to God in the combat of ordeal. Take heed! for the Holy Church is awakened to watch her sheepfold, and to extirpate heresy by fire and steel; so much I warn thee of."

Catharine uttered a suppressed exclamation, and with

difficulty compelling herself to assume an appearance of composure, promised her father, that if he would spare her any farther discussion of the subject till to-morrow morning, she would then meet him, determined to make a full discovery of her sentiments.

With this promise, Simon Glover was obliged to remain contented, though extremely anxious for the postponed explanation. It could not be levity or fickleness of character which induced his daughter to act with so much apparent inconsistency towards the man of his choice, and whom she had so lately unequivocally owned to be also the man of her own. What external force there could exist, of a kind powerful enough to change the resolutions she had so decidedly expressed within twenty-four hours, was a matter of complete mystery.

"But I will be as obstinate as she can be," thought the Glover, "and she shall either marry Henry Smith without farther delay, or old Simon Glover will know an excellent reason to the contrary."

The subject was not renewed during the evening; but early on the next morning, just at sunrising, Catharine knelt before the bed in which her parent still slumbered. Her heart sobbed as if it would burst, and her tears fell thick upon her father's face. The good old man awoke, looked up, crossed his child's forehead, and kissed her affectionately.

"I understand thee, Kate," he said; "thou art come to confession, and, I trust, art desirous to escape a heavy penance by being sincere."

Catharine was silent for an instant.

"I need not ask, my father, if you remember the Carthusian monk, Clement, and his preachings and lessons; at which indeed you assisted so often, that you cannot be ignorant men called you one of his converts, and with greater justice termed me so likewise?"

"I am aware of both," said the old man, raising himself on his elbow; "but I defy foul fame to show that I ever owned him in any heretical proposition, though I loved to hear him talk of the corruptions of the church, the misgovernment of the nobles, and the wild ignorance of the poor, proving, as it seemed to me, that the sole virtue of our commonweal, its strength, and its estimation, lay among the burgher craft of the better class, which I received as comfortable doctrine, and creditable to the town. And if he preached other than right doctrine, wherefore did his superiors in the Carthusian convent permit it? If the shepherds turn a wolf in sheep's clothing into the flock, they should not blame the sheep for being worried."

"They endured his preaching, nay, they encouraged it," said Catharine, "while the vices of the laity, the contentions of the nobles, and the oppression of the poor, were the subject of his censure, and they rejoiced in the crowds, who, attracted to the Carthusian church, forsook those of the other convents. But the hypocrites—for such they are—joined with the other fraternities in accusing their preacher Clement, when, passing from censuring the crimes of the state, he began to display the pride, ignorance, and luxury of the churchmen themselves; their thirst of power, their usurpation over men's consciences, and their desire to augment their worldly wealth."

"For God's sake, Catharine," said her father, "speak within doors; your voice rises in tone, and your speech in bitterness, —your eyes sparkle. It is owing to this zeal in what concerns you no more than others, that malicious persons fix upon you the odious and dangerous name of a heretic."

"You know I speak no more than what is truth," said Catharine, "and which you yourself have avouched often."

"By needle and buck-skin, no!" answered the Glover, hastily; "wouldst thou have me avouch what might cost me life and limb, land and goods? For a full commission hath been granted for taking and trying heretics, upon whom is laid the cause of all late tumults and miscarriages; wherefore, few words are best, wench. I am ever of mind with the old Maker,—

> "Since word is thrall, and thought is free
> Keep well thy tongue, I counsel thee." [1]

"The counsel comes too late, father," answered Catharine, sinking down on a chair by her father's bedside. "The words have been spoken and heard; and it is indited against Simon Glover, burgess in Perth, that he hath spoken irreverent discourses of the doctrines of holy Church——"

"As I live by knife and needle," interrupted Simon, "it is a lie! I never was so silly as to speak of what I understood not."

[1] These lines are still extant in the ruinous house of an Abbot, and are said to be allusive to the holy man having kept a mistress.

"And hath slandered the anointed of the Church, both regular and secular," continued Catharine.

"Nay, I will never deny the truth," said the Glover; "an idle word I may have spoken at the ale-bench, or over a pottle pot of wine, or in right sure company; but else, my tongue is not one to run my head into peril."

"So you think, my dearest father; but your slightest language has been espied, your best-meaning phrases have been perverted, and you are in dittay as a gross railer against church and churchmen, and for holding discourse against them with loose and profligate persons, such as the deceased Oliver Proudfute, the Smith Henry of the Wynd, and others, set forth as commending the doctrines of Father Clement, whom they charge with seven rank heresies, and seek for with staff and spear, to try him to the death.—But that," said Catharine, kneeling, and looking upwards with the aspect of one of those beauteous saints whom the Catholics have given to the fine arts,—"that they shall never do.—He hath escaped from the net of the fowler; and, I thank Heaven, it was by my means."

"Thy means, girl—art thou mad?" said the amazed Glover.

"I will not deny what I glory in," answered Catharine; "it was by my means that Conachar was led to come hither with a party of men, and carry off the old man, who is now far beyond the Highland line."

"O my rash—my unlucky child!" said the Glover; "hast thou dared to aid the escape of one accused of heresy, and to invite Highlanders in arms to interfere with the administration of justice within burgh? Alas! thou hast offended both against the laws of the church and those of the realm. What would become of us, were this known!"

"It *is* known, my dear father," said the maiden, firmly; "known even to those who will be the most willing avengers of the deed."

"This must be some idle notion, Catharine, or some trick of those cogging priests and nuns; it accords not with thy late cheerful willingness to wed Henry Smith."

"Alas! dearest father, remember the dismal surprise occasioned by his reported death, and the joyful amazement at finding him alive; and deem it not wonder if I permitted myself, under your protection, to say more than my reflection justified. But then, I knew not the worst, and thought the danger exaggerated. Alas! I was yesterday fearfully undeceived, when the Abbess herself came hither, and with her the Dominican. They showed me the commission, under the broad seal of Scotland, for enquiring into and punishing heresy; they showed me your name, and my own, in a list of suspected persons; and it was with tears, real tears, that the Abbess conjured me to avert a dreadful fate, by a speedy retreat into the cloister; and that the monk pledged his word that you should not be molested, if I complied."

"The foul fiend take them both for weeping crocodiles!" said the Glover.

"Alas!" replied Catharine, "complaint or anger will little help us; but you see I have had real cause for this present alarm."

"Alarm! call it utter ruin.—Alas! my reckless child, where was your prudence when you ran headlong into such a snare?"

"Hear me, father," said Catharine; "there is still one mode of safety held out; it is one which I have often proposed, and for which I have in vain supplicated your permission."

"I understand you—the convent," said her father. "But Catharine, what abbess or prioress would dare——"

"That I will explain to you, father, and it will also show the circumstances which have made me seem unsteady of resolution to a degree which has brought censure upon me from yourself and others. Our confessor, old Father Francis, whom I chose from the Dominican convent at your command——"

"Ay, truly," interrupted the Glover; "and I so counselled and commanded thee, in order to take off the report that thy conscience was altogether under the direction of Father Clement."

"Well, this Father Francis has at different times urged and provoked me to converse on such matters as he judged I was likely to learn something of from the Carthusian preacher. Heaven forgive me my blindness! I fell into the snare, spoke freely, and, as he argued gently, as one who would fain be convinced, I even spoke warmly in defence of what I believed devoutly. The confessor assumed not his real aspect, and betrayed not his secret purpose, until he had learned all that I had to tell him. It was then that he threatened me with temporal punishment, and with eternal condemnation. Had his threats reached me alone, I could have stood firm; for their cruelty on earth I could have endured, and their power beyond this life I have no belief in."

"For Heaven's sake!" said the Glover, who was wellnigh beside himself at perceiving at every new word the increasing extremity of his daughter's danger, "beware of blaspheming the Holy Church—whose arms are as prompt to strike as her ears are sharp to hear."

"To me," said the Maid of Perth, again looking up, "the terrors of the threatened denunciations would have been of little avail; but when they spoke of involving thee, my father, in the charge against me, I own I trembled, and desired to compromise. The Abbess Martha, of Elcho nunnery, being my mother's kinswoman, I told her my distresses, and obtained her promise that she would receive me, if, renouncing worldly love and thoughts of wedlock, I would take the veil in her sisterhood. She had conversation on the topic, I doubt not, with the Dominican Francis, and both joined in singing the same song. 'Remain in the world,' said they, 'and thy father and thou shalt be brought to trial as heretics— assume the veil, and the errors of both shall be forgiven and cancelled.' They spoke not even of recantation of errors of doctrine; all should be peace if I would but enter the convent."

"I doubt not—I doubt not," said Simon; "the old Glover is thought rich, and his wealth would follow his daughter to the convent of Elcho, unless what the Dominicans might claim as their own share. So this was thy call to the veil— these thy objections to Henry Wynd?"

"Indeed, father, the course was urged on all hands, nor did my own mind recoil from it. Sir John Ramorny threatened me with the powerful vengeance of the young Prince, if I continued to repel his wicked suit—and as for poor Henry, it is but of late that I have discovered, to my own surprise— that—that I love his virtues more than I dislike his faults. Alas! the discovery has only been made to render my quitting the world more difficult than when I thought I had thee only to regret!"

She rested her head on her hand, and wept bitterly.

"All this is folly," said the Glover. "Never was there an extremity so pinching, but what a wise man might find counsel if he was daring enough to act upon it. This has never been the land or the people over whom priests could rule in the name of Rome, without their usurpation being controlled. If they are to punish each honest burgher who says the monks love gold, and that the lives of some of them cry shame upon the doctrines they teach, why truly, Stephen Smotherwell will not lack employment—and if all foolish maidens are to be secluded from the world because they follow the erring doctrines of a popular preaching friar, they must enlarge the nunneries and receive their inmates on slighter composition. Our privileges have been often defended against the Pope himself, by our good monarchs of yore, and when he pretended to interfere with the temporal government of the kingdom, there wanted not a Scottish Parliament, who told him his duty in a letter that should have been written in letters of gold. I have seen the epistle myself, and though I could not read it, the very sight of the seals of the right reverend prelates, and noble and true barons, which hung at it, made my heart leap for joy. Thou shouldst not have kept this secret, my child; but it is no time to tax thee with thy fault. Go down, get me some food. I will mount instantly, and go to our Lord Provost, and have his advice, and, as I trust, his protection and that of other true-hearted Scottish nobles, who will not see a true man trodden down for an idle word."

"Alas, my father," said Catharine, "it was even this impetuosity which I dreaded. I knew if I made my plaint to you there would soon be fire and feud, as if religion, though sent to us by the Father of peace, were fit only to be the mother of discord—and hence I could now—even now—give up the world, and retire with my sorrow among the sisters of Elcho, would you but let me be the sacrifice. Only, father,—comfort poor Henry when we are parted for ever—and do not—do not let him think of me too harshly—Say Catharine will never vex him more by her remonstrances, but that she will never forget him in her prayers."

"The girl hath a tongue that would make a Saracen weep," said her father, his own eyes sympathizing with those of his daughter. "But I will not yield way to this combination between the nun and the priest, to rob me of my only child.—Away with you, girl, and let me don my clothes; and prepare yourself to obey me in what I may have to recommend for your safety. Get a few clothes together, and what valuables thou hast—also, take the keys of my iron box, which poor Henry Smith gave me, and divide what gold you find into two portions,—put the one into a purse for thyself, and the other into the quilted girdle which I made on purpose to wear on journeys. Thus both shall be provided, in case fate should sunder us; in which event, God send the whirlwind may take the withered leaf, and spare the green one! Let them make ready my horse instantly, and the white jennet that I bought for thee but a day since, hoping to see thee ride to St. John's Kirk with maids and matrons, as blithe a bride as ever crossed the holy threshold. But it skills not talking—Away, and remember that the saints help those who are willing to help themselves. Not a word in answer—begone, I say,—no wilfulness now. The pilot, in calm weather, will let a sea-boy trifle with the rudder; but, by my soul, when winds howl, and waves arise, he stands by the helm himself. Away; no reply."

Catharine left the room to execute, as well as she might, the commands of her father, who, gentle in disposition, and devotedly attached to his child, suffered her often, as it seemed, to guide and rule both herself and him; yet who, as she knew, was wont to claim filial obedience, and exercise parental authority, with sufficient strictness, when the occasion seemed to require an enforcement of domestic discipline.

While the fair Catharine was engaged in executing her father's behests, and the good old Glover was hastily attiring himself, as one who was about to take a journey, a horse's tramp was heard in the narrow street. The horseman was wrapped in his riding cloak, having the cape of it drawn up, as if to hide the under part of his face, while his bonnet was pulled over his brows, and a broad plume obscured his upper features. He sprung from the saddle, and Dorothy had scarce time to reply to his enquiries that the Glover was in his bedroom, ere the stranger had ascended the stairs and entered the sleeping apartment. Simon, astonished and alarmed, and disposed to see in this early visitant an apparitor or sumner, come to attach him and his daughter, was much relieved, when, as the stranger doffed the bonnet, and threw the skirt of the mantle from his face, he recognized the knightly Provost of the Fair City, a visit from whom, at any time, was a favour of no ordinary degree; but being made at such an hour, had something marvellous, and, connected with the circumstances of the times, even alarming.

"Sir Patrick Charteris!"—said the Glover—"this high honour done to your poor beadsman—"

"Hush!" said the Knight, "there is no time for idle civilities. I came hither, because a man is, in trying occasions, his own safest page, and I can remain no longer than to bid thee fly, good Glover, since warrants are to be granted this day in council for the arrest of thy daughter and thee, under charge of heresy; and delay will cost you both your liberty for certain, and perhaps your lives."

"I have heard something of such a matter," said the Glover, "and was this instant setting forth to Kinfauns, to plead my innocence of this scandalous charge, to ask your lordship's counsel, and to implore your protection."

"Thy innocence, friend Simon, will avail thee but little before prejudiced judges; my advice is, in one word, to fly, and wait for happier times. As for my protection, we must tarry till the tide turns ere it will in any sort avail thee. But if thou canst lie concealed for a few days or weeks, I have little doubt that the churchmen, who, by siding with the Duke of Albany in court intrigue, and by alleging the decay of the purity of Catholic doctrine as the sole cause of the present national misfortunes, have, at least for the present hour, an irresistible authority over the King, will receive a check. In the meanwhile, however, know that King Robert hath not only given way to this general warrant for inquisition after heresy, but hath confirmed the Pope's nomination of Henry Wardlaw, to be Archbishop of St. Andrews, and Primate of Scotland;[1] thus yielding to Rome those freedoms and immunities of the Scottish church, which his ancestors, from the time of

---

[1] Mastere Henry of Wardlaw
That like til Vertue was to draw,
Chantour that time of Glasgu,
Commendit of alkyn Vertew,
The Pape had in affectioun,
Baith for his fame and his resoun.

*   *   *   *   *   *

Sua by his resoun speciale
Of the threttinth Benet Pape,
This Master Henry was Bischape
Of Sanct Andrewis with honoure.
Of Canon he was then Doctour.
                Wyntoun, B. ix. chap. 23.

Malcolm Canmore, have so boldly defended. His brave fathers would have rather subscribed a covenant with the devil, than yielded in such a matter to the pretensions of Rome."

"Alas, and what remedy?"

"None, old man, save in some sudden court change," said Sir Patrick. "The King is but like a mirror, which, having no light itself, reflects back with equal readiness any which is placed near to it for the time. Now, although the Douglas is banded with Albany, yet the Earl is unfavourable to the high claims of those domineering priests, having quarrelled with them about the exactions which his retinue hath raised on the Abbot of Arbroath. He will come back again with a high hand, for report says, the Earl of March hath fled before him. When he returns we shall have a changed world, for his presence will control Albany; especially as many nobles, and I myself, as I tell you in confidence, are resolved to league with him to defend the general right. Thy exile, therefore, will end with his return to our court. Thou hast but to seek thee some temporary hiding-place."

"For that, my lord," said the Glover, "I can be at no loss, since I have just title to the protection of the high Highland Chief, Gilchrist MacIan, Chief of the Clan Quhele."

"Nay, if thou canst take hold of his mantle thou needs no help of any one else—neither lowland churchman nor layman finds a free course of justice beyond the Highland frontier."

"But then my child, noble sir—my Catharine?" said the Glover.

"Let her go with thee, man. The graddan cake will keep her white teeth in order, the goat's whey will make the blood spring to her cheek again, which these alarms have banished; and even the Fair Maiden of Perth may sleep soft enough on a bed of Highland breckan."

"It is not from such idle respects, my lord, that I hesitate," said the Glover. "Catharine is the daughter of a plain burgher, and knows not nicety of food or lodging. But the son of MacIan hath been for many years a guest in my house, and I am obliged to say, that I have observed him looking at my daughter (who is as good as a betrothed bride) in a manner that, though I cared not for it in this lodging in Curfew Street, would give me some fear of consequences in a Highland glen, where I have no friend, and Conachar many."

The knightly Provost replied by a long whistle.—"Whew! whew!—Nay, in that case, I advise thee to send her to the nunnery at Elcho, where the Abbess, if I forget not, is some relation of yours. Indeed she said so herself, adding, that she loved her kinswoman well, together with all that belongs to thee, Simon."

"Truly, my lord, I do believe that the Abbess hath so much regard for me, that she would willingly receive the trust of my daughter, and my whole goods and gear into her sisterhood—Marry, her affection is something of a tenacious character, and would be loath to unloose its hold, either upon the wench or her tocher."

"Whew—whew!" again whistled the Knight of Kinfauns; "by the Thane's Cross, man, but this is an ill-favoured pirn to wind. Yet it shall never be said the fairest maid in the Fair City was cooped up in a convent, like a kain-hen in a cavey, and she about to be married to the bold burgess Henry Wynd. That tale shall not be told while I wear belt and spurs, and am called Provost of Perth."

"But what remede, my lord?" asked the Glover.

"We must all take our share of the risk. Come, get you and your daughter presently to horse. You shall ride with me, and we'll see who dare gloom at you. The summons is not yet served on thee, and if they send an apparitor to Kinfauns, without a warrant under the King's own hand, I make mine avow, by the Red Rover's soul! that he shall eat his writ, both wax and wether-skin. To horse, to horse! and," addressing Catharine, as she entered at the moment, "you too, my pretty maid,

> 'To horse, and fear not for your quarters;
> They thrive in law that trust in Charters.'"

In a minute or two the father and daughter were on horseback, both keeping an arrow's flight before the Provost, by his direction, that they might not seem to be of the same company. They passed the eastern gate in some haste, and rode forward roundly until they were out of sight. Sir Patrick followed leisurely; but, when he was lost to the view of the warders, he spurred his mettled horse, and soon came up with the Glover and Catharine, when a conversation ensued which throws light upon some previous passages of this history.

CHAPTER XXVI

Hail, land of bowmen ! seed of those who scorn'd
To stoop the neck to wide imperial Rome—
O dearest half of Albion sea-walled!

Albania (1737).

"I HAVE been devising a mode," said the well-meaning Provost, "by which I may make you both secure for a week or two from the malice of your enemies, when I have little doubt I may see a changed world at court. But that I may the better judge what is to be done, tell me frankly, Simon, the nature of your connexion with Gilchrist MacIan, which leads you to repose such implicit confidence in him. You are a close observer of the rules of the city, and are aware of the severe penalties which they denounce against such burghers as have covine and alliance with the Highland clans."

"True, my lord; but it is also known to you, that our craft, working in skins of cattle, stags, and every other description of hides, have a privilege, and are allowed to transact with those Highlanders, as with the men who can most readily supply us with the means of conducting our trade, to the great profit of the burgh. Thus it hath chanced with me to have great dealings with these men; and I can take it on my salvation, that you nowhere find more just and honourable traffickers, or by whom a man may more easily make an honest penny. I have made in my day several distant journeys into the far Highlands, upon the faith of their chiefs; nor did I ever meet with a people more true to their word, when you can once prevail upon them to plight it in your behalf. And as for the Highland Chief, Gilchrist MacIan, saving that he is hasty in homicide and fire-raising towards those with whom he hath deadly feud, I have nowhere seen a man who walketh a more just and upright path."

"It is more than ever I heard before," said Sir Patrick Charteris. "Yet I have known something of the Highland runagates too."

"They show another favour, and a very different one, to their friends than to their enemies, as your lordship shall understand," said the Glover. "However, be that as it may, it chanced me to serve Gilchrist MacIan in a high matter. It is now about eighteen years since, that it chanced, the Clan Quhele and Clan Chattan being at feud, as indeed they are seldom at peace, the former sustained such a defeat, as wellnigh extirpated the family of their chief, MacIan. Seven of his sons were slain in battle and after it, himself put to flight, and his castle taken and given to the flames. His wife, then near the time of giving birth to an infant, fled into the forest, attended by one faithful servant and his daughter. Here, in sorrow and care enough, she gave birth to a boy; and as the misery of the mother's condition rendered her little able to suckle the infant, he was nursed with the milk of a doe, which the forester who attended her contrived to take alive in a snare. It was not many months afterwards, that, in a second encounter of these fierce clans, MacIan defeated his enemies in his turn, and regained possession of the district which he had lost. It was with unexpected rapture, that he found his wife and child were in existence, having never expected to see more of them than the bleached bones, from which the wolves and wild-cats had eaten the flesh.

"But a strong and prevailing prejudice, such as is often entertained by these wild people, prevented their Chief from enjoying the full happiness arising from having thus regained his only son in safety. An ancient prophecy was current among them, that the power of the tribe should fall by means of a boy born under a bush of holly, and suckled by a white doe. The circumstance, unfortunately for the Chief, tallied exactly with the birth of the only child which remained to him, and it was demanded of him by the elders of the clan, that the boy should be either put to death, or at least removed from the dominions of the tribe, and brought up in obscurity. Gilchrist MacIan was obliged to consent; and having made choice of the latter proposal, the child, under the name of Conachar, was brought up in my family, with the purpose, as was at first intended, of concealing from him all knowledge who or what he was, or of his pretensions to authority over a numerous and warlike people. But as years rolled on, the elders of the tribe, who had exerted so much authority, were removed by death, or rendered incapable of interfering in the public affairs by age; while, on the other hand, the influence of Gilchrist MacIan was increased by his successful struggles against the Clan Chattan, in which he restored the equality betwixt the two contending confederacies, which had existed before the calamitous defeat of which I told your honour. Feeling himself thus firmly seated, he naturally became desirous to bring home his only son to his bosom and family, and for that purpose caused me to send the young Conachar, as he was called, more than once to the Highlands. He was a youth expressly made, by his form and gallantry of bearing, to gain a father's heart. At length, I suppose the lad either guessed the secret of his birth, or something of it was communicated to him; and the disgust which the paughty Hieland varlet had always shown for my honest trade, became more manifest; so that I dared not so much as lay my staff over his costard, for fear of receiving a stab with a dirk, as an answer in Gaelic to a Saxon remark. It was then that I wished to be well rid of him, the rather that he showed so much devotion to Catharine, who, forsooth, set herself up to wash the Ethiopian, and teach a wild Hielandman mercy and morals. She knows herself how it ended."

"Nay, my father," said Catharine, "it was surely but a point of charity to snatch the brand from the burning."

"But a small point of wisdom," said her father, "to risk the burning of your own fingers for such an end.—What says my lord to the matter?"

"My lord would not offend the Fair Maid of Perth," said Sir Patrick; "and he knows well the purity and truth of her mind. And yet I must needs say, that had this nurslin; of the doe been shrivelled, haggard, cross-made, and redhaired, like some Highlanders I have known, I question if the Fair Maiden of Perth would have bestowed so much zeal upon his conversion; and if Catharine had been as aged, wrinkled, and bent by years, as the old woman that opened the door to me this morning, I would wager my gold spurs against a pair of Highland brogues, that this wild roebuck would never have listened to a second lecture.—You laugh, Glover, and Catharine blushes a blush of anger. Let it pass, it is the way of the world."

"The way in which the men of the world esteem their neighbours, my lord," answered Catharine, with some spirit.

"Nay, fair saint, forgive a jest," said the knight; "and thou, Simon, tell us how this tale ended—with Conachar's escape to the Highlands I suppose?"

"With his return thither," said the Glover. "There was, for some two or three years, a fellow about Perth, a sort of messenger, who came and went under divers pretences, but was in fact the means of communication between Gilchrist MacIan and his son, young Conachar, or, as he is now called, Hector. From this gillie, I learned, in general, that the banishment of the Dault an Neigh Dheil, or foster child of the

White Doe, was again brought under consideration of the tribe. His foster father, Torquil of the Oak, the old forester, appeared with eight sons, the finest men of the clan, and demanded that the doom of banishment should be revoked. He spoke with the greater authority, as he was himself Taishatar, or a Seer, and supposed to have communication with the invisible world. He affirmed that he had performed a magical ceremony, termed *Tine-Egan*,[1] by which he evoked a fiend, from whom he extorted a confession that Conachar, now called Eachin, or Hector MacIan, was the only man in the approaching combat between the two hostile clans, who should come off without blood or blemish. Hence, Torquil of the Oak argued that the presence of the fated person was necessary to insure the victory. 'So much I am possessed of this,' said the forester, 'that unless Eachin fight in his place in the ranks of the Clan Quhele, neither I, his foster father, nor any of my eight sons, will lift a weapon in the quarrel.'

"This speech was received with much alarm; for the defection of nine men, the stoutest of their tribe, would be a serious blow, more especially if the combat, as begins to be rumoured, should be decided by a small number from each side. The ancient superstition concerning the foster son of the White Doe was counterbalanced by a new and later prejudice, and the father took the opportunity of presenting to the clan his long-hidden son, whose youthful, but handsome and animated countenance, haughty carriage, and active limbs, excited the admiration of the clansmen, who joyfully received him as the heir and descendant of their Chief, notwithstanding the ominous presage attending his birth and nurture.

"From this tale, my lord," continued Simon Glover, "your lordship may easily conceive why I myself should be secure of a good reception among the Clan Quhele; and you may also have reason to judge that it would be very rash in me to carry Catharine thither. And this, noble lord, is the heaviest of my troubles."

"We shall lighten the load, then," said Sir Patrick; "and, good Glover, I will take risk for thee and this damsel. My alliance with the Douglas gives me some interest with Marjory,

[1] *Tine-egan*, or *Neidfyre, i.e.* forced fire. All the fires in the house being extinguished, two men produced a flame of potent virtue by the friction of wood. This charm was used, within the memory of living persons, in the Hebrides, in cases of murrain among cattle.

Duchess of Rothsay, his daughter, the neglected wife of our wilful Prince. Rely on it, good Glover, that in her retinue thy daughter will be as secure as in a fenced castle. The Duchess keeps house now at Falkland, a castle which the Duke of Albany, to whom it belongs, has lent to her for her accommodation. I cannot promise you pleasure, Fair Maiden; for the Duchess Marjory of Rothsay is unfortunate, and therefore splenetic, haughty, and overbearing; conscious of the want of attractive qualities, therefore jealous of those women who possess them. But she is firm in faith, and noble in spirit, and would fling Pope or prelate into the ditch of her castle, who should come to arrest any one under her protection. You will therefore have absolute safety, though you may lack comfort."

"I have no title to more," said Catharine; "and deeply do I feel the kindness that is willing to secure me such honourable protection. If she be haughty, I will remember she is a Douglas, and hath right, as being such, to entertain as much pride as may become a mortal—if she be fretful, I will recollect that she is unfortunate—and if she be unreasonably captious, I will not forget that she is my protectress. Heed no longer for me, my lord, when you have placed me under the noble lady's charge.—But my poor father, to be exposed amongst these wild and dangerous people!"

"Think not of that, Catharine," said the Glover; "I am as familiar with brogues and bracken as if I had worn them myself. I have only to fear that the decisive battle may be fought before I can leave this country: and if the Clan Quhele lose the combat, I may suffer by the ruin of my protectors."

"We must have that cared for," said Sir Patrick; "rely on my looking out for your safety—But which party will carry the day, think you?"

"Frankly, my Lord Provost, I believe the Clan Chattan will have the worse; these nine children of the forest form a third nearly of the band surrounding the Chief of Clan Quhele, and are redoubted champions."

"And your apprentice, will he stand to it, thinkest thou?"

"He is hot as fire, Sir Patrick," answered the Glover; "but he is also unstable as water. Nevertheless, if he is spared, he seems likely to be one day a brave man."

"But, as now, he has some of the White Doe's milk still lurking about his liver, ha, Simon?"

"He has little experience, my lord," said the Glover, "and I need not tell an honoured warrior like yourself, that danger must be familiar to us ere we can dally with it like a mistress."

This conversation brought them speedily to the Castle of Kinfauns, where, after a short refreshment, it was necessary that the father and the daughter should part, in order to seek their respective places of refuge. It was then first, as she saw that her father's anxiety on her account had drowned all recollections of his friend, that Catharine dropped, as if in a dream, the name of "Henry Gow."

"True, most true," continued her father; "we must possess him of our purposes."

"Leave that to me," said Sir Patrick. "I will not trust to a messenger, nor will I send a letter, because, if I could write one, I think he could not read it. He will suffer anxiety in the meanwhile, but I will ride to Perth to-morrow by times, and acquaint him with your designs."

The time of separation now approached. It was a bitter moment; but the manly character of the old burgher, and the devout resignation of Catharine to the will of Providence, made it lighter than might have been expected. The good Knight hurried the departure of the burgess, but in the kindest manner; and even went so far as to offer him some gold pieces in loan, which might, where specie was so scarce, be considered as the *ne plus ultra* of regard. The Glover, however, assured him he was amply provided, and departed on his journey in a north-westerly direction. The hospitable protection of Sir Patrick Charteris was no less manifested towards his fair guest. She was placed under the charge of a duenna, who managed the good Knight's household, and was compelled to remain several days in Kinfauns, owing to the obstacles and delays interposed by a Tay boatman, named Kitt Stenshaw, to whose charge she was to be committed, and whom the Provost highly trusted.

Thus were severed the child and parent in a moment of great danger and difficulty, much augmented by circumstances of which they were then ignorant, and which seemed greatly to diminish any chance of safety that remained for them.

CHAPTER XXVII

"This Austin humbly did."—"Did he?" quoth he.
"Austin may do the same again for me."
POPE's *Prologue to Canterbury Tales from Chaucer.*

THE course of our story will be best pursued by attending that of Simon Glover. It is not our purpose to indicate the exact local boundaries of the two contending clans, especially since they are not clearly pointed out by the historians who have transmitted accounts of this memorable feud. It is sufficient to say, that the territory of the Clen Chattan extended far and wide, comprehending Caithness and Sutherland, and having for their paramount chief the powerful Earl of the latter shire, thence called *Mohr ar chat.*[1] In this general sense, the Keiths, the Sinclairs, the Guns, and other families and clans of great power, were included in the confederacy. These, however, were not engaged in the present quarrel, which was limited to that part of the Clan Chattan occupying the extensive mountainous districts of Perthshire and Inverness-shire, which form a large portion of what is called the north-eastern Highlands. It is well known that two large septs, unquestionably known to belong to the Clan Chattan, the MacPhersons and the MacIntoshes, dispute to this day which of their chieftains was at the head of this Badenoch branch of the great confederacy, and both have of later times assumed the title of Captain of Clan Chattan. *Non nostrum est*—But, at all events, Badenoch must have been in the centre of the confederacy, so far as involved in the feud of which we treat.

Of the rival league of Clan Quhele we have a still less distinct account, for reasons which will appear in the sequel. Some authors have identified them with the numerous and powerful sept of MacKay. If this is done on good authority, which is to be doubted, the MacKays must have shifted their settlements greatly since the reign of Robert III., since they are now to be found (as a clan) in the extreme northern

---

[1] *i.e.* The Great Cat. The County of Caithness is supposed to have its name from Teutonic settlers of the race of the *Gatti,* and heraldry has not neglected so fair an occasion for that species of painted punning in which she used to delight. *Touch not the cat but a glove,* is the motto of Mackintosh, alluding to his crest, which, as with most of the now scattered septs of the old Clan Chattan, is the Mountain Cat.

parts of Scotland, in the counties of Ross and Sutherland.[1]
We cannot, therefore, be so clear as we would wish in the
geography of the story. Suffice it, that directing his course
in a north-westerly direction, the Glover travelled for a day's
journey in the direction of the Breadalbane country, from
which he hoped to reach the Castle where Gilchrist MacIan,
the Captain of the Clan Quhele, and the father of his
pupil Conachar, usually held his residence, with a barbarous
pomp of attendance and ceremonial, suited to his lofty
pretensions.

We need not stop to describe the toil and terrors of such
a journey, where the path was to be traced among wastes and
mountains, now ascending precipitous ravines, now plunging
into inextricable bogs, and often intersected with large brooks,
and even rivers. But all these perils Simon Glover had
before encountered, in quest of honest gain; and it was not
to be supposed that he shunned or feared them where liberty,
and life itself, were at stake.

The danger from the warlike and uncivilized inhabitants
of these wilds would have appeared to another at least
as formidable as the perils of the journey. But Simon's
knowledge of the manners and language of the people assured
him on this point also. An appeal to the hospitality of
the wildest Gael was never unsuccessful; and the kern, that
in other circumstances would have taken a man's life for
the silver button of his cloak, would deprive himself of a meal
to relieve the traveller who implored hospitality at the door
of his bothy. The art of travelling in the Highlands was to
appear as confident and defenceless as possible; and accordingly the Glover carried no arms whatever, journeyed without
the least appearance of precaution, and took good care to
exhibit nothing which might excite cupidity. Another rule
which he deemed it prudent to observe, was to avoid communication with any of the passengers whom he might chance
to meet, except in the interchange of the common civilities of
salutation, which the Highlanders rarely omit. Few opportunities occurred of exchanging even such passing greetings.
The country, always lonely, seemed now entirely forsaken;
and even in the little straths or valleys which he had occasion
to pass or traverse, the hamlets were deserted, and the

---

[1] Their territory, commonly called, after the chief of the Mackays, *Lord
Reay's* country, has lately passed into the possession of the noble family
of Stafford-Sutherland.

inhabitants had betaken themselves to woods and caves. This was easily accounted for, considering the imminent dangers of a feud, which all expected would become one of the most general signals for plunder and ravage that had ever distracted that unhappy country.

Simon began to be alarmed at this state of desolation. He had made a halt since he left Kinfauns, to allow his nag some rest; and now he began to be anxious how he was to pass the night. He had reckoned upon spending it at the cottage of an old acquaintance, called Niel Booshalloch, (or the Cowherd,) because he had charge of numerous herds of cattle belonging to the Captain of Clan Quhele, for which purpose he had a settlement on the banks of the Tay, not far from the spot where it leaves the lake of the same name. From this his old host and friend, with whom he had transacted many bargains for hides and furs, the old Glover hoped to learn the present state of the country, the prospect of peace or war, and the best measures to be taken for his own safety. It will be remembered that the news of the indentures of battle entered into for diminishing the extent of the feud had only been communicated to King Robert the day before the Glover left Perth, and did not become public till some time afterwards.

"If Niel Booshalloch hath left his dwelling like the rest of them, I shall be finely holped up," thought Simon, "since I want not only the advantage of his good advice, but also his interest with Gilchrist MacIan; and, moreover, a night's quarters and a supper."

Thus reflecting, he reached the top of a swelling green hill, and saw the splendid vision of Loch Tay lying beneath him, an immense plate of polished silver, its dark heathy mountains and leafless thickets of oak serving as an arabesque frame to a magnificent mirror.

Indifferent to natural beauty at any time, Simon Glover was now particularly so; and the only part of the splendid landscape on which he turned his eye was the angle or loop of meadow land, where the river Tay, rushing in full-swoln dignity from its parent lake, and wheeling around a beautiful valley of about a mile in breadth, begins his broad course to the south-eastward, like a conqueror and a legislator, to subdue and to enrich remote districts. Upon the sequestered spot, which is so beautifully situated between lake, mountain, and river, arose afterwards the feudal castle of The Ballough, which in our time has been succeeded by the splendid palace of the Earls of Breadalbane.

But the Campbells, though they had already attained very great power in Argyleshire, had not yet extended themselves so far eastward as Loch Tay, the banks of which were, either by right, or by mere occupancy, possessed for the present by the Clan Quhele, whose choicest herds were fattened on the margin of the lake. In this valley, therefore, between the river and the lake, amid extensive forests of oak-wood, hazel, rowan-tree, and larches, arose the humble cottage of Niel Booshalloch, a village Eumæus whose hospitable chimneys were seen to smoke plentifully, to the great encouragement of Simon Glover, who might otherwise have been obliged to spend the night in the open air, to his no small discomfort.

He reached the door of the cottage, whistled, shouted, and made his approach known. There was a baying of hounds and collies, and presently the master of the hut came forth. There was much care on his brow, and he seemed surprised at the sight of Simon Glover, though the herdsman covered both as well as he might; for nothing in that region could be reckoned more uncivil, than for the landlord to suffer any thing to escape him in look or gesture, which might induce the visitor to think that his arrival was an unpleasing, or even an unexpected incident. The traveller's horse was conducted to a stable, which was almost too low to receive him, and the Glover himself was led into the mansion of the Booshalloch, where, according to the custom of the country, bread and cheese was placed before the wayfarer, while more solid food was preparing. Simon, who understood all their habits, took no notice of the obvious marks of sadness on the brow of his entertainer, and on those of the family, until he had eaten somewhat for form's sake; after which he asked the general question, Was there any news in the country?

"Bad news as ever were told," said the herdsman; "our father is no more."

"How?" said Simon, greatly alarmed, "is the Captain of the Clan Quhele dead?"

"The Captain of the Clan Quhele never dies," answered the Booshalloch; "but Gilchrist MacIan died twenty hours since, and his son, Eachin MacIan, is now captain."

"What, Eachin—that is Conachar—my apprentice?"

"As little of that subject as you list, brother Simon," said the herdsman. "It is to be remembered, friend, that your craft, which doth very well for a living in the douce city of Perth, is something too mechanical to be much esteemed at the foot of Ben Lawers, and on the banks of Loch Tay. We have not a Gaelic word by which we can even name a maker of gloves."

"It would be strange if you had, friend Niel," said Simon, dryly, "having so few gloves to wear. I think there be none in the whole Clan Quhele, save those which I myself gave to Gilchrist MacIan, whom God assoilzie, who esteemed them a choice propine. Most deeply do I regret his death, for I was coming to him on express business."

"You had better turn the nag's head southward with morning light," said the herdsman. "The funeral is instantly to take place, and it must be with short ceremony; for there is a battle to be fought by the Clan Quhele and the Clan Chattan, thirty champions on a side, as soon as Palm Sunday next, and we have brief time either to lament the dead or honour the living.

"Yet are my affairs so pressing, that I must needs see the young Chief, were it but for a quarter of an hour," said the Glover."

"Hark thee, friend," replied his host, "I think thy business must be either to gather money or to make traffic. Now, if the Chief owe thee any thing for upbringing or otherwise, ask him not to pay it when all the treasures of the tribe are called in for making gallant preparation of arms and equipment for their combatants, that we may meet these proud hill-cats in a fashion to show ourselves their superiors. But if thou comest to practise commerce with us, thy time is still worse chosen. Thou knowest that thou art already envied of many of our tribe, for having had the fosterage of the young Chief, which is a thing usually given to the best of the clan."

"But, St. Mary, man!" exclaimed the Glover, "men should remember the office was not conferred on me as a favour which I courted, but that it was accepted by me on importunity and entreaty, to my no small prejudice. This Conachar, or Hector of yours, or whatever you call him, has destroyed me doe-skins to the amount of many pounds Scots."

"There again, now," said the Booshalloch, "you have

spoken a word to cost your life;—any allusion to skins or hides, or especially to deer and does, may incur no less a forfeit. The Chief is young, and jealous of his rank—none knows the reason better than thou, friend Glover. He will naturally wish that everything concerning the opposition to his succession, and having reference to his exile, should be totally forgotten; and he will not hold him in affection who shall recall the recollection of his people, or force back his own, upon what they must both remember with pain. Think how, at such a moment, they will look on the old Glover of Perth, to whom the Chief was so long apprentice!—Come, come, old friend, you have erred in this. You are in over great haste to worship the rising sun, while his beams are yet level with the horizon. Come thou when he has climbed higher in the heavens, and thou shalt have thy share of the warmth of his noonday height."

"Niel Booshalloch," said the Glover, "we have been old friends, as thou say'st; and as I think thee a true one, I will speak to thee freely, though what I say might be perilous if spoken to others of thy clan. Thou think'st I come hither to make my own profit of thy young Chief, and it is natural thou shouldst think so. But I would not, at my years, quit my own chimney corner in Curfew Street, to bask me in the beams of the brightest sun that ever shone upon Highland heather. The very truth is, I come hither in extremity—my foes have the advantage of me, and have laid things to my charge whereof I am incapable, even in thought. Nevertheless, doom is like to go forth against me, and there is no remedy but that I must up and fly, or remain and perish. I come to your young Chief, as one who had refuge with me in his distress; who ate of my bread and drank of my cup. I ask of him refuge, which, as I trust, I shall need but a short time."

"That makes a different case," replied the herdsman. "So different, that if you came at midnight to the gate of MacIan, having the King of Scotland's head in your hand, and a thousand men in pursuit for the avenging of his blood, I could not think it for his honour to refuse you protection. And for your innocence or guilt, it concerns not the case,—or rather, he ought the more to shelter you if guilty, seeing your necessity and his risk are both in that case the greater. I must straightway to him, that no hasty tongue tell him of your arriving hither without saying the cause."

" A pity of your trouble," said the Glover ; "but where lies the Chief ? "

" He is quartered about ten miles hence, busied with the affairs of the funeral, and with preparations for the combat— the dead to the grave, and the living to battle."

" It is a long way, and will take you all night to go and come," said the Glover ; "and I am very sure that Conachar, when he knows it is I who—"

" Forget Conachar," said the herdsman, placing his finger on his lips. " And as for the ten miles, they are but a Highland leap, when one bears a message between his friend and his Chief."

So saying, and committing the traveller to the charge of his eldest son and his daughter, the active herdsman left his house two hours before midnight, to which he returned long before sunrise. He did not disturb his wearied guest, but when the old man had arisen in the morning, he acquainted him that the funeral of the late Chieftain was to take place the same day, and that, although Eachin MacIan could not invite a Saxon to the funeral, he would be glad to receive him at the entertainment which was to follow.

" His will must be obeyed," said the Glover, half smiling at the change of relation between himself and his late apprentice. " The man is the master now, and I trust he will remember, that, when matters were otherwise between us, I did not use my authority ungraciously."

" Troutsho, friend ! " exclaimed the Booshalloch, "the less of that you say the better. You will find yourself a right welcome guest to Eachin, and the deil a man dares stir you within his bounds. But fare you well, for I must go, as beseems me, to the burial of the best Chief the clan ever had, and the wisest Captain that ever cocked the sweet gale (bog-myrtle) in his bonnet. Farewell to you for a whlle, and if you will go to the top of the Tom-an-Lonach behind the house, you will see a gallant sight, and hear such a coronach as will reach the top of Ben Lawers. A boat will wait for you, three hours hence, at a wee bit creek about half a mile westward from the head of the Tay."

With these words he took his departure, followed by his three sons, to man the boat in which he was to join the rest of the mourners, and two daughters, whose voices were wanted to join in the Lament, which was chanted, or rather screamed, on such occasions of general affliction.

Simon Glover, finding himself alone, resorted to the stable to look after his nag, which, he found, had been well served with graddan, or bread made of scorched barley. Of this kindness he was fully sensible, knowing that, probably, the family had little of this delicacy left to themselves, until the next harvest should bring them a scanty supply. In animal food they were well provided, and the lake found them abundance of fish for their lenten diet, which they did not observe very strictly; but bread was a delicacy very scanty in the Highlands. The bogs afforded a soft species of hay, none of the best to be sure, but Scottish horses, like their riders, were then accustomed to hard fare. Gauntlet, for this was the name of the palfrey, had his stall crammed full of dried fern for litter, and was otherwise as well provided for as Highland hospitality could contrive.

Simon Glover being thus left to his own painful reflections, nothing better remained, after having seen after the comforts of the dumb companion of his journey, than to follow the herdsman's advice; and ascending towards the top of an eminence called Tom-an-Lonach, or the Knoll of Yew Trees, after a walk of half an hour he reached the summit, and could look down on the broad expanse of the lake, of which the height commanded a noble view. A few aged and scattered yew-trees, of great size, still vindicated for the beautiful green hill the name attached to it. But a far greater number had fallen a sacrifice to the general demand for bow-staves in that warlike age, the bow being a weapon much used by the mountaineers, though those which they employed, as well as their arrows, were, in shape and form, and especially in efficacy, far inferior to the archery of merry England. The dark and shattered individual yews which remained, were like the veterans of a broken host, occupying in disorder some post of advantage, with the stern purpose of resisting to the last. Behind this eminence, but detached from it, arose a higher hill, partly covered with copsewood, partly opening into glades of pasture, where the cattle strayed, finding, at this season of the year, a scanty sustenance, among the spring-heads and marshy places, where the fresh grass began first to arise.

The opposite, or northern shore of the lake presented a far more Alpine prospect than that upon which the Glover was stationed. Woods and thickets ran up the sides of the mountains, and disappeared among the sinuosities formed by the winding ravines which separated them from each other; but far above these specimens of a tolerable natural soil, arose the swart and bare mountains themselves, in the dark grey desolation proper to the season.

Some were peaked, some broad-crested, some rocky and precipitous, others of a tamer outline; and the clan of Titans seemed to be commanded by their appropriate chieftains—the frowning mountain of Ben Lawers, and the still more lofty eminence of Ben Mohr, arising high above the rest, whose peaks retain a dazzling helmet of snow far into the summer season, and sometimes during the whole year. Yet the borders of this wild and silvan region, where the mountains descended upon the lake, intimated, even at that early period, many traces of human habitation. Hamlets were seen, especially on the northern margin of the lake, half hid among the little glens that poured their tributary streams into Loch Tay, which, like many earthly things, made a fair show at a distance, but, when more closely approached, were disgustful and repulsive, from their squalid want of the conveniences which attend even Indian wigwams. They were inhabited by a race who neither cultivated the earth, nor cared for the enjoyments which industry procures. The women, although otherwise treated with affection, and even delicacy of respect, discharged all the absolutely necessary domestic labour. The men, excepting some reluctant use of an ill-formed plough, or more frequently a spade, grudgingly gone through, as a task infinitely beneath them, took no other employment than the charge of the herds of black cattle, in which their wealth consisted. At all other times, they hunted, fished, or marauded, during the brief intervals of peace, by way of pastime; plundering with bolder license, and fighting with embittered animosity, in time of war, which, public or private, upon a broader or more restricted scale, formed the proper business of their lives, and the only one which they esteemed worthy of them.

The magnificent bosom of the lake itself was a scene to gaze on with delight. Its noble breadth, with its termination in a full and beautiful run, was rendered yet more picturesque by one of those islets which are often happily situated in the Scottish lakes.[1] The ruins upon that isle, now almost shape-less, being overgrown with wood, rose, at the time we speak

[1] Note XVII.

of, into the towers and pinnacles of a priory where slumbered the remains of Sibilla, daughter of Henry I. of England, and consort of Alexander the First of Scotland. This holy place had been deemed of dignity sufficient to be the deposit of the remains of the Captain of the Clan Quhele, at least till times when the removal of the danger, now so imminently pressing, should permit of his body being conveyed to a distinguished convent in the north, where he was destined ultimately to repose with all his ancestry.

A number of boats pushed off from various points of the near and more distant shore, many displaying sable banners, and others having their several pipers in the bow, who from time to time poured forth a few notes of a shrill, plaintive, and wailing character, and intimated to the Glover that the ceremony was about to take place. These sounds of lamentation were but the tuning as it were of the instruments, compared with the general wail which was speedily to be raised.

A distant sound was heard from far up the lake, even as it seemed from the remote and distant glens out of which the Dochart and the Lochy pour their streams into Loch Tay. It was in a wild inaccessible spot, where the Campbells at a subsequent period founded their strong fortress of Finlayrigg, that the redoubted commander of the Clan Quhele drew his last breath ; and, to give due pomp to his funeral, his corpse was now to be brought down the Loch to the island assigned for his temporary place of rest. The funeral fleet, led by the chieftain's barge, from which a huge black banner was displayed, had made more than two thirds of its voyage ere it was visible from the eminence on which Simon Glover stood to overlook the ceremony. The instant the distant wail of the coronach was heard proceeding from the attendants on the funeral barge, all the subordinate sounds of lamentation were hushed at once, as the raven ceases to croak and the hawk to whistle, whenever the scream of the eagle is heard. The boats, which had floated hither and thither upon the lake, like a flock of water-fowl dispersing themselves on its surface, now drew together with an appearance of order, that the funeral flotilla might pass onward, and that they themselves might fall into their proper places. In the meanwhile the piercing din of the war-pipes became louder and louder, and the cry from the numberless boats which followed that from which the black banner of the Chief was displayed, rose in wild unison up to the Tom-an-Lonach, from which the

Glover viewed the spectacle. The galley which headed the procession, bore on its poop a species of scaffold, upon which, arrayed in white linen, and with the face bare, was displayed the corpse of the deceased Chieftain. His son, and the nearest relatives, filled the vessel, while a great number of boats, of every description that could be assembled, either on Loch Tay itself, or brought by land carriage from Loch Earn and otherwise, followed in the rear, some of them of very frail materials. There were even curraghs, composed of ox-hides stretched over hoops of willow, in the manner of the ancient British; and some committed themselves to rafts formed for the occasion, from the readiest materials that occurred, and united in such a precarious manner as to render it probable, that, before the accomplishment of the voyage, some of the clansmen of the deceased might be sent to attend their Chieftain in the world of spirits.

When the principal flotilla came in sight of the smaller group of boats collected towards the foot of the lake, and bearing off from the little island, they hailed each other with a shout so loud and general, and terminating in a cadence so wildly prolonged, that not only the deer started from their glens for miles around, and sought the distant recesses of the mountains, but even the domestic cattle, accustomed to the voice of man, felt the full panic which the human shout strikes into the wilder tribes, and like them fled from their pasture into morasses and dingles.

Summoned forth from their convent by those sounds, the monks who inhabited the little islet, began to issue from their lowly portal, with cross and banner, and as much of ecclesiastical state as they had the means of displaying; their bells at the same time, of which the edifice possessed three, pealing the death-toll over the long lake, which came to the ears of the now silent multitude, mingled with the solemn chant of the Catholic church, raised by the monks in their procession. Various ceremonies were gone through, while the kindred of the deceased carried the body ashore, and, placing it on a bank long consecrated to the purpose, made the Deasil [1] around the departed. When the corpse

---

[1] A very ancient custom, which consists in going three times round the body of a dead or living person, imploring blessings upon him. The Deasil must be performed sunways, that is, by moving from right to left. If misfortune is imprecated, the party moves withershins (German, WIDDERSINS), that is *against the sun*, from left to right.

was uplifted to be borne into the church, another united yell burst from the assembled multitude, in which the deep shout of warriors, and the shrill wail of females, joined their notes with the tremulous voice of age, and the babbling cry of childhood. The coronach was again, and for the last time, shrieked, as the body was carried into the interior of the church, where only the nearest relatives of the deceased, and the most distinguished of the leaders of the clan, were permitted to enter.[1] The last yell of woe was so terribly loud, and answered by so many hundred echoes, that the Glover instinctively raised his hands to his ears, to shut out, or deaden at least, a sound so piercing. He kept this attitude, while the hawks, owls, and other birds, scared by the wild scream, had begun to settle in their retreats, when, as he withdrew his hands, a voice close by him, said,—

"Think you this, Simon Glover, the hymn of penitence and praise, with which it becomes poor forlorn man, cast out from his tenement of clay, to be wafted into the presence of his Maker?"

The Glover turned, and in the old man, with a long white beard, who stood close beside him, had no difficulty, from the clear mild eye, and the benevolent cast of features, to recognize the Carthusian monk Father Clement, no longer wearing his monastic habiliments, but wrapped in a frieze mantle, and having a Highland cap on his head.

It may be recollected that the Glover regarded this man with a combined feeling of respect and dislike—respect, which his judgment could not deny to the monk's person and character, and dislike, which arose from Father Clement's peculiar doctrines being the cause of his daughter's exile and his own distress. It was not, therefore, with sentiments of unmixed satisfaction, that he returned the greetings of the Father, and replied to the reiterated question, What he thought of the funeral rites, which were discharged in so wild a manner,—"I know not, my good Father; but these men do their duty to their deceased Chief according to the fashion of their ancestors; they mean to express their regret for their friend's loss, and their prayers to Heaven in his behalf; and that which is done of good-will, must, to my thinking, be accepted favourably. Had it been otherwise, methinks they had ere now been enlightened to do better."

[1] Note XVIII.

"Thou art deceived," answered the Monk. "God has sent his light amongst us all, though in various proportions; but man wilfully shuts his eyes and prefers darkness. This benighted people mingle with the ritual of the Roman Church, the old heathen ceremonies of their own fathers, and thus unite with the abominations of a church corrupted by wealth and power, the cruel and bloody ritual of savage Paynims."

"Father," said Simon, abruptly, "methinks your presence were more useful in yonder chapel, aiding your brethren in the discharge of their clerical duties, than in troubling and unsettling the belief of an humble, though ignorant Christian, like myself."

"And wherefore say, good brother, that I would unfix thy principles of belief?" answered Clement. "So Heaven deal with me, as, were my life-blood necessary to cement the mind of any man to the holy religion he professeth, it should be freely poured out for the purpose."

"Your speech is fair, Father, I grant you," said the Glover; "but if I am to judge the doctrine by the fruits, Heaven has punished me by the hand of the Church, for having hearkened thereto. Ere I heard you, my confessor was little moved, though I might have owned to have told a merry tale upon the ale-bench, even if a friar or a nun were the subject. If at a time I had called Father Hubert a better hunter of hares than of souls, I confessed me to the Vicar Vinesauf, who laughed and made me pay a reckoning for penance—or if I had said that the Vicar Vinesauf was more constant to his cup than to his breviary, I confessed me to Father Hubert, and a new hawking-glove made all well again; and thus I, my conscience, and Mother Church, lived together on terms of peace, friendship, and mutual forbearance. But since I have listened to you, Father Clement, this goodly union is broke to pieces, and nothing is thundered in my ear but burgatory in the next world, and fire and fagot in this. Therefore, avoid you, Father Clement, or speak to those who can understand your doctrine. I have no heart to be a martyr; I have never in my whole life had courage enough so much as to snuff a candle with my fingers; and, to speak the truth, I am minded to go back to Perth, sue out my pardon in the spiritual court, carry my fagot to the gallows' foot, in token of recantation, and purchase myself once more the name of a good Catholic, were it at the price of all the worldly wealth that remains to me."

prepared to return with displayed banners, and every demonstration of mirth and joy; for there was but brief time to celebrate festivals, when the awful conflict betwixt the Clan Quhele and their most formidable rivals so nearly approached. It had been agreed, therefore, that the funeral feast should be blended with that usually given at the inauguration of the young Chief.

Some objections were made to this arrangement, as containing an evil omen. But, on the other hand, it had a species of recommendation, from the habits and feelings of the Highlanders, who, to this day, are wont to mingle a degree of solemn mirth with their mourning, and something resembling melancholy with their mirth. The usual aversion to speak or think of those who have been loved and lost, is less known to this grave and enthusiastic race, than it is to others. You hear not only the young mention (as is everywhere usual) the merits and the character of parents, who have, in the course of nature, predeceased them; but the widowed partner speaks, in ordinary conversation, of the lost spouse, and, what is still stranger, the parents allude frequently to the beauty or valour of the child whom they have interred. The Scottish Highlanders appear to regard the separation of friends by death, as something less absolute and complete than is generally esteemed in other countries, and converse of the dear connexions, who have sought the grave before them, as if they had gone upon a long journey in which they themselves must soon follow. The funeral feast, therefore, being a general custom throughout Scotland, was not, in the opinion of those who were to share it, unseemingly mingled, on the present occasion, with the festivities which hailed the succession to the Chieftainship.

The barge which had lately borne the dead to the grave, now conveyed the young MacIan to his new command; and the minstrels sent forth their gayest notes to gratulate Eachin's succession, as they had lately sounded their most doleful dirges when carrying Gilchrist to his grave. From the attendant flotilla rang notes of triumph and jubilee, instead of those yells of lamentation, which had so lately disturbed the echoes of Loch Tay; and a thousand voices hailed the youthful Chieftain as he stood on the poop, armed at all points, in the flower of early manhood, beauty and activity, on the very spot where his father's corpse had so

"You are angry, my dearest brother," said Clement; "and repent you on the pinch of a little worldly danger, and a little worldly loss, for the good thoughts which you once entertained."

"You speak at ease, Father Clement, since I think you have long forsworn the wealth and goods of the world, and are prepared to yield up your life, when it is demanded, in exchange for the doctrine you preach and believe. You are as ready to put on your pitched shirt and brimstone head-gear, as a naked man is to go to his bed, and it would seem you have not much more reluctance to the ceremony. But I still wear that which clings to me. My wealth is still my own, and I thank Heaven it is a decent pittance whereon to live— my life, too, is that of a hale old man of sixty, who is in no haste to bring it to a close—and if I were poor as Job, and on the edge of the grave, must I not still cling to my daughter, whom your doctrines have already cost so dear?"

"Thy daughter, friend Simon," said the Carthusian, "may be truly called an angel upon earth."

"Ay; and by listening to your doctrines, Father, she is now like to be called on to be an angel in heaven, and to be transported thither in a chariot of fire."

"Nay, my good brother," said Clement, "desist, I pray you, to speak of what you little understand. Since it is wasting time to show thee the light that thou chafest against, yet listen to that which I have to say touching thy daughter, whose temporal felicity, though I weigh it not even for an instant in the scale against that which is spiritual, is, nevertheless, in its order, as dear to Clement Blair as to her own father."

The tears stood in the old man's eyes as he spoke, and Simon Glover was in some degree mollified as he again addressed him.

"One would think thee, Father Clement, the kindest and most amiable of men; how comes it then that thy steps are haunted by general ill-will, wherever thou chancest to turn them? I could lay my life thou hast contrived already to offend yonder half score of poor friars in their water-girdled cage, and that you have been prohibited from attendance on the funeral?"

"Even so, my son," said the Carthusian, "and I doubt whether their malice will suffer me to remain in this country. I did but speak a few sentences about the superstition and folly of frequenting St. Fillian's church, to detect theft by means of his bell—of bathing mad patients in his pool, to cure their infirmity of mind—and lo! the persecutors have cast me forth of their communion, as they will speedily cast me out of this life."

"Lo you there now," said the Glover, "see what it is for a man that cannot take a warning! Well, Father Clement, men will not cast me forth unless it were as a companion of yours. I pray you, therefore, tell me what you have to say of my daughter, and let us be less neighbours than we have been."

"This then, brother Simon, I have to acquaint you with. This young Chief, who is swoln with contemplation of his own power and glory, loves one thing better than it all, and that is thy daughter."

"He, Conachar!" exclaimed Simon. "My runagate apprentice look up to my daughter!"

"Alas!" said Clement, "how close sits our worldly pride, even as ivy clings to the wall, and cannot be separated!— Look *up* to thy daughter, good Simon? Alas, no! The Captain of Clan Quhele, great as he is, and greater as he soon expects to be, looks *down* to the daughter of the Perth burgess, and considers himself demeaned in doing so. But, to use his own profane expression, Catharine is dearer to him than life here, and Heaven hereafter—he cannot live without her."

"Then he may die, if he lists," said Simon Glover, "for she is betrothed to an honest burgess of Perth; and I would not break my word to make my daughter bride to the Prince of Scotland."

"I thought it would be your answer," replied the Monk; "I would, worthy friend, thou couldst carry into thy spiritual concerns some part of that daring and resolved spirit with which thou canst direct thy temporal affairs."

"Hush thee—hush, Father Clement!" answered the Glover; "when thou fallest into that vein of argument, thy words savour of blazing tar, and that is a scent I like not. As to Catharine, I must manage as I can, so as not to displease the young dignitary; but well is it for me that she is far beyond his reach."

"She must then be distant indeed," said the Carthusian. "And now, brother Simon, since you think it must be perilous to own me and my opinions, I must walk alone with my own doctrines, and the dangers they draw on me. But should your eye, less blinded than it now is by worldly hopes and fears, ever turn a glance back on him, who soon may be snatched from you, remember, that by nought, save a deep

sense of the truth and importance of the doctrine which he taught, could Clement Blair have learned to encounter, nay, to provoke, the animosity of the powerful and inveterate, to alarm the fears of the jealous and timid, to walk in the world as he belonged not to it, and to be accounted mad of men, that he might, if possible, win souls to God. Heaven be my witness, that I would comply in all lawful things, to conciliate the love and sympathy of my fellow-creatures! It is no light thing to be shunned by the worthy as an infected patient; to be persecuted by the Pharisees of the day as an unbelieving heretic; to be regarded with horror at once and contempt by the multitude, who consider me as a madman, who may be expected to turn mischievous. But were all those evils multiplied an hundred-fold, the fire within must not be stifled, the voice which says within me—Speak, must receive obedience. Woe unto me if I preach not the Gospel, even should I at length preach it from amidst the pile of flames!"

So spoke this bold witness; one of those whom Heaven raised up from time to time, to preserve amidst the most ignorant ages, and to carry down to those which succeed them, a manifestation of unadulterated Christianity, from the time of the Apostles to the age when, favoured by the invention of printing, the Reformation broke out in full splendour. The selfish policy of the Glover was exposed in his own eyes; and he felt himself contemptible as he saw the Carthusian turn from him in all the hallowedness of resignation. He was even conscious of a momentary inclination to follow the example of the preacher's philanthropy and disinterested zeal; but it glanced like a flash of lightning through a dark vault, where there lies nothing to catch the blaze; and he slowly descended the hill in a direction different from that of the Carthusian, forgetting him and his doctrines, and buried in anxious thoughts about his child's fate and his own.

CHAPTER XXVIII

What want these outlaws conquerors should have,
But History's purchased page to call them great,
A wider space, an ornamented grave?
Their hopes were not less warm, their souls were full as brave.
                                                    BYRON.

THE funeral obsequies being over, the same flotilla which had proceeded in solemn and sad array down the lake,

lately been extended, and surrounded by triumphant friends, as that had been by desolate mourners. One boat kept closest of the flotilla to the honoured galley. Torquil of the Oak, a grizzled giant, was steersman; and his eight sons, each exceeding the ordinary stature of mankind, pulled the oars. Like some powerful and favourite wolf-hound, unloosed from his couples, and frolicking around a liberal master, the boat of the foster brethren passed the Chieftain's barge, now on one side, and now on another, and even rowed around it, as if in extravagance of joy; while, at the same time, with the jealous vigilance of the animal we have compared it to, they made it dangerous for any other of the flotilla to approach so near as themselves, from the risk of being run down by their impetuous and reckless manœuvres. Raised to an eminent rank in the clan by the succession of their foster brother to the command of the Clan Quhele, this was the tumultuous and almost terrible mode in which they testified their peculiar share in their Chief's triumph.

Far behind, and with different feelings, on the part of one at least of the company, came the small boat, in which, manned by the Booshalloch and one of his sons, Simon Glover was a passenger.

"If we are bound for the head of the lake," said Simon to his friend, "we shall hardly be there for hours."

But as he spoke, the crew of the boat of the foster brethren, or Leichtach, on a signal from the Chief's galley, lay on their oars until the Booshalloch's boat came up, and throwing on board a rope of hides, which Niel made fast to the head of his skiff, they stretched to their oars once more; and, notwithstanding they had the small boat in tow, swept through the lake with almost the same rapidity as before. The skiff was tugged on with a velocity which seemed to hazard the pulling her under water, or the separation of her head from her other timbers.

Simon Glover saw with anxiety the reckless fury of their course, and the bows of the boat occasionally brought within an inch or two of the level of the water; and though his friend Niel Booshalloch assured him it was all done in especial honour, he heartily wished his voyage might have a safe termination. It had so, and much sooner than he apprehended; for the place of festivity was not four miles distant from the sepulchral island, being chosen to suit the Chieftain's course, which lay to the south-east, so soon as the banquet should be concluded.

A bay on the southern side of Loch Tay presented a beautiful beach of sparkling sand, on which the boats might land with ease, and a dry meadow, covered with turf, verdant considering the season, behind and around which rose high banks, fringed with copsewood, and displaying the lavish preparations which had been made for the entertainment.

The Highlanders, well known for ready hatchet-men, had constructed a long arbour or silvan banqueting-room, capable of receiving two hundred men, while a number of smaller huts around seemed intended for sleeping apartments. The uprights, the couples, and rooftree of the temporary hall, were composed of mountain-pine, still covered with its bark. The frame-work of the sides was of planks or spars of the same material, closely interwoven with the leafy boughs of the fir and other evergreens, which the neighbouring woods afforded, while the hills had furnished plenty of heath to form the roof. Within this silvan palace the most important personages present were invited to hold high festival. Others of less note were to feast in various long sheds, constructed with less care; and tables of sod, or rough planks, placed in the open air, were allotted to the numberless multitude. At a distance were to be seen piles of glowing charcoal or blazing wood, around which countless cooks toiled, bustled, and fretted, like so many demons working in their native element. Pits, wrought in the hillside, and lined with heated stones, served as ovens for stewing immense quantities of beef, mutton, and venison—wooden spits supported sheep and goats, which were roasted entire; others were cut into joints, and seethed in caldrons made of the animals' own skins, sewed hastily together and filled with water; while huge quantities of pike, trout, salmon, and char, were broiled with more ceremony on glowing embers. The Glover had seen many a Highland banquet, but never one the preparations for which were on such a scale of barbarous profusion.

He had little time, however, to admire the scene around him; for, as soon as they landed on the beach, the Booshalloch observed with some embarrassment, that as they had not been bidden to the table of the dais, to which he seemed to have expected an invitation, they had best secure a place in one of the inferior bothies, or booths; and was leading the way in that direction, when he was stopped by one of the bodyguards, seeming to act as master of ceremonies, who whispered something in his ear.

"I thought so," said the herdsman, much relieved, "I thought neither the stranger, nor the man that has my charge, would be left out at the high table."

They were conducted accordingly into the ample lodge, within which were long ranges of tables already mostly occupied by the guests, while those who acted as domestics were placing upon them the abundant though rude materials of the festival. The young Chief, although he certainly saw the Glover and the herdsman enter, did not address any personal salute to either, and their places were assigned them in a distant corner, far beneath the Salt, (a huge piece of antique silver-plate,) the only article of value that the table displayed, and which was regarded by the Clan as a species of palladium, only produced and used on the most solemn occasions, such as the present.

The Booshalloch, somewhat discontented, muttered to Simon as he took his place—"These are changed days, friend. His father, rest his soul, would have spoken to us both; but these are bad manners which he has learned among the Sassenachs in the Low Country."

To this remark the Glover did not think it necessary to reply; instead of which he adverted to the evergreens, and particularly to the skins and other ornaments with which the interior of the bower was decorated. The most remarkable part of these ornaments was a number of Highland shirts of mail, with steel-bonnets, battle-axes, and two-handed swords to match, which hung around the upper part of the room, together with targets highly and richly embossed. Each mail shirt was hung over a well-dressed stag's hide, which at once displayed the armour to advantage, and saved it from suffering by damp.

"These," whispered the Booshalloch, "are the arms of the chosen champions of the Clan Quhele. They are twenty-nine in number, as you see, Eachin himself being the thirtieth, who wears his armour to-day, else had there been thirty. And he has not got such a good hauberk after all, as he should wear on Palm Sunday. These nine suits of harness, of such large size, are for the Leichtach from whom so much is expected."

"And these goodly deer-hides," said Simon, the spirit of his profession awakening at the sight of the goods in which he traded,—"think you the Chief will be disposed to chaffer for them?—they are in demand for the doublets which knights wear under their armour."

"Did I not pray you," said Niel Booshalloch, "to say nothing on that subject?"

"It is the mail shirts I speak of," said Simon,—"may I ask if any of them were made by our celebrated Perth armourer, called Henry of the Wynd?"

"Thou art more unlucky than before," said Niel; "that man's name is to Eachin's temper like a whirlwind upon the lake; yet no man knows for what cause."

"I can guess," thought our Glover, but gave no utterance to the thought; and, having twice lighted on unpleasant subjects of conversation, he prepared to apply himself, like those around him, to his food, without starting another topic.

We have said as much of the preparations as may lead the reader to conclude that the festival, in respect of the quality of the food, was of the most rude description, consisting chiefly of huge joints of meat, which were consumed with little respect to the fasting season, although several of the friars of the Island Convent graced and hallowed the board by their presence. The platters were of wood, and so were the hooped cogues or cups, out of which the guests quaffed their liquor, as also the broth or juice of the meat, which was held a delicacy. There were also various preparations of milk which were highly esteemed, and were eaten out of similar vessels. Bread was the scarcest article at the banquet, but the Glover and his patron Niel were served with two small loaves expressly for their own use. In eating, as indeed was then the case all over Britain, the guests used their knives called skenes, or the large poniards named dirks, without troubling themselves by the reflection that they might occasionally have served different or more fatal purposes.

At the upper end of the table stood a vacant seat, elevated a step or two above the floor. It was covered with a canopy of holly boughs and ivy, and there rested against it a sheathed sword and a folded banner. This had been the seat of the deceased Chieftain, and was left vacant in honour of him. Eachin occupied a lower chair on the right hand of the place of honour.

The reader would be greatly mistaken who should follow out this description, by supposing that the guests behaved like a herd of hungry wolves, rushing upon a feast rarely offered to them. On the contrary, the Clan Quhele conducted themselves with that species of courteous reserve and attention to the wants of others, which is often found in primitive nations, especially such as are always in arms; because a general observance of the rules of courtesy is necessary to prevent quarrels, bloodshed, and death. The guests took the places assigned them by Torquil of the Oak, who acting as Marischal *Taeh*, i.e. sewer of the mess, touched with a white wand, without speaking a word, the place where each was to sit. Thus placed in order, the company patiently waited for the portion assigned them, which was distributed among them by the Leichtach; the bravest men, or more distinguished warriors of the tribe, being accommodated with a double mess, emphatically called *bieyfir*, or the portion of a man. When the sewers themselves had seen every one served, they resumed their places at the festival, and were each served with one of these larger messes of food. Water was placed within each man's reach, and a handful of soft moss served the purposes of a table-napkin, so that, as at an Eastern banquet, the hands were washed as often as the mess was changed. For amusement, the bard recited the praises of the deceased Chief, and expressed the clan's confidence in the blossoming virtues of his successor. The Seanachie recited the genealogy of the tribe, which they traced to the race of the Dalriads; the harpers played within, while the war-pipes cheered the multitude without. The conversation among the guests was grave, subdued, and civil—no jest was attempted beyond the bounds of a very gentle pleasantry, calculated only to excite a passing smile. There were no raised voices, no contentious arguments; and Simon Glover had heard a hundred times more noise at a guild-feast in Perth, than was made on this occasion by two hundred wild mountaineers.

Even the liquor itself did not seem to raise the festive party above the same tone of decorous gravity. It was of various kinds—wine appeared in very small quantities, and was served out only to the principal guests, among which honoured number Simon Glover was again included. The wine and the two wheaten loaves were indeed the only marks of notice which he received during the feast; but Niel Booshalloch, jealous of his master's reputation for hospitality, failed not to enlarge on them as proofs of high distinction. Distilled liquors, since so generally used in the Highlands, were then comparatively unknown. The usquebaugh was circulated in small quantities, and was highly flavoured with a decoction of saffron and other herbs, so as to resemble a medicinal potion, rather than a festive cordial. Cider and mead were seen at the entertainment, but ale, brewed in great quantities for the purpose, and flowing round without restriction, was the liquor generally used, and that was drunk with a moderation much less known among the more modern Highlanders. A cup to the memory of the deceased Chieftain was the first pledge solemnly proclaimed after the banquet was finished; and a low murmur of benedictions was heard from the company, while the monks alone, uplifting their united voices, sung *Requiem eternam dona.* An unusual silence followed, as if something extraordinary was expected, when Eachin arose, with a bold and manly yet modest grace, and ascended the vacant seat or throne, saying with dignity and firmness—

"This seat and my father's inheritance, I claim as my right—so prosper me God and St. Barr!"

"How will you rule your father's children?" said an old man, the uncle of the deceased.

"I will defend them with my father's sword, and distribute justice to them under my father's banner."

The old man, with a trembling hand, unsheathed the ponderous weapon, and holding it by the blade, offered the hilt to the young Chieftain's grasp; at the same time Torquil of the Oak unfurled the pennon of the tribe, and swung it repeatedly over Eachin's head, who, with singular grace and dexterity, brandished the huge claymore as in its defence. The guests raised a yelling shout, to testify their acceptance of the patriarchal Chief who claimed their allegiance, nor was there any who, in the graceful and agile youth before them, was disposed to recollect the subject of sinister vaticinations. As he stood in glittering mail, resting on the long sword, and acknowledging by gracious gestures the acclamations which rent the air within, without, and around, Simon Glover was tempted to doubt whether this majestic figure was that of the same lad whom he had often treated with little ceremony, and began to have some apprehension of the consequences of having done so. A general burst of minstrelsy succeeded to the acclamations, and rock and greenwood rang to harp and pipes, as lately to shout and yell of woe.

It would be tedious to pursue the progress of the inaugural

feast, or detail the pledges that were quaffed to former heroes of the clan, and above all to the twenty-nine brave Gallow-glasses who were to fight in the approaching conflict, under the eye and leading of their young Chief. The bards, assuming, in old times, the prophetic character combined with their own, ventured to assure them of the most distinguished victory, and to predict the fury with which the Blue Falcon, the emblem of the Clan Quhele, should rend to pieces the Mountain-cat, the well-known badge of the Clan Chattan.

It was approaching sunset, when a bowl, called the grace-cup, make of oak, hooped with silver, was handed round the table as the signal of dispersion, although it was left free to any who chose a longer carouse to retreat to any of the outer bothies. As for Simon Glover, the Booshalloch conducted him to a small hut, contrived, it would seem, for the use of a single individual, where a bed of heath and moss was arranged as well as the season would permit, and an ample supply of such delicacies as the late feast afforded, showed that all care had been taken for the inhabitant's accommodation.

"Do not leave this hut," said the Booshalloch, taking leave of his friend and protégé ; "this is your place of rest. But apartments are lost on such a night of confusion, and if the badger leaves his hole the tod will creep into it."

To Simon Glover this arrangement was by no means disagreeable. He had been wearied by the noise of the day, and felt desirous of repose. After eating, therefore, a morsel, which his appetite scarce required, and drinking a cup of wine to expel the cold, he muttered his evening prayer, wrapt himself in his cloak, and lay down on a couch which old acquaintance had made familiar and easy to him. The hum and murmur, and even the occasional shouts, of some of the festive multitude who continued revelling without, did not long interrupt his repose ; and in about ten minutes he was as fast asleep as if he had lain in his own bed in Curfew Street.

CHAPTER XXIX

Still harping on my daughter.

Hamlet.

Two hours before the black-cock crew, Simon Glover was wakened by a well-known voice, which called him by name.

"What, Conachar!" he replied, as he started from sleep, "is the morning so far advanced?" and raising his eyes, the person of whom he was dreaming stood before him; and at the same moment, the events of yesterday rushing on his recollection, he saw with surprise that the vision retained the form which sleep had assigned it, and it was not the mail-clad Highland Chief, with claymore in hand, as he had seen him the preceding night, but Conachar of Curfew Street, in his humble apprentice's garb, holding in his hand a switch of oak. An apparition would not more have surprised our Perth burgher. As he gazed with wonder, the youth turned upon him a piece of lighted bog-wood which he carried in a lantern, and to his waking exclamation replied,—

"Even so, father Simon; it is Conachar, come to renew our old acquaintance, when our intercourse will attract least notice."

So saying, he sat down on a trestle which answered the purpose of a chair, and placing the lantern beside him, proceeded in the most friendly tone.

"I have tasted of thy good cheer many a day, father Simon—I trust thou hast found no lack in my family?"

"None whatever, Eachin MacIan," answered the Glover,— for the simplicity of the Celtic language and manners rejects all honorary titles; "it was even too good for this fasting season, and much too good for me, since I must be ashamed to think how hard you fared in Curfew Street."

"Even too well, to use your own word," said Conachar, "for the deserts of an idle apprentice, and for the wants of a young Highlander. But yesterday, if there was, as I trust, enough of food, found you not, good Glover, some lack of courteous welcome? Excuse it not,—I know you did so. But I am young in authority with my people, and I must not too early draw their attention to the period of my residence in the Lowlands, which, however, I can never forget."

"I understand the cause entirely," said Simon; "and therefore it is unwillingly, and as it were by force, that I have made so early a visit hither."

"Hush, father, hush! It is well you are come to see some of my Highland splendour while it yet sparkles— Return after Palm-Sunday, and who knows whom or what you may find in the territories we now possess! The Wild-cat may have made his lodge where the banqueting bower of MacIan now stands."

The young Chief was silent, and pressed the top of the rod to his lips, as if to guard against uttering more.

"There is no fear of that, Eachin," said Simon, in that vague way in which lukewarm comforters endeavour to turn the reflections of their friends from the consideration of inevitable danger.

"There *is* fear, and there is peril of utter ruin," answered Eachin; "and there is positive certainty of great loss I marvel my father consented to this wily proposal of Albany. I would MacGillie Chattachan would agree with me, and then, instead of wasting our best blood against each other, we would go down together to Strathmore, and kill and take possession. I would rule at Perth, and he at Dundee, and all the Great Strath should be our own to the banks of the Frith of Tay. Such is the policy I have caught from your old grey head, father Simon, when holding a trencher at thy back, and listening to thy evening talk with Bailie Craigdallie."

"The tongue is well called an unruly member," thought the Glover. "Here have I been holding a candle to the devil, to show him the way to mischief."

But he only said aloud, "These plans come too late."

"Too late indeed!" answered Eachin. "The indentures of battle are signed by our marks and seals; the burning hate of the Clan Quhele and Clan Chattan is blown up to an inextinguishable flame by mutual insults and boasts. Yes, the time is passed by.—But to thine own affairs, father Glover. It is religion that has brought thee hither, as I learn from Niel Booshalloch. Surely, my experience of thy prudence did not lead me to suspect thee of any quarrel with Mother Church. As for my old acquaintance, Father Clement, he is one of those who hunt after the crown of martyrdom, and think a stake, surrounded with blazing fagots, better worth embracing than a willing bride. He is a very knight-errant, in defence of his religious notions, and does battle wherever he comes. He hath already a quarrel with the monks of Sibyl's Isle yonder, about some point of doctrine—Hast seen him?"

"I have," answered Simon; "but we spoke little together, the time being pressing."

"He may have said that there is a third person—one more likely, I think, to be a true fugitive for religion, than either you, a shrewd citizen, or he, a wrangling preacher,—who would be right heartily welcome to share our protection?—Thou art dull, man, and wilt not guess my meaning—Thy daughter, Catharine?"

These last words the young Chief spoke in English; and he continued the conversation in that language, as if apprehensive of being overheard; and, indeed, as if under the sense of some involuntary hesitation.

"My daughter Catharine," said the Glover, remembering what the Carthusian had told him, "is well and safe."

"But where, or with whom?" said the young Chief. "And wherefore came she not with you? Think you the Clan Quhele have no cailliachs as active as old Dorothy, whose hand has warmed my haffits before now, to wait upon the daughter of their Chieftain's master."

"Again I thank you," said the Glover, "and doubt neither your power nor your will to protect my daughter, as well as myself. But an honourable lady, the friend of Sir Patrick Charteris, hath offered her a safe place of refuge, without the risk of a toilsome journey through a desolate and distracted country."

"Oh, ay,—Sir Patrick Charteris," said Eachin, in a more reserved and distant tone—"he must be preferred to all men, without doubt; he is your friend I think?"

Simon Glover longed to punish this affectation of a boy, who had been scolded four times a-day for running into the street to see Sir Patrick Charteris ride past; but he checked his spirit of repartee, and simply said,—

"Sir Patrick Charteris has been Provost of Perth for seven years; and it is likely is so still, since the magistrates are elected, not in Lent, but at St. Martinmas."

"Ah, father Glover," said the youth, in his kinder and more familiar mode of address, "you are so used to see the sumptuous shows and pageants of Perth, that you would but little relish our barbarous festival in comparison. What didst thou think of our ceremonial of yesterday?"

"It was noble and touching," said the Glover; "and to me, who knew your father, most especially so. When you rested on the sword, and looked around you, methought I saw mine old friend Gilchrist MacIan arisen from the dead, and renewed in years and in strength."

"I played my part there boldly, I trust; and showed little of that paltry apprentice boy, whom you used to—use just as he deserved."

"Eachin resembles Conachar," said the Glover, "no more

than a salmon resembles a par, though men say they are the same fish in a different state ; or than a butterfly resembles a grub."

"Thinkest thou that while I was taking upon me the power which all women love, I would have been myself an object for a maiden's eye to rest upon?—To speak plain, what would Catharine have thought of me in the ceremonial?"

"We approach the shallows now," thought Simon Glover ; "and without nice pilotage, we drive right on shore."

"Most women like show, Eachin ; but I think my daughter Catharine be an exception. She would rejoice in the good fortune of her household friend and playmate ; but she would not value the splendid MacIan, Captain of Clan Quhele, more than the orphan Conachar."

"She is ever generous and disinterested," replied the young Chief. "But yourself, father, have seen the world for many more years than she has done, and can better form a judgment what power and wealth do for those who enjoy them. Think, and speak sincerely, what would be your own thoughts, if you saw your Catharine standing under yonder canopy, with the command over an hundred hills, and the devoted obedience of ten thousand vassals ; and as the price of these advantages, her hand in that of the man who loves her the best in the world?"

"Meaning in your own, Conachar?" said Simon.

"Ay, Conachar call me—I love the name, since it was by that I have been known to Catharine."

"Sincerely, then," said the Glover, endeavouring to give the least offensive turn to his reply, "my inmost thought would be the earnest wish that Catharine and I were safe in our humble booth in Curfew Street, with Dorothy for our only vassal."

"And with poor Conachar also, I trust? You would not leave him to pine away in solitary grandeur?"

"I would not," answered the Glover, "wish so ill to the Clan Quhele, mine ancient friends, as to deprive them, at the moment of emergency, of a brave young Chief, and that Chief of the fame which he is about to acquire at their head in the approaching conflict."

Eachin bit his lip, to suppress his irritated feelings, as he replied,—"Words—words,—empty words, father Simon. You fear the Clan Quhele more than you love them, and you suppose their indignation would be formidable, should their Chief marry the daughter of a burgess of Perth."

"And if I do fear such an issue, Hector MacIan, have I not reason? How have ill-assorted marriages had issue in the House of MacCallanmore, in that of the powerful Macleans, nay, of the Lords of the Isles themselves? What has ever come of them but divorce and exheredation—sometimes worse fate, to the ambitious intruder? You could not marry my child before a priest, and you could only wed her with your left hand; and I"—he checked the strain of impetuosity which the subject inspired, and concluded,— "And I am an honest, though humble burgher of Perth, who would rather my child were the lawful and undoubted spouse of a citizen in my own rank, than the licensed concubine of a monarch."

"I will wed Catharine before the priest and before the world,—before the altar and before the black stones of Iona," said the impetuous young man. "She is the love of my youth, and there is not a tie in religion or honour, but I will bind myself by them! I have sounded my people. If we do but win this combat—and, with the hope of gaining Catharine, we SHALL win it—my heart tells me so—I shall be so much lord over their affections, that were I to take a bride from the almshouse, so it was my pleasure, they would hail her as if she were a daughter of MacCallanmore.—But you reject my suit?" said Eachin, sternly.

"You put words of offence in my mouth," said the old man, "and may next punish me for them, since I am wholly in your power. But with my consent my daughter shall never wed, save in her own degree. Her heart would break amid the constant wars and scenes of bloodshed which connect themselves with your lot. If you really love her, and recollect her dread of strife and combat, you would not wish her to be subjected to the train of military horrors in which you, like your father, must needs be inevitably and eternally engaged. Choose a bride amongst the daughters of the mountain-chiefs, my son, or fiery Lowland nobles. You are fair, young, rich, high-born, and powerful, and will not woo in vain. You will readily find one who will rejoice in your conquests, and cheer you under defeat. To Catharine, the one would be as frightful as the other. A warrior must wear a steel gauntlet—a glove of kid-skin would be torn to pieces in an hour."

A dark cloud passed over the face of the young Chief, lately animated with so much fire.

"Farewell," he said, "the only hope, which could have lighted me to fame or victory!"—He remained for a space silent, and intensely thoughtful, with downcast eyes, a lowering brow, and folded arms. At length he raised his hands, and said, "Father,—for such you have been to me,—I am about to tell you a secret. Reason and Pride both advise me to be silent, but Fate urges me, and must be obeyed. I am about to lodge in you the deepest and dearest secret that man ever confided to man. But beware—end this conference how it will—beware how you ever breathe a syllable of what I am now to trust to you; for know, that were you to do so in the most remote corner of Scotland, I have ears to hear it even there, and a hand and poniard to reach a traitor's bosom.—I am—but the word will not out!"

"Do not speak it then," said the prudent Glover; "a secret is no longer safe when it crosses the lips of him who owns it; and I desire not a confidence so dangerous as you menace me with.

"Ay, but I must speak, and you must hear," said the youth. "In this age of battle, father, you have yourself been a combatant?"

"Once only," replied Simon, "when the Southron assaulted the Fair City. I was summoned to take my part in the defence, as my tenure required, like that of other craftsmen, who are bound to keep watch and ward."

"And how felt you upon that matter?" enquired the young Chief.

"What can that import to the present business?" said Simon, in some surprise.

"Much, else I had not asked the question," answered Eachin, in the tone of haughtiness which from time to time he assumed.

"An old man is easily brought to speak of olden times," said Simon, not unwilling, on an instant's reflection, to lead the conversation away from the subject of his daughter, "and I must needs confess, my feelings were much short of the high cheerful confidence, nay, the pleasure, with which I have seen other men go to battle. My life and profession were peaceful, and though I have not wanted the spirit of a man, when the time demanded it, yet I have seldom slept worse than the night before that onslaught. My ideas were harrowed by the tales we were told (nothing short of the truth) about the Saxon archers; how they drew shafts of a cloth-yard length, and used bows a third longer than ours. When I fell into a broken slumber, if but a straw in the mattress pricked my side, I started and waked, thinking an English arrow was quivering in my body. In the morning, as I began for very weariness to sink into some repose, I was waked by the tolling of the common bell, which called us burghers to the walls;—I never heard its sound peal so like a passing knell before or since."

"Go on—what further chanced?" demanded Eachin.

"I did on my harness," said Simon, "such as it was—took my mother's blessing, a high-spirited woman, who spoke of my father's actions for the honour of the Fair Town. This heartened me, and I felt still bolder when I found myself ranked among the other crafts, all bowmen, for thou knowest the Perth citizens have good skill in archery. We were dispersed on the walls, several knights and squires in armour of proof being mingled amongst us, who kept a bold countenance, confident perhaps in their harness, and informed us, for our encouragement, that they would cut down with their swords and axes, any of those who should attempt to quit their post. I was kindly assured of this myself by the old Kempe of Kinfauns, as he was called, this good Sir Patrick's father, then our Provost. He was a grandson of the Red Rover, Tom of Longueville, and a likely man to keep his word, which he addressed to me in especial, because a night of much discomfort may have made me look paler than usual; and besides, I was but a lad."

"And did his exhortation add to your fear, or your resolution?" said Eachin, who seemed very attentive.

"To my resolution," answered Simon; "for I think nothing can make a man so bold to face one danger at some distance in his front, as the knowledge of another close behind him, to push him forward. Well—I mounted the walls in tolerable heart, and was placed with others on the Spey Tower, being accounted a good bowman. But a very cold fit seized me as I saw the English, in great order, with their archers in front, and their men-at-arms behind, marching forward to the attack in strong columns, three in number. They came on steadily, and some of us would fain have shot at them; but it was strictly forbidden, and we were obliged to remain motionless, sheltering ourselves behind the battlement as we best might. As the Southron formed their long ranks into lines, each man occupying his place as by magic, and preparing to cover

themselves by large shields, called pavesses, which they planted
before them, I again felt a strange breathlessness, and some
desire to go home for a glass of distilled waters. But as I
looked aside, I saw the worthy Kempe of Kinfauns bending
a large crossbow, and I thought it pity he should waste the
bolt on a true-hearted Scotsman, when so many English were
in presence; so I e'en staid where I was, being in a comfortable angle, formed by two battlements. The English then
strode forward, and drew their bowstrings,—not to the breast,
as your Highland kerne do, but to the ear,—and sent off their
volleys of swallow-tails before we could call on St. Andrew.
I winked when I saw them haul up their tackle, and I believe
I started as the shafts began to rattle against the parapet.
But looking round me, and seeing none hurt but John
Squallit, the town-crier, whose jaws were pierced through
with a cloth-yard shaft, I took heart of grace, and shot in my
turn with good will and good aim. A little man I shot at,
who had just peeped out from behind his target, dropt with a
shaft through his shoulder. The Provost cried—'Well stitched,
Simon Glover!'—'Saint John, for his own town,—my fellow-
craftsmen!'—shouted I, though I was then but an apprentice.
And if you will believe me, in the rest of the skirmish, which
was ended by the foes drawing off, I drew bowstring and
loosed shaft as calmly as if I had been shooting at butts
instead of men's breasts. I gained some credit, and I have
ever afterwards thought, that in case of necessity, (for with me
it had never been matter of choice,) I should not have lost it
again.—And this is all I can tell of warlike experience in
battle. Other dangers I have had, which I have endeavoured
to avoid like a wise man, or, when they were inevitable, I
have faced them like a true one. Upon other terms a man
cannot live or hold up his head in Scotland."

"I understand your tale," said Eachin; "but I shall find it
difficult to make you credit mine, knowing the race of which
I am descended, and especially that I am the son of him
whom we have this day laid in the tomb—well that he lies
where he will never learn what you are now to hear! Look,
my father—the light which I bear grows short and pale, a few
minutes will extinguish it—but before it expires, the hideous
tale will be told.—Father, I am—a COWARD!—It is said
at last, and the secret of my disgrace is in keeping of
another!"

The young man sunk back in a species of syncope, produced

by the agony of his mind as he made the fatal communication. The Glover, moved as well by fear as by compassion, applied himself to recall him to life, and succeeded in doing so, but not in restoring him to composure. He hid his face with his hands, and his tears flowed plentifully and bitterly.

"For Our Lady's sake, be composed," said the old man, "and recall the vile word! I know you better than yourself— you are NO coward, but only too young and inexperienced, ay, and somewhat too quick of fancy, to have the steady valour of a bearded man. I would hear no other man say that of you, Conachar, without giving him the lie—You are no coward—I have seen high sparks of spirit fly from you even on slight enough provocation."

"High sparks of pride and passion!" said the unfortunate youth; "but when saw you them supported by the resolution that should have backed them? the sparks you speak of, fell on my dastardly heart as on a piece of ice which could catch fire from nothing—if my offended pride urged me to strike, my weakness of mind prompted me the next moment to fly."

"Want of habit," said Simon; "it is by clambering over walls that youths learn to scale precipices. Begin with slight feuds—exercise daily the arms of your country in tourney with your followers."

"And what leisure is there for this?" exclaimed the young Chief, starting as if something horrid had occurred to his imagination. "How many days are there betwixt this hour and Palm Sunday, and what is to chance then?—A list enclosed, from which no man can stir, more than the poor bear who is chained to his stake. Sixty living men, the best and fiercest, (one alone excepted!) which Albyn can send down from her mountains, all athirst for each other's blood, while a King and his nobles, and shouting thousands besides, attend, as at a theatre, to encourage their demoniac fury! Blows clang, and blood flows, thicker, faster, redder—they rush on each other like madmen—they tear each other like wild beasts—the wounded are trodden to death amid the feet of their companions! Blood ebbs, arms become weak—but there must be no parley, no truce, no interruption, while any of the maimed wretches remain alive! Here is no crouching behind battlements, no fighting with missile weapons,—all is hand to hand, till hands can no longer be raised to maintain the ghastly conflict!—If such a field is so horrible in idea, what think you it will be in reality?"

The Glover remained silent.

"I say again, what think you?"

"I can only pity you, Conachar," said Simon. "It is hard to be the descendant of a lofty line—the son of a noble father—the leader by birth of a gallant array—and yet to want, or think you want (for still I trust the fault lies much in a quick fancy, that over-estimates danger), to want that dogged quality, which is possessed by every game-cock that is worth a handful of corn, every hound that is worth a mess of offal. But how chanced it, that with such a consciousness of inability to fight in this battle, you proffered even now to share your chiefdom with my daughter? Your power must depend on your fighting this combat, and in that Catharine cannot help you."

"You mistake, old man," replied Eachin; "were Catharine to look kindly on the earnest love I bear her, it would carry me against the front of the enemies with the mettle of a war-horse. Overwhelming as my sense of weakness is, the feeling that Catharine looked on would give me strength. Say yet—oh, say yet—she shall be mine if we gain the combat, and not the *Gow Chrom* himself, whose heart is of a piece with his anvil, ever went to battle so light as I shall do! One strong passion is conquered by another."

"This is folly, Conachar. Cannot the recollections of your interest, your honour, your kindred, do as much to stir your courage, as the thoughts of a brent-browed lass? Fie upon you, man!"

"You tell me but what I have told myself—but it is in vain," replied Eachin, with a sigh. "It is only whilst the timid stag is paired with the doe, that he is desperate and dangerous. Be it from constitution—be it, as our Highland cailliachs will say, from the milk of the White Doe—be it from my peaceful education, and the experience of your strict restraint—be it, as you think, from an overheated fancy, which paints danger yet more dangerous and ghastly than it is in reality, I cannot tell. But I know my failing, and—yes, it must be said!—so sorely dread that I cannot conquer it, that, could I have your consent to my wishes on such terms, I would even here make a pause, renounce the rank I have assumed, and retire into humble life."

"What, turn glover at last, Conachar?" said Simon; "this beats the legend of St. Crispin. Nay, nay, your hand was not framed for that; you shall spoil me no more doe-skins."

"Jest not," said Eachin, I am serious. If I cannot labour, I will bring wealth enough to live without it. They will proclaim me recreant with horn and war-pipe—Let them do so—Catharine will love me the better that I have preferred the paths of peace to those of bloodshed, and Father Clement shall teach us to pity and forgive the world, which will load us with reproaches that wound not. I shall be the happiest of men—Catharine will enjoy all that unbounded affection can confer upon her, and will be freed from apprehension of the sights and sounds of horror, which your ill-assorted match would have prepared for her; and you, Father Glover, shall occupy your chimney-corner, the happiest and most honoured man, that ever——"

"Hold, Eachin—I prithee, hold," said the Glover; "the fir light, with which this discourse must terminate, burns very low, and I would speak a word in my turn, and plain dealing is best. Though it may vex, or perhaps enrage you, let me end these visions by saying at once—Catharine can never be yours. A glove is the emblem of faith, and a man of my craft should therefore less than any other break his own. Catharine's hand is promised—promised to a man whom you may hate, but whom you must honour—to Henry the Armourer. The match is fitting by degree, agreeable to their mutual wishes, and I have given my promise. It is best to be plain at once—resent my refusal as you will—I am wholly in your power—But nothing shall make me break my word."

The Glover spoke thus decidedly, because he was aware from experience that the very irritable disposition of his former apprentice yielded in most cases to stern and decided resolution. Yet recollecting where he was, it was with some feelings of fear that he saw the dying flame leap up, and spread a flash of light on the visage of Eachin, which seemed pale as the grave, while his eye rolled like that of a maniac in his fever fit. The light instantly sunk down and died, and Simon felt a momentary terror, lest he should have to dispute for his life with the youth, whom he knew to be capable of violent actions when highly excited, however short a period his nature could support the measures which his passion commenced. He was relieved by the voice of Eachin, who muttered in a hoarse and altered tone,—

"Let what we have spoken this night rest in silence for ever—If thou bring'st it to light, thou wert better dig thine own grave."

Thus speaking, the door of the hut opened, admitting a

gleam of moonshine. The form of the retiring Chief crossed it for an instant, the hurdle was then closed, and the shieling left in darkness.

Simon Glover felt relieved, when a conversation, fraught with offence and danger, was thus peaceably terminated. But he remained deeply affected by the condition of Hector MacIan, whom he had himself bred up.

"The poor child," said he, "to be called up to a place of eminence, only to be hurled from it with contempt! What he told me I partly knew, having often remarked that Conachar was more prone to quarrel than to fight. But this overpowering faintheartedness, which neither shame nor necessity can overcome, I, though no Sir William Wallace, cannot conceive. And to propose himself for a husband to my daughter, as if a bride were to find courage for herself and the bridegroom! No, no—Catharine must wed a man to whom she may say,— 'Husband, spare your enemy'—not one in whose behalf she must cry,—'Generous enemy, spare my husband.'"

Tired out with these reflections, the old man at length fell asleep. In the morning, he was awakened by his friend the Booshalloch, who, with something of a blank visage, proposed to him to return to his abode on the meadow at the Ballough. He apologized, that the Chief could not see Simon Glover that morning, being busied with things about the expected combat; and that Eachin MacIan thought the residence at the Ballough would be safest for Simon Glover's health, and had given charge that every care should be taken for his protection and accommodation.

Niel Booshalloch dilated on these circumstances, to gloss over the neglect implied in the Chief's dismissing his visitor without a particular audience.

"His father knew better," said the herdsman. "But where should he have learned manners, poor thing, and bred up among your Perth burghers, who, excepting yourself, neighbour Glover, who speak Gaelic as well as I do, are a race incapable of civility?"

Simon Glover, it may be well believed, felt none of the want of respect which his friend resented on his account. On the contrary, he greatly preferred the quiet residence of the good herdsman, to the tumultuous hospitality of the daily festival of the Chief, even if there had not just passed an interview with Eachin upon a subject which it would be most painful to revive.

To the Ballough, therefore, he quietly retreated, where, could he have been secure of Catharine's safety, his leisure was spent pleasantly enough. His amusement was sailing on the lake, in a little skiff, which a Highland boy managed, while the old man angled. He frequently landed on the little island, where he mused over the tomb of his old friend Gilchrist MacIan, and made friends with the monks, presenting the prior with gloves of marten's fur, and the superior officers with each of them a pair made from the skin of the wild-cat. The cutting and stitching of these little presents, served to beguile the time after sunset, while the family of the herdsman crowded around, admiring his address, and listening to the tales and songs with which the old man had skill to pass away a heavy evening.

It must be confessed that the cautious Glover avoided the conversation of Father Clement, whom he erroneously considered as rather the author of his misfortunes, than the guiltless sharer of them. "I will not," he thought, "to please his fancies, lose the good-will of these kind monks, which may be one day useful to me. I have suffered enough by his preachments already, I trow. Little the wiser and much the poorer have they made me. No, no, Catharine and Clement may think as they will; but I will take the first opportunity to sneak back like a rated hound at the call of his master, submit to a plentiful course of hair-cloth and whip-cord, disburse a lusty mulct, and become whole with the church again."

More than a fortnight had passed since the Glover had arrived at Ballough, and he began to wonder that he had not heard news of Catharine or of Henry Wynd, to whom he concluded the Provost had communicated the plan and place of his retreat. He knew the stout Smith dared not come up into the Clan Quhele country, on account of various feuds with the inhabitants, and with Eachin himself, while bearing the name of Conachar; but yet the Glover thought Henry might have found means to send him a message, or a token, by some one of the various couriers who passed and repassed between the court and the headquarters of the Clan Quhele, in order to concert the terms of the impending combat, the march of the parties to Perth, and other particulars requiring previous adjustment. It was now the middle of March, and the fatal Palm Sunday was fast approaching.

Whilst time was thus creeping on, the exiled Glover had not even once set eyes upon his former apprentice. The care that was taken to attend to his wants and convenience in every respect, showed that he was not forgotten; but yet when he heard the Chieftain's horn ringing through the woods, he usually made it a point to choose his walk in a different direction. One morning, however, he found himself unexpectedly in Eachin's close neighbourhood, with scarce leisure to avoid him; and thus it happened.

As Simon strolled pensively through a little silvan glade, surrounded on either side with tall forest trees, mixed with underwood, a white aoe broke from the thicket, closely pursued by two deer greyhounds, one of which griped her haunch, the other her throat, and pulled her down within half a furlong of the Glover, who was something startled at the suddenness of the incident. The near and piercing blast of a horn, and the baying of a slowhound, made Simon aware that the hunters were close behind, and on the trace of the deer. Hallooing and the sound of men running through the copse, were heard close at hand. A moment's recollection would have satisfied Simon, that his best way was to stand fast, or retire slowly, and leave it to Eachin to acknowledge his presence or not, as he should see cause. But his desire of shunning the young man had grown into a kind of instinct, and in the alarm of finding him so near, Simon hid himself in a bush of hazels mixed with holly, which altogether concealed him. He had hardly done so, ere Eachin, rosy with exercise, dashed from the thicket into the open glade, accompanied by his foster-father, Torquil of the Oak. The latter, with equal strength and address, turned the struggling hind on her back, and holding her fore feet in his right hand, while he knelt on her body, offered his skene with the left, to the young Chief, that he might cut the animal's throat.

"It may not be, Torquil; do thine office, and take the assay thyself. I must not kill the likeness of my foster-mother."

This was spoken with a melancholy smile, while a tear at the same time stood in the speaker's eye. Torquil stared at his young Chief for an instant, then drew his sharp wood-knife across the creature's throat, with a cut so swift and steady, that the weapon reached the back-bone. Then rising on his feet, and again fixing a long piercing look on his Chief, he said,—"As much as I have done to that hind, would I do to any living man whose ears could have heard my dault (foster-son) so much as name a white doe, and couple the word with Hector's name!"

If Simon had no reason before to keep himself concealed, this speech of Torquil furnished him with a pressing one.

"It cannot be concealed, father Torquil," said Eachin; "it will all out to the broad day."

"What will out? what will to broad day?" asked Torquil in surprise.

"It is the fatal secret," thought Simon; "and now, if this huge privy counsellor cannot keep silence, I shall be made answerable, I suppose, for Eachin's disgrace having been blown abroad."

Thinking thus anxiously, he availed himself, at the same time, of his position to see as much as he could of what passed between the afflicted Chieftain and his confidant, impelled by that spirit of curiosity which prompts us in the most momentous, as well as the most trivial occasions of life, and which is sometimes found to exist in company with great personal fear.

As Torquil listened to what Eachin communicated, the young man sank into his arms, and, supporting himself on his shoulder, concluded his confession by a whisper into his ear. Torquil seemed to listen with such amazement as to make him incapable of crediting his ears. As if to be certain that it was Eachin who spoke, he gradually roused the youth from his reclining posture, and holding him up in some measure by a grasp on his shoulder, fixed on him an eye that seemed enlarged, and at the same time turned to stone, by the marvels he listened to. And so wild waxed the old man's visage after he had heard the murmured communication, that Simon Glover apprehended he would cast the youth from him as a dishonoured thing, in which case he might have lighted among the very copse in which he lay concealed, and occasioned his discovery in a manner equally painful and dangerous. But the passions of Torquil, who entertained for his foster-child even a double portion of that passionate fondness which always attends that connexion in the Highlands, took a different turn.

"I believe it not!"—he exclaimed; "it is false of thy father's child;—false of thy mother's son; falsest of MY *dault!*

I offer my gage to heaven and hell, and will maintain the combat with him that shall call it true! Thou hast been spell-bound by an evil eye, my darling, and the fainting which you call cowardice is the work of magic. I remember the bat that struck the torch out on the hour that thou wert born,—that hour of grief and of joy. Cheer up, my beloved! Thou shalt with me to Iona, and the good St. Columbus, with the whole choir of blessed saints and angels, who ever favoured thy race, shall take from thee the heart of the white doe, and return that which they have stolen from thee."

Eachin listened, with a look as if he would fain have believed the words of the comforter.

"But, Torquil," he said, "supposing this might avail us, the fatal day approaches, and if I go to the lists, I dread me we shall be shamed."

"It cannot be—it shall not!" said Torquil,—"Hell shall not prevail so far—we will steep thy sword in holy water,—place vervain, St. John's-wort, and rowan-tree in thy crest. We will surround thee, I and thy eight brethren—thou shalt be safe as in a castle."

Again the youth helplessly muttered something, which, from the dejected tone in which it was spoken, Simon could not understand, while Torquil's deep tones in reply fell full and distinct upon his ear.

"Yes, there may be a chance of withdrawing thee from the conflict. Thou art the youngest who is to draw blade. Now, hear me, and thou shalt know what it is to have a foster-father's love, and how far it exceeds the love even of kinsmen. The youngest on the indenture of the Clan Chattan is Ferquhard Day. His father slew mine, and the red blood is seething hot between us—I looked to Palm Sunday as the term that should cool it—But mark!—Thou wouldst have thought that the blood in the veins of this Ferquhard Day and in mine would not have mingled, had they been put into the same vessel, yet hath he cast the eyes of his love upon my only daughter Eva—the fairest of our maidens. Think with what feelings I heard the news. It was as if a wolf from the skirts of Ferragon had said, 'Give me thy child in wedlock, Torquil.' My child thought not thus, she loves Ferquhard, and weeps away her colour and strength in dread of the approaching battle. Let her give him but a sign of favour, and well I know he will forget kith and kin, forsake the field, and fly with her to the desert."

"He, the youngest of the champions of Clan Chattan, being absent, I, the youngest of the Clan Quhele, may be excused from combat," said Eachin, blushing at the mean chance of safety thus opened to him.

"See now, my Chief," said Torquil, "and judge my thoughts towards thee—others might give thee their own lives and that of their sons—I sacrifice to thee the honour of my house."

"My friend, my father," repeated the Chief, folding Torquil to his bosom, "what a base wretch am I that have a spirit dastardly enough to avail myself of your sacrifice!"

"Speak not of that—Green woods have ears. Let us back to the camp, and send our gillies for the venison.—Back, dogs, and follow at heel."

The slowhound, or lyme-dog, luckily for Simon, had drenched his nose in the blood of the deer, else he might have found the Glover's lair in the thicket; but its more acute properties of scent being lost, it followed tranquilly with the gaze-hounds.

When the hunters were out of sight and hearing, the Glover arose, greatly relieved by their departure, and began to move off, in the opposite direction, as fast as his age permitted. His first reflection was on the fidelity of the foster-father.

"The wild mountain heart is faithful and true. Yonder man is more like the giants in romaunts, than a man of mould like ourselves; and yet Christians might take an example from him for his lealty. A simple contrivance this though, to finger a man from off their enemies' chequer, as if there would not be plenty of the Wild-cats ready to supply his place."

Thus thought the Glover, not aware that the strictest proclamations were issued, prohibiting any of the two contending clans, their friends, allies, and dependents, from coming within fifty miles of Perth, during a week before and a week after the combat, which regulation was to be enforced by armed men.

So soon as our friend Simon arrived at the habitation of the herdsman, he found other news awaiting him. They were brought by Father Clement, who came in a pilgrim's cloak, or dalmatic, ready to commence his return to the southward, and desirous to take leave of his companion in exile, or to accept him as a travelling companion.

"But what," said the citizen, "has so suddenly induced you to return within the reach of danger?"

"Have you not heard," said Father Clement, "that March and his English allies having retired into England before the Earl of Douglas, the good Earl has applied himself to redress the evils of the commonwealth, and hath written to the court letters, desiring that the warrant for the High Court of Commission against heresy be withdrawn, as a trouble to men's consciences—that the nomination of Henry of Wardlaw to be Prelate of St. Andrews, be referred to the Parliament, with sundry other things pleasing to the Commons? Now, most of the nobles that are with the King at Perth, and with them Sir Patrick Charteris, your worthy Provost, have declared for the proposals of the Douglas. The Duke of Albany hath agreed to them; whether from good-will or policy I know not. The good King is easily persuaded to mild and gentle courses. And thus are the jaw-teeth of the oppressors dashed to pieces in their sockets, and the prey snatched from their ravening talons. Will you with me to the Lowlands, or do you abide here a little space?"

Niel Booshalloch saved his friend the trouble of reply.

"He had the Chief's authority," he said, "for saying that Simon Glover should abide until the champions went down to the battle." In this answer the citizen saw something not quite consistent with his own perfect freedom of volition; but he cared little for it at the time, as it furnished a good apology for not travelling along with the clergyman.

"An exemplary man," he said to his friend Niel Booshalloch, as soon as Father Clement had taken leave, "a great scholar, and a great saint. It is a pity almost he is no longer in danger to be burned, as his sermon at the stake would convert thousands. O, Niel Booshalloch! Father Clement's pile would be a sweet savouring sacrifice, and a beacon to all devout Christians. But what would the burning of a borrell ignorant burgess like me serve? Men offer not up old glove leather for incense, nor are beacons fed with undressed hides, I trow? Sooth to speak, I have too little learning and too much fear to get credit by the affair, and, therefore, I should, in our homely phrase, have both the scathe and the scorn."

"True for you," answered the herdsman.

CHAPTER XXX

We must return to the characters of our dramatic narrative, whom we left at Perth, when we accompanied the Glover and his fair daughter to Kinfauns, and from that hospitable mansion traced the course of Simon to Loch Tay ; and the Prince, as the highest personage, claims our immediate attention.

This rash and inconsiderate young man endured with some impatience his sequestered residence with the Lord High Constable, with whose company, otherwise in every respect satisfactory, he became dissatisfied, from no other reason than that he held in some degree the character of his warder. Incensed against his uncle, and displeased with his father, he longed, not unnaturally, for the society of Sir John Ramorny, on whom he had been so long accustomed to throw himself for amusement, and, though he would have resented the imputation as an insult, for guidance and direction. He, therefore, sent him a summons to attend him, providing his health permitted ; and directed him to come by water to a little pavilion in the High Constable's garden, which, like that of Sir John's own lodgings, ran down to the Tay. In renewing an intimacy so dangerous, Rothsay only remembered that he had been Sir John Ramorny's munificent friend ; while Sir John, on receiving the invitation, only recollected, on his part, the capricious insults he had sustained from his patron, the loss of his hand, and the lightness with which he had treated the subject, and the readiness with which Rothsay had abandoned his cause in the matter of the Bonnet-maker's slaughter. He laughed bitterly when he read the Prince's billet.

"Eviot," he said, "man a stout boat with six trusty men,—trusty men, mark me—lose not a moment ; and bid Dwining instantly come hither.—Heaven smiles on us, my trusty friend," he said to the mediciner. "I was but beating my brains how to get access to this fickle boy, and here he sends to invite me."

"Hem !—I see the matter very clearly," said Dwining. "Heaven smiles on some untoward consequences—he ! he ! he !"

"No matter, the trap is ready ; and it is baited, too, my friend, with what would lure the boy from a sanctuary, though a troop with drawn weapons waited him in the churchyard.

Yet is it scarce necessary. His own weariness of himself would have done the job. Get thy matters ready—thou goest with us. Write to him, as I cannot, that we come instantly to attend his commands, and do it clerkly. He reads well, and that he owes to me."

"He will be your valiancy's debtor for more knowledge before he dies—he! he! he! But is your bargain sure with the Duke of Albany?"

"Enough to gratify my ambition, thy avarice, and the revenge of both. Aboard, aboard, and speedily; let Eviot throw in a few flasks of the choicest wine, and some cold baked meats."

"But your arm, my lord, Sir John? Does it not pain you?"

"The throbbing of my heart silences the pain of my wound. It beats as it would burst my bosom."

"Heaven forbid!"—said Dwining; adding, in a low voice, "it would be a strange sight if it should. I should like to dissect it, save that its stony case would spoil my best instruments."

In a few minutes they were in the boat, while a speedy messenger carried the note to the Prince.

Rothsay was seated with the Constable, after their noontide repast. He was sullen and silent; and the Earl had just asked whether it was his pleasure that the table should be cleared, when a note, delivered to the Prince, changed at once his aspect.

"As you will," he said. "I go to the pavilion in the garden,—always with permission of my Lord Constable,—to receive my late Master of the Horse."

"My lord?" said Lord Errol.

"Ay, my lord; must I ask permission twice?"

"No, surely, my lord," answered the Constable; "but has your royal Highness recollected that Sir John Ramorny——"

"Has not the plague, I hope?" replied the Duke of Rothsay. "Come, Errol, you would play the surly turnkey; but it is not in your nature,—farewell for half an hour."

"A new folly!" said Errol, as the Prince, flinging open a lattice of the ground-parlour in which they sat, stept out into the garden. "A new folly, to call back that villain to his councils. But he is infatuated."

The Prince, in the meantime, looked back, and said hastily,—

"Your lordship's good housekeeping will afford us a flask or two of wine, and a slight collation in the pavilion? I love the al fresco of the river."

The Constable bowed, and gave the necessary orders; so that Sir John found the materials of good cheer ready displayed, when, landing from his barge, he entered the pavilion.

"It grieves my heart to see your Highness under restraint," said Ramorny, with a well executed appearance of sympathy.

"That grief of thine will grieve mine," said the Prince. "I am sure here has Errol, and a right true-hearted lord he is, so tired me with grave looks, and something like grave lessons, that he has driven me back to thee, thou reprobate, from whom, as I expect nothing good, I may perhaps obtain something entertaining. Yet ere we say more, it was foul work, that upon the Fastern's Even, Ramorny. I well hope thou gavest not aim to it."

"On my honour, my lord, a simple mistake of the brute Bonthron. I did but hint to him that a dry beating would be due to the fellow by whom I had lost a hand; and lo you, my knave makes a double mistake. He takes one man for another, and instead of the baton he uses the axe."

"It is well that it went no farther. Small matter for the Bonnet-maker; but I had never forgiven you had the Armourer fallen—there is not his match in Britain.—But I hope they hanged the villain high enough?"

"If thirty feet might serve," replied Ramorny.

"Pah! no more of him," said Rothsay; "his wretched name makes the good wine taste of blood.—And what are the news in Perth, Ramorny?—How stands it with the bona robas and the galliards?"

"Little galliardise stirring, my lord," answered the Knight. "All eyes are turned to the motions of the Black Douglas, who comes with five thousand chosen men to put us all to rights, as if he were bound for another Otterburn. It is said he is to be Lieutenant again. It is certain many have declared for his faction."

"It is time, then, my feet were free," said Rothsay, "otherwise I may find a worse warder than Errol."

"Ah, my lord! were you once away from this place, you might make as bold a head as Douglas."

"Ramorny," said the Prince, gravely, "I have but a confused remembrance of your once having proposed something horrible to me. Beware of such counsel. I would be free—

I would have my person at my own disposal; but I will never levy arms against my father, nor those it pleases him to trust."

"It was only for your Royal Highness's personal freedom that I was presuming to speak," answered Ramorny. "Were I in your Grace's place, I would get me into that good boat which hovers on the Tay, and drop quietly down to Fife, where you have many friends, and make free to take possession of Falkland. It is a royal castle; and though the King has bestowed it in gift on your uncle, yet surely even if the grant were not subject to challenge, your Grace might make free with the residence of so near a relative."

"He hath made free with mine," said the Duke, "as the Stewartry of Renfrew can tell. But stay, Ramorny—hold— Did I not hear Errol say that the Lady Marjory Douglas, whom they call Duchess of Rothsay, is at Falkland? I would neither dwell with that lady, nor insult her by dislodging her."

"The lady was there, my lord," replied Ramorny; "but I have sure advice that she is gone to meet her father."

"Ha! to animate the Douglas against me? or perhaps to beg him to spare me, providing I come on my knees to her bed, as pilgrims say the Emirs and Amirals, upon whom a Saracen Soldan bestows a daughter in marriage, are bound to do? Ramorny, I will act by the Douglas's own saying, 'It is better to hear the lark sing than the mouse squeak.' [1] I will keep both foot and hand from fetters."

"No place fitter than Falkland," replied Ramorny. "I have enough of good yeomen to keep the place; and should your Highness wish to leave it, a brief ride reaches the sea in three directions."

"You speak well. But we shall die of gloom yonder. Neither mirth, music, nor maidens—Ha!" said the heedless Prince.

"Pardon me, noble Duke; but though the Lady Marjory Douglas be departed, like an errant dame in romance, to implore succour of her doughty sire, there is, I may say, a lovelier, I am sure a younger maiden, either presently at Falkland, or who will soon be on the road thither. Your Highness has not forgotten the Fair Maid of Perth?"

"Forget the prettiest wench in Scotland!—No—any more than thou hast forgotten the hand that thou hadst in the Curfew Street onslaught on St. Valentine's Eve."

---

[1] Implying, that it was better to keep the forest than shut themselves up in fortified places.

"The hand that I *had*?—Your Highness would say, the hand that I lost. As certain as I shall never regain it, Catharine Glover is, or will soon be, at Falkland. I will not flatter your Highness by saying she expects to meet you— in truth, she proposes to place herself under the protection of the Lady Marjory."

"The little traitress," said the Prince—"she too to turn against me? She deserves punishment, Ramorny."

"I trust your Grace will make her penance a gentle one," replied the knight.

"Faith, I would have been her Father Confessor long ago, but I have ever found her coy."

"Opportunity was lacking, my lord," replied Ramorny; "and time presses even now."

"Nay, I am but too apt for a frolic ; but my father——"

"He is personally safe," said Ramorny, "and as much at freedom as ever he can be ; while your Highness——"

"Must brook fetters, conjugal or literal—I know it.— Yonder comes Douglas, with his daughter in his hand, as haughty, and as harsh-featured as himself, bating touches of age."

"And at Falkland, sits in solitude the fairest wench in Scotland," said Ramorny. "Here is penance and restraint, yonder is joy and freedom."

"Thou hast prevailed, most sage counsellor," replied Rothsay ; "but mark you, it shall be the last of my frolics."

"I trust so," replied Ramorny ; "for, when at liberty, you may make a good accommodation with your royal father."

"I will write to him, Ramorny—get the writing-materials —No, I cannot put my thoughts in words—do thou write."

"Your Royal Highness forgets," said Ramorny, pointing to his mutilated arm.

"Ah! that cursed hand of yours. What can we do?"

"So please your Highness," answered his counsellor, "if you would use the hand of the mediciner, Dwining—He writes like a clerk."

"Hath he a hint of the circumstances? Is he possessed of them?"

"Fully," said Ramorny ; and stepping to the window, he called Dwining from the boat.

He entered the presence of the Prince of Scotland,

creeping as if he trode upon eggs, with downcast eyes, and a frame that seemed shrunk up by a sense of awe produced by the occasion.

"There, fellow, are writing-materials. I will make trial of you—thou know'st the case—place my conduct to my father in a fair light."

Dwining sat down, and in a few minutes wrote a letter, which he handed to Sir John Ramorny.

"Why, the devil has aided thee, Dwining," said the Knight. "Listen, my dear lord.—'Respected father and liege Sovereign,—Know that important considerations induce me to take my departure from this your court, purposing to make my abode at Falkland, both as the seat of my dearest uncle Albany, with whom I know your Majesty would desire me to use all familiarity, and as the residence of one from whom I have been too long estranged, and with whom I haste to exchange vows of the closest affection from henceforward.'"

The Duke of Rothsay and Ramorny laughed aloud; and the physician, who had listened to his own scroll as if it were a sentence of death, encouraged by their applause, raised his eyes, uttered faintly his chuckling note of He! he! and was again grave and silent, as if afraid he had transgressed the bounds of reverent respect.

"Admirable!" said the Prince—"Admirable! The old man will apply all this to the Duchess, as they call her, of Rothsay.—Dwining, thou should'st be *a secretis* to his Holiness the Pope, who sometimes, it is said, wants a scribe that can make one word record two meanings. I will subscribe it, and have the praise of the device."

"And now, my lord," said Ramorny, sealing the letter, and leaving it behind, "will you not to boat?"

"Not till my chamberlain attends, with some clothes and necessaries—and you may call my sewer also."

"My lord," said Ramorny, "time presses, and preparation will but excite suspicion. Your officers will follow with the mails to-morrow. For to-night, I trust my poor service may suffice to wait on you at table and chamber."

"Nay, this time it is thou who forgets," said the Prince, touching the wounded arm with his walking-rod. "Recollect, man, thou canst neither carve a capon, nor tie a point— a goodly sewer, or valet of the mouth!"

Ramorny grinned with rage and pain; for his wound,

though in a way of healing, was still highly sensitive, and even the pointing a finger towards it made him tremble.

"Will your Highness now be pleased to take boat?"

"Not till I take leave of the Lord Constable. Rothsay must not slip away, like a thief from a prison, from the house of Errol. Summon him hither."

"My Lord Duke," said Ramorny, "it may be dangerous to our plan."

"To the devil with danger, thy plan and thyself!—I must and will act to Errol as becomes us both."

The Earl entered, agreeable to the Prince's summons.

"I gave you this trouble, my lord," said Rothsay, with the dignified courtesy which he knew so well how to assume, "to thank you for your hospitality and your good company. I can enjoy them no longer, as pressing affairs call me to Falkland."

"My lord," said the Lord High Constable, "I trust your Grace remembers that you are under ward."

"How!—under ward? If I am a prisoner, speak plainly—if not, I will take my freedom to depart."

"I would, my lord, your Highness would request his Majesty's permission for this journey. There will be much displeasure."

"Mean you displeasure against yourself, my lord, or against me?"

"I have already said your Highness lies in ward here; but if you determine to break it, I have no warrant—God forbid—to put force on your inclinations. I can but entreat your Highness, for your own sake——"

"Of my own interests I am the best judge—Good evening to you, my lord."

The wilful Prince stepped into the boat with Dwining and Ramorny, and, waiting for no other attendance, Eviot pushed off the vessel, which descended the Tay rapidly by the assistance of sail and oar, and of the ebb-tide.

For some space the Duke of Rothsay appeared silent and moody, nor did his companions interrupt his reflections He raised his head at length, and said, "My father loves a jest, and when all is over, he will take this frolic at no more serious rate than it deserves—a fit of youth, with which he will deal as he has with others.—Yonder, my masters, shows the old Hold of Kinfauns, frowning above the Tay. Now, tell me, John Ramorny, how thou hast dealt to get the Fair Maid of Perth out of the hands of yonder bull-headed Provost; for Errol told me it was rumoured that she was under his protection."

"Truly she was, my lord, with the purpose of being transferred to the patronage of the Duchess,—I mean of the Lady Marjory of Douglas. Now, this beetle-headed Provost, who is after all but a piece of blundering valiancy, has, like most such, a retainer of some slyness and cunning, whom he uses in all his dealings, and whose suggestions he generally considers as his own ideas. Whenever I would possess myself of a landward baron, I address myself to such a confidant, who, in the present case, is called Kitt Henshaw, an old skipper upon the Tay, and who, having in his time sailed as far as Campvere, holds with Sir Patrick Charteris the respect due to one who has seen foreign countries. This his agent I have made my own, and by his means have insinuated various apologies, in order to postpone the departure of Catharine for Falkland."

"But to what good purpose?"

"I know not if it is wise to tell your Highness, lest you should disapprove of my views—I meant the officers of the Commission for enquiry into heretical opinions should have found the Fair Maid at Kinfauns, for our beauty is a peevish, self-willed swerver from the Church; and certes, I designed that the Knight should have come in for his share of the fines and confiscations that were about to be inflicted. The monks were eager enough to be at him, seeing he hath had frequent disputes with them about the salmon-tithe."

"But wherefore wouldst thou have ruined the Knight's fortunes, and brought the beautiful young woman to the stake, perchance?"

"Pshaw, my Lord Duke!—Monks never burn pretty maidens. An old woman might have been in some danger; and as for my Lord Provost, as they call him, if they had clipped off some of his fat acres, it would have been some atonement for the needless brave he put on me in Saint John's church."

"Methinks, John, it was but a base revenge," said Rothsay.

"Rest ye contented, my lord. He that cannot right himself by the hand, must use his head.—Well, that chance was over by the tender-hearted Douglas's declaring in favour of tender conscience; and then, my lord, old Henshaw found no

further objections to carrying the Fair Maid of Perth to
Falkland,—not to share the dulness of the Lady Marjory's
society, as Sir Patrick Charteris and she herself doth opine,
but to keep your Highness from tiring when we return from
hunting in the park."

There was again a long pause, in which the Prince seemed
to muse deeply. At length he spoke.—"Ramorny, I have a
scruple in this matter; but if I name it to thee, the devil of
sophistry, with which thou art possessed, will argue it out of
me, as it has done many others. This girl is the most beautiful,
one excepted, whom I ever saw or knew; and I like her the
more that she bears some features of—Elizabeth of Dunbar.
But she, I mean Catharine Glover, is contracted, and presently
to be wedded, to Henry the Armourer, a craftsman unequalled
for skill, and a man-at-arms yet unmatched in the barrace.
To follow out this intrigue would do a good fellow too much
wrong."

"Your Highness will not expect me to be very solicitous of
Henry Smith's interest," said Ramorny, looking at his wounded
arm.

"By Saint Andrew with his shored cross, this disaster of
thine is too much harped upon, John Ramorny! Others are
content with putting a finger into every man's pie, but thou
must thrust in thy whole gory hand. It is done, and cannot
be undone—let it be forgotten."

"Nay, my lord, you allude to it more frequently than I,"
answered the Knight,—"in derision, it is true; while I—but
I can be silent on the subject if I cannot forget it."

"Well, then, I tell thee that I have scruple about this intrigue. Dost thou remember, when we went in a frolic to
hear Father Clement preach, or rather to see this fair heretic,
that he spoke as touchingly as a minstrel about the rich man
taking away the poor man's only ewe lamb?"

"A great matter, indeed," answered Sir John, "that this
churl's wife's eldest son should be fathered by the Prince of
Scotland! How many earls would covet the like fate for their
fair countesses? and how many that have had such good luck
sleep not a grain the worse for it?"

"And if I might presume to speak," said the mediciner,
"the ancient laws of Scotland assigned such a privilege to
every feudal lord over his female vassals, though lack of spirit
and love of money hath made many exchange it for gold."

"I require no argument to urge me to be kind to a pretty

woman : But this Catharine has been ever cold to me," said the Prince.

"Nay, my lord," said Ramorny, "if, young, handsome, and a Prince, you know not how to make yourself acceptable to a fine woman, it is not for me to say more."

"And if it were not far too great audacity in me to speak again, I would say," quoth the leech, "that all Perth knows that the *Gow Chrom* never was the maiden's choice, but fairly forced upon her by her father. I know for certain that she refused him repeatedly."

"Nay, if thou canst assure us of that, the case is much altered," said Rothsay. "Vulcan was a smith as well as Harry Wynd ; he would needs wed Venus, and our Chronicles tell us what came of it."

"Then long may Lady Venus live and be worshipped," said Sir John Ramorny ; "and success to the gallant knight Mars, who goes a-wooing to her goddess-ship ! "

The discourse took a gay and idle turn for a few minutes ; but the Duke of Rothsay soon dropped it. "I have left," he said, "yonder air of the prison-house behind me, and yet my spirits scarce revive. I feel that drowsy, not unpleasing, yet melancholy mood, that comes over us when exhausted by exercise, or satiated with pleasure. Some music now, stealing on the ear, yet not loud enough to make us lift the eye, were a treat for the gods."

"Your Grace has but to speak your wishes, and the nymphs of the Tay are as favourable as the fair ones upon the shore.— Hark—it is a lute."

"A lute ! " said the Duke of Rothsay, listening ; "it is, and rarely touched. I should remember that dying fall. Steer towards the boat from whence the music comes."

"It is old Henshaw," said Ramorny, "working up the stream.—How, skipper ! "

The boatmen answered the hail, and drew up alongside of the Prince's barge.

"Oh, ho ! my old friend ! " said the Prince, recognizing the figure as well as the appointments of the French glee-woman, Louise. "I think I owe thee something for being the means of thy having a fright, at least, upon St. Valentine's day. Into this boat with thee, lute, puppy dog, scrip and all —I will prefer thee to a lady's service, who shall feed thy very cur on capons and canary."

"I trust your Highness will consider "—said Ramorny.

"I will consider nothing but my pleasure, John. Pray, do thou be so complying as to consider it also."

"Is it indeed to a lady's service you would promote me?" said the glee-maiden. "And where does she dwell?"

"At Falkland," answered the Prince.

"Oh, I have heard of that great lady!" said Louise; "and will you indeed prefer me to your right royal consort's service?"

"I will, by my honour—whenever I receive her as such—Mark that reservation, John," said he aside to Ramorny.

The persons who were in the boat caught up the tidings, and concluding a reconciliation was about to take place betwixt the royal couple, exhorted Louise to profit by her good fortune, and add herself to the Duchess of Rothsay's train. Several offered her some acknowledgment for the exercise of her talents.

During this moment of delay, Ramorny whispered to Dwining, "Make in, knave, with some objection. This addition is one too many. Rouse thy wits, while I speak a word with Henshaw."

"If I might presume to speak," said Dwining, "as one who have made my studies both in Spain and Arabia, I would say, my lord, that the sickness has appeared in Edinburgh, and that there may be risk in admitting this young wanderer into your Highness's vicinity."

"Ah! and what is it to thee," said Rothsay, "whether I choose to be poisoned by the pestilence or the pothecary? Must thou, too, needs thwart my humour?"

While the Prince thus silenced the remonstrances of Dwining, Sir John Ramorny had snatched a moment to learn from Henshaw that the removal of the Duchess of Rothsay from Falkland was still kept profoundly secret, and that Catharine Glover would arrive there that evening or the next morning, in expectation of being taken under the noble lady's protection.

The Duke of Rothsay, deeply plunged in thought, received this intimation so coldly, that Ramorny took the liberty of remonstrating. "This, my lord," he said, "is playing the spoilt child of fortune. You wish for liberty—it comes. You wish for beauty—it awaits you, with just so much delay as to render the boon more precious. Even your slightest

desires seem a law to the Fates; for you desire music when
it seems most distant, and the lute and song are at your
hand. These things, so sent, should be enjoyed, else we
are but like petted children, who break and throw from them
the toys they have wept themselves sick for."

"To enjoy pleasure, Ramorny," said the Prince, "a man
should have suffered pain, as it requires fasting to gain a
good appetite. We, who can have all for a wish, little
enjoy that all when we have possessed it. Seest thou yonder
thick cloud, which is about to burst to rain? It seems to
stifle me—the waters look dark and lurid—the shores have
lost their beautiful form——"

"My lord, forgive your servant," said Ramorny. "You
indulge a powerful imagination, as an unskilful horseman
permits a fiery steed to rear until he falls back on
his master and crushes him. I pray you shake off this lethargy.
Shall the glee-maiden make some music?"

"Let her—but it must be melancholy; all mirth would at
this moment jar on my ear."

The maiden sung a melancholy dirge in Norman French;
the words, of which the following is an imitation, were united
to a tune as doleful as they are themselves.

I

Yes, thou mayst sigh,
And look once more at all around,
At stream and bank, and sky and ground.
Thy life its final course has found,
And thou must die.

2

Yes, lay thee down,
And while thy struggling pulses flutter,
Bid the grey monk his soul-mass mutter,
And the deep bell its death-tone utter—
Thy life is gone.

3

Be not afraid.
'Tis but a pang, and then a thrill,
A fever fit, and then a chill;
And then an end of human ill,
For thou art dead.

The Prince made no observation on the music; and the
maiden, at Ramorny's beck, went on from time to time with
her minstrel craft, until the evening sunk down into rain,

first soft and gentle, at length in great quantities, and accompanied by a cold wind. There was neither cloak nor covering for the Prince, and he sullenly rejected that which Ramorny offered.

"It is not for Rothsay to wear your cast garments, Sir John—this melted snow, which I feel pierce me to the very marrow, I am now encountering by your fault. Why did you presume to put off the boat without my servants and apparel?"

Ramorny did not attempt an exculpation; for he knew the Prince was in one of those humours, when to enlarge upon a grievance was more pleasing to him than to have his mouth stopped by any reasonable apology. In sullen silence, or amid unsuppressed chiding, the boat arrived at the fishing village of Newburgh. The party landed, and found horses in readiness, which indeed Ramorny had long since provided for the occasion. Their quality underwent the Prince's bitter sarcasm, expressed to Ramorny sometimes by direct words, oftener by bitter gibes. At length they were mounted, and rode on through the closing night and the falling rain, the Prince leading the way with reckless haste. The glee-maiden, mounted by his express order, attended them; and well for her that, accustomed to severe weather, and exercise both on foot and horseback, she supported as firmly as the men the fatigues of the nocturnal ride. Ramorny was compelled to keep at the Prince's rein, being under no small anxiety lest, in his wayward fit, he might ride off from him entirely, and, taking refuge in the house of some loyal baron, escape the snare which was spread for him. He therefore suffered inexpressibly during the ride, both in mind and in body.

At length the forest of Falkland received them, and a glimpse of the moon showed the dark and huge tower, an appendage of royalty itself, though granted for a season to the Duke of Albany. On a signal given the drawbridge fell. Torches glared in the court-yard, menials attended, and the Prince, assisted from horseback, was ushered into an apartment, where Ramorny waited on him, together with Dwining, and entreated him to take the leech's advice. The Duke of Rothsay repulsed the proposal, haughtily ordered his bed to be prepared, and having stood for some time shivering in his dank garments beside a large blazing fire, he retired to his apartment without taking leave of any one.

"You see the peevish humour of this childish boy, now," said Ramorny to Dwining; "can you wonder that a servant, who has done so much for him as I have, should be tired of such a master ? "

" No, truly," said Dwining, " that and the promised Earldom of Lindores would shake any man's fidelity.   But shall we commence with him this evening ?   He has, if eye and cheek speak true, the foundation of a fever within him, which will make our work easy, while it will seem the effect of nature."

" It is an opportunity lost," said Ramorny ; " but we must delay our blow till he has seen this beauty, Catharine Glover. She may be hereafter a witness that she saw him in good health, and master of his own motions, a brief space before— you understand me ? "

Dwining nodded assent, and added,

" There is no time lost ; for there is little difficulty in blighting a flower, exhausted from having been made to bloom too soon."

CHAPTER XXXI

Ah me ! in sooth he was a shameless wight,
Sore given to revel and ungodly glee :
Few earthly things found favour in his sight,
Save concubines and carnal companie,
And flaunting wassailers of high and low degree.

BYRON.

WITH the next morning the humour of the Duke of Rothsay was changed.   He complained, indeed, of pain and fever, but they rather seemed to stimulate than to overwhelm him. He was familiar with Ramorny, and though he said nothing on the subject of the preceding night, it was plain he remembered what he desired to obliterate from the memory of his followers—the ill-humour he had then displayed.   He was civil to every one, and jested with Ramorny on the subject of Catharine's arrival.

" How surprised will the pretty prude be at seeing herself in a family of men, when she expects to be admitted amongst the hoods and pinners of Dame Marjory's waiting-women ! Thou hast not many of the tender sex in thy household, I take it, Ramorny ? "

" Faith, none except the minstrel wench, but a household drudge or two whom we may not dispense with.   By the way, she is anxiously enquiring after the mistress your Highness promised to prefer her to.—Shall I dismiss her, to hunt for her new mistress at leisure?"

"By no means, she will serve to amuse Catharine—And, hark you, were it not well to receive that coy jillet with something of a mumming?"

"How mean you, my lord?·

"Thou art dull, man.—We will not disappoint her, since she expects to find the Duchess of Rothsay—I will be Duke and Duchess in my own person."

"Still I do not comprehend."

"No one so dull as a wit," said the Prince, "when he does not hit off the scent at once. My Duchess, as they call her, has been in as great a hurry to run away from Falkland, as I to come hither. We have both left our apparel behind. There is as much female trumpery in the wardrobe adjoining to my sleeping-room as would equip a whole carnival. Look you, I will play Dame Marjory, disposed on this day-bed here with a mourning veil and a wreath of willow, to show my forsaken plight; thou, John, wilt look starch and stiff enough for her Galwegian maid of honour, the Countess Hermigild; and Dwining shall present the old Hecate, her nurse,—only she hath more beard on her upper lip than Dwining on his whole face, and skull to boot. He should have the commodity of a beard to set her forth comfortably. Get thy kitchen drudges, and what passable pages thou hast with thee, to make my women of the bedroom. Hearest thou?—about it instantly."

Ramorny hasted into the anteroom, and told Dwining the Prince's device.

"Do thou look to humour the fool," he said; "I care not how little I see him, knowing what is to be done."

"Trust all to me," said the physician, shrugging his shoulders. "What sort of a butcher is he that can cut the lamb's throat, yet is afraid to hear it bleat?"

"Tush, fear not my constancy—I cannot forget that he would have cast me into the cloister with as little regard as if he threw away the truncheon of a broken lance. Begone— yet stay—ere you go to arrange this silly pageant something must be settled to impose on the thick-witted Charteris. He is like enough, should he be left in the belief that the Duchess of Rothsay is still here, and Catharine Glover in attendance on her, to come down with offers of service, and the like, when, as I need scarce tell thee, his presence would be inconvenient—Indeed, this is the more likely, that some folks have given a warmer name to the iron-headed Knight's great and tender patronage of this damsel."

"With that hint, let me alone to deal with him. I will send him such a letter, that for this month he shall hold himself as ready for a journey to hell as to Falkland.—Can you tell me the name of the Duchess's confessor?"

"Waltheof, a grey friar."

"Enough—then here I start."

In a few minutes, for he was a clerk of rare celerity, Dwining finished a letter, which he placed in Ramorny's hands.

"This is admirable, and would have made thy fortune with Rothsay—I think I should have been too jealous to trust thee in his household, save that his day is closed."

"Read it aloud," said Dwining, "that we may judge if it goes trippingly off." And Ramorny read as follows :—
"By command of our high and mighty Princess Marjory, Duchess of Rothsay, and so forth, we Waltheof, unworthy brother of the order of St Francis, do thee, Sir Patrick Charteris, Knight, of Kinfauns, to know that her Highness marvels much at the temerity with which you have sent to her presence a woman, of whose fame she can judge but lightly, seeing she hath made her abode, without any necessity, for more than a week in thine own castle, without company of any other female saving menials ; of which foul cohabitation the savour is gone up through Fife, Angus, and Perthshire. Nevertheless, her Highness, considering the case as one of human frailty, hath not caused this wanton one to be scourged with nettles, or otherwise to dree penance ; but as two good brethren of the convent of Lindores, the Fathers Thickscull and Dundermore, have been summoned up to the Highlands upon an especial call, her Highness hath committed to their care this maiden Catharine, with charge to convey her to her father, whom she states to be residing beside Loch Tay, under whose protection she will find a situation more fitting her qualities and habits, than the Castle of Falkland, while her Highness the Duchess of Rothsay abides there. She hath charged the said reverend brothers so to deal with the young woman, as may give her a sense of the sin of incontinence, and she commendeth thee to confession and penitence.— Signed, Waltheof, by command of an high and mighty Princess "—and so forth.

When he had finished, "Excellent—excellent !" Ramorny

exclaimed. "This unexpected rebuff will drive Charteris mad! He hath been long making a sort of homage to this lady, and to find himself suspected of incontinence, when he was expecting the full credit of a charitable action, will altogether confound him; and, as thou say'st, it will be long enough ere he come hither to look after the damsel, or do honour to the dame.—But away to thy pageant, while I prepare that which shall close the pageant for ever."

It was an hour before noon, when Catharine, escorted by old Henshaw, and a groom of the Knight of Kinfauns, arrived before the lordly tower of Falkland. The broad banner which was displayed from it bore the arms of Rothsay, the servants who appeared wore the colours of the Prince's houshold, all confirming the general belief that the Duchess still resided there. Catharine's heart throbbed, for she had heard that the Duchess had the pride as well as the high courage of the house of Douglas, and felt uncertain touching the reception she was to experience. On entering the Castle, she observed that the train was smaller than she had expected, but as the Duchess lived in close retirement, she was little surprised at this. In a species of anteroom she was met by a little old woman, who seemed bent double with age, and supported herself upon an ebony staff.

"Truly thou art welcome, fair daughter," said she, saluting Catharine, "and, as I may say, to an afflicted house; and I trust (once more saluting her) thou wilt be a consolation to my precious and right royal daughter the Duchess. Sit thee down, my child, till I see whether my lady be at leisure to receive thee. Ah, my child, thou art very lovely indeed, if Our Lady hath given to thee a soul to match with so fair a body."

With that the counterfeit old woman crept into the next apartment, where she found Rothsay in the masquerading habit he had prepared, and Ramorny, who had evaded taking part in the pageant, in his ordinary attire.

"Thou art a precious rascal, Sir Doctor," said the Prince; "by my honour I think thou couldst find in thy heart to play out the whole play thyself, lover's part and all."

"If it were to save your Highness trouble," said the leech, with his usual subdued laugh.

"No, no," said Rothsay, "I'll never need thy help, man—and tell me now, how look I, thus disposed on the couch—languishing and ladylike, ha?"

"Something too fine-complexioned and soft-featured for the Lady Marjory of Douglas, if I may presume to say so," said the leech.

"Away, villain, and marshal in this fair frost-piece—fear not she will complain of my effeminacy—and thou, Ramorny, away also."

As the Knight left the apartment by one door, the fictitious old woman ushered in Catharine Glover by another. The room had been carefully darkened to twilight, so that Catharine saw the apparently female figure stretched on the couch without the least suspicion.

"Is that the maiden?" asked Rothsay, in a voice naturally sweet, and now carefully modulated to a whispering tone—"Let her approach, Griselda, and kiss our hand."

The supposed nurse led the trembling maiden forward to the side of the couch, and signed to her to kneel. Catharine did so, and kissed with much devotion and simplicity the gloved hand which the counterfeit Duchess extended to her.

"Be not afraid," said the same musical voice; "in me you only see a melancholy example of the vanity of human greatness—happy those, my child, whose rank places them beneath the storms of state."

While he spoke, he put his arms around Catharine's neck and drew her towards him, as if to salute her in token of welcome. But the kiss was bestowed with an earnestness which so much over-acted the part of the fair patroness, that Catharine, concluding the Duchess had lost her senses, screamed aloud.

"Peace, fool! it is I—David of Rothsay."

Catharine looked around her—the nurse was gone, and the Duke tearing off his veil, she saw herself in the power of a daring young libertine.

"Now be present with me, Heaven!" she said; "and thou wilt, if I forsake not myself."

As this resolution darted through her mind, she repressed her disposition to scream, and, as far as she might, strove to conceal her fear.

"The jest hath been played," she said, with as much firmness as she could assume; "may I entreat that your Highness will now unhand me," for he still kept hold of her arm.

"Nay, my pretty captive, struggle not—why should you fear?"

"I do not struggle, my lord. As you are pleased to detain me, I will not, by striving, provoke you to use me ill, and give pain to yourself, when you have time to think."

"Why, thou traitress, thou hast held me captive for months," said the Prince · "and wilt thou not let me hold thee for a moment?"

"This were gallantry, my lord, were it in the streets of Perth, where I might listen or escape as I listed—it is tyranny here."

"And if I did let thee go, whither wouldst thou fly?" said Rothsay. "The bridges are up—the portcullis down—and the men who follow me are strangely deaf to a peevish maiden's squalls. Be kind, therefore, and you shall know what it is to oblige a Prince."

"Unloose me, then, my lord, and hear me appeal from thyself to thyself—from Rothsay to the Prince of Scotland.— I am the daughter of an humble but honest citizen. I am, I may wellnigh say, the spouse of a brave and honest man. If I have given your Highness any encouragement for what you have done, it has been unintentional. Thus forewarned, I entreat you to forego your power over me, and suffer me to depart. Your Highness can obtain nothing from me, save by means equally unworthy of knighthood or manhood."

"You are bold, Catharine," said the Prince, "but neither as a knight nor a man can I avoid accepting a defiance. I must teach you the risk of such challenges."

While he spoke, he attempted to throw his arms again around her; but she eluded his grasp, and proceeded in the same tone of firm decision.

"My strength, my lord, is as great to defend myself in an honourable strife, as yours can be to assail me with a most dishonourable purpose. Do not shame yourself and me by putting it to the combat. You may stun me with blows, or you may call aid to overpower me; but otherwise you will fail of your purpose."

"What a brute you would make me!" said the Prince. "The force I would use is no more than excuses women in yielding to their own weakness."

He sat down in some emotion.

"Then keep it," said Catharine, "for those women who desire such an excuse. My resistance is that of the most determined mind, which love of honour and fear of shame ever inspired. Alas! my lord, could you succeed, you would but break every bond between me and life—between yourself and honour. I have been trained fraudulently here, by what decoys I know not; but were I to go dishonoured hence, it would be to denounce the destroyer of my happiness to every quarter of Europe. I would take the palmer's staff in my hand, and wherever chivalry is honoured, or the word Scotland has been heard, I would proclaim the heir of a hundred kings, the son of the godly Robert Stewart, the Heir of the heroic Bruce—a truthless, faithless man, unworthy of the crown he expects, and of the spurs he wears. Every lady in wide Europe would hold your name too foul for her lips—every worthy knight would hold you a baffled, forsworn caitiff, false to the first vow of arms, the protection of woman, and the defence of the feeble."

Rothsay resumed his seat, and looked at her with a countenance in which resentment was mingled with admiration. "You forget to whom you speak, maiden. Know, the distinction I have offered you is one for which hundreds, whose trains you are born to bear, would feel gratitude."

"Once more, my lord," resumed Catharine, "keep these favours for those by whom they are prized; or rather reserve your time and your health for other and nobler pursuits,—for the defence of your country and the happiness of your subjects. Alas, my lord! how willingly would an exulting people receive you for their chief!—How gladly would they close around you, did you show desire to head them against the oppression of the mighty, the violence of the lawless, the seduction of the vicious, and the tyranny of the hypocrite!"

The Duke of Rothsay, whose virtuous feelings were as easily excited as they were evanescent, was affected by the enthusiasm with which she spoke. "Forgive me if I have alarmed you, maiden," he said; "thou art too noble-minded to be the toy of passing pleasure, for which my mistake destined thee; and I, even were thy birth worthy of thy noble spirit and transcendent beauty, have no heart to giv thee; for by the homage of the heart only should such as thou be wooed. But my hopes have been blighted, Catharine —the only woman I ever loved has been torn from me in the very wantonness of policy, and a wife imposed on me whom I must ever detest, even had she the loveliness and softness which alone can render a woman amiable in my eyes. My health is fading even in early youth; and all that is left for me is to snatch such flowers as the short passage from life to the grave will now present. Look at my hectic cheek —feel, if you will, my intermitting pulse ; and pity me, and excuse me, if I, whose rights as a Prince and as a man have been trampled upon and usurped, feel occasional indifference towards the rights of others, and indulge a selfish desire to gratify the wish of the passing moment."

" Oh, my lord !" exclaimed Catharine, with the enthusiasm which belonged to her character—" I will call you my dear lord,—for dear must the Heir of Bruce be to every child of Scotland,—let me not, I pray, hear you speak thus ! Your glorious ancestor endured exile, persecution, the night of famine, and the day of unequal combat, to free his country, —do you practise the like self-denial to free yourself. Tear yourself from those who find their own way to greatness smoothed by feeding your follies. Distrust yon dark Ramorny ! —you know it not, I am sure—you could not know ; but the wretch who could urge the daughter to courses of shame by threatening the life of the aged father, is capable of all that is vile—all that is treacherous !"

" Did Ramorny do this ?" said the Prince.

" He did indeed, my lord, and he dares not deny it."

" It shall be looked to," answered the Duke of Rothsay. " I have ceased to love him ; but he has suffered much for my sake, and I must see his services honourably requited."

" *His* services ! Oh, my lord, if chronicles speak true, such services brought Troy to ruins, and gave the infidels possession of Spain."

" Hush, maiden ; speak within compass, I pray you," said the Prince, rising up ; " our conference ends here."

" Yet one word, my Lord Duke of Rothsay," said Catharine, with animation, while her beautiful countenance resembled that of an admonitory angel—" I cannot tell what impels me to speak thus boldly ; but the fire burns within me and will break out. Leave this castle without an hour's delay ! the air is unwholesome for you. Dismiss this Ramorny, before the day is ten minutes older ! his company is most dangerous."

" What reason have you for saying this ?"

" None in especial," answered Catharine, abashed at her own eagerness,—" none, perhaps, excepting my fears for your safety."

" To vague fears, the Heir of Bruce must not listen,—what, ho ! who waits without ? "

Ramorny entered, and bowed low to the Duke and to the maiden, whom, perhaps, he considered as likely to be preferred to the post of favourite Sultana, and therefore entitled to a courteous obeisance.

"Ramorny," said the Prince, "is there in the household any female of reputation, who is fit to wait on this young woman, till we can send her where she may desire to go?"

"I fear," replied Ramorny, "if it displease not your Highness to hear the truth, your household is indifferently provided in that way; and that, to speak the very verity, the glee-maiden is the most decorous amongst us."

"Let her wait upon this young person, then, since better may not be.—And take patience, maiden, for a few hours."

Catharine retired.

"So, my lord,—part you so soon from the Fair Maid of Perth? This is, indeed, the very wantonness of victory."

"There is neither victory nor defeat in the case," returned the Prince, dryly. "The girl loves me not; nor do I love her well enough to torment myself concerning her scruples."

"The chaste Malcolm the Maiden revived in one of his descendants!" said Ramorny.

"Favour me, sir, by a truce to your wit, or by choosing a different subject for its career. It is noon, I believe, and you will oblige me by commanding them to serve up dinner."

Ramorny left the room, but Rothsay thought he discovered a smile upon his countenance; and to be the subject of this man's satire, gave him no ordinary degree of pain. He summoned, however, the Knight to his table, and even admitted Dwining to the same honour. The conversation was of a lively and dissolute cast, a tone encouraged by the Prince; as if designing to counterbalance the gravity of his morals in the morning, which Ramorny, who was read in old chronicles, had the boldness to liken to the continence of Scipio.

The banquet, notwithstanding the Duke's indifferent health, was protracted in idle wantonness, far beyond the rules of temperance; and, whether owing simply to the strength of the wine which he drank, or the weakness of his constitution, or, as it is probable, because the last wine which he quaffed had been adulterated by Dwining, it so happened that the Prince, towards the end of the repast, fell into a lethargic sleep, from which it seemed impossible to rouse him. Sir John Ramorny and Dwining carried him to his chamber, accepting no other assistance than that of another person, whom we will afterwards give name to.

Next morning, it was announced that the Prince was taken ill of an infectious disorder ; and to prevent its spreading through the household, no one was admitted to wait on him save his late Master of Horse, the physician Dwining, and the domestic already mentioned ; one of whom seemed always to remain in the apartment, while the others observed a degree of precaution respecting their intercourse with the rest of the family, so strict as to maintain the belief that he was dangerously ill of an infectious disorder.

CHAPTER XXXII

In winter's tedious nights, sit by the fire,
With good old folks ; and let them tell thee tales
Of woeful ages, long ago betid :
And, ere thou bid good-night, to quit their grief,
Tell thou the lamentable fall of me.
King Richard II. Act 5, *Scene* 1.

FAR different had been the fate of the misguided Heir of Scotland, from that which was publicly given out in the town of Falkland. His ambitious uncle had determined on his death, as the means of removing the first and most formidable barrier betwixt his own family and the throne. James, the younger son of the King, was a mere boy, who might at more leisure be easily set aside. Ramorny's views of aggrandizement, and the resentment which he had latterly entertained against his master, made him a willing agent in young Rothsay's destruction. Dwining's love of gold, and his native malignity of disposition, rendered him equally forward. It had been resolved, with the most calculating cruelty, that all means which might leave behind marks of violence were to be carefully avoided, and the extinction of life suffered to take place of itself, by privation of every kind acting upon a frail and impaired constitution. The Prince of Scotland was not to be murdered, as Ramorny had expressed himself on another occasion,—he was only to cease to exist.

Rothsay's bedchamber in the Tower of Falkland was well adapted for the execution of such a horrible project. A small narrow staircase, scarce known to exist, opened from thence by a trap-door to the subterranean dungeons of the castle, through a passage by which the feudal lord was wont to visit, in private, and in disguise, the inhabitants of those miserable regions. By this staircase the villains conveyed the insensible Prince to the lowest dungeon of the castle, so deep in the bowels of the earth, that no cries or groans, it was supposed, could possibly be heard, while the strength of its door and fastenings must for a long time have defied force, even if the entrance could have been discovered. Bonthron, who had been saved from the gallows for the purpose, was the willing agent of Ramorny's unparalleled cruelty to his misled and betrayed patron.

This wretch revisited the dungeon at the time when the Prince's lethargy began to wear off, and when, awaking to sensation, he felt himself deadly cold, unable to move, and oppressed with fetters, which scarce permitted him to stir from the dank straw on which he was laid. His first idea was, that he was in a fearful dream—his next brought a confused augury of the truth. He called, shouted,—yelled at length in frenzy,—but no assistance came, and he was only answered by the vaulted roof of the dungeon. The agent of Hell heard these agonized screams, and deliberately reckoned them against the taunts and reproaches with which Rothsay had expressed his instinctive aversion to him. When, exhausted and hopeless, the unhappy youth remained silent, the savage resolved to present himself before the eyes of his prisoner. The locks were drawn, the chain fell; the Prince raised himself as high as his fetters permitted—a red glare against which he was fain to shut his eyes, streamed through the vault; and when he opened them again, it was on the ghastly form of one whom he had reason to think dead. He sunk back in horror. "I am judged and condemned!" he exclaimed; "and the most abhorred fiend in the infernal regions is sent to torment me!"

"I live, my lord," said Bonthron; "and that you may live and enjoy life, be pleased to sit up and eat your victuals."

"Free me from these irons," said the Prince,—"release me from this dungeon,—and, dog as thou art, thou shalt be the richest man in Scotland."

"If you would give me the weight of your shackles in gold," said Bonthron, "I would rather see the iron on you than have the treasure myself!—But look up—you were wont to love delicate fare—behold how I have catered for you." The wretch, with fiendish glee, unfolded a piece of raw hide covering the bundle which he bore under his arm, and, passing the light to and fro before it, showed the unhappy Prince a bull's head recently hewn from the trunk, and known in Scotland as the certain signal of death. He placed it at the foot of the bed, or rather lair on which the Prince lay. "Be moderate in your food," he said; "it is like to be long ere thou get'st another meal."

"Tell me but one thing, wretch," said the Prince. "Does Ramorny know of this practice?"

"How else hadst thou been decoyed hither? Poor woodcock, thou art snared!" answered the murderer.

With these words the door shut, the bolts resounded, and the unhappy Prince was left to darkness, solitude, and misery. "Oh, my father!—my prophetic father!—The staff I leaned on has indeed proved a spear!"—We will not dwell on the subsequent hours, nay days, of bodily agony and mental despair.

But it was not the pleasure of Heaven that so great a crime should be perpetrated with impunity.

Catharine Glover and the glee-woman, neglected by the other inmates, who seemed to be engaged with the tidings of the Prince's illness, were, however, refused permission to leave the Castle, until it should be seen how this alarming disease was to terminate, and whether it was actually an infectious sickness. Forced on each other's society, the two desolate women became companions, if not friends; and the union drew somewhat closer, when Catharine discovered that this was the same female minstrel on whose account Henry Wynd had fallen under her displeasure. She now heard his complete vindication, and listened with ardour to the praises which Louise heaped on her gallant protector. On the other hand, the minstrel, who felt the superiority of Catharine's station and character, willingly dwelt upon a theme which seemed to please her, and recorded her gratitude to the stout Smith in the little song of "Bold and True," which was long a favourite in Scotland.

> Oh, Bold and True,
> In bonnet blue,
> That fear or falsehood never knew;
> Whose heart was loyal to his word,
> Whose hand was faithful to his sword—
> Seek Europe wide from sea to sea,
> But bonny Blue-cap still for me!

I've seen Almain's proud champions prance—
Have seen the gallant knights of France,
Unrivall'd with the sword and lance—
Have seen the sons of England true,
Wield the brown bill and bend the yew.
Search France the fair, and England free,
But bonny Blue-cap still for me !

In short, though Louise's disreputable occupation would have
been in other circumstances an objection to Catharine's
voluntarily frequenting her company, yet, forced together as
they now were, she found her a humble and accommodating
companion.

They lived in this manner for four or five days, and, in
order to avoid as much as possible the gaze, and perhaps
the incivility, of the menials in the offices, they prepared
their food in their own apartment.   In the absolutely
necessary intercourse with domestics, Louise, more accustomed to expedients, bolder by habit, and desirous to
please Catharine, willingly took on herself the trouble of
getting from the pantler the materials of their slender meal,
and of arranging it with the dexterity of her country.

The glee-woman had been abroad for this purpose upon
the sixth day, a little before noon ; and the desire of fresh
air, or the hope to find some sallad or pot-herbs, or at least
an early flower or two, with which to deck their board, had
carried her into the small garden appertaining to the
castle.   She re-entered her apartment in the tower with a
countenance pale as ashes, and a frame which trembled
like an aspen-leaf.   Her terror instantly extended itself to
Catharine, who could hardly find words to ask what new
misfortune had occurred.

" Is the Duke of Rothsay dead ? "

" Worse ! they are starving him alive."

" Madness, woman ! "

" No, no, no, no ! " said Louise, speaking under her breath,
and huddling her words so thick upon each other, that
Catharine could hardly catch the sense.   " I was seeking
for flowers to dress your pottage, because you said you
loved them yesterday—my poor little dog, thrusting himself
into a thicket of yew and holly bushes that grow out of
some old ruins close to the castle-wall, came back whining
and howling.   I crept forward to see what might be the
cause—and, oh ! I heard a groaning as of one in extreme
pain, but so faint, that it seemed to arise out of the very

depth of the earth. At length, I found it proceeded from a small rent in the wall, covered with ivy; and when I laid my ear close to the opening, I could hear the Prince's voice distinctly say,—'It cannot now last long;' and then it sunk away in something like a prayer."

"Gracious Heaven !—did you speak to him ? "

"I said, 'Is it you, my lord ? ' and the answer was, 'Who mocks me with that title ? '—I asked him if I could help him, and he answered with a voice I shall never forget,— 'Food !—food !—I die of famine ! ' So I came hither to tell you.—What is to be done ?—Shall we alarm the house ? "——

"Alas ! that were more likely to destroy than to aid him," said Catharine.

"And what then shall we do ? " said Louise.

"I know not yet," said Catharine, prompt and bold on occasions of moment, though yielding to her companion in ingenuity of resource on ordinary occasions. "I know not yet—but something we will do—the blood of Bruce shall not die unaided."

So saying, she seized the small cruise which contained their soup, and the meat of which it was made, wrapped some thin cakes which she had baked, into the fold of her plaid, and, beckoning her companion to follow with a vessel of milk, also part of their provisions, she hastened towards the garden.

"So, our fair vestal is stirring abroad ? " said the only man she met, who was one of the menials; but Catharine passed on without notice or reply, and gained the little garden without farther interruption.

Louise indicated to her a heap of ruins, which, covered with underwood, was close to the castle-wall. It had probably been originally a projection from the building ; and the small fissure, which communicated with the dungeon, contrived for air, had terminated within it. But the aperture had been a little enlarged by decay, and admitted a dim ray of light to its recesses, although it could not be observed by those who visited the place with torch-light aids.

"Here is dead silence," said Catharine, after she had listened attentively for a moment.—"Heaven and earth, he is gone ! "

"We must risk something," said her companion, and ran her fingers over the strings of her guitar.

A sigh was the only answer from the depth of the dungeon. Catharine then ventured to speak. "I am here, my lord— I am here, with food and drink."

"Ha! Ramorny?—the jest comes too late—I am dying," was the answer.

His brain is turned, and no wonder, thought Catharine; but whilst there is life, there may be hope.

"It is I, my lord, Catharine Glover—I have food, if I could pass it safely to you."

"Heaven bless thee, maiden! I thought the pain was over, but it glows again within me at the name of food."

"The food is here, but how, ah how, can I pass it to you? the chink is so narrow, the wall is so thick! Yet there is a remedy—I have it.—Quick, Louise; cut me a willow bough, the tallest you can find."

The glee-maiden obeyed, and by means of a cleft in the top of the wand, Catharine transmitted several morsels of the soft cakes, soaked in broth, which served at once for food and for drink.

The unfortunate young man ate little, and with difficulty, but prayed for a thousand blessings on the head of his comforter. "I had destined thee to be the slave of my vices," he said, "and yet thou triest to become the preserver of my life! But away, and save thyself."

"I will return with food as I shall see opportunity," said Catharine, just as the glee-maiden plucked her sleeve, and desired her to be silent, and stand close.

Both couched among the ruins, and they heard the voices of Ramorny and the mediciner in close conversation.

"He is stronger than I thought," said the former in a low croaking tone. "How long held out Dalwolsy, when the Knight of Liddesdale prisoned him in his Castle of Hermitage?"

"For a fortnight," answered Dwining; "but he was a strong man, and had some assistance by grain which fell from a granary above his prison-house," [1]

"Were it not better end the matter more speedily? The

---

[1] Sir Alexander Ramsay of Dalhousie having irritated William Douglas, Lord of Galloway, by obtaining the Sheriffship of Teviotdale, which the haughty baron considered due to himself, was surprised in Hawick while exercising his office, and confined in Hermitage Castle until he died of famine in June, A.D. 1342. Godscroft mentions the circumstance of the grain dropping from the cornloft.—P. 75.

Black Douglas comes this way. He is not in Albany's secret. He will demand to see the Prince, and all *must* be over ere he comes."

They passed on in their dark and fatal conversation.

"Now gain we the tower," said Catharine to her companion, when she saw they had left the garden. "I had a plan of escape for myself—I will turn it into one of rescue for the Prince. The dey-woman enters the castle about vesper time, and usually leaves her cloak in the passage as she goes into the pantler's office with the milk. Take thou the cloak, muffle thyself close, and pass the warder boldly; he is usually drunken at that hour, and thou wilt go, as the dey-woman, unchallenged through gate and along bridge, if thou bear thyself with confidence. Then away to meet the Black Douglas; he is our nearest and only aid."

"But," said Louise, "is he not that terrible lord who threatened me with shame and punishment?"

"Believe it," said Catharine, "such as thou or I never dwelt an hour in the Douglas's memory, either for good or evil. Tell him that his son-in-law, the Prince of Scotland, dies—treacherously famished—in Falkland Castle, and thou wilt merit not pardon only, but reward."

"I care not for reward," said Louise; "the deed will reward itself. But methinks to stay is more dangerous than to go—Let me stay then, and nourish the unhappy Prince; and do you depart to bring help. If they kill me before you return, I leave you my poor lute, and pray you to be kind to my poor Charlot."

"No, Louise," replied Catharine, "you are a more privileged and experienced wanderer than I—do you go—and if you find me dead on your return, as may well chance, give my poor father this ring, and a lock of my hair, and say, Catharine died in endeavouring to save the blood of Bruce. And give this other lock to Henry; say, Catharine thought of him to the last; and that if he has judged her too scrupulous touching the blood of others, he will then know it was not because she valued her own."

They sobbed in each other's arms, and the intervening hours till evening were spent in endeavouring to devise some better mode of supplying the captive with nourishment, and in the construction of a tube, composed of hollow reeds, slipping into each other, by which liquids might be conveyed to him. The bell of the village church of Falkland tolled to vespers. The dey,[1] or farm-woman, entered with her pitchers, to deliver the milk for the family, and to hear and tell the news stirring. She had scarcely entered the kitchen, when the female minstrel, again throwing herself in Catharine's arms, and assuring her of her unalterable fidelity, crept in silence downstairs, the little dog under her arm. A moment after, she was seen by the breathless Catharine, wrapt in the dey-woman's cloak, and walking composedly across the drawbridge.

"So," said the warder, "you return early to-night, May Bridget? Small mirth towards in the hallf—Ha, wench!—Sick times are sad times!"

"I have forgotten my tallies," said the ready-witted French-woman, "and will return in the skimming of a bowie." [2]

She went onward, avoiding the village of Falkland, and took a footpath which led through the park. Catharine breathed freely, and blessed God when she saw her lost in the distance. It was another anxious hour for Catharine, which occurred before the escape of the fugitive was discovered. This happened so soon as the dey-girl, having taken an hour to perform a task which ten minutes might have accomplished, was about to return, and discovered that some one had taken away her grey frieze cloak. A strict search was set on foot; at length the women of the house remembered the glee-maiden, and ventured to suggest her as one not likely to exchange an old cloak for a new one. The warder, strictly questioned, averred he saw the dey-woman depart immediately after vespers; and on this being contradicted by the party herself, he could suggest, as the only alternative, that it must needs have been the devil.

As, however, the glee-woman could not be found, the real circumstances of the case were easily guessed at; and the steward went to inform Sir John Ramorny and Dwining, who were now scarcely ever separate, of the escape of one of their female captives. Every thing awakens the suspicions of the guilty. They looked on each other with faces of dismay, and then went together to the humble apartment of Catharine, that they might take her as much as possible by surprise, while they enquired into the facts attending Louise's disappearance.

---

[1] Hence, perhaps, dairy-woman and dairy.

[2] *i.e.* A small milk-pail.—One of the sweetest couplets in The Gentle Shepherd is—

> "To bear the milk-bowie no pain was to me,
> When I at the buchting forgather'd wi' thee."

"Where is your companion, young woman?" said Ramorny, in a tone of austere gravity.

"I have no companion here," answered Catharine.

"Trifle not," replied the Knight; "I mean the glee-maiden, who lately dwelt in this chamber with you."

"She is gone, they tell me"—said Catharine, "gone about an hour since."

"And whither?" said Dwining.

"How," answered Catharine, "should I know which way a professed wanderer may choose to travel? She was tired no doubt of a solitary life, so different from the scenes of feasting and dancing which her trade leads her to frequent. She is gone, and the only wonder is that she should have stayed so long."

"This, then," said Ramorny, "is all you have to tell us?"

"All that I have to tell you, Sir John," answered Catharine, firmly; "and if the Prince himself enquire I can tell him no more."

"There is little danger of his again doing you the honour to speak to you in person," said Ramorny, "even if Scotland should escape being rendered miserable by the sad event of his decease."

"Is the Duke of Rothsay so very ill?" asked Catharine.

"No help, save in Heaven," answered Ramorny, looking upward.

"Then may there yet be help there," said Catharine, "if human aid prove unavailing!"

"Amen!" said Ramorny, with the most determined gravity; while Dwining adopted a face fit to echo the feeling, though it seemed to cost him a painful struggle to suppress his sneering yet soft laugh of triumph, which was peculiarly excited by any thing having a religious tendency.

"And it is men—earthly men, and not incarnate devils, who thus appeal to heaven, while they are devouring by inches the life-blood of their hapless master!" muttered Catharine, as her two baffled inquisitors left the apartment.—"Why sleeps the thunder?—But it will roll ere long, and oh! may it be to preserve as well as to punish!"

The hour of dinner alone afforded a space, when, all in the Castle being occupied with that meal, Catharine thought she had the best opportunity of venturing to the breach in the wall, with the least chance of being observed. In waiting for the hour, she observed some stir in the Castle, which had been silent as the grave ever since the seclusion of the Duke of Rothsay. The portcullis was lowered and raised, and the creaking of the machinery was intermingled with the tramp of horse, as men-at-arms went out and returned with steeds hard-ridden and covered with foam. She observed, too, that such domestics as she casually saw from her window were in arms. All this made her heart throb high, for it augured the approach of rescue; and besides, the bustle left the little garden more lonely than ever. At length, the hour of noon arrived; she had taken care to provide, under pretence of her own wishes, which the pantler seemed disposed to indulge, such articles of food as could be the most easily conveyed to the unhappy captive. She whispered to intimate her presence —there was no answer—she spoke louder, still there was silence.

"He sleeps"—she muttered these words half aloud, and with a shuddering which was succeeded by a start and a scream, when a voice replied behind her,—

"Yes, he sleeps—but it is for ever."

She looked round—Sir John Ramorny stood behind her in complete armour, but the visor of his helmet was up, and displayed a countenance more resembling one about to die than to fight. He spoke with a grave tone, something between that of a calm observer of an interesting event, and of one who is an agent and partaker in it.

"Catharine," he said, "all is true which I tell you. He is dead—you have done your best for him—you can do no more."

"I will not—I cannot believe it," said Catharine. "Heaven be merciful to me! it would make one doubt of Providence, to think so great a crime has been accomplished."

"Doubt not of Providence, Catharine, though it has suffered the profligate to fall by his own devices. Follow me—I have that to say which concerns you. I say follow," (for she hesitated,) "unless you prefer being left to the mercies of the brute Bonthron, and the mediciner Henbane Dwining."

"I will follow you," said Catharine. "You cannot do more to me than you are permitted."

He led the way into the tower, and mounted staircase after staircase, and ladder after ladder.

Catharine's resolution failed her. "I will follow no farther," she said. "Whither would you lead me?—If to my death, I can die here."

"Only to the battlements of the castle, fool," said Ramorny, throwing wide a barred door which opened upon the vaulted roof of the castle, where men were bending mangonels, as they called them, (military engines, that is, for throwing arrows or stones,) getting ready cross-bows, and piling stones together. But the defenders did not exceed twenty in number, and Catharine thought she could observe doubt and irresolution amongst them.

"Catharine," said Ramorny, "I must not quit this station, which is necessary for my defence; but I can speak with you here as well as elsewhere."

"Say on," answered Catharine,—"I am prepared to hear you."

"You have thrust yourself, Catharine, into a bloody secret. Have you the firmness to keep it?"

"I do not understand you, Sir John," answered the maiden.

"Look you. I have slain—murdered, if you will—my late master, the Duke of Rothsay. The spark of life which your kindness would have fed was easily smothered. His last words called on his father. You are faint—bear up—you have more to hear. You know the crime, but you know not the provocation. See! this gauntlet is empty—I lost my right hand in his cause; and when I was no longer fit to serve him, I was cast off like a worn-out hound, my loss ridiculed, and a cloister recommended, instead of the halls and palaces in which I had my natural sphere! Think on this—pity and assist me."

"In what manner can you require my assistance?" said the trembling maiden: "I can neither repair your loss, nor cancel your crime."

"Thou canst be silent, Catharine, on what thou hast seen and heard in yonder thicket. It is but a brief oblivion I ask of you, whose word will, I know, be listened to, whether you say such things were or were not. That of your mountebank companion, the foreigner, none will hold to be of a pin-point's value. If you grant me this, I will take your promise for my security, and throw the gate open to those who now approach it. If you will not promise silence, I defend this Castle till every one perishes, and I fling you headlong from these battlements. Ay, look at them—it is not a leap to be rashly braved. Seven courses of stairs brought you up hither with fatigue and shortened breath; but you shall go from the top to the bottom in briefer time than you can breathe a sigh! Speak the word, fair maid; for you speak to one unwilling to harm you, but determined in his purpose."

Catharine stood terrified, and without power of answering a man who seemed so desperate; but she was saved the necessity of reply, by the approach of Dwining. He spoke with the same humble congés which at all times distinguished his manner, and with his usual suppressed ironical sneer, which gave that manner the lie.

" I do you wrong, noble sir, to intrude on your valiancy when engaged with a fair damsel. But I come to ask a trifling question."

"Speak, tormentor!" said Ramorny; "ill news are sport to thee even when they affect thyself, so that they concern others also."

" Hem!—he, he!—I only desired to know if your knight-hood proposed the chivalrous task of defending the Castle with your single hand—I crave pardon—I meant your single arm? The question is worth asking, for I am good for little to aid the defence, unless you could prevail on the besiegers to take physic—He, he, he!—and Bonthron is as drunk as ale and strong waters can make him—and you, he, and I, make up the whole garrison who are disposed for resistance."

" How!—Will the other dogs not fight?" said Ramorny.

" Never saw men who showed less stomach to the work," answered Dwining, " never. But here come a brace of them— *Venit extrema dies.*—He, he, he!"

Eviot and his companion Buncle now approached with sullen resolution in their faces, like men who had made their minds up to resist that authority which they had so long obeyed.

" How now!" said Ramorny, stepping forward to meet them. " Wherefore from your posts?"—Why have you left the barbican, Eviot?—And you other fellow, did I not charge you to look to the mangonels?"

" We have something to tell you, Sir John Ramorny," answered Eviot. " We will not fight in this quarrel."

" How—my own squires control me?" exclaimed Ramorny.

" We were your squires and pages, my lord, while you were master of the Duke of Rothsay's household—It is bruited about the Duke no longer lives—we desire to know the truth."

" What traitor dares spread such falsehoods?" said Ramorny.

" All who have gone out to skirt the forest, my lord, and

I myself among others, bring back the same news. The minstrel woman who left the Castle yesterday has spread the report everywhere, that the Duke of Rothsay is murdered, or at death's door. The Douglas comes on us with a strong force——"

"And you, cowards, take advantage of an idle report to forsake your master?" said Ramorny, indignantly.

"My lord," said Eviot, "let Buncle and myself see the Duke of Rothsay, and receive his personal orders for defence of this Castle, and if we do not fight to the death in that quarrel, I will consent to be hanged on its highest turret. But if he be gone by natural disease, we will yield up the Castle to the Earl of Douglas, who is, they say, the King's Lieutenant—Or if,—which Heaven forefend!—the noble Prince has had foul play, we will not involve ourselves in the guilt of using arms in defence of the murderers, be they who they will."

"Eviot," said Ramorny, raising his mutilated arm, "had not that glove been empty, thou hadst not lived to utter two words of this insolence."

"It is as it is"—answered Eviot, "and we do but our duty. I have followed you long, my lord, but here I draw bridle."

"Farewell, then, and a curse light on all of you!" exclaimed the incensed Baron. "Let my horse be brought forth!"

"Our Valiancy is about to run away," said the mediciner, who had crept close to Catharine's side before she was aware. "Catharine, thou art a superstitious fool, like most women; nevertheless thou hast some mind, and I speak to thee as one of more understanding than the buffaloes which are herding about us. These haughty barons who overstride the world, what are they in the day of adversity?—chaff before the wind. Let their sledge-hammer hands, or their column-resembling legs, have injury, and bah!—the men-at-arms are gone—heart and courage is nothing to them, lith and limb every thing—give them animal strength, what are they better than furious bulls—take that away, and your hero of chivalry lies grovelling like the brute when he is hamstrung. Not so the Sage; while a grain of sense remains in a crushed or mutilated frame, his mind shall be strong as ever.—Catharine, this morning I was practising your death; but methinks I now rejoice that you may survive, to tell how the poor mediciner, the pill-gilder, the mortar-pounder, the poison-vender, met his fate, in company with the gallant Knight of Ramorny, Baron in possession, and Earl of Lindores in expectation—God save his lordship!"

"Old man," said Catharine, "if thou be indeed so near the day of thy deserved doom, other thoughts were far wholesomer than the vain-glorious ravings of a vain philosophy.—Ask to see a holy man——"

"Yes," said Dwining, scornfully, "refer myself to a greasy monk, who does not—he! he! he!—understand the barbarous Latin he repeats by rote. Such would be a fitting counsellor to one who has studied both in Spain and Arabia! No, Catharine, I will choose a confessor that is pleasant to look upon, and you shall be honoured with the office.—Now, look yonder at his Valiancy—his eyebrow drops with moisture, his lip trembles with agony; for his Valiancy,—he! he! he!—is pleading for his life with his late domestics, and has not eloquence enough to persuade them to let him slip. See how the fibres of his face work as he implores the ungrateful brutes, whom he has heaped with obligations, to permit him to get such a start for his life as the hare has from the grey-hounds, when men course her fairly. Look also at the sullen, downcast, dogged faces with which, fluctuating between fear and shame, the domestic traitors deny their lord this poor chance for his life. These things thought themselves the superior of a man like me! and you, foolish wench, think so meanly of your Deity, as to suppose wretches like them are the work of Omnipotence!"

"No! man of evil, no!" said Catharine, warmly; "the God I worship created these men with the attributes to know and adore him, to guard and defend their fellow-creatures, to practise holiness and virtue. Their own vices, and the temptations of the Evil One, have made them such as they now are. Oh, take the lesson home to thine own heart of adamant! Heaven made thee wiser than thy fellows, gave thee eyes to look into the secrets of nature, a sagacious heart, and a skilful hand; but thy pride has poisoned all these fair gifts, and made an ungodly Atheist of one who might have been a Christian sage!"

"Atheist, say'st thou?" answered Dwining; "perhaps I have doubts on that matter—but they will be soon solved. Yonder comes one who will send me, as he has done thousands, to the place where all mysteries shall be cleared."

Catharine followed the mediciner's eye up one of the forest glades, and beheld it occupied by a body of horsemen advancing at full gallop. In the midst was a pennon displayed, which, though its bearings were not visible to Catharine, was, by a murmur around, acknowledged as that of the Black Douglas. They halted within arrow-shot of the Castle, and a herald with two trumpets advanced up to the main portal, where, after a loud flourish, he demanded admittance for the high and dreaded Archibald Earl of Douglas, Lord Lieutenant of the King, and acting for the time with the plenary authority of his Majesty; commanding, at the same time, that the inmates of the Castle should lay down their arms, all under penalty of high treason.

"You hear?" said Eviot to Ramorny, who stood sullen and undecided. "Will you give orders to render the Castle, or must I——"

"No, villain!" interrupted the Knight, "to the last I will command you. Open the gates, drop the bridge, and render the Castle to the Douglas."

"Now, that's what may be called a gallant exertion of free-will," said Dwining. "Just as if the pieces of brass that were screaming a minute since, should pretend to call those notes their own, which are breathed through them by a frowsy trumpeter."

"Wretched man," said Catharine, "either be silent, or turn thy thoughts to the eternity on the brink of which thou art standing."

"And what is that to thee?" answered Dwining. "Thou canst not, wench, help hearing what I say to thee, and thou wilt tell it again, for thy sex cannot help that either. Perth and all Scotland shall know, what a man they have lost in Henbane Dwining!"

The clash of armour now announced that the new comers had dismounted and entered the Castle, and were in the act of disarming the small garrison. Earl Douglas himself appeared on the battlements, with a few of his followers, and signed to them to take Ramorny and Dwining into custody. Others dragged from some nook the stupified Bonthron.

"It was to these three that the custody of the Prince was solely committed, during his alleged illness?" said the Douglas, prosecuting an enquiry which he had commenced in the hall of the Castle.

"No other saw him, my lord," said Eviot, "though I offered my services."

"Conduct us to the Duke's apartment, and bring the prisoners with us—Also there should be a female in the Castle, if she hath not been murdered or spirited away—the companion of the glee-maiden who brought the first alarm."

"She is here, my lord," said Eviot, bringing Catharine forward.

Her beauty and her agitation made some impression even upon the impassible Earl.

"Fear nothing, maiden," he said; "thou hast deserved both praise and reward. Tell to me, as thou wouldst confess to Heaven, the things thou hast witnessed in this Castle?"

Few words served Catharine to unfold the dreadful story.

"It agrees," said the Douglas, "with the tale of the glee-maiden, from point to point.—Now show us the Prince's apartment."

They passed to the room which the unhappy Duke of Rothsay had been supposed to inhabit; but the key was not to be found, and the Earl could only obtain entrance by forcing the door. On entering, the wasted and squalid remains of the unhappy Prince were discovered, flung on the bed as if in haste. The intention of the murderers had apparently been to arrange the dead body, so as to resemble a timely parted corpse, but they had been disconcerted by the alarm occasioned by the escape of Louise. Douglas looked on the body of the misguided youth, whose wild passions and caprices had brought him to this fatal and premature catastrophe.

"I had wrongs to be redressed," he said; "but to see such a sight as this banishes all remembrance of injury!"

"He! he!—It should have been arranged," said Dwining, "more to your omnipotence's pleasure; but you came suddenly on us, and hasty masters make slovenly service."

Douglas seemed not to hear what his prisoner said, so closely did he examine the wan and wasted features, and stiffened limbs, of the dead body before him. Catharine, overcome by sickness and fainting, at length obtained permission to retire from the dreadful scene, and, through confusion of every description, found her way to her former apartment, where she was locked in the arms of Louise, who had returned in the interval.

The investigations of Douglas proceeded. The dying hand

of the Prince was found to be clenched upon a lock of hair, resembling, in colour and texture, the coal-black bristles of Bonthron. Thus, though famine had begun the work, it would seem that Rothsay's death had been finally accomplished by violence. The private stair to the dungeon, the keys of which were found at the subaltern assassin's belt,— the situation of the vault, its communication with the external air by the fissure in the walls, and the wretched lair of straw, with the fetters which remained there,—fully confirmed the story of Catharine and of the glee-woman.

"We will not hesitate an instant," said the Douglas to his near kinsman, the Lord Balveny, as soon as they returned from the dungeon. "Away with the murderers! hang them over the battlements."

"But, my lord, some trial may be fitting," answered Balveny.

"To what purpose?" answered Douglas. "I have taken them red-hand;[1] my authority will stretch to instant execution. Yet stay—have we not some Jedwood men in our troop?"

"Plenty of Turnbulls, Rutherfords, Ainslies, and so forth," said Balveny.

"Call me an inquest of these together; they are all good men and true, saving a little shifting for their living. Do you see to the execution of these felons, while I hold a court in the great hall, and we'll try whether the jury or the provost-marshal do their work first; we will have Jedwood justice,—hang in haste, and try at leisure."

"Yet stay, my lord," said Ramorny, "you may rue your haste—Will you grant me a word out of ear-shot?"

"Not for worlds!" said Douglas; "speak out what thou hast to say before all that are here present."

"Know all, then," said Ramorny, aloud, "that this noble Earl had letters from the Duke of Albany and myself, sent him by the hand of yon cowardly deserter, Buncle—let him deny it if he dare,—counselling the removal of the Duke for a space from court, and his seclusion in this Castle of Falkland."

"But not a word," replied Douglas, sternly smiling, "of his being flung into a dungeon—famished—strangled.— Away with the wretches, Balveny, they pollute God's air too long!"

[1] Note XIX.—Red-hand.

The prisoners were dragged off to the battlements. But while the means of execution were in the act of being prepared, the apothecary expressed so ardent a desire to see Catharine once more, and, as he said, for the good of his soul, that the maiden, in hopes his obduracy might have undergone some change even at the last hour, consented again to go to the battlements, and face a scene which her heart recoiled from. A single glance showed her Bonthron, sunk in total and drunken insensibility; Ramorny, stripped of his armour, endeavouring in vain to conceal fear, while he spoke with a priest, whose good offices he had solicited; and Dwining, the same humble, obsequious-looking, crouching individual she had always known him. He held in his hand a little silver pen, with which he had been writing on a scrap of parchment.

"Catharine," he said,—"he, he, he!—I wish to speak to thee on the nature of my religious faith."

"If such be thy intention, why lose time with me?—Speak with this good father."

"The good father," said Dwining, "is—he, he!—already a worshipper of the Deity whom I have served. I therefore prefer to give the altar of mine idol a new worshipper in thee, Catharine. This scrap of parchment will tell thee how to make your way into my chapel, where I have worshipped so often in safety. I leave the images which it contains to thee as a legacy, simply because I hate and contemn thee something less than any of the absurd wretches whom I have hitherto been obliged to call fellow-creatures. And now away! —or remain and see if the end of the quacksalver belies his life."

"Our Lady forbid!" said Catharine.

"Nay," said the mediciner, "I have but a single word to say, and yonder nobleman's valiancy may hear it if he will."

Lord Balveny approached, with some curiosity; for the undaunted resolution of a man who never wielded sword or bore armour, and was in person a poor dwindled dwarf, had to him an air of something resembling sorcery.

"You see this trifling implement," said the criminal, showing the silver pen. "By means of this I can escape the power even of the Black Douglas."

"Give him no ink nor paper," said Balveny, hastily, "he will draw a spell."

"Not so, please your wisdom and valiancy,—he, he, he!" —said Dwining, with his usual chuckle, as he unscrewed the top of the pen, within which was a piece of sponge, or some such substance, no bigger than a pea. "Now, mark this——" said the prisoner, and drew it between his lips. The effect was instantaneous. He lay a dead corpse before them, the contemptuous sneer still on his countenance.

Catharine shrieked and fled, seeking, by a hasty descent, an escape from a sight so appalling. Lord Balveny was for a moment stupified, and then exclaimed, "This may be glamour! hang him over the battlements, quick or dead. If his foul spirit hath only withdrawn for a space, it shall return to a body with a dislocated neck."

His commands were obeyed. Ramorny and Bonthron were then ordered for execution. The last was hanged before he seemed quite to comprehend what was designed to be done with him. Ramorny, pale as death, yet with the same spirit of pride which had occasioned his ruin, pleaded his knighthood, and demanded the privilege of dying by decapitation by the sword, and not by the noose.

"The Douglas never alters his doom," said Balveny. "But thou shalt have all they rights.—Send the cook hither with a cleaver." The menial whom he called appeared at his summons. "What shakest thou for, fellow?" said Balveny; "here, strike me this man's gilt spurs from his heels with thy cleaver.—And now, John Ramorny, thou art no longer a knight, but a knave—To the halter with him, provost-marshal! hang him betwixt his companions, and higher than them if it may be."

In a quarter of an hour afterwards, Balveny descended to tell the Douglas that the criminals were executed.

"Then there is no further use in the trial," said the Earl. "How say you, good men of inquest, were these men guilty of high-treason—ay or no?"

"Guilty," exclaimed the obsequious inquest, with edifying unanimity, "we need no farther evidence."

"Sound trumpets, and to horse then, with our own train only; and let each man keep silence on what has chanced here, until the proceedings shall be laid before the King, which cannot conveniently be till the battle of Palm Sunday shall be fought and ended. Select our attendants, and tell each man who either goes with us or remains behind, that he who prates dies."

In a few minutes the Douglas was on horseback, with the followers selected to attend his person. Expresses were sent to his daughter, the widowed Duchess of Rothsay, directing her to take her course to Perth, by the shores of Lochleven, without approaching Falkland, and committing to her charge Catharine Glover and the glee-woman, as persons whose safety he tendered.

As they rode through the forest, they looked back, and beheld the three bodies hanging, like specks darkening the walls of the old castle.

"The hand is punished," said Douglas; "but who shall arraign the head by whose direction the act was done!"

"You mean the Duke of Albany?" said Balveny.

"I do, kinsman; and were I to listen to the dictates of my heart, I would charge him with the deed, which I am certain he has authorized. But there is no proof of it beyond strong suspicion, and Albany has attached to himself the numerous friends of the House of Stewart, to whom, indeed, the imbecility of the King, and the ill-regulated habits of Rothsay, left no other choice of a leader. Were I, therefore, to break the band which I have so lately formed with Albany, the consequence must be civil war, an event ruinous to poor Scotland, while threatened by invasion from the activity of the Percy, backed by the treachery of March. No, Balveny—the punishment of Albany must rest with Heaven, which, in its own good time, will execute judgment on him and on his house."

CHAPTER XXXIII

The hour is nigh: now hearts beat high:
Each sword is sharpen'd well;
And who dares die, who stoops to fly,
To-morrow's light shall tell.

Sir Edwald.

WE are now to recall to our reader's recollection, that Simon Glover and his fair daughter had been hurried from their residence without having time to announce to Henry Smith, either their departure or the alarming cause of it. When, therefore, the lover appeared in Curfew Street, on the morning of their flight, instead of the hearty welcome of the honest burgher, and the April reception, half joy half censure, which he had been promised on the part of his lovely daughter, he received only the astounding intelligence, that her father and she had set off early, on the summons of a stranger, who had kept himself carefully muffled from observation. To this, Dorothy, whose talents for forestalling evil, and communicating her views of it, are known to the reader, chose to add, that she had no doubt her master and young mistress were bound for the Highlands, to avoid a visit which had been made since their departure, by two or three apparitors, who, in the name of a Commission appointed by the King, had searched the house, put seals upon such places as were supposed to contain papers, and left citations for father and daughter to appear before the Court of Commission on a day certain, under pain of outlawry. All these alarming particulars Dorothy took care to state in the gloomiest colours, and the only consolation which she afforded the alarmed lover was, that her master had charged her to tell him to reside quietly at Perth, and that he should soon hear news of them. This checked the Smith's first resolve, which was to follow them instantly to the Highlands, and partake the fate which they might encounter.

But when he recollected his repeated feuds with divers of the Clan Quhele, and particularly his personal quarrel with Conachar, who was now raised to be a high chief, he could not but think, on reflection, that his intrusion on their place of retirement was more likely to disturb the safety which they might otherwise enjoy there, than be of any service to them. He was well acquainted with Simon's habitual intimacy with the Chief of the Clan Quhele, and justly augured that the Glover would obtain protection, which his own arrival might be likely to disturb, while his personal prowess could little avail him in a quarrel with a whole tribe of vindictive mountaineers. At the same time his heart throbbed with indignation, when he thought of Catharine being within the absolute power of young Conachar, whose rivalry he could not doubt, and who had now so many means of urging his suit. What if the young Chief should make the safety of the father depend on the favour of the daughter. He distrusted not Catharine's affections : but then her mode of thinking was so disinterested, and her attachment to her father so tender, that, if the love she bore her suitor was weighed against his security, or perhaps his life, it was matter of deep and awful doubt, whether it might not be found light in the balance. Tormented by thoughts on which we need not dwell, he resolved nevertheless to remain at home, stifle his anxiety as he might, and await the promised intelligence from the old man. It came, but it did not relieve his concern.

Sir Patrick Charteris had not forgotten his promise to communicate to the Smith the plans of the fugitives But amid the bustle occasioned by the movement of troops, he could not himself convey the intelligence. He therefore intrusted to his agent, Kitt Henshaw, the task of making it known. But this worthy person, as the reader knows, was in the interest of Ramorny, whose business it was to conceal from every one, but especially from a lover so active and daring as Henry, the real place of Catharine's residence. Henshaw therefore announced to the anxious Smith, that his friend the Glover was secure in the Highlands; and though he affected to be more reserved on the subject of Catharine, he said little to contradict the belief, that she as well as Simon shared the protection of the Clan Quhele. But he reiterated, in the name of Sir Patrick, assurances that father and daughter were both well, and that Henry would best consult his own interest and their safety, by remaining quiet, and waiting the course of events.

With an agonized heart, therefore, Henry Gow determined to remain quiet till he had more certain intelligence, and employed himself in finishing a shirt of mail, which he intended should be the best tempered, and the most finely polished, that his skilful hands had ever executed. This exercise of his craft pleased him better than any other occupation which he could have adopted, and served as an apology for secluding himself in his workshop, and shunning society, where the idle reports which were daily circulated, served only to perplex and disturb him. He resolved to trust in the warm regard of Simon, the faith of his daughter, and the friendship of the Provost, who, having so highly commended his valour in the combat with Bonthron, would never, he thought, desert him at this extremity of his fortunes. Time, however, passed on day by day; and it was not till Palm Sunday was near approaching, that Sir Patrick Charteris, having entered the city to make some arrangements for the ensuing combat, bethought himself of making a visit to the Smith of the Wynd.

He entered his work-shop with an air of sympathy unusual to him, and which made Henry instantly augur that he brought bad news. The Smith caught the alarm, and the uplifted hammer was arrested in its descent upon the heated iron, while the agitated arm that wielded it, strong before as that of a giant, became so powerless, that it was with difficulty Henry was able to place the weapon on the ground, instead of dropping it from his hand.

"My poor Henry," said Sir Patrick, "I bring you but cold news—they are uncertain, however; and, if true, they are such as a brave man like you should not take too deeply to heart."

"In God's name, my lord," said Henry, "I trust you bring no evil news of Simon Glover or his daughter?"

"Touching themselves," said Sir Patrick, "no; they are safe and well. But as to thee, Henry, my tidings are more cold. Kitt Henshaw has, I think, apprized thee that I had endeavoured to provide Catharine Glover with a safe protection in the house of an honourable lady, the Duchess of Rothsay. But she hath declined the charge; and Catharine hath been sent to her father in the Highlands. What is worst is to come. Thou mayest have heard that Gilchrist MacIan is dead, and that his son Eachin, who was known in Perth as the apprentice of old Simon, by the name of Conachar, is now the Chief of Clan Quhele; and I heard from one of my domestics, that there is a strong rumour among the MacIans, that the young Chief seeks the hand of Catharine in marriage. My domestic learned this (as a secret, however) while in the Breadalbane country, on some arrangements touching the ensuing combat. The thing is uncertain; but, Henry, it wears a face of likelihood."

"Did your lordship's servant see Simon Glover and his daughter?" said Henry, struggling for breath, and coughing, to conceal from the Provost the excess of his agitation.

"He did not," said Sir Patrick; "the Highlanders seemed jealous, and refused to permit him to speak to the old man, and he feared to alarm them by asking to see Catharine. Besides he talks no Gaelic, nor had his informer much English, so there may be some mistake in the matter. Nevertheless there *is* such a report, and I thought it best to tell it you. But you may be well assured, that the wedding cannot go on till the affair of Palm Sunday be over; and I advise you to take no step till we learn the circumstances of the matter, for certainty is most desirable, even when it is painful.—Go you to the Council-House," he added, after a pause, "to speak about the preparations for the lists in the North Inch? You will be welcome there."

"No, my good lord."

"Well, Smith, I judge by your brief answer, that you are discomposed with this matter; but after all, women are weathercocks, that is the truth on't. Solomon and others have proved it before you."

And so Sir Patrick Charteris retired, fully convinced he had discharged the office of a comforter in the most satisfactory manner.

With very different impressions did the unfortunate lover regard the tidings, and listen to the consoling commentary.

"The Provost," he said bitterly to himself, "is an excellent man; marry, he holds his knighthood so high, that if he speaks nonsense, a poor man must hold it sense, as he must praise dead ale if it be handed to him in his lordship's silver flagon. How would all this sound in another situation? Suppose I were rolling down the steep descent of the Corrichie Dhu, and before I came to the edge of the rock, comes my Lord Provost, and cries, 'Henry, there is a deep precipice, and I grieve to say you are in the fair way of rolling over it. But be not downcast, for Heaven may send a stone or a bush to stop your progress. However, I thought it would be comfort to you to know the worst, which you will be presently aware of. I do not know how many hundred feet deep the precipice descends, but you may form a judgment when you are at the bottom, for certainty is certainty. And hark ye, when come you to take a game at bowls?' And this gossip is to serve instead of any friendly attempt to save the poor wight's neck! When I think of this, I could go mad, seize my hammer, and break and destroy all around me. But I will be calm; and if this Highland kite, who calls himself a falcon, should stoop at my turtle dove, he shall know whether a burgess of Perth can draw a bow or not."

It was now the Thursday before the fated Palm Sunday, and the champions on either side were expected to arrive the next day, that they might have the interval of Saturday to rest, refresh themselves, and prepare for the combat. Two or three of each of the contending parties were detached to receive directions about the encampment of their little band, and such other instructions as might be necessary to the proper ordering of the field. Henry was not, therefore, surprised at seeing a tall and powerful Highlander peering anxiously about the wynd in which he lived, in the manner in which the natives of a wild country examine the curiosities of one that is more civilized. The Smith's heart rose against the man, on account of his country, to which our Perth burgher bore natural prejudice, and more especially as he observed the individual wear the plaid peculiar to the Clan Quhele. The sprig of oak-leaves, worked in silk, intimated also that the individual was one of those personal guards of young Eachin, upon whose exertions in the future battle so much reliance was placed by those of their clan.

Having observed so much, Henry withdrew into his smithy, for the sight of the man raised his passion; and knowing that the Highlander came plighted to a solemn combat, and could not be the subject of any inferior quarrel, he was resolved at least to avoid friendly intercourse with him. In a few minutes, however, the door of the smithy flew open, and, fluttering in his tartans, which greatly magnified his actual size, the Gael entered with the haughty step of a man conscious of a personal dignity superior to anything which he is likely to meet with. He stood looking around him, and seemed to expect to be received with courtesy, and regarded with wonder. But Henry had no sort of inclination to indulge his vanity, and kept hammering away at a breast-plate, which was lying upon his anvil, as if he were not aware of his visitor's presence.

"You are the *Gow Chrom?*" (the bandy-legged smith,) said the Highlander.

"Those that wish to be crook-backed call me so," answered Henry.

"No offence meant," said the Highlander; "but her own self comes to buy an armour."

"Her own self's bare shanks may trot hence with her," answered Henry,—"I have none to sell."

"If it was not within two days of Palm Sunday, herself would make you sing another song," retorted the Gael.

"And being the day it is," said Henry with the same contemptuous indifference, "I pray you to stand out of my light."

"You are an uncivil person; but her own self is *fir nan ord*[1] too; and she knows the smith is fiery when the iron is hot."

"If her nainsell be hammer-man hersell, her nainsell may make her nain harness," replied Henry.

"And so her nainsell would, and never fash you for the

[1] *i.e.* A man of the hammer.

matter; but it is said, *Gow Chrom*, that you sing and whistle tunes over the swords and harnishes that you work, that have power to make the blades cut steel-links as if they were paper, and the plate and mail turn back steel-lances as if they were boddle prins?"

"They tell your ignorance any nonsense that Christian men refuse to believe," said Henry. "I whistle at my work whatever comes uppermost, like an honest craftsman, and commonly it is the Highlandman's 'Och hone for Houghmanstares!'[1] My hammer goes naturally to that tune."

"Friend, it is but idle to spur a horse when his legs are hamshackled," said the Highlander, haughtily. "Her own self cannot fight even now, and there is little gallantry in taunting her thus."

"By nails and hammer, you are right there," said the Smith, altering his tone. "But speak out at once, friend, what is it thou wouldst have of me? I am in no humour for dallying."

"A hauberk for her Chief, Eachin MacIan," said the Highlander.

"You are a hammerman, you say? Are you a judge of this?" said our Smith, producing from a chest the mail shirt on which he had been lately employed.

The Gael handled it with a degree of admiration which had something of envy in it. He looked curiously at every part of its texture, and at length declared it the very best piece of armour that he had ever seen.

"A hundred cows and bullocks, and a good drift of sheep, would be e'en ower cheap an offer," said the Highlandman, by way of tentative; "but her nainsell will never bid thee less, come by them how she can."

"It is a fair proffer," replied Henry; "but gold nor gear will never buy that harness. I want to try my own sword on my own armour; and I will not give that mail-coat to any one but who will face me for the best of three blows and a thrust in the fair field; and it is your Chief's upon these terms."

"Hut, prut, man—take a drink, and go to bed," said the Highlander, in great scorn. "Are ye mad? Think ye the Captain of the Clan Quhele will be brawling and battling with a bit Perth burgess body like you? Whisht, man, and hearken. Her nainsell will do ye mair credit than ever belonged to your kin. She will fight you for the fair harness hersell."

"She must first show that she is my match," said Henry, with a grim smile.

"How! I, one of Eachin MacIan's Leichtach, and not your match!"

"You may try me, if you will. You say you are a *fir nan ord*—Do you know how to cast a sledge-hammer?"

"Ay, truly—ask the eagle if he can fly over Ferragon."

"But before you strive with me, you must first try a cast with one of *my* Leichtach.—Here, Dunter, stand forth for the honour of Perth!—And now, Highlandman, there stands a row of hammers—choose which you will, and let us to the garden."

The Highlander, whose name was Norman nan Ord, or Norman of the Hammer, showed his title to the epithet by selecting the largest hammer of the set, at which Henry smiled. Dunter, the stout journeyman of the Smith, made what was called a prodigious cast; but the Highlander, making a desperate effort, threw beyond it by two or three feet, and looked with an air of triumph to Henry, who again smiled in reply.

"Will you mend that?" said the Gael, offering our Smith the hammer.

"Not with that child's toy," said Henry, "which has scarce weight to fly against the wind.—Janniken, fetch me Sampson; or one of you help the boy, for Sampson is somewhat ponderous."

The hammer now produced was half as heavy again as that which the Highlander had selected as one of unusual weight. Norman stood astonished; but he was still more so when Henry, taking his position, swung the ponderous implement far behind his right haunch joint, and dismissed it from his hand as if it had flown from a warlike engine. The air groaned and whistled as the mass flew through it. Down at length it came, and the iron head sunk a foot into the earth, a full yard beyond the cast of Norman.

The Highlander, defeated and mortified, went to the spot where the weapon lay, lifted it, poised it in his hand with great wonder, and examined it closely, as if he expected to discover more in it than a common hammer. He at length returned it to the owner with a melancholy smile, shrugging his shoulders and shaking his head, as the Smith asked him whether he would not mend his cast.

"Norman has lost too much at the sport already," he replied. "She has lost her own name of the Hammerer. But does her ownself, the *Gow Chrom*, work at the anvil with that horse's load of iron?"

"You shall see, brother," said Henry, leading the way to the smithy. "Dunter," he said, "rax me that bar from the furnace;" and uplifting Sampson, as he called the monstrous hammer, he plied the metal with a hundred strokes from right to left—now with the right hand, now with the left, now with both, with so much strength at once and dexterity, that he worked off a small but beautifully proportioned horse-shoe in half the time that an ordinary smith would have taken for the same purpose, using a more manageable implement.

"Oigh, oigh!" said the Highlander, "and what for would you be fighting with our young Chief, who is far above your standard, though you were the best smith ever wrought with wind and fire?"

"Hark you!" said Henry—"You seem a good fellow, and I'll tell you the truth. Your master has wronged me, and I give him this harness freely for the chance of fighting him myself."

"Nay, if he hath wronged you, he must meet you," said the life-guardsman. "To do a man wrong takes the eagle's feather out of the Chief's bonnet; and were he the first in the Highlands, and to be sure so is Eachin, he must fight the man he has wronged, or else a rose falls from his chaplet."

"Will you move him to this," said Henry, "after the fight on Sunday?"

"Oh, her nainsell will do her best, if the hawks have not got her nainsell's bones to pick; for you must know, brother, that Clan Chattan's claws pierce rather deep."

"The armour is your Chief's on that condition," said Henry; "but I will disgrace him before King and Court if he does not pay me the price."

"Deil a fear, deil a fear; I will bring him in to the barrace myself," said Norman, "assuredly."

"You will do me a pleasure," replied Henry; "and that you may remember your promise, I will bestow on you this dirk. Look—if you hold it truly, and can strike between the mail-hood and the collar of your enemy, the surgeon will be needless."

The Highlander was lavish in his expressions of gratitude, and took his leave.

"I have given him the best mail harness I ever wrought," said the Smith to himself, rather repenting his liberality, "for the poor chance that he will bring his Chief into a fair field with me; and then let Catharine be his who can win her fairly. But much I dread the youth will find some evasion, unless he have such luck on Palm Sunday as may induce him to try another combat. That is some hope, however; for I have often, ere now, seen a raw young fellow shoot up after his first fight, from a dwarf into a giant-queller."

Thus, with little hope, but with the most determined resolution, Henry Smith awaited the time that should decide his fate. What made him augur the worst, was the silence both of the Glover and of his daughter. They are ashamed, he said, to confess the truth to me, and therefore they are silent.

Upon the Friday at noon, the two bands of thirty men each, representing the contending Clans, arrived at the several points where they were to halt for refreshments.

The Clan Quhele was entertained hospitably at the rich Abbey of Scone, while the Provost regaled their rivals at his Castle of Kinfauns; the utmost care being taken to treat both parties with the most punctilious attention, and to afford neither an opportunity of complaining of partiality. All points of etiquette were, in the meanwhile, discussed and settled by the Lord High Constable Errol, and the young Earl of Crawford, the former acting on the part of the Clan Chattan, and the latter patronising the Clan Quhele. Messengers were passing continually from the one Earl to the other, and they held more than six meetings within thirty hours, before the ceremonial of the field could be exactly arranged.

Meanwhile, in case of revival of ancient quarrel, many seeds of which existed betwixt the burghers and their mountain neighbours, a proclamation commanded the citizens not to approach within half a mile of the place where the Highlanders were quartered; while on their part the intended combatants were prohibited from approaching Perth without special license. Troops were stationed to enforce this order, who did their charge so scrupulously, as to prevent Simon Glover himself, burgess and citizen of Perth, from approaching the town, because he owned having come thither at the same time with the champions of Eachin MacIan, and wore a plaid around him of their check or pattern. This interruption prevented Simon from seeking out Henry Wynd, and possessing him with a true knowledge of all that had happened since their separation, which intercourse, had it taken place, must have materially altered the catastrophe of our narrative.

On Saturday afternoon another arrival took place, which interested the city almost as much as the preparations for the expected combat. This was the approach of the Earl Douglas, who rode through the town with a troop of only thirty horse, but all of whom were knights and gentlemen of the first consequence. Men's eyes followed this dreaded peer as they pursue the flight of an eagle through the clouds, unable to ken the course of the bird of Jove, yet silent, attentive, and as earnest in observing him, as if they could guess the object for which he sweeps through the firmament. He rode slowly through the city, and passed out at the northern gate. He next alighted at the Dominican Convent, and desired to see the Duke of Albany. The Earl was introduced instantly, and received by the Duke with a manner which was meant to be graceful and conciliatory, but which could not conceal both art and inquietude. When the first greetings were over, the Earl said with great gravity, " I bring you melancholy news. Your Grace's royal Nephew, the Duke of Rothsay, is no more, and I fear hath perished by some foul practices."

" Practices ! " said the Duke, in confusion, " what practices ?—who dared practise on the heir of the Scottish throne ? "

" 'Tis not for me to state how these doubts arise," said Douglas—" but men say the eagle was killed with an arrow fledged from his own wing, and the oak trunk rent by a wedge of the same wood."

" Earl of Douglas," said the Duke of Albany, " I am no reader of riddles."

" Nor am I a propounder of them," said Douglas, haughtily. " Your Grace will find particulars in these papers worthy of perusal. I will go for half an hour to the cloister garden,[1] and then rejoin you."

" You go not to the King, my lord ? " said Albany.

" No," answered Douglas ; " I trust your Grace will agree

[1] Note XXI.—Gardens of the Dominican Convent.

with me that we should conceal this great family misfortune from our Sovereign till the business of to-morrow be decided."

"I willingly agree," said Albany. "If the King heard of this loss, he could not witness the combat; and if he appear not in person, these men are likely to refuse to fight, and the whole work is cast loose. But I pray you sit down, my lord, while I read these melancholy papers respecting poor Rothsay."

He passed the papers through his hands, turning some over with a hasty glance, and dwelling on others as if their contents had been of the last importance. When he had spent nearly a quarter of an hour in this manner, he raised his eyes, and said very gravely, "My lord, in these most melancholy documents, it is yet a comfort to see nothing which can renew the divisions in the King's councils, which were settled by the last solemn agreement between your lordship and myself. My unhappy nephew was by that agreement to be set aside, until Time should send him a graver judgment. He is now removed by Fate, and our purpose in that matter is anticipated and rendered unnecessary."

"If your Grace," replied the Earl, "sees nothing to disturb the good understanding which the tranquillity and safety of Scotland require should exist between us, I am not so ill a friend of my country as to look closely for such."

"I understand you, my Lord of Douglas," said Albany, eagerly. "You hastily judged that I should be offended with your lordship for exercising your powers of Lieutenancy, and punishing the detestable murderers within my territory of Falkland. Credit me, on the contrary, I am obliged to your lordship for taking out of my hands the punishment of these wretches, as it would have broken my heart even to have looked on them. The Scottish Parliament will enquire, doubtless, into this sacrilegious deed; and happy am I that the avenging sword has been in the hand of a man so important as your lordship. Our communication together, as your lordship must well recollect, bore only concerning a proposed restraint of my unfortunate nephew, until the advance of a year or two had taught him discretion?"

"Such was certainly your Grace's purpose, as expressed to me," said the Earl; "I can safely avouch it."

"Why, then, noble Earl, we cannot be censured, because villains, for their own revengeful ends, appear to have engrafted a bloody termination on our honest purpose?"

"The Parliament will judge it after their wisdom," said Douglas. "For my part, my conscience acquits me."

"And mine assoilzies *me*," said the Duke, with solemnity. "Now, my lord, touching the custody of the boy James,[1] who succeeds to his father's claims of inheritance?"

"The King must decide it," said Douglas, impatient of the conference. "I will consent to his residence anywhere save at Stirling, Doune, or Falkland."

With that he left the apartment abruptly.

"He is gone," muttered the crafty Albany, "and he must be my ally—yet feels himself disposed to be my mortal foe. No matter—Rothsay sleeps with his fathers—James may follow in time, and then—a crown is the recompense of my perplexities."

CHAPTER XXXIV

——Thretty for thretty faucht in Barreris,
At Sanct Johnstoun on a day besyde the Black Freris.
Wyntoun.

PALM SUNDAY now dawned. At an earlier period of the Christian Church, the use of any of the days of Passion Week for the purpose of combat, would have been accounted a profanity worthy of excommunication. The Church of Rome, to her infinite honour, had decided, that during the holy season of Easter, when the redemption of man from his fallen state was accomplished, the sword of war should be sheathed, and angry monarchs should respect the season termed the Truce of God. The ferocious violence of the latter wars betwixt Scotland and England had destroyed all observance of this decent and religious ordinance. Very often the most solemn occasions were chosen by one party for an attack, because they hoped to find the other engaged in religious duties, and unprovided for defence. Thus the truce, once considered as proper to the season, had been discontinued; and it became not unusual even to select the sacred festivals of the church for decision of the trial by combat, to which this intended contest bore a considerable resemblance.

On the present occasion, however, the duties of the day were observed with the usual solemnity, and the combatants

[1] Second son of Robert III., brother of the unfortunate Duke of Rothsay, and afterwards King James I. of Scotland.

themselves took share in them. Bearing branches of yew in their hands, as the readiest substitute for palm boughs, they marched respectively to the Dominican and Carthusian convents, to hear High Mass, and by a show at least of devotion, to prepare themselves for the bloody strife of the day. Great care had of course been taken, that, during this march, they should not even come within the sound of each other's bagpipes ; for it was certain that, like game-cocks exchanging mutual notes of defiance, they would have sought out and attacked each other before they arrived at the place of combat.

The citizens of Perth crowded to see the unusual procession on the streets, and thronged the churches where the two clans attended their devotions, to witness their behaviour, and to form a judgment from their appearance which was most likely to obtain the advantage in the approaching conflict. Their demeanour in the church, although not habitual frequenters of places of devotion, was perfectly decorous ; and, notwithstanding their wild and untamed dispositions, there were few of the mountaineers who seemed affected either with curiosity or wonder. They appeared to think it beneath their dignity of character to testify either curiosity or surprise at many things which were probably then presented to them for the first time.

On the issue of the combat, few even of the most competent judges dared venture a prediction ; although the great size of Torquil and his eight stalwart sons, induced some who professed themselves judges of the thews and sinews of men, to incline to ascribe the advantage to the party of the Clan Quhele. The opinion of the female sex was much decided by the handsome form, noble countenance, and gallant demeanour of Eachin MacIan. There were more than one who imagined they had recollection of his features ; but his splendid military attire rendered the humble Glover's apprentice unrecognizable in the young Highland Chief, saving by one person.

That person, as may well be supposed, was the Smith of the Wynd, who had been the foremost in the crowd that thronged to see the gallant champions of Clan Quhele. It was with mingled feelings of dislike, jealousy, and something approaching to admiration, that he saw the Glover's apprentice stripped of his mean slough, and blazing forth as a chieftain, who, by his quick eye and gallant demeanour, the noble shape of his brow and throat, his splendid arms and well-proportioned limbs, seemed well worthy to hold the foremost rank among men selected to live or die for the honour of their race. The Smith could hardly think that he looked upon the same passionate boy, whom he had brushed off as he might a wasp that stung him, and, in mere compassion, forebore to despatch by treading on him.

"He looks it gallantly with my noble hauberk," thus muttered Henry to himself, "the best I ever wrought. Yet if he and I stood together where there was neither hand to help nor eye to see, by all that is blessed in this holy church, the good harness should return to its owner! All that I am worth would I give for three fair blows on his shoulders to undo my own best work; but such happiness will never be mine. If he escape from the conflict, it will be with so high a character for courage, that he may well disdain to put his fortune, in its freshness, to the risk of an encounter with a poor burgess like myself. He will fight by his champion, and turn me over to my fellow-craftsman the Hammerer, when all I can reap will be the pleasure of knocking a Highland bullock on the head. If I could but see Simon Glover!—I will to the other church in quest of him, since for sure he must have come down from the Highlands."

The congregation was moving from the church of the Dominicans, when the Smith formed this determination, which he endeavoured to carry into speedy execution, by thrusting through the crowd as hastily as the solemnity of the place and occasion would permit. In making his way through the press, he was at one instant carried so close to Eachin that their eyes encountered. The Smith's hardy and embrowned countenance coloured up like the heated iron on which he wrought, and retained its dark-red hue for several minutes. Eachin's features glowed with a brighter blush of indignation, and a glance of fiery hatred was shot from his eyes. But the sudden flush died away in ashy paleness, and his gaze instantly avoided the unfriendly but steady look with which it was encountered.

Torquil, whose eye never quitted his foster-son, saw his emotion, and looked anxiously around to discover the cause. But Henry was already at a distance, and hastening on his way to the Carthusian convent. Here also the religious service of the day was ended; and those who had so lately borne palms in honour of the great event which brought peace on earth, and good-will to the children of men, were now streaming to the place of combat; some prepared to take the lives of their fellow-creatures, or to lose their own; others to view the deadly strife, with the savage delight which the heathens took in the contests of their gladiators.

The crowd was so great that any other person might well have despaired of making way through it. But the general deference entertained for Henry of the Wynd, as the Champion of Perth, and the universal sense of his ability to force a passage, induced all to unite in yielding room for him, so that he was presently quite close to the warriors of the Clan Chattan. Their pipers marched at the head of their column. Next followed the well-known banner, displaying a mountain cat rampant, with the appropriate caution,—"Touch not the cat but (i.e. without) the glove." The Chief followed with his two-handed sword advanced, as if to protect the emblem of the tribe. He was a man of middle stature, more than fifty years old, but betraying, neither in features nor form, any decay of strength, or symptoms of age. His dark-red close-curled locks were in part chequered by a few grizzled hairs, but his step and gesture were as light in the dance in the chase, or in the battle, as if he had not passed his thirtieth year. His grey eye gleamed with a wild light expressive of valour and ferocity mingled; but wisdom and experience dwelt on the expression of his forehead, eyebrows, and lips. The chosen champions followed by two and two. There was a cast of anxiety on several of their faces, for they had that morning discovered the absence of one of their appointed number; and, in a contest so desperate as was expected, the loss seemed a matter of importance to all save to their high-mettled Chief, MacGillie Chattanach.

"Say nothing to the Saxons of his absence," said this bold leader, when the diminution of his force was reported to him. "The false Lowland tongues might say that one of Clan Chattan was a coward, and perhaps that the rest favoured his escape, in order to have a pretence to avoid the battle. I am sure that Ferquhard Day will be found in the ranks ere we are ready for battle; or, if he should not, am not I man enough for two of the Clan Quhele? or would we not fight them fifteen to thirty, rather than lose the renown that this day will bring us?"

The tribe received the brave speech of their leader with applause, yet there were anxious looks thrown out in hopes of espying the return of the deserter ; and perhaps the Chief himself was the only one of the determined band who was totally indifferent on the subject.

They marched on through the streets without seeing any thing of Ferquhard Day, who, many a mile beyond the mountains, was busied in receiving such indemnification as successful love could bestow for the loss of honour. MacGillie Chattanach marched on without seeming to observe the absence of the deserter, and entered upon the North Inch, a beautiful and level plain, closely adjacent to the city, and appropriated to the martial exercises of the inhabitants.

The plain is washed on one side by the deep and swelling Tay. There was erected within it a strong palisade, enclosing on three sides a space of one hundred and fifty yards in length, and seventy-four yards in width. The fourth side of the lists was considered as sufficiently fenced by the river. An amphitheatre for the accommodation of spectators surrounded the palisade, leaving a large space free to be occupied by armed men on foot and horseback, and for the more ordinary class of spectators. At the extremity of the lists, which was nearest to the city, there was a range of elevated galleries for the King and his courtiers, so highly decorated with rustic treillage, intermingled with gilded ornaments, that the spot retains to this day the name of the Golden, or Gilded Arbour.

The mountain minstrelsy, which sounded the appropriate pibrochs or battle-tunes of the rival confederacies, was silent when they entered on the Inch, for such was the order which had been given. Two stately, but aged warriors, each bearing the banner of his tribe, advanced to the opposite extremities of the lists, and pitching their standards into the earth, prepared to be spectators of a fight in which they were not to join. The pipers, who were also to be neutral in the strife, took their places by their respective *brattachs*.

The multitude received both bands with the same general shout, with which on similar occasions they welcome those from whose exertion they expect amusement, or what they term sport. The destined combatants returned no answer to this greeting, but each party advanced to the opposite extremities of the lists, where were entrances by which they were to be admitted to the interior. A strong body of men-at-arms guarded either access; and the Earl Marshal at the one, and the Lord High Constable at the other, carefully examined each individual, to see whether he had the appropriate arms, being steel-cap, mail-shirt, two-handed sword, and dagger. They also examined the numbers of each party; and great was the alarm among the multitude, when the Earl of Errol held up his hand and cried,—"Ho!—The combat cannot proceed, for the Clan Chattan lack one of their number."

"What reck of that?" said the young Earl of Crawford; "they should have counted better ere they left home."

The Earl Marshal, however, agreed with the Constable, that the fight could not proceed until the inequality should be removed; and a general apprehension was excited in the assembled multitude, that after all the preparation there would be no battle.

Of all present, there were only two perhaps who rejoiced at the prospect of the combat being adjourned; and these were, the Captain of the Clan Quhele, and the tender-hearted King Robert. Meanwhile the two Chiefs, each attended by a special friend and adviser, met in the midst of the lists, having, to assist them in determining what was to be done, the Earl Marshal, the Lord High Constable, the Earl of Crawford, and Sir Patrick Charteris. The Chief of the Clan Chattan declared himself willing and desirous of fighting upon the spot, without regard to the disparity of numbers.

"That," said Torquil of the Oak, "Clan Quhele will never consent to. You can never win honour from us with the sword, and you seek but a subterfuge, that you may say when you are defeated, as you know you will be, that it was for want of the number of your band fully counted out. But I make a proposal—Ferquhard Day was the youngest of your band, Eachin MacIan is the youngest of ours—we will set him aside in place of the man who has fled from the combat."

"A most unjust and unequal proposal," exclaimed Toshach Beg, the second, as he might be termed, of MacGillie Chattanach. "The life of the Chief is to the clan the breath of our nostrils, nor will we ever consent that our Chief shall be exposed to dangers which the Captain of Clan Quhele does not share."

Torquil saw with deep anxiety that his plan was about to fail, when the objection was made to Hector's being withdrawn from the battle; and he was meditating how to support his proposal, when Eachin himself interfered. His timidity, it must be observed, was not of that sordid and selfish nature which induces those who are infected by it calmly to submit to dishonour rather than risk danger. On the contrary, he was morally brave, though constitutionally timid, and the shame of avoiding the combat became at the moment more powerful than the fear of facing it.

"I will not hear," he said, "of a scheme which will leave my sword sheathed during this day's glorious combat. If I am young in arms, there are enough of brave men around me, whom I may imitate if I cannot equal."

He spoke these words in a spirit which imposed on Torquil, and perhaps on the young Chief himself.

"Now, God bless his noble heart!" said the foster-father to himself. "I was sure the foul spell would be broken through, and that the tardy spirit which besieged him would fly at the sound of the pipe, and the first flutter of the Brattach!"

"Hear me, Lord Marshal," said the Constable. "The hour of combat may not be much longer postponed, for the day approaches to high noon. Let the Chief of Clan Chattan take the half hour which remains, to find, if he can, a substitute for this deserter; if he cannot, let them fight as they stand."

"Content I am," said the Marshal, "though, as none of his own clan are nearer than fifty miles, I see not how MacGillie Chattanach is to find an auxiliary."

"That is his business," said the High Constable; "but if he offers a high reward, there are enough of stout yeomen surrounding the lists, who will be glad enough to stretch their limbs in such a game as is expected. I myself, did my quality and charge permit, would blithely take a turn of work amongst these wild fellows, and think it fame won."

They communicated their decision to the Highlanders, and the Chief of the Clan Chattan replied,—"You have judged impartially and nobly, my lords, and I deem myself obliged to follow your direction.—So make proclamation, heralds, that if any one will take his share with Clan Chattan of the honours and chances of this day, he shall have present payment of a gold crown, and liberty to fight to the death in my ranks."

"You are something chary of your treasure, Chief," said the Earl Marshal; "a gold crown is poor payment for such a campaign as is before you."

" If there be any man willing to fight for honour," replied MacGillie Chattanach, " the price will be enough ; and I want not the service of a fellow who draws his sword for gold alone."

The heralds had made their progress, moving half way round the lists, stopping from time to time, to make proclamation as they had been directed, without the least apparent disposition on the part of any one to accept of the proffered enlistment. Some sneered at the poverty of the Highlanders, who set so mean a price upon such a desperate service. Others affected resentment, that they should esteem the blood of citizens so lightly. None showed the slightest intention to undertake the task proposed, until the sound of the proclamation reached Henry of the Wynd, as he stood without the barrier, speaking from time to time with Bailie Craigdallie, or rather listening vaguely to what the magistrate was saying to him.

" Ha ! what proclaim they ? " he cried out.

" A liberal offer on the part of MacGillie Chattanach," said the Host of the Griffin, " who proposes a gold crown to any one who will turn wild cat for the day, and be killed a little in his service ! That's all."

" How ! " exclaimed the Smith, eagerly, " do they make proclamation for a man to fight against the Clan Quhele ? "

" Ay, marry do they," said Griffin ; " but I think they will find no such fools in Perth."

He had hardly said the word, when he beheld the Smith clear the barriers at a single bound, and alight in the lists, saying, " Here am I, Sir Herald, Henry of the Wynd, willing to do battle on the part of the Clan Chattan."

A cry of admiration ran through the multitude, while the grave burghers, not being able to conceive the slightest reason for Henry's behaviour, concluded that his head must be absolutely turned with the love of fighting. The Provost was especially shocked.

" Thou art mad," he said, " Henry ! Thou hast neither two-handed sword nor shirt of mail."

" Truly no," said Henry, " for I parted with a mail-shirt, which I had made for myself, to yonder gay Chief of the Clan Quhele, who will soon find on his shoulders with what sort of blows I clink my rivets ! As for two-handed sword, why this boy's brand will serve my turn till I can master a heavier one."

"This must not be," said Errol. "Hark thee, armourer, by Saint Mary, thou shalt have my Milan hauberk and good Spanish sword."

"I thank your noble earlship, Sir Gilbert Hay; but the yoke with which your brave ancestor turned the battle at Loncarty, would serve my turn well enough. I am little used to sword or harness that I have not wrought myself, because I do not well know what blows the one will bear out without being cracked, or the other lay on without snapping."

The cry had in the meanwhile run through the multitude, and passed into the town, that the dauntless Smith was about to fight without armour, when, just as the fated hour was approaching, the shrill voice of a female was heard screaming for passage through the crowd. The multitude gave place to her importunity, and she advanced, breathless with haste, under the burden of a mail hauberk and a large two-handed sword. The widow of Oliver Proudfute was soon recognized, and the arms which she bore were those of the Smith himself, which, occupied by her husband on the fatal evening when he was murdered, had been naturally conveyed to his house with the dead body, and were now, by the exertions of his grateful widow, brought to the lists at a moment when such proved weapons were of the last consequence to their owner. Henry joyfully received the well-known arms, and the widow with trembling haste assisted in putting them on, and then took leave of him, saying, "God for the champion of the widow and orphan, and ill-luck to all who come before him!"

Confident at feeling himself in his well-proved armour, Henry shook himself as if to settle the steel shirt around him, and, unsheathing the two-handed sword, made it flourish over his head, cutting the air through which it whistled in the form of the figure eight, with an ease and sleight of hand, that proved how powerfully and skilfully he could wield the ponderous weapon. The champions were now ordered to march in their turns around the lists, crossing so as to avoid meeting each other, and making obeisance as they passed the Golden Arbour where the King was seated.

While this course was performing, most of the spectators were again curiously comparing the stature, limbs, and sinews of the two parties, and endeavouring to form a conjecture as to the probable issue of the combat. The feud of a hundred years, with all its acts of aggression and retaliation, was concentrated in the bosom of each combatant. Their countenances seemed fiercely writhen into the wildest expression of pride, hate, and a desperate purpose of fighting to the very last.

The spectators murmured a joyful applause, in high-wrought expectation of the bloody game. Wagers were offered and accepted both on the general issue of the conflict, and on the feats of particular champions. The clear, frank, and elated look of Henry Smith, rendered him a general favourite among the spectators, and odds, to use the modern expression, were taken, that he would kill three of his opponents before he himself fell. Scarcely was the Smith equipped for the combat, when the commands of the Chiefs ordered the champions into their places ; and at the same moment Henry heard the voice of Simon Glover issuing from the crowd, who were now silent with expectation, and calling on him, " Harry Smith, Harry Smith, what madness hath possessed thee ? "

" Ay, he wishes to save his hopeful son-in-law, that is, or is to be, from the Smith's handling," was Henry's first thought—his second, was to turn and speak with him—and his third, that he could on no pretext desert the band which he had joined, or even seem desirous to delay the fight, consistently with honour.

He turned himself, therefore, to the business of the hour. Both parties were disposed by the respective Chiefs in three lines, each containing ten men. They were arranged with such intervals between each individual, as offered him scope to wield his sword, the blade of which was five feet long, not including the handle. The second and third lines were to come up as reserves, in case the first experienced disaster. On the right of the array of Clan Quhele, the Chief, Eachin MacIan, placed himself in the second line betwixt two of his foster-brothers. Four of them occupied the right of the first line, whilst the father and two others protected the rear of the beloved chieftain. Torquil, in particular, kept close behind, for the purpose of covering him. Thus Eachin stood in the centre of nine of the strongest men of his band, having four especial defenders in front, one on each hand, and three in his rear.

The line of the Clan Chattan was arranged in precisely the same order, only that the Chief occupied the centre of the middle rank, instead of being on the extreme right. This induced Henry Smith, who saw in the opposing bands only one enemy, and that was the unhappy Eachin, to propose placing himself on the left of the front rank of the Clan Chattan. But the leader disapproved of this arrangement; and having reminded Henry that he owed him obedience, as having taken wages at his hand, he commanded him to occupy the space in the third line, immediately behind himself,—a post of honour, certainly, which Henry could not decline, though he accepted of it with reluctance.

When the clans were thus drawn up opposed to each other, they intimated their feudal animosity, and their eagerness to engage, by a wild scream, which, uttered by the Clan Quhele, was answered and echoed back by the Clan Chattan, the whole at the same time shaking their swords, and menacing each other, as if they meant to conquer the imagination of their opponents ere they mingled in the actual strife.

At this trying moment, Torquil, who had never feared for himself, was agitated with alarm on the part of his Dault, yet consoled by observing that he kept a determined posture; and that the few words which he spoke to his clan were delivered boldly, and well calculated to animate them to combat, as expressing his resolution to partake their fate in death or victory. But there was no time for further observation. The trumpets of the King sounded a charge, the bagpipes blew up their screaming and maddening notes, and the combatants, starting forward in regular order, and increasing their pace till they came to a smart run, met together in the centre of the ground, as a furious land torrent encounters an advancing tide.

For an instant or two the front lines, hewing at each other with their long swords, seemed engaged in a succession of single combats; but the second and third ranks soon came up on either side, actuated alike by the eagerness of hatred and the thirst of honour, pressed through the intervals, and rendered the scene a tumultuous chaos, over which the huge swords rose and sunk, some still glittering, others streaming with blood, appearing, from the wild rapidity with which they were swayed, rather to be put in motion by some complicated machinery, than to be wielded by human hands. Some of the combatants, too much crowded together to use those long weapons, had already betaken themselves to their poniards, and endeavoured to get within the sword-sweep of those opposed to them. In the meantime, blood flowed fast, and the groans of those who fell began to mingle with the cries of those who fought; for, according to the manner of the Highlanders at all times, they could hardly be said to shout, but to yell. Those of the spectators, whose eyes were best accustomed to such scenes of blood and confusion, could nevertheless discover no advantage yet acquired by either party. The conflict swayed, indeed, at different intervals forwards or backwards, but it was only in momentary superiority, which the party who acquired it almost instantly lost by a corresponding exertion on the other side. The wild notes of the pipers were still heard above the tumult, and stimulated to farther exertions the fury of the combatants.

At once, however, and as if by mutual agreement, the instruments sounded a retreat; it was expressed in wailing notes, which seemed to imply a dirge for the fallen. The two parties disengaged themselves from each other, to take breath for a few minutes. The eyes of the spectators greedily surveyed the shattered array of the combatants as they drew off from the contest, but found it still impossible to decide what had sustained the greater loss. It seemed as if the Clan Chattan had lost rather fewer men than their antagonists; but in compensation, the bloody plaids and shirts of their party (for several on both sides had thrown their mantles away) showed more wounded men than the Clan Quhele. About twenty of both sides lay on the field dead or dying; and arms and legs lopped off, heads cleft to the chin, slashes deep through the shoulder into the breast, showed at once the fury of the combat, the ghastly character of the weapons used, and the fatal strength of the arms which wielded them. The Chief of the Clan Chattan had behaved himself with the most determined courage, and was slightly wounded. Eachin also had fought with spirit, surrounded by his body-guard. His sword was bloody; his bearing bold and warlike; and he smiled when old Torquil, folding him in his arms, loaded him with praises and with blessings.

The two Chiefs, after allowing their followers to breathe for the space of about ten minutes, again drew up in their files, diminished by nearly one third of their original number. They now chose their ground nearer to the river than that on which they had formerly encountered, which was encum-bered with the wounded and the slain. Some of the former were observed, from time to time, to raise themselves to gain a glimpse of the field, and sink back, most of them to die from the effusion of blood which poured from the terrific gashes inflicted by the claymore.

Harry Smith was easily distinguished by his Lowland habit, as well as his remaining on the spot where they had first encountered, where he stood leaning on a sword beside a corpse, whose bonneted head, carried to ten yards' distance from the body by the force of the blow which had swept it off, exhibited the oak-leaf, the appropriate ornament of the bodyguard of Eachin MacIan. Since he slew this man, Henry had not struck a blow, but had contented himself with warding off many that were dealt at himself, and some which were aimed at the Chief. MacGillie Chattanach became alarmed, when, having given the signal that his men should again draw together, he observed that his powerful recruit remained at a distance from the ranks, and showed little disposition to join them.

" What ails thee, man ? " said the Chief. " Can so strong a body have a mean and cowardly spirit ? Come, and make in to the combat."

" You as good as called me hireling but now," replied Henry—" If I am such," pointing to the headless corpse, " I have done enough for my day's wage."

" He that serves me without counting his hours," replied the Chief, " I reward him without reckoning wages."

" Then," said the Smith, " I fight as a volunteer, and in the post which best likes me."

" All that is at your own discretion," replied MacGillie Chattanach, who saw the prudence of humouring an auxiliary of such promise.

" It is enough," said Henry ; and shouldering his heavy weapon, he joined the rest of the combatants with alacrity, and placed himself opposite to the Chief of the Clan Quhele.

It was then, for the first time, that Eachin showed some uncertainty. He had long looked up to Henry as the best combatant which Perth and its neighbourhood could bring into the lists. His hatred to him as a rival was mingled with recollection of the ease with which he had once, though unarmed, foiled his own sudden and desperate attack ; and when he beheld him with his eyes fixed in his direction, the dripping sword in his hand, and obviously meditating an attack on him individually, his courage fell, and he gave symptoms of wavering which did not escape his foster-father.

It was lucky for Eachin, that Torquil was incapable, from the formation of his own temper, and that of those with whom he had lived, to conceive the idea of one of his own tribe, much less of his Chief and foster-son, being deficient in animal courage. Could he have imagined this, his grief and rage might have driven him to the fierce extremity of taking Eachin's life, to save him from staining his honour. But his mind rejected the idea that his Dault was a personal coward, as something which was monstrous and unnatural. That he was under the influence of enchantment, was a solution which superstition had suggested, and he now anxiously, but in a whisper, demanded of Hector, "Does the spell now darken thy spirit, Eachin?"

"Yes, wretch that I am," answered the unhappy youth; "and yonder stands the fell enchanter!"

"What!" exclaimed Torquil, "and you wear harness of his making?—Norman, miserable boy, why brought you that accursed mail?"

"If my arrow has flown astray, I can but shoot my life after it," answered Norman-nan-Ord. "Stand firm, you shall see me break the spell."

"Yes, stand firm," said Torquil. "He may be a fell enchanter; but my own ear has heard, and my own tongue has told, that Eachin shall leave the battle whole, free, and unwounded—let us see the Saxon wizard who can gainsay that. He may be a strong man, but the fair forest of the oak shall fall, stock and bough, ere he lay a finger on my Dault. Ring around him, my sons,—*Bas air son Eachin!*"

The sons of Torquil shouted back the words, which signify, "Death for Hector."

Encouraged by their devotion, Eachin renewed his spirit, and called boldly to the minstrels of his clan, "*Seid suas*," that is, Strike up.

The wild pibroch again sounded the onset; but the two parties approached each other more slowly than at first, as men who knew and respected each other's valour. Henry Wynd, in his impatience to begin the contest, advanced before the Clan Chattan, and signed to Eachin to come on. Norman, however, sprang forward to cover his foster-brother, and there was a general, though momentary pause, as if both parties were willing to obtain an omen of the fate of the day, from the event of this duel. The Highlander advanced, with his large sword uplifted, as in act to strike; but just as he came within sword's length, he dropt the long and cumbrous weapon, leapt lightly over the Smith's sword, as he fetched a cut at him, drew his dagger, and being thus within Henry's guard, struck him with the weapon (his own gift) on the side of the throat, directing the blow downwards into the chest, and calling aloud, at the same time, "You taught me the stab!"

But Henry Wynd wore his own good hauberk, doubly defended with a lining of tempered steel. Had he been less surely armed, his combats had been ended for ever. Even as it was, he was slightly wounded.

"Fool!" he replied, striking Norman a blow with the pommel of his long sword, which made him stagger backwards, "you were taught the thrust, but not the parry;" and fetching a blow at his antagonist, which cleft his skull through the steel-cap, he strode over the lifeless body to engage the young chief, who now stood open before him.

But the sonorous voice of Torquil thundered out, "*Far eil air son Eachin!*" (Another for Hector!) and the two brethren who flanked their Chief on each side, thrust forward upon Henry, and, striking both at once, compelled him to keep the defensive.

"Forward, race of the Tiger Cat!" cried MacGillie Chattanach; "save the brave Saxon; let these kites feel your talons!"

Already much wounded, the Chief dragged himself up to the Smith's assistance, and cut down one of the *Leichtach*, by whom he was assailed. Henry's own good sword rid him of the other.

"*Reist air son Eachin!*" (Again for Hector,) shouted the faithful foster-father.

"*Bas air son Eachin!*" (Death for Hector,) answered two more of his devoted sons, and opposed themselves to the fury of the Smith and those who had come to his aid; while Eachin, moving towards the left wing of the battle, sought less formidable adversaries, and again, by some show of valour, revived the sinking hopes of his followers. The two children of the oak, who had covered this movement, shared the fate of their brethren; for the cry of the Clan Chattan Chief had drawn to that part of the field some of his bravest warriors. The sons of Torquil did not fall unavenged, but left dreadful marks of their swords on the persons of the dead and living. But the necessity of keeping their most distinguished soldiers around the person of their Chief told to disadvantage on the general event of the combat; and so few were now the number who remained fighting, that it was easy to see that the Clan Chattan had fifteen of their number left, though most of them wounded; and that of the Clan Quhele, only about ten remained, of whom there were four of the Chief's body-guard, including Torquil himself.

They fought and struggled on, however, and as their strength decayed, their fury seemed to increase. Henry Wynd, now wounded in many places, was still bent on breaking through, or exterminating, the band of bold hearts who continued to fight around the object of his animosity. But still the father's shout of, "Another for Hector!" was cheerfully answered by the fatal counter-sign, "Death for Hector!" and though the Clan Quhele were now outnumbered, the combat seemed still dubious. It was bodily lassitude alone that again compelled them to another pause.

The Clan Chattan were then observed to be twelve in number, but two or three were scarce able to stand without leaning on their swords. Five were left of the Clan Quhele; Torquil and his youngest son were of the number, both slightly wounded. Eachin alone had, from the vigilance used to intercept all blows levelled against his person, escaped without injury. The rage of both parties had sunk, through exhaustion, into sullen desperation. They walked staggering, as if in their sleep, through the carcasses of the slain, and gazed on them, as if again to animate their hatred towards their surviving enemies, by viewing the friends they had lost.

The multitude soon after beheld the survivors of the desperate conflict drawing together to renew the exterminating feud on the banks of the river, as the spot least slippery with blood, and less encumbered with the bodies of the slain.

"For God's sake—for the sake of the mercy which we daily pray for," said the kind-hearted old King to the Duke of Albany, "let this be ended! Wherefore should these wretched rags and remnants of humanity be suffered to complete their butchery?—Surely they will now be ruled, and accept of peace on moderate terms?"

"Compose yourself, my liege," said his brother. "These men are the pest of the Lowlands. Both Chiefs are still living—if they go back unharmed, the whole day's work is cast away. Remember your promise to the council, that you would not cry hold."

"You compel me to a great crime, Albany, both as a King, who should protect his subjects, and as a Christian man, who respects the brother of his faith."

"You judge wrong, my lord," said the Duke; "these are not loving subjects, but disobedient rebels, as my Lord of Crawford can bear witness; and they are still less Christian men, for the Prior of the Dominicans will vouch for me, that they are more than half heathen."

The King sighed deeply. "You must work your pleasure, and are too wise for me to contend with. I can but turn away, and shut my eyes from the sights and sounds of a carnage which makes me sicken. But well I know that God will punish me even for witnessing this waste of human life."

"Sound, trumpets," said Albany; "their wounds will stiffen if they dally longer."

While this was passing, Torquil was embracing and encouraging his young Chief.

"Resist the witchcraft but a few minutes longer! Be of good cheer—you will come off without either scar or scratch, wem or wound. Be of good cheer!"

"How can I be of good cheer," said Eachin, "while my brave kinsmen have one by one died at my feet?—died all for me, who could never deserve the least of their kindness!"

"And for what were they born, save to die for their Chief?" said Torquil composedly. "Why lament that the arrow returns not to the quiver, providing it hit the mark? Cheer up yet—Here are Tormot and I but little hurt, while the wild-cats drag themselves through the plain as if they were half throttled by the terriers—Yet one brave stand, and the day shall be your own, though it may well be that you alone remain alive.—Minstrels, sound the gathering!"

The pipers on both sides blew their charge, and the combatants again mingled in battle, not indeed with the same strength, but with unabated inveteracy. They were joined by those whose duty it was to have remained neuter, but who now found themselves unable to do so. The two old champions who bore the standards, had gradually advanced from the extremity of the lists, and now approached close to the immediate scene of action. When they beheld the carnage more nearly, they were mutually impelled by the desire to revenge their brethren, or not to survive them. They attacked each other furiously with the lances to which the standards were attached, closed after exchanging several deadly thrusts, then grappled in close strife, still holding their banners, until at length, in the eagerness of their conflict, they fell together into the Tay, and were found drowned after the combat, closely locked in each other's arms. The fury of battle, the frenzy of rage and despair, infected next the minstrels. The two pipers, who, during the conflict, had done their utmost to keep up the spirits of their brethren, now saw the dispute wellnigh terminated for want of men to support it. They threw down their instruments, rushed desperately upon each other with their daggers, and each being more intent on despatching his opponent than in defending himself, the piper of Clan Quhele was almost instantly slain, and he of Clan Chattan mortally wounded. The last, nevertheless, again grasped his instrument, and the pibroch of the clan yet poured its expiring notes over the Clan Chattan, while the dying minstrel had breath to inspire it. The instrument which he used, or at least that part of it called the chanter, is preserved in the family of a Highland Chief to this day, and is much honoured under the name of the *Federan Dhu*, or Black Chanter.[1]

Meanwhile, in the final charge, young Tormot, devoted, like his brethren, by his father Torquil to the protection of his Chief, had been mortally wounded by the unsparing sword of the Smith. The other two remaining of the Clan Quhele had also fallen, and Torquil, with his foster-son and the wounded Tormot, forced to retreat before eight or ten of the Clan Chattan, made a stand on the bank of the river, while their enemies were making such exertions as their wounds would permit to come up with them. Torquil had just reached the spot where he had resolved to make the stand, when the youth Tormot dropped and expired. His death drew from his father the first and only sigh which he had breathed throughout the eventful day.

[1] The present Cluny MacPherson, Chief of his Clan, is in possession of this ancient trophy of their presence at the North Inch. Another account of it is given by a tradition, which says, that an aerial minstrel appeared over the heads of the Clan Chattan, and having played some wild strains, let the instrument drop from his hand. Being made of glass, it was broken by the fall, excepting only the chanter, which, as usual, was of lignum vitæ. The MacPherson piper secured this enchanted pipe, and the possession of it is still considered as ensuring the prosperity of the clan.

"My son Tormot!" he said, "my youngest and dearest! But if I save Hector, I save all.—Now, my darling Dault, I have done for thee all that man may, excepting the last. Let me undo the clasps of that ill-omened armour, and do thou put on that of Tormot; it is light, and will fit thee well. While you do so, I will rush on these crippled men, and make what play with them I can. I trust I shall have but little to do, for they are following each other like disabled steers. At least, darling of my soul, if I am unable to save thee, I can show thee how a man should die."

While Torquil thus spoke, he unloosed the clasps of the young Chief's hauberk, in the simple belief that he could thus break the meshes which fear and necromancy had twined about his heart.

"My father, my father, my more than parent!" said the unhappy Eachin—"Stay with me!—with you by my side, I feel I can fight to the last."

"It is impossible," said Torquil. "I will stop them coming up, while you put on the hauberk. God eternally bless thee, beloved of my soul!"

And then, brandishing his sword, Torquil of the Oak rushed forward with the same fatal war-cry, which had so often sounded over that bloody field, *Bas air son Eachin*!—The words rung three times in a voice of thunder; and each time that he cried his war-shout, he struck down one of the Clan Chattan, as he met them successively straggling towards him.—"Brave battle, hawk—well flown, falcon!" exclaimed the multitude, as they witnessed exertions which seemed, even at this last hour, to threaten a change of the fortunes of the day. Suddenly these cries were hushed into silence, and succeeded by a clashing of swords so dreadful, as if the whole conflict had recommenced in the person of Henry Wynd and Torquil of the Oak. They cut, foined, hewed and thrust, as if they had drawn their blades for the first time that day; and their inveteracy was mutual, for Torquil recognized the foul wizard, who, as he supposed, had cast a spell over his child; and Henry saw before him the giant, who, during the whole conflict, had interrupted the purpose for which alone he had joined the combatants—that of engaging in single combat with Hector. They fought with an equality which, perhaps, would not have existed, had not Henry, more wounded than his antagonist, been somewhat deprived of his usual agility

Meanwhile Eachin, finding himself alone, after a disorderly and vain attempt to put on his foster-brother's harness, became animated by an emotion of shame and despair, and hurried forward to support his foster-father in the terrible struggle, ere some other of the Clan Chattan should come up. When he was within five yards, and sternly determined to take his share in the death-fight, his foster-father fell, cleft from the collar-bone well-nigh to the heart, and murmuring with his last breath, *Bas air son Eachin!*—The unfortunate youth saw the fall of his last friend, and at the same moment beheld the deadly enemy who had hunted him through the whole field, standing within sword's point of him, and brandishing the huge weapon which had hewed its way to his life through so many obstacles. Perhaps this was enough to bring his constitutional timidity to its highest point ; or perhaps he recollected at the same moment that he was without defensive armour, and that a line of enemies, halting indeed and crippled, but eager for revenge and blood, were closely approaching. It is enough to say, that his heart sickened, his eyes darkened, his ears tingled, his brain turned giddy—all other considerations were lost in the apprehension of instant death ; and drawing one ineffectual blow at the Smith, he avoided that which was aimed at him in return, by bounding backward ; and ere the former could recover his weapon, Eachin had plunged into the stream of the Tay. A roar of contumely pursued him as he swam aeross the river, although, perhaps, not a dozen of those who joined in it would have behaved otherwise in the like circumstances. Henry looked after the fugitive in silence and surprise, but could not speculate on the consequences of his flight, on account of the faintness which seemed to overpower him as soon as the animation of the contest had subsided. He sat down on the grassy bank, and endeavoured to stanch such of his wounds as were pouring fastest.

The victors had the general meed of gratulation. The Duke of Albany and others went down to survey the field ; and Henry Wynd was honoured with particular notice.

" If thou wilt follow me, good fellow," said the Black Douglas, " I will change thy leathern apron for a knight's girdle, and thy burgage tenement for an hundred-pound-land to maintain thy rank withal."

" I thank you humbly, my lord," said the Smith, dejectedly, " but I have shed blood enough already ; and Heaven has punished me, by foiling the only purpose for which I entered the combat."

" How, friend?" said Douglas. "Didst thou not fight for the Clan Chattan, and have they not gained a glorious conquest?"

"*I fought for my own hand,*" said the Smith, indifferently; and the expression is still proverbial in Scotland.[1]

The good King Robert now came up on an ambling palfrey, having entered the barriers for the purpose of causing the wounded to be looked after.

"My Lord of Douglas," he said, "you vex the poor man with temporal matters, when it seems he may have short time to consider those that are spiritual. Has he no friends here who will bear him where his bodily wounds, and the health of his soul, may be both cared for?"

" He hath as many friends as there are good men in Perth," said Sir Patrick Charteris; "and I esteem myself one of the closest."

"A churl will savour of churl's kind"—said the haughty Douglas, turning his horse aside; "the proffer of knighthood from the sword of Douglas had recalled him from death's door, had there been a drop of gentle blood in his body."

Disregarding the taunt of the mighty Earl, the Knight of Kinfauns dismounted to take Henry in his arms, as he now sunk back from very faintness. But he was prevented by Simon Glover, who, with other burgesses of consideration, had now entered the barrace.

" Henry, my beloved son Henry!" said the old man. " O, what tempted you to this fatal affray!—Dying—speechless?"

" No—not speechless," said Henry.—" Catharine——"

He could utter no more.

" Catharine is well, I trust: and shall be thine—that is, if——"

" If she be safe, thou wouldst say, old man," said the Douglas, who, though something affronted at Henry's rejection of his offer, was too magnanimous not to interest himself in what was passing,—"She is safe, if Douglas's banner can protect her—safe, and shall be rich. Douglas can give wealth to those who value it more than honour."

" For her safety, my lord, let the heartfelt thanks and blessings of a father go with the noble Douglas. For wealth,

[1] Meaning, I did such a thing for my own pleasure, not for your profit.

we are rich enough—Gold cannot restore my beloved son."

"A marvel!" said the Earl—"a churl refuses nobility—a citizen despises gold!"

"Under your lordship's favour," said Sir Patrick, "I, who am knight and noble, take license to say, that such a brave man as Henry Wynd may reject honourable titles— such an honest man as this reverend citizen may dispense with gold."

"You do well, Sir Patrick, to speak for your town, and I take no offence," said the Douglas. "I force my bounty on no one.—But," he added, in a whisper to Albany, "your Grace must withdraw the King from this bloody sight, for he must know *that* to-night which will ring over broad Scotland when to-morrow dawns. This feud is ended. Yet even *I* grieve that so many brave Scottish men lie here slain, whose brands might have decided a pitched field in their country's cause."

With difficulty King Robert was withdrawn from the field; the tears running down his aged cheeks and white beard, as he conjured all around him, nobles and priests, that care should be taken for the bodies and souls of the few wounded survivors, and honourable burial rendered to the slain. The priests who were present answered zealously for both services, and redeemed their pledge faithfully and piously.

Thus ended this celebrated conflict of the North Inch of Perth. Of sixty-four brave men (the minstrels and standard-bearers included) who strode manfully to the fatal field, seven alone survived, who were conveyed from thence in litters, in a case little different from the dead and dying around them, and mingled with them in the sad procession which conveyed them from the scene of their strife. Eachin alone had left it void of wounds, and void of honour.

It remains but to say, that not a man of the Clan Quhele survived the bloody combat, except the fugitive Chief; and the consequence of the defeat was the dissolution of their confederacy. The clans of which it consisted are now only matter of conjecture to the antiquary, for, after this eventful contest they never assembled under the same banner. The Clan Chattan, on the other hand, continued to increase and flourish; and the best families of the Northern High- lands boast their descent from the race of the Cat-a-Mountain.[1]

' Note XXII.

CHAPTER XXXV

WHILE the King rode slowly back to the convent which he then occupied, Albany, with a discomposed aspect, and faltering voice, asked the Earl of Douglas, "Will not your lordship, who saw this most melancholy scene at Falkland, communicate the tidings to my unhappy brother?"

"Not for broad Scotland," said the Douglas. "I would sooner bare my breast, within flight-shot, as a butt to an hundred Tynedale bowmen. No, by St. Bride of Douglas! I could but say I saw the ill-fated youth dead. How he came by his death, your Grace can perhaps better explain. Were it not for the rebellion of March, and the English war, I would speak my own mind of it." So saying, and making his obeisance to the King, the Earl rode off to his own lodgings, leaving Albany to tell his tale as he best could.

"The rebellion and the English war?" said the Duke to himself,—"Ay, and thine own interest, haughty Earl, which, imperious as thou art, thou darest not separate from mine. Well, since the task falls on me, I must and will discharge it."

He followed the King into his apartment. The King looked at him with surprise after he had assumed his usual seat.

"Thy countenance is ghastly, Robin," said the King. "I would thou wouldst think more deeply when blood is to be spilled, since its consequences affect thee so powerfully. And yet, Robin, I love thee the better that thy kind nature will sometimes show itself, even through thy reflecting policy."

"I would to Heaven, my royal brother," said Albany, with a voice half choked, "that the bloody field we have seen were the worst we had to see or hear of this day. I should waste little sorrow on the wild kerne who lie piled on it like carrion. But——" he paused.

"How!" exclaimed the King, in terror,—"What new evil? —Rothsay?—It must be—it is Rothsay!—Speak out!—What new folly has been done?—What fresh mischance?"

"My lord—my liege—folly and mischance are now ended with my hapless nephew."

"He is dead!—he is dead!" screamed the agonized parent. "Albany, as thy brother, I conjure thee—But no—I am thy brother no longer! As thy King, dark and subtle man, I charge thee to tell the worst!"

Albany faltered out,—"The details are but imperfectly known to me—but the certainty is, that my unhappy nephew was found dead in his apartment last night from sudden illness —as I have heard."

"O, Rothsay!—O, my beloved David!—Would to God I had died for thee, my son—my son!"

So spoke, in the emphatic words of Scripture, the helpless and bereft father, tearing his grey beard and hoary hair, while Albany, speechless and conscience-struck, did not venture to interrupt the tempest of his grief. But the agony of the King's sorrow almost instantly changed to fury—a mood so contrary to the gentleness and timidity of his nature, that the remorse of Albany was drowned in his fear.

"And this is the end," said the King, " of thy moral saws and religious maxims!—But the besotted father, who gave the son into thy hands, who gave the innocent lamb to the butcher, is a King! and thou shalt know it to thy cost. Shall the murderer stand in presence of his brother—stained with the blood of that brother's son? No!—What ho, without there!—Mac-Louis!—Brandanes!—Treachery!—Murder!—Take arms, if you love the Stewart!"

MacLouis, with several of the guards, rushed into the apartment.

"Murder and treason!" exclaimed the miserable King. "Brandanes—your noble Prince"—here his grief and agitation interrupted for a moment the fatal information it was his object to convey. At length he resumed his broken speech,—"An axe and a block instantly into the courtyard!—Arrest"—The word choked his utterance.

"Arrest whom, my noble liege?" said MacLouis, who, observing the King influenced by a tide of passion so different from the gentleness of his ordinary demeanour, almost conjectured that his brain had been disturbed by the unusual horrors of the combat he had witnessed,—"Whom shall I arrest, my liege?" he replied. "Here is none but your Grace's royal brother of Albany."

"Most true," said the King, his brief fit of vindictive passion soon dying away. "Most true—none but Albany— none but my parent's child—none but my brother. O God! enable me to quell the sinful passion which glows in this bosom—*Sancta Maria, ora pro nobis!*"

MacLouis cast a look of wonder towards the Duke of Albany, who endeavoured to hide his confusion under an affectation of deep sympathy, and muttered to the officer,—

"The great misfortune has been too much for his understanding."

"What misfortune, please your Grace?" replied MacLouis. "I have heard of none."

"How!—not heard of the death of my nephew Rothsay?"

"The Duke of Rothsay dead, my Lord of Albany!" exclaimed the faithful Brandane, with the utmost horror and astonishment,—"When, how, and where?"

"Two days since—the manner as yet unknown—at Falkland."

MacLouis gazed at the Duke for an instant; then, with a kindling eye and determined look, said to the King, who seemed deeply engaged in his mental devotion,—"My liege! a minute or two since you left a word—one word—unspoken. Let it pass your lips, and your pleasure is law to your Brandanes!"

"I was praying against temptation, MacLouis," said the heart-broken King, "and you bring it to me. Would you arm a madman with a drawn weapon?—But oh, Albany! my friend, my brother, my bosom counsellor!—how—how camest thou by the heart to do this!"

Albany, seeing that the King's mood was softening, replied with more firmness than before,—"My castle has no barrier against the power of death—I have not deserved the foul suspicions which your Majesty's words imply. I pardon them, from the distraction of a bereaved father. But I am willing to swear by cross and altar—by my share in salvation, by the souls of our royal parents——"

"Be silent, Robert!" said the King; "add not perjury to murder. And was this all done to gain a step nearer to a crown and sceptre? Take them to thee at once, man; and mayst thou feel as I have done, that they are both of red-hot iron!—Oh Rothsay, Rothsay! thou hast at least escaped being a king!"

"My liege," said MacLouis, "let me remind you, that the crown and sceptre of Scotland are, when your Majesty ceases to bear them, the right of Prince James, who succeeds to his brother's rights."

"True, MacLouis," said the King, eagerly, "and will succeed, poor child, to his brother's perils! Thanks, MacLouis, thanks—You have reminded me that I have still work upon earth. Get thy Brandanes under arms with what speed thou canst. Let no man go with us whose truth is not known to thee. None in especial who has trafficked with the Duke of Albany—that man, I mean, who calls himself my brother! —and order my litter to be instantly prepared. We will to Dunbarton, MacLouis, or to Bute. Precipices, and tides, and my Brandanes' hearts, shall defend the child till we can put oceans betwixt him and his cruel uncle's ambition.— Farewell, Robert of Albany—farewell for ever, thou hard-hearted bloody man! Enjoy such share of power as the Douglas may permit thee—But seek not to see my face again, far less to approach my remaining child! for, that hour thou dost, my guards shall have orders to stab thee down with their partisans!—MacLouis, look it be so directed."

The Duke of Albany left the presence without attempting further justification or reply.

What followed is matter of history. In the ensuing Parliament, the Duke of Albany prevailed on that body to declare him innocent of the death of Rothsay, while, at the same time, he showed his own sense of guilt by taking out a remission or pardon for the offence. The unhappy and aged monarch secluded himself in his Castle of Rothsay, in Bute, to mourn over the son he had lost, and watch with feverish anxiety over the life of him who remained. As the best step for the youthful James's security, he sent him to France to receive his education at the court of the reigning sovereign. But the vessel in which the Prince of Scotland sailed, was taken by an English cruiser, and although there was a truce for the moment betwixt the kingdoms, Henry IV. ungenerously detained him a prisoner. This last blow completely broke the heart of the unhappy King Robert III. Vengeance followed, though with a slow pace, the treachery and cruelty of his brother. Robert of Albany's own grey hairs went, indeed, in peace to the grave, and he transferred the regency which he had so foully acquired, to his son Murdoch. But, nineteen years after the death of the old King, James I. returned to Scotland, and Duke Murdoch of Albany, with his sons, was brought to the scaffold, in expiation of his father's guilt and his own.[1]

[1] Note XXIII.

CHAPTER XXXVI

The honest heart that's free frae a'
    Intended fraud or guile,
However Fortune kick the ba,'
    Has aye some cause to smile.

                                        BURNS.

We now return to the Fair Maid of Perth, who had been sent from the horrible scene at Falkland, by order of the Douglas, to be placed under the protection of his daughter, the now widowed Duchess of Rothsay. That lady's temporary residence was a religious house called Campsie, the ruins of which still occupy a striking situation on the Tay. It arose on the summit of a precipitous rock, which descends on the princely river, there rendered peculiarly remarkable by the cataract called Campsie Linn, where its waters rush tumultuously over a range of basaltic rock, which intercepts the current, like a dike erected by human hands. Delighted with a site so romantic, the monks of the Abbey of Cupar reared a structure there, dedicated to an obscure Saint, named St. Hunnand, and hither they were wont themselves to retire for pleasure or devotion. It had readily opened its gates to admit the noble lady who was its present inmate, as the country was under the influence of the powerful Lord Drummond, the ally of the Douglas. There the Earl's letters were presented to the Duchess by the leader of the escort which conducted Catharine and the glee-maiden to Campsie. Whatever reason she might have to complain of Rothsay, his horrible and unexpected end greatly shocked the noble lady, and she spent the greater part of the night in indulging her grief, and in devotional exercises.

On the next morning, which was that of the memorable Palm Sunday, she ordered Catharine Glover and the minstrel into her presence. The spirits of both the young women had been much sunk and shaken by the dreadful scenes in which they had so lately been engaged ; and the outward appearance of the Duchess Marjory was, like that of her father, more calculated to inspire awe than confidence. She spoke with kindness, however, though apparently in deep affliction, and learned from them all which they had to tell concerning the fate of her erring and inconsiderate husband. She appeared grateful for the efforts which Catharine and the glee-maiden had made, at their own extreme peril, to save Rothsay from his horrible fate. She invited them to join in her devotions; and at the hour of dinner gave them her hand to kiss, and dismissed them to their own refection, assuring both, and Catharine in particular, of her efficient protection, which should include, she said, her father's, and be a wall around them both, so long as she herself lived.

They retired from the presence of the widowed Princess, and partook of a repast with her duennas and ladies, all of whom, amid their profound sorrow, showed a character of stateliness, which chilled the light heart of the Frenchwoman, and imposed restraint even on the more serious character of Catharine Glover. The friends, for so we may now term them, were fain, therefore, to escape from the society of these persons, all of them born gentlewomen, who thought themselves but ill-assorted with a burgher's daughter and a strolling glee-maiden, and saw them with pleasure go out to walk in the neighbourhood of the convent. A little garden, with its bushes and fruit-trees, advanced on one side of the convent, so as to skirt the precipice, from which it was only separated by a parapet built on the ledge of the rock, so low that the eye might easily measure the depth of the crag, and gaze on the conflicting waters which foamed, struggled, and chafed over the reef below.

The Fair Maiden of Perth and her companion walked slowly on a path that ran within this parapet, looked at the romantic prospect, and judged what it must be when the advancing summer should clothe the grove with leaves. They observed for some time a deep silence. At length the gay and bold spirit of the glee-maiden rose above the circumstances in which she had been and was now placed.

"Do the horrors of Falkland, fair May, still weigh down your spirits? Strive to forget them as I do; we cannot tread life's path lightly, if we shake not from our mantles the rain-drops as they fall."

"These horrors are not to be forgotten," answered Catharine. "Yet my mind is at present anxious respecting my father's safety; and I cannot but think how many brave men may be at this instant leaving the world, even within six miles of us, or little farther."

"You mean the combat betwixt sixty champions, of which the Douglas's equerry told us yesterday? It were a sight for a minstrel to witness. But out upon these womanish eyes of mine—they could never see swords cross each other, without being dazzled. But see,—look yonder, May Catharine, look yonder! That flying messenger certainly brings news of the battle."

"Methinks I should know him who runs so wildly," said Catharine—"But if it be he I think of, some wild thoughts are urging his speed."

As she spoke, the runner directed his course to the garden. Louise's little dog ran to meet him, barking furiously, but came back, to cower, creep, and growl behind its mistress; for even dumb animals can distinguish when men are driven on by the furious energy of irresistible passion, and dread to cross or encounter them in their career. The fugitive rushed into the garden at the same reckless pace. His head was bare, his hair dishevelled; his rich acton, and all his other vestments, looked as if they had been lately drenched in water. His leathern buskins were cut and torn, and his feet marked the sod with blood. His countenance was wild, haggard, and highly excited, or, as the Scottish phrase expresses it, much *raised*.

"Conachar!" said Catharine, as he advanced, apparently without seeing what was before him, as hares are said to do when severely pressed by the greyhounds. But he stopped short when he heard his own name.

"Conachar," said Catharine, "or rather Eachin MacIan—what means all this?—Have the Clan Quhele sustained a defeat?"

"I *have* borne such names as this maiden gives me," said the fugitive, after a moment's recollection. "Yes, I was called Conachar when I was happy, and Eachin when I was powerful. But now I have no name, and there is no such clan as thou speak'st of; and thou art a foolish maid to speak of that which is not, to one who has no existence."

"Alas! unfortunate——"

"And why unfortunate, I pray you?" exclaimed the youth. "If I am coward and villain, have not villainy and cowardice command over the elements?—Have I not braved the water without its choking me, and trod the firm earth without its opening to devour me? And shall a mortal oppose my purpose?"

"He raves, alas!" said Catharine. "Haste to call some help. He will not harm me; but I fear he will do evil to himself. See how he stares down on the roaring waterfall!"

The glee-woman hastened to do as she was ordered;

and Conachar's half-frenzied spirit seemed relieved by her absence. "Catharine," he said, "now she is gone, I will say I know thee—I know thy love of peace and hatred of war. But hearken—I have, rather than strike a blow at my enemy, given up all that a man calls dearest—I have lost honour, fame, and friends ; and such friends ! " (he placed his hands before his face,)—"Oh ! their love surpassed the love of woman ! Why should I hide my tears ?—All know my shame —all should see my sorrow. Yes, all might see, but who would pity it ?—Catharine, as I ran like a madman down the strath, man and woman called shame on me !—The beggar to whom I flung an alms that I might purchase one blessing, threw it back in disgust, and with a curse upon the coward ! Each bell that tolled rung out, Shame on the recreant caitiff ! The brute beasts in their lowing and bleating—the wild winds in their rustling and howling—the hoarse waters in their dash and roar, cried, Out upon the dastard !—The faithful nine are still pursuing me ; they cry with feeble voice, 'Strike but one blow in our revenge, we all died for you ! ' "

While the unhappy youth thus raved, a rustling was heard in the bushes. "There is but one way ! " he exclaimed, springing upon the parapet, but with a terrified glance towards the thicket, through which one or two attendants were stealing, with the purpose of surprising him. But the instant he saw a human form emerge from the cover of the bushes, he waved his hands wildly over his head, and shrieking out, "*Bas air Eachin !*" plunged down the precipice into the raging cataract beneath.

It is needless to say, that aught save thistledown must have been dashed to pieces in such a fall. But the river was swelled, and the remains of the unhappy youth were never seen. A varying tradition has assigned more than one supplement to the history. It is said by one account, that the young Captain of Clan Quhele swam safe to shore, far below the Linns of Campsie; and that, wandering disconsolately in the deserts of Rannoch, he met with Father Clement, who had taken up his abode in the wilderness as a hermit, on the principle of the old Culdees. He converted, it is said, the heart-broken and penitent Conachar, who lived with him in his cell, sharing his devotion and privations, till death removed them in succession.

Another wilder legend supposes that he was snatched from death by the *Daione-Shie*, or fairy-folk ; and that he continues to wander through wood and wild, armed like an ancient Highlander, but carrying his sword in his left hand. The phantom appears always in deep grief. Sometimes he seems about to attack the traveller, but, when resisted with courage, always flies. These legends are founded on two peculiar points in his story—his evincing timidity, and his committing suicide; both of them circumstances almost unexampled in the history of a Mountain Chief.

When Simon Glover, having seen his friend Henry duly taken care of in his own house in Curfew Street, arrived that evening at the place of Campsie, he found his daughter extremely ill of a fever, in consequence of the scenes to which she had lately been a witness, and particularly the catastrophe of her late playmate. The affection of the glee-maiden rendered her so attentive and careful a nurse, that the Glover said it should not be his fault if she ever touched lute again, save for her own amusement

It was some time ere Simon ventured to tell his daughter of Henry's late exploits, and his severe wounds ; and he took care to make the most of the encouraging circumstance, that her faithful lover had refused both honour and wealth, rather than become a professed soldier, and follow the Douglas. Catharine sighed deeply, and shook her head at the history of bloody Palm Sunday on the North Inch. But apparently she had reflected that men rarely advance in civilisation or refinement beyond the ideas of their own age, and that a headlong and exuberant courage, like that of Henry Smith, was, in the iron days in which they lived, preferable to the deficiency which had led to Conachar's catastrophe. If she had any doubts on the subject, they were removed in due time by Henry's protestations, so soon as restored health enabled him to plead his own cause.

" I should blush to say, Catharine, that I am even sick at the thoughts of doing battle. Yonder last field showed carnage enough to glut a tiger. I am therefore resolved to hang up my broadsword, never to be drawn more unless against the enemies of Scotland."

" And should Scotland call for it," said Catharine, "I will buckle it round you."

" And, Catharine," said the joyful Glover, "we will pay largely for soul masses for those who have fallen by Henry's sword ; and that will not only cure spiritual flaws, but make us friends with the Church again."

"For that purpose, father," said Catharine, "the hoards of the wretched Dwining may be applied. He bequeathed them to me, but I think you would not mix his base blood-money with your honest gains!"

"I would bring the plague into my house as soon," said the resolute Glover.

The treasures of the wicked apothecary were distributed accordingly among the four monasteries; nor was there ever after a breath of suspicion concerning the orthodoxy of old Simon or his daughter.

Henry and Catharine were married within four months after the battle of the North Inch, and never did the corporations of the glovers and hammermen trip their sword-dance so featly as at the wedding of the boldest burgess and brightest maiden in Perth. Ten months after, a gallant infant filled the well-spread cradle, and was rocked by Louise, to the tune of

> Bold and True
> In bonnet blue.

The names of the boy's sponsors are recorded, as "Ane Hie and Michty Lord, Archibald Erl of Douglas, ane Honorabil and gude Knicht, Schir Patrick Charteris of Kinfauns, and ane Gracious Princess, Marjory, Dowaire of his Serene Highness David, umquhile Duke of Rothsay." Under such patronage a family rises fast; and several of the most respected houses in Scotland, but especially in Perthshire, and many individuals, distinguished both in arts and arms, record with pride their descent from the *Gow Chrom* and the *Fair Maid of Perth.*

NOTES

Note I. p. 19.—VIEW FROM THE WICKS OF BAIGLIE

The following note is supplied by a distinguished local antiquary ;—

" The modern method of conducting the highways through the valleys and along the bases, instead of over the tops of the mountains, as in the days when Chrystal Croftangry travelled, has deprived the stranger of two very striking points of view on the road from Edinburgh to Perth. The first of these presented itself at the summit of one of the Ochills ; and the second, which was, in fact, but a nearer view of a portion of the first, was enjoyed on attaining the western shoulder of the hill of Moredun, or Moncreiff. This view from Moncreiff (that which, it is said, made the Romans exclaim that they had found another field of Mars on the bank of another Tiber) now opens to the traveller in a less abrupt and striking manner than formerly, but it still retains many of those features which Pennant has so warmly eulogized. The view from the Ochills has been less fortunate, for the road here winds through a narrow but romantic valley amongst these eminences, and the passing stranger is ushered into Strathern, without an opportunity being offered to him of surveying the magnificent scene which in days of no ancient date every traveller from the South had spread out before him at the Wicks of Baiglie.

" But in seeking out this spot—and it will repay the toil of the ascent a thousandfold—the admirer of such scenes should not confine his researches to the Wicks of Baiglie, strictly so called, but extend them westward until he gain the old road from Kinross to the Church of Drone, being that by which Mr. Croftangry must have journeyed. The point cannot be mistaken ; it is the only one from which Perth itself is visible. To this station, for reasons that the critic will duly appreciate, might with great propriety be applied the language of one of the guides at Dunkeld, on reaching a bold projecting rock on Craig Vinean—" Ah, sirs, this is the *decisive point !* "

Note II. p. 21.

David II., after the death of his .... married his .... " ane lusty woman, Catharine Logie," an .... a would fain have repudiated her, the Pope .... favour, he found himself bound. As to the ...., Boece tells us that, " After King Robert (II.) marryit the .... Rossis dochter, he had Elizabeth Mure (of Rowallan, in place of his wife. In the thrid year of King Robert, deceasit Euphame his Queen ; and he incontinent marryit Elizabeth, lemman afore rehearsit, for the affection that he had to her bairnis."—BELLENDEN, Vol. i. p. 452.

Robert III. himself was a son of Elizabeth Mure.

Note III. p. 36.—ROBERT BRUCE

The story of Bruce, when in sore straits, watching a spider near his bed, as it made repeated unsuccessful efforts to attach its thread, but, still persevering, at last attained the object, and drawing from this an augury which encouraged him to proceed in spite of fortune's hard usage, is familiar to the reader of Barbour. It was ever after held a foul crime in any of the name of Bruce, or inheriting Gentle King Robert's blood, to injure an insect of this tribe; but indeed it is well known that compassion towards the weak formed part of his character through life; and the beautiful incident of his stopping his army when on the march in circumstances of pressing difficulty in the Ulster campaign, because a poor *lavendere* (washerwoman) was taken with the pains of childbirth, and must have been left, had he proceeded, to the mercy of the Irish Kernes, is only one of many anecdotes, that to this day keep up a peculiar tenderness, as well as pride of feeling, in the general recollection of this great man, now five hundred years mingled with the dust.

Note. IV. p. 44.—GLUNE-AMIE

This word has been one of the torments of the lexicographers. There is no doubt that in Perthshire, and wherever the Highlanders and the Lowlanders bordered on each other, it was a common term, whereby, whether in scorn or honour, the Gaelic race used to be designated. Whether the *etymon* be, as Celtic scholars say, *Gluineamach*—i.e. *the Gartered*—(and certainly the garter has always been a marking feature in "the Garb of old Gaul")—or, as Dr. Jamieson seems to insinuate, the word originally means *black cattle*, and had been contemptuously applied by the Sassenach to the herdsman, as on an intellectual level with his herd—I shall not pretend to say, more than that *adhuc sub judice lis est.*

Note V. p. 50.—HIGH STREET

The two following notes are furnished by a gentleman well versed in the antiquities of bonny St. Johnston :—

" Some confusion occasionally occurs in the historical records of Perth, from there having been two high or principal streets in that city : the North High Street, still called *the* High Street, and the South High Street, now known only as the South Street, or Shoegate. An instance of this occurs in the evidence of one of the witnesses on the Gowrie Conspiracie, who deponed that the Earl of Gowrie ran in from ' the High Street ;' whereas the Earl's House stood in that part of the town now known as the South Street. This circumstance will explain how the Smith had to pass St. Anne's Chapel and St. John's Church on his way from the High Street to Curfew Row, which edifices he would not have approached if his morning walk had been taken through the more northerly of the two principal streets."

Note VI. p. 50—Curfew Street

Curfew Street, or Row, must, at a period not much earlier than that of the story, have formed part of the suburbs of Perth. It was the Wynd or Row immediately surrounding the Castle Yard, and had probably been built, in part at least, soon after the Castle was raised, and its moat filled up, by Robert Bruce. There is every probability that in the days of Robert the Third, it was of greater extent than at present,—the *Castle Gable*, which now terminates it to the eastward, having then run in a line with the Skinnergate, as the ruins of some walls still bear witness. The shops, as well as the houses of the Glovers, were then, as the name implies, chiefly in the Skinnergate ; but the charters in possession of the incorporation show that the members had considerable property in or adjacent to the Curfew Row, consisting not only of fields and gardens, but of dwelling-houses.

" In the wall of the corner house of the Curfew Row, adjacent to Blackfriar's Vennel, there is still to be seen a niche in the wall where the Curfew bell hung. This house formed at one time a part of a chapel dedicated to Saint Bartholomew, and in it at no very distant period the members of the Glover incorporation held their meetings."

Note VII. p. 71.—The Glovers

Our local antiquary says, " The Perth artisans of this craft were of great repute, and numbered amongst them, from a very early period, men of considerable substance. There are still extant among their records many charters and grants of money and lands to various religious purposes, in particular to the upholding of the altar of St. Bartholomew, one of the richest of the many shrines within the parish church of St. John.

" While alluding to these evidences of the rich possessions of the old Glovers of Perth, it ought not to pass unnoticed—as Henry pinched Simon on the subject of his rival artificers in leather, the cordwainers—that the chaplain ' aikers of St. Crispin,' on the Leonardhall property, were afterwards bought up by the Glovers.

" The avocations of this incorporation were not always of a peaceful nature. They still show a banner under which their forefathers fought in the troubles of the 17th century. It bears this inscription. ' *The perfect honour of a craft, or beauty of a trade, is not in wealthe but in moral worth, whereby virtue gains renowne :* ' and surmounted by the words, ' Grace and Peace,' the date 1604.

" The only other relic in the archives of this body which calls for notice in this place, is a leathern lash, called ' The whip of St. Bartholomew,' which the craft are often admonished in the records to apply to the back of refractory apprentices. It cannot have existed in the days of our friend the Glover, otherwise its frequent application to the shoulders of Conachar, would have been matter of record in the history of that family."

Note VIII. p. 90.—East Port

The following is extracted from a kind communication of the well-known antiquary, Mr. Morrison of Perth :—

"'The port at which the deputation for Kinfauns must have met, was a strongly fortified gate at the east end of the High Street, opening to the Bridge. On the north side of the street adjoining the gate, stood the chapel of the Virgin, from which the monks had access to the river by a flight of steps still called 'Our Lady's Stairs.' Some remains of this chapel are yet extant, and one of the towers is in a style of architecture which most antiquaries consider peculiar to the age of Robert III. Immediately opposite, on the south side of the street, a staircase is still to be seen, evidently of great antiquity, which is said to have formed part o '*Gowrie's Palace.*' But as Gowrie House stood at the other end of the Watergate—as most of the houses of the nobility were situated *between* the staircase we now refer to and Gowrie House ; and as, singularly enough, this stair is built upon ground, which, although in the middle of the town, is not within the burgh lands, some of the local antiquaries do not hesitate to say, that it formed part of the Royal Palace, in which the Kings of Scotland resided, until they found more secluded, and probably more comfortable, lodging in the Blackfriars' Monastery. Leaving the determination of this question to those who have more leisure for solving it, thus far is certain, that the place of rendezvous for the hero of the tale and his companions was one of some consequence in the town, where their bearing was not likely to pass unobserved. The bridge to which they passed through the gate, was a very stately edifice. Major calls it, 'Pontem Sancti Joannis ingentem apud Perth.' The date of its erection is not known, but it was extensively repaired by Robert Bruce, in whose reign it suffered by the repeated sieges to which Perth was subjected, as well as by some of those inundations of the Tay to which it was frequently exposed, and one of which eventually swept it away in 1621."

Note IX. p. 232.—St. Johnston's Hunt is up

This celebrated Slogan or War Cry was often accompanied by a stirring strain of music, which was of much repute in its day, but which has long eluded the search of musical antiquaries. It is described by the local poet, Mr. Adamson, as a great inspirer of courage.

> "Courage to give, was mightily then blown
> Saint Johnston's Hunt's up, since most famous known
> By all musicians——"
>
> *Muses' Threnodie, 5th Muse.*

From the description which follows, one might suppose that it had also been accompanied by a kind of war-dance.

> "O ! how they bend their backs and fingers tirle !
> Moving their quivering heads, their brains do whirle
> With divers moods ; and as with uncouth rapture
> Transported, so do shake their bodies' structure ;
> Their eyes do reele, heads, arms, and shoulders move ;
> Feet, legs, and hands, and all parts approve
> That heavenly harmonie ; while as they threw
> Their browes, O mighty strain ! that's brave ! they shew
> Great fantasie : "——
>
> *Ibid. Id.*

Mr. Morrison says :—" The various designations by which Henry or Hal of the Wynd, the Gow Chrom or Bandy-legged Smith of St. Johnston, was known, have left the field open to a great variety of competitors for the honour of being reckoned among his descendants. The want of early registers, and various other circumstances, prevent our venturing to pronounce any verdict on the comparative strength of these claims, but we shall state them all fairly and briefly.

" First, we have the Henry or Hendrie families, who can produce many other instances besides their own, in which a Christian name has become that of a family or tribe, from the celebrity attached to it through the great deeds of some one of their ancestors by whom it was borne. Then follow the Hals, Halls, and Halleys, among whom even some of the ancient and honourable race of the Halkets have ranged themselves. All these claims are, however, esteemed very lightly by the Wynds, who to this day pride themselves on their thewes and sinews, and consider that their ancestor being styled ' Henrie Winde ' by the metrical historian of the town, is of itself proof sufficient that their claim is more solid than the name would altogether imply.

" It is rather singular that, in spite of all the ill-will which Henry seems to have borne to the Celts, and the contemptuous terms in which he so often speaks of them in the text, the Gows should be found foremost among the claimants, and that the strife should lie mainly between them and their Saxon namesakes the Smiths, families whose number, opulence, and respectability, will render it an extremely difficult matter to say which of them are in the direct line, even if it should be clearer than it is, that the children of the hero were known by their father's occupation, and not by his residence.

" It only remains to notice the pretensions of the Chroms, Crooms, Crambs, or Crombies, a name which every schoolboy will associate, if not with the athletic, at least with the gymnastic exercises for which the Gow Chrom and the grammar school of Perth were equally celebrated. We need scarcely add, that while the Saxon name corresponding with the word Gow, has brought a host of competitors into the field, there has not yet started any claimant resting his pretensions on the quality expressed in the epithet *Chrom, i.e.* bandy-legged."

Note XI. p. 250.—THE COUNCIL-ROOM

Mr. Morrison says, " The places where the public assemblies of the citizens, or their magistrates, were held, were so seldom changed in former times, that there seems every reason to conclude that the meetings of the town-council of Perth were always held in or near the place where they still convene. The room itself is evidently modern, but the adjoining building, which seems to have been reared close to, if it did not actually form a part of the Chapel of the Virgin, bears many marks of antiquity. The room, in which it is not improbable the council meetings were held about the period of our story, had been relieved of part of its gloomy aspect in the reign of the third James, by the addition of one of those octagonal towers which distinguish the architecture of his favourite Cochran. The upper part of it and the spire are modern, but the lower structure is a good specimen of that artist's taste.

"The power of trying criminal cases of the most serious kind, and of inflicting the highest punishment of the law, was granted by Robert III. to the magistrates of Perth, and was frequently exercised by them, as the records of the town abundantly prove.

Note XII. p. 252.—MORRICE-DANCERS

Considerable diversity of opinion exists respecting the introduction of the Morrice dance into Britain. The name points it out as of Moorish origin; and so popular has this leaping kind of dancing for many centuries been in this country, that when Handel was asked to point out the peculiar taste in dancing and music of the several nations of Europe—to the French he ascribed the minuet; to the Spaniard, the saraband; to the Italian, the arietta; to the English, the hornpipe, or Morrice dance.

The local antiquary whose kindness has already been more than once acknowledged, says—

"It adds not a little interest to such an enquiry, in connexion with a story in which the fortunes of a Perth glover form so prominent a part—to find that the Glover Incorporation of Perth have preserved entire among their relics, the attire of one of the Morrice dancers, who, on some festive occasion, exhibited his paces 'to the jocose recreatment' of one of the Scottish monarchs, while on a visit to the Fair City.

"This curious vestment is made of fawn-coloured silk, in the form of a tunic, with trappings of green and red satin. There accompany it *two hundred and fifty-two* small circular bells, formed into twenty-one sets of twelve bells each, upon pieces of leather, made to fasten to various parts of the body. What is most remarkable about these bells, is the perfect intonation of each set, and the regular musical *intervals* between the tone of each. The twelve bells on each piece of leather are of various sizes, yet all combining to form one perfect intonation in concord with the leading note in the set. These concords are maintained not only in each set, but also in the intervals between the various pieces. The performer could thus produce, if not *a tune*, at least a pleasing and musical chime, according as he regulated with skill the movements of his body. This is sufficient evidence that the Morrice dance was not quite so absurd and unmeaning as might at first be supposed; but that a tasteful performer could give pleasure by it to the skilful, as well as amusement to the vulgar."

Note XIII. p. 257.—CHURCH OF ST. JOHN

"There is," says Mr. Morrison, "a simplicity in the internal architecture of the building which bespeaks a very ancient origin, and makes us suspect that the changes it has undergone have in a great measure been confined to its exterior. Tradition ascribes its foundation to the Picts, and there is no doubt that in the age immediately subsequent to the termination of that monarchy it was famed throughout all Scotland. It is probable that the western part of it was built about that period, and the eastern not long afterwards, and in both divisions there is still to be seen a unity and beauty of design, which is done little justice to by the broken, irregular, and paltry manner in which the exterior has at various times been patched up. When the three churches into which it is now cut down were in one, the ceilings high and decorated, the aisles enriched by the offerings of the devotees to the various altars which were reared around it, and the arches free from the galleries which now deform all these Gothic buildings,—it must have formed a splendid theatre for such a spectacle as that of the trial by bier-right."

Note XIV. p. 287.—Ordeal by Fire

In a volume of miscellanies published in Edinburgh in 1825, under the name of *Janus*, there is included a very curious paper illustrative of the solemnity with which the Catholic Church in the dark ages superintended the appeal to heaven by the ordeal of *fire*; and as the ceremonial on occasions such as that in the text was probably much the same as what is there described, an extract may interest the reader.

"Church-Service for the Ordeal by Fire

"We are all well aware that the ordeal by fire had, during many centuries, the sanction of the church, and moreover, that, considering in what hands the knowledge of those times lay, this blasphemous horror could never have existed without the connivance, and even actual co-operation, of the priesthood.

"It is only a few years ago, however, that any actual form of ritual, set apart by ecclesiastical authority for this atrocious ceremony of fraud, has been recovered. Mr. Büsching, the well-known German antiquary, has the merit of having discovered a most extraordinary document of this kind in the course of examining the charter-chest of an ancient Thuringian monastery; and he has published it in a periodical work entitled '*Die Vorzeit*,' in 1817. We shall translate the *prayers*, as given in that work, as literally as possible To those who suspected no deceit, there can be no doubt this service must have been as awfully impressive as any that is to be found in the formularies of any church; but words are wanting to express the abject guilt of those who, well knowing the base trickery of the whole matter, who, having themselves assisted in preparing all the appliances of legerdemain behind the scenes of the sanctuary-stage, dared to clothe their iniquity in the most solemn phraseology of religion.

"A fire was kindled within the church, not far from the great altar. The person about to undergo the ordeal was placed in front of the fire, surrounded by his friends, by all who were in any way interested in the result of the trial, and by the whole clergy of the vicinity. Upon a table near the fire, the coulter over which he was to walk, the bar he was to carry, or, if he were a knight, the steel-gloves which, after they had been made red-hot, he was to put on his hands, were placed in view of all.

"Part of the usual service of the day being performed, a priest advances, and places himself in front of the fire, uttering at the same moment, the following prayer, which is the first Mr. Büsching gives:—

"'O Lord God, bless this place, that herein there may be health, and holiness, and purity, and sanctification, and victory, and humility, and meekness, fulfilment of the law, and obedience to God the Father, the Son, and the Holy Ghost. May thy blessing, O God of purity and justice, be upon this place, and upon all that be therein ; for the sake of Christ the Redeemer of the world.'

" A second priest now lifts the iron, and bears it towards the fire. A series of prayers follows ; all to be repeated ere the iron is laid on the fire.

" *These are the Prayers to be said over the Fire and the Iron*

" ' 1. Lord God, Almighty Father, Fountain of Light, hear us :—enlighten us, O thou that dwellest in light unapproachable. Bless this fire, O God ; and as from the midst of the fire thou didst of old enlighten Moses, so from this flame enlighten and purify our hearts, that we may be worthy, through Christ our Lord, to come unto thee, and unto the life eternal.

" ' 2. Our Father which art in Heaven, &c.

" ' 3. O Lord, save thy servant. Lord God, send him help out of Zion, thy holy hill. Save him, O Lord. Hear us, O Lord. O Lord, be with us.

" ' 4. O God, Holy and Almighty, hear us. By the majesty of thy most holy name, and by the coming of thy dear Son, and by the gift of the comfort of thy Holy Spirit, and by the justice of thine eternal seat, hear us, good Lord. Purify this metal, and sanctify it, that all falsehood and deceit of the devil may be cast out of it, and utterly removed ; and that the truth of thy righteous judgment may be opened and made manifest to all the faithful that cry unto thee this day, through Jesus Christ, our Lord.'

" The iron is now placed in the fire, and sprinkled with consecrated water, both before and after it is so placed. The mass is said while the iron is heating,—the introductory scripture being,—' O Lord, thou art just, and righteous are all thy judgments.' The priest delivers the wafer to the person about to be tried, and, ere he communicates, the following prayer is said by the priest and congregation :—

" ' We pray unto thee, O God, that it may please thee to absolve this thy servant, and to clear him from his sins. Purify him, O heavenly Father, from all the stains of the flesh, and enable him, by thy all-covering and atoning grace, to pass through this fire,—thy creature—triumphantly, being justified in Christ our Lord.'

" Then the Gospel :—' Then there came one unto Jesus, who fell upon his knees, and cried out, Good Master, what must I do that I may be saved? Jesus said, Why callest thou me good ? ' &c.

" The chief priest, from the altar, now addresses the accused, who is still kneeling near the fire :—

" ' By the name of the Father, and of the Son, and of the Holy Ghost, and by the Christianity whose name thou bearest, and by the baptism in which thou wert born again, and by all the blessed relics of the saints of God that are preserved in this church, I conjure thee, Come not unto this altar, nor eat of this body of Christ, if thou beest guilty in the things that are laid to thy charge ; but if thou beest innocent therein, come, brother, and come freely.'

" The accused then comes forward and communicates,—the priest saying,—' This day may the body and blood of Jesus Christ, which were given and shed for thee, be thy protection and thy succour, yea, even in the midst of the flame.'

" The priest now reads this prayer :—'O Lord, it hath pleased thee to accept our spiritual sacrifice. May the joyful partaking in this holy sacrament be comfortable and useful to all that are here present, and serviceable to the removing of the bondage and thraldom of whatsoever sins do most easily beset us. Grant also, that to this thy servant it may be of exceeding comfort, gladdening his heart, until the truth of thy righteous judgment be revealed.'

" The organ now peals, and *Kyrie Eleeison* and the Litany are sung in full chorus.

" After this comes another prayer :—

"'O God ! thou that through fire hast shown forth so many signs of thy almighty power ! thou that didst snatch Abraham, thy servant, out of the brands and flames of the Chaldeans, wherein many were consumed ! thou that didst cause the bush to burn before the eyes of Moses, and yet not to be consumed ! God, that didst send thy Holy Spirit in the likeness of tongues of fiery flame, to the end that thy faithful servants might be visited and set apart from the unbelieving generation ; God, that didst safely conduct the three children through the flame of the Babylonians ; God, that didst waste Sodom with fire from heaven, and preserve Lot, thy servant, as a sign and a token of thy mercy : O God, show forth yet once again thy visible power, and the majesty of thy unerring judgment : that truth may be made manifest, and falsehood avenged, make thou this fire thy minister before us ; powerless be it where is the power of purity, but sorely burning, even to the flesh and the sinews, the hand that hath done evil, and that hath not feared to be lifted up in false swearing. O God ! from whose eye nothing can be concealed, make thou this fire thy voice to us thy servants, that it may reveal innocence, or cover iniquity with shame. Judge of all the earth ! hear us : hear us, good Lord, for the sake of Jesus Christ thy Son.'

" The priest now dashes once more the holy water over the fire, saying, 'Upon this fire be the blessing of the Father, and of the Son, and of the Holy Ghost, that it may be a sign to us of the righteous judgment of God.'

" The priest pauses ; instantly the accused approaches to the fire, and lifts the iron, which he carries nine yards from the flame. The moment he lays it down he is surrounded by the priests, and borne by them into the vestry ; there his hands are wrapped in linen cloths, sealed down with the signet of the church : these are removed on the third day, when he is declared innocent or guilty, according to the condition in which his hands are found. ' *Si sinus rubescens in vestigio ferri reperiatur, culpabilis ducatur. Sin autem mundus reperiatur, Laus Deo referatur.*'

" Such is certainly one of the most extraordinary records of the craft, the audacity, and the weakness of mankind."

The belief that the corpse of a murdered person would bleed on the touch, or at the approach of the murderer, was universal among the northern nations. We find it seriously urged in the High Court of Justiciary at Edinburgh, so late as 1688, as an evidence of guilt. The case was that of Philip Standsfield, accused of the murder of his father, and this part of the evidence against him is thus stated in the " libel," or indictment. "And when his father's dead body was sighted and inspected by chirurgeons, and the clear and evident signs of the murder had appeared, the body was sewed up, and most carefully cleaned, and his nearest relations and friends were desired to lift his body to the coffin ; and accordingly, James Row, merchant, (who was in Edinburgh in the time of the murder,) having lifted the left side of Sir James his head and shoulder, and the said Philip the right side, his father's body, though carefully cleaned, as said is, so as the least blood was not on it, did (according to God's usual method of discovering murders) blood afresh upon him, and defiled all his hands, which struck him with such a terror, that he immediately let his father's head and body fall with violence, and fled from the body, and in consternation and confusion cried, 'Lord, have mercy upon me!' and bowed himself down over a seat in the church (where the corp was inspected), wiping his father's innocent blood off his own murdering hands upon his cloaths." To this his counsel replied, that, "this is but a superstitious observation, without any ground either in law or reason ; and Carpzovius relates that several persons upon that ground had been unjustly challenged." It was, however, insisted on as a link in the chain of evidence, not as a merely singular circumstance, but as a miraculous interposition of Providence; and it was thus animadverted upon by Sir George Mackenzie, the king's counsel, in his charge to the jury. "But they, fully persuaded that Sir James was murdered by his own son, sent out some chirurgeons and friends, who, having raised the body, did see it bleed miraculously upon his touching it. In which God Almighty himself was pleased to bear a share in the testimonies we produce ; that Divine power, which makes the blood circulate during life, has oft times, in all nations, opened a passage to it after death upon such occasions, but most in this case."

Note XV. p. 289.—SKINNERS' YARDS

"The Skinners' Yard," says Mr. Morrison, "is still in the possession of that fraternity, and is applied to the purpose which its name implies. Prior to the time of the peaceable Robert, it was the court-yard of the castle. Part of the gate which opened from the town, to the drawbridge of the castle, is still to be seen, as well as some traces of the foundation of the Keep or Donjon, and of the towers which surrounded the Castle-yard. The Curfew-row, which now encloses the Skinners'-yard, at that time formed the avenue or street leading from the northern part of th town to the Dominican Monastery."

Note XVI. p. 294.—EARL OF ERROL'S LODGINGS

"The Constable's, or Earl of Errol's lodgings," says Mr. Morrison, "stood near the south end of the Watergate, the quarter of the town in which most of the houses of the nobility were placed, amidst gardens which extended to the wall of the city adjoining the river. The families of the Hays had many rich possessions in the neighbourhood, and other residences in the town besides that commonly known as the Constable's Lodgings. Some of these subsequently passed, along with a considerable portion of the Carse, to the Ruthven or Gowrie family. The last of those noble residences in Perth which retained any part of its former magnificence, (and on that account styled the Palace,) was the celebrated

Gowrie House, which was nearly entire in 1805, but of which not a vestige now remains. On the confiscation of the Gowrie estates, it merged into the public property of the town; and, in 1746, was presented by the magistrates to the Duke of Cumberland. His Royal Highness, on receiving this mark of the attachment or servility of the Perth rulers, asked, with sarcastic nonchalance, 'If the *piece of ground* called the Carse of Gowrie went along with it?'"

Note XVII. p. 334

The security no less than the beauty of the situations led to the choice of these lake islands for religious establishments. Those in the Highlands were generally of a lowly character, and in many of them the monastic orders were tolerated, and the rites of the Romish Church observed, long after the Reformation had swept both "the rooks and their nests" out of the Lowlands. The Priory on Loch Tay was founded by Alexander I., and the care of it committed to a small body of monks; but the last residents in it were three nuns, who, when they did emerge into society, seemed determined to enjoy it in its most complicated and noisy state, for they came out only once a year, and that to *a market* at Kenmore. Hence that Fair is still called "Fiell na m'hau maomb," or Holy Woman's market.

Note XVIII. p. 337

The installation, the marriage, and the funeral of a chieftain, were the three periods of his course observed with the highest ceremony by all the clan. The latter was perhaps the most imposing of the three spectacles, from the solemnity of the occasion, and the thrilling effect produced by the coronach, sung by hundreds of voices, its melancholy notes undulating through the valleys, or reverberating among the hills. All these observances are fading away, and the occasional attempt at a gathering, for the funeral of a chief, now resembles the dying note of the coronach, faintly echoed for the last time among the rocks.

Note XIX. p. 406.—RED-HAND

Mr. Morrison says, "the case of a person taken *red-hand* by the magistrates of Perth and immediately executed, was the main cause of the power of trying cases of life and death being taken from them and from all subordinate judicatories. A young English officer connected with some families of rank and influence, who was stationed with a recruiting party at Perth, had become enamoured of a lady there, so young as still to be under the tuition of a dancing-master. Her admirer was in the habit of following her into the school, to the great annoyance of the teacher, who, on occasion of a ball given in his class-room in the Kirkgate, stationed himself at the door, determined to resist the entrance of the officer, on account of the scandal to which his visits had given rise. The officer came as a matter of course, and a scuffle ensued, which at last bore so threatening an aspect, that the poor dancing-master fled through the passage, or *close*, as it is called, by which there was access to the street.

He was pursued by the officer with his drawn sword, and was run through the body ere he could reach the street, where the crowd usually assembled on such occasions might have protected him. The officer was instantly apprehended and executed, it is understood, even without any form of trial; at least there is no notice of it in any of the records where it would with most probability have been entered. But the sword is still in the possession of a gentleman whose ancestors held official situations in the town at the time, and the circumstances of the murder and of the execution have been handed down with great minuteness and apparent truth of description from father to son. It was immediately afterwards that the power of the civic magistrates in matters criminal was abridged,—it is thought chiefly through the influence of the friends of this young officer."

Note XX. p. 415.—Ploughman Stares

" This place, twice referred to in the course of our story as hateful to the Highlanders, lies near the *Staredam*, a collection of waters in a very desolate hollow between the hill of Birnam, and the road from Perth to Dunkeld. The *eeriness* of the place is indescribable, and is rendered yet more striking from its being within a furlong of one of the loveliest and richest scenes in Scotland—the north-west opening of Strathmore. The " dam " has been nearly drained within these few years, but the miserable patches of sickly corn which have with vast labour and cost been obtained, look still more melancholy than the solitary tarn which the barren earth seems to have drunk up. The whole aspect of the place fitted it for being the scene of the trial and punishment of one of the most notorious bands of thieves and outlaws that ever laid the Low Country under contribution. Ruthven, the Sheriff, is said to have held his court on a rising ground to the north, still called the Court-hill; and there were lately, or there still may be, at the east end of the Roch-in-roy wood, some oaks on which the Highlanders were hung, and which long went by the name of the Hanged-men's-trees. The hideous appearance of the bodies hanging in chains gave the place a name which to this day grates on the ear of a Celt."—Morrison.

Note XXI. p. 419.—Gardens of the Dominicans

" The gardens of the Dominicans surrounded the monastery on all sides, and were of great extent and beauty. Part of them immediately adjoined the North Inch, and covered all that space of ground now occupied by Atholl Place, the Crescent, and Rose Terrace, besides a considerable extent of ground to the west and south, still known by the name of the Black Friars. On a part of these grounds overlooking the North Inch, probably near the south end of the Terrace, a richly decorated summer-house stood, which is frequently mentioned in old writings as the Gilten Arbour. From the balconies of this edifice King Robert is supposed to have witnessed the conflict of the clans. What the peculiar forms, construction, or ornaments of this building were, which gained for it this title, is not even hinted at by any or the local chroniclers. It may be mentioned, however, although it is a matter of mere tradition, that the ornaments on the ceiling of the Monks' Tower (a circular watch-tower at the south-east angle of the town) were said to have been copied from those on the Gilten Arbour, by orders of the first Earl of Gowrie, at the corner of whose Garden the Monks' Tower stood. This tower was taken down at the same time with Gowrie House, and many yet remember the general appearance of the paintings on the ceiling, yet it does not seem to have occurred to any one to have had them copied. They were allegorical and astronomical, representing the virtues and vices, the seasons, the zodiac, and other subjects commonplace enough ; yet even the surmise that they might have been copied from others still more ancient, if it could not save them from destruction, should have entitled them to a greater share than they seem to have possessed of the notice of their contemporaries. The patience with which the antiquaries of Perth have submitted to the removal (in many cases the wanton and useless removal) of the historical monuments with which they were at one time surrounded, is truly wonderful."—Morrison.

Note XXII. p. 442.

The reader may be amused with the account of this onslaught in Boece, as translated by Bellenden.

" At this time, mekil of all the north of Scotland was hevely trublit be two clannis of Irsmen, namit Clankayis and Glenquhattanis ; invading the cuntre, be thair weris, with ithand slauchter and reif. At last, it was appointit betwix the heidis-men of thir two clannis, be avise of the Erlis of Murray and Crawfurd, that xxx of the principall men of the ta clan sal cum, with othir xxx of the tothir clan, arrayit in thair best avise ; and sall convene afore the king at Perth, for decision of al pleis ; and fecht with scharp swerdis to the deith, but ony harnes ; and that clan quhare the victory succedit, to have perpetuall empire above the tothir. Baith thir clannis, glaid of this condition, come to the North Inche, beside Perth, with jugis set in scaffaldis, to discus the verite. Ane of thir clannis wantit ane man to perfurnis furth the nowmer, and wagit ane carll, for money, to debait thair actioun, howbeit this man pertenit na thing to thaim in blud nor kindnes. Thir two clannis stude arrayit with gret hatrent aganis othir ; and, be sound of trumpet, ruschit togidder ; takand na respect to thair woundis, sa that thay micht distroy thair ennimes ; and faucht in this maner lang, with uncertane victory ; quhen ane fel, ane othir was put in his rowme. At last, the Clankayis war al slane except ane, that swam throw the watter of Tay. Of Glenquhattannis, was left xi personis on live ; bot thay war sa hurt, that thay micht nocht hald thair swerdis in thair handis. This debait was fra the incarnation, MCCCXCVI yeiris."

Note XXIII. p. 446.

The death of the Duke of Rothsay is not accompanied with the circumstances detailed by later writers in Wyntoun. The Chronicler of Lochleven says simply :—

> "A thousand foure hundyr yeris and twa,
> All before as ye herd done,
> Our lord the king is eldest sone,

"Suete and vertuous, yong and fair,
And his nerast lauchful ayr,
Honest, habil, and avenand,
Our Lorde, our Prynce, in all plesand,
Cunnand into letterature,
A seymly persone in stature,
Schir Davy Duke of Rothesay,
Of Marche the sevyn and twenty day
Yauld his Saule til his Creatoure,
His corse til hallowit Sepulture.
In Lundoris his Body lies,
His Spirite intil Paradys."—B. ix. chap. 23.

The Continuator of Fordun is far more particular, and though he does not positively pronounce on the guilt of Albany, says enough to show that, when he wrote, the suspicion against him was universal; and that Sir John Ramorny was generally considered as having followed the dark and double course ascribed to him in the novel.

"Anno Domini millesimo quadringentesimo primo, obiit columna ecclesiæ robustissima, vas eloquentiæ, thesaurus scientæ, ac defensor catholicæ fidei. dominus Walterus Treyl episcopus S. Andreæ; et etiam domina Anabella regina apud Sconam decessit, et sepulta est in Dunfermelyn. Hi enim duo, dum viverent, honorem quasi regni exaltabant; videlicet, principes et magnates in discordiam concitatos ad concordiam revocantes, alienigenas et extraneos egregiè susceptantes et conviviantes, ac munificè dimossos lætificantes. Unde quasi proverbialiter tunc dictum exstitit, quòd mortuis reginâ Scotiæ, comite de Douglas, et episcopo Sancti Andreæ, abiit decus, recessit honor, et honestas obiit Scotiæ. Eodem anno quarta mortalitas exstitit in regno. Paulo ante dominus rex in consilio deputavit certos consiliarios; valentes barones et milites, juratos ad regendum et consiliandum dominum David Stewart ducem Rothsaiensem, comitem de Carrik, et principem regni, quia videbatur regi et consilio quòd immiscebat se sæpiùs effrænatis lusibus et levioribus ludicris. Propter quod et ipse consilio astrictis saniori, juravit se regimini eorum et consilio conformare. Sed mortuâ reginâ ipsius nobili matre, quæ eum in multis refrænabat, tanquam laqueus contritus fuisset, speravit se liberatum, et, spreto proborum consilio, denuo in priori levitate se totum dedit. Propter quod consilium procerum sibi assignatum quitabit se regi, et si voluisset, non tamen posse se eum ad gravitatem morum flexisse attestatur. Unde rex impotens et decrepitus scripsit fratri suo duci Albaniæ, gubernatori regni, ut arrestaretur, et ad tempus custodiæ deputaretur, donec virgâ disciplinæ castigatus, seipsum meliùs cognosceret. Non enim osculatur filium pater, quod aliquando castigat. Sed quod rex proposuit ad filii emendam, tendit ei ad noxam. Nam uterque bajulus literæ regalis ad gubernatorem de facto ostendit, se incentorem et instigatorem regi ut taliter demandaret, quod honori alterius obviaret, sicut experientiâ exitus rei patefecit. Domini enim Willelmus Lindesay de Rossy et Johannes Remorgeney milites, regis familiares et consiliarii, nuncii et portatores erant literarum regis gubernatori: quique etiam, ut dicitur, duci Rothsaiensi priùs suggesserunt, ut, post obitum episcopi Sancti Andreæ, castrum suum ad usum regis, quousque novus episcopus, institueretur, reciperet et servaret: quique ipsum ducem, nihil mali præmeditatum, ad castrum Sancti Andreæ simpliciter, et cum moderata familia, equitantem, inter villam de Nidi et Stratyrum arrestaverunt, et per potentiam eundem ducem ad ipsum castrum Sancti Andreæ, sibi ad deliberandum paratum, induxerunt, et ibidem in custodia tenuerunt, quousque dux Albaniæ cum suo consilio apud Culros tento, quid de eo facerent, deliberaverunt. Qui quidem dux Albaniæ, cum domino Archibaldo II. comite de Douglas, manu validâ ipsum ad turrim de Faulkland, jumento impositum et russeto collobio chlamidatum transvexerunt: ubi in quadam honesta camerula eum servandum deputaverunt. In qua tam diu custoditus, scilicet per Johannem Selkirk et Johannem Wrycht, donec dyssenteriâ, sive, ut alii volunt, fame tabefactus, finem vitæ dedit vij. Kal. Aprilis, in vigilia Paschæ serò, sive in die Paschæ summo mane, et sepultus est in Londoris. Præmissus verò Johannes Remorgeney tam principi, quàm domino regi, erat consiliarius, audax spiritu, et pronunciatione eloquent-issimus, ac in arduis causis prolocutor regis, et causidicus disertissimus: qui, ut dicitur, ante hæc suggessit ipsi principi duci Rothsaiensi, ut patruum suum ducem Albaniæ arrestaret, et, qualicunque occasione nactâ, statim de medio tolleret: quod facere omnino princeps refutavit. Istud atten-dens miles, malitiæ suæ fuligine occæcatus, à cœptis desistere nequivit, hujusmodi labe attachiatus; quia, ut ait Chrysostomus, 'Coërceri omnino nequit animus pravâ semel voluntate vitiatus.' Et ideo, vice versâ, pallium in alterum humerum convertens, hoc idem maleficium ducem Albaniæ de nepote suo duce Rothsaiensi facere instruxit; aliàs fine fallo, ut asseruit, dux Rothsaiensis de ipso finem facturus fuisset. Dictus insuper D. Willelmus Lindesay cum ipso Johanne Remorgeney in eandem sententiam fortè con-sentivit, pro eo quòd dictus dux Rothsaiensis sororem ipsius D. Willelmi Euphemiam de Lindesay affidavit, sed per sequentia aliarum matrimonia attemptata, sicut et filiam comitis Marchiæ, sic eandem repudiavit. Ipse enim, ut æstimo, est ille David, de quo vates de Breclyngton sic vaticinatus est, dicens;

> Psalletur gestis David luxuria festis,
> Quòd tenet uxores uxore suâ meliores,
> Deficient mores regales, perdet honores.

Paulo ante captionem suam apparuit mirabilis cometes, emitens ex se radios crinitos ad Aquilonem tendentes. Ad quam visendum cùm primò appareret, quodam vespere in castro de Edinburgh cum aliis ipse dux secedens, fertur ipsum sic de stella disseruisse, dicens; 'Ut à mathe-maticis audivi hujusomodi cometes, cùm apparet, signat mortem vel mutationem alicujus principis, vel alicujus patriæ destructionem.' Et sic evenit ut prædixit. Nam, duce capto, statim in præjacentem materiam, sicut Deus voluit, redit stella. In hoc potuit iste dux Sibyllæ prophetissæ comparari, de qua sic loquitur Claudianus:

> Miror, cur aliis quæ fata pandere soles,
> Ad propriam cladem cæca Sibylla taces.

The narrative of Boece attaches murder distinctly to Albany. After mentioning the death of Queen Annabella Drummond, he thus proceeds:—
"Be quhais deith, succedit gret displeseir to hir son, David, Duk of Rothesay: for, during hir life, he wes haldin in virtewis and honest occupa-tion: eftir hir deith, he began to rage in all maner of insolence; and fulyeit virginis, matronis, and nunnis, be his unbridillit lust. At last, King Robert, informit of his young and insolent maneris, send letteris to his brothir, the Duke of Albany, to intertene his said son, the Duk of Rothesay, and to leir him honest and civill maneris. The Duk of Albany, glaid of thir writtingis, tuk the Duk of Rothesay betwix Dunde and Sanct Androis, and brocht him to Falkland, and inclusit him in the tour hairof, but ony meit or drink. It is said, ane woman, havand commisera-tioun on this Duk, leit meill fall doun throw the loftis of the toure: be

quhilkis, his life was certane dayis savit. This woman, fra it wes knawin, wes put to deith. On the same maner, ane othir woman gaif him milk of hir paup, throw ane lang reid; and wes slane with gret cruelte, fra it wes knawin. Than wes the Duke destitute of all mortall supplie; and brocht, finalie, to sa miserable and hungry appetite, that he eit, nocht allanerlie the filth of the toure quhare he wes, bot his awin fingaris; to his gret marterdome. His body was beryit in Lundoris, and kithit miraklis mony yeris eftir; quhil, at last, King James the First began to punis his slayaris; and fra that time furth, the miraclis ceissit."

The *Remission*, which Albany and Douglas afterwards received at the hands of Robert III., was first printed by Lord Hailes; and is as follows:—

"Robertus, Dei gratiâ, Rex Scottorum, Universis, ad quorum notitiam præsentes literæ pervenerint, Salutem in Domino sempiternam: Cum nuper carissimi nobis, Robertus Albaniæ Dux, Comes de Fife et de Menteth, frater noster germanus, et Archibaldus Comes de Douglas, et Dominus Galwidiæ, filius noster secundum legem, ratione filiæ nostræ quam duxit in uxorem, præcarissimum filium nostrum primogenitum David, quondam Ducem Rothsaye ac Comitem de Carrick et Atholiæ, capi fecerunt, et personaliter arrestari, et in castro Sancti Andreæ primo custodiri, deindeque apud Faucland in custodia detineri, ubi ab hac luce, divinâ providentiâ, et non aliter, migrasse dignoscitur. Quibus comparentibus coram nobis, in concilio nostro generali apud Edinburgh, decimo sexto die mensis Maii, anno Domini millesimo quadringentesimo secundo, inchoato, et nonnullis diebus continuato, et super hoc interrogatis ex officio nostro regali, sive accusatis, hujusmodi captionem, arrestationem, mortem, ut superius est expressum, confitentes, causas ipsos ad hoc moventes, pro publica, ut asseruerunt, utilitate arctantes, in præsentia nostra assignârunt, quas non duximus præsentibus inserendas, et ex causâ: Habitâ deinde super hoc diligenti inquisitione, consideratis omnibus et singulis in hac parte considerandis, hujusmodi causam tangentibus, et maturâ deliberatione concilii nostri præhabitâ discussis, prænotatos Robertum fratrem nostrum germanum, Archibaldumque filium nostrum secundum jura, et eorum in hac parte participes quoscunque, viz. arresta-tores, detentores, custodes, consiliarios, et omnes alios consilium, videlicet, auxilium, vel favorem eisdem præstantes, sive eorum jussum aut mandatum qualitercunque exsequentes, excusatos habemus; necnon et ipsos, et eorum quemlibet, a crimine læsæ majestatis nostræ, vel alio quocunque crimine, culpa, injuria, rancore, et offensa, quæ eis occasione præmissorum imputari possent qualitercunque, in dicto consilio nostro palam et publicè declaravimus, pronunciavimus, et diffinivimus, tenoreque præsentium declaramus, pronunciamus, et per hanc diffinitivam nostram sententiam diffinimus, innocentes, innoxios, inculpabiles, quietos, liberos, et immunes, penitus et omnimodo: Et si quam contra ipsos, sive eorum aliquem, aut aliquam vel aliquos, in hoc facto qualitercunque participes, vel eis quomodolibet adhærentes, indignationem, iram, rancorem, vel offensionem, concepimus qualitercunque, illos proprio motu, ex certa scientia, et etiam ex deliberatione concilii nostri jam dicti, annullamus, removemus, et adnullatos volumus haberi, in perpetuum. Quare omnibus et singulis subditis nostris, cujuscunque statûs aut conditionis exstiterint, districtè præcipimus et mandamus, quatenus sæpe dictis Roberto et Archibaldo, eorumque in hoc facto participibus, consentientibus, seu adhærentibus, ut præmittitur, verbo non detrahent, neque facto, nec contra eosdem murmurent qualitercunque, unde possit eorum bona fama lædi, vel aliquod

præjudicium generari, sub omni pœna quæ exinde competere poterit
quomodolibet ipso jure. Datum, sub testimonio magni sigilli nostri, in
monasterio Sanctæ Crucis de Edinburgh, vicesimo die mensis Maii
prædicti, anno Domini millesimo quadringentesimo secundo, et regni nostri
anno tertio decimo."

Lord Hailes sums up his comment on the document with words which,
as Pinkerton says, leave no doubt that he considered the prince as having
been murdered : viz. "The Duke of Albany and the Earl of Douglas
obtained a remission in terms as ample as if they had actually murdered
the heir apparent."

GLOSSARY

A', *all.*

AIN, *own.*

AMERCIAMENTS, *penalties not fixed by law, but at the discretion of the Courts.*

AN, *if.*

AN, *respecting, concerning.*

ANE ANOTHER, *one another.*

APPARITOR, *ghost, apparition.*

ASSOILZIED, ASSOILIZED, *acquited.*

ASSYTHMENT, *a money-payment to the nearest relatives in atonement for bloodshed.*

AULD, *old.*

AWA', *away.*

AWEEL, *ah, well!*

BACK-BEARAND, *lawful rights of retaliation against grievous wrong.*

BAILIE, *magistrate.*

BAIRN, *child.*

BALDRICK, *girdle.*

BALLOCK, *glen,* also *discharge of a lake into a river.*

BAN-DOG, *house dog, mastiff.*

BARBER-CHIRURGEON, *barber-surgeon.*

BARRACE, *bounds, lists for combatants.*

BEADSMAN, BEDESMAN, *a poor pensioner, one who is supported on condition of praying for a deceased patron.*

BIELDED, *sheltered.*

BIER-RIGHT, *an ancient ordeal of discovering the guilt of an alleged murderer by contact with the dead body of the victim.*

BIEYFIR, *allotted portion of a man at mess or the banquet-table.*

BIGGEN, *cap.*

BINK, *kitchen shelves for plates and dishes.*

BIT, *little, tiny.*

BLADE, *sword.*

BLITHE, *pleasant, glad.*

BLOOD-SUIT VENDETTA, *a family vengeance for murder.*

BOGGED, *sunk in a bog.*

BOGGLED, *hesitated, wavered.*

BOLT, *the arrow of a cross-bow.*

BOOSHALLOCK, *cow-herd.*

BORDEL, *brothel.*

BORDELLER, *frequenter of a brothel debauchee.*

BORREL LOONS, *low rustic rogues.*

BOSKETS, *thickets, underwood.*

BOTHY, *hut, hovel.*

BOUNTITH, *the bounty given in addition to stipulated wages.*

BOWIE, *small milk-pail.*

BRACKEN, *fern.*

BRAGS, *boastings.*

BRATTACH, *standard,* literally *cloth.*

BRENT-BROWED LASS, *girl with a high forehead.*

BREWIS, BROSE, *stirabout.*

BROGUES, *shoes; in the Lowlands, shoes of half-tanned leather.*

BURN-THE-WIND, *blacksmith.*

BUSK, *dress, arrange.*

BUT, *without.*

CAILLIACHS, *old women.*

CAITIFF, *slave; mean despicable person.*

CALABASH, *wine-gourd.*

CANNA, *cannot.*

CARLE, *fellow.*

CARTEL, *challenge, note of defiance.*

CATERAN, CATHERAN, *Highland robber, freebooter.*

CAUDLE, *a warm drink for sick persons.*

CERTES, *certainly, in truth.*

CHEEK BY JOUL, *side by side.*

CHEVRON, *zigzag ornament.*

CHIRURGEON, *surgeon.*

CHROM, *bandy-legged.*

COGUES, *wooden drinking cups.*

COMMON GOOD, *the public property of the Burgh.*

CORBIE, *raven.*

CORONACH, *dirge.*

CROSS-BOW BOLTS, *cross-bow arrows.*

CUMMER, *gossip, neighbour.*

CURRAGHS, *small boats of wicker-work or willow hoops, covered with hides.*

CURTAL-AXES, *broadswords.*

DAULT, *foster-child.*

DEASIL, *a Scottish superstitious practice of walking three times round a person in the direction of the sun.*

DEBOSHED, *debased, debauched.*

DEVOIR, *respect, act of civility.*

DEY-WOMAN, *farm-woman.*

DINGING, *striking, beating, hammering.*

DINK, *contemptuous.*

DIRK, *Scotch dagger.*

DOUCE, *quiet, sedate.*

DOURLACH, *satchels of arrows.*

DROMOND, *vessel of the largest kind; in this particular instance, wooden figure of a soldan or common enemy.*

DUENNA, *chaperon, governess.*

E'EN, *even, evening.*

ENEUGH, *enough.*

ERRANT DAMSEL, *adventurous maid.*

FAITOUR, *rascal.*

FASTERN'S E'EN, *Shrove Tuesday.*

FEE AND BOUNTITH, *wages and an additional reward.*

FORE-HAMMER, *forge-hammer, blacksmith's hammer.*

FOU, *full, satisfied.*

FRENCH MUTTON, *a French gold coin, "mouton," so called because impressed with the figure of a lamb.*

GAGE, *pledge.*

GAILLARD, GALLIARD, *a reveller.*

GAIT, *way, road.*

GALLO-GLASSES, *heavily armed men.*

GANG, *go.*

GEAR, *property, possessions.*

GIE, *give.*

GILLIE, *Highland man-servant.*

GIRDLES, *iron plates for firing cakes on.*

GLEE-WOMAN, *minstrel-woman.*

GOUGE, *wench.*

GOW, *smith.*

GOW CHROM, *bandy-legged smith.*

GULLS, *fools, persons easily deceived.*

HABERGEON *v.* HAUBERK.

HAE, *have.*

HAFFITS, *sides of the head, cheeks.*

HAILL, *whole.*

HANK, *rope, coil.*

HAUBERK, HABERGEON, *a shirt of mail formed of steel rings interwoven.*

HERSELL, *herself.*

HIELANDMAN, *Highlander.*

HIELANDS, *Highlands.*

HINNY, *honey, my dear.*

HOBBLESHOW, *confused kick-up, uproar.*

HOLIDAME, *Holy Mother, the Virgin.*

HOLYTIDE, *festival time, season of the Carnival.*

ILK *v.* OF THAT ILK.

INDOCTRINATE, *instruct in the principles of a system, institution, or religion.*

INFANG, *a thief taken on one's lands or premises.*

IN TROTH, *in truth.*

I'SE, *I will.*

JACKMAN, *retainer.*

JEDWOOD JUSTICE, *Jedburgh justice,* i.e. *hang a man and try him afterwards.*

JENNET, *small Spanish horse.*

JILLET, *giddy girl.*

KEN, *know.*

KENN'D, *knew.*

KENS NAETHING, *knows nothing.*

KERNE, *freebooters.*

KIRSTENING, *christening.*

LAIRD, *squire.*

LANDLOUPER, *one who passes from one country to another.*

LANDWARD, *the country.*

LANG-LEGGED LOONS, *long-legged rascals.*

LAWING, *reckoning.*

LEECH, *physician.*

LEICHTACH, *body-guard.*

LEMAN, *sweetheart, lover.*

LIEGEMAN, *faithful follower.*

LIGHT O' LOVE, *mistress.*

LIMMERS, *women of loose character.*

LIPPING, *making notches in a sword or knife.*

LOCHABAR-AXE, *formidable weapon of defence, peculiar to the Highlands.*

LOCK, *ladleful.*

LOCKMAN, *executioner, so called because he receives as one of his dues a "lock" of meal out of every caskful exposed in open market.*

LOON, *rascal.*

LOW COUNTRY, *the Lowlands,* also *England.*

LURDANE, *fool.*

LURE, *an object similar to a jowl, held out by a falconer to call a hawk.*

MAIR, *more.*

MAKER, *poet.*

MALTALENT, *a grudge, hatred.*

MALVOISE, *Malmsey wine.*

MAMMOCKS, *large pieces.*

MARTIALIST, *soldier.*

MASKERS, *masqueraders, revellers.*

MASSAMORE, MASSY MORE, *principal dungeon of the feudal castle.*

MAUN, *must.*

MERK, *an old Scottish coin, value* 13s. 4d.

MISERS, *literally* miserable persons.

MUTTON *v.* FRENCH MUTTON.

NAETHING, *nothing.*

NAINSELL, *ownself.*

NEIDFYRE, *forced fire, produced by the friction of wood after all* the lights and fires are extinguished.

NIGHT GEAR, *night clothes.*

NO, *not.*

OF THAT ILK, *of the place of the same name, e.g. " Waverley of Waverley."*

ONY MAIR, *any more.*

OUTFANG, *a thief caught on another's lands or premises.*

PANTLER, *kitchen steward in charge of the pantry.*

PELLACH, *porpoise.*

PIBROCH, *music peculiar to the Highland bagpipes.*

PIPKIN, *small earthern boiler.*

PLAID, *tartan mantle.*

POINTS, *latchets for tying the doublet to the hose.*

POTTERCARRIER, *apothecary.*

POTTLE-POT, *a vessel containing four quarts of liquid.*

POUNCET-BOX, *ornamental smelling box.*

PRECISIAN, *a formalist, one strictly exact in the observance of rules.*

PRETTY FELLOW, *smart fellow.*

PRITHEE, *I pray thee.*

PROVOST, *Mayor.*

QUACKSALVER, *quack doctor.*

QUEAN, *wench.*

REBECK, *a species of violin.*

REDE, *advice.*

REIVING, *robbing.*

ROUPING LIKE A CORBIE, *as hoarse as a raven.*

ROWAN-TREE, *mountain ash.*

SACK, *hot spiced wine of sherry or canary.*

SAIR, *sore, very much.*

SASSENACHS, *Saxons, English.*

SCATHE, *harm, injury.*

SHAMOY, *chamois.*

SHIELING, *hut, temporary summer milk-house.*

SKENES, *knives.*

SLOGAN, *war-cry, gathering word of the clans.*

SOLDAN v. DROMOND.

SORNERS, *obtrusive guests, sturdy beggars.*

SOUTHLAND, *England,* also *the Lowlands.*

SPORRAN, *Highland pouch or goat-skin purse.*

SPORRAN-MOULLACH, *Highland shaggy pouch worn at the belt with the rough side outwards.*

STICKLERS, *the seconds in ancient single combats, so called from the white sticks they carried.*

STITHY, *anvil.*

STOUTHREIF, *robbery.*

STRATH, *glen, watered valley.*

STYPTIC, *astringent to arrest hæmorrhage.*

SWASH-BUCKLER, *bully; sword-player; swaggering, boastful fellow.*

SWINGED, *driven.*

THIGGERS, *mannerly beggars who ask a benevolence but refuse an alms.*

THRALL, *enslaved.*

THRAW, *twist.*

TIRRIVIE, *tantrum.*

TOD, *fox.*

TOYS, *female finery.*

TROTH, *truth, faith.*

TUILZIE, *scuffle.*

UPHAULD, *uphold, maintain.*

VALENTINE, *sweetheart, lover.*

VALIANCIE, VALIANCY, *bravery, brave self.*

VAUNT, *boast.*

VESTIARY, *robing-room.*

VIOL, *ancient form of violin, having six strings.*

WAR FOU, *was full, was satisfied.*

WARK, *work.*

WARSTLE, *wrestle.*

WEAN, *infant, child.*

WEAPON-SHAWING, *duelling.*

WELKED, *withered.*

WHASE, *whose.*

WHINGER, *large wood knife.*

WITHERSHINS, *against the sun,* i.e. *from left to right; wrong ways about.*

WOODCRAFT, *knowledge of the rules of the chase.*

WYND, *lane, turning.*

YESTERNIGHT, *last night.*

EVERYMAN'S LIBRARY: A Selected List

1

FICTION

2

3

4

HISTORY

LEGENDS AND SAGAS

POETRY AND DRAMA

REFERENCE

Reader's Guide to Everyman's Library. Compiled by *A. J. Hoppé*. This volume is a new compilation and gives in one alphabetical sequence the names of all the authors, titles and subjects in Everyman's Library. (An Everyman Paperback, 1889). *Many volumes formerly included in Everyman's Library reference section are now included in Everyman's Reference Library and are bound in larger format.*

RELIGION AND PHILOSOPHY